A PHILIP ROTH READER

Philip Roth was born in Newark, New Jersey, in 1933 and educated at Bucknell University and the University of Chicago. His first book, *Goodbye, Columbus*, won the US National Book Award 1960 and was made into a highly successful film. His other books include the international bestseller *Portnoy's Complaint*, *The Ghost Writer*, *Zuckerman Unbound*, *The Anatomy Lesson*, *The Prague Orgy*, *The Counterlife* (winner of the 1987 National Book Critics' Circle Award), *Deception* and *Patrimony*.

His latest book, *Operation Shylock*, is published by Jonathan Cape.

BY THE SAME AUTHOR

Operation Shylock
Patrimony
Deception
The Facts
The Counterlife
The Prague Orgy
The Anatomy Lesson
Zuckerman Unbound
The Ghost Writer
The Professor of Desire
Reading Myself and Others
My Life as a Man
The Great American Novel
The Breast
Our Gang
Portnoy's Complaint
When She Was Good
Letting Go
Goodbye, Columbus

PORTNOY'S COMPLAINT

'One of the funniest books I have ever read... more than a novel, it is a genuine piece of contemporary American folklore. No – universal'

Anthony Burgess, *Sunday Times*

THE BREAST

'The Breast is one of the funniest books to appear for a long time. Philip Roth's prose is elegant and intelligent'

Margaret Drabble, *Listener*

THE GREAT AMERICAN NOVEL

'Roth has an immense talent for making a single unlikely metaphor speak volumes. That talent has never been more hugely, iconoclastically employed'

Jacky Gillott, *The Times*

My Life as a Man

'As long as he remains willing to stay on duty as a sexual satirist, in which case he again mans the sentry-box in *My Life as a Man*, he may help us to retain a toe-hold on sanity'

Norman Shrapnel, *Guardian*

The Professor of Desire

'A profound and commanding book. There is a great beauty in it, humanity and tenderness'

Janice Elliot, *Sunday Telegraph*

The Ghost Writer

'This is a brilliant, witty and extremely elegant book... as Philip Roth has demonstrated, fantasy and reality can be handled together only with a very delicate touch'

Emma Tennant, *Guardian*

A Philip Roth Reader

VINTAGE

VINTAGE
20 Vauxhall Bridge Road, London SW1V 2SA

London Melbourne Sydney Auckland Johannesburg
and agencies throughout the world

First published in Great Britain by
Jonathan Cape Ltd, 1981

Vintage edition 1993

2 4 6 8 10 9 7 5 3 1

Printed and bound in Great Britain by
Cox & Wyman, Reading, Berkshire

ISBN 0 09 922521 2

Contents

Introduction

Philip Roth seems to me the most gifted novelist now writing, at least if one puts a stress on tradition in using the word "novelist." He translates his intelligence and his feelings into the terms specific to serious fiction, with more firmness than Bellow, more richness than Mailer, more patience and steadiness and taste and tact than anyone else. That is the case I shall argue.

He has at least one special claim on all serious readers, that he is himself the serious reader as writer. Of course, most good novelists have always read seriously; though their reading (as reflected in their critical judgments) has often been weirdly distorted by compulsions deriving from their needs as writers. But what makes Roth special is not only that his critical sense is not so distorted, but that it plays a part, a big part, in his imaginative creations. His stories are full of beautiful insights into books and authors, into the business of teaching and criticizing, and into living with works of literature over time.

I know no other novelist, for instance, who makes the discussion of books such a valuable part of his story's action—with critical comments quite substantial in themselves and yet not an obstacle to the flow of dramatized life. These comments are appreciation rather than analysis—much less exegesis—but they are none the less critical in the best sense. And if this is possible because so much of his novels' action takes place among different parts of the protagonist's mind, nevertheless it *is* dramatized life —and there are more external exchanges.

For instance, in *Letting Go* (1962), James's *Portrait of a Lady* immediately becomes a point at issue between Gabe Wallach, the hero, and Libby, the woman with whom he gets most deeply entangled. He sends her a copy that has between its pages a letter from his dying mother. And there is in both Libby and his mother a kind of strained idealism, imposing strain as well as charm on those around them, which reminds the reader of Isabel Archer. And the decorum of James's novel (in both the art of narrative and the life narrated) contrasts with the indecorousness of Libby's plight. The burden of these (unspoken) comparisons and contrasts bears on Libby, but if the reader, at a second reading, reverses the arrow, toward Isabel, he will find that rewarding and relevant too. Points are being made about Isabel, and James, which shade in the picture of Libby and Roth. There is a penumbra of such implications, a halo of literary critical meanings, which surrounds and sets off the central icon.

Then, in *The Professor of Desire,* David Kepesh goes to Prague largely because he is devoted to Kafka, visits the latter's home, discusses him with a Czech professor (himself devoted to Melville) and finally dreams about him. In the discussion he has talked about his own sexual impotence, and waywardly suggested that *The Castle* is a story of similar sexual oppression. (The Czech professor, who suffers the political oppression of state Communism, interprets *Moby Dick* in terms relevant to *that* suffering.) In Kepesh's dream, he visits Kafka's still-surviving whore, and hears all about his sexual practices, even has them performed before him. Kafka's face and fate having been evoked in our mind before, the contrast is poignant and cruel—the contrast between Kepesh and Kafka, but also that between Kepesh's devotion to, and his desecration of, Kafka's image.

It is, typically, a presence and a contrast that are evoked each time. In an essay-story of 1973, "Looking at Kafka," Roth imagines a Kafka who had survived his tuberculosis and come to America, to be Hebrew teacher to the American author in Newark in 1942 (when Roth was nine). This Kafka would have destroyed his manuscripts and ceased to be a writer. His remarkableness would be all suppressed, his quality unnamed and unrecognized, except for a something the boy Roth would apprehend without comprehending. And he would be involved in the Roth family affairs by an attempted match between him and Roth's aunt—yet another foredoomed failure in Kafka's series of attempts to marry. (It is worth noting that Roth's father was himself an insurance agent, whose parents emigrated from Austria-Hungary.) The contrast—left to the reader to develop—is between the self-denying and self-defeating Czech, spiritual athlete and ascetic, and the brash and greedy son of immigrants, the Jew who got away, whose writings embody the all-voracious culture around him, even as they bitterly criticize it.

In his most recent novel, *The Ghost Writer* (1979), he makes a similar fantasy-use of Anne Frank, who appears in the life of the author's representative, having survived the holocaust. She represents to him the life of suffering and denial, of moral dignity and achieved beauty, to contrast with his own anxious egotism and overprivilege—to feed his anxiety about (among other things) his assigned task of creating equal beauty out of privilege. This use of her, and even more that of Kafka, which makes the reader turn, at every pause in Roth's lifelong self-analysis, to compare him with the other man, strikes me as wholly original and wholly successful.

It therefore comes as no surprise that Roth is unusually susceptible to literary influence, which means, to some degree, literary fashion, and leads, in some cases, to unsuccess. There is some writing of Roth's as epitaph on which we might take his own line from the very successful *My Life as a Man* (1974): "I leave it to those writers who live in the flamboyant American present, and whose extravagant fictions I sample from afar, to treat the implausible, the preposterous, and the bizarre in something other than a straightforward and recognizable manner." That mode was not indeed right for Roth, but his susceptibility to influence does not necessarily lead to disaster. Frequently it leads to success, as we have seen, and most often it stamps individual works with their special character.

Goodbye, Columbus (1959) surely bears the mark of Salinger's influence. Obviously, *The Breast* (1972) was conceived because of Kafka's precedent—and Gogol's—and the contrast between this metamorphosis and Kafka's is an important part of its statement about the author and his culture. In *My Life as a Man* the story "Courting Disaster" was surely conceived by the aid of Nabokov's precedent in *Lolita*—though I see no significant contrast there. While Mailer (the Mailer of "The Time of Her Time") may be responsible for certain of Roth's scenes, or stresses within those scenes, especially a kind of sexual anger; and Bellow is a pervasive presence throughout Roth's oeuvre, though most notably in the early works.

Perhaps Roth's cultivation of his susceptibility to influence, and the weaknesses it brings, are more obvious than the strengths. But it seems to me that Roth consummates and combines the tendencies of these other writers, and produces a classical concentration of the literary imagination of our time. As I read him I find Salinger combined with Mailer, and Nabokov combined with Malamud, and I feel I am getting the best of each of them —when Roth is at his best. And it strikes me as a significant coincidence that a gifted novelist should cultivate this particular gift just when a school of criticism was arising which focused its attention on "the anxiety of influence."

However, the most poignant literary context into which to put Roth is a quite different one. It is the most poignant because it is more than, but not other than, literary. I mean the Polish and Czech writers he has published in the Penguin series of which he is the General Editor, Writers from the Other Europe. Obviously, his interest in these writers, all (except Bruno Schulz) postwar names, and essentially Roth's contemporaries, represents a questioning of himself comparable to that embodied in his cult of Kafka. But this time the question is, more transparently, What would have happened to me and what kind of writer would I have become if my grandparents had not come to America from Eastern Europe? Moreover, the project of finding these writers and publishing their books is a kind of action of intervention; it makes a difference to their lives; it involves, conceivably, some risk to them, as well as at least some effort for him; he steps out of the charmed circle that threatens to imprison a writer of his type—the charmed circle of popular success, of purely literary effort, and of merely erotic subject matter.

A glance at two of those Eastern European writers will show what Roth is saying—or rather, what he now no longer needs to say—about himself, his work, and his culture. Tadeusz Borowski, who was born in the Ukraine in 1922, was a student in Poland when the Germans marched in; he spent time in Auschwitz and Dachau, and after 1945 wrote for the Communist Party in Poland until he committed suicide (apparently out of shame or guilt) in 1951. His collection of stories, *This Way for the Gas, Ladies and Gentlemen,* is about the life of prisoners in concentration camps, and focuses on the ugliness of their behavior to each other as well as the horror of their oppression by the guards. Milan Kundera, a Czech born in 1929, the son of a famous musician, presents a different sort of contrast to Roth, because essentially like him in talent, temperament, and subject matter. Another child of fortune, he writes stories of erotic intrigue so elegant and playful they can remind one of Chekhov or Boccaccio. But just because he is a parallel figure to Roth, the difference between their fates is striking. Kundera has been expelled from the Communist Party of Czechoslovakia twice, and is—or was when Roth wrote about him in introduction to a collection of his stories—relegated to the provinces, forbidden to travel, not allowed to teach at the Prague Film School, his books removed from libraries and bookstores, his plays banned from theaters. Roth compares Kundera to Mailer, to bring out his light, humorous, and unmelodramatic eroticism; and mentions also the very limited social freedom of Kundera's protagonists. The reader is bound to reflect that that freedom is to be found again in the scope of Mailer's (and Roth's) eroticism—their moral and imaginative scope in general. Kundera and Roth show similar talents molded into different forms and directed toward different fates by the forces of history.

It is perhaps notable that it was certain contemporaries, rather than Flaubert, Mann, James, or other of Roth's oracles, whom I was reminded of, who are for me the relevant surround to his work. Those grander and as it were more official sponsors I feel as living presences only in reading *When She Was Good* (1967).

There one *can* feel Flaubert and James, standing to the left and right of the author's chair, and bending over his shoulder to read each paragraph he completes. But when, in *The Ghost Writer,* we are aware of Henry James, and in *The Professor of Desire,* of Chekhov, it is as part of the subject matter. As "influences"—as rivals the author must measure up to, face up to—they have been successfully distanced, just by being incorporated. The reader feels no anxiety of influence. And their absence or their distance from most of his work fits in, as a part of Roth's treatment of the general theme, the grandeur and misery of ideas, the comedy and tragedy of their influence and non-influence upon behavior. In *My Life as a Man,* Peter Tarnopol remarks that he has just used one of his father's phrases, "what one owes oneself," and adds that his effective thinking owes more to his father than to, say, Aristotle. The same point is made more incisively in an interview printed in *Reading Myself and Others* (1975).

Roth says there that he should have defended himself (against charges that his early work was vulgarly anti-Semitic) by citing, not as he did the precedent of Flaubert and the value of objectivity, but the precedent of Henny Youngman, the comic he enjoyed as a boy, and the value of Jewish vaudeville. He adds that as much as *The Wings of the Dove* it was Jake the Snake he'd admired and learned from, growing up—the owner of his corner candy store, a lewd anecdotalist and local satirist.

Or take the parallel contrast, in *My Life as a Man,* between Caroline Benson, the hero's college English teacher (Virginia Woolf, on whom he writes his thesis, standing behind her), and Sharon Shatzky (daughter of Al "the Zipper King" Shatzky), whom he inducts into sexual shamelessness. Peter Tarnopol is intoxicated by his success with Miss Benson quite as much as by that with Sharon. The two affairs proceed in tandem, twin flowerings of his youthful talent, and though the two women cannot be brought together, and the two sides to his nature are dangerously dissociated, neither of those facts is the point the story makes. Its point is just the diversity of pasture on which his pride so greedily and happily crops. Tarnopol has no inhibiting shames and guilts—until much later in the story. And it is that comic, and earthy, and bawdy strain of his native culture, so unlike the austere, the noble, and the exquisite artists he admires, which Roth employs in his fiction to set it at a distance from its "classical" sponsors.

All this, of course, Roth is perfectly aware of, draws our attention to, makes use of. For him it is only a starting point, but for the critic—at least for me—it's still a source of wonderment; in the work of other Jewish-American writers, too, but Roth gives the phenomenon a classical completeness. How can any writer be so in tune with Mann, Woolf, James and still so raucous and raunchy in word and deed? Even more, how can any writer pass so surefootedly and unembarrassedly from one to the other? No English novelist has ever been able to do that. Roth's work does reveal some of the limits of the process (his heroes are deeply upset by other people's vulgarity, and their vigor of language finds only a feeble counterpart in their behavior). But his stress is on the zest of it, and his stress is convincing. The range of his movement is an achievement, and a vivid case of his interest in the limited powers of "ideas" and "literature."

Roth's world of vulgarity is Jewish. To be a Jewish child, however, an experience Roth makes much of, is to grow up in a world of refinement. His heroes' families are the heart of all refinement. In *Portnoy's Complaint* (1969) we read, "The guilt, the fears—the terror bred into my bones! What in their world was not charged with danger, dripping with germs, fraught with peril? Oh, where was the gusto, where was the boldness and courage?" But, the reader might reply, you know where they were—down at the corner candy store, in Jake the Snake's sardonic judgment on all refinement. When Portnoy, grown up, declares that "to be bad and enjoy it makes men of us boys," he is reciting Jake's lesson. He grows up, as Jewish, with a map of life in which areas of refinement and vulgarity are marked off from each other clearly, but with the routes of passage, and the visiting hours, equally clear.

To be Jewish was also to embody the Protestant work ethic. In *My Life as a Man* we are told, of the Zuckermans, "A strong character, not a big bankroll, was to them the evidence of one's worth." And, by a natural extension, to be Jewish was to be a good husband and father and family man. In Roth's novels, wives constantly praise and protect husbands, mothers admire and idolize sons, sisters love and support brothers. As a boy, watching the men play softball on weekends, Portnoy longed to grow up to be a Jewish husband and father. As a man, he found that even Gentile girls wanted a Jew for a husband, because he could be relied on to stay around the house, to give them kids to rear and Kafka to read.

In fact, to be Jewish, according to Roth, is to be middle class. The goyim are characteristically upper, like Susan McCall in *My Life as a Man,* or lower, like Mary Jane Reed, The Monkey in *Portnoy's Complaint.* Of course, there *are* middle-class WASP girls in his novels—it's a type that fascinates Roth—the point is not that the Gentiles are never middle class, but that the Jews always are. Characteristically, non-Jewish Americans appear to Roth's Jews as either vulgar and violent, or else desiccated and heartless. So to be Jewish is to be called, quite specially, to uphold social values and embody social faith.

But Roth's work also records a rebellion, an exasperation with, a blasphemy against, that piety. That has seemed, especially to Jewish readers, the main thrust of his work, from *Goodbye, Columbus* on. The story "Epstein," for instance, is built around the scene in which the father stands naked before his wife and child, his genitals apparently marked with venereal disease; a scene that outrages the piety taught in Leviticus against "uncovering the nakedness" of a father.

Roth has always claimed that there was nothing anti-Jewish in this, nothing more than the artist's need to find pungent means of expression, and that seems plausible to me. On the other hand, that artist's need is, in our present phase of culture, for a pungency offensive to piety; to be an artist is to be in a state of inflamed exasperation, and it is not philistine to sympathize with those who protested.

However, from Roth's point of view, he was in those days socially pious himself because in sympathy with his society's criteria of seriousness. The big fact of his development, as he describes it, has been that he came to doubt even those criteria. In his early work, he tells us, he was always trying to be mature and responsible, to be manly, in whatever he wrote. If we may take Peter Tarnopol to represent Philip Roth, he translates his parents' values into literary terms, *seemingly* different, just as Peter's brother Morris translates those values into radical political terms. The brothers, being intellectuals, belong to a different branch of American culture from their parents, but one quite parallel in direction. Peter's position then, however he quarrels with his parents, is very different from his position after being defeated by Maureen, when he becomes unable and unwilling to be a man any more.

It is, nevertheless, in terms like manliness that Roth's heroes continue to measure themselves, despite his attempts to escape them. In an interview he said that his work changed with *Portnoy,* because of an increased responsiveness to what was unsocialized in himself. And Tarnopol tells Karen Oakes that now he's been broken by Maureen, he'll take Genet, Miller, and Céline as his literary heroes, and write like them. But he realizes immediately that he is sensitive to nothing so much as to his moral reputation. And Roth's later work, including *The Breast* and *The Professor of Desire,* has a strain of moral suffering that sounds deeper than anything else.

For that reason, one precedent I am always reminded of in reading Roth is George Eliot. Of course, a concern with conscience is hardly enough to isolate these two from the general run of serious novelists. But when one adds the special relation in each of them of conscience to comedy, the practiced irony of transition from the one mode to the other, the crowd of contenders thins out remarkably. That habit of transition is expressed in the elaborate sentences that come naturally to the pair of them. The irony is just sardonic enough to sanitize the tears—and which other authors' representatives spend so much time in tears?

And there is a similar pathos of ineffectiveness in both writers in their non-fiction, especially in political matters, so crucial to the kind of seriousness they speak for. Both are gifted essay writers, but—being so very intelligent as they are—their non-fiction is a sad comedown from their fiction, where their intelligence so overflows its immediate functions that it seems all-encompassing and omni-competent. The satire, just because it denies itself the full freedom of fiction, is a bit of a disappointment. *Our Gang,* for instance, seems to me the least exciting of his books (merely a duty done, dues paid by the writer as citizen), and one is as puzzled as in Eliot's case to say why it should be so forceless, why their strength as thinkers is limited to "personal relations."

But in *that* field, in saying exactly how personal concerns run with and against political ones, and exactly what life-gestures mean—what, say, the life styles of Susan McCall and Maureen Johnson signify—as in finding the exact word, syntax, intonation for his characters, Roth is supreme. By comparison Doris Lessing, in other ways George Eliot's heir, does *not* know the exact word, and lacks the broadly humorous gamut of feeling.

But of course to see likenesses between Roth and Eliot can only be preliminary to seeing differences. Roth is much more strenuously autobiographical in his stories, for one thing (I mean he invites the reader to wonder how autobiographical he is being). In this aspect he reminds me of Kingsley Amis, and the comparison brings out the weightier character of the American's work. The Englishman's talent expresses itself quite strikingly in acts of self-limitation, renunciations of the sort of seriousness we associate with George Eliot. Whereas the American won't stop trying, won't give up the great tradition. It is typical that whereas Amis announces as a saving truth that nice things are nicer than nasty ones, Roth (or at least Tarnopol) tells his analyst, "You're very hung up on the pleasure principle." Roth's heroes acknowledge that the women who give them the most pleasure fail to engage their imaginations; but though they curse themselves for that perversity, they pursue no illusion that they can just choose "nice things" henceforth.

Which brings us to that other, and largest, difference between Roth and Eliot—the character and intensity of his erotic preoccupation. This is of course a general difference between nineteenth- and twentieth-century novelists, between nineteenth- and twentieth-century culture; but that difference too is exemplified in classical form by Roth. If novelists now can write only about personal relations, *they* are nowadays only erotic, or almost so. Out of that subject matter he makes his farce, comedy of manners, moral tragedy, satire, sociology, everything. But what is most striking, to my eye, are the signs that our eroticism has seriously scarred Roth's conscience, and even his imagination. Take conscience first: in *My Life as a Man,* Tarnopol ends his relationship with Susan in a scene at her mother's house in which she (hitherto strikingly modest) "comes on very shameless," and when he says the final goodbye she reaches up from her chair and takes hold of his genitals. Her mother has just accused him of debauching Susan—"Must she be driven crazy with sex too?"—and though she quite misses the moral intention of his relations with Susan, the reader is left feeling that she was accidentally right. Tarnopol *has* taught Susan to "try to be bold, to be shameless, to be greedy"—for character-building purposes; and since it is after he has dismissed the mother's accusations that the daughter makes her final grotesque gesture, the story seems to confirm them for us.

As for the scar on Roth's imagination, that is what is announced by the episode I described in *The Professor of Desire,* where Kepesh's long love of Kafka finds expression in a pornographic fantasy. Roth is implying something very similar to what Susan Sontag said in "The Pornographic Imagination" (1967). "There is, demonstrably, something incorrectly designed and potentially disorienting in the human sexual capacity—at least in the capacities of man-in-civilization. Man, the sick animal, bears within him an appetite which can drive him mad." Sontag's dissent from the sexual orthodoxies of liberal humanism is like that of Norman O. Brown, and leads her, like Brown, to a choice between accepting pornography, obscenity, abjection and accepting the ideal of chastity. "Human sexuality is, quite apart from Christian repressions, a highly questionable phenomenon, and belongs, at least potentially, among the extreme rather than the ordinary experiences of humanity. . . . [It is] . . . one of the demonic forces in human consciousness. . . . Even on the level of simple physical sensation and mood, making love surely resembles having an epileptic fit at least as much, if not more, than it does eating a meal or conversing with someone."

It is no accident that Susan Sontag sees modern art as "a spiritual project," and that her culture heroes are "perverse spiritual athletes" who drive their art and thought toward "silence," like Artaud, Wittgenstein, Beckett, or like Roth's Kafka.

There is another critic who can, I think, be profitably placed beside Roth, and that is Lionel Trilling. I am thinking of two essays in particular, "The Fate of Pleasure" and "The Teaching of Modern Literature." The first discusses, as a feature of modern culture in general, that turning away from pleasure, that cult of the sublime, which we noted in Roth's eroticism. The second lists the modernist books Trilling taught at Columbia (Roth's teacher-heroes often draw up similar lists), and discusses the false position of the teacher who encourages in his students a kind of spiritual revolt, a pursuit of the extreme and intractable, the anti-social, which he himself does not live by. In *The Professor of Desire* the whole narrative is a self-explanation by a teacher of a course in erotic literature, composed in order to escape that false position and meet his students in sincerity. But it is in *My Life as a Man* that the most moving parallel occurs between Trilling's essay and Roth's fiction.

The crux of that book is Tarnopol's destruction by a crazy wife, and his passive participation in the process. Why did I do this, or let this happen? he asks a hundred times, and the main answer comes on p. 194 of the novel (p. 26 here). "My trouble in my middle twenties was that. . . . Stuffed to the gills with great fiction —entranced not by cheap romances, like Madame Bovary, but by *Madame Bovary*—I now expected to find in everyday experience that same sense of the difficult and the deadly earnest that informed the novels I admired most. My model of reality, deduced from reading the masters, had at its heart *intractability.*" And hence it was that crazy Maureen could impose herself upon him as authentic, as more real than the girls he liked, as his spiritual equal and mate. This is, I think, exactly what Trilling was talking about.

Of course, Roth grew up under Trilling's aegis, for he was a child of the fifties, as he has often told us. In an interview with himself, he says he first saw writing as "something like a religious calling, and literature a kind of sacrament." In the fifties, he says, cultural loyalties divided the young as political ones were to do, and the young Roth, *choosing* literature, felt he had committed himself to every noble value. Tarnopol (or his alter ego, Zuckerman) says that then "Everything that was a part of getting older seemed to me to be a pleasure: . . . the refinement and strengthening of one's moral nature—to be magnanimous where one had been selfish and carping. . . . Oh, how I wanted a soul that was pure and spotless!" That aspiration was part of the manhood, the maturity, of his Life as a Man. The major part was marriage. "For those young men who reached their maturity in the fifties . . . there was considerable moral prestige in taking a wife." He describes his proposal to Maureen as "manly," and she accuses him of not being a man when he doesn't want to be a husband to her. She calls him a boy: "A real woman and you're in tears, Peter." At a climactic moment he puts on her underwear, to renounce manhood and end the struggle.

These are events in a novel, not in a biography. But in Roth's development as a writer we find something parallel. In the late sixties, on his own theory, he rebelled against social piety. He had belonged, he said, to the most propagandized generation in American history, but the sixties had been a demythologizing decade. In *My Life as a Man,* Tarnopol's story, "Salad Days," gets praised by a critic ten years younger for "flirting with the playful, the perverse, and the disreputable," and escaping from the propriety of his early work. In *The Great American Novel,* his protagonist, Roth says, imagined a myth of an *ailing* America, though in grotesquely comic terms.

Roth's career therefore is a vivid case of the changes that have come over American literary culture from the fifties through the seventies. But it is also a vivid case of continuity, for if his "desire to be good" was replaced by a "desire to be bad," both are there, in conflict, from the beginning. His early autobiographical hero, Gabe Wallach in *Letting Go,* is full of that conflict. And its terms are not so different in *The Professor of Desire,* though the protagonist is much battered, saddened, almost silenced.

To place him evaluatively, I should put Roth beside Bellow, an author he much admires and much resembles, for Bellow too is an artist of conscience and comedy, with political responsibilities and autobiographical tendencies. One crucial likeness is between their senses of themselves as overprivileged, burdened with others' love or envy, too lucky by half. (This is a leading trait of all our Jewish novelists' heroes, and the crux of this genre of fiction.) Roth seems to me demonstrably the better in his handling of this central theme. In Bellow there is a softness of self-definition, a queasiness of self-love, which spoils a good deal. Roth's superiority is in fictional taste (in knowing what to omit), in the richer realism of his specification, and in the firmer personal center to the extravaganzas of fantasy and the structures of reasoning. All in all, it seems to me, Roth is the central novelist of his generation, the one who sums up and dramatizes our central concerns.

What this Reader ought to do is to make clear the nature of Roth's achievement, at mid-career, after twenty years of writing, and to win for him that central place on the map of our literary culture which is his due. The three parts of the Reader, arranged and selected by Roth himself, reflect each one a major aspect of his work; and of his sense of himself, which is the main subject of his fiction, and of his sense of his work, which is also—to an unusual degree—the subject of his fiction. Part I is made up of episodes that derive from his feelings about other writers and their bearing upon himself—as writer and as man—but also his feelings about literature as a whole, and *its* bearing—what it means that he is a writer. The second set of episodes represents the aspect of Roth that is perhaps best known, or most often thought to be typical of him: the wild extravaganza upon the theme of a serious moral dilemma, which is quite grimly true as well as very funny—the farce that is a by-product of the progress toward moral authenticity, and also, more strikingly, a brake upon that progress when it becomes overweening. And it is to be noted that two of the passages presented are of political satire, and so situate their author within a great historical tradition of humanist writing. The last part ("You Must Change Your Life") reminds us of the process of self-indictment which lies at the root of everything else in Roth. Here it is worth stressing his concern with virtue, with the choice to be virtuous, and the constraints and distortions which that imposes upon the personality and the feelings; and also the choice (for Roth, something closely related) to be a realistic writer, writing about painful and unexhilarating situations, with unremitting attention to detail; and finally (because Roth has been accused of not doing well by women in his fiction) the fact that often the protagonists of such episodes are female.

As for Roth's future, the direction in which he will turn his talents, I at least cannot read that in the Reader. It is perhaps especially the fate of this kind of writer, who steers between other writers' Scyllae and Charybdes, to know where he's going only when he has got there. Other writers embody single ideas, long-term projects, huge acts of will. Roth is essentially modest in those regards, largely anonymous seen from those points of view. He follows in a number of wakes and plots his course by them as well as by the fixed stars. We can foreknow only that he will make something absolutely his own out of these various materials, and that he will set the stamp of the highest quality upon it.

MARTIN GREEN

“Literature Got Me into This and Literature Is Gonna Have to Get Me Out”

I

Marriage à la Mode

For those young men who reached their maturity in the fifties, and who aspired to be grown-up during that decade, when as one participant has written, everyone *wanted* to be thirty, there was considerable moral prestige in taking a wife, and hardly because a wife was going to be one's maidservant or "sexual object." Decency and Maturity, a young man's "seriousness," were at issue precisely because it was thought to be the other way around: in that the great world was so obviously a man's, it was only within marriage that an ordinary woman could hope to find equality and dignity. Indeed, we were led to believe by the defenders of womankind of our era that we were exploiting and degrading the women we *didn't* marry, rather than the ones we did. Unattached and on her own, a woman was supposedly not even able to go to the movies or out to a restaurant by herself, let alone perform an appendectomy or drive a truck. It was up to us then to give them the value and the purpose that society at large withheld—by marrying them. If we didn't marry women, who would? Ours, alas, was the only sex available for the job: the draft was on.

No wonder then that a young college-educated bourgeois male

In this chapter from *My Life as a Man* (1974), Peter Tarnopol, a novelist, describes what drew him into a disastrous marriage with Maureen Johnson Mezik Walker. He is now separated from her and conducting a love affair with a rich, uncertain, and vulnerable young widow, Susan Seabury McCall.

of my generation who scoffed at the idea of marriage for himself, who would just as soon eat out of cans or in cafeterias, sweep his own floor, make his own bed, and come and go with no binding legal attachments, finding female friendship and sexual adventure where and when he could and for no longer than he liked, laid himself open to the charge of "immaturity," if not "latent" or blatant "homosexuality." Or he was just plain "selfish." Or he was "frightened of responsibility." Or he could not "commit himself" (nice institutional phrase, that) to "a permanent relationship." Worst of all, most shameful of all, the chances were that this person who thought he was perfectly able to take care of himself on his own was in actuality "unable to love."

An awful lot of worrying was done in the fifties about whether people were able to love or not—I venture to say, much of it by young women in behalf of the young men who didn't particularly *want* them to wash their socks and cook their meals and bear their children and then tend them for the rest of their natural days. "But aren't you capable of loving anyone? Can't you think of anyone but yourself?" when translated from desperate fifties-feminese into plain English, generally meant "I want to get married and I want you to get married to."

Now I am sure that many of the young women of that period who set themselves up as specialists in loving hadn't a very clear idea of how strong a charge their emotions got from the instinct for survival—or how much those emotions arose out of the yearning to own and be owned, rather than from a reservoir of pure and selfless love that was the special property of themselves and their gender. After all, how lovable *are* men? Particularly men "unable to love"? No, there was more to all that talk about "commitment" and "permanent relationships" than many young women (and their chosen mates) were able to talk about or able at that time fully to understand: the more was the fact of female dependence, defenselessness, and vulnerability.

This hard fact of life was of course experienced and dealt with by women in accordance with personal endowments of intelligence and sanity and character. One imagines that there were brave and genuinely self-sacrificing decisions made by women who refused to accede to those profoundest of self-delusions, the ones that come cloaked in the guise of love; likewise, there was much misery in store for those who were never able to surrender their romantic illusions about the arrangement they had made in behalf of their helplessness, until they reached the lawyer's office, and he threw their way that buoy known as alimony. It has been said that those ferocious alimony battles that have raged in the courtrooms of this country during the last few decades, the way religious wars raged throughout Europe in the seventeenth century, were really "symbolic" in nature. My guess is that rather than serving as a symbol around which to organize other grievances and heartaches, the alimony battle frequently tended to clarify what was generally obscured by the metaphors with which marital arrangements were camouflaged by the partners themselves. The extent of the panic and rage aroused by the issue of alimony, the ferocity displayed by people who were otherwise sane and civilized enough, testifies, I think, to the shocking—and humiliating—realization that came to couples in the courtroom about the fundamental role that each may actually have played in the other's life. "So, it has descended to this," the enraged contestants might say, glaring in hatred at one another—but even that was only an attempt to continue to hide from the most humiliating fact of all: that it really *was* this, all along.

Now I realize that it is possible to dismiss these generalizations as a manifestation of my bitterness and cynicism, an unfortunate consequence of my own horrific marriage and of the affair that recently ended so unhappily. Furthermore, it can be said that, having chosen women like Maureen and Susan (or, if you prefer, having had them chosen for me by my own aberrant, if not pathological, nature), I for one should not generalize, even loosely, about what men want (and get) from women, or what women want and get out of men. Well, I grant that I do not find myself feeling very "typical" at this moment, nor am I telling this story in order to argue that my life is representative of anything; nonetheless, I am naturally interested in looking around to see how much of my experience with women has been special to me and—if you must have it that way—my pathology, and how much is symptomatic of a more extensive social malaise. And looking around, I conclude this: in Maureen and Susan I came in contact with two of the more virulent strains of a virus to which only a few women among us are immune.

Outwardly, of course, Maureen and Susan couldn't have been more dissimilar, nor could either have had a stronger antipathy for the "type" she took the other to be. However, what drew them together as women—which is to say, what drew me to them, for that is the subject here—was that in her own extreme and vivid way, each of these antipathetic originals demonstrated that sense of defenselessness and vulnerability that has come to be a mark of their sex and is often at the core of their relations with men. That I came to be bound to Maureen by *my* helplessness does not mean that either of us ever really stopped envisioning *her* as the helpless victim and myself as the victimizer who had only to desist in his brutishness for everything to be put right and sexual justice to be done. So strong was the myth of male inviolability, of male dominance and potency, not only in Maureen's mind but in mine, that even when I went so far as to dress myself in a woman's clothes and thus concede that as a man I surrendered, even *then* I could never fully assent to the idea that in our household conventional assumptions about the strong and the weak did not adequately describe the situation. Right down to the end, I still saw Maureen, and she saw herself, as the damsel in distress; and in point of fact, beneath all that tough exterior, all those claims to being "in business for herself" and nobody's patsy, Maureen was actually more of a Susan than Susan was, *and to herself no less than to me.*

There is a growing body of opinion which maintains that by and large marriages, affairs, and sexual arrangements generally are made by masters in search of slaves: there are the dominant and the submissive, the brutish and the compliant, the exploiters and the exploited. What this formula fails to explain, among a million other things, is why so many of the "masters" appear themselves to be in bondage, oftentimes to their "slaves." I do not contend—to make the point yet again—that my story furnishes anything like an explanation or a paradigm; it is only an instance, a postchivalric instance to be sure, of what might be described as the Prince Charming phenomenon. In this version of the fairy tale the part of the maiden locked in the tower is played consecutively by Maureen Johnson Tarnopol and Susan Seabury McCall. I of course play the prince. My performance, as described here, may give rise to the sardonic suggestion that I should have played his horse. But, you see, it was not as an animal that I wished to be a star—it was decidedly *not* horsiness, goatishness, foxiness, lionliness, or beastliness in any form that I aspired to. I wanted to be humanish: manly, a man.

At the time when all this began, I would never even have thought it necessary to announce that as an aspiration—I was too confident at twenty-five that success was all but at hand—nor did I foresee a career in which being married and then trying to get unmarried would become my predominant activity and obsession. I would have laughed had anyone suggested that struggling with a woman over a marriage would come to occupy me in the way that exploring the South Pole had occupied Admiral Byrd—or writing *Madame Bovary* had occupied Flaubert. Clearly the last thing I could have imagined was myself, a dissident and skeptical member of my generation, succumbing to all that moralizing rhetoric about "permanent relationships." And, in truth, it did take something more than the rhetoric to do me in. It took a Maureen, wielding it. Yet the humbling fact remains: when the dissident and skeptical member of his generation was done in, it was on the same grounds as just about everyone else.

I was fooled by appearances, largely my own.

As a young writer already publishing stories in literary quarterlies, as one who resided in a Lower East Side basement apartment between Second Avenue and the Bowery, living on army savings and a twelve-hundred-dollar publisher's advance that I doled out to myself at thirty dollars a week, I did not think of myself as an ordinary or conventional university graduate of those times. My college acquaintances were all off becoming lawyers and doctors; a few who had been friends on the Brown literary magazine were working on advanced degrees in literature—prior to my induction into the army, I had myself served a year and a half in the Ph.D. program at the University of Chicago, before falling by the wayside, a casualty of "Bibliography" and "Anglo-Saxon"; the rest—the fraternity boys, the athletes, the business majors, those with whom I'd had little association at school—were by now already married and holding down nine-to-five jobs. Of course I dressed in blue button-down oxford shirts and wore my hair clipped short, but what else was I to wear, a serape? long curls? This was 1958. Besides, there were other ways in which it seemed to me I was distinguishable from the mass of my contemporaries: I read books and I wanted to write them. My master was not Mammon or Fun or Propriety, but Art, and Art of the earnest moral variety. I was by then already well into writing a novel about a retired Jewish haberdasher from the Bronx who on a trip to Europe with his wife nearly strangles to death a rude German housewife in his rage over "the six million." The haberdasher was modeled upon my own kindly, excitable, hardworking Jewish father who had had a similar urge on a trip he and my mother had taken to visit me in the army; the haberdasher's GI son was modeled upon myself, and his experiences closely paralleled mine in Germany during my fourteen months as a corporal in Frankfurt. I had had a German girl friend, a student nurse, large and blonde as a Valkyrie, but sweet to the core, and all the confusion that she had aroused in my parents, and in me, was to be at the heart of the novel that eventually became *A Jewish Father.*

Over my desk I did not have a photograph of a sailboat or a dream house or a diapered child or a travel poster from a distant land, but words from Flaubert, advice to a young writer that I had copied out of one of his letters: "Be regular and orderly in your life like a bourgeois, so that you may be violent and original in your work." I appreciated the wisdom in this, and coming from Flaubert, the wit, but at twenty-five, for all my dedication to the art of fiction, for all the discipline and seriousness (and *awe*) with which I approached the Flaubertian vocation, I still wanted my life to be *somewhat* original, and if not violent, at least interesting, when the day's work was done. After all, hadn't Flaubert himself, before he settled down at his round table to become the tormented anchorite of modern literature, gone off as a gentleman-vagabond to the Nile, to climb the pyramids and sow his oats with dusky dancing girls?

So: Maureen Johnson, though not exactly Egyptian, struck me

as someone who might add a little outside interest to my dedicated writer's life. Did she! Eventually she *displaced* the writing, she was so interesting. To begin with, she was twenty-nine years of age, that temptingly unknown creature of a young man's eroto-heroic imaginings, *an older woman.* Moreover, she had the hash marks to prove it. Not one but two divorces: first from the husband in Rochester, a Yugoslav saloonkeeper named Mezik, whose sixteen-year-old barmaid she had been; she claimed that Mezik, a heavy drinker with a strong right hook, had once "forced" her to go down on a friend of his, the manager of an upholstery factory—later she changed the story somewhat and said that the three of them had been drunk at the time, and that the men had drawn straws to see which of them young Maureen would go off with to the bedroom; she had decided to blow Mezik's buddy, rather than have intercourse with him, because it had seemed to her, in the circumstances and in her innocence, less demeaning. "It wasn't," she added. Then the marriage and divorce from Walker, a handsome young actor with a resonant voice and a marvelous profile who turned out to be a homosexual—that is to say, he'd "promised" Maureen he'd get over it after the wedding, but only got worse. Twice then she had been "betrayed" by men—nonetheless there was plenty of the scrapper in her when we met. And plenty of tough wit. "I am Duchess of Malfi still," was a line she pulled on me our first night in bed—not bad, I thought, not bad, even if it was obviously something her actor husband had taught her. She had the kind of crisp good looks that are associated with "dark Irishmen"—only a little marred in her case by a lantern jaw—a lithe, wiry little body (the body of a tomboyish prepubescent, except for the sizable conical breasts) and terrific energy and spirit. With her quick movements and alert eyes, she was like one of nature's undersized indefatigables, the bee or the hummingbird, who are out working the flowers from sunup to sundown, sipping from a million stamens in order to meet their minimum daily nutritional requirements. She jocularly boasted of having been the fastest runner, male or female, of her era in the Elmira, New York, grade-school system, and that (of all she told me) may well have been the truth. The night we met—at a poet's party uptown—she had challenged me to a footrace from the Astor Place subway station to my apartment two blocks away on East Ninth: "Winner calls the shots!" she cried, and off we went—I triumphed, but only by the length of a brownstone, and at the apartment, breathless from the race she'd run me, I said, "Okay, the spoils: take off your clothes," which she gladly (and rapidly) proceeded to do in the hallway where we stood, panting. Hot stuff, this (thought I); very *interesting.* Oh yes, she was fast, that girl—but I was faster, was I not? . . . Also, I should mention here, Maureen had these scores to settle with my sex, and rather large delusions about her gifts, which she had come to believe lay somewhere, anywhere, in the arts.

At the age of sixteen, an eleventh-grader, she had run away from her family's home in Elmira—a runaway, that got me too. I'd never met a real one before. What did her father do? "Everything. Nothing. Handyman. Night watchman. Who remembers any more?" Her mother? "Kept house. Drank. Oh, Christ, Peter, I forgot them long ago. And they, me." She ran off from Elmira to become—of course, an actress . . . but of all places, to Rochester. "What did I know?" she said, dismissing her innocence with a wave of the hand; a dead issue, that innocence. In Rochester she met Mezik ("married the brute—and then met his buddy"), and after three years of frustration with the second-raters in the local avant-garde theater group, switched to art school to become—an abstract painter. Following her divorce, she gave up painting—and the painter whose mistress she had become during her separation from Mezik and who had broken his "promise" to help get her in with his dealer in Detroit—and took harpsichord lessons while waiting on tables in Cambridge, Massachusetts, a town she'd heard had fewer types like Mezik in residence. There, just twenty-one, she married Walker of the Brattle Theater; five long years followed, of him and his Harvard boys. By the time we met, she had already tried wood sculpture in Greenwich Village (her teacher's wife was fiercely jealous of her, so she dropped it) and was back "in the theater," temporarily "in the production end"—that is, taking tickets and ushering at an off-Broadway theater on Christopher Street.

As I say, I believed all these reversals and recoveries, all this *movement* of hers, to be evidence of a game, audacious, and determined little spirit; and it was, it was. So too did this mess of history argue for a certain instability and lack of focus in her life. On the other hand, there was so much focus to my own, and always had been, that Maureen's chaotic, daredevil background had a decidedly exotic and romantic appeal. She had been around—and around. I liked that idea; I hadn't been anywhere really, not quite yet.

She was also something of a rough customer, and that was new to me too. At the time I took up with Maureen, I had for nearly a year been having a passionate affair with a college girl named Dina Dornbusch, a senior at Sarah Lawrence and the daughter of a wealthy Jewish family from Long Island. She was an ambitious literature and language major, and we met when she came to my basement apartment, along with four other coeds and a *Mademoiselle* editor, to interview me about my work. I had just gotten out of the army, and my "work" at the time consisted only of the six short stories that had been published in the quarterlies while I had been stationed in Frankfurt; that they had been read by these awed young girls was very nice to know. I already knew of course that they had been read with interest by New York book publishers and literary agents, for their numerous letters of inquiry had reached me in Germany, and upon returning to the U.S. after my discharge, I had chosen an agent and subsequently signed a publisher's contract that provided me with a modest advance for the novel I was writing. But that I had, while serving as a draftee in Germany, achieved enough "fame" for these girls to settle on me as the young American writer they wished to interview for a feature in the magazine, well, needless to say, that opened up a fantasy or two in my head. To be sure, I talked to them about Flaubert, about Salinger, about Mann, about my experiences in Germany and how I thought I might put them to use in fiction, but nonetheless I was wondering throughout how to get the girl with the marvelous legs and the earnest questions to stay behind when the others left.

Oh, why did I forsake Dina Dornbusch—for Maureen! Shall I tell you? Because Dina was still in college writing papers on "the technical perfection" of "Lycidas." Because Dina listened to me so intently, was so much my student, taking my opinions for her own. Because Dina's father gave us front-row seats to Broadway musicals that we had to go to see for fear of offending him. Because—yes, this is true, too; incredible, but true—because when Dina came in to visit me from school, practically all we did, from the moment she stepped into the doorway, was fuck. In short, because she was rich, pretty, protected, smart, sexy, adoring, young, vibrant, clever, confident, ambitious—that's why I gave her up for Maureen! She was a girl still, who had just about everything. I, I decided at twenty-five, was beyond "that." I wanted something called "a woman."

At twenty-nine, with two unhappy marriages behind her, with no rich, doting father, no gorgeous clothes, and no future, Maureen seemed to me to have earned all that was implied by that noun; she was certainly the first person of her sex I had ever known intimately to be so completely adrift and on her own. "I've always been more or less in business for myself," she'd told me at the party where we'd met—straight, unsentimental talk, and I liked it. With Dina, everybody seemed always to be in business for her. Likewise with myself.

Prior to Maureen, the closest I had come to a girl who had known real upheaval in her life was Grete, the student nurse in Frankfurt, whose family had been driven from Pomerania by the advancing Russian army. I used to be fascinated by whatever she could tell me about her experience of the war, but that turned out to be next to nothing. Only a child of eight when the war ended, all she could remember of it was living in the country with her brothers and sisters and her mother, on a farm where they had eggs to eat, animals to play with, and spelling and arithmetic to learn in the village school. She remembered that when the family, in flight in the spring of '45, finally ran into the American army, a GI had given her an orange; and on the farm sometimes, when the children were being particularly noisy, her mother used to put her hands up to her ears and say, "Children, quiet, quiet, you sound like a bunch of Jews." But that was as much contact as she seemed to have had with the catastrophe of the century. This did not make it so simple for me as one might think, nor did I in turn make it easy for Grete. Our affair frequently bewildered her because of my moodiness, and when she then appeared to be innocent of what it was that had made me sullen or short-tempered, I became even more difficult. Of course, she *had* been only eight when the European war ended —nonetheless, I could never really believe that she was simply a big, sweet, good-natured, commonsensical eighteen-year-old girl who did not care very much that I was a dark Jew and she a blonde Aryan. This suspiciousness, and my self-conscious struggle with it, turned up in the affair between the two young lovers depicted in *A Jewish Father.*

What I liked, you see, was something taxing in my love affairs, something problematical and puzzling to keep the imagination going even while I was away from my books; I liked most being with young women who gave me something to think about, and not necessarily because we talked together about "ideas."

So, Maureen was a rough customer—I thought about that. I wondered if I was "up"—nice word—to someone with her history and determination. It would seem by the way I hung in there that I decided that I at least ought to be. I had been up to Grete and the problems she raised for me, had I not? Why back away from difficulties, or disorder, or even turbulence—what was there to be afraid of? I honestly didn't know.

Besides, for a very long time, the overwhelming difficulty—Maureen's helplessness—was largely obscured by the fight in her and by the way in which she cast herself as the victim always of charlatans and ingrates, rather than as a person who hadn't the faintest idea of the relationship of beginning, middle, and end. When she fought me, I was at first so busy fighting back I didn't have time to see her defiance as the measure of her ineptitude and desperation. Till Maureen I had never even fought a man in anger—with my hands, that is; but I was much more combative at twenty-five than I am now and learned quickly enough how to disarm her of her favorite weapon, the spike of a high-heeled shoe. Eventually I came to realize that not even a good shaking such as parents administer to recalcitrant children was sufficient to stop her once she was on the warpath—it required a slap in the face to do that. "Just like Mezik!" screamed Maureen, dropping dramatically to the floor to cower before my violence (and pretending as best she could that it did not give her pleasure to have uncovered the brute in the high-minded young artist).

Of course by the time I got around to hitting her I was already in over my head and looking around for a way out of an affair that grew more distressing and bewildering—and frightening—practically by the hour. It was not only the depths of acrimony between us that had me reeling, but the shocking realization of this helplessness of hers, that which *drove* her to the episodes of wild and reckless rage. As the months passed I had gradually come to see that nothing she did ever worked—or, rather, I had finally come to penetrate the obfuscating rhetoric of betrayal and victimization in order to see it *that way:* the Christopher Street producer went back on his "promise" to lift her from the ticket office into the cast; the acting teacher in the West Forties who needed an assistant turned out to be a "a psychotic"; her boss at one job was "a slave driver," at the next, "a fool," at the next, "a lecher," and invariably, whenever she quit in disgust or was fired and came home in angry tears—whenever yet another of those "promises" that people were forever making to her had been broken—she would return to my basement apartment in the middle of the day to find me over the typewriter, pouring sweat—as happens when I'm feeling fluent—and reeking through my button-down oxford shirt like a man who'd been out all day with the chain gang. At the sight of me working away feverishly at what I wanted most to do, her rage at the world of oppressors was further stoked by jealousy of me—even though, as it happened, she greatly admired my few published stories, defended them vehemently against all criticism, and enjoyed vicariously the small reputation that I was coming to have. But then vicariousness was her nemesis: what she got through men was all she got. No wonder she could neither forgive nor forget him who had wronged her by "forcing" her at sixteen into bed with his buddy, or him who preferred the flesh of Harvard freshmen to her own; and if she could not relinquish the bartender Mezik or the bit player Walker, imagine the meaning she must have found in one whose youthful earnestness and single-minded devotion to a high artistic calling might magically become her own if only she could partake forever of his flesh and blood.

Our affair was over (except that Maureen wouldn't move out, and I hadn't the sense, or the foresight, to bequeath to her my two rooms of secondhand furniture and take flight; having never before been defeated in my life in anything that mattered, I simply could not recognize defeat as a possibility for me, certainly not at the hands of someone seemingly so inept)—our affair was over, but for the shouting, when Maureen told me . . . Well, you can guess what she told me. Anybody could have seen it coming a mile away. Only I didn't. Why would a woman want to fool Peter Tarnopol? Why would a woman want to tell me a lie in order to get me to marry her? What chance for happiness in such a union? No, no, it just could not be. No one would be so silly and stupid as to do a thing like that *and certainly not to me.* I Had Just Turned Twenty-Six. I Was Writing A Serious Novel. I Had My Whole Life Ahead Of Me. No—the way *I* pictured it, I would tell Maureen that this affair of ours had obviously been a mistake from the beginning and by now had become nothing but a nightmare for both of us. "As much my fault as yours, Maureen" —I didn't believe it, but I would say it, for the sake of getting out without further altercation; the only sensible solution, I would say, was for each now to go his own separate way. How could we be anything but better off without all this useless conflict and demeaning violence in our lives? "We just"—I would tell her, in straight, unsentimental talk such as she liked to use herself—"we just don't have any business together any more." Yes, that's what I would say, and she would listen and nod in acquiescence (she would have to—I would be so decent about it, and so sensible) and she would go, with me wishing her good luck.

It didn't work out that way. Actually it was in the midst of one of the ten or fifteen quarrels that we had per day, now that she had decided to stay at home and take up writing herself, that I told her to leave. The argument, which began with her accusing me of trying to prevent her from writing fiction because I was "frightened" of competition from a woman, ended with her sinking her teeth into my wrist—whereupon, with my free hand, I bloodied her nose. "You and Mezik! No difference *at all!*" The barkeeper, she claimed, used to draw blood from her every single day during the last year of their married life—he had turned her nose "into a faucet." For me it was a first, however—and a shock. Likewise her teeth in my flesh was like nothing I had ever known before in my stable and unbloody past. I had been raised to be fearful and contemptuous of violence as a means of settling disputes or venting anger— my idea of manliness had little to do with dishing out physical punishment or being able to absorb it. Nor was I ashamed that I could do neither. To find Maureen's blood on my hand was in fact *un*manning, as disgraceful as her teeth marks on my wrist. "Go!" I screamed, "Get out of here!" And because she had never seen me in such a state before—I was so unhinged by rage that while she packed her suitcase I stood over her tearing the shirt off my own body—she left, borrowing my spare typewriter, however, so she could write a story about "a heartless infantile son-of-a-bitch so-called artist just like you!"

"Leave that typewriter where it is!" "But what will I write on then?" "Are you kidding? Are you *crazy?* You're going to 'expose' me, and you want me to give you the weapon to do it with?" "But you have *two* of them! Oh, I'm going to tell the world, Peter, I'll tell them just what a selfish, self-important, egomaniacal baby you are!" "Just go, Maureen—and *I'll* tell them! But I won't have any more fucking screaming and arguing and *biting* around here when I am trying to do my work!" "Oh fuck your high and mighty work! What about *my life!"* "Fuck your life, it's not my affair any longer! Get out of here! Oh, take it—take it and just go!" Maybe she thought (now that my shirt was hanging off me in strips) that I might start in next tearing *her* to shreds—for all at once she backed off and was out of the apartment, taking with her, to be sure, the old gray Remington Royal portable that had been my parents' bar mitzvah present to the hotshot assistant sports editor of the *Yonkers High Broadcaster.*

Three days later she was back at the door, in blue duffel coat and knee socks, wan and scrappy-looking as a street urchin. Because she could not face her top-floor room on Carmine Street alone, she had spent the three days with friends of hers, a Village couple in their early fifties whom I couldn't stand, who in turn considered me and my narratives "square." The husband (advertised by Maureen as "an old friend of Kenneth Patchen's") had been Maureen's teacher when she first came to New York and went into wood sculpture. Months back she had declared that she had been badly misled by these two "schizorenos," but never explained how.

As was her way the morning after even the most horrendous scenes, she laughed off the violent encounter of three days earlier, asking me (in wonderment at my naiveté) how I could take seriously anything she may have said or done in anger. One aspect of my squareness (according to those who worked in wood) was that I had no more tolerance for the irregular or the eccentric than George F. Babbitt of Zenith, Middle America. I was not open to experience in my basement apartment on East Ninth the way those middle-aged beatniks were in their Bleecker Street loft. I was a nice Jewish boy from Westchester who cared only about Success. I was their Dina Dornbusch.

"Lucky I am," I told her, "otherwise you'd be at the bottom of the East River." She was sitting in a chair, still in her duffel coat; I had given no sign that I had any intention of allowing her to move back in. When she had gone to peck me on the cheek in the doorway, I had—again, to her amusement—pulled my head away. "Where's the typewriter?" I asked, my way of saying that as far as I was concerned the only excuse Maureen could have to be visiting me was to return what she had borrowed. "You middle-class monster!" she cried. "You throw me out into the street. I have to go sleep on somebody's floor with sixteen cats lapping my face all night long—and all you can think about is your portable typewriter! Your *things.* It's a thing, Peter, *a thing*—and I'm a human being!" "You could have slept at your own place, Maureen." "I was *lonely.* You don't understand that because you have ice in your heart instead of feelings. And my own place isn't a 'place,' as you so blithely put it—it's a shithole of an attic and you know it! *You* wouldn't sleep there for half an hour." "Where's the typewriter?" "The typewriter is a *thing,* damn it, an inanimate object! What about *me?"* and leaping from the chair, she charged, swinging her pocketbook like a shillelagh. "CLIP ME WITH THAT, MAUREEN, AND I'LL KILL YOU!" "Do it!" was her reply. "Kill me! Some man's going to—why not a 'civilized' one like you! Why not a follower of Flaubert!" Here she collapsed against me, and with her arms around my neck, began to sob. "Oh, Peter, I don't have anything. Nothing at all. I'm really lost, baby. I didn't want to go to them—I *had* to. Please, don't make me go away again right now. I haven't even had a shower in three days. Let me just take a shower. Let me just calm down—and this time I'll go forever, I promise." She then explained that the loft on Bleecker Street had been burglarized one night when all except the cats were out eating spaghetti on Fourteenth Street; my typewriter had been stolen, along with all of her friends' wood-carving tools, their recorders, and their Blatstein, which sounded to me like an automatic rifle but was a painting.

I didn't believe a word of it. She went off to the bathroom, and when I heard the shower running, I put my hand into the pocket of her duffel coat and after just a little fishing around in the crumpled Kleenex and the small change came up with a pawn ticket. If I hadn't been living half a block from the Bowery, I don't imagine it would have occurred to me that Maureen had taken the typewriter up the street for the cash. But I was learning —though not quite fast enough.

Now, an even worldlier fellow than myself—George F. Babbitt, say, of Zenith—would have remembered the old business adage, "Cut your losses," and after finding the pawn ticket, would have dropped it back into her pocket and said nothing. Shower her, humor her, and get her the hell out, George F. Babbitt would have said to himself, and peace and quiet will reign once again. Instead I rushed into the bathroom—no Babbitt I—where we screamed at each other with such ferocity that the young married couple upstairs, whose life we made a misery during these months (the husband, an editor at a publishing house, cuts me to this day), began to pound on the floor above with a broom handle. "You petty little thief! You *crook!*" "But I did it for you!" "For me? You pawned my typewriter for *me?*" "Yes!" "What are you *talking* about?" Here, with the water still beating down on her, she slumped to the bottom of the bathtub, and sitting on her haunches, began actually to keen in her woe. Unclothed, she would sometimes make me think of an alley cat —quick, wary, at once scrawny and strong; now, as she rocked and moaned with grief under the full blast of the shower, something about the weight and pointiness of her large conical breasts, and her dark hair plastered to her head, made her look to me like some woman out of the bush, a primitive whose picture you might come upon in *National Geographic,* praying to the sun-god to roll back the waters. "Because—" she howled, "because I'm pregnant. Because—because I wasn't going to tell you. Because I was going to get the money however I could and get an abortion and never bother you again. Peter, I've been shoplifting too." "Stealing? Where?" "Altman's—a little from Klein's. I *had* to!" "But you *can't* be pregnant, Maureen—*we haven't slept together for weeks!*" "BUT I AM! TWO MONTHS PREGNANT!" "Two months?" "Yes! And I never said a word, because I didn't want to interfere with your ART!" "Well, you should have, goddam it, because I would have given you the money to go out and get an abortion!" "Oh, you are so generous—! But it's too late—I've taken enough from men like you in my life! You're going to marry me or I'm going to kill myself! And I will do it!" she cried, hammering defiantly on the rim of the tub with her two little fists. "This is no empty threat, Peter—I cannot take you people any more! You selfish, spoiled, immature, irresponsible Ivy League bastards, born with those spoons in your mouths!" The silver spoon was somewhat hyperbolic, and even she knew that much, but she was hysterical, and in hysteria, as she eventually made clear to me, anything goes. "With your big fat advance and your high Art—oh, you make me sick the way you hide from life behind that *Art* of yours! I hate you and I hate that fucking Flaubert, and you are going to marry me, Peter, because I have had enough! I'm not going to be another man's helpless victim! You are not going to dump me the way you dumped that girl!"

"That girl" was how she referred to Dina, toward whom she had never until that moment been anything but dismissive; now, all at once, she invoked in her own behalf not just Dina, but Grete *and* the Pembroke undergraduate who had been my girl friend during my senior year at Brown. All of them shared with Maureen the experience of being "discarded" when I had finished having my "way" with them. "But we are not leftovers, Peter; we're not trash or scum and we will not be treated that way! We are human beings, and we will not be thrown into a garbage pail by *you!*" "You're not pregnant, Maureen, and you know damn well you're not. That's what all this 'we' business is about," I said, suddenly, with perfect confidence. And with that, she all but collapsed—"We're not *talking* about me right now," she said, "we're talking about *you.* Don't you know *yet* why you got rid of your Pembroke pal? Or your German girl friend? Or that girl who had everything? Or why you're getting rid of me?" I said, "You're not pregnant, Maureen. That is a lie." "It is not—and listen to me! Do you have no idea at all why it is you are so afraid of marriage and children and a family and treat women the way that you do? Do you know what you really are, Peter, aside from being a heartless, selfish writing machine?" I said, "A fag." "That's right! And making light of it doesn't make it any less true!" "I would think it makes it more true." "It does! You are the most transparent latent homosexual I have ever run across in my life! Just like big brave Mezik who forced me to blow his buddy —*so that he could watch.* Because it's really what he wanted to do himself—but he didn't even have the guts for that!" *"Forced* you? Oh, come on, pal, you've got pointy teeth in that mouth of yours—I've felt your fangs. Why didn't you bite it off and teach them both a lesson, if you were being *forced* to?" "I should have! Don't you think I didn't think of it! Don't you think a woman doesn't think of it every time! And don't you worry, mister, if they weren't twelve inches taller than me, I would have bitten the thing off at the root! And spit on the bleeding stump—just like I spit on you, you high and mighty Artist, for throwing me two months pregnant out into the street!" But she was weeping so, that the spittle meant for me just rolled down her lips onto her chin.

She slept in the bed that night (first bed in three days, I was reminded) and I sat at my desk in the living room, thinking about running away—not because she continued to insist she had missed two periods in a row, but because she was so tenaciously hanging on to what I was certain was a lie. I could leave right then for any number of places. I had friends up in Providence, a young faculty couple who'd gladly put me up for a while. I had an army buddy in Boston, graduate-school colleagues still out in

Chicago, there was my sister Joan in California. And of course brother Morris uptown, if I should require spiritual comfort and physical refuge near at hand. He would take me in for as long as was necessary, no questions asked. Since I'd settled in New York, I had been getting phone calls from Moe every couple of weeks checking to see if there was anything I needed and reminding me to come to dinner whenever I was in the mood. At his invitation I had even taken Maureen up to their apartment one Sunday morning for bagels and the smoked fish spread. To my surprise, she had appeared rather cowed by my brother's bearish manner (Moe is a great one to cross-examine strangers), and the general intensity of the family life seemed to make her morose; she did not have much to say after we left, except that Moe and I were very different people. I agreed; Moe was very much the public man (the university, the UN commissions, political meetings and organizations ever since high school) and very much the paterfamilias . . . She said, "I meant he's a brute." "A what?" "The way he treats that wife of his. It's unspeakable." "He's nuts about her, for Christ's sake." "Oh? Is that why he walks all over her? What a little sparrow *she* is! Has she ever had an idea of her own in her life? She just sits there, eating his crumbs. And that's her life." "Oh, that's not her life, Maureen." "Sorry, I don't like him—or her."

Moe didn't like Maureen either, but at the outset said nothing, assuming it was my affair not his, and that she was just the girl of the moment. As I had assumed myself. But when combat between Maureen and me stepped up dramatically, and I apparently began to look and sound as confused and embattled as I'd become, Moe tried on a couple of occasions to give me some brotherly advice; each time I shook him off. As I still couldn't imagine any long-range calamity befalling me, I objected strenuously to being "babied," as I thought of it—particularly by someone whose life, though admirable, was *grounded* in ways I was just too young to be concerned about. As I saw it, it was essential for me to be able to confront whatever troubles I'd made for myself without his, or anyone else's, assistance. In brief, I was as arrogant (and blind) as youth and luck and an aristocratic literary bent could make me, and so, when he invited me up to Columbia for lunch I told him, "I'll work it all out, don't worry." "But why should it be 'work'? Your *work* is your work, not this little Indian." "I take it that's some kind of euphemism. For the record, the mother's family was Irish, the father's German." "Yeah? She looks a little Apache to me, with those eyes and that hair. There's something savage there, Peppy. No? All right, don't answer. Sneer now, pay later. You weren't brought up for savagery, kid." "I know. Nice boy. Jewish." "What's so bad about that? You are a nice civilized Jewish boy, with some talent and some brains. How much remains to be seen. Why don't you attend to that and leave the lions to Hemingway." "What is that supposed to mean, Moey?" "You. You look like you've been sleeping in the jungle." "Nope. Just down on Ninth Street." "I thought girls were for fun, Pep. Not to scare the shit out of you." I was offended both by his low-mindedness and his meddling and refused to talk further about it. Afterward I looked in the mirror for the signs of fear—or doom. I saw nothing: still looked like Tarnopol the Triumphant to me.

The morning after Maureen had announced herself pregnant, I told her to take a specimen of urine to the pharmacy on Second and Ninth; that way, said I without hiding my skepticism, we could shortly learn just how pregnant she was. "In other words, you don't believe me. You want to close your eyes to the whole thing!" "Just take the urine and shut up." So she did as she was told: took a specimen of urine to the drugstore for the pregnancy test—only it wasn't her urine. I did not find this out until three years later, when she confessed to me (in the midst of a suicide attempt) that she had gone from my apartment to the drugstore by way of Tompkins Square Park, lately the hippie center of the East Village, but back in the fifties still a place for the neighborhood poor to congregate and take the sun. There she approached a pregnant Negro woman pushing a baby carriage and told her she represented a scientific organization willing to pay the woman for a sample of her urine. Negotiations ensued. Agreement reached, they retired to the hallway of a tenement building on Avenue B to complete the transaction. The pregnant woman pulled her underpants down to her knees, and squatting in a corner of the unsavory hallway—still heaped with rubbish (just as Maureen had described it) when I paid an unsentimental visit to the scene of the crime upon my return to New York only a few years later—delivered forth into Maureen's preserve jar the stream that sealed my fate. Here Maureen forked over two dollars and twenty-five cents. She drove a hard bargain, my wife.

During the four days that we had to wait—according to Maureen—for the result of the pregnancy test, she lay on my bed recalling scenes and conversations out of her wasted past: delirious (or feigning delirium—or both), she quarreled once again with Mezik, screamed her hatred at Mezik's buddy from the upholstery factory, and choked and wept with despair to discover Walker in their bathroom in Cambridge, dressed in her underwear, his own white sweat socks stuffed into the cups of the brassiere. She would not eat; she would not converse; she refused to let me telephone the psychiatrist who had once tried treating her for a couple of months; when I called her friends over on Bleecker Street, she refused to talk to them. I went ahead anyway and suggested to them that they might want to come over and see her—maybe they at least could get her to eat something—whereupon the wife grabbed the phone away from the husband and said, "We don't want to see that one again *ever,*" and hung up. So, all was not well with the "schizorenos" on Bleecker Street either, after Maureen's brief visit . . . And I was afraid now to leave the apartment for fear that she would try to kill herself when I was gone. I had never lived through three such days before in my life, though I was to know a hundred more just as grim and frightening in the years to come.

The night before we were to learn the test results, Maureen abruptly stopped "hallucinating" and got up from bed to wash her face and drink some orange juice. At first she wouldn't speak directly to me, but for an hour sat perfectly still, calm and controlled, in a chair in the living room, wrapped in my bathrobe. Finally I told her that as she was up and around, I was going out to take a walk around the block. "Don't try anything," I said, "I'm just going to get some air." Her tone, in response, was mild and sardonic. "Air? Oh, where, I wonder?" "I'm taking a walk around the block." "You're about to leave me, Peter, I know that. Just the way you've left every girl you've ever known. Find 'em-fuck 'em-and-forget 'em Flaubert." "I'll be right back." When I unlatched the door to go out, she said, as though addressing a judge from the witness stand—prophetic bitch!—"And I never saw him again, Your Honor."

I went around to the drugstore and asked the pharmacist if by any chance the result of Mrs. Tarnopol's pregnancy test—so Maureen had identified herself, just a bit prematurely—due back tomorrow might have come in that night. He told me the result had come in that morning. Maureen had gotten it wrong—we hadn't to wait four days, only three. Was the error inadvertent? Just one of her "mistakes"? ("So I make mistakes!" she'd cry. "I'm not perfect, damn it! Why must everybody in this world be a perfect robot—a compulsive little middle-class success machine, like you! Some of us are *human.*") But if not a mistake, if intentional, why? Out of habit? An addiction to falsification? Or was this *her* art of action, "creativity" gone awry . . . ?

Harder to fathom was the result. How could Maureen be pregnant for two whole months and manage to keep it from me? It made no sense. Such restraint was beyond her—represented everything she was *not.* Why would she have let me throw her out that first time without striking back with this secret? It made no sense. *It could not be.*

Only it was. Two months pregnant, by me.

Only *how?* I could not even remember the last time we two had had intercourse. Yet she was pregnant, *somehow,* and if I didn't marry her, she would take her life rather than endure the humiliation of an abortion or an adoption or of abandoning a fatherless child. It went without saying that she, who could not hold a job for more than six months, was incapable of raising a child on her own. And it went without saying—to me, to me—that the father of this fatherless child-to-be was Peter Tarnopol. Never once did it occur to me that if indeed she were pregnant, someone other than I might have done it. Yes, I already knew what a liar she was, yet surely not so thoroughgoing as to want to deceive me about something as serious as fatherhood. *That* I couldn't believe. This woman was not a character out of a play by Strindberg or a novel by Hardy, but someone with whom I'd been living on the Lower East Side of Manhattan, sixty minutes by subway and bus from Yonkers, where I'd been born.

Now, unduly credulous as I may have been, I still needn't have married her; had I been so independent, so manly, so "up" to travail as I aspired to be in my middle twenties, she would never have become my wife, even if a laboratory test had "scientifically" proved that she was with child and even if I had been willing to accept on faith that mine was the penis responsible. I could still have said this: "You want to kill yourself, that's your business. You don't want an abortion, also up to you. But I'm not getting married to you, Maureen, under any circumstances. Marrying you would be insane."

But instead of going home to tell her just that, I walked from Ninth Street all the way up to Columbia and back, concluding on upper Broadway—only two blocks from Morris's building—that the truly manly way to face up to my predicament was to go back to the apartment, pretending that I still did not know the result of the pregnancy test, and deliver the following oration: "Maureen, what's been going on here for three days makes no sense. I don't care if you're pregnant or not. I want you to marry me, regardless of how the test comes out tomorrow. I want you to be my wife." You see, I just couldn't believe, given her behavior during the past three days, that she was bluffing about doing herself in; I was sure that if I walked out on her for good, she would kill herself. And that was unthinkable—I could not be the cause of another's death. Such a suicide was murder. So I would marry her instead. And, further, I would do my best to make it appear that in marrying her I had acted out of choice rather than necessity, for if our union were to be anything other than a nightmare of recrimination and resentment, it would have to appear to Maureen—and even, in a way, to me—that I had married her because I had decided that I wanted to, rather than because I had been blackmailed, or threatened, or terrorized into it.

But why ever would I want to? The whole thing made no sense—especially as we had not copulated in God only knew how long! And I never wanted to again! I hated her.

Yes, it was indeed one of those grim and unyielding predicaments such as I had read about in fiction, such as Thomas Mann might have had in mind when he wrote in an autobiographical sketch the sentence that I had already chosen as one of the two portentous epigraphs for *A Jewish Father:* "All actuality is deadly earnest, and it is morality itself that, one with life, forbids us to be true to the guileless unrealism of our youth."

It seemed then that I was making one of those moral decisions that I had heard so much about in college literature courses. But how different it all had been up in the Ivy League, when it was happening to Lord Jim and Kate Croy and Ivan Karamazov instead of to me. Oh, what an authority on dilemmas I had been in the senior honors seminar! Perhaps if I had not fallen so in love with these complicated fictions of moral anguish, I never would have taken that long anguished walk to the Upper West Side and back, and arrived at what seemed to me the only "honorable" decision for a young man as morally "serious" as myself. But then I do not mean to attribute my ignorance to my teachers, or my delusions to books. Teachers and books are still the best things that ever happened to me, and probably had I not been so grandiose about my honor, my integrity, and my manly duty, about "morality itself," I would never have been so susceptible to a literary education and its attendant pleasures to begin with. Nor would I have embarked upon a literary career. And it's too late now to say that I shouldn't have, that by becoming a writer I only exacerbated my debilitating obsession. Literature got me into this and literature is gonna have to get me out. My writing is all I've got now, and though it happens not to have made life easy for me either in the years since my auspicious debut, it is really all I trust.

My trouble in my middle twenties was that rich with confidence and success, I was not about to settle for complexity and depth in books alone. Stuffed to the gills with great fiction—entranced not by cheap romances, like Madame Bovary, but by *Madame Bovary*—I now expected to find in everyday experience that same sense of the difficult and the deadly earnest that informed the novels I admired most. My model of reality, deduced from reading the masters, had at its heart *intractability.* And here it was, a reality as obdurate and recalcitrant and (in addition) as awful as any I could have wished for in my most bookish dreams. You might even say that the ordeal that my daily life was shortly to become was only Dame Fortune smiling down on "the golden boy of American literature" (*New York Times Book Review,* September 1959) and dishing out to her precocious favorite whatever literary sensibility required. Want complexity? Difficulty? Intractability? Want the deadly earnest? Yours!

Of course what I also wanted was that my intractable existence should take place at an appropriately lofty moral altitude, an elevation somewhere, say, between *The Brothers Karamazov* and *The Wings of the Dove.* But then not even the golden can expect to have everything: instead of the intractability of serious fiction, I got the intractability of soap opera. Resistant enough, but the wrong genre. Though maybe not, given the leading characters in the drama, of which Maureen, I admit, was only one.

I returned to Ninth Street a little after eleven; I had been gone nearly three hours. Maureen, to my surprise, was now completely dressed and sitting at my desk in her duffel coat.

"You didn't do it," she said, and lowering her face to the desk, began to cry.

"Where were you going, Maureen?" Probably back to her room; *I* assumed to the East River, to jump in.

"I thought you were on a plane to Frankfurt."

"What were you going to do, Maureen?"

"What's the difference . . ."

"Maureen! Look up at me."

"Oh, what's the difference any more, Peter. Go, go back to that Long Island girl, with her pleated skirts and her cashmere sweaters."

"Maureen, listen to me: I want to marry you. I don't care whether you're pregnant or not. I don't care what the test says tomorrow. I want to marry you." I sounded to myself about as convincing as the romantic lead in a high-school play. I think it may have been in that moment that my face became the piece of stone I was to carry around on my neck for years thereafter. "Let's get married," I said, as if saying it yet again, another way, would fool anyone about my real feelings.

Yet it fooled Maureen. I could have proposed in Pig Latin and fooled Maureen. She could of course carry on in the most bizarre and unpredictable ways, but in all those years of surprises, I would never be so stunned by her wildest demonstration of rage, her most reckless public ravings, as I was by the statement with which she greeted this proposal so obviously delivered without heart or hope.

She erupted, "Oh, darling, we'll be happy as kings!"

That was the word—"kings," plural—uttered wholly ingenuously. I don't think she was lying this time. She believed that to be so. We would be happy as kings. Maureen Johnson and Peter Tarnopol.

She threw her arms around me, as happy as I had ever seen her —and for the first time I realized that she *was* truly mad. I had just proposed marriage to a madwoman. In deadly earnest.

"Oh, I always knew it," she said joyously.

"Knew what?"

"That you loved me. That you couldn't hold out forever against that kind of love. Not even you."

She was crazy.

And what did that make of me? A "man"? *How?*

She went on and on about the paradise that lay before us. We could move to the country and save money by growing our own vegetables. Or continue to live in the city where she could become my agent (I had an agent, but no matter). Or she could just stay home and bake bread and type my manuscripts (I typed my own, but no matter) and get back to her wood sculpture.

"You'll have to stay at home anyway," I said. "The baby."

"Oh, lovey," she said. "I'll do it—for you. Because you *do* love me. You see, that's all I had to find out—that you loved me. That you weren't Mezik, that you weren't Walker. *That I could trust you.* Don't you understand? Now that I know, I'll do anything."

"Meaning?"

"Peter, stop being suspicious—you don't *have* to be any more. I'll have an abortion. If the test comes back tomorrow saying that I'm pregnant—and it will, I've never missed two periods before in my life, never—but don't worry, I'll go off and get an abortion. Whatever you want, I'll do it. I know of a doctor. In Coney Island. And I'll go to him, if you want me to."

I wanted her to, all right. I'd wanted her to right at the outset, and had she agreed then, I would never have made my "manly" proposal of marriage. But better now than not at all. And so the next day, after I phoned the drugstore and pretended to be hearing for the first time the lab report verifying Mrs. Tarnopol's pregnancy, I went to the bank and withdrew ten weeks' worth of advance and another twenty dollars for the round-trip taxi fare to Coney Island. And on Saturday morning, I put Maureen in a taxi and she went off to Coney Island by herself, which she said was the only way the abortionist would receive his patients. I stood out on Second Avenue watching the cab move south, and I thought: "Now get out. Take a plane to anywhere, but go while the going is good." But I didn't, because that isn't what a man like myself did. Or so I "reasoned."

Besides, in bed the night before, Maureen had wept in fearful anticipation of the illegal operation (had she had the abortion, it would actually have been her third, I eventually found out) and clinging to me, she begged, "You won't desert, me, will you? You'll be here when I get home—won't you? Because I couldn't take it if you weren't . . ." "I'll be here," said I, manfully.

And there I was when she returned at four that afternoon, my fond lover, pale and wan (the strain of sitting six hours at the movies), wearing a Kotex between her legs to absorb the blood (said she), and still in pain from the abortion she had undergone (said she) without an anesthetic. She went immediately to bed to ward off the hemorrhage that she feared was coming on, and there she lay, on into the night, teeth chattering, limbs trembling, in an old, washed-out sweatshirt of mine and a pair of my pajamas. I piled blankets on top of her, but that still didn't stop her shaking. "He just stuck his knife up there," she said, "and wouldn't give me anything for the pain but a tennis ball to squeeze. He promised he would put me out, on the phone he promised me, and then when I was on the table and said, 'Where's the anesthetic?', he said, 'What do you think, girlie, I'm out of my mind?' I said, 'But you promised. How else can I possibly stand the pain?' And you know what he told me, that smelly old bastard? 'Look, you want to get up and go, fine with me. You want me to get rid of the baby, then squeeze the magic ball and shut up. You had your fun, now you're going to have to pay.' So I stayed, I stayed and I squeezed down on the ball, and I tried to think just about you and me, but it hurt, oh, he hurt me so much."

A horrifying tale of humiliation and suffering at the hands of yet another member of my sex, and a lie from beginning to end. Only it took me a while to find out. In actuality, she had pocketed the three hundred dollars (against the day I would leave her penniless) and after disembarking from the cab when it got to Houston Street, had gone back up to Times Square by subway to see Susan Hayward in *I Want to Live,* saw it three times over, the morbid melodrama of a cocktail waitress (if I remember correctly—I had already taken her to see it once myself) who gets the death penalty in California for a crime she didn't commit: right up Maureen's alley, that exemplary little tale. Then she'd donned a Kotex in the washroom and had come on home, weak in the knees and white around the gills. As who wouldn't be, after a day in a Times Square movie house?

All this she confessed three years later in Wisconsin.

The next morning I went alone to a booth—Maureen charging, as I left the apartment, that I was running away, leaving her bleeding and in pain while I disappeared forever with "that girl" —and telephoned my parents to tell them I was getting married.

"Why?" my father demanded to know.

"Because I want to." I was not about to tell my father, in whom I had not confided anything since I was ten, what I had been through in the past week. I had loved him dearly as a child, but he was only a small-time haberdasher, and I now wrote short stories published in the high-brow magazines and had a publisher's advance on a serious novel dense with moral ambiguity. So which of us could be expected to understand the principle involved? Which was what again? Something to do with my duty, my courage, my word.

"Peppy," my mother said, after having received the news in silence, "Peppy, I'm sorry, but I have to say it—there's something wrong with that woman. Isn't there?"

"She's over thirty years old," said my father.

"She's twenty-nine."

"And you're just twenty-six, you're a babe in the woods. Son, she's kicked around too long for my money. Your mother is right —something ain't right there with her."

My parents had met my intended just once, in my apartment; on the way home from a Wednesday matinee, they had stopped off to say hello, and there was Maureen, on my sofa, reading the script of a TV serial in which someone had "promised" her a part. Ten minutes of amiable, if self-conscious talk, and then they took the train back home. What they were saying about Maureen I assumed grew out of conversations with Morris and Lenore. I was wrong. Morris had never mentioned Maureen to them. They had figured her out on their own—after only ten minutes.

I tried acting lighthearted; laughing, I said, "She's not the girl across the street, if that's what you mean."

"What does she even do for a living? Anything?"

"She told you. She's an actress."

"Where?"

"She's looking for work."

"Son, listen to me: you're a college graduate. You're a summa cum laude. You had a four-year scholarship. The army is behind you. You've traveled in Europe. The world is before you, *and it's all yours.* You can have anything, *anything*—why are you settling for this? Peter, are you listening?"

"I'm listening."

"Peppy," asked my mother, "do you—love her?"

"Of course I do." And what did I want to shout into the phone at that very moment? *I'm coming home. Take me home. This isn't what I want to do. You're right, there's something wrong with her: the woman is mad. Only I gave my word!*

My father said, "Your voice don't sound right to me."

"Well, I didn't expect this kind of reaction, frankly, when I said I would be getting married."

"We want you to be happy, that's all," said my mother.

"This is going to make you happy, marrying her?" asked my father. "I'm not talking about that she's Gentile. I'm not a narrowminded dope, I never was. I don't live in a dead world. The German girl in Germany was something else, and her I never disliked personally, you know that. But that's water under the bridge."

"I know. I agree."

"I'm talking about happiness now, with another human being."

"Yes, I follow you."

"You don't sound right," he said, his own voice getting huskier with emotion. "You want me to come down to the city? I'll come in a minute—"

"No, don't be silly. Good Christ, no. I know what I'm doing. I'm doing what I want."

"But why so sudden?" my father asked, fishing. "Can you answer me that? I'm sixty-five years old, Peppy, I'm a grown man —you can talk to me, and the truth."

"What's 'sudden' about it? I've known her nearly a year. Please, don't fight me on this."

"Peter," said my mother, teary now, "we don't fight you on anything."

"I know, I know. I appreciate that. So let's not start now. I just called to tell you. A judge is marrying us on Wednesday at City Hall."

My mother's voice was weak now, almost a whisper, when she asked, "You want us to come?" It didn't sound as though she cared to be told yes. What a shock that was!

"No, there's no need for you to be there. It's just a formality. I'll call you afterwards."

"Peppy, are you still on the outs with your brother?"

"I'm not on the outs with him. He lives his life and I live mine."

"Peter, have you spoken to him about this? Peppy, your older brother is a brother boys dream about having. He adores you. Call him, at least."

"Look, it's not a point I want to debate with Moe. He's a great arguer—and I'm not. There's nothing to argue over."

"Maybe he wouldn't argue. Maybe at least he'd like to know, to come to whatever it is—the wedding ceremony."

"He won't want to come."

"And you won't talk to him, only for a few minutes? Or to Joan?"

"What does Joan know about my life? Dad, just let me get married, okay?"

"You make it sound like nothing, like marrying a person for the rest of your life is an everyday affair. It ain't."

"I'm summa cum laude. I know that."

"Don't joke. You left us when you were too young, that's the problem. You always had your way. The apple of your mother's eye—you could have anything. The last of her babies . . ."

"Look, look—"

"You thought you already knew everything at fifteen—remember? We should never have let you skip all those grades and get ahead of yourself—that was our first mistake."

On the edge of tears now, I said, "That may be. But I would have been out of grade school by now anyway. Look, I'm getting married. It'll be all right." And I hung up, before I lost control and told my father to come down and take back to his home his twenty-six-year-old baby boy.

"[illegible] out of your life [illegible] affair," [illegible].

[illegible]

"Don't joke. [illegible] problem. You always had your way. The apple of your mother's eye—you could have anything. The last of her babies."

"Look, [illegible]—"

"You thought you always knew everything [illegible]—remember? We should never have let you skip all those grades and get ahead of yourself—that was your father's idea."

On the edge of tears now, I said, "That may be. But I would have been [illegible] grade-school [illegible] by now [illegible] getting married. I'll be all right." [illegible] and told my father to come down [illegible] the twenty-[illegible]-year-old baby [illegible].

Portrait of the Artist

I first met Dr. Spielvogel the year Maureen and I were married. We had moved out of my Lower East Side basement apartment to a small house in the country near New Milford, Connecticut, not far from where Spielvogel and his family were summering at Candlewood Lake. Maureen was going to grow vegetables and I was going to write the final chapters of *A Jewish Father.* As it turned out, the seeds never got in the ground (or the bread in the oven, or the preserves in the jar), but because there was a twelve-by-twelve shack at the edge of the woods back of the house *with a bolt on the door,* somehow the book got finished. I saw Spielvogel maybe three times that summer at parties given by a New York magazine editor who was living nearby. I don't remember that the doctor and I had much to say to each other. He wore a yachting cap, this New York analyst summering in rural Connecticut, but otherwise he seemed at once dignified and without airs—a tall, quiet, decorous man, growing stout in his middle forties, with a mild German accent and that anomalous yachting cap. I never even noticed which woman was his wife; I discovered later that he had noticed which was mine.

When, in June of '62, it became necessary, according to my brother, for me to remain in New York and turn myself over to a psychiatrist, I came up with Spielvogel's name; friends in Con-

This selection from *My Life as a Man* comprises the bulk of the chapter that follows "Marriage à la Mode."

necticut that summer had spoken well of him, and, if I remembered right, treating "creative" people was supposed to be his specialty. Not that that made much difference to me in the shape I was in. Though I continued to write every day, I had really stopped thinking of myself as capable of creating anything other than misery for myself. I was not a writer any longer, no matter how I filled the daylight hours—I was Maureen's husband, and I could not imagine how I could get to be anything else ever again.

His appearance, like mine, had changed for the worse in three years. While I had been battling with Maureen, Spielvogel had been up against cancer. *He* had survived, though the disease appeared to have shrunk him down some. I remembered him of course in the yachting cap and with a summer tan; in his office, he wore a drab suit bought to fit a man a size larger, and an unexpectedly bold striped shirt whose collar now swam around his neck. His skin was pasty, and the heavy black frames of the glasses he wore tended further to dramatize this shrinkage he had undergone—beneath them, behind them, his head looked like a skull. He also walked now with a slight dip, or list, to the left, the cancer having apparently damaged his hip or leg. In all, the doctor he reminded me of most was Dr. Roger Chillingworth in Hawthorne's *Scarlet Letter.* Appropriate enough, because I sat facing him as full of shameful secrets as the Reverend Arthur Dimmesdale.

Maureen and I had lived a year in western Connecticut, a year at the American Academy in Rome, and a year at the university in Madison, and as a result of all that moving around I had never been able to find anyone in whom I was willing to confide. By the end of three years I had convinced myself that it would be "disloyal," a "betrayal," to tell even the closest friends I had made in our wanderings what went on between Maureen and me in private, though I imagined they could guess plenty from what often took place right out on the street or in other people's houses. Mostly I didn't open up to anyone because I was so ashamed of my defenselessness before her wrath and frightened of what she might do either to herself or to me, or to the person in whom I'd confided, if she ever found out what I had said. Sitting in a chair immediately across from Spielvogel, looking in embarrassment from his shrunken skull to the framed photograph of the Acropolis that was the only picture on his cluttered desk, I realized that I still couldn't do it: indeed, to tell *this* stranger the whole sordid story of my marriage seemed to me as reprehensible as committing a serious crime.

"You remember Maureen?" I asked. "My wife?"

"I do. Quite well." His voice, in contrast to his appearance, was strong and vigorous, causing me to feel even more puny and self-conscious . . . the little stool pigeon about to sing. My impulse was to get up and leave, my shame and humiliation (and my disaster) still my own—and simultaneously to crawl into his lap. "A small, pretty, dark-haired young woman," he said. "Very determined looking."

"Very."

"A lot of spunk there, I would think."

"She's a lunatic, Doctor!" I began to cry. For fully five minutes I sobbed into my hands—until Spielvogel asked, "Are you finished?"

There are lines from my five years of psychoanalysis as memorable to me as the opening sentence of *Anna Karenina*—"Are you finished?" is one of them. The perfect tone, the perfect tactic. I turned myself over to him, then and there, for good or bad.

Yes, yes, I was finished. "All I do these days is collapse in tears . . ." I wiped my face with a Kleenex from a box that he offered me and proceeded to "spill"—though not about Maureen (I couldn't, right off) but about Karen Oakes, the Wisconsin coed with whom I had been maniacally in love during the winter and early spring of that year. I had been watching her bicycle around the campus for months before she showed up in my undergraduate writing section in the second semester to become the smartest girl in the class. Good-natured, gentle, a beguiling mix of assertive innocence and shy adventurousness, Karen had a small lyrical gift as a poet and wrote clever, somewhat magisterial literary analyses of the fiction that we read in class; her candor and lucidity, I told Spielvogel, were as much a balm to me as her mild temperament, her slender limbs, her pretty and composed American girl's face. Oh, I went on and on about Ka-reen (the pet name for the pillow talk), growing increasingly intoxicated, as I spoke, with memories of our ardent "passion" and brimming "love"—I did not mention that in all we probably had not been alone with one another more than forty-eight hours over the course of the three months, and rarely for more than forty-five minutes at a clip; we were together either in the classroom with fifteen undergraduates for chaperones, or in her bed. Nonetheless she was, I said, "the first good thing" to happen in my private life since I'd been discharged from the army and come to New York to write. I told Spielvogel how she had called herself "Miss Demi-Womanhood of 1962"; he did not appear to be one-hundredth as charmed by the remark as I had been, but then he had not just disrobed for the first time the demiwoman who had said it. I recounted to him the agonies of doubt and longing that I had experienced before I went ahead, three weeks into the semester, and wrote "See me" across the face of one of her A+ papers. She came, as directed, to my office, and accepted my courtly, professorial invitation to be seated. In the first moments, courtliness was rampant, as a matter of fact. "You wanted to see me?" "Yes, I did, Miss Oakes." A silence ensued, long and opaquely eloquent enough to satisfy Anton Chekhov. "Where do you come from, Miss Oakes?" "Racine." "And what does your father do?" "He's a physician." And then, as though hurling myself off a bridge, I did it: reached forward and laid a hand upon her straw-colored hair. Miss Oakes swallowed and said nothing. "I'm sorry," I told her, "I couldn't help it." She said: "Professor Tarnopol, I'm not a sophisticated person." Whereupon I proceeded to apologize profusely. "Oh, please, don't worry," she said, when I wouldn't stop, "a lot of teachers do it." "Do they?" the award-winning novelist asked. "Every semester so far," said she, nodding a little wearily; "and usually it's English." "What happens then, usually?" "I tell them I'm not a sophisticated person. Because I'm not." "And then?" "That's it, generally." "They get conscience-stricken and apologize profusely." "They have second thoughts, I suppose." "Just like me." "And me," she said, without blinking; "the doctrine of *in loco parentis* works both ways." "Look, look —" "Yes?" "Look, I'm *taken* with you. Terribly." "You don't even know me, Professor Tarnopol." "I don't and I do. I've read your papers. I've read your stories and poems." "I've read yours." Oh my God, Dr. Spielvogel, how can you sit there like an Indian? Don't you appreciate the *charm* of all this? Can't you see what a conversation like that meant to me in my despair? "Look, Miss Oakes, I want to see you—I *have* to see you!" "Okay." *"Where?"* "I have a room—" "I can't go into a dormitory, you know that." "I'm a senior. I don't live in the dorm any more. I moved out." "You did?" "I have my own room in town." "Can I come to talk to you there?" "Sure."

Sure! Oh, what a wonderful, charming, disarming, engaging little word that one is! I went around sibilating it to myself all through the rest of the day. "What are you so bouncy about?" asked Maureen. *Shoor. Shewer. Shur.* Now just how did that beautiful and clever and willing and healthy young girl say it anyway? *Sure!* Yes, like that—crisp and to the point. *Sure!* Oh yes, sure as sure is sure, Miss Oakes is going to have an adventure, and Professor Tarnopol is going to have a breakdown . . . How many hours before I decided that when the semester was over we would run off together? Not that many. The second time we were in bed I proposed the idea to Ka-reen. We would go to Italy in June—catch the Pan Am flight from Chicago (I'd checked on it by phone) the evening of the day she'd taken her last exam; I could send my final grades in from Rome. Wouldn't that be terrific? Oh, I would say to her, burying my face in her hair, I want to take you somewhere, Ka-reen, I want to go away with you! And she would murmur softly, "Mmmmmm, mmmmmm," which I interpreted as delicious acquiescence. I told her about all the lovely Italian piazzas in which Maureen and I had screamed bloody murder at one another: the Piazza San Marco in Venice, the Piazza della Signoria in Florence, the Piazza del Campo in Siena . . . Karen went home for spring vacation and never came back. That's how overbearing and frightening a character I had become. That murmuring was just the sound her good mind gave off as it gauged the dreadful consequences of having chosen this particular member of the conscience-stricken English faculty to begin sophisticated life with outside of a college dorm. It was one thing reading Tolstoy in class, another playing Anna and Vronsky with the professor.

After she failed to return from spring recess, I made desperate phone calls to Racine practically daily. When I call at lunchtime I am told she is "out." I refuse to believe it—where does she eat then? "Who is this, please?" I am asked. I mumble, "A friend from school . . . are you *sure* she isn't . . . ?" "Would you care to leave your name?" "No." After dinner each night I last about ten minutes in the living room with Maureen before I begin to feel myself on the brink of cracking up; rising from my reading chair, I throw down my pencil and my book—as though I am Rudolph Hess, twenty years in Spandau Prison, I cry, "I have to take a walk! I have to see some faces! I'm suffocating in here!" Once out the door, I break into a sprint, and crossing back lawns and leaping low garden fences, I head for the dormitory nearest our apartment, where there is a telephone booth on the first floor. I will catch Karen at the dinner hour and beg her at least to come back to school for the rest of this semester, even if she will not run away in June to live in Trastevere with me. She says, "Hang on a sec—let me take it on another phone." A few moments later I hear her call, "Will you hang up the downstairs phone, please, Mom?" "Karen! Karen!" "Yes, I'm back." "Kareen, I can't bear it—I'll meet you somewhere in Racine! I'll hitch! I can be there by nine-thirty!" But she *was* the smartest girl in my class and had no intention of letting some overwrought creative writing teacher with a bad marriage and a stalled career ruin her life. She could not save me from my wife, she said, I would have to do that myself. She had told her family she had had an unhappy love affair, but, she assured me, she had not and would not tell them with whom. "But what about your degree?" I demanded, as though I were the dean of students. "That's not important right now," said Karen, speaking as calmly from her bedroom in Racine as she did in class. "But I love you! I want you!" I shouted at the slender girl who only the week before had bicycled in sneakers and a poplin skirt to English 312, her straw-colored hair in braids and her innards still awash with semen from our lunchtime assignation in her rented room. "You just can't leave, Karen! Not now! Not after how marvelous it's been!" "But I can't save you, Peter. I'm only twenty years old." In tears I cried, "I'm only twenty-nine!" "Peter, I should never have started up. I had no idea what was at stake. That's my fault. Forgive me. I'm as sorry as I can be." "Christ, don't be 'sorry'—*just come back!*" One night Maureen followed me out of the house and across the backyards to the dormitory, and after standing out of sight for a minute with her ear to the telephone booth, threw back the door while I was pleading with Karen yet again to change her mind and come with me to Europe on the Pan Am night flight from O'Hare. "Liar!" screamed Maureen, "whoremongering liar!" and ran back to the apartment to swallow a small handful of sleeping pills. Then, on hands and knees, she crawled into the living room in her underwear and knelt there on the floor with my Gillette razor in her hand, waiting patiently for me to finish talking with my undergraduate harlot and come on home so that she could get on with the job of almost killing herself.

I told Spielvogel what Maureen had confessed to me from the living-room floor. Because this had happened only two months earlier, I found with Spielvogel, as I had that morning with Moe in the taxi back from the airport, that I could not recount the story of the false urine specimen without becoming woozy and weak, as though once the story surfaced in my mind, it was only a matter of seconds before the fires of rage had raced through me, devouring all vitality and strength. It is not that easy for me to tell it today without at least a touch of vertigo. And I have never been able to introduce the story into a work of fiction, not that I haven't repeatedly tried and failed in the five years since I received Maureen's confession. I cannot seem to make it credible—probably because I still don't entirely believe it myself. How could she? To me! No matter how I may contrive to transform low actuality into high art, that is invariably what is emblazoned across the face of the narrative, in blood: HOW COULD SHE? TO ME!

"And then," I told Spielvogel, "do you know what she said next? She was on the floor with the blade of the razor right on her wrist. In her panties and bra. And I was just standing over her. Dumbstruck. *Dumbstruck.* I could have kicked her head in. I should have!"

"And what did she say?"

"Say? She said, 'If you forgive me for the urine, I'll forgive you for your mistress. I'll forgive you for deceiving me with that girl on the bicycle and begging her to run away with you to Rome.' "

"And what did you do?" asked Spielvogel.

"Did I kick her, you mean? No. No, no, no, no, no. I didn't do anything—to her. Just stood there for a while. I couldn't right off get over the *ingenuity* of it. The *relentlessness.* That she had thought of such a thing *and then gone ahead and done it.* I actually felt *admiration.* And pity, *pity!* That's true. I thought, 'Good Christ, what *are* you? To do this thing, *and then to keep it a secret for three years!'* And then I saw my chance to get out. As though it required this, you see, nothing less, for me to feel free to go. Not that I went. Oh, I *told* her I was going, all right. I said, I'm leaving, Maureen, I can't live any more with somebody who would do such a thing, and so on. But she was crying by then and she said, 'Leave me and I'll cut my wrists. I'm full of sleeping pills already.' And I said, and this is true, I said, 'Cut them, why should I care?' And so she pressed down with the razor—and blood came out. It turned out that she had only scratched herself, but what the hell did I know? She could have gone through to the bone. I started shouting, 'Don't—don't do that!' and I began wrestling with her for the razor. I was terrified that I was going to get my own veins slashed in the rolling around, but I kept trying to get it away, grabbing at the damn thing—and I was crying. That goes without saying. All I do now is cry, you know—and she was crying, of course, and finally I got the thing away from her and she said, 'Leave me, and I'll ruin that girl of yours! I'll have that pure little face in every paper in Wisconsin!' And then she began to scream about my 'deceiving' her and how I couldn't be trusted and she always knew it—and this is just three minutes after describing in detail to me buying the urine from that Negro woman on Avenue B!"

"And what did you do then?"

"Did I slit her throat from ear to ear? No. No! I fell apart. Completely. I went into a tantrum. The two of us were smeared with blood—my left palm had been cut, up by the thumb, and her wrist was dripping, and God only knows what we looked like—like a couple of Aztecs, fucking up the sacrificial rites. I mean, it's comical when you think about it. I am the Dagwood Bumstead of fear and trembling!"

"You had a tantrum."

"That's not the *half* of it. I got down on my knees—I *begged* her to let me go. I banged my head on the floor, Doctor. I began running from room to room. Then—then I did what she told me Walker used to do. Maybe Walker never even did it; that was probably a lie too. Anyway, *I* did it. At first I was just running around looking for some place to hide the razor from her. I remember unscrewing the head and dropping the blade into the toilet and flushing and flushing and the damn thing just lying there at the bottom of the bowl. Then I ran into our bedroom—I was screaming all this time, you see, 'Let me go! Let me go!' and sobbing, and so on. And all the while I was tearing my clothes off. I'd done that before, in a rage with her, but this time I actually tore everything off me. And I put on Maureen's underwear. I pulled open her dresser and I put on a pair of her underpants—I could just get them up over my prick. Then I tried to get into one of her brassieres. I put my arms through the shoulder loops, that is. And then I just stood there like that, crying—and bleeding. Finally she came into the room—no, she just got as far as the doorway and stood there, looking at me. And, you see, that's all she was wearing, too, her underwear. She saw me and she broke into sobs again, and she cried, 'Oh, sweetheart, no, no . . .' "

"Is that all she said?" asked Spielvogel. "Just called you 'sweetheart'?"

"No. She said, 'Take that off. I'll never tell anybody. Just take that off right now.' "

"That was two months ago," said Dr. Spielvogel, when it appeared that I had nothing more to say.

"Yes."

"And?"

"It's not been good, Doctor."

"What do you mean?"

"I've done some other strange things."

"Such as?"

"Such as staying with Maureen—that's the strangest thing of all! Three years of it, and now I know what I know, and I'm still living with her! And if I don't fly back tomorrow, she says she's going to tell the world 'everything.' That's what she told my brother to tell me on the phone. And she will. *She will do it.*"

"Any other 'strange things'?"

". . . with my sperm."

"I didn't hear you. Your sperm? What about your sperm?"

"My semen—I leave it places."

"Yes?"

"I smear it places. I go to people's houses and I leave it—places."

"You break into people's houses?"

"No, no," I said sharply—what did he think I was, a madman? "I'm invited. I go to the bathroom. I leave it somewhere . . . on the tap. In the soap dish. Just a few drops . . ."

"You masturbate in their bathrooms."

"Sometimes, yes. And leave . . ."

"Your signature."

"Tarnopol's silver bullet."

He smiled at my joke; I did not. I had still more to tell. "I've done it in the university library. Smeared it on the bindings of books."

"Of books? Which books?"

"Books! Any books! Whatever books are handy!"

"Anywhere else?"

I sighed.

"Speak up, please," said the doctor.

"I sealed an envelope with it," I said in a loud voice. "My bill to the telephone company."

Again Spielvogel smiled. "Now that is an original touch, Mr. Tarnopol."

And again I broke into sobs. "What does it mean!"

"Come now," said Dr. Spielvogel, "what do you think it 'means'? You don't require a soothsayer, as far as I can see."

"That I'm completely out of control!" I said, sobbing. "That I don't know what I'm doing any more!"

"That you're angry," he said, slapping the arm of his chair. "That you are furious. You are not *out* of control—you are *under* control. Maureen's control. You spurt the anger everywhere, except where it belongs. There you spurt tears."

"But she'll ruin Karen! She will! She knows who she is—she

used to check out my students like a hawk! She'll destroy that lovely innocent girl!"

"Karen sounds as if she can take care of herself."

"But you don't know Maureen once she gets going. She could *murder* somebody. She used to grab the wheel of our VW in Italy and try to run us off the side of a mountain—because I hadn't opened a door for her leaving the hotel in Sorrento! She could carry a grudge like that for days—then she would erupt with it, in the car, weeks later! You can't imagine what it's like when she goes wild!"

"Well, then, Karen should be properly warned, if that is the case."

"It *is* the case! It's hair-raising! Grabbing the wheel from my hands and spinning it the other way when we're winding down a mountain road! You must believe what I've been through—I am not exaggerating! To the contrary, I'm leaving things *out!*"

Now, with my avenger dead and her ashes scattered from a plane into the Atlantic Ocean, now with all that rage *stilled,* it seems to me that I simply could not have been so extensively unmanned by Maureen Johnson Mezik Walker Tarnopol, drop-out from Elmira High, as I indicated (and demonstrated) to Spielvogel during our first hour together. I was, after all, bigger than she was, more intelligent than she was, better educated than she was, and far more accomplished. What then (I asked the doctor) had made me such a willing, or will-less, victim? Why couldn't I find the strength, or just the simple survival mechanism, to leave her once it became obvious that it was no longer she who needed rescuing from her disasters, but I from mine? Even after she had confessed to committing the urine fraud, even *then* I couldn't get up and go! Now why? Why should someone who had battled so determinedly all his life to be independent—his own child, his own adolescent, his own man—why should someone with my devotion to "seriousness" and "maturity" knuckle under like a defenseless little boy to this cornball Clytemnestra?

Dr. Spielvogel invited me to look to the nursery for the answer. The question with which he began our second session was, "Does your wife remind you of your mother?"

My heart sank. Psychoanalytic reductivism was not going to

save me from the IRT tracks, or worse, from returning to Wisconsin at the end of the week to resume hostilities with Maureen. In reply to the question I said, no, she did not. My wife reminded me of no one I had ever known before, anywhere. Nobody in my entire lifetime had ever dared to deceive, insult, threaten, or blackmail me the way she did—certainly no woman I had ever known. Nor had anyone ever hollered at me like that, except perhaps the basic training cadre at Fort Dix. I suggested to Spielvogel that it wasn't because she was like my mother that I couldn't deal with her, but, if anything, because she was so *unlike* her. My mother was not aggrieved, contentious, resentful, violent, helpless, or suicidal, and she did not ever want to see me humbled—far from it. Certainly, for our purposes, the most telling difference between the two was that my mother *adored* me, worshipped me across the board, and I had basked in that adoration. Indeed, it was her enormous belief in my perfection that had very likely helped to spawn and nourish whatever gifts I had. I supposed that it could be said that I had knuckled under to my mother when I was still a little boy—but in a little boy that is not knuckling under, is it? That is just common sense and a feel for family life: childhood realpolitik. One does not expect to be treated like a thirty-year-old at five. But at fifteen I certainly did expect deferential treatment of a kind, and from my mother I got it. As I remember it, I could sweet-talk that lady into just about anything during my high-school years, without too much effort get her to agree to the fundamental soundness of my position on just about every issue arising out of my blooming sense of prerogatives; in fact, it was with demonstrable delight (as I recalled it) that she acquiesced to the young prince whom she had been leading all these years toward the throne.

It was the supernumerary father I'd had to struggle with back then. He was anxious for me in my ambitiousness and cockiness. He had seen less of me as a child—off in the store all day, and in bad times selling roofing and siding for his brother-in-law door to door at night—and understandably he had some trouble when he first discovered that the little bird's beak he'd been feeding all those years had been transformed overnight into a yapping adolescent mouth that could outtalk him, outreason him, and generally outsmart him with the aid of "logic," "analogy," and assorted techniques of condescension. But then came my four-year scholarship to Brown, and that crown of crowns, straight A's in college, and gradually he too gave in and left off even trying to tell me what to think and do. By my seventeenth year it was already pretty clear that I did not mean to use my freedom from parental constraint and guidance to become a bum, and so, to his credit, he did the best an aggressive entrepreneur and indestructible breadwinner and loving father could, to let me be.

Spielvogel wouldn't see it that way. He questioned my "fairly happy childhood," suggesting that people could of course delude themselves about the good old days that had never been. There might be a harsher side to it all that I was conveniently forgetting—the *threatening* aspect of my mother's competence and vigor and attentiveness, and the "castration anxiety," as he called it, that it had fostered in her baby boy, the last, and emotionally the most fragile, of her offspring. From my descriptions of Morris's life and my few vivid childhood recollections of him, Dr. Spielvogel concluded that my brother had been "constitutionally" a much tougher specimen than I to begin with, and that this biological endowment had been reinforced in his formative years when he had virtually to raise himself while my mother was off working most of each day in the store with my father. As for Joan, it was Spielvogel's educated guess that as the ugly duckling and the girl in the family she had hardly been in danger of being overwhelmed by my mother's attention; to the contrary, she had probably felt herself at the periphery of the family circle, neglected and useless as compared with the hearty older brother and the clever younger one. If so (he continued, writing his Tarnopol family history), it would not be surprising to find her in her forties still so avid to *have*—famous friends, modish beauty, exotic travels, fancy and expensive clothes: to have, in a word, the admiration and envy of the crowd. He shocked me by asking if my sister also took lovers with such avidity. "Joannie? It never occurred to me." "Much hasn't," the doctor assured the patient.

Now I for one had never denied that my mother might have been less than perfect; of course I remembered times when she seemed to have scolded me too severely or needlessly wounded my pride or hurt my feelings; of course she had said and done her share of thoughtless things while bringing me up, and at times, in anger or uncertainty, had like any parent taken the tyrannical way out. But not until I came under the influence of Dr. Spielvogel could I possibly have imagined a child any more valued or loved than Mrs. Tarnopol's little boy. Any more, in fact, and I really *would* have been in trouble. My argument with this line the doctor began to take on my past was that if I had suffered anything serious from having had a mother like my own, it was because she had nourished in me a boundless belief in my ability to *win* whatever I wanted, an optimism and innocence about my charmed life that (now that I thought about it) could very well have left me less than fortified against the realities of setback and frustration. Yes, perhaps what made me so pathetic at dealing with Maureen in her wildest moments was that I simply could not believe that anybody like her could exist in the world that had been advertised to me as Peter's oyster. It wasn't the repetition of an ancient "trauma" that rendered me so helpless with my defiant wife—it was its uniqueness. I might as well have been dealing with a Martian, for all the familiarity I had with female rage and resentment.

I admitted readily to Dr. Spielvogel that of course I had been reduced in my marriage to a bewildered and defenseless little boy, but that, I contended, was because I had never been a *bewildered* little boy before. I did not see how we could account for my downfall in my late twenties without accounting simultaneously for all those years of success and good fortune that had preceded it. Wasn't it possible that in my "case," as I willingly called it, triumph *and* failure, conquest *and* defeat derived from an indestructible boyish devotion to a woman as benefactress and celebrant, protectress and guide? Could we not conjecture that what had made me so available to the Bad Older Woman was the reawakening in me of that habit of obedience that had stood me in such good stead with the Good Older Woman of my childhood? A small boy, yes, most assuredly, no question about it—but not at all, I insisted, because the protecting, attentive, and regulating mother of my fairly happy memories had been Spielvogel's "phallic threatening mother figure" to whom I submitted out of fear and whom a part of me secretly loathed. To be sure, whoever held absolute power over a child had inevitably to inspire hatred in him at times, but weren't we standing the relationship on its head by emphasizing her fearsome aspect, real as it may have been, over the lovingness and tenderness of the mother who dominated the recollections of my first ten years? And weren't we drastically exaggerating my submissiveness as well, when all available records seemed to indicate that in fact I had been a striving, spirited little boy, nicknamed Peppy, who hardly behaved in the world like a whipped dog? Children, I told Spielvogel (who I assumed knew as much), had undergone far worse torment than I ever had for displeasing adults.

Spielvogel wouldn't buy it. It was hardly unusual, he said, to have felt loved by the "threatening mother"; what was distressing was that at this late date I should continue to depict her in this "idealized" manner. That to him was a sign that I was still very much "under her spell," unwilling so much as to utter a peep of protest for fear *yet* of reprisal. As he saw it, it was my vulnerability as a sensitive little child to the pain such a mother might so easily inflict that accounted for "the dominance of narcissism" as my "primary defense." To protect myself against the "profound anxiety" engendered by my mother—by the possibilities of rejection and separation, as well as the helplessness that I experienced in her presence—I had cultivated a strong sense of superiority, with all the implications of "guilt" and "ambivalence" over being "special."

I argued that Dr. Spielvogel had it backwards. My sense of superiority—if he wanted to call it that—was not a "defense" against the threat of my mother, but rather my altogether willing acceptance of her estimation of me. I just agreed with her, that's all. As what little boy wouldn't? I was not pleading with Spielvogel to believe that I had ever in my life felt like an ordinary person or wished to be one; I was only trying to explain that it did not require "profound anxiety" for my mother's lastborn to come up with the idea that he was somebody to conjure with.

Now, when I say that I "argued" or "admitted," and Spielvogel "took issue," etc., I am drastically telescoping a dialectic that was hardly so neat and narrow, or so pointed, as it evolved from session to session. A summary like this tends to magnify considerably my own resistance to the archaeological reconstruction of my childhood that began to take shape over the first year or so of therapy, as well as to overdraw the subtle enough means by which the doctor communicated to me his hypotheses about the origin of my troubles. If I, in fact, had been less sophisticated about "resistance"—and he'd had less expertise—I might actually have been able to resist him more successfully. (On the basis of this paragraph, Dr. Spielvogel would undoubtedly say that my resistance, far from being overcome by my "sophistication," has triumphed over all in the end. For why do I assign to him, rather than myself, the characterization of my mother as "a phallic threatening figure," if not because I am *still* unwilling to be responsible for thinking such an unthinkable thought?) Also, had I been less desperate to be cured of whatever was ailing me, and ruining me, I probably could have held out somewhat longer—though being, as of old, the most willing of pupils, I would inevitably, I think, have seriously entertained his ideas just out of schoolboy habit. But as it was, because I so wanted to get a firm grip upon myself and to stop being so susceptible to Maureen, I found that once I got wind of Dr. Spielvogel's bias, I became increasingly willing to challenge my original version of my fairly happy childhood with rather Dickensian recollections of my mother as an overwhelming and frightening person. Sure enough, memories began to turn up of cruelty, injustice, and of offenses against my innocence and integrity, and as time passed, it was as though the anger that I felt toward Maureen had risen over its banks and was beginning to rush out across the terrain of my childhood. If I would never wholly relinquish my benign version of our past, I nonetheless so absorbed Spielvogel's that when, some ten months into analysis, I went up to Yonkers to have Passover dinner with my parents and Morris's family, I found myself crudely abrupt and cold with my mother, a performance almost as bewildering afterward to me as to this woman who so looked forward to each infrequent visit that I made to her dinner table. Peeved, and not about to hide it, my brother took me aside at one point in the meal and said, "Hey, what's going on here tonight?" I could not give him anything but a shrug for a reply. And try as I might, when I later kissed her goodbye at the door, I did not seem to have the wherewithal to feign even a little filial affection—as though my mother, who had been crestfallen the very first time she had laid eyes on Maureen, and afterward had put up with the fact of her solely to please me, was somehow an accomplice to Maureen's vindictive rage.

Somewhere along in my second year of therapy, when relations with my mother were at their coolest, it occurred to me that rather than resenting Spielvogel, as I sometimes did, for provoking this perplexing change in behavior and attitude toward her, I should see it rather as a strategy, harsh perhaps but necessary, designed to deplete the fund of maternal veneration on which Maureen had been able to draw with such phenomenal results. To be sure, it was no fault of my mother's that I had blindly transferred the allegiance she had inspired through the abundance of her love to someone who was in actuality my enemy; it could be taken, in fact, as a measure of just how gratifying a mother she had been, what a *genius* of a mother she had been, that a son of hers, decades later, had found himself unable to "wrong" a woman with whom his mother shared nothing except a common gender, and a woman whom actually he had come to *despise.* Nonetheless, if my future as a man required me to sever at long last the reverential bonds of childhood, then the brutal and bloody surgery on the emotions would have to proceed, and without blaming the physician in charge for whatever pain the operation might cause the blameless mother or for the disorientation it produced in the apron-strung idolatrous son . . . Thus did I try to rationalize the severity with which I was coming to judge my mother, and to justify and understand the rather patriarchal German-Jewish doctor, whose insistence on "the phallic threatening mother" I sometimes thought revealed more about some bête noire of his than of my own.

But that suspicion was not one that I cared, or dared, to pursue. I was far too much the needy patient to presume to be my doctor's doctor. I had to trust someone if I hoped ever to recover from my defeat, and I chose him.

I had, of course, no real idea what kind of man Dr. Spielvogel was outside of his office, or even in the office with other patients.

Where exactly he had been born, raised, and educated, when and under what circumstances he had emigrated to America, what his wife was like, whether he had children—I knew no more about these simple facts of his life than I did about the man who sold me my morning paper; and I was too obedient to what I understood to be the rules of the game to ask, and too preoccupied with my own troubles to be anything more than sporadically curious about this stranger in whose presence I lay down on a couch in a dimly lit room for fifty minutes, three afternoons a week, and spoke as I had never spoken even to those who had proved themselves worthy of my trust. My attitude toward the doctor was very much like that of the first-grader who accepts on faith the wisdom, authority, and probity of his teacher, and is unable to grasp the idea that his teacher also lives in the ambiguous and uncertain world beyond the blackboard.

I had myself been just such a youngster, and experienced my first glimpse of my doctor riding a Fifth Avenue bus with the same stunned disbelief and embarrassment that I had felt at age eight when, in the company of my sister, I had passed the window of a neighborhood barbershop one day and saw the man who taught "shop" in my school getting a shine and a shave. I was four months into my analysis on the drizzly morning when I looked up from the bus stop in front of Doubleday's on Fifth Avenue and saw Spielvogel, in a rainhat and a raincoat, looking out from a seat near the front of the No. 5 bus and wearing a decidedly dismal expression on his face. Of course years before I had seen him in his yachting cap sipping a drink at a summer party, so I knew for a fact that he did not really cease to exist when he was not practicing psychoanalysis on me; I happened too to have been acquainted with several young training analysts during my year of graduate work at Chicago, people with whom I'd gotten along easily enough during evenings in the local student bar. But then Spielvogel was no casual beer-drinking acquaintance: he was the repository of my intimate history, he was to be the instrument of my psychic—my *spiritual*—recovery, and that a person entrusted with that responsibility should actually go out into the street and board a public vehicle such as carried the common herd from point A to point B—well, it was beyond my comprehension. How could I have been so stupid as to confide my darkest secrets to a person who went out in public and took a bus? How could I ever have believed that this gaunt, middle-aged man, looking so done in and defenseless beneath his olive-green rainhat, this unimpressive stranger on a *bus,* could possibly free me from my woes? And just what in God's name was I expected to do now—climb aboard, pay my fare, proceed down the aisle, tap him on the shoulder, and say—say what? "Good day, Dr. Spielvogel, it's me—you remember, the man in his wife's underwear."

I turned and walked rapidly away. When he saw me move off, the bus driver, who had been waiting patiently for me to rise from my reverie and enter the door he held open, called out, in a voice weary of ministering to the citizenry of Manhattan, "*Another* screwball," and drove off, bearing through an orange light my shaman and savior, bound (I later learned, incredulously) for an appointment with his dentist.

It was in September of 1964, at the beginning of my third year of analysis, that I had a serious falling out with Dr. Spielvogel. . . . My dispute with him arose over an article he had written for the *American Forum for Psychoanalytic Studies* and published in a special number focusing on "The Riddle of Creativity." I happened to catch sight of the magazine on his desk as I was leaving the office one evening in the third year of my analysis—noticed the symposium title on the cover and then his name among the contributors listed below. I asked if I might borrow it to read his paper. He answered, "Of course," though it seemed to me that before issuing gracious consent, a look of distress, or alarm, had crossed his face—as though anticipating (correctly) what my reaction to the piece would be . . . But if so, why had the magazine been displayed so conspicuously on the desk I passed every evening leaving his office? Since he knew that like most literary people I as a matter of course scan the titles of all printed matter lying out in the open—by now he had surely observed that reading-man's tic in me a hundred times—it would seem that either he didn't care one way or another whether I noticed the *Forum,* or that he actually wanted me to see his name on the magazine's cover and read his contribution. Why then the split second of alarm? Or was I, as he was inevitably to suggest later, merely "projecting" my own "anticipatory anxiety" onto him?

"Am I submitted in evidence?" I asked, speaking in a mild, jesting tone, as though it was as unlikely as it was likely and didn't matter to me either way. "Yes," answered Spielvogel. "Well," said I, and pretended to be taken aback a little in order to hide just how surprised I was. "I'll read it tonight." Spielvogel's polite smile now obscured entirely whatever that might really mean to him. . . .

On the evening that I arrived at Susan's with the *American Forum for Psychoanalytic Studies* in my hand, I called hello from the door, but instead of going to the kitchen, as was my habit—how I habituated myself during those years! how I coveted whatever orderliness I had been able to reestablish in my life!—to chat with her from a stool while she prepared our evening's delicacies, I went into the living room and sat on the edge of Jamey's flame-stitch ottoman, reading quickly through Spielvogel's article, entitled "Creativity: The Narcissism of the Artist." Somewhere in the middle of the piece I came upon what I'd been looking for—at least I *supposed* this was it: "A successful Italian-American poet in his forties entered into therapy because of anxiety states experienced as a result of his enormous ambivalence about leaving his wife. . . ." Up to this point in the article, the patients described by Spielvogel had been "an actor," "a painter," and "a composer"—so this *had* to be me. Only I had not been in my forties when I first became Spielvogel's patient; I'd come to him at age twenty-nine, wrecked by a mistake I'd made at twenty-six. Surely between a man in his forties and a man in his twenties there are differences of experience, expectation, and character that cannot be brushed aside so easily as this . . . And "successful"? Does that word (in my mind, I immediately began addressing Spielvogel directly), does that word describe to you the tenor of my life at that time? A "successful" apprenticeship, absolutely, but when I came to you in 1962, at age twenty-nine, I had for three years been writing fiction I couldn't stand, and I could no longer even teach a class without fear of Maureen rushing in to "expose" me to my students. Successful? His forties? And surely it goes without saying that to disguise (in my brother's words) "a nice civilized Jewish boy" as something called "an Italian-American," well, that is to be somewhat dim-witted about matters of social and cultural background that might well impinge upon a person's psychology and values. And while we're at it, Dr. Spielvogel, a poet and a novelist have about as much in common as a jockey and a diesel driver. Somebody ought to tell you that, especially since "creativity" is your subject here. Poems and novels arise out of radically different sensibilities and resemble each other not at all, and you cannot begin to make sense about "creativity" or "the artist" or even "narcissism" if you are are going to be so insensitive to fundamental distinctions having to do with age, accomplishment, background, and vocation. And if I may, sir—his *self* is to many a novelist what his own physiognomy is to a painter of portraits: the closest subject at hand demanding scrutiny, a problem for his art to solve—given the enormous obstacles to truthfulness, *the* artistic problem. He is not simply looking into the mirror because he is transfixed by what he sees. Rather, the artist's success depends as much as anything on his powers of detachment, on *de-*narcissizing himself. That's where the excitement comes in. That hard *conscious* work that makes it *art!* Freud, Dr. Spielvogel, studied his own dreams not because he was a "narcissist," but because he was a student of dreams. And whose were at once the least and most accessible of dreams, if not his own?

. . . And so it went, my chagrin renewed practically with each word. I could not read a sentence in which it did not seem to me that the observation was off, the point missed, the nuance blurred—in short, the evidence rather munificently distorted so as to support a narrow and unilluminating thesis at the expense of the ambiguous and perplexing actuality. In all there were only two pages of text on the "Italian-American poet," but so angered and disappointed was I by what seemed to me the unflagging wrongness of the description of my case that it took me ten minutes to get from the top of page 85 to the bottom of 86. ". . . enormous ambivalence about leaving his wife. . . . It soon became clear that the poet's central problem here as elsewhere was his castration anxiety vis-à-vis a phallic mother figure. . . ." Not so! His central problem here as elsewhere derives from nothing of the sort. That will not serve to explain his "enormous ambivalence" about leaving his wife any more than it describes the prevailing emotional tone of his childhood years, which was one of intense *security.* "His father was a harassed man, ineffectual and submissive to his mother. . . ." What? Now where did you get that idea? My father was harassed, all right, but not by his wife—any child who lived in the same house with them knew that much. He was harassed by his own adamant refusal to allow his three children or his wife to do without: he was harassed by his own vigor, by his ambitions, by his business, by the times. By his overpowering commitment to the idea of Family and the religion he made of Doing A Man's Job! My "ineffectual" father happened to have worked twelve hours a day, six and seven days a week, often simultaneously at two exhausting jobs, with the result that not even when the store was as barren of customers as the Arctic tundra, did his loved ones lack for anything essential. Broke and overworked, no better off than a serf or an indentured servant in the America of the thirties, he did not take to drink, jump out of the window, or beat his wife and kids—and by the time he sold Tarnopol's Haberdashery and retired two years ago, he was making twenty thousand bucks a year. Good Christ, Spielvogel, from whose example did I come to associate virility with hard work and self-discipline, if not from my father's? Why did I like to go down to the store on Saturdays and spend all day in the stockroom arranging and stacking the boxes of goods? In order to hang around an ineffectual father? Why did I listen like Desdemona to Othello when he used to lecture the customers on Interwoven socks and McGregor shirts—because he was *bad* at it? Don't kid yourself—and the other psychiatrists. It was because I was so *proud* of his affiliation with those big brand names—because his pitch was so *convincing.* It wasn't his wife's hostility he had to struggle against, but the world's! And he did it, with splitting headaches to be sure, *but without giving in.* I've told you that a hundred times. Why don't you believe me? Why, to substantiate your "ideas," do you want to create this fiction about me and my family, when your gift obviously lies elsewhere? Let *me* make up stories—you make sense! ". . . in order to avoid a confrontation with his dependency needs toward his wife the poet acted out sexually with other women almost from the beginning of his marriage." But that just is not so! You must be thinking of some other poet. Look, is this supposed to be an amalgam of the ailing, or me alone? Who was there to "act out" with other than Karen? Doctor, I had a desperate *affair* with that girl—hopeless and ill-advised and adolescent, that may well be, but also passionate, also painful, also *warm-hearted,* which was what the whole thing was about to begin with: I was dying for some *humanness* in my life, *that's* why I reached out and touched her hair! And oh yes, I fucked a prostitute in Naples after a forty-eight-hour fight with Maureen in our hotel. And another in Venice, correct—making two in all. Is that what you call "acting out" with "other women almost from the beginning of his marriage"? The marriage only lasted three years! It was *all* "almost" the beginning. And why don't you mention how it began? ". . . he once picked up a girl at a party. . . ." But that was here in New York, months and months *after* I had left Maureen in Wisconsin. The marriage was *over,* even if the state of New York refused to allow that to be so! ". . . the poet acted out his anger in his relationships with women, reducing all women to masturbatory sexual objects. . . ." Now, do you really mean to say that? All women? Is that what Karen Oakes was to me, "a masturbatory sexual object"? Is that what Susan McCall is to me now? Is that why I have encouraged and cajoled and berated her into going back to finish her schooling, because she is "a masturbatory sexual object"? Is that why I nearly give myself a stroke each night trying to help her to come? Look, let's get down to the case of cases: Maureen. Do you think that's what *she* was to me, "a masturbatory sexual object"? Good God, what a reading of my story *that* is! Rather than reducing that lying, hysterical bitch to an object of any kind, I made the grotesque mistake of *elevating* her to the status of a human being toward whom I had a *moral responsibility.* Nailed myself with my romantic morality to the cross of her desperation! Or, if you prefer, caged myself in with my cowardice! And don't tell me that was out of "guilt" for having *already* made of her "a masturbatory sexual object," because you just can't have it both ways! Had I actually been able to treat her as some goddam "object," or simply to see her for what she was, I would never have done my manly duty and married her! Did it ever occur to you, Doctor, in the course of your ruminations, that maybe *I* was the one who was made into a sexual object? You've got it all backwards, Spielvogel—inside out! And how can that be? How can you, who have done me so much good, have it all so wrong? Now *there* is something to write an article about! *That* is a subject for a symposium! Don't you see, it isn't that women mean too little to me—what's caused the trouble is that they mean so much. The testing ground, not for potency, but *virtue!* Believe me, if I'd listened to my prick instead of to my upper organs, I would never have gotten into this mess to begin with! I'd still be fucking Dina Dornbusch! And she'd have been my wife!

What I read next brought me up off the ottoman and to my feet, as though in a terrifying dream my name had finally been called—then I remembered that blessedly it was not a Jewish novelist in his late twenties or early thirties called Tarnopol, but a nameless Italian-American poet in his forties that Spielvogel claimed to be describing (and diagnosing) for his colleagues. ". . . leaving his semen on fixtures, towels, etc., so completely libidinized was his anger; on another occasion, he dressed himself in nothing but his wife's underpants, brassiere, and stockings. . . . ?" Stockings? Oh, I didn't put on her stockings, damn it! Can't you get anything right? And it was not at all "another occasion"! One, she had just drawn blood from her wrist with my razor; two, she had just confessed (a) to perpetrating a fraud to get me to marry her and (b) to keeping it secret from me for three wretched years of married life; three, she had just threatened to put Karen's "pure little face" in every newspaper in Wisconsin—

Then came the worst of it, what made the protective disguise of the Italian-American poet so ludicrous . . . In the very next paragraph Spielvogel recounted an incident from my childhood that I had myself narrated somewhat more extensively in the autobiographical *New Yorker* story published above my name the previous month.

It had to do with a move we had made during the war, when Moe was off in the merchant marine. To make way for the landlord's newlywed daughter and her husband, we had been dispossessed from the second-floor apartment of the two-family house where we had been living ever since the family had moved to Yonkers from the Bronx nine years earlier, when I'd been born. My parents had been able to find a new apartment very like our old one, and fortunately only a little more expensive, some six blocks away in the same neighborhood; nonetheless, they had been infuriated by the high-handed treatment they had received from the landlord, particularly given the loving, proprietary care that my mother had taken of the building, and my father of the little yard, over the years. For me, being uprooted after a lifetime in the same house was utterly bewildering; to make matters even worse, the first night in our new apartment I had gone to bed with the room in a state of disarray that was wholly foreign to our former way of life. Would it be this way forevermore? Eviction? Confusion? Disorder? Were we on the skids? Would this somehow result in my brother's ship, off in the dangerous North Atlantic, being sunk by a German torpedo? The day after the move, when it came time to go home from school for lunch, instead of heading off for the new address, I "unthinkingly" returned to the house in which I had lived all my life in perfect safety with brother, sister, mother, and father. At the second-floor landing I was astonished to find the door to our apartment wide open and to hear men talking loudly inside. Yet standing in the hallway on that floor planed smooth over the years by my mother's scrub brush, I couldn't seem to get myself to remember that we had moved the day before and now lived elsewhere. "It's Nazis!" I thought. The Nazis had parachuted into Yonkers, made their way to our street, and taken everything away. *Taken my mother away.* So I suddenly perceived it. I was no braver than the ordinary nine-year-old, and no bigger, and so where I got the courage to peek inside I don't know. But when I did, I saw that "the Nazis" were only the housepainters sitting on a drop cloth on what used to be our living-room floor, eating their sandwiches out of wax-paper wrappings. I ran—down that old stairwell, the feel of the rubber treads on each stair as familiar to me as the teeth in my head, and through the neighborhood to our new family sanctum, and at the sight of my mother in her apron (unbeaten, unbloodied, unraped, though visibly distressed from imagining what might have happened to delay her punctual child on his way home from school), I collapsed into her arms in a fit of tears.

Now, as Spielvogel interpreted this incident, I cried in large part because of "guilt over the aggressive fantasies directed toward the mother." As I construed it—in the short story in journal form, entitled "The Diary of Anne Frank's Contemporary"—I cry with relief to find that my mother is alive and well, that the new apartment has been transformed during the morning I have been in school into a perfect replica of the old one—and that we are Jews who live in the haven of Westchester County, rather than in our ravaged, ancestral, Jew-hating Europe.

Susan finally came in from the kitchen to see what I was doing off by myself.

"Why are you standing there like that? Peter, what's happened?"

I held the journal in the air. "Spielvogel has written an article about something he calls 'creativity.' And I'm in it."

"By *name?*"

"No, but identifiably me. *Me* coming home to the wrong house when I was nine. He *knew* I was using it. I talked about that story to him, and still he goes ahead and has some fictitious Italian-American poet—!"

"Who? I can't follow you."

"Here!" I handed her the magazine. "Here! This straw patient is supposed to be me! Read it! Read this thing!"

She sat down on the ottoman and began to read. "Oh, Peter."

"Keep going."

"It says . . ."

"What?"

"It says here—you put on Maureen's underwear and stockings. Oh, he's out of his mind."

"He's not—I did. Keep reading."

Her tear appeared. "You *did?*"

"Not the stockings, *no*—that's him, writing his banal fucking fiction! *He* makes it sound like I was dressing up for the drag-queen ball! All I was doing, Susan, was saying, 'Look, I wear the panties in this family and don't you forget it!' That's all it boils down to! Keep reading! He doesn't get *anything* right. It's all perfectly *off!*"

She read a little further, then put the magazine in her lap. "Oh, sweetheart."

"What? *What?*"

"It says . . ."

"My sperm?"

"Yes."

"I did that too. But I don't any more! Keep reading!"

"Well," said Susan, wiping away her tear with a fingertip, "don't shout at *me.* I think it's awful that he's written this and put it in print. It's unethical, it's reckless—and I can't even believe he would do such a thing. You tell me he's so smart. You make him sound so *wise.* But how could anybody wise do something so insensitive and uncaring as *this?*"

"Just read on. Read the whole hollow pretentious meaningless thing, right on down to the footnotes from Goethe and Baudelaire to prove a connection between 'narcissism' and 'art'! So what else is new? Oh, Jesus, what this man thinks of as *evidence!* 'As Sophocles has written,'—and that constitutes *evidence!* Oh, you ought to go through this thing, line by line, and watch the ground shift beneath you! Between every paragraph there's a hundred-foot drop!"

"What are you going to do?"

"What *can* I do? It's printed—it's out."

"Well, you just can't sit back and take it. He's betrayed your confidence!"

"I know that."

"Well, that's terrible."

"I know that!"

"Then *do* something!" she pleaded.

On the phone Spielvogel said that if I was as "distressed" as I sounded—"I am!" I assured him—he would stay after his last patient to see me for the second time that day. So, leaving Susan (who had much to be distressed about, too), I took a bus up

Madison to his office and sat in the waiting room until seven-thirty, constructing in my mind angry scenes that could only culminate in leaving Spielvogel forever.

The argument between us was angry, all right, and it went on unabated through my sessions for a week, but it was Spielvogel, not I, who finally suggested that I leave him. Even while reading his article, I hadn't been so shocked—so unwilling to believe in what he was doing—as when he suddenly rose from his chair (even as I continued my attack on him from the couch) and took a few listing steps around to where I could see him. Ordinarily I addressed myself to the bookcase in front of the couch, or to the ceiling overhead, or to the photograph of the Acropolis that I could see on the desk across the room. At the sight of him at my side, I sat straight up. "Look," he said, "this has gone far enough. I think either you will have now to forget this article of mine, or leave me. But we cannot proceed with treatment under these conditions."

"What kind of choice is that?" I asked, my heart beginning to beat wildly. He remained in the middle of the room, supporting himself now with a hand on the back of a chair. "I have been your patient for over two years. I have an investment here—of effort, of time, of hope, of money. I don't consider myself recovered. I don't consider myself able to go at my life alone just yet. And neither do you."

"But if as a result of what I have written about you, you find me so 'untrustworthy' and so 'unethical,' so absolutely 'wrong' and, as you put it, 'off' about relations between you and your family, then why would you want to stay on as a patient any longer? It is clear that I am too flawed to be your doctor."

"Come off it, please. Don't hit me over the head with the 'narcissism' again. You know why I want to stay on."

"Why?"

"Because I'm scared to be out there alone. But also because I *am* stronger—things in my life *are* better. Because staying with you, I was finally able to leave Maureen. That was no inconsequential matter for me, you know. If I hadn't left her, I'd be dead —dead or in jail. You may think that's an exaggeration, but I happen to know that it's true. What I'm saying is that on the practical side, on the subject of my everyday life, you have been a considerable help to me. You've been with me through some bad times. You've prevented me from doing some wild and foolish things. Obviously I haven't been coming here three times a week for two years for no reason. But all that doesn't mean that this article is something I can just forget."

"But there is really nothing more to be said about it. We have discussed it now for a week. We have been over it thoroughly. There is nothing new to add."

"You could add that you were wrong."

"I have answered the charge already and more than once. I don't find anything I did 'wrong.' "

"It was wrong, it was at the very least imprudent, for you to use that incident in your article, knowing as you did that I was using it in a story."

"We were writing simultaneously, I explained that to you."

"But I told you I was using it in the Anne Frank story."

"You are not remembering correctly. I did not know you had used it until I read the story last month in *The New Yorker.* By then the article was at the printer's."

"You could have changed it then—left that incident out. And I am not remembering incorrectly."

"First you complain that by disguising your identity I misrepresent you and badly distort the reality. You're a Jew, not an Italian-American. You're a novelist, not a poet. You came to me at twenty-nine, not at forty. Then in the next breath you complain that I fail to disguise your identity enough—rather, that I have *revealed* your identity by using this particular incident. This of course is your ambivalence again about your 'specialness.' "

"It is not of course my ambivalence again! You're confusing the argument again. You're blurring important distinctions—just as you do in that piece! Let's at least take up each issue in turn."

"We have taken up each issue in turn, three and four times over."

"But you still refuse to get it. Even if your article was at the printer, once you had read the Anne Frank story you should have made every effort to protect my privacy—and my trust in you!"

"It was impossible."

"You could have withdrawn the article."

"You are asking the impossible."

"What is more important, publishing your article or keeping my trust?"

"Those were not my alternatives."

"But they *were.*"

"That is the way you see it. Look here, we are clearly at an impasse, and under these conditions treatment cannot be continued. We can make no progress."

"But I did not just walk in off the street last week. *I am your patient.*"

"True. And I cannot be under attack from my patient any longer."

"Tolerate it," I said bitterly—a phrase of his that had helped me through some rough days. "Look, given that you must certainly have had an *inkling* that I might be using that incident in a piece of fiction, since you in fact *knew* I was working on a story to which that incident was the conclusion, mightn't you at the very least have thought to ask my permission, ask if it was all right with me . . ."

"Do you ask permission of the people you write about?"

"But I am not a psychoanalyst! The comparison won't work. I write fiction—or did, once upon a time. *A Jewish Father* was not 'about' my family, or about Grete and me, as you certainly must realize. It may have originated there, but it was finally a contrivance, an artifice, a *rumination* on the real. A self-avowed work of imagination, Doctor! I do not write 'about' people in a strict factual or historical sense."

"But then you think," he said, with a hard look, "that I don't either."

"Dr. Spielvogel, please, that is just not a good enough answer. And you must know it. First off, you are bound by ethical considerations that happen not to be the ones that apply to my profession. Nobody comes to me with confidences the way they do to you, and if they tell me stories, it's not so that I can cure what ails them. That's obvious enough. It's in the nature of being a novelist to make private life public—that's a part of what a novelist is up to. But certainly it is not what I thought *you* were up to when I came here. I thought your job was to treat me! And second, as to accuracy—you are *supposed* to be accurate, after all, even if you haven't been as accurate as I would want you to be in this thing here."

"Mr. Tarnopol, 'this thing here' is a scientific paper. None of us could write such papers, none of us could share our findings with one another, if we had to rely upon the permission or the approval of our patients in order to publish. You are not the only patient who would want to censor out the unpleasant facts or who would find 'inaccurate' what he doesn't like to hear about himself."

"Oh, that won't wash, and you know it! I'm willing to hear anything about myself—and always have been. My problem, as I see it, isn't my impenetrability. As a matter of fact, I tend to rise to the bait, Dr. Spielvogel, as Maureen, for one, can testify."

"Oh, do you? Ironically, it is the narcissistic defenses discussed here that prevent you from accepting the article as something other than an assault upon your dignity or an attempt to embarrass or belittle you. It is precisely the blow to your narcissism that has swollen the issue out of all proportion for you. Simultaneously, you act as though it is about nothing *but* you, when actually, of the fifteen pages of text, your case takes up barely two. But then you do not like at all the idea of yourself suffering from 'castration anxiety.' You do not like the idea of your aggressive fantasies vis-à-vis your mother. You never have. You do not like me to describe your father, and by extension you, his son and heir, as 'ineffectual' and 'submissive,' though you don't like when I call you 'successful' either. Apparently that tends to dilute a little too much your comforting sense of victimized innocence."

"Look, I'm sure there are in New York City such people as you've just described. Only I ain't one of 'em! Either that's some model you've got in your head, some kind of patient for all seasons, or else it's some other patient of yours you're thinking about; I don't know what the hell to make of it, frankly. Maybe what it comes down to is a problem of self-expression; maybe it's that the writing isn't very precise."

"Oh, the writing is also a problem?"

"I don't like to say it, but maybe writing isn't your strong point."

He smiled. "Could it be, in your estimation? Could I be precise enough to please you? I think perhaps what so disturbs you about the incident in the Anne Frank story is not that by using it I may have disclosed your identity, but that in your opinion I plagiarized and abused your material. You are made so very angry by this piece of writing that I have dared to publish. But if I am such a weak and imprecise writer as you suggest, then you should not feel so threatened by my little foray into English prose."

"I don't feel 'threatened.' Oh, please, don't argue like Maureen, will you? That is just more of that language again, which doesn't at all express what you mean and doesn't get anyone anywhere."

"I assure you, unlike Maureen, I said 'threatened' because I meant 'threatened.' "

"But maybe writing *isn't* your strong point. Maybe that is an objective statement of fact and has nothing to do with whether I am a writer or a tightrope walker."

"But why should it matter so much to you?"

"Why? Why?" That he could seriously ask this question just took the heart out of me; I felt the tears welling up. "Because, among other things, I am the subject of that writing! I am the one your imprecise language has misrepresented! Because I come here each day and turn over the day's receipts, every last item out of my most personal life, and in return I expect an accurate accounting!" I had begun to cry. "You were my friend, and I told you the truth. I told you everything."

"Look, let me disabuse you of the idea that the whole world is waiting with bated breath for the newest issue of our little journal in which you claim you are misrepresented. I assure you that is not the case. It is not *The New Yorker* magazine, or even the *Kenyon Review.* If it is any comfort to you, most of my colleagues don't even bother to read it. But this is your narcissism again. Your sense that the whole world has nothing to look forward to but the latest information about the secret life of Peter Tarnopol."

The tears had stopped. "And that is your reductivism again, if

I may say so, and your obfuscation. Spare me that word 'narcissism,' will you? You use it on me like a club."

"The word is purely descriptive and carries no valuation," said the doctor.

"Oh, is that so? Well, you be on the receiving end and see how little 'valuation' it carries! Look, can't we grant that there is a difference between self-esteem and vanity, between pride and megalomania? Can we grant that there actually is an ethical matter at stake here, and that my sensitivity to it, and your apparent indifference to it, cannot be explained away as a psychological aberration of *mine?* You've got a psychology too, you know. You do this with me all the time, Dr. Spielvogel. First you shrink the area of moral concern, you say that what I, for instance, call my responsibility toward Susan is so much camouflaged narcissism—and then if I consent to see it that way, and I leave off with the moral implications of my conduct, you tell me I'm a narcissist who thinks only about his own welfare. Maureen, you know, used to do something similar—only she worked the hog-tying game from the other way round. She made the kitchen *sink* into a moral issue! Everything in the whole wide world was a test of my decency and honor—and the moral ignoramus you're looking at believed her! If driving out of Rome for Frascati, I took a wrong turn, she had me pegged within half a mile as a felon, as a fiend up from Hell by way of Westchester and the Ivy League. And I believed her! . . . Look, look—let's *talk* about Maureen a minute, let's talk about the possible consequences of all this for me, 'narcissistic' as that must seem to you. Suppose Maureen were to get hold of this issue and read what you've written here. It's not unlike her, after all, to be on her toes where I'm concerned—where *alimony* is concerned. I mean it won't do, to go back a moment to what you just said—it won't do to say that nobody reads the magazine anyway. Because if you really believed that, then you wouldn't publish your paper there to begin with. What good are your findings published in a magazine that has no readers? The magazine is around, and it's read by somebody, surely here in New York it is—and if it somehow came to Maureen's attention . . . well, just imagine how happy she would be to read those pages about me to the judge in the courtroom. Just imagine a New York municipal judge taking that stuff in. Do you see what I'm saying?"

"Oh, I see very well what you're saying."

"Where you write, for instance, that I was 'acting out' sexually with other women 'almost from the beginning of the marriage.' First off, that is not accurate either. Stated like that, you make it seem as though I'm just another Italian-American who sneaks off after work each day for a quick bang on the way home from the poetry office. Do you follow me? You make me sound like somebody who is simply fucking around with women all the time. And that is not so. God knows, what you write here is not a proper description of my affair with Karen. That was nothing if it wasn't earnest—and earnest in part because I was so *new* at it!"

"And the prostitutes?"

"Two prostitutes—in three years. That breaks down to about half a prostitute a year, which is probably, among miserably married men, a national record for *not* acting out. Have you forgotten? *I was miserable!* See the thing in context, will you? You seem to forget that the wife I was married to was Maureen. You seem to forget the circumstances under which we married. You seem to forget that we had an argument in every piazza, cathedral, museum, trattoria, pensione, and hotel on the Italian peninsula. Another man would have beaten her head in! My predecessor Mezik, the Yugoslav barkeep, would have 'acted out' with a right to the jaw. I am a literary person. I went forth and did the civilized thing—I laid a three-thousand-lire whore! Ah, and that's how you came up with 'Italian-American' for me, isn't it?"

He waved a hand to show what he thought of my *aperçu*—then said, "Another man might have confronted his wife more directly, that is true, rather than libidinizing his anger."

"But the only direct way to confront that woman was *to kill her!* And you yourself have told me that killing people is against the law, crazy wives included. I was not 'sexually acting out,' whatever that means—I was trying to stay alive in all that madness. Stay *me!* 'Let me shun that,' and so on!"

"And," he was saying, "you conveniently forget once again the wife of your young English department colleague in Wisconsin."

"Good Christ, who are you, Cotton Mather? Look, I may be childish and a weakling, I may even be the narcissist of your fondest professional dreams—*but I am not a slob!* I am not a bum or a lecher or a gigolo or some kind of walking penis. Why do you want to portray me that way? Why do you want to characterize me in your writing as some sort of heartless rapist manqué? Surely, surely there is another way to describe my affair with Karen—"

"But I said nothing about Karen. I only reminded you of the wife of your colleague, whom you ran into that afternoon at the shopping center in Madison."

"You've got such a good memory, why don't you also remember that I didn't even fuck her! She blew me, in the car. So what? *So what?* I tell you, it was a surprise to the two of us. And what's it to you, anyway? I mean that! We were friends. She wasn't so happily married either. That, for Christ's sake, wasn't 'sexually acting out.' It was friendship! It was heartbrokenness! It was generosity! It was tenderness! It was despair! It was being adolescents together for ten secret minutes in the rear of a car before we both went nobly back into Adulthood! It was a sweet and harmless game of Let's Pretend! Smile, if you like, smile from your pulpit, but that's still closer to a proper description of what was going on there than what *you* call it. And we did not let it go any further, which was a possibility, you know; we let it remain a kind of happy, inconsequential accident and returned like good soldiers to the fucking front lines. Really, Your Holiness, really, Your Excellency, does that in your mind add up to 'acting out sexually with other women from the beginning of the marriage'?"

"Doesn't it?"

"Two street whores in Italy, a friend in a car in Madison . . . and Karen? No! I call it practically *monkish,* given the fact of my marriage. I call it pathetic, that's what! From the beginning of his marriage, the Italian-American poet had some crazy idea that now that he was a husband his mission in life was to be *faithful* —to whom never seemed to cross his mind. It was like *keeping his word* and *doing his duty*—what had gotten him married to this shrew in the first place! Once again the Italian-American poet did what he thought to be 'manly' and 'upright' and 'principled'—which, needless to say, was only what was cowardly and submissive. Pussywhipped, as my brother so succinctly puts it! As a matter of fact, Dr. Spielvogel, those two Italian whores and my colleague's wife back of the shopping center, and Karen, constituted the only praiseworthy, the only manly, the only *moral* . . . oh, the hell with it."

"I think at this point we are only saying the same thing in our different vocabularies. Isn't that what you just realized?"

"No, no, no, no, no. I just realized that you are never going to admit to me that you could be mistaken in any single particular of diction, or syntax, let alone in the overriding idea of that paper. Talk about narcissism as a defense!"

He did not bristle at my tone, contemptuous as it had become. His voice throughout had been strong and even—a touch of sarcasm, some irony, but no outrage, and certainly no tears. Which was as it should be. What did he have to lose if I left?

"I am not a student any longer, Mr. Tarnopol. I do not look to my patients for literary criticism. You would prefer that I leave the professional writing to you, it would seem, and confine my activities to this room. You remember how distressed you were several years ago to discover that I occasionally went out into the streets to ride the bus."

"That was awe. Don't worry, I'm over it."

"Good. No reason for you to think I'm perfect."

"I don't."

"On the other hand, the alternative is not necessarily to think I am another Maureen, out to betray and deceive you for my own sadistic and vengeful reasons."

"I didn't say you were."

"You may nonetheless think that I am."

"If you mean do I think that I have been misused by you, the answer is yes. Maureen is not the issue—that article is."

"All right, that is your judgment. Now you must decide what you are going to do about the treatment. If you want to continue with your attack upon me, treatment will be impossible—it would be foolish even to try. If you want to return to the business at hand, then of course I am prepared to go forward. Or perhaps there is a third alternative that you may wish to consider—perhaps you will choose to take up treatment with somebody else. This is for you to decide before the next session."

Susan was enraged by the decision I did reach. I never had heard her argue about anything as she did against Spielvogel's "brutal" handling of me, nor had she ever dared to criticize me so forthrightly either. Of course her objections were in large part supplied by Dr. Golding, who, she told me, had been "appalled" by the way Spielvogel had dealt with me in the article in the *Forum;* however, she would never even have begun to communicate Golding's position to me if it were not for startling changes that were taking place in her attitude toward herself. Now, maybe reading about me walking around in Maureen's underwear did something to boost her confidence with me, but whatever had triggered it, I found myself delighted by the emergence of the vibrant and emphatic side so long suppressed in her—at the same time that I was greatly troubled by the possibility that what she and her doctor were suggesting about my decision to stay with Spielvogel constituted more of the humbling truth. Certainly in my defense I offered up to Susan what sounded even to me like the feeblest of arguments.

"You should leave him," she said.

"I can't. Not at this late date. He's done me more good than harm."

"But he's got you all wrong. How could that do anybody any good?"

"I don't know—but it did me. Maybe he's a lousy analyst and a good therapist."

"That makes no sense, Peter."

"Look, I'm not getting into bed with my worst enemy any more, am I? I am out of that, am I not?"

"But any doctor would have helped you to leave her. Any doctor who was the least bit competent would have seen you through that."

"But he happens to be the one who did it."

"Does that mean he can just get away with anything as a result? His sense of what you are is all wrong. Publishing that article without consulting you about it first was all wrong. His attitude when you confronted him with what he had done, the way he said, 'Either shut up or go'—that was as wrong as wrong can be. And you know it! Dr. Golding said that was as reprehensible as anything he had ever heard of between a doctor and his patient. Even his writing stinks—you said it was just jargon and crap."

"Look, I'm staying with him. I don't want to talk about it any more."

"If *I* answered *you* like that, you'd hit the ceiling. You'd say, 'Stop backing away! Stand up for yourself, twerp!' Oh, I don't understand why you are acting like this, when the man has so clearly abused you. Why do you let people get away with such things?"

"Which people?"

"Which people? People like Maureen. People like Spielvogel. People who . . ."

"What?"

"Well, walk all over you like that."

"Susan, I cannot put in any more time thinking of myself as someone who gets walked over. It gets me nowhere."

"Then don't be one! Don't let them get away with it!"

"It doesn't seem to me that in this case anybody is getting away with anything."

"Oh, Lambchop, that isn't what Dr. Golding says."

Spielvogel simply shrugged off what Dr. Golding said, when I passed it on to him. "I don't know the man," he grunted, and that was that. Settled. As though if he did know him, he could tell me Golding's motives for taking such a position—otherwise, why bother? As for Susan's anger, and her uncharacteristic vehemence about my leaving him, well, I understood that, did I not? She hated Spielvogel for what Spielvogel had written about the Peter who was to *her* so inspirational and instructive, the man she had come to adore for the changes he was helping to bring about in her life. Spielvogel had demythologized her Pygmalion—of course Galatea was furious. Who expected otherwise?

I must say, his immunity to criticism *was* sort of dazzling. Indeed, the imperviousness of this pallid doctor with the limping gait seemed to me, in those days of uncertainty and self-doubt, a condition to aspire to: *I am right and you are wrong, and even if I'm not, I'll just hold out and hold out and not give a single inch, and that will make it so.* And maybe that's why I stayed on with him—out of admiration for his armor, in the hope that some of that impregnability would rub off on me. Yes, I thought, he is teaching me by example, the arrogant German son of a bitch. Only I won't give him the satisfaction of telling him. Only who is to say he doesn't know it? Only who is to say he does, other than I?

As the weeks passed and Susan continued to grimace at the mention of Spielvogel's name, I sometimes came close to making what seemed to me the best possible defense of him—and thereby of myself, for if it turned out that I had been as deluded about Spielvogel as about Maureen, it was going to be awfully hard ever to believe in my judgment again. In order to substantiate my own claim to sanity and intelligence, and to protect my sense of trust from total collapse (or was it just to perpetuate my childish illusions? to cherish and protect my naiveté right on down to the last good drop?), I felt I had to make as strong a case as I could for him. And even if that meant accepting as valid his obfuscating defense—even if it meant looking back myself with psychoanalytic skepticism upon my own valid objections! "Look," I wanted to say to Susan, "if it weren't for Spielvogel, I wouldn't even be here. If it weren't for Spielvogel saying 'Why not stay?' every time I say 'Why not leave?' I would have been out of this affair long ago. We have him to thank for whatever exists between us—he's the one who was your advocate, not me." But that it was largely because of Spielvogel's encouragement that I had continued to visit her almost nightly during that first year, when I was so out of sympathy with her way of living, was really not her business, even if she wouldn't let up about his "reprehensible" behavior; nor would it do her fragile sense of self-esteem any good to know that even now, several years into our affair—with me her Lambchop and her my Suzie Q., with all that tender lovers' playfulness between us—that it was Spielvogel who prevented me from leaving her whenever I became distressed about those burgeoning dreams of marriage and family that I did not share. "But she wants to have children—and now, before she gets any older." "But you don't want to." "Right. And I can't allow her to nurse these expectations. That just won't do." "Then tell her not to." "I *do.* I *have.* She can't bear hearing it any more. She says, 'I know, I know, you're not going to marry me—do you have to tell me that every *hour?*' " "Well, every hour is perhaps a little more frequent than necessary." "Oh, it isn't every hour—it just sounds that way to her. You see, because I tell her where things stand doesn't mean she takes it to heart." "Yes, but what more can you do?" "Go. I should." "I wouldn't think she thinks you should." "But if I stay . . ." "You might *really* fall in love with her. Does it ever occur to you that maybe this is what you are running away from? Not the children, not the marriage . . . but the love?" "Oh, Doctor, don't start practicing psychoanalysis. No, that doesn't occur to me. I don't think it should, because I don't think it's true." "No? But you are somewhat in love already—are you not? You tell me how sweet she is, how kind she is. How gentle. You tell me how beautiful she is when she sits there reading. You tell me what a touching person she is. Sometimes you are positively lyrical about her." "Am I?" "Yes, yes, and you know that." "But there is still too much that's wrong there, *you* know *that.*" "Yes, well, this I could have warned you about at the outset." "Please, the husband of Maureen Tarnopol understands that the other gender is also imperfect." "Knowing this, the husband of Maureen Tarnopol should be grateful perhaps for a woman, who despite her imperfections, happens to be tender and appreciative and absolutely devoted to him. She is all these things, am I right?" "She is all these things. She also turns out to be smart and charming and funny." "And in love with you." "And in love with me." "And a cook—such a cook. You tell me about her dishes, you make my mouth water." "You're very hung up on the pleasure principle, Dr. Spielvogel." "And you? Tell me, where are you running again? To what? To whom? Why?" "To no one, to nothing—but *'why?'* I've told you why: suppose she tries to commit suicide!" "Still with the suicide?" "But what if she does it!" "Isn't that her responsibility? And Dr. Golding's? She is in therapy after all. Are you going to run for fear of this remote possibility?" "I can't take it hanging over my head. Not after all that's gone on. Not after Maureen."

"Maybe you are too thin-skinned, you know? Maybe it is time at thirty to develop a thicker hide." "No doubt. I'm sure you rhinoceroses lead a better life. But my hide is my hide. I'm afraid you can shine a flashlight through it. So give me some other advice." "What other advice is there? The choice is yours. Stay or run." "This choice that is mine you structure oddly." "All right, *you* structure it." "The point, you see, is that if I do stay, she must realize that I am marrying no one unless and until *I want to do it.* And everything conspires to make me think that *I don't want to do it.*" "Mr. Tarnopol, somehow I feel I can rely on you to put that proviso before her from time to time."

Why did I stay with Spielvogel? Let us not forget his Mosaic prohibitions and what they meant to a thin-skinned man at the edge of he knew not what intemperate act.

Thou shalt not covet thy wife's underwear.

Thou shalt not drop thy seed upon thy neighbor's bathroom floor or dab it upon the bindings of library books.

Thou shalt not be so stupid as to buy a Hoffritz hunting knife to slay your wife and her matrimonial lawyer.

"But why can't I? What's the difference any more? They're driving me crazy! They're ruining my life! First she tricked me into marrying her with that urine, now they're telling the judge I can write movies and make a fortune! She tells the court that I 'obstinately' refuse to go out to Hollywood and do an honest day's work! Which is true! I obstinately refuse! *Because that is not my work!* My work is writing fiction! And I can't even do *that* any more! Only when I say I can't, they say, right, so just get your ass out to Hollywood where you can earn yourself a thousand bucks a day! Look! Just look at this affidavit she filed! Look what she calls me here, Doctor—'a well-known seducer of college girls'! That's how she spells 'Karen'! Read this document, will you please? I brought it so you can see with your own eyes that I am not exaggerating! Just look at *this* version of me! 'A seducer of college girls'! They're trying to hold me up, Doctor Spielvogel—this is legalized extortion!" "To be sure," said my Moses, gently, "but still you cannot buy that knife and stick it in her heart. You must not buy a knife, Mr. Tarnopol." "WHY NOT? GIVE ME ONE GOOD REASON WHY NOT!" "Because killing is against the law." "FUCK THE LAW! THE LAW IS WHAT IS KILLING ME!" "Be that as it may, kill her and they will put you in jail." "So what!" "You wouldn't like it there." "I wouldn't care—she'd be dead. *Justice* would come into this world!" "Ah, but Just as the world would become following her death, for you it still wouldn't be paradise. You did not even like the army that much, remember? Well, jail is worse. I don't believe you would be happy there." "I'm not exactly happy *here.*" "I understand that. But there you would be even less happy."

So, with him to restrain me (or with him to pretend to restrain me, while I pretend to be unrestrained), I did not buy the knife in Hoffritz's Grand Central window (her lawyer's office was just across the street, twenty flights up). And a good thing too, for when I discovered that the reporter from the *Daily News* who sat in a black raincoat at the back of the courtroom throughout the separation proceedings had been alerted to the hearing by Maureen's lawyers, I lost all control of myself (no pretending now), and out in the corridor during the lunch recess, I took a swing at the dapper, white-haired attorney in his dark three-piece suit with the Phi Beta Kappa key dangling conspicuously from a chain. He was obviously a man of years (though in my state, I might even have attacked a somewhat younger man), but he was agile and easily blocked my wild blow with his briefcase. "Watch out, Egan, watch out for me!" It was pure playgroundese I shouted at him, language dating back to the arm's-length insolence of grade-school years; my eyes were running with rage, as of old, but before I could swing out at his briefcase again, my own lawyer had grabbed me around the middle and was dragging me backward down the corridor. "You jackass," said Egan coldly, "we'll fix your wagon." "You goddam thief! You publicity hound! What more can you do, you bastard!" "Wait and see," said Egan, unruffled, and even smiling at me now, as a small crowd gathered around us in the hall. "She tricked me," I said to him, "and you know it! With that urine!" "You've got quite an imagination, son. Why don't you put it to work for you?" Here my lawyer managed to turn me completely around, and running and pushing at me from behind, shoved me a few paces farther down the courthouse corridor and into the men's room.

Where we were promptly joined by the stout, black-coated Mr. Valducci of the *Daily News.* "Get out of here, you," I said, "leave me alone." "I just want to ask you some questions. I want to ask about your wife, that's all. I'm a reader of yours. I'm a real fan." "I'll bet." "Sure. *The Jewish Merchant.* My wife read it too. Terrific ending. Ought to be a movie." "Look, I've heard enough about the movies today!" "Take it easy, Pete—I just want to ask you, for instance, what did the missus do before you were married?" "The missus was a show girl! She was in the line at the Latin Quarter! Fuck off, will you!" "Whatever you say, whatever you say," and with a bow to my attorney, who had now interposed himself between the two of us, Valducci stepped back a ways and asked, deferentially, "You don't mind if I take a leak, do you? Since I'm already here?" While Valducci voided, we looked on in silence. "Just shut up," my lawyer whispered to me. "See you, Pete," said Valducci, after meticulously washing and drying his hands, "see you, Counselor."

The next morning, over Valducci's by-line, in the lower half of page five, ran this three-column head—

PRIZE-WINNING AUTHOR TURNS
COURTROOM PRIZEFIGHTER

The story was illustrated with my book-jacket photo, dark-eyed, thin-faced innocence, circa 1959, and a photograph of Maureen taken the day before, her lantern jaw slicing the offending air as she strides down the courthouse steps on the arm of Attorney Dan P. Egan, who, the story noted (with relish) was seventy years old and formerly middleweight boxing champion at Fordham; in his heyday, I learned, he was known as "Red," and was still a prized toastmaster at Fordham alumni functions. The tears I had shed during my contretemps with Red did not go unreported. "Oh, I should never have listened to you about that knife. I could have killed Valducci too." "You are not satisfied with page five?" "I should have done it. And that judge too. Cut his self-righteous gizzard out, sitting there pitying poor Maureen!" "Please," said Spielvogel, laughing lightly, "the pleasure would have been momentary." "Oh, no, it wouldn't." "Oh, yes, believe me. Murder four people in a courtroom, and before you know it, it's over and you're behind bars. This way, you see, you have it always to imagine when your spirit needs a lift."

So I stayed on as Spielvogel's patient, at least so long as Maureen drew breath (and breathed fire), and Susan McCall was my tender, appreciative, and devoted mistress.

Nathan Dedalus

Who could sleep after that? I didn't even turn the lamp off to try. For the longest time I just stared at E. I. Lonoff's tidy desk: neat piles of typing paper, each stack a different pale color—for different drafts, I assumed. Finally I got up and, sacrilege though it surely was, sat on his typing chair in my undershorts. No wonder his back hurt. It wasn't a chair made for relaxing in, not if you were his size. Lightly I touched my fingers to his portable typewriter keys. Why a portable for a man who went nowhere? Why not a machine on the order of a cannonball, black and big and built to write for all time? Why not a comfortable padded executive's chair to lean back in and think? Why not indeed.

Pinned to the bulletin board beside his desk—the cell's only real embellishments—were a little wall calendar from the local bank and two annotated index cards. One card bore a fragmentary sentence ascribed to "Schumann, on Chopin's Scherzo No. 2 in B flat minor, Op. 31." It read, ". . . so overflowing with tenderness, boldness, love, and contempt that it may be compared, not inappropriately, to a poem by Byron." I didn't know

---

The second chapter of *The Ghost Writer* (1979). Nathan Zuckerman, a twenty-three-year-old writer, retires—on a snowy December night in 1956—to the study of a semi-reclusive fifty-six-year-old writer, E. I. Lonoff, whom he idolizes. Over brandy after dinner, the older man had praised Zuckerman's as yet meager output of fiction. Amy Bellette is a young woman of indeterminate foreign origin, a former student of Lonoff's, who will also be staying the night. Hope, of an old New England family, has been Mrs. Lonoff for thirty-five years.

what to make of it there, or rather, what Lonoff made of it, until I remembered that Amy Bellette could play Chopin with great charm. Maybe it was she who had typed it out for him, scrupulous attribution and all—enclosing it, perhaps, with the gift of a record so that in the late afternoons he could listen to Chopin even when she was no longer around. Perhaps it was this very line she'd been musing upon when I first saw her on the study floor: musing because the description seemed as pertinent to herself as to the music . . .

If displaced, what had become of her family? Murdered? Did that explain her "contempt"? But for whom the overflowing love, then? Him? If so, the contempt might well be for Hope. If so, if so.

It required no ingenuity to guess the appeal of the quotation typed on the other card. After what Lonoff had been telling me all evening, I could understand why he might want these three sentences hanging over his head while beneath them he sat turning his own sentences around. "We work in the dark—we do what we can—we give what we have. Our doubt is our passion and our passion is our task. The rest is the madness of art." Sentiments ascribed to a story I did not know by Henry James called "The Middle Years." But "the madness of art"? I would have thought the madness of everything but art. The art was what was sane, no? Or was I missing something? Before the night was over I was to read "The Middle Years" twice through, as though preparing to be examined on it in the morning. But that was canon law to me then: ready to write a thousand words on "What does Henry James mean by 'the madness of art'?" if the question should happen to turn up on my paper napkin at breakfast.

Photographs of Lonoff's children were set out on a bookshelf behind the typing chair: one male, two females, not a trace of the paternal genes in any of their bones. One of the girls, a fair, freckled maiden in horn-rimmed glasses, looked, in fact, much as her shy, studious mother probably did back in her art-school days. Beside her photo in the twin frame was a postcard that had been mailed from Scotland to Massachusetts one August day nine years earlier, addressed to the writer alone. This perhaps accounted for its status as a memento to be preserved under glass. Much about his life indicated that communicating with his children had been no easier for him than having enough opinions for Manhattan in the thirties. "Dear Pop, We are now in Banffshire (Highlands) and I am standing amidst the wreck of Balvenie Castle, Dufftown, where Mary Stuart once stayed. Yesterday we biked to Cawdor (Thane of Cawdor, *ca.* 1050, Shakespeare's Macbeth), where Duncan was murdered. See you soon, Love, Becky."

Also directly behind his desk were several shelves of his works in foreign translation. Seating myself on the floor I tried translating from French and German sentences that I had read first in Lonoff's English. With the more exotic tongues the most I could do was try to spot his characters' names in the hundreds of indecipherable pages. Pechter. Marcus. Littman. Winkler. There they were, surrounded on all sides by Finnish.

And which language was hers? Portuguese? Italian? Hungarian? In which did she overflow like a poem by Byron?

On a large lined pad that I took from my briefcase, a bulging *Bildungsroman* briefcase—ten pounds of books, five obscure magazines, and easily enough paper to write the whole of my first novel if it should happen to come to me while riding back and forth on the bus—I began methodically to list everything on his bookshelves I had not read. There was more German philosophy than I had been expecting, and only halfway down the page I already seemed to have sentenced myself to a lifetime at hard labor. But, worthily, I kept going—to the accompaniment of the words with which he had commended me before going up to his reading. That, and the toast, had been echoing in my head for an hour. On a clean sheet of paper I finally wrote down what he'd said so as to see exactly what he'd meant. All he'd meant.

As it turned out, I wanted someone else to see as well, for soon I had forgotten the forthcoming ordeal with Heidegger and Wittgenstein, and was seated with my pad at Lonoff's desk, struggling to explain to my father—the foot-doctor father, the first of my fathers—the "voice" that, according to no less a vocalist than E. I. Lonoff, started back of my knees and reached above my head. The letter was overdue. Three weeks now he had been waiting for some enlightened sign of contrition for the offenses I had begun to commit against my greatest supporters. And for three weeks I had let him stew, if that is how you describe being yourself unable to think of little else upon awakening from bad dreams at 4 A.M.

Our trouble had begun when I gave my father the manuscript of a story based on an old family feud in which he had played peacemaker for nearly two years before the opponents ended up shouting in court. The story was the most ambitious I had written—some fifteen thousand words—and, as I saw it, my motives for sending it to him were no less benign than those I'd had in college, when I mailed home poems for the family to read even before they appeared in the student verse magazine. It wasn't trouble I was looking for but admiration and praise. Out of the oldest and most ingrained of habits, I wanted to please them and make them proud.

That wasn't hard either. For years I had been making him proud just by sending along clippings for his "files," a voluminous accumulation of magazine and newspaper articles—including an unbroken series of transcripts of "America's Town Meeting of the Air"—on what he called "vital issues." Whenever I was home on a visit, my mother, who could repeat herself, would invariably remind me—with her own deeply satisfied look—of the thrill it gave him to say to his patients (after working them around to the vital issue on his mind), "I just got something in the mail this morning on that subject. My son Nathan saw it at college. He's out at the University of Chicago. Straight A's in everything. Went out there when he was sixteen—special program. Well, he saw it in one of the Chicago papers and sent it on for my files."

Oh, what sitting ducks I had for parents! A son of theirs would have had to be a half-wit or a sadist *not* to make them proud. And I was neither; I was dutiful and thoughtful, and too excited with myself in flight to be ungrateful for the boost I'd begun with. Despite the flaming wrangles of my adolescence—weekend night hours, fashions in footwear, the unhygienic high-school hangout, my alleged but ceaselessly disavowed penchant for the last word—we had emerged from our fifty textbook scenes of domestic schism much the same close family bound by the same strong feelings. I'd slammed a lot of doors and declared a few wars, but still I loved them like their child. And whether or not I wholly knew just how extensive the addiction, I was much in need of their love for me, of which I assumed there was an inexhaustible supply. That I couldn't—wouldn't?—assume otherwise goes a long way toward explaining why I was naïve enough to expect nothing more than the usual encouragement for a story that borrowed from our family history instances of what my exemplary father took to be the most shameful and disreputable transgressions of family decency and trust.

The facts I had begun my story with were these:

A great-aunt of mine, Meema Chaya, had left for the education of two fatherless grandsons the pot of money she had diligently hoarded away as a seamstress to Newark's upper crust. When Essie, the widowed mother of the twin boys, attempted to invade the trust to send them from college to medical school, her younger brother, Sidney, who was to inherit the money remaining in Meema Chaya's estate upon conclusion of the boys' higher education, had sued to stop her. For four years Sidney had been waiting for Richard and Robert to graduate from Rutgers—waiting mostly in pool rooms and saloons, to hear the family tell it—so he could buy a downtown parking lot with his legacy. Loudly—his way—Sidney proclaimed that he was not about to postpone the good life just so there could be two more fancy doctors driving Caddies around South Orange. Those in the family who detested Sidney's womanizing and his shady friends immediately lined up in support of the boys and their dignified aspirations, leaving Sidney with a phalanx consisting of his ill-used, timid wife Jenny, and his mysterious Polish tootsie Annie, whose scandalously florid *shmatas* were much discussed, if never once seen, at family weddings, funerals, etc. Also in the phalanx, for all it was worth to him, was me. My admiration was long-standing, dating back to Sidney's Navy days, when he had won four thousand dollars on the homeward journey of the battleship *Kansas*, and was said to have thrown into the South Pacific, for the sharks to dispose of, a Mississippi sore loser who at the end of an all-night poker game had referred to the big winner as a dirty Jew. The lawsuit, whose outcome hinged on how exhaustive Meema Chaya had meant to be in her will with the ringing words "higher education," was eventually decided by the judge—a *goy*—in Sidney's favor, though within only a few years the Raymond Boulevard parking lot bought with his inheritance became such a hot piece of real estate that it was nationalized out from under him by the Mob. For his trouble they gave Sidney a tenth of what it was worth, and shortly thereafter his heart broke like a balloon in the bed of yet another overdressed bimbo not of our persuasion. My cousins Richard and Robert were meanwhile being put through medical school by their iron-willed mother. After she lost the lawsuit, Essie quit her job at a downtown department store and for the next ten years went to work on the road selling shingles and siding. So iron-willed was she that by the time she had finally bought carpeting and venetians for the new offices leased for Richard and Robert in suburban North Jersey, there was hardly a working-class neighborhood in the state that she hadn't left encased in asphalt. Out canvassing one hot afternoon during the twins' internship, Essie had decided to spend an hour in an air-cooled Passaic movie theater. In her thousands of days and nights finding leads and closing deals, this was said to be the first time ever that she stopped to do anything other than eat and call the boys. But now residencies in orthopedics and dermatology were only just around the corner, and the thought of their advent, combined with the August heat, made her just a little light-headed. In the dark movie theater, however, Essie hadn't even time to mop her brow before a fellow in the next seat put his hand on her knee. He must have been a very lonely fellow—it was a very stout knee; nonetheless, she broke the hand for him, at the wrist, with the hammer carried in her purse all these years to protect herself and the future of two fatherless sons. My story, entitled "Higher Education," concluded with Essie taking aim.

"Well, you certainly didn't leave anything out, did you?"

Thus began my father's critique on the Sunday I'd come to say goodbye before leaving for the winter at Quahsay. Earlier in the day, along with a favorite aunt and uncle and a childless neighbor couple—also called "Aunt" and "Uncle" by me since the cradle—I had partaken of our family's traditional Sunday brunch. Fifty-two Sundays a year, for most of my lifetime, my father went out to the corner for the smoked fish and the warm rolls, my brother and I set the table and squeezed the juice, and for three hours my mother was unemployed in her own house. "Like a queen" was how she described the predicament. Then, after my parents had read the Newark Sunday papers and listened on the radio to "The Eternal Light"—great moments from Jewish history in weekly half-hour dramatizations—we two boys were rounded up and the four of us set off in the car to visit relatives. My father, long in contention with an opinionated older brother for the vacant position of family patriarch, generally delivered a hortatory sermon somewhere along the way to somebody who seemed to him to need it, and then we drove home. And always at dusk, before we reassembled around the kitchen table to observe the Sunday-evening rites—to partake of the sacred delicatessen supper, washed down with sacramental soda pop; to await together the visitation from heaven of Jack Benny, Rochester, and Phil Harris—the "men," as my mother called us, went off for their brisk walk to the nearby park. "Hi, Doc—how are you?" So the neighbors we passed along the way always greeted my popular and talkative father, and though he seemed never to be bothered by it, for a time his class-conscious little boy used to think that if only there had been no quotas and he'd become a *real* physician, they would have greeted him as "Doctor Zuckerman." "Doc" was what they called the pharmacist who made milk shakes and sold cough drops.

"Well, Nathan," began my father, "you certainly didn't leave anything out, did you?"

I was by then a little weary from doing my duty and anxious to leave for New York to pack for Quahsay. My brunch-time visit had now lasted the entire day and, to my surprise, had been marked by the comings and goings of numerous relatives and old family friends dropping by seemingly just to see me. Kibitzing, reminiscing, swapping dialect jokes, and munching too much fruit, I had hung around until the company began to leave, and then had stayed on, at my father's request, so that he could give me his thoughts on my story. Portentously he said he wanted an hour with me alone.

At four that afternoon, in our coats and scarves, the two of us set out for the park. Every half hour a New York bus stopped just by the park gateway on Elizabeth Avenue, and my plan was to catch one after he'd had his say.

"I left a lot of things out." I pretended to be innocent of what he meant—as innocent as when I'd sent him the story, though the moment he'd spoken in the house of giving me his "thoughts" (rather than his pat on the head), I realized immediately how mindless I had been. Why hadn't I waited to see if I could even get it published, and then shown him the story already in print? Or would that only have made it worse? "Things had to be left out—it's only fifty pages."

"I mean," he said sadly, "you didn't leave anything disgusting out."

"Did I? Didn't I? I wasn't thinking along those lines, exactly."

"You make everybody seem awfully greedy, Nathan."

"But everybody was."

"That's one way of looking at it, of course."

"That's the way you looked at it yourself. That's why you were so upset that they wouldn't compromise."

"The point is, there is far more to our family than this. And you know that. I hope that today reminded you of the kind of people we are. In case in New York you've forgotten."

"Dad, I had a good time seeing everybody. But you didn't have to give me a refresher course in the family's charms."

But on he went. "And people who are crazy about you. Is there anybody who came into the house today whose face didn't light up when they laid eyes on you? And you couldn't have been kinder, you couldn't have been a sweeter boy. I watched you with your family and with all our old dear friends, and I thought to myself, Then what is this story all about? Why is he going on like this about ancient history?"

"It wasn't ancient history when it happened."

"No, then it was nonsense."

"You didn't seem to think so. You were running from Essie to Sidney for over a year."

"The fact remains, son, there is more to the family, much much more, than is in this story. Your great-aunt was as kind and loving and hard-working a woman as you could ever meet in this world.

Your grandmother and all her sisters were, every last one of them. They were women who thought only of others."

"But the story is not about them."

"But they are *part* of the story. They are the *whole* story as far as I'm concerned. Without them there would be no story at all! Who the hell was Sidney? Does anybody in his right mind even think about him any longer? To you, as a boy, I suppose he was an amusing character, somebody to get a kick out of, who came and went. I can understand how that would be: a big six-foot ape in bellbottom trousers, clanking his I.D. bracelet and talking a mile a minute as though he was Admiral Nimitz and not just the nobody who swabbed the deck. Which is all he ever was, of course. I remember how he came to the house and got down on the floor and taught you and your little brother to roll dice. As a joke. I wanted to throw the lummox out on his ear."

"I don't even remember that."

"Well, I do. I remember plenty. I remember it all. To Meema Chaya, Sidney was never anything but heartache. Little children don't realize that underneath the big blowhard who rolls on the floor and makes them laugh there can be somebody who makes other people cry. And he made your great-aunt cry plenty, and from the time he was old enough to go into the street, looking for grief to give her. And still, *still,* that woman left him that chunk of her hard-earned dough, and prayed that somehow it would help. She rose above all the misery and the shame he had caused her—just like the wonderful woman that she was. 'Chaya' means life, and that is what she had in her to give to everybody. But that you leave out."

"I didn't leave it out. I suggest as much about her on the first page. But you're right—I don't go into Meema Chaya's life."

"Well, that would be some story."

"Well, that isn't this story."

"And do you fully understand what a story like this story, when it's published, will mean to people who don't know us?"

We had by now descended the long incline of our street and reached Elizabeth Avenue. No lawn we passed, no driveway, no garage, no lamppost, no little brick stoop was without its power over me. Here I had practiced my sidearm curve, here on my sled I'd broken a tooth, here I had copped my first feel, here for teasing a friend I had been slapped by my mother, here I had learned that my grandfather was dead. There was no end to all I could remember happening to me on this street of one-family brick houses more or less like ours, owned by Jews more or less like us, to whom six rooms with a "finished" basement and a screened-in porch on a street with shade trees was something never to be taken for granted, given the side of the city where they'd started out.

Across the wide thoroughfare was the entrance to the park. There my father used to seat himself—each Sunday the same bench—to watch my brother and me play tag, yelling our heads off after hours of good behavior with grandparents, great-aunts and great-uncles, ordinary aunts and uncles—sometimes it seemed to me that there were more Zuckermans in Newark than Negroes. I wouldn't see as many of them in a year as I saw cousins on an ordinary Sunday driving around the city with my father. "Oh," he used to say, "how you boys love to shout" and with one hand for each son's head would smooth back our damp hair as we started out of the park and back up the familiar hill where we lived. "Any game with shouting in it," he would tell our mother, "and these two are in seventh heaven." Now my younger brother was knuckling under to the tedium of a pre-dental course, having surrendered (to my father's better judgment) a halfhearted dream of a career as an actor, and I—? I apparently was shouting again.

I said, "I think maybe I'll just get the bus. Maybe we should skip the park. It's been a long day, and I have to go home and get ready to leave for Quahsay tomorrow."

"You haven't answered my question."

"It wouldn't be useful, Dad. The best thing now is to put the story in the mail and send it back to me—and try to forget it."

My suggestion triggered a light sardonic laugh from my father.

"All right," I said sharply, "then don't forget it."

"Calm down," he replied. "I'll walk you to the bus. I'll wait with you."

"You really ought to go home. It's getting cold."

"I'm plenty warm," he informed me.

We waited in silence at the bus stop.

"They take their time on Sundays," he finally said. "Maybe you should come home and have dinner. You could catch one first thing in the morning."

"I've got to go to Quahsay first thing in the morning."

"They can't wait?"

"I can't," I said.

I stepped out into the street to watch for the bus.

"You're going to get yourself killed out there."

"Perhaps."

"So," he said, when at last, in my own sweet time, I came back up on the curb, "what do you do with the story now? Send it to a magazine?"

"It's long for a magazine. Probably no magazine will publish it."

"Oh, they'll publish it. The *Saturday Review* has put you on the map. That was a wonderful write-up, a terrific honor to be chosen like that at your age."

"Well, we'll see."

"No, no. You're on your way. The *Saturday Review* never sold so many copies in North Jersey as when your picture was in it. Why do you think everybody came by today, Frieda and Dave, Aunt Tessie, Birdie, Murray, the Edelmans? Because they saw your picture and they're proud."

"They all told me."

"Look, Nathan, let me have my say. Then you can go, and up there at the artists' colony maybe you'll think over in peace and quiet what I'm trying to get you to understand. If you were going to turn out to be nobody, I wouldn't be taking this seriously. But I do take you seriously—and you have to take yourself seriously, and what you are doing. Stop looking for that goddam bus and listen to me, *please.* You can catch the *next* bus! Nathan, you are not in school any more. You are the older brother and you are out in the world and I am treating you accordingly."

"I understand that. But that doesn't mean that we can't disagree. That's what it *does* mean."

"But from a lifetime of experience I happen to know what ordinary people will think when they read something like this story. And you don't. You can't. You have been sheltered from it all your life. You were raised here in this neighborhood where you went to school with Jewish children. When we went to the shore and had the house with the Edelmans, you were always among Jews, even in the summertime. At Chicago your best friends who you brought home were Jewish boys, always. It's not your fault that you don't know what Gentiles think when they read something like this. But I can tell you. They don't think about how it's a great work of art. They don't know about art. Maybe I don't know about art myself. Maybe none of our family does, not the way that you do. But that's my point. People don't read art—they read about *people.* And they judge them as such. And how do you think they will judge the people in your story, what conclusions do you think they will reach? Have you thought about that?"

"Yes."

"And what have you concluded?"

"Oh, I can't put it into one word, not out here in the street. I didn't write fifteen thousand words so as now to put it into one word."

"Well, I can. And the street isn't a bad place for it. Because I know the word. I wonder if you fully understand just how very little love there is in this world for Jewish people. I don't mean in Germany, either, under the Nazis. I mean in run-of-the-mill Americans, Mr. and Mrs. Nice Guy, who otherwise you and I consider perfectly harmless. Nathan, it is there. I guarantee you it is there. I *know* it is there. I have seen it, I have felt it, even when they do not express it in so many words."

"But I'm not *denying* that. Why did Sidney throw that redneck off his ship—?"

"Sidney," he said furiously, "never threw any redneck off any ship! Sidney threw the bull, Nathan! Sidney was a petty hoodlum who cared about nobody and nothing in this world but the good of Sidney!"

"And who actually existed, Dad—and no better than I depict him!"

"Better? He was worse! How rotten he was you don't *begin* to know. I could tell you stories about that bastard that would make your hair stand on end."

"Then where *are* we? If he was *worse*—Oh, look, we're not getting anywhere. Please, it's getting dark, it's going to snow—*go home.* I'll write when I get up there. But there is no more to say on this subject. We just disagree, period."

"All right!" he said crisply, "all right!" But only, I knew, to defuse me for the moment.

"Dad, go home, please."

"It won't hurt if I wait with you. I don't like you waiting out here by yourself."

"I can manage perfectly well out here by myself. I have for years now."

Some five minutes later, blocks away, we saw what looked like the lights of the New York bus.

"Well," I said, "I'll be back down in a few months. I'll keep in touch—I'll phone—"

"Nathan, your story, as far as Gentiles are concerned, is about one thing and one thing only. Listen to me, before you go. It is about kikes. Kikes and their love of money. That is all our good Christian friends will see, I guarantee you. It is not about the scientists and teachers and lawyers they become and the things such people accomplish for others. It is not about the immigrants like Chaya who worked and saved and sacrificed to get a decent footing in America. It is not about the wonderful peaceful days and nights you spent growing up in our house. It is not about the lovely friends you always had. No, it's about Essie and her hammer, and Sidney and his chorus girls, and that shyster of Essie's and his filthy mouth, and, as best I can see, about what a jerk I was begging them to reach a decent compromise before the whole family had to be dragged up in front of a *goyisher* judge."

"I didn't depict you as a jerk. Christ, far from it. I thought," I said angrily, "I was administering a bear hug, to tell you the truth."

"Oh, did you? Well, it didn't come out that way. Look, son, maybe I *was* a jerk, trying to talk sense to such people. I don't mind being made a little fun of—that couldn't bother me less. I've been around in life. But what I can't accept is what you don't see—what you don't *want* to see. This story isn't us, and what is worse, it isn't even *you.* You are a loving boy. I watched you like a hawk all day. I've watched you all your life. You are a good and kind and considerate young man. You are not somebody who writes this kind of story and then pretends it's the truth."

"But I *did* write it." The light changed, the New York bus started toward us across the intersection—and he threw his arms onto my shoulders. Making me all the more belligerent. "I *am* the kind of person who writes this kind of story!"

"You're not," he pleaded, shaking me just a little.

But I hopped up onto the bus, and then behind me the pneumatic door, with its hard rubber edge, swung shut with what I took to be an overly appropriate thump, a symbol of the kind you leave out of fiction. It was a sound that suddenly brought back to me the prize fights at the Laurel Garden, where once a year my brother and I used to wager our pennies with one another, each of us alternately backing the white fighter or the colored fighter, while Doc Zuckerman waved hello to his few acquaintances in the sporting crowd, among them, on one occasion, Meyer Ellenstein, the dentist who became the city's first Jewish mayor. What I heard was the heartrending thud that follows the roundhouse knockout punch, the sound of the stupefied heavyweight hitting the canvas floor. And what I saw, when I looked out to wave goodbye for the winter, was my smallish, smartly dressed father—turned out for my visit in a new "fingertip" car coat that matched the coffee-toned slacks and the checkered peaked cap, and wearing, of course, the same silver-rimmed spectacles, the same trim little mustache that I had grabbed at from the crib; what I saw was my bewildered father, alone on the darkening street-corner by the park that used to be our paradise, thinking himself and all of Jewry gratuitously disgraced and jeopardized by my inexplicable betrayal.

Nor was that the end. So troubled was he that several days later, against the counsel of my mother, and after an unpleasant phone conversation with my younger brother, who warned him from Ithaca that I wasn't going to like it when I found out, he decided to seek an audience with Judge Leopold Wapter, after Ellenstein and Rabbi Joachim Prinz perhaps the city's most admired Jew.

Wapter had been born of Galician Jews in the slums adjacent to the city's sweatshops and mills some ten years before our family arrived there from Eastern Europe in 1900. My father still remembered having been rescued by one of the Wapter brothers —it could have been the future jurist himself—when a gang of Irish hooligans were having some fun throwing the seven-year-old mocky up into the air in a game of catch. I had heard this story more than once in my childhood, usually when we drove by the landscaped gardens and turreted stone house on Clinton Avenue where Wapter lived with a spinster daughter—one of the first Jewish students at Vassar College to earn the esteem of her Christian teachers—and his wife, the department-store heiress, whose philanthropic activities had given her family name the renown among the Jews of Essex County that it was said to have in her native Charleston. Because the Wapters occupied a position of prestige and authority rather like that accorded in our household to President and Mrs. Roosevelt, I used to imagine her, when I was a small boy, going around wearing Mrs. Roosevelt's dowager hats and dresses, and, oddly for a Jewish woman, speaking in the First Lady's awesome Anglified tones. It did not seem to me that, coming from South Carolina, she could really *be* Jewish. Which was exactly what she thought about me, after reading my story.

To approach the judge, my father had first to contact a lofty cousin of ours—an attorney, a suburbanite, and a former Army colonel who had been president for several years of the judge's Newark temple. Cousin Teddy had already helped him to the judge once before, back when my father had gotten it into his head that I should be one of the five youngsters for whom each year Wapter wrote letters of recommendation to college-admissions officers which—it was said—never failed to do the trick. To go up before Judge Wapter I had to wear a blue suit on a bus in broad daylight and then, from where the bus left me off at the Four Corners (our Times Square), to walk all the way up Market Street through throngs of shoppers, whom I imagined dropping in their tracks at the sight of me out in my only dress suit at that hour. I was to be interviewed at the Essex County Courthouse, in his "chambers," a word that had been intoned to relatives on the phone so frequently and with such reverence by my mother during the preceding week that it may well have accounted for the seven visits I made to our bathroom before I could get myself buttoned for good into the blue suit.

Teddy had telephoned the night before to give me some tips on how to conduct myself. This explained the suit and my father's black silk socks, which I was wearing held up with a pair of his garters, and also the initialed briefcase, a grade-school graduation present that I had never removed from the back of my closet. In the gleaming briefcase I carried ten typewritten pages I had written for International Relations the year before on the Balfour Declaration.

As instructed, I "spoke up" right away and offered to show the judge the essay. To my relief, his chambers had turned out to be one room, not ten—and a room no more grand than the principal's office in our high school. Nor did the tanned, plumpish, cheery judge have the shock of white hair I had been expecting. And though not as small as my father, he still was easily a foot shorter than Abraham Lincoln, whose bronze statue you pass coming into the courthouse. He actually looked years younger than my own anxious father, and not half as serious. Reputedly an excellent golfer, he was probably either on his way to or from a game; that's how I later came to terms with his argyle socks. But when I first noticed them—as he leaned back in his leather chair to flip through my essay—I was shocked. It was as though he were the callow, unworldly applicant, and I, with my father's garters pulled tight as a tourniquet, were the judge. "May I keep this for now, Nathan?" he asked, turning with a smile through my pages of *op. cits* and *ibids.* "I'd like to take it home for my wife to see." Then began the inquiry. I had prepared myself the night before (at Teddy's suggestion) by reading through the Constitution of the United States, the Declaration of Independence, and the editorial page of the Newark *Evening News.* The members of Truman's Cabinet and the majority and minority leaders of both Houses of Congress I of course knew already by heart, though before bed I had gone over them out loud with my mother just to help her relax.

To the judge's questions I gave the following answers:

Journalist. The University of Chicago. Ernie Pyle. One brother, younger. Reading—and sports. The Giants in the National

League and the Tigers in the American. Mel Ott and Hank Greenberg. Li'l Abner. Thomas Wolfe. Canada; Washington, D.C.; Rye, New York; New York City itself; Philadelphia; and the Jersey shore. No, sir, never to Florida.

When the judge's secretary made public the names of Newark's five Jewish boys and girls whose college applications Wapter would endorse, mine was one.

I never saw the judge again, though to please my father I had sent my sponsor a letter from the University of Chicago during orientation week of my freshman year, thanking him again for all he had done on my behalf. The letter I received from Wapter some seven years later, during my second week as a guest at Quahsay, was the first I knew of their meeting to talk about "Higher Education."

> Dear Nathan:
>
> My familiarity with your fine family goes back, as you must know, to the turn of the century on Prince Street, where we were all poor people in a new land, struggling for our basic needs, our social and civil rights, and our spiritual dignity. I still remember you as one of the outstanding Jewish graduates of our Newark public-school system. I was most pleased to hear from your father that your college record was at the same high level of achievement that you had maintained throughout your school career here, and that you are already beginning to gain recognition in the field of short-story writing. Since there is nothing a judge likes better than to be right from time to time, I was delighted to know that my confidence in you as a high-school senior has already been substantiated in the larger world. I expect that your family and your community can look forward to great achievements from you in the not too distant future.
>
> Your father, knowing of my interest in the development of our outstanding young people, recently asked if I would take time out from my judicial duties to write you with my candid opinion of one of your short stories. He informed me that you are soon to submit the short story entitled "Higher Education" to a leading national magazine, and he wanted

to know whether I thought the story contained material suitable for such a publication.

In our lengthy and interesting conversation here in my chambers, I informed him that classically, down through the ages and in all countries, the artist has always considered himself beyond the mores of the community in which he lived. Great artists, as history reveals, have been harshly persecuted time and again by the frightened and ill-educated, who do not understand that the artist is a special individual with a unique contribution to make to mankind. Socrates was considered an enemy of the people and a corrupter of the young. The Norwegian playwright and Nobel Prize winner, Henrik Ibsen, was forced into exile because his countrymen failed to understand the profound truth of his great dramas. I explained to your father that I for one would never want to be allied with the intolerance shown by the Greeks towards Socrates, or by the Norwegians towards Ibsen. On the other hand, I do believe that, like all men, the artist has a responsibility to his fellow man, to the society in which he lives, and to the cause of truth and justice. With that responsibility and that alone as my criterion, I would attempt to give him an opinion on the suitability for publication in a national magazine of your latest fictional effort.

Attached you will find a questionnaire about your story, prepared jointly by my wife and myself. Because of Mrs. Wapter's interest in literature and the arts—and because I did not think it fair to rely solely upon my reading—I have taken the liberty of securing her opinion. These are serious and difficult questions to which Mrs. Wapter and I would like you to give just one hour of your time. We don't want you to answer them to our satisfaction—we want you to answer them to your own. You are a young man of great promise and, we all think, of potentially great talent. But with great talent come great responsibilities, and an obligation to those who have stood behind you in the early days so that your talent might come to fruition. I would like to think that if and when the day should dawn that you receive *your* invitation to Stockholm to accept a Nobel Prize, we will have had some small share in awakening your conscience to the responsibilities of your calling.

Sincerely yours,
Leopold Wapter

P.S. If you have not yet seen the Broadway production of *The Diary of Anne Frank,* I strongly advise that you do so. Mrs. Wapter and I were in the audience on opening night; we wish that Nathan Zuckerman could have been with us to benefit from that unforgettable experience.

The sheet of questions prepared for me by the Wapters read as follows:

TEN QUESTIONS FOR NATHAN ZUCKERMAN

1. If you had been living in Nazi Germany in the thirties, would you have written such a story?
2. Do you believe Shakespeare's Shylock and Dickens's Fagin have been of no use to anti-Semites?
3. Do you practice Judaism? If so, how? If not, what credentials qualify you for writing about Jewish life for national magazines?
4. Would you claim that the characters in your story represent a fair sample of the kinds of people that make up a typical contemporary community of Jews?
5. In a story with a Jewish background, what reason is there for a description of physical intimacy between a married Jewish man and an unmarried Christian woman? Why in a story with a Jewish background must there be (a) adultery; (b) incessant fighting within a family over money; (c) warped human behavior in general?
6. What set of aesthetic values makes you think that the cheap is more valid than the noble and the slimy is more truthful than the sublime?
7. What in your character makes you associate so much of life's ugliness with Jewish people?
8. Can you explain why in your story, in which a rabbi

appears, there is nowhere the grandeur of oratory with which Stephen S. Wise and Abba Hillel Silver and Zvi Masliansky have stirred and touched their audiences?

9. Aside from the financial gain to yourself, what benefit do you think publishing this story in a national magazine will have for (a) your family; (b) your community; (c) the Jewish religion; (d) the well-being of the Jewish people?
10. Can you honestly say that there is anything in your short story that would not warm the heart of a Julius Streicher or a Joseph Goebbels?

Three weeks after hearing from the judge and Mrs. Wapter, and only days before my visit to Lonoff, I was interrupted around noon by the Colony secretary. She had come out to my cabin in her coat, apologizing for the disturbance, but saying that I had a long-distance phone call that had been described by the other party as an emergency.

When my mother heard my voice she began to cry. "I know it's wrong to bother you," she said, "but I can't take any more. I can't take another night of it. I can't sit through another meal."

"What is it? What's the matter?"

"Nathan, did you or didn't you get a letter from Judge Wapter?"

"Oh, I got it all right."

"But"—she was flabbergasted—"then why didn't you answer it?"

"He should not have gone to Wapter with that story, Mother."

"Oh, darling, maybe he shouldn't. But he did. He did because he knows you respect the judge—"

"I don't even *know* the judge."

"That's not *true.* He did so much for you when you were ready for college. He gave you such a wonderful boost. It turns out that in his files he still had the essay you wrote on the Balfour Declaration in high school. His secretary took out the files and there it was. Daddy saw it, right in his chambers. Why you haven't given him the courtesy of a reply . . . Daddy is beside himself. He can't believe it."

"He'll have to."

"But all he wanted was for you not to bring yourself harm. You know that."

"I thought it was the harm I was going to do the Jews that you're all worried about."

"Darling, please, for my sake, why won't you answer Judge Wapter? Why won't you give him the hour he asks for? Surely you have an hour where you are to write a letter. Because you cannot, at the age of twenty-three, ignore such a person. You cannot make enemies at twenty-three of people who are so admired and loved, and by Gentiles, too."

"Is that what my father says?"

"He says so much, Nathan. It's been three *weeks* now."

"And how does he even know I haven't answered?"

"From Teddy. He didn't hear from you, so finally he called him. You can well imagine. Teddy is a little fit to be tied. He's not used to this treatment, either. After all, he also extended himself on our behalf when you wanted to go to Chicago."

"Ma, I hate to suggest this, but it could be that the judge's famous letter, procured after great ass-kissing all around, had about as much effect on the University of Chicago as a letter about my qualifications from Rocky Graziano."

"Oh, Nathan, where's your humility, where's your modesty—where's the courtesy you have always had?"

"Where are my father's *brains!*"

"He only wants to *save* you."

"From what?"

"Mistakes."

"Too late, Mother. Didn't you read the Ten Questions for Nathan Zuckerman?"

"Dear, I did. He sent us a copy—and the letter, too."

"The Big Three, Mama! Streicher, Goebbels, and your son! What about the *judge's* humility? Where's *his* modesty?"

"He only meant that what happened to the Jews—"

"In Europe—not in Newark! We are not the wretched of Belsen! We were not the victims of that crime!"

"But we *could* be—in their place we *would* be. Nathan, violence is nothing new to Jews, you *know* that!"

"Ma, you want to see physical violence done to the Jews of

Newark, go to the office of the plastic surgeon where the girls get their noses fixed. That's where the Jewish blood flows in Essex County, that's where the blow is delivered—with a mallet! To their bones—and to their pride!"

"Please don't shout at me. I'm not up to all of this, please—that's why I'm calling. Judge Wapter did not mean *you* were Goebbels. God forbid. He was only a little shocked still from reading your story. We all were, you can understand that."

"Oh, maybe then you all shock a little too easily. Jews are heirs to greater shocks than I can possibly deliver with a story that has a sharpie in it like Sidney. Or Essie's hammer. Or Essie's lawyer. You know as much yourself. You just *said* as much."

"Oh, darling, then tell the judge that. Just tell him that, the way you told it to me, and that'll do it. Your father will be happy. Write him *something.* You can write such wonderful and beautiful letters. When Grandma was dying, you wrote her a letter that was like a poem. It was like—like listening to French, it was so beautiful. What you wrote about the Balfour Declaration was so beautiful when you were only fifteen years old. The judge gave it back to Daddy and said he still remembered how much it had impressed him. He's not against you, Nathan. But if you get your back up and show disrespect, then he will be. And Teddy too, who could be such a help."

"Nothing I could write Wapter would convince him of anything. Or his wife."

"You could tell him you went to see *The Diary of Anne Frank.* You could at least do that."

"I didn't see it. I read the book. *Everybody* read the book."

"But you liked it, didn't you?"

"That's not the issue. How can you *dis*like it? Mother, I will not prate in platitudes to please the adults!"

"But if you just said that, about reading the book, and liking it . . . Because Teddy told Daddy—well, Nathan, is this true?—that to him it looks like you don't really like Jews very much."

"No, Teddy's got it confused. It's him I don't like very much."

"Oh, darling, don't be clever. Don't start that last-word business, please. Just answer me, I'm so confused in the middle of all this. Nathan, tell me something."

"What?"

"I'm only quoting Teddy. Darling . . ."

"What is it, Ma?"

"Are you really anti-Semitic?"

"I'll leave it to you. What do you think?"

"Me? I never heard of such a thing. But Teddy . . ."

"I know, he's a college graduate and lives with wall-to-wall carpeting in Millburn. But they come pretty stupid too."

"Nathan!"

"Sorry, but that's my opinion."

"Oh, I don't know anything any more—all this from that story! Please, if you will not do anything else I ask, at least phone your father. He's been waiting for something for three whole weeks now. And he's a doer, your father, he's not a man who knows how to wait. Darling, phone him at his office. Phone him now. For me."

"No."

"I beg of you."

"No."

"Oh, I can't believe this is you."

"It *is* me!"

"But—what about your father's love?"

"I am on my own!"

In Lonoff's study that night I began letter after letter explaining myself to my father, but each time I got to the point of repeating E. I. Lonoff's praise for my work, I tore the thing up in a rage. I owed no explanations, and he wouldn't buy those I offered anyway, if he even understood them. Because my voice started back of my knees and reached above my head wasn't going to make him any happier about my informing on those unsavory family miscreants who were nobody's business but our own. Nor would it help to argue that Essie wielding her hammer came off in my story as something more impressive than an embarrassment; that wasn't what other people were going to say about a woman who behaved like that, and then expressed herself in a court of law like a man in a barroom brawl. Nor would a spin through the waxworks of my literary museum—from Babel's

Odessa gangsters to Abravanel's Los Angeles worldlings—convince him that I was upholding the responsibilities placed on me by his hero, the judge. Odessa? Why not Mars? He was talking about what people would say when they read that story in North Jersey, where we happened to come from. He was talking about the *goyim,* who looked down on us with enough unearned contempt already, and who would be only too pleased to call us all kikes because of what I had written for the whole world to read about Jews fighting over money. It was not for me to leak the news that such a thing could possibly happen. That was worse than informing—that was collaborating.

Oh, this is useless, I thought, this is idiotic—and tore up yet another half-finished letter in my defense. That the situation between us had deteriorated so rapidly—by his going to Wapter with my story, and by my refusal to justify myself to my elders—was as it had to be, sooner or later. Hadn't Joyce, hadn't Flaubert, hadn't Thomas Wolfe, the romantic genius of my high-school reading list, all been condemned for disloyalty or treachery or immorality by those who saw themselves as slandered in their works? As even the judge knew, literary history was in part the history of novelists infuriating fellow countrymen, family, and friends. To be sure, our dispute hadn't achieved the luster of literary history quite yet, but still, writers weren't writers, I told myself, if they didn't have the strength to face the insolubility of that conflict and go on.

But what about sons? It wasn't Flaubert's father or Joyce's father who had impugned me for my recklessness—it was my own. Nor was it the Irish he claimed I had maligned and misrepresented, but the Jews. Of which I was one. Of which, only some five thousand days past, there had been millions more.

Yet each time I tried again to explain my motives, the angrier with him I became. It's you who humiliated yourself—now live with it, you moralizing ass! Wapter, that know-nothing windbag! That dopey pillar! And the pious belle with her love for the arts! Worth ten million and she chides *me* about "financial gain"! And Abba Hillel Silver on top of that! Oh, don't waste time on prodigal me about Rabbi Silver's grandeur, lady, tell my late cousin Sidney and his friends in the Mob—quote Zvi Masliansky to them, like you do at the country club on the eighteenth hole!

At around eleven I heard the town snowplow clearing the unpaved road beyond the apple orchard. Later a pickup truck with a snowblade clamped to the front end charged into the driveway and shoved the evening's snowfall into the orchard atop the snowfall of the previous thirty nights. The little Renault arrived last, swerving slowly into the driveway about half an hour later, one beam on high, the other dim, and with half-dead windshield wipers.

At the first sound of her car returning, I had flipped off all my lights and crawled to the study window on my knees so as to watch her make her way toward the house. For I had not stayed awake simply because I couldn't forget my father's disapproval or E. I. Lonoff's toast—I also had no intention of being unconscious when the enchanting and mysterious houseguest (all the more alluring, of course, as Hope's imagined erotic rival) got back to change into her nightdress on the floor above me. What I would be able to do about this, I had no idea. However, just to be awake and unclothed in one bed while she was awake and nearly unclothed in another was better than nothing. It was a start.

But predictably, it was worse than nothing and the start of little that was new. The lantern on the half-buried lamppost between the house and the car shed went dark, and then, from where I was kneeling beside the study door, I heard her enter the house. She moved through the hallway and up the carpeted stairs—and that was the last of her that I saw or heard until about an hour later, when I was privileged to audit another astounding course, this one in the adult evening division of the Lonoff School of the Arts. The rest of what I'd been waiting up for I had, of course, to imagine. But that is easier work by far than making things up at the typewriter. For that kind of imagining you don't have to have your picture in the *Saturday Review.* You don't even have to know the alphabet. Being young will usually get a fellow through with flying colors. You don't even have to be young. You don't have to be anything.

Virtuous reader, if you think that after intercourse all animals are sad, try masturbating on the daybed in E. I. Lonoff's study and see how you feel when it's over. To expiate my sense of utter shabbiness, I immediately took to the high road and drew from Lonoff's bookshelves the volume of Henry James stories containing "The Middle Years," the source of one of the two quotations pinned to the bulletin board. And there where I had indulged myself in this most un-Jamesian lapse from the amenities, I read the story two times through, looking to discover what I could about the doubt that's the writer's passion, the passion that's his task, and the madness of—of all things—art.

Dencombe, a novelist "who had a reputation," is convalescing from a debilitating ailment at an English health resort when a copy of his latest book, *The Middle Years,* arrives from his publisher. Seated alone on a bench looking out to sea, Dencombe reluctantly opens the book—to discover what he believes is the artistic distinction that had always evaded him. His genius has flowered, however, just when he no longer has the strength to develop a " 'last manner' . . . to which his real treasure would be gathered." That would require a second existence, and everything tells him that the first one is nearly over.

While fearfully contemplating the end of his life, Dencombe is joined on the bench by a garrulous young stranger carrying his own copy of *The Middle Years.* He begins to speak ardently of Dencombe's achievement to the mild gentleman who he finds has also been reading the new novel. The admirer—"the greatest admirer . . . whom it was supposable he might boast"—is Dr. Hugh, physician to a rich, eccentric English countess who is at the hotel, like Dencombe, to recover from some grave illness. Inflamed with passion for *The Middle Years,* Dr. Hugh opens the book to read aloud a particularly beautiful passage; but, having mistakenly seized Dencombe's copy rather than his own, he discovers that the printed text has been altered in a dozen places by a pencil. With this, the anonymous and ailing author on the brink of being discovered—"a passionate corrector" never able to arrive at a final form—feels his sickness sweeping over him and loses consciousness.

In the days that follow, Dencombe, bedridden, hopes that some remedy miraculously concocted by the attentive young physician will restore his strength. However, when he learns that the countess plans to disinherit Dr. Hugh of a magnificent fortune if he continues to neglect her for the novelist, Dencombe encourages Dr. Hugh to follow her to London. But Dr. Hugh cannot overcome his passionate idolatry, and by the time he acts on Dencombe's advice to hurry to his employer, he has already suffered "a terrible injury" for which Dencombe almost believes himself to be responsible: the countess has died, in a relapse brought on by her jealousy, bequeathing to the young physician not a penny. Says Dr. Hugh, returning from her grave to the dying soul whom he adores, "I had to choose."

> "You chose to let a fortune go?"
>
> "I chose to accept, whatever they might be, the consequences of my infatuation," smiled Doctor Hugh. Then, as a larger pleasantry: "The fortune be hanged! It's your own fault if I can't get your things out of my head."

A thin black line had been drawn beneath the "pleasantry" in Lonoff's book. In script so tiny it was almost unreadable, the writer had noted beside it a droll pleasantry of his own: "And also your fault if I can."

From there on, down both margins of the final page describing Dencombe's death, Lonoff had penned three vertical lines. Nothing resembling drollery here. Rather, the six surgically precise black lines seemed to simulate the succession of fine impressions that James's insidious narrative about the novelist's dubious wizardry had scored upon Lonoff's undeluded brain.

After Dencombe has learned the consequences of the young man's infatuation—consequences so utterly irreconcilable with his own honorable convictions that, upon hearing of his place in it all, Dencombe utters "a long bewildered moan"—he lies "for many hours, many days . . . motionless and absent."

> At the last he signed to Doctor Hugh to listen and, when he was down on his knees by the pillow, brought him very near. "You've made me think it all a delusion."
>
> "Not your glory, my dear friend," stammered the young man.
>
> "Not my glory—what there is of it! It *is* glory—to have

been tested, to have had our little quality and cast our little spell. The thing is to have made somebody care. You happen to be crazy of course, but that doesn't affect the law."

"You're a great success!" said Doctor Hugh, putting into his young voice the ring of a marriage-bell.

Dencombe lay taking this in; then he gathered strength to speak once more. "A second chance—*that's* the delusion. There never was to be but one. We work in the dark—we do what we can—we give what we have. Our doubt is our passion and our passion is our task. The rest is the madness of art."

"If you've doubted, if you've despaired, you've always 'done' it," his visitor subtly argued.

"We've done something or other," Dencombe conceded.

"Something or other is everything. It's the feasible. It's *you!*"

"Comforter!" poor Dencombe ironically sighed.

"But it's true," insisted his friend.

"It's true. It's frustration that doesn't count."

"Frustration's only life," said Doctor Hugh.

"Yes, it's what passes." Poor Dencombe was barely audible, but he had marked with the words the virtual end of his first and only chance.

Within moments of hearing muffled voices coming from above my head, I stood up on the daybed—my finger still holding my place in the book—and, stretching to my full height, tried to make out what was being said up there and by whom. When that didn't help, I thought of climbing onto Lonoff's desk; it was easily a foot or so higher than the daybed and would put my ear only inches from the room's low ceiling. But if I should fall, if I should alter by a millimeter the placement of his typing paper, if somehow I should leave footprints—no, I couldn't risk it and shouldn't even have been thinking of it. I had gone far enough already by expropriating the corner of the desk to compose my half dozen unfinished letters home. My sense of propriety, not to mention the author's gracious hospitality, required me to restrain myself from committing such a sordid, callow little indecency.

But in the meantime I had done it.

A woman was crying. Which one, over what, who was there comforting her—or causing the tears? Just a little higher and maybe I could find out. A thick dictionary would have been perfect, but Lonoff's Webster's was down on a shelf of fat reference books level with the typing chair, and the best I could manage under pressure was to gain another couple of inches by kneeling to insert between the desk and my feet the volume of stories by Henry James.

Ah, the unreckoned consequences, the unaccountable uses of art! Dencombe would understand. James would understand. But would Lonoff? *Don't fall.*

"Now you're being sensible." Lonoff was the speaker. "You had to see for yourself, and so you saw."

A light thud directly overhead. Someone had dropped into a chair. The weary writer? In his bathrobe now, or still in suit and tie and polished shoes?

Then I heard Amy Bellette. And what was *she* wearing at this hour? "I saw nothing—only more misery either way. Of course I can't live here—but I can't keep living there, either. I can't live anywhere. I can't *live.*"

"Quiet down. She's had it for today. Let her rest, now that she's asleep."

"She's ruining everyone's life."

"Don't blame her for what you hold against me. I'm the one who says no around here. Now *you* go to sleep."

"I can't. I don't want to. We can talk."

"We've talked."

Silence. Were they down on their knees listening through the old floorboards for *me?* Then they had long since heard my drumming heart.

Bedsprings! Lonoff climbing in beside her!

But it was Amy getting out of bed I heard, not Lonoff climbing in. Her feet lightly crossed the floor only inches above my lips.

"I love you. I love you so, Dad-da. There's no one else like you. They're all such dopes."

"You're a good girl."

"Let me sit on your lap. Just hold me a little and I'll be fine."

"You're fine now. You're always fine in the end. You're the great survivor."

"No, just the world's strongest weakling. Oh, tell me a story. Sing me a song. Oh, imitate the great Durante, I really need it tonight."

At first it sounded like somebody coughing. But then I could hear that, yes, he was singing to her, very quietly, in the manner of Jimmy Durante—"So I ups to him, and he ups to me"—I could catch just the one line, but that was enough for me to recall the song itself being sung by Durante on his radio show, in the celebrated raffish voice, and with the hoarse, endearing simple-hearted delivery that the famous author was now impersonating overhead.

"More," said Amy.

Was she now on his lap? Amy in her nightie and Lonoff in his suit?

"You go to sleep," he told her.

"More. Sing 'I Can Do Without Broadway.' "

" 'Oh, I know don well I can do widout Broadway—*but*... can Broadway do widout meeeee? . . .' "

"Oh, Manny, we could be so happy—in Florence, my sweetest, we could come out of hiding."

"We're not in hiding. We never have been."

"No, not when it's like this. But otherwise it's all so false and wrong and lonely. We could make each other so happy. I wouldn't be your little girl over there. I would when we played, but otherwise I'd be your wife."

"We'd be what we've always been. Stop dreaming."

"No, not so. Without her—"

"You want a corpse on your conscience? She would be dead in a year."

"But I have a corpse on my conscience." The floor creaked where her two feet had suddenly landed. So she *had* been on his lap! "Look!"

"Cover yourself."

"My corpse."

Scuffling on the floorboards. The heavy tread of Lonoff on the move.

"Good night."

"Look at it."

"Melodrama, Amy. Cover up."

"You prefer tragedy?"

"Don't wallow. You're not convincing. Decide not to lose hold—and then don't."

"But I'm going crazy! I cannot live apart from you! I don't know how. Oh, why didn't I take that job—and move back! And the hell with her!"

"You did the right thing. You know just what to do."

"Yes, give things up!"

"Dreamy things, correct."

"Oh, Manny, would it kill you just to kiss my breasts? Is that dreamy, too? Would it cause the death of anyone if you just did that?"

"You cover yourself now."

"Dad-da, *please.*"

But next I heard Lonoff's carpet slippers—yes, he was out of his suit, dressed for bed—padding through the upstairs corridor. Soundlessly as I could, I slipped down from the desk and made my way on my toes to the daybed, where, from the sheer physical effort that had gone into my acrobatic eavesdropping, I collapsed. My astonishment at what I'd overheard, my shame at the unpardonable breach of his trust, my relief at having escaped undiscovered—all that turned out to be nothing, really, beside the frustration I soon began to feel over the thinness of my imagination and what that promised for the future. Dad-da, Florence, the great Durante; her babyishness and desire, his mad, heroic restraint—Oh, if only I could have imagined the scene I'd overheard! If only I could invent as presumptuously as real life! If one day I could just *approach* the originality and excitement of what actually goes on! But if I ever did, what then would they think of me, my father and his judge? How would my elders hold up against that? And if they couldn't, if the blow to their sentiments was finally too wounding, just how well would I hold up against being hated and reviled and disowned?

The Professor in Prague

And then the summer after I return East I meet a young woman altogether unlike this small band of counsolers, counselors, tempters, and provocateurs—the "influences," as my father would have it—off whom my benumbed and unsexed carcass has been careening since I've been a womanless, pleasureless, passionless man on his own.

I am invited for a weekend on Cape Cod by a faculty couple I have just gotten to know, and there I am introduced to Claire Ovington, their young neighbor, who is renting a tiny shingled bungalow in a wild-rose patch near the Orleans beach for herself and her golden Labrador. Some ten days after the morning we spend talking together on the beach—after I have sent her a painfully charming letter from New York, and consulted for several clammy hours with Klinger—I take the impulse by the horns and return to Orleans, where I move into the local inn. I am drawn at first by the same look of soft voluptuousness that had (against all seemingly reasonable reservations) done so much to draw me to Helen, and which has touched off, for the first time in over a year, a spontaneous surge of warm feeling. Back in New

---

From the 1977 novel, *The Professor of Desire.* At the beginning of this selection, the narrator, David Kepesh, a teacher of literature, is in a state of spiritual despair and physical impotence after the failure of his marriage to the flamboyant Helen Baird. Herbie Bratasky, who appears in the dream sequence, was the ebullient, shameless social director at the Catskill Mountains resort hotel owned by Kepesh's parents, where David grew up.

York after my brief weekend visit, I had thought only about her. Do I sense the renewal of desire, of confidence, of capacity? Not quite yet. During my week at the inn, I cannot stop behaving like an overzealous child at dancing class, unable to go through a door or to raise a fork without the starchiest display of good manners. And after the *self*-display of that letter, that bravura show of wit and self-assurance! Why did I listen to Klinger? "Of course, go—what can you lose?" But what does *he* have to lose if I fail? Where's his tragic view of life, damn it? Impotence is no joke—it's a plague! People kill themselves! And alone in my bed at the inn, after yet another evening of keeping my distance from Claire, I can understand why. In the morning, just before I am to leave for New York once again, I arrive at her bungalow for an early breakfast, and midway through the fresh blueberry pancakes try to redeem myself a little by admitting to my shame. I don't know how else to get out of this with at least some self-esteem intact, though why I will ever have to care about self-esteem again I cannot imagine. "I seem to have come all the way up here—after writing to you like that, and then arriving out of nowhere—well, after all that fanfare, I seem to have come upon the scene and . . . disappeared." And now moving over me—moving right up to the roots of my hair—I feel something very like the shame that I must have imagined I could avoid *by* disappearing. "I must seem odd to you. At this point I seem odd to myself. I've seemed odd to myself for some time now. I'm only trying to say that it's nothing you've done or said that's made me behave so coldly." "But," she says, before I can begin another round of apology about this "oddity" that I am, "it's been so pleasant. In a way it's been the sweetest thing." "It has?" I say, fearful that I am about to be humbled in some unforeseen way. "*What* has?" "Seeing somebody shy for a change. It's nice to know it still exists in the Age of Utter Abandon."

God, as tender within as without! The tact! The calm! The *wisdom!* As physically alluring to me as Helen—but there the resemblance ends. Poise and confidence and determination, but, in Claire, all of it marshaled in behalf of something more than high sybaritic adventure. At twenty-four, she has earned a degree from Cornell in experimental psychology, a master's from

Columbia in education, and is on the faculty of a private school in Manhattan, where she teaches eleven- and twelve-year-olds, and, as of the coming semester, will be in charge of the curriculum-review committee. Yet, for someone who, as I come to learn, emanates in her professional role a strong aura of reserve, a placid, coolheaded, and seemingly unassailable presence, she is surprisingly innocent and guileless about the personal side of her life, and, as regards her friends, her plants, her herb garden, her dog, her cooking, her sister Olivia, who summers on Martha's Vineyard, and Olivia's three children, she has about as much reserve as a healthy ten-year-old girl. In all, this translucent mix of sober social aplomb and domestic enthusiasms and youthful susceptibility is simply irresistible. What I mean is *no resistance is necessary.* A tempter of a kind to whom I can at last succumb.

Now it is as if a gong has been struck in my stomach when I recall—and I do, daily—that I had written Claire my clever, flirtatious letter, and then had very nearly been content to leave it at that. Had even told Klinger that writing out of the blue to a voluptuous young woman I had spoken with casually on a beach for two hours was a measure of just how hopeless my prospects had become. I had almost decided against showing up for breakfast that last morning on the Cape, so fearful was I of what my convalescent desire might have in store for me were I, with a suitcase in one hand and my plane ticket in the other, to try to put it to a crazy last-minute test. How ever *did* I manage to make it past my shameful secret? Do I owe it to sheer luck, to ebullient, optimistic Klinger, or do I owe everything I now have to those breasts of hers in that bathing suit? Oh, if so, then bless each breast a thousand times! For now, now I am positively exultant, thrilled, astonished—grateful for everything about her, for the executive dispatch with which she orders her life as for the patience that she brings to our lovemaking, that canniness of hers that seems to sense exactly how much raw carnality and how much tender solicitude it is going to require to subdue my tenacious anxiety and renew my faith in coupling and all that may come in its wake. All the pedagogic expertise bestowed upon those sixth-graders is now bestowed upon *me* after school—such a gentle, tactful tutor comes to my apartment each day, and yet always the hungry woman with her! And those breasts, those breasts—large and soft and vulnerable, each as heavy as an udder upon my face, as warm and heavy in my hand as some fat little animal fast asleep. Oh, the look of this large girl above me when she is still half stripped! And, mind you, an assiduous keeper of records as well! Yes, the history of each passing day in calendar books going back through college, her life's history in the photographs she has been taking since childhood, first with a Brownie, now with the best equipment from Japan. And those lists! Those wonderful, orderly lists! I too write out on a yellow pad what I plan to accomplish each day, but by bedtime I seem never to find a soothing little check mark beside each item, confirming that the letter has been dispatched, the money withdrawn, the article xeroxed, the call made. Despite my own strong penchant for orderliness, passed along through the maternal chromosomes, there are still mornings when I can't even locate the list I drew up the night before, and, usually, what I don't feel like doing one day, I am able to put off to the next without too many qualms. Not so with Mistress Ovington—to every task that presents itself, regardless of how difficult or dreary, she gives her complete attention, taking each up in its turn and steadfastly following it through to its conclusion. And, to my great good luck, reconstituting my life is apparently just such a task. It is as though at the top of one of her yellow pads she has spelled out my name and then, beneath, in her open spherical hand, written instructions to herself, as follows: "Provide DK with— 1. Loving kindness. 2. Impassioned embraces. 3. Sane surroundings." For within a year the job is somehow done, a big check mark beside each life-saving item. I give up the anti-depressants, and no abyss opens beneath me. I sublet the sublet apartment, and, without being wracked too much by memories of the handsome rugs, tables, dishes, and chairs once jointly owned by Helen and me and now hers alone, I furnish a new place of my own. I even accept an invitation to a dinner party at the Schonbrunns', and at the end of the evening politely kiss Debbie's cheek while Arthur paternally kisses Claire's. Easy as that. Meaningless as that. At the door, while Arthur and Claire conclude the conversation they'd been having at dinner—about the curriculum that

Claire is now devising for the upper grades—Debbie and I have a moment to chat privately. For some reason—alcoholic intake on both sides, I think—we are holding hands! "Another of your tall blondes," says Debbie, "but this one seems a bit more sympathetic. We both find her very sweet. And very bright. Where did you meet?" "In a brothel in Marrakesh. Look, Debbie, isn't it about time you got off my ass? What does that mean, my 'tall blondes'?" "It's a fact." "No, it is not even a fact. Helen's hair was auburn. But suppose it was cut from the same bolt as Claire's—the fact is that 'blondes,' in that context, and that tone, is, as you may even know, a derogatory term used by intellectuals and other serious people to put down pretty women. I also believe it is dense with unsavory implication when addressed to men of my origin and complexion. I remember how fond you used to be at Stanford of pointing out to people the anomaly of a literate chap like myself coming from the 'Borscht Belt.' That too used to strike me as a bit reductive." "Oh, you take yourself too seriously. Why don't you just admit you have a penchant for these big blondes and leave it at that? It's nothing to be ashamed of. They do look lovely up on water skis with all that hair streaming. I bet they look lovely everywhere." "Debbie, I'll make a deal with you. I'll admit I know nothing about you, if you'll admit you know nothing about me. I'm sure you have a whole wondrous being and inner life that I know nothing about." "Nope," she says, "this is it. This is the whole thing. Take it or leave it." Both of us begin to laugh. I say, "Tell me, what does Arthur see in you? It's really one of the mysteries of life. What do you have that I'm blind to?" "Everything," she replies. Out in the car, I give Claire an abridged version of the conversation. "The woman is warped," I say. "Oh, no," says Claire, "just silly, that's all." "She tricked you, Clarissa. Silly is the cover—assassination is the game." "Ah, sweetie," says Claire, "it's *you* she's tricked."

So much for my rehabilitation back into society. As for my father and his awesome loneliness, well, now he takes the train from Cedarhurst to have dinner in Manhattan once a month; he can't be coaxed in any more often, but in truth, before there was the new apartment, and Claire to help with the conversation and the cooking, I didn't work at coaxing him that hard, no, not so each of us could sit and peer sadly at the other picking at his spareribs, two orphans in Chinatown . . . not so I could wait to hear him ask over the lichee nuts, "And that guy, he hasn't come back to bother you, has he?"

And, to be sure, from the maw of that maelstrom called Baumgarten I withdraw my toes a little. We still have lunch together from time to time, but the grander feasts I leave him to partake of on his own. And I do not introduce him to Claire.

My, how easy life is when it's easy, and how hard when it's hard!

One night, after dinner at my apartment, while Claire is preparing her next day's lessons at the cleared dining table, I finally get up the nerve, or no longer seem to need "nerve," to reread what there is of my Chekhov book, shelved now for more than two years. In the midst of the laborious and deadly competence of those fragmentary chapters intended to focus upon the subject of romantic disillusionment, I find five pages that are somewhat readable—reflections growing out of Chekhov's comic little story, "Man in a Shell," about the tyrannical rise and celebrated fall—"I confess," says the goodhearted narrator after the tyrant's funeral, "it is a great pleasure to bury people like Belikov"—the rise and fall of a provincial high school official whose love of prohibitions and hatred of all deviations from the rules manages to hold a whole town of "thoughtful, decent people" under his thumb for fifteen years. I go back to reread the story, then to reread "Gooseberries" and "About Love," written in sequence with it and forming a series of anecdotal ruminations upon the varieties of pain engendered by spiritual imprisonment—by petty despotism, by ordinary human complacency, and finally, even by the inhibitions upon feeling necessary to support a scrupulous man's sense of decency. For the next month, with a notebook on my lap, and some tentative observations in mind, I return to Chekhov's fiction nightly, listening for the anguished cry of the trapped and miserable socialized being, the well-bred wives who during dinner with the guests wonder "Why do I smile and lie?", and the husbands, seemingly settled and secure, who are "full of conventional truth and conventional deception." Simultaneously I am watching how Chekhov, simply and clearly, though not quite so pitilessly as Flaubert, reveals the humiliations and failures—worst of all, the destructive power—of those who seek a way *out* of the shell of restrictions and convention, out of the pervasive boredom and the stifling despair, out of the painful marital situations and the endemic social falsity, into what they take to be a vibrant and desirable life. There is the agitated young wife in "Misfortune" who looks for "a bit of excitement" against the grain of her own offended respectability; there is the lovesick landowner in "Ariadne," confessing with Herzogian helplessness to a romantic misadventure with a vulgar trampy tigress who gradually transforms him into a hopeless misogynist, but whom he nonetheless waits on hand and foot; there is the young actress in "A Boring Story," whose bright hopeful enthusiasm for a life on the stage, and a life with men, turns bitter with her first experiences of the stage and of men, and of her own lack of talent—"I have no talent, you see, I have no talent and . . . and lots of vanity." And there is "The Duel." Every night for a week (with Claire only footsteps away) I reread Chekhov's masterpiece about the weaseling, slovenly, intelligent, literary-minded seducer Layevsky, immersed in his lies and his self-pity, and Layevsky's antagonist, the ruthless punitive conscience who all but murders him, the voluble scientist Von Koren. Or so it is that I come to view the story: with Von Koren as the ferociously rational and merciless prosecutor called forth to challenge the sense of shame and sinfulness that is nearly all that Layevsky has become, and from which, alas, he no longer can flee. It is this immersion in "The Duel" that finally gets me writing, and within four months the five pages extracted from the old unfinished rehash of my thesis on romantic disillusionment are transformed into some forty thousand words entitled *Man in a Shell,* an essay on license and restraint in Chekhov's world—longings fulfilled, pleasures denied, and the pain occasioned by both; a study, at bottom, of what makes for Chekhov's pervasive pessimism about the methods—scrupulous, odious, noble, dubious—by which the men and women of his time try in vain to achieve "that sense of personal freedom" to which Chekhov himself is so devoted. My first book! With a dedication page that reads "To C.O."

"She is to steadiness," I tell Klinger (and Kepesh, who must never, never, never forget), "what Helen was to impetuosity. She is to common sense what Birgitta was to indiscretion. I have never seen such devotion to the ordinary business of daily life. It's awesome, really, the way she deals with each day as it comes, the attention she pays minute by minute. There's no dreaming going on there—just steady, dedicated *living.* I trust her, that's the point I'm making. That's what's done it," I announce triumphantly, "trust."

To all of which Klinger eventually replies goodbye then and good luck. At the door of his office on the spring afternoon of our parting, I have to wonder if it can really be that I no longer need bucking up and holding down and hearing out, warning, encouragement, consent, consolation, applause, and opposition—in short, professional doses of mothering and fathering and simple friendship three times a week for an hour. *Can* it be that I've come through? Just like that? Just because of Claire? What if I awaken tomorrow morning once again a man with a crater instead of a heart, once again without a man's capacity and appetite and strength and judgment, without the least bit of mastery over my flesh or my intelligence or my feelings . . .

"Stay in touch," says Klinger, shaking my hand. Just as I could not look squarely at him the day I neglected to mention the impact on my conscience of his daughter's snapshot—as though suppressing that fact I might be spared his unuttered judgment, or my own—so I cannot let his eyes engage mine when we say farewell. But now it is because I would prefer not to give vent to my feelings of elation and indebtedness in an outburst of tears. Sniffing all sentiment back up my nose—and firmly, for the moment, suppressing all doubt—I say, "Let's hope I don't have to," but once out on the street by myself, I repeat the incredible words aloud, only now to the accompaniment of the appropriate emotions: "I've come through!"

The following June, when the teaching year is over for the two of us, Claire and I fly to the north of Italy, my first time back in Europe since I'd gone prowling there with Birgitta a decade earlier. In Venice we spend five days at a quiet pensione near the

Accademia. Each morning we eat breakfast in the pensione's aromatic garden and then, in our walking shoes, weave back and forth across the bridges and alleyways that lead to the landmarks Claire has marked on the map for us to visit that day. Whenever she takes her pictures of these palazzos and piazzas and churches and fountains I wander off always, but always looking back to get a picture of her and her unadorned beauty.

Each evening after dinner under the arbor in the garden, we treat ourselves to a little gondola ride. With Claire beside me in the armchair that Mann describes as "the softest, most luxurious, most relaxing seat in the world," I ask myself yet again if this serenity truly exists, if this contentment, this wonderful accord is real. *Is* the worst over? Have I no more terrible mistakes to make? And no more to pay on those behind me? Was all that only so much Getting Started, a longish and misguided youth out of which I have finally aged? "Are you sure we didn't die," I say, "and go to heaven?" "I wouldn't know," she replies; "you'll have to ask the gondolier."

Our last afternoon I blow us to lunch at the Gritti. On the terrace I tip the headwaiter and point to the very table where I had imagined myself sitting with the pretty student who used to lunch on Peanut Chews in my classroom; I order exactly what I ate that day back in Palo Alto when we were studying Chekhov's stories about love and I felt myself on the edge of a nervous collapse—only this time I am not imagining the delicious meal with the fresh, untainted mate, this time both are real and I am well. Settling back—I with a cold glass of wine; Claire, the teetotaling daughter of parents who overimbibed, with her *acqua minerale*—I look out across the gleaming waters of this indescribably beautiful toy town and I say to her, "Do you think Venice is really sinking? The place seems in vaguely the same position as last time I was here."

"Who were you with then? Your wife?"

"No. It was my Fulbright year. I was with a girl."

"Who was that?"

Now, how endangered or troubled would she feel, what, if anything, do I risk awakening if I go ahead and tell her all? Oh, how dramatically put! What did "all" consist of—any more, really, than a young sailor goes out to find in his first foreign port? A sailor's taste for a little of the lurid, but, as things turned out, neither a sailor's stomach nor strength . . . Still, to someone so measured and orderly, someone who has turned all her considerable energy to making normal and ordinary what had for her been heartbreakingly irregular in her childhood home, I think it best to answer, "Oh, nobody, really," and let the matter drop.

Whereupon the nobody who has been no part of my life for over ten years is all I can think of. In that Chekhov class the mismatched husband had recalled sunnier days on the terrace of the Gritti, an unbruised, audacious, young Kepesh still running around Europe scot-free; now on the terrace of the Gritti, where I have come to celebrate the triumphant foundation of a sweet and stable new life, to celebrate the astonishing renewal of health and happiness, I am recalling the earliest, headiest hours of my sheikdom, the night in our London basement when it is my turn to ask Birgitta what it is *she* most wants. What I most want the two girls have given me; what Elisabeth most wants we are leaving for last—she does not know . . . for in her heart, as we are to discover when the truck knocks her down, she wants none of it. But Birgitta has desires about which she is not afraid to speak, and which we proceed to satisfy. Yes, sitting across from Claire, who has said that my semen filling her mouth makes her feel that she is drowning, that this is something she just doesn't care to do, I am remembering the sight of Birgitta kneeling before me, her face upturned to receive the strands of flowing semen that fall upon her hair, her forehead, her nose. *"Här!"* she cries, *"här!"*, while Elisabeth, wearing her pink woolen robe, and reclining on the bed, looks on in frozen fascination at the naked masturbator and his half-clothed suppliant.

As if such a thing matters! As if Claire is withholding anything that *matters!* But admonish myself as I will for amnesia, stupidity, ingratitude, callowness, for a lunatic and suicidal loss of all perspective, the rush of greedy lust I feel is not for this lovely young woman with whom I have only recently emerged into a life promising the most profound sort of fulfillment, but for the smallish buck-toothed comrade I last saw leaving my room at midnight some thirty kilometers outside Rouen over ten years ago, desire for my own lewd, lost soul mate, who, back before my sense of the permissible began its inward collapse, welcomed as feverishly and gamely as did I the uncommon act and the alien thought. Oh, Birgitta, go away! But this time we are in our room right here in Venice, a hotel on a narrow alleyway off the Zattere, not very far from the little bridge where Claire had taken my picture earlier in the day. I tie a kerchief around her eyes, careful to knot it tightly at the back, and then I am standing over the blindfolded girl and—ever so lightly to begin with—whipping her between her parted legs. I watch as she strains upward with her hips to catch the bite of each stroke of my belt on her genital crease. I watch this as I have never watched anything before in my life. "Say all the things," Birgitta whispers, and I do, in a low, subdued growl such as I have never used before to address anyone or anything.

For Birgitta then—for what I would now prefer to dismiss as a "longish and misguided youth"—a surging sense of lascivious kinship . . . and for Claire, for this truly passionate and loving rescuer of mine? Anger; disappointment; disgust—contempt for all she does so marvelously, resentment over that little thing she will not deign to do. I see how very easily I could have no use for her. The snapshots. The lists. The mouth that will not drink my come. The curriculum-review committee. Everything.

The impulse to fly up from the table and telephone Dr. Klinger I suppress. I will not be one of those hysterical patients at the other end of the overseas line. No, not that. I eat the meal when it is served, and sure enough, by the time the dessert is to be ordered, yearnings for Birgitta begging me and Birgitta beneath me and Birgitta below me, all such yearnings have begun to subside, as left to themselves those yearnings will. And the anger disappears too, to be replaced by shame-filled sadness. If Claire senses the rising and ebbing of all this distress—and how can she not? how else understand my silent, icy gloom?—she decides to pretend ignorance, to talk on about her plans for the curriculum-review committee until whatever has cast us apart has simply passed away.

From Venice we drive a rented car to Padua to look at the Giottos. Claire takes more pictures. She will have them developed when we get home and then, sitting cross-legged on the floor—the posture of tranquillity, of concentration, the posture of a very good girl indeed—paste them, in their proper sequence, into the album for this year. Now northern Italy will be in the bookcase at the foot of the bed where her volumes of photographs are stored, now northern Italy will be forever *hers,* along with Schenectady, where she was born and raised, Ithaca, where she went to college, and New York City, where she lives and works and lately has fallen in love. And I will be there at the foot of the bed, along with her places, her family, and her friends.

Though so many of her twenty-five years have been blighted by the squabbling of contentious parents—arguments abetted, as often as not, by too many tumblers of Scotch—she regards the past as worth recording and remembering, if only because she has outlasted the pain and disorder to establish a decent life of her own. As she likes to say, it is the only past she has got to remember, hard as it may have been when the bombs were bursting around her and she was trying her best to grow up in one piece. And then, of course, that Mr. and Mrs. Ovington put more energy into being adversaries than into being the comforters of their children does not mean that their daughter must deny *herself* the ordinary pleasures that ordinary families (if such there be) take as a matter of course. To all the pleasant amenities of family life—the exchanging of photographs, the giving of gifts, the celebration of holidays, the regular phone calls—both Claire and her older sister are passionately devoted, as though in fact she and Olivia are the thoughtful parents and their parents the callow offspring.

From a hotel in a small mountain town where we find a room with a terrace and a bed and an Arcadian view, we make day trips to Verona and Vicenza. Pictures, pictures, pictures. What is the opposite of a nail being driven into a coffin? Well, that is what I hear as Claire's camera clicks away. Once again I feel I am being sealed up into something wonderful. One day we just walk with a picnic lunch up along the cowpaths and through the flowering fields, whole nations of minute bluets and lacquered little buttercups and unreal poppies. I can walk silently with Claire for hours on end. I am content just to lie on the ground propped up on one elbow and watch her pick wild flowers to take back to our room and arrange in a water glass to place beside my pillow. I feel no need for anything more. "More" has no meaning. Nor does Birgitta appear to have meaning any longer, as though "Birgitta" and "more" are just different ways of saying the same thing. Following the performance at the Gritti, she has failed to put in anything like such a sensational appearance again. For the next few nights she does come by to pay me a visit each time Claire and I make love—kneeling, always kneeling, and begging for what thrills her most—but then she is gone, and I am above the body I am above, and with that alone partake of all the "more" I now could want, or want to want. Yes, I just hold tight to Claire and the unbeckoned visitor eventually drifts away, leaving me to enjoy once again the awesome fact of my great good luck.

On our last afternoon, we carry our lunch to the crest of a field that looks across high green hills to the splendid white tips of the Dolomites. Claire lies stretched out beside where I am sitting, her ample figure gently swelling and subsiding with each breath she draws. Looking steadily down at this large, green-eyed girl in her thin summer clothes, at her pale, smallish, oval, unmarred face, her scrubbed, unworldly prettiness—the beauty, I realize, of a young Amish or Shaker woman—I say to myself, "Claire is enough. Yes, 'Claire' and 'enough'—they, too, are one word."

From Venice we fly by way of Vienna—and the house of Sigmund Freud—to Prague. During this last year I have been teaching the Kafka course at the university—the paper that I am to read a few days from now in Bruges has Kafka's preoccupations with spiritual starvation as its subject—but I have not as yet seen his city, other than in books of photographs. Just prior to our departure I had graded the final examinations written by my fifteen students in the seminar, who had read all of the fiction, Max Brod's biography, and Kafka's diaries and his letters to Milena and to his father. One of the questions I had asked on the examination was this—

> In his "Letter to His Father" Kafka writes, "My writing is all about you; all I did there, after all, was to bemoan what I could not bemoan upon your breast. It was an intentionally

> long-drawn-out leave-taking from you, yet, although it was enforced by you, it did take its course in the direction determined by me . . ." What does Kafka mean when he says to his father, "My writing is all about you," and adds, "yet it did take its course in the direction determined by me"? If you like, imagine yourself to be Max Brod writing a letter of your own to Kafka's father, explaining what it is your friend has in mind . . .

I had been pleased by the number of students who had taken my suggestion and decided to pretend to be the writer's friend and biographer—and, in describing the inner workings of a most unusual son to a most conventional father, had demonstrated a mature sensitivity to Kafka's moral isolation, to his peculiarities of perspective and temperament, and to those imaginative processes by which a fantasist as entangled as Kafka was in daily existence transforms into fable his everyday struggles. Hardly a single benighted literature major straying into ingenious metaphysical exegesis! Oh, I am pleased, all right, with the Kafka seminar and with myself for what I've done there. But these first months with Claire, what hasn't been a source of pleasure?

Before leaving home I had been given the name and telephone number of an American spending the year teaching in Prague, and, happily, as it turns out (and what doesn't these days?), he and a Czech friend of his, another literature professor, have the afternoon free and are able to give us a tour of old Prague. From a bench in the Old Town Square we gaze across at the palatial building where Franz Kafka attended Gymnasium. To the right of the columned entryway is the ground-floor site of Hermann Kafka's business. "He couldn't even get away from him at school," I say. "All the worse for him," the Czech professor replies, "and all the better for the fiction." In the imposing Gothic church nearby, high on one wall of the nave, a small square window faces an apartment next door where, I am informed, Kafka's family had once lived. So Kafka, I say, could have sat there furtively looking down on the sinner confessing and the faithful at prayer . . . and the interior of this church, might it not have furnished, if not every last detail, at least the atmosphere for the Cathedral of *The Trial?* And those steep angular streets across the river leading circuitously to the sprawling Hapsburg castle, surely they must have served as inspiration for him too . . . Perhaps so, says the Czech professor, but a small castle village in northern Bohemia that Kafka knew from his visits to his grandfather is thought to have been the principal model for the topography of *The Castle.* Then there is the little country village where his sister had spent a year managing a farm and where Kafka had gone to stay with her during a spell of illness. Had we time, says the Czech professor, Claire and I might benefit from an overnight visit to the countryside. "Visit one of those xenophobic little towns, with its smoky taverna and its buxom barmaid, and you will see what a thoroughgoing realist this Kafka was."

For the first time I sense something other than geniality in this smallish, bespectacled, neatly attired academic—I sense all that the geniality is working to suppress.

Near the wall of the castle, on cobbled Alchemist Street—and looking like a dwelling out of a child's bedtime story, the fit habitation for a gnome or elf—is the tiny house that his youngest sister had rented one winter for Kafka to live in, another of her efforts to help separate the bachelor son from father and family. The little place is now a souvenir shop. Picture postcards and Prague mementos are being sold on the spot where Kafka had meticulously scribbled variants of the same paragraph ten times over in his diary, and where he had drawn his sardonic stick figures of himself, the "private ideograms" he hid, along with practically everything else, in a drawer. Claire takes a picture of the three literature professors in front of the perfectionist writer's torture chamber. Soon it will be in its place in one of the albums at the foot of her bed.

While Claire goes off with the American professor, and her camera, for a tour of the castle grounds, I sit over tea with Professor Soska, our Czech guide. When the Russians invaded Czechoslovakia and put an end to the Prague Spring reform movement, Soska was fired from his university post and at age thirty-nine placed in "retirement" on a minuscule pension. His wife, a research scientist, also was relieved of her position for political reasons and, in order to support the family of four, has been working for a year now as a typist in a meat-packing plant. How has the retired professor managed to keep up his morale, I wonder. His three-piece suit is impeccable, his gait quick, his speech snappy and precise—how does he do it? What gets him up in the morning and to sleep at night? What gets him through each day?

"Kafka, of course," he says, showing me that smile again. "Yes, this is true; many of us survive almost solely on Kafka. Including people in the street who have never read a word of his. They look at one another when something happens, and they say, 'It's Kafka.' Meaning, 'That's the way it goes here now.' Meaning, 'What else did you expect?' "

"And anger? Is it abated any when you shrug your shoulders and say, 'It's Kafka'?"

"For the first six months after the Russians came to stay with us I was myself in a continuous state of agitation. I went every night to secret meetings with my friends. Every other day at least I circulated another illegal petition. And in the time remaining I wrote, in my most precise and lucid prose, in my most elegant and thoughtful sentences, encyclopedic analyses of the situation which then circulated in *samizdat* among my colleagues. Then one day I keeled over and they sent me to the hospital with bleeding ulcers. I thought at first, all right, I will lie here on my back for a month, I will take my medicine and eat my slops, and then—well, then *what?* What will I do when I stop bleeding? Return to playing K. to their Castle and their Court? This can all go on interminably, as Kafka and his readers so well know. Those pathetic, hopeful, striving K.'s of his, running madly up and down all those stairwells looking for their solution, feverishly traversing the city contemplating the new development that will lead to, of all things, their success. Beginnings, middles, and, most fantastical of all, endings—that is how they believe they can force events to unfold."

"But, Kakfa and his readers aside, will things change if there is no opposition?"

The smile, disguising God only knows the kind of expression he would *like* to show to the world. "Sir, I have made my position known. The entire country has made its position known. This way we live now is not what we had in mind. For myself, I cannot burn away what remains of my digestive tract by continuing to make this clear to our authorities seven days a week."

"And so what do you do instead?"

"I translate *Moby Dick* into Czech. Of course, a translation happens already to exist, a very fine one indeed. There is absolutely no need for another. But it is something I have always thought about, and now that I have nothing else pressing to be accomplished, well, why not?"

"Why that book? Why Melville?" I ask him.

"In the fifties I spent a year on an exchange program, living in New York City. Walking the streets, it looked to me as if the place was aswarm with the crew of Ahab's ship. And at the helm of everything, big or small, I saw yet another roaring Ahab. The appetite to set things right, to emerge at the top, to be declared a 'champ.' And by dint, not just of energy and will, but of enormous rage. And *that,* the rage, that is what I should like to translate into Czech . . . if"—smiling—"that *can* be translated into Czech.

"Now, as you might imagine, this ambitious project, when completed, will be utterly useless for two reasons. First, there is no need for another translation, particularly one likely to be inferior to the distinguished translation we already have; and second, no translation of mine can be published in this country. In this way, you see, I am able to undertake what I would not otherwise have dared to do, without having to bother myself any longer worrying whether it is sensible or not. Indeed, some nights when I am working late, the futility of what I am doing would appear to be my deepest source of satisfaction. To you perhaps this may appear to be nothing but a pretentious form of capitulation, of self-mockery. It may even appear that way to me on occasion. Nonetheless, it remains the most serious thing I can think to do in my retirement. And you," he asks, so very genially, "what draws you so to Kafka?"

"It's a long story too."

"Dealing with?"

"Not with political hopelessness."

"I would think not."

"Rather," I say, "in large part, with sexual despair, with vows of chastity that seem somehow to have been taken by me behind my back, and which I lived with against my will. Either I turned against my flesh, or it turned against me—I still don't know quite how to put it."

"From the look of things, you don't seem to have suppressed its urgings entirely. That is a very attractive young woman you are traveling with."

"Well, the worst is over. *May* be over. At least is over for *now.* But while it lasted, while I couldn't be what I had always just assumed I was, well, it wasn't quite like anything I had ever known before. Of course you are the one on intimate terms with totalitarianism—but if you'll permit me, I can only compare the body's utter singlemindedness, its cold indifference and absolute contempt for the well-being of the spirit, to some unyielding, authoritarian regime. And you can petition it all you like, offer up the most heartfelt and dignified and logical sort of appeal—and get no response at all. If anything, a kind of laugh is what you get. I submitted my petitions through a psychoanalyst; went to his office every other day for an hour to make my case for the restoration of a robust libido. And, I tell you, with arguments and perorations no less involuted and tedious and cunning and abstruse than the kind of thing you find in *The Castle.* You think poor K. is clever—you should have heard me trying to outfox impotence."

"I can imagine. That's not a pleasant business."

"Of course, measured against what you—"

"Please, you needn't say things like that. It is *not* a pleasant business, and the right to vote provides, in this matter, little in the way of compensation."

"That is true. I did vote during this period, and found it made me no happier. What I started to say about Kafka, about reading Kafka, is that stories of obstructed, thwarted K.'s banging their heads against invisible walls, well, they suddenly had a disturbing new resonance for me. It was all a little less remote, suddenly, than the Kafka I'd read in college. In my own way, you see, I had come to know that sense of having been summoned—or of imagining yourself summoned—to a calling that turns out to be beyond you, yet in the face of every compromising or farcical consequence, being unable to wise up and relinquish the goal. You see, I once went about living as though sex were sacred ground."

"So to be 'chaste' . . ." he says, sympathetically. "Most unpleasant."

"I sometimes wonder if *The Castle* isn't in fact linked to Kafka's own erotic blockage—a book engaged at every level with not reaching a climax."

He laughs at my speculation, but as before, gently and with that unrelenting amiability. Yes, just so profoundly compromised is the retired professor, caught, as in a mangle, between conscience and the regime—between conscience and searing abdominal pain. "Well," he says, putting a hand on my arm in a kind and fatherly way, "to each obstructed citizen his own Kafka."

"And to each angry man his own Melville," I reply. "But then what are bookish people to do with all the great prose they read—"

"—but sink their teeth into it. Exactly. Into the books, instead of into the hand that throttles them."

Late that afternoon, we board the streetcar whose number Professor Soska had written in pencil on the back of a packet of postcards ceremoniously presented to Claire at the door of our hotel. The postcards are illustrated with photographs of Kafka, his family, and Prague landmarks associated with his life and his work. The handsome little set is no longer in circulation, Soska explained to us, now that the Russians occupy Czechoslovakia and Kafka is an outlawed writer, *the* outlawed writer. "But you do have another set, I hope," said Claire, "for yourself—?" "Miss Ovington," he said, with a courtly bow, "I have Prague. Please, permit me. I am sure that everyone who meets you wants to give you a gift." And here he suggested the visit to Kafka's grave, to which it would not, however, be advisable for him to accompany us . . . and motioning with his hand, he drew our attention to a man standing with his back to a parked taxicab some fifty feet up the boulevard from the door of the hotel: the plainclothesman, he informs us, who used to follow him and Mrs. Soska around in the months after the Russian invasion, back when the professor was helping to organize the clandestine opposition to the new puppet regime and his duodenum was still intact. "Are you sure that's him, here?" I had asked. "Sufficiently sure," said Soska, and stooping quickly to kiss Claire's hand, he moved with a rapid, comic stride, rather like a man in a walking race, into the crowd descending the wide stairs of the passageway to the underground. "My God," said Claire, "it's too awful. All that terrible smiling. And that getaway!"

We are both a little stunned, not least of all, in my case, for feeling myself so safe and inviolable, what with the passport in my jacket and the young woman at my side.

The streetcar carries us from the center of Prague to the outlying district where Kafka is buried. Enclosed within a high wall, the Jewish graveyard is bounded on one side by a more extensive Christian cemetery—through the fence we see visitors tending the graves there, kneeling and weeding like patient gardeners—and on the other by a wide bleak thoroughfare bearing truck traffic to and from the city. The gate to the Jewish cemetery is chained shut. I rattle the chain and call toward what seems a watchman's house. In time a woman with a little boy appears from somewhere inside. I say in German that we have flown all the way from New York to visit Franz Kafka's grave. She appears to understand, but says no, not today. Come back Tuesday, she says. But I am a professor of literature and a Jew, I explain, and pass a handful of crowns across to her between the bars. A key appears, the gate is opened, and inside the little boy is assigned to accompany us as we follow the sign that points the way. The sign is in five different tongues—so many peoples fascinated by the fearful inventions of this tormented ascetic, so many fearful millions: Khrobu / К могиле / Zum Grabe / To the Grave of / à la tombe de / FRANZE KAFKY.

Of all things, marking Kafka's remains—and unlike anything else in sight—a stout, elongated, whitish rock, tapering upward to its pointed glans, a tombstone phallus. That is the first surprise. The second is that the family-haunted son is buried forever—still!—between the mother and the father who outlived him. I take a pebble from the gravel walk and place it on one of the little mounds of pebbles piled there by the pilgrims who've preceded me. I have never done so much for my own grandparents, buried with ten thousand others alongside an expressway twenty minutes from my New York apartment, nor have I made such a visit to my mother's tree-shaded Catskill grave site since I accompanied my father to the unveiling of her stone. The dark rectangular slabs beyond Kafka's grave bear familiar Jewish names. I might be thumbing through my own address book, or at the front desk looking over my mother's shoulder at the roster of registered guests at the Hungarian Royale: Levy, Goldschmidt, Schneider, Hirsch . . . The graves go on and on, but only Kafka's appears to be properly looked after. The other dead are without survivors hereabouts to chop away the undergrowth and to cut back the ivy that twists through the limbs of the trees and forms a heavy canopy joining the plot of one extinct Jew to the next. Only the childless bachelor appears to have living progeny. Where better for irony to abound than à la tombe de Franze Kafky?

Set into the wall facing Kafka's grave is a stone inscribed with the name of his great friend Brod. Here too I place a small pebble. Then for the first time I notice the plaques affixed to the length of cemetery wall, inscribed to the memory of Jewish citizens of Prague exterminated in Terezin, Auschwitz, Belsen, and Dachau. There are not pebbles enough to go around.

With the silent child trailing behind, Claire and I head back to the gate. When we get there Claire snaps a picture of the shy little boy and, using sign language, instructs him to write down his name and address on a piece of paper. Pantomiming with broad gestures and stagy facial expressions that make me wonder suddenly just how childish a young woman she is—just how childlike and needy a man I have become—she is able to inform the little boy that when the photograph is ready she will send a copy to him. In two or three weeks Professor Soska is also to receive a photograph from Claire, this one taken earlier in the day outside the souvenir shop where Kafka had once spent a winter.

Now why do I want to call what joins me to her childish? Why do I want to call this happiness names? Let it happen! Let it be! Stop the challenging before it even starts! You need what you need! Make peace with it!

The woman has come from the house to open the gate. Again we exchange some remarks in German.

"There are many visitors to Kafka's grave?" I ask.

"Not so many. But always distinguished people, Professor, like yourself. Or serious young students. He was a very great man. We had many great Jewish writers in Prague. Franz Werfel. Max Brod. Oskar Baum. Franz Kafka. But now," she says, casting her first glance, and a sidelong, abbreviated one at that, toward my companion, "they are all gone."

"Maybe your little boy will grow up to be a great Jewish writer."

She repeats my words in Czech. Then she translates the reply the boy has given while looking down at his shoes. "He wants to be an aviator."

"Tell him people don't always come from all over the world to visit an aviator's grave."

Again words are exchanged with the boy, and, smiling pleasantly at me—yes, it is only to the Jewish professor that she will address herself with a gracious smile—she says, "He doesn't mind that so much. And, sir, what is the name of your university?"

I tell her.

"If you would like, I will take you to the grave of the man who was Dr. Kafka's barber. He is buried here too."

"Thank you, that is very kind."

"He was also the barber of Dr. Kafka's father."

I explain to Claire what the woman has offered. Claire says, "If you want, go ahead."

"Better not to," I say. "Start with Kafka's barber, and by midnight we may end up by the grave of his candlestick maker."

To the graveyard attendant I say, "I'm afraid that's not possible right now."

"Of course your wife may come too," she starchily informs me.

"Thank you. But we have to get back to our hotel."

Now she looks me over with undisguised suspiciousness, as though it well may be that I am not from a distinguished American university at all. She has gone out of her way to unlock the gate on a day other than the one prescribed for tourists, and I have turned out to be less than serious, probably nothing but a curiosity seeker, a Jew perhaps, but in the company of a woman quite clearly Aryan.

At the streetcar stop I say to Claire, "Do you know what Kafka said to the man he shared an office with at the insurance company? At lunchtime he saw the fellow eating his sausage and Kafka is supposed to have shuddered and said, 'The only fit food for a man is half a lemon.' "

She sighs, and says, sadly, "Poor dope," finding in the great writer's dietary injunction a disdain for harmless appetites that is just plain silly to a healthy girl from Schenectady, New York.

That is all—yet, when we board the streetcar and sit down beside each other, I take her hand and feel suddenly purged of yet another ghost, as de-Kafkafied by my pilgrimage to the cemetery as I would appear to have been de-Birgittized once and for all by that visitation on the terrace restaurant in Venice. My obstructed days are behind me—along with the *un*obstructed ones: no more "more," and no more nothing, either!

"Oh, Clarissa," I say, bringing her hand to my lips, "it's as though the past can't do me any more harm. I just don't have any more regrets. And my fears are gone, too. And it's all from finding you. I'd thought the god of women, who doles them out to you, had looked down on me and said, 'Impossible to please —the hell with him.' And then he sends me Claire."

That evening, after dinner in our hotel, we go up to the room to prepare for our early departure the next day. While I pack a suitcase with my clothes and with the books I have been reading on the airplanes and in bed at night, Claire falls asleep amid the clothing she has laid out on the comforter. Aside from the Kafka diaries and Brod's biography—my supplemental guidebooks to old Prague—I have with me paperbacks by Mishima, Gombrowicz, and Genet, novels for next year's comparative literature class. I have decided to organize the first semester's reading around the subject of erotic desire, beginning with these disquieting contemporary novels dealing with prurient and iniquitous sexuality (disquieting to students because they are the sort of books admired most by a reader like Baumgarten, novels in which the author is himself pointedly implicated in what is morally most alarming) and ending the term's work with three masterworks concerned with illicit and ungovernable passions, whose assault is made by other means: *Madame Bovary, Anna Karenina,* and "Death in Venice."

Without awakening her, I pick Claire's clothes off the bed and pack them in her suitcase. Handling her things, I feel overwhelmingly in love. Then I leave her a note saying that I have gone for a walk and will be back in an hour. Passing through the lobby I notice that there are now some fifteen or twenty pretty young prostitutes seated singly, and in pairs, beyond the glass doorway of the hotel's spacious café. Earlier in the day there had been just three of them, at a single table, gaily chatting together. When I asked Professor Soska how all this is organized under socialism, he had explained that most of Prague's whores are secretaries and shopgirls moonlighting with tacit government approval; a few are employed full-time by the Ministry of the Interior to get what information they can out of the various delegations from East and West that pass through the big hotels. The covey of miniskirted girls I see seated in the café are probably there to greet the members of the Bulgarian trade mission who occupy most of the floor beneath ours. One of them, who is stroking the belly of a brown dachshund puppy that lies cuddled in her arms, smiles my way. I smile back (costs nothing) and then am off to the Old Town Square, where Kafka and Brod used to take their evening stroll. When I get there is is after nine and the spacious melancholy plaza is empty of everything except the shadows of the aged façades enclosing it. Where the tourist buses had been parked earlier in the day there is now only the smooth, worn, cobblestone basin. The place is empty—of all, that is, except mystery and enigma. I sit alone on a bench beneath a street lamp and, through the thin film of mist, look past the looming figure of Jan Hus to the church whose most sequestered proceedings the Jewish author could observe by peering through his secret aperture.

It is here that I begin to compose in my head what at first strikes me as no more than a bit of whimsy, the first lines of an introductory lecture to my comparative literature class inspired by Kafka's "Report to an Academy," the story in which an ape addresses a scientific gathering. It is only a little story of a few thousand words, but one that I love, particularly its opening, which seems to me one of the most enchanting and startling in literature: "Honored Members of the Academy! You have done me the honor of inviting me to give your Academy an account of the life I formerly led as an ape."

"Honored Members of Literature 341," I begin . . . but by the time I am back at the hotel and have seated myself, with pen in hand, at an empty table in a corner of the café, I have penetrated the veneer of donnish satire with which I began, and on hotel stationery am writing out in longhand a formal introductory lecture (not uninfluenced by the ape's impeccable, professorial prose) that I want with all my heart to deliver—and to deliver not in September but at this very moment!

Seated two tables away is the prostitute with the little dachshund; she has been joined by a friend, whose favorite pet seems to be her own hair. She strokes away at it as though it is somebody else's. Looking up from my work, I tell the waiter to bring a cognac to each of these petite and pretty working girls, neither of them as old as Claire, and order a cognac for myself.

"Cheers," says the prostitute pleasing her puppy, and after the three of us smile at one another for a brief, enticing moment, I go back to writing what seem to me then and there somehow to be sentences of the most enormous consequence for my happy new life.

> Rather than spend the first day of class talking about the reading list and the general idea behind this course, I would like to tell you some things about myself that I have never before divulged to any of my students. I have no business doing this, and until I came into the room and took my seat I wasn't sure I would go through with it. And I may change my mind yet. For how do I justify disclosing to you the most intimate facts of my personal life? True, we will be meeting to discuss books for three hours a week during the coming two semesters, and from experience I know, as you do, that under such conditions a strong bond of affection can develop. However, we also know that this does not give me license to indulge what may only be so much impertinence and bad taste.
>
> As you may already have surmised—by my style of dress,

as easily as from the style of my opening remarks—the conventions traditionally governing the relationship between student and teacher are more or less those by which I have always operated, even during the turbulence of recent years. I have been told that I am one of the few remaining professors who address students in the classroom as "Mr." and "Miss," rather than by their given names. And however you may choose to attire yourselves—in the getup of garage mechanic, panhandler, tearoom gypsy, or cattle rustler—I still prefer to appear before you to teach wearing a jacket and a tie . . . though, as the observant will record, generally it will be the same jacket and the same tie. And when women students come to my office to confer, they will see, if they should even bother to look, that throughout the meeting I will dutifully leave open to the outside corridor the door to the room where we sit side by side. Some of you may be further amused when I remove my watch from my wrist, as I did only a moment ago, and place it beside my notes at the beginning of each class session. By now I no longer remember which of my own professors used to keep careful track of the passing hour in this way, but it would seem to have made its impression on me, signaling a professionalism with which I like still to associate myself.

All of which is not to say that I shall try to keep hidden from you the fact that I am flesh and blood—or that I understand that you are. By the end of the year you may even have grown a little weary of my insistence upon the connections between the novels you read for this class, even the most eccentric and off-putting of novels, and what you know so far of life. You will discover (and not all will approve) that I do not hold with certain of my colleagues who tell us that literature, in its most valuable and intriguing moments, is "fundamentally non-referential." I may come before you in my jacket and my tie, I may address you as madam and sir, but I am going to request nonetheless that you restrain yourselves from talking about "structure," "form," and "symbols" in my presence. It seems to me that many of you have been intimidated sufficiently by your junior year of college and should be allowed to recover and restore to respectability those interests and enthusiasms that more than likely drew you to reading fiction to begin with and which you oughtn't to be ashamed of now. As an experiment you might even want during the course of this year to try living without any classroom terminology at all, to relinquish "plot" and "character" right along with those very exalted words with which not a few of you like to solemnize your observations, such as "epiphany," "persona," and, of course, "existential" as a modifier of everything existing under the sun. I suggest this in the hope that if you talk about *Madame Bovary* in more or less the same tongue you use with the grocer, or your lover, you may be placed in a more intimate, a more interesting, in what might even be called a more *referential* relationship with Flaubert and his heroine.

In fact, one reason the novels to be read during the first semester are all concerned, to a greater or lesser degree of obsessiveness, with erotic desire is that I thought that readings organized around a subject with which you all have some sort of familiarity might help you even better to locate these books in the world of experience, and further to discourage the temptation to consign them to that manageable netherworld of narrative devices, metaphorical motifs, and mythical archetypes. Above all, I hope that by reading these books you will come to learn something of value about life in one of its most puzzling and maddening aspects. I hope to learn something myself.

All right. This much said by way of stalling, the time has come to begin to disclose the undisclosable—the story of the *professor's* desire. Only I can't, not quite yet, not until I have explained to my own satisfaction, if not to your parents', why I would even think to cast you as my voyeurs and my jurors and my confidants, why I would expose my secrets to people half my age, almost all of whom I have never previously known even as students. Why for me an audience, when most men and women prefer either to keep such matters entirely to themselves or to reveal them only to their most trusted confessors, secular or devout? What makes it compellingly necessary, or at all appropriate, that I present myself to you young strangers in the guise not of your teacher but as the first of this semester's texts?

Permit me to reply with an appeal to the heart.

I love teaching literature. I am rarely ever so contented as when I am here with my pages of notes, and my marked-up texts, and with people like yourselves. To my mind there is nothing quite like the classroom in all of life. Sometimes when we are in the midst of talking—when one of you, say, has pierced with a single phrase right to the heart of the book at hand—I want to cry out, "Dear friends, cherish this!" Why? Because once you have left here people are rarely, if ever, going to talk to you or listen to you the way you talk and listen to one another and to me in this bright and barren little room. Nor is it likely that you will easily find opportunities elsewhere to speak without embarrassment about what has mattered most to men as attuned to life's struggles as were Tolstoy, Mann, and Flaubert. I doubt that you know how very affecting it is to hear you speak thoughtfully and in all earnestness about solitude, illness, longing, loss, suffering, delusion, hope, passion, love, terror, corruption, calamity, and death . . . moving because you are nineteen and twenty years old, from comfortable middle-class homes most of you, and without much debilitating experience in your dossiers yet—but also because, oddly and sadly, this may be the last occasion you will ever have to reflect in any sustained and serious way upon the unrelenting forces with which in time you will all contend, like it or not.

Have I made any clearer why I should find our classroom to be, in fact, the *most* suitable setting for me to make an accounting of my erotic history? Does what I have just said render any more legitimate the claim I should like to make upon your time and patience and tuition? To put it as straight as I can—what a church is to the true believer, a classroom is to me. Some kneel at Sunday prayer, others don phylacteries each dawn . . . and I appear three times each week, my tie around my neck and my watch on my desk, to teach the great stories to you.

Class, oh, students, I have been riding the swell of a very large emotion this year. I'll get to that too. In the meantime, if possible, bear with my mood of capaciousness. Really, I only wish to present you with my credentials for teaching Literature 341. Indiscreet, unprofessional, unsavory as portions of these disclosures will surely strike some of you, I nonetheless would like, with your permission, to go ahead now and give an open account to you of the life I formerly led as a human being. I am devoted to fiction, and I assure you that in time I will tell you whatever I may know about it, but in truth nothing lives in me like my life.

The two pretty young prostitutes are still unattended, still sitting across from me in their white angora sweaters, pastel miniskirts, dark net stockings, and elevating high-heel shoes—rather like children who have ransacked Mamma's closet to dress as usherettes for a pornographic movie house—when I rise with my sheaf of stationery to leave the café.

"A letter to your wife?" says the one who strokes the dog and speaks some English.

I cannot resist the slow curve she has thrown me. "To the children," I say.

She nods to the friend who is stroking her hair: yes, they know my type. At eighteen they know all the types.

Her friend says something in Czech and they have a good laugh.

"Goodbye, sir; nighty-night," says the knowing one, offering a harmless enough smirk for me to carry away from the encounter. I am thought to have gotten my kick by buying two whores a drink. Maybe I did. Fair enough.

In our room I find that Claire has changed into her nightdress and is sleeping now beneath the blankets. A note for me on the pillow: "Dear One—I loved you so much today. I *will* make you happy. C."

Oh, I *have* come through—on my pillow is the proof!

And the sentences in my hands? They hardly seem now to be so laden with implication for my future as they did when I was hurrying back to the hotel from the Old Town Square, dying to get my hands on a piece of paper so as to make *my* report to *my* academy. Folding the pages in two, I put them with the paperbacks at the bottom of my suitcase, there along with Claire's note that promises to make her dear one happy. I feel absolutely triumphant: capacious indeed.

When I am awakened in the early morning by a door slamming beneath our room—down where the Bulgarians are sleeping, one of them no doubt with a little Czech whore and a dachshund puppy—I find I cannot begin to reconstruct the meandering maze of dreams that had so challenged and agitated me throughout the night. I had expected I would sleep marvelously, yet I awaken perspiring and, for those first timeless seconds, with no sense at all of where I am in bed or with whom. Then, blessedly, I find Claire, a big warm animal of my own species, my very own mate of the other gender, and encircling her with my arms—drawing her sheer creatureliness up against the length of my body—I begin to recall the long, abusive episode that had unfolded more or less along these lines:

I am met at the train by a Czech guide. He is called X, "as in the alphabet," he explains. I am sure he is really Herbie Bratasky, our master of ceremonies, but I do nothing to tip my hand. "And what have you seen so far?" asks X as I disembark.

"Why, nothing. I am just arriving."

"Then I have just the thing to start you off. How would you like to meet the whore Kafka used to visit?"

"There is such a person? And she is still alive?"

"How would you like to be taken to talk with her?"

I speak only after I have looked to be sure that no one is eavesdropping. "It is everything I ever hoped for."

"And how was Venice without the Swede?" X asks as we step aboard the cemetery streetcar.

"Dead."

The apartment is four flights up, in a decrepit building by the river. The woman we have come to see is nearly eighty: arthritic hands, slack jowls, white hair, clear and sweet blue eyes. Lives in a rocking chair on the pension of her late husband, an anarchist. I ask myself, "An anarchist's widow receiving a government pension?"

"Was he an anarchist all his life?" I ask.

"From the time he was twelve," X replies. "That was when his father died. He once explained to me how it happened. He saw his father's dead body, and he thought, 'This man who smiles at me and loves me is no more. Never again will any man smile at me and love me as he did. Wherever I go I will be a stranger and an enemy all my life.' That's how anarchists are made, apparently. I take it you are not an anarchist."

"No. My father and I love each other to this day. I believe in the rule of law."

From the window of the apartment I can see the gliding force of the famous Moldau. "Why, there, boys and girls, at the edge of the river"—I am addressing my class—"is the *piscine* where Kafka and Brod would go swimming together. See, it is as I told you: Franz Kafka was real, Brod was not making him up. And so am I real, nobody is making me up, other than myself."

X and the old woman converse in Czech. X says to me, "I told her that you are a distinguished American authority on the works of the great Kafka. You can ask her whatever you want."

"What did she make of him?" I ask. "How old was he when she knew him? How old was she? When exactly was all this taking place?"

X (interpreting): "She says, 'He came to me and I took a look at him and I thought, "What is this Jewish boy so depressed about?" ' She thinks it was in 1916. She says she was twenty-five. Kafka was in his thirties."

"Thirty-three," I say. "Born, class, in 1883. And as we know from all our years of schooling, three from six is three, eight from one doesn't go, so we must borrow one from the preceding digit; eight from eleven is three, eight from eight is zero, and one from one is zero—and that is why thirty-three is the correct answer to the question: How old was Kafka when he paid his visits to this whore? Next question: What, if any, is the relationship between Kafka's whore and today's story, 'The Hunger Artist'?"

X says, "And what else would you like to know?"

"Was he regularly able to have an erection? Could he usually reach orgasm? I find the diaries inconclusive."

Her eyes are expressive when she answers, though the crippled hands lie inert in her lap. In the midst of the indecipherable Czech I catch a word that makes my flesh run: Franz!

X nods gravely. "She says that was no problem. She knew what to do with a boy like him."

Shall I ask? Why not? I have come not just from America, after all, but out of oblivion, to which I shall shortly return. "What was that?"

Matter-of-fact still, she tells X what she did to arouse the author of—"Name Kafka's major works in the order of their composition. Grades will be posted on the department bulletin board. All those who wish recommendations for advanced literary studies will please line up outside my office to be whipped to within an inch of their lives."

X says, "She wants money. American money, not crowns. Give her ten dollars."

I give over the money. What use will it be in oblivion? "No, that will not be on the final."

X waits until she is finished, then translates: "She blew him."

Probably for less than it cost me to find out. There is such a thing as oblivion, and there is such a thing as fraud, which I am also against. Of course! This woman is nobody, and Bratasky gets half.

"And what did Kafka talk about?" I ask, and yawn to show just how seriously I now take these proceedings.

X translates the old woman's reply word for word: "I don't remember any more. I didn't remember the next day probably. Look, these Jewish boys would sometimes say nothing at all. Like little birds, not even a squeak. I'll tell you one thing, though—they never hit me. And they were clean boys. Clean underwear. Clean collars. They would never dream to come here with so much as a soiled handkerchief. Of course everybody I always would wash with a rag. I was always hygienic. But they didn't even need it. They were clean and they were gentlemen. As God is my witness, they never beat on my backside. Even in bed they had manners."

"But is there anything about Kafka in particular that she remembers? I didn't come here, to her, to Prague, to talk about nice Jewish boys."

She gives some thought to the question; or, more likely, no thought. Just sits there trying out being dead.

"You see, he wasn't so special," she finally says. "I don't mean he wasn't a gentleman. They were all gentlemen."

I say to Herbie (refusing to pretend any longer that he is some Czech named X), "Well, I don't really know what to ask next, Herb. I have the feeling she may have Kafka confused with somebody else."

"The woman's mind is razor-sharp," Herbie replies.

"Still, she's not exactly Brod on the subject."

The aged whore, sensing perhaps that I have had it, speaks again.

Herbie says, "She wants to know if you would like to inspect her pussy."

"To what possible end?" I reply.

"Shall I inquire?"

"Oh, please do."

Eva (for this, Herbie claims, is the lady's name) replies at length. "She submits that it might hold some literary interest for you. Others like yourself, who have come to her because of her relationship with Kafka, have been most anxious to see it, and, providing of course that their credentials established them as serious, she has been willing to show it to them. She says that because you are here on my recommendation she would be delighted to allow you to have a quick look."

"I thought she only blew him. Really, Herb, of what possible interest could her pussy be to me? You know I am not in Prague alone."

Translation: "Again, she frankly admits she doesn't know of what interest anything about her is to anyone. She says she is grateful for the little money she is able to make from her friendship with young Franz, and she is flattered that her callers are themselves distinguished and learned men. Of course, if the gentleman does not care to examine it—"

But why not? Why come to the battered heart of Europe if not to examine just this? Why come into the world at all? "Students of literature, you must conquer your squeamishness once and for all! You must face the unseemly thing itself! You must come off your high horse! There, *there* is your final exam."

It would cost me five more American dollars. "This is a flourishing business, this Kafka business," I say.

"First of all, given your field of interest, the money is tax-deductible. Second, for only a fiver, you are striking a decisive blow against the Bolsheviks. She is one of the last in Prague still in business for herself. Third, you are helping preserve a national literary monument—you are doing a service for our suffering writers. And last but not least, think of the money you have given to Klinger. What's five more to the cause?"

"I beg your pardon. What cause?"

"Your happiness. We only want to make you happy, to make you finally you, David dear. You have denied yourself too much as it is."

Despite her arthritic hands Eva is able on her own to tug her dress up until it is bunched in her lap. Herbie, however, has to hold her around with one arm, shift her on her buttocks, and draw down her underpants for her. I reluctantly help by steadying the rocking chair.

Accordioned kidskin belly, bare ruined shanks, and, astonishingly, a triangular black patch, pasted on like a mustache. I find myself rather doubting the authenticity of the pubic hair.

"She would like to know," says Herbie, "if the gentleman would care to touch it."

"And how much does that go for?"

Herbie repeats my question in Czech. Then to me, with a courtly bow, "Her treat."

"Thanks, no."

But again she assures the gentleman that it will cost him nothing. Again the gentleman courteously declines.

Now Eva smiles—between her parted lips, her tongue, still red. The pulp of the fruit, still red!

"Herb, what did she say just then?"

"Don't think I ought to repeat it, not to you."

"What was it, Herbie? I demand to know!"

"Something indecent," he says, chuckling, "about what Kafka liked the most. His big thrill."

"What was it?"

"Oh, I don't think your dad would want you to hear that, Dave. Or your dad's dad, and so on, all the way back to the Father of the Faithful and the Friend of God. Besides, it may just have been a malicious remark, gratuitously made, with no foundation in fact. She may only have said it because you insulted her. You see, by refusing to touch a finger to her famous vizz you have cast doubt—perhaps not entirely inadvertently either—on the very meaning of her life. Moreover, she is afraid you will go back to America now and tell your colleagues that she is a fraud. And then serious scholars will no longer come to pay their respects—which, of course, would mark the end for her, and if I may say so, the end too for private enterprise in our country. It would constitute nothing less than the final victory of the Bolsheviks over free men."

"Well, except for this new Czech routine of yours—which, I have to admit, could have fooled just about anybody but me—you haven't changed, Bratasky, not a bit."

"Too bad I can't say the same about you."

Here Herbie approaches the old woman, her face now sadly tear-streaked, and cupping his fingers as though to catch the trickle of a stream, he places his hands between her bare legs.

"Coo," she gurgles. "Coo. Coo." And closing her blue eyes, she rubs her cheek against Herbie's shoulder. The tip of her tongue I see protruding from her mouth. The pulp of the fruit, still red.

"I Always Wanted You to Admire My Fasting"; or, Looking at Kafka

"I always wanted you to admire my fasting," said the hunger artist. "We do admire it," said the overseer, affably. "But you shouldn't admire it," said the hunger artist. "Well, then we don't admire it," said the overseer, "but why shouldn't we admire it?" "Because I have to fast, I can't help it," said the hunger artist. "What a fellow you are," said the overseer, "and why can't you help it?" "Because," said the hunger artist, lifting his head a little and speaking, with his lips pursed, as if for a kiss, right into the overseer's ear, so that no syllable might be lost, "because I couldn't find the food I liked. If I had found it, believe me, I should have made no fuss and stuffed myself like you or anyone else." These were his last words, but in his dimming eyes remained the firm though no longer proud persuasion that he was still continuing to fast.

—FRANZ KAFKA, "A HUNGER ARTIST"

1.

I am looking, as I write of Kafka, at the photograph taken of him at the age of forty (my age)—it is 1924, as sweet and hopeful a year as he may ever have known as a man, and the year of his death. His face is sharp and skeletal, a burrower's face: pro-

---

Published first in 1973 in *American Review 17;* reprinted here from *Reading Myself and Others* (1975).

nounced cheekbones made even more conspicuous by the absence of sideburns; the ears shaped and angled on his head like angel wings; an intense, creaturely gaze of startled composure—enormous fears, enormous control; a black towel of Levantine hair pulled close around the skull the only sensuous feature; there is a familiar Jewish flare in the bridge of the nose, the nose itself is long and weighted slightly at the tip—the nose of half the Jewish boys who were my friends in high school. Skulls chiseled like this one were shoveled by the thousands from the ovens; had he lived, his would have been among them, along with the skulls of his three younger sisters.

Of course it is no more horrifying to think of Franz Kafka in Auschwitz than to think of anyone in Auschwitz—it is just horrifying in its own way. But he died too soon for the holocaust. Had he lived, perhaps he would have escaped with his good friend Max Brod, who found refuge in Palestine, a citizen of Israel until his death there in 1968. But *Kafka* escaping? It seems unlikely for one so fascinated by entrapment and careers that culminate in anguished death. Still, there is Karl Rossmann, his American greenhorn. Having imagined Karl's escape to America and his mixed luck here, could not Kafka have found a way to execute an escape for himself? The New School for Social Research in New York becoming *his* Great Nature Theatre of Oklahoma? Or perhaps, through the influence of Thomas Mann, a position in the German department at Princeton . . . But then, had Kafka lived, it is not at all certain that the books of his which Mann celebrated from *his* refuge in New Jersey would ever have been published; eventually Kafka might either have destroyed those manuscripts that he had once bid Max Brod to dispose of at his death or, at the least, continued to keep them his secret. The Jewish refugee arriving in America in 1938 would not then have been Mann's "religious humorist" but a frail and bookish fifty-five-year-old bachelor, formerly a lawyer for a government insurance firm in Prague, retired on a pension in Berlin at the time of Hitler's rise to power—an author, yes, but of a few eccentric stories, mostly about animals, stories no one in America had ever heard of and only a handful in Europe had read; a homeless K., but without K.'s willfulness and purpose, a homeless Karl, but without Karl's youthful spirit and resilience; just a Jew lucky enough to have escaped with his life, in his possession a suitcase containing some clothes, some family photos, some Prague mementos, and the manuscripts, still unpublished and in pieces, of *Amerika, The Trial, The Castle,* and (stranger things happen) three more fragmented novels, no less remarkable than the bizarre masterworks that he keeps to himself out of oedipal timidity, perfectionist madness, and insatiable longings for solitude and spiritual purity.

July 1923: Eleven months before he will die in a Vienna sanatorium, Kafka somehow finds the resolve to leave Prague and his father's home for good. Never before has he even remotely succeeded in living apart, independent of his mother, his sisters, and his father, nor has he been a writer other than in those few hours when he is not working in the legal department of the Workers' Accident Insurance Office in Prague; since taking his law degree at the university, he has been by all reports the most dutiful and scrupulous of employees, though he finds the work tedious and enervating. But in June of 1923—having some months earlier been pensioned from his job because of his illness—he meets a young Jewish girl of nineteen at a seaside resort in Germany, Dora Dymant, an employee at the vacation camp of the Jewish People's Home of Berlin. Dora has left her Orthodox Polish family to make a life of her own (at half Kafka's age); she and Kafka —who has just turned forty—fall in love . . . Kafka has by now been engaged to two somewhat more conventional Jewish girls —twice to one of them—hectic, anguished engagements wrecked largely by his fears. "I am mentally incapable of marrying," he writes his father in the forty-five-page letter he gave to his mother to deliver. ". . . the moment I make up my mind to marry I can no longer sleep, my head burns day and night, life can no longer be called life." He explains why. "Marrying is barred to me," he tells his father, "because it is your domain. Sometimes I imagine the map of the world spread out and you stretched diagonally across it. And I feel as if I could consider living in only those regions that are not covered by you or are not within your reach. And in keeping with the conception I have of your magnitude, these are not many and not very comforting regions—and marriage is not among them." The letter explaining what is wrong between this father and this son is dated November 1919; the mother thought it best not even to deliver it, perhaps for lack of courage, probably, like the son, for lack of hope.

During the following two years, Kafka attempts to wage an affair with Milena Jesenká-Pollak, an intense young woman of twenty-four who has translated a few of his stories into Czech and is most unhappily married in Vienna; his affair with Milena, conducted feverishly, but by and large through the mails, is even more demoralizing to Kafka than the fearsome engagements to the nice Jewish girls. They aroused only the paterfamilias longings that he dared not indulge, longings inhibited by his exaggerated awe of his father—"spellbound," says Brod, "in the family circle"—and the hypnotic spell of his own solitude; but the Czech Milena, impetuous, frenetic, indifferent to conventional restraints, a woman of appetite and anger, arouses more elemental yearnings and more elemental fears. According to a Prague critic, Rio Preisner, Milena was "psychopathic"; according to Margaret Buber-Neumann, who lived two years beside her in the German concentration camp where Milena died following a kidney operation in 1944, she was powerfully sane, extraordinarily humane and courageous. Milena's obituary for Kafka was the only one of consequence to appear in the Prague press; the prose is strong, so are the claims she makes for Kafka's accomplishment. She is still only in her twenties, the dead man is hardly known as a writer beyond his small circle of friends—yet Milena writes: "His knowledge of the world was exceptional and deep, and he was a deep and exceptional world in himself. . . . [He had] a delicacy of feeling bordering on the miraculous and a mental clarity that was terrifyingly uncompromising, and in turn he loaded on to his illness the whole burden of his mental fear of life. . . . He wrote the most important books in recent German literature." One can imagine this vibrant young woman stretched diagonally across the bed, as awesome to Kafka as his own father spread out across the map of the world. His letters to her are disjointed, unlike anything else of his in print; the word "fear" appears on page after page. "We are both married, you in

Vienna, I to my Fear in Prague." He yearns to lay his head upon her breast; he calls her "Mother Milena"; during at least one of their two brief rendezvous, he is hopelessly impotent. At last he has to tell her to leave him be, an edict that Milena honors, though it leaves her hollow with grief. "Do not write," Kafka tells her, "and let us not see each other; I ask you only to quietly fulfill this request of mine; only on those conditions is survival possible for me; everything else continues the process of destruction."

Then, in the early summer of 1923, during a visit to his sister, who is vacationing with her children by the Baltic Sea, he finds young Dora Dymant, and within a month Franz Kafka has gone off to live with her in two rooms in a suburb of Berlin, out of reach at last of the "claws" of Prague and home. How can it be? How can he, in his illness, have accomplished so swiftly and decisively the leave-taking that was beyond him in his healthiest days? The impassioned letter writer who could equivocate interminably about which train to catch to Vienna to meet with Milena (if he should meet with her for the weekend at all); the bourgeois suitor in the high collar, who, during his drawn-out agony of an engagement with the proper Fräulein Bauer, secretly draws up a memorandum for himself, countering the arguments "for" marriage with the arguments "against"; the poet of the ungraspable and the unresolved, whose belief in the immovable barrier separating the wish from its realization is at the heart of his excruciating visions of defeat; the Kafka whose fiction refutes every easy, touching, humanish daydream of salvation and justice and fulfillment with densely imagined counterdreams that mock all solutions and escapes—this Kafka *escapes.* Overnight! K. penetrates the Castle walls—Joseph K. evades his indictment—"a breaking away from it altogether, a mode of living completely outside the jurisdiction of the Court." Yes, the possibility of which Joseph K. has just a glimmering in the Cathedral, but can neither fathom nor effectuate—"not . . . some influential manipulation of the case, but . . . a circumvention of it"—Kafka realizes in the last year of his life.

Was it Dora Dymant or was it death that pointed the new way? Perhaps it could not have been one without the other. We know that the "illusory emptiness" at which K. gazed, upon first entering the village and looking up through the mist and the darkness to the Castle, was no more vast and incomprehensible than the idea of himself as husband and father was to the young Kafka; but now, it seems, the prospect of a Dora forever, of a wife, home, and children everlasting, is no longer the terrifying, bewildering prospect it would once have been, for now "everlasting" is undoubtedly not much more than a matter of months. Yes, the dying Kafka is determined to marry, and writes to Dora's Orthodox father for his daughter's hand. But the imminent death that has resolved all contradictions and uncertainties in Kafka is the very obstacle placed in his path by the young girl's father. The request of the dying man Franz Kafka to bind to him in his invalidism the healthy young girl Dora Dymant is—denied!

If there is not one father standing in Kafka's way, there is another—and another behind him. Dora's father, writes Max Brod in his biography of Kafka, "set off with [Kafka's] letter to consult the man he honored most, whose authority counted more than anything else for him, the 'Gerer Rebbe.' The rabbi read the letter, put it to one side, and said nothing more than the single syllable, 'No.' " *No.* Klamm himself could have been no more abrupt—or any more removed from the petitioner. *No.* In its harsh finality, as telling and inescapable as the curselike threat delivered by his father to Georg Bendemann, that thwarted fiancé: "Just take your bride on your arm and try getting in my way. I'll sweep her from your very side, you don't know how!" *No.* Thou shalt not have, say the fathers, and Kafka agrees that he shall not. The habit of obedience and renunciation; also, his own distaste for the diseased and reverence for strength, appetite, and health. " 'Well, clear this out now!' said the overseer, and they buried the hunger artist, straw and all. Into the cage they put a young panther. Even the most insensitive felt it refreshing to see this wild creature leaping around the cage that had so long been dreary. The panther was all right. The food he liked was brought him without hesitation by the attendants; he seemed not even to miss his freedom; his noble body, furnished almost to the bursting point with all that it needed, seemed to carry freedom around with it too; somewhere in his jaws it seemed to lurk; and the joy of life streamed with such ardent passion from his throat that for the onlookers it was not easy to stand the shock of it. But they braced themselves, crowded round the cage, and did not want ever to move away." So no is no; he knew as much himself. A healthy young girl of nineteen cannot, *should* not, be given in matrimony to a sickly man twice her age, who spits up blood ("I sentence you," cries Georg Bendemann's father, "to death by drowning!") and shakes in his bed with fevers and chills. What sort of un-Kafka-like dream had Kafka been dreaming!

And those nine months spent with Dora have still other "Kafkaesque" elements: a fierce winter in quarters inadequately heated; the inflation that makes a pittance of his own meager pension, and sends into the streets of Berlin the hungry and needy whose suffering, says Dora, turns Kafka "ash-gray"; and his tubercular lungs, flesh transformed and punished. Dora cares for the diseased writer as devotedly and tenderly as Gregor Samsa's sister does for her brother, the bug. Gregor's sister plays the violin so beautifully that Gregor "felt as if the way were opening before him to the unknown nourishment he craved"; he dreams, in his condition, of sending his gifted sister to the Conservatory! Dora's music is Hebrew, which she reads aloud to Kafka, and with such skill that, according to Brod, "Franz recognized her dramatic talent; on his advice and under his direction she later educated herself in the art . . ."

Only Kafka is hardly vermin to Dora Dymant, *or to himself*. Away from Prague and his father's home, Kafka, at forty, seems at last to have been delivered from the self-loathing, the self-doubt, and those guilt-ridden impulses to dependence and self-effacement that had nearly driven him mad throughout his twenties and thirties; all at once he seems to have shed the pervasive sense of hopeless despair that informs the great punitive fantasies of *The Trial*, "In the Penal Colony," and "The Metamorphosis." Years earlier, in Prague, he had directed Max Brod to destroy all his papers, including three unpublished novels, upon his death; now, in Berlin, when Brod introduces him to a German publisher interested in his work, Kafka consents to the publication of a volume of four stories, and consents, says Brod, "without much need of long arguments to persuade him." With Dora to help, he diligently resumes the study of Hebrew; despite his illness and the harsh winter, he travels to the Berlin Academy for Jewish Studies to attend a series of lectures on the Talmud—a very different Kafka from the estranged melancholic who once wrote in his diary, "What have I in common with the Jews? I have hardly anything in common with myself and should stand very quietly in a corner, content that I can breathe." And to further mark the change, there is ease and happiness with a woman: with this young and adoring companion, he is playful, he is pedagogical, and, one would guess, in light of his illness (*and* his happiness), he is chaste. If not a husband (such as he had striven to be to the conventional Fräulein Bauer), if not a lover (as he struggled hopelessly to be with Milena), he would seem to have become something no less miraculous in his scheme of things: a father, a kind of father to this sisterly, mothering daughter. *As Franz Kafka awoke one morning from uneasy dreams he found himself transformed in his bed into a father, a writer, and a Jew.*

"I have completed the construction of my burrow," begins the long, exquisite, and tedious story that he wrote that winter in Berlin, "and it seems to be successful. . . . Just at the place where, according to my calculations, the Castle Keep should be, the soil was very loose and sandy and had literally to be hammered and pounded into a firm state to serve as a wall for the beautifully vaulted chamber. But for such tasks the only tool I possess is my forehead. So I had to run with my forehead thousands and thousands of times, for whole days and nights, against the ground, and I was glad when the blood came, for that was proof that the walls were beginning to harden; in that way, as everybody must admit, I richly paid for my Castle Keep."

"The Burrow" is the story of an animal with a keen sense of peril whose life is organized around the principle of defense, and whose deepest longings are for security and serenity; with teeth and claws—*and* forehead—the burrower constructs an elaborate and ingeniously intricate system of underground chambers and corridors that are designed to afford it some peace of mind; however, while this burrow does succeed in reducing the sense of danger from without, its maintenance and protection are equally fraught with anxiety: "these anxieties are different from ordinary ones, prouder, richer in content, often long repressed, but in their destructive effects they are perhaps much the same as the anxieties that existence in the outer world gives rise to." The story (whose ending is lost) terminates with the burrower fixated upon distant subterranean noises that cause it "to assume the existence of a great beast," itself burrowing in the direction of the Castle Keep.

Another grim tale of entrapment, and of obsession so grand that no distinction is possible between character and predicament. Yet this fiction imagined in the last "happy" months of his life is touched by a spirit of personal reconciliation and sardonic self-acceptance, by a tolerance of one's own brand of madness, that is not apparent in "The Metamorphosis." The piercing masochistic irony of the earlier animal story—as of "The Judgment" and *The Trial*—has given way here to a critique of the self and its preoccupations that, though bordering on mockery, no longer seeks to resolve itself in images of the uttermost humiliation and defeat . . . Yet there is more here than a metaphor for the insanely defended ego, whose striving for invulnerability produces a defensive system that must in its turn become the object of perpetual concern—there is also a very unromantic and hardheaded fable about how and why art is made, a portrait of the artist in all his ingenuity, anxiety, isolation, dissatisfaction, relentlessness, obsessiveness, secretiveness, paranoia, and self-addiction, a portrait of the magical thinker at the end of his tether, Kafka's Prospero . . . It is an endlessly suggestive story, this story of life in a hole. For, finally, remember the proximity of Dora Dymant during the months that Kafka was at work on "The Burrow" in the two underheated rooms that were their illicit home. Certainly a dreamer like Kafka need never have entered the young girl's body for her tender presence to kindle in him a fantasy of a hidden orifice that promises "satisfied desire," "achieved ambition," and "profound slumber," but that, once penetrated and in one's possession, arouses the most terrifying and heartbreaking fears of retribution and loss. "For the rest I try to unriddle the beast's plans. Is it on its wanderings, or is it working on its own burrow? If it is on its wanderings then perhaps an understanding with it might be possible. If it should really break through to the burrow I shall give it some of my stores and it will go on its way again. It will go on its way again, a fine story! Lying in my heap of earth I can naturally dream of all sorts of things, even of an understanding with the beast, though I know well enough that no such thing can happen, and that at the instant when we see each other, more, at the moment when we merely guess at each other's presence, we shall blindly bare our claws and teeth . . ."

He died of tuberculosis of the lungs and larynx on June 3, 1924, a month before his forty-first birthday. Dora, inconsolable, whispers for days afterward, "My love, my love, my good one . . ."

2.

1942. I am nine; my Hebrew-school teacher, Dr. Kafka, is fifty-nine. To the little boys who must attend his "four-to-five" class each afternoon, he is known—in part because of his remote and melancholy foreignness, but largely because we vent on him our resentment at having to learn an ancient calligraphy at the very hour we should be out screaming our heads off on the ball field—he is known as Dr. Kishka. Named, I confess, by me. His sour breath, spiced with intestinal juices by five in the afternoon, makes the Yiddish word for "insides" particularly telling, I think. Cruel, yes, but in truth I would have cut out my tongue had I ever imagined the name would become legend. A coddled child, I do not yet think of myself as persuasive, or, quite yet, as a literary force in the world. My jokes don't hurt, how could they, I'm so adorable. And if you don't believe me, just ask my family and the teachers in my school. Already at nine, one foot in college, the other in the Catskills. Little borscht-belt comic that I am outside the classroom, I amuse my friends Schlossman and Ratner on the dark walk home from Hebrew school with an imitation of Kishka, his precise and finicky professorial manner, his German accent, his cough, his gloom. "Doctor *Kishka!*" cries Schlossman, and hurls himself savagely against the newsstand that belongs to the candy-store owner whom Schlossman drives just a little crazier each night. "Doctor Franz—Doctor Franz—Doctor Franz—*Kishka!*" screams Ratner, and my chubby little friend who lives upstairs from me on nothing but chocolate milk and Mallomars does not stop laughing until, as is his wont (his mother has asked me "to keep an eye on him" for just this reason), he wets his pants. Schlossman takes the occasion of Ratner's humiliation to pull the little boy's paper out of his notebook and wave it in the air—it is the assignment Dr. Kafka has just returned to us, graded; we were told to make up an alphabet of our own, out of straight lines and curved lines and dots. "That is all an alphabet is," he had explained. "That is all Hebrew is. That is all English is. Straight lines and curved lines and dots." Ratner's alphabet, for which he received a C, looks like twenty-six skulls strung in a row. I received my A for a curlicued alphabet, inspired largely (as Dr. Kafka seems to have surmised, given his comment at the top of the page) by the number eight. Schlossman received an F for forgetting even to do it—and a lot he seems to care. He is content—he is *overjoyed*—with things as they are. Just waving a piece of paper in the air and screaming, "Kishka! Kishka!" makes him deliriously happy. We should all be so lucky.

At home, alone in the glow of my goose-necked "desk" lamp (plugged after dinner into an outlet in the kitchen, my study), the vision of our refugee teacher, sticklike in a fraying three-piece blue suit, is no longer very funny—particularly after the entire beginners' Hebrew class, of which I am the most studious member, takes the name Kishka to its heart. My guilt awakens redemptive fantasies of heroism, I have them often about the "Jews in Europe." I must save him. If not me, who? The demonic Schlossman? The babyish Ratner? And if not now, when? For I have learned in the ensuing weeks that Dr. Kafka lives in a room in the house of an elderly Jewish lady on the shabby lower stretch of Avon Avenue, where the trolley still runs and the poorest of Newark's Negroes shuffle meekly up and down the street, for all they seem to know, still back in Mississippi. A *room*. And *there!* My family's apartment is no palace, but it is ours at least, so long as we pay the $38.50 a month in rent; and though our neighbors are not rich, they refuse to be poor and they refuse to be meek. Tears of shame and sorrow in my eyes, I rush into the living room to tell my parents what I have heard (though not that I heard it during a quick game of "aces up" played a minute before class against the synagogue's rear wall—worse, played directly beneath a stained-glass window embossed with the names of the dead): "My Hebrew teacher lives in a *room.*"

My parents go much further than I could imagine anybody going in the real world. Invite him to dinner, my mother says. *Here?* Of course here—Friday night; I'm sure he can stand a home-cooked meal, she says, and a little pleasant company. Meanwhile, my father gets on the phone to call my Aunt Rhoda, who lives with my grandmother and tends her and her potted plants in the apartment house at the corner of our street. For nearly two decades my father has been introducing my mother's "baby" sister, now forty, to the Jewish bachelors and widowers of north Jersey. No luck so far. Aunt Rhoda, an "interior decorator" in the dry-goods department of the Big Bear, a mammoth merchandise and produce market in industrial Elizabeth, wears falsies (this information by way of my older brother) and sheer frilly blouses, and family lore has it that she spends hours in the bathroom every day applying powder and sweeping her stiffish hair up into a dramatic pile on her head; but despite all this dash and display, she is, in my father's words, "still afraid of the facts of life." He, however, is undaunted, and administers therapy regularly and gratis: "Let 'em squeeze ya, Rhoda—it *feels* good!" I am his flesh and blood, I can reconcile myself to such scandalous talk in our kitchen—*but what will Dr. Kafka think?* Oh, but it's too late to do anything now. The massive machinery of matchmaking has been set in motion by my undiscourageable father, and the smooth engines of my proud homemaking mother's hospitality are already purring away. To throw my body into the works in an attempt to bring it all to a halt—well, I might as well try to bring down the New Jersey Bell Telephone Company by leaving our receiver off the hook. Only Dr. Kafka can save me now. But to my muttered invitation, he replies, with a formal bow that turns me scarlet—who has ever seen a person do such a thing outside of a movie house?—he replies that he would be *honored* to be my family's dinner guest. "My aunt," I rush to tell him, "will be there too." It appears that I have just said something mildly humorous; odd to see Dr. Kafka smile. Sighing, he says, "I will be delighted to meet her." Meet her? He's supposed to *marry* her. How do I warn him? And how do I warn Aunt Rhoda (a very great admirer of me and my marks) about his sour breath, his roomer's pallor, his Old World ways, so at odds with her up-to-dateness? My face feels as if it will ignite of its own—and spark the fire that will engulf the synagogue, Torah and all—when I see Dr. Kafka scrawl our address in his notebook, and beneath it, some words *in German.* "Good night, Dr. Kafka!" "Good night, and thank you, thank you." I turn to run, I go, but not fast enough: out on the street I hear Schlossman—that fiend!—announcing to my classmates, who are punching one another under the lamplight down from the synagogue steps (where a card game is also in progress, organized by the bar mitzvah boys): "Roth invited Kishka to his *house!* To *eat!*"

Does my father do a job on Kafka! Does he make a sales pitch for familial bliss! What it means to a man to have two fine boys and a wonderful wife! Can Dr. Kafka imagine what it's like? The thrill? The satisfaction? The pride? He tells our visitor of the network of relatives on his mother's side that are joined in a "family association" of over two hundred people located in seven states, including the state of Washington! Yes, relatives even in the Far West: here are their photographs, Dr. Kafka; this is a beautiful book we published entirely on our own for five dollars a copy, pictures of every member of the family, including infants, and a family history by "Uncle" Lichtblau, the eighty-five-year-old patriarch of the clan. This is our family newsletter, which is published twice a year and distributed nationwide to all the relatives. This, in the frame, is the menu from the banquet of the family association, held last year in a ballroom of the "Y" in Newark, in honor of my father's mother on her seventy-fifth birthday. My mother, Dr. Kafka learns, has served *six consecutive years* as the secretary-treasurer of the family association. My father has served a two-year term as president, as have each of his three brothers. We now have fourteen boys in the family in uniform. Philip writes a letter on V-mail stationery to five of his cousins in the army every single month. "Religiously," my mother puts in, smoothing my hair. "I firmly believe," says my father, "that the family is the cornerstone of everything."

Dr. Kafka, who has listened with close attention to my father's spiel, handling the various documents that have been passed to him with great delicacy and poring over them with a kind of rapt absorption that reminds me of myself over the watermarks of my stamps, now for the first time expresses himself on the subject of family; softly he says, "I agree," and inspects again the pages of our family book. "Alone," says my father, in conclusion, "alone, Dr. Kafka, is a stone." Dr. Kafka, setting the book gently down upon my mother's gleaming coffee table, allows with a nod that that is so. My mother's fingers are now turning in the curls behind my ears; not that I even know it at the time, or that she does. Being stroked is my life; stroking me, my father, and my brother is hers.

My brother goes off to a Boy Scout meeting, but only after my father has him stand in his neckerchief before Dr. Kafka and describe to him the skills he has mastered to earn each of his badges. I am invited to bring my stamp album into the living room and show Dr. Kafka my set of triangular stamps from Zanzibar. "Zanzibar!" says my father rapturously, as though I, not even ten, have already been there and back. My father accompanies Dr. Kafka and me into the "sun parlor," where my tropical fish swim in the aerated, heated, and hygienic paradise I have made for them with my weekly allowance and my Hanukkah *gelt.* I am encouraged to tell Dr. Kafka what I know about the temperament of the angelfish, the function of the catfish, and the family life of the black mollie. I know quite a bit. "All on his own he does that," my father says to Kafka. "He gives me a lecture on one of those fish, it's seventh heaven, Dr. Kafka." "I can imagine," Kafka replies.

Back in the living room my Aunt Rhoda suddenly launches into a rather recondite monologue on "Scotch plaids," intended, it would appear, for the edification of my mother alone. At least she looks fixedly at my mother while she delivers it. I have not yet seen her look directly at Dr. Kafka; she did not even turn his way at dinner when he asked how many employees there were at the Big Bear. "How would I know?" she had replied, and then continued right on conversing with my mother, about a butcher who would take care of her "under the counter" if she could find him nylons for his wife. It never occurs to me that she will not look at Dr. Kafka because she is shy—nobody that dolled up could, in my estimation, be shy. I can only think that she is outraged. *It's his breath. It's his accent. It's his age.*

I'm wrong—it turns out to be what Aunt Rhoda calls his "superiority complex." "Sitting there, sneering at us like that," says my aunt, somewhat superior now herself. "Sneering?" repeats my father, incredulous. "Sneering and laughing, yes!" says Aunt Rhoda. My mother shrugs. "*I* didn't think he was laughing." "Oh, don't worry, by himself there he was having a very good time—*at our expense.* I know the European-type man. Underneath they think they're all lords of the manor," Rhoda says. "You know something, Rhoda?" says my father, tilting his head and pointing a finger, "I think you fell in love." "With *him?* Are you *crazy?*" "He's too quiet for Rhoda," my mother says. "I think maybe he's a little bit of a wallflower. Rhoda is a very lively person, she needs lively people around her." "Wallflower? He's not a wallflower! He's a gentleman, that's all. And he's lonely," my father says assertively, glaring at my mother for going over his head like this *against* Kafka. My Aunt Rhoda is forty years old—it is not exactly a shipment of brand-new goods that he is trying to move. "He's a gentleman, he's an educated man, and I'll tell you something, he'd give his eyeteeth to have a nice home and a wife." "Well," says my Aunt Rhoda, "let him find one then, if he's so educated. Somebody who's his equal, who he doesn't have to look down his nose at with his big sad refugee eyes!" "Yep, she's in love," my father announces, squeezing Rhoda's knee in triumph. "With him?" she cries, jumping to her feet, taffeta crackling around her like a bonfire. "With *Kafka?*" she snorts. "I wouldn't give an old man like him the time of day!"

Dr. Kafka calls and takes my Aunt Rhoda to a movie. I am astonished, both that he calls and that she goes; it seems there is more desperation in life than I have come across yet in my fish tank. Dr. Kafka takes my Aunt Rhoda to a play performed at the "Y." Dr. Kafka eats Sunday dinner with my grandmother and my Aunt Rhoda and, at the end of the afternoon, accepts with that formal bow of his the mason jar of barley soup that my grandmother presses him to carry back to his room with him on the No.

8 bus. Apparently he was very taken with my grandmother's jungle of potted plants—and she, as a result, with him. Together they spoke in Yiddish about gardening. One Wednesday morning, only an hour after the store has opened for the day, Dr. Kafka shows up at the dry-goods department of the Big Bear; he tells Aunt Rhoda that he just wants to see where she works. That night he writes in his diary: "With the customers she is forthright and cheery, and so managerial about 'taste' that when I hear her explain to a chubby young bride why green and blue do not 'go,' I am myself ready to believe that Nature is in error and R. is correct."

One night, at ten, Dr. Kafka and Aunt Rhoda come by unexpectedly, and a small impromptu party is held in the kitchen—coffee and cake, even a thimbleful of whiskey all around, to celebrate the resumption of Aunt Rhoda's career on the stage. I have only heard tell of my aunt's theatrical ambitions. My brother says that when I was small she used to come to entertain the two of us on Sundays with her puppets—she was at that time employed by the W.P.A. to travel around New Jersey and put on marionette shows in schools and even in churches; Aunt Rhoda did all the voices and, with the help of a female assistant, manipulated the manikins on their strings. Simultaneously she had been a member of the Newark Collective Theater, a troupe organized primarily to go around to strike groups to perform *Waiting for Lefty.* Everybody in Newark (as I understood it) had had high hopes that Rhoda Pilchik would go on to Broadway—everybody except my grandmother. To me this period of history is as difficult to believe in as the era of the lake dwellers, which I am studying in school; people say it was once so, so I believe them, but nonetheless it is hard to grant such stories the status of the real, given the life I see around me.

Yet my father, a very avid realist, is in the kitchen, schnapps glass in hand, toasting Aunt Rhoda's success. She has been awarded one of the starring roles in the Russian masterpiece *The Three Sisters,* to be performed six weeks hence by the amateur group at the Newark "Y." Everything, announces Aunt Rhoda, everything she owes to Franz and his encouragement. One conversation—"One!" she cries gaily—and Dr. Kafka had apparently talked my grandmother out of her lifelong belief that actors are not serious human beings. And what an actor *he* is, in his own right, says Aunt Rhoda. How he had opened her eyes to the meaning of things, by reading her the famous Chekhov play—yes, read it to her from the opening line to the final curtain, all the parts, and actually left her in tears. Here Aunt Rhoda says, "Listen, listen—this is the first line of the play—it's the key to everything. Listen—I just think about what it was like the night Pop passed away, how I wondered and wondered what would become of us, what would we all do—and, and, *listen—*"

"We're listening," laughs my father. So am *I* listening, from my bed.

Pause; she must have walked to the center of the kitchen linoleum. She says, sounding a little surprised, " 'It's just a year ago today that father died.' "

"Shhh," warns my mother, "you'll give the little one nightmares."

I am not alone in finding my aunt a "changed person" during the weeks of rehearsal. My mother says this is just what she was like as a little girl. "Red cheeks, always those hot, red cheeks—and everything exciting, even taking a bath." "She'll calm down, don't worry," says my father, "and then he'll pop the question." "Knock on wood," says my mother. "Come on," says my father, "he knows what side his bread is buttered on—he sets foot in this house, he sees what a family is all about, and believe me, he's licking his chops. Just look at him when he sits in that club chair. This is his dream come true." "Rhoda says that in Berlin, before Hitler, he had a young girl friend, years and years it went on, and then she left him. For somebody else. She got tired of waiting." "Don't worry," says my father, "when the time comes I'll give him a little nudge. He ain't going to live forever, either, and he knows it."

Then one weekend, as a respite from the "strain" of nightly rehearsals—which Dr. Kafka regularly visits, watching in his hat and coat at the back of the auditorium until it is time to accompany Aunt Rhoda home—they take a trip to Atlantic City. Ever since he arrived on these shores Dr. Kafka has wanted to see the famous boardwalk and the horse that dives from the high board.

But in Atlantic City something happens that I am not allowed to know about; any discussion of the subject conducted in my presence is in Yiddish. Dr. Kafka sends Aunt Rhoda four letters in three days. She comes to us for dinner and sits till midnight crying in our kitchen. She calls the "Y" on our phone to tell them (weeping) that her mother is still ill and she cannot come to rehearsal again—she may even have to drop out of the play. No, she can't, she can't, her mother is too ill, she herself is too upset! goodbye! Then back to the kitchen table to cry. She wears no pink powder and no red lipstick, and her stiff brown hair, down, is thick and spiky as a new broom.

My brother and I listen from our bedroom, through the door that silently he has pushed ajar.

"Have you ever?" says Aunt Rhoda, weeping. "Have you *ever?*"

"Poor soul," says my mother.

"Who?" I whisper to my brother. "Aunt Rhoda or—"

"Shhhh!" he says. "Shut *up!*"

In the kitchen my father grunts. "Hmm. Hmm." I hear him getting up and walking around and sitting down again—and then grunting. I am listening so hard that I can hear the letters being folded and unfolded, stuck back into their envelopes, then removed to be puzzled over one more time.

"Well?" demands Aunt Rhoda. *"Well?"*

"Well what?" answers my father.

"Well, what do you want to say *now?*"

"He's *meshugeh,*" admits my father. "Something is wrong with him all right."

"But," sobs Aunt Rhoda, "no one would believe me when *I* said it!"

"Rhody, Rhody," croons my mother in that voice I know from those times that I have had to have stitches taken, or when I have awakened in tears, somehow on the floor beside my bed. "Rhody, don't be hysterical, darling. It's over, kitten, it's all over."

I reach across to my brother's twin bed and tug on the blanket. I don't think I've ever been so confused in my life, not even by death. The speed of things! Everything good undone in a moment! By what? *"What?"* I whisper. *"What is it?"*

My brother, the Boy Scout, smiles leeringly and, with a fierce hiss that is no answer and enough answer, addresses my bewilderment: "Sex!"

Years later, a junior at college, I receive an envelope from home containing Dr. Kafka's obituary, clipped from *The Jewish News*, the tabloid of Jewish affairs that is mailed each week to the homes of the Jews of Essex County. It is summer, the semester is over, but I have stayed on at school, alone in my room in the town, trying to write short stories. I am fed by a young English professor and his wife in exchange for babysitting; I tell the sympathetic couple, who are also loaning me the money for my rent, why it is I can't go home. My tearful fights with my father are all I can talk about at their dinner table. "Keep him away from me!" I scream at my mother. "But, darling," she asks me, "what is going on? What is this all about?"—the very same question with which I used to plague my older brother, asked now of me and out of the same bewilderment and innocence. "He *loves* you," she explains.

But that, of all things, seems to me precisely what is blocking my way. Others are crushed by paternal criticism—I find myself oppressed by his high opinion of me! Can it possibly be true (and can I possibly admit) that I am coming to hate him for loving me so? praising me so? But that makes no sense—the ingratitude! the stupidity! the contrariness! Being loved is so obviously a blessing, *the* blessing, praise such a rare bequest. Only listen late at night to my closest friends on the literary magazine and in the drama society—they tell horror stories of family life to rival *The Way of All Flesh*, they return shell-shocked from vacations, drift back to school as though from the wars. What they would give to be in my golden slippers! "What's going on?" my mother begs me to tell her; but how can I, when I myself don't fully believe that this is happening to us, or that I am the one who is making it happen. That they, who together cleared all obstructions from my path, should seem now to be my final obstruction! No wonder my rage must filter through a child's tears of shame, confusion, and loss. All that we have constructed together over the course of two century-long decades, and look how I must bring it down—in the name of this tyrannical need that I call my "independence"! My mother, keeping the lines of communication open, sends a note to me at school: "We miss you"—and encloses the brief obituary notice. Across the margin at the bottom of the clipping, she has written (in the same hand with which she wrote notes to my teachers and signed my report cards, in that very same handwriting that once eased my way in the world), "Remember poor Kafka, Aunt Rhoda's beau?"

"Dr. Franz Kafka," the notice reads, "a Hebrew teacher at the Talmud Torah of the Schley Street Synagogue from 1939 to 1948, died on June 3 in the Deborah Heart and Lung Center in Browns Mills, New Jersey. Dr. Kafka had been a patient there since 1950. He was 70 years old. Dr. Kafka was born in Prague, Czechoslovakia, and was a refugee from the Nazis. He leaves no survivors."

He also leaves no books: no *Trial,* no *Castle,* no Diaries. The dead man's papers are claimed by no one, and disappear—all except those four *"meshugeneh"* letters that are, to this day, as far as I know, still somewhere in among the memorabilia accumulated by my spinster aunt, along with a collection of Broadway Playbills, sales citations from the Big Bear, and transatlantic steamship stickers.

Thus all trace of Dr. Kafka disappears. Destiny being destiny, how could it be otherwise? Does the Land Surveyor reach the Castle? Does K. escape the judgment of the Court, or Georg Bendemann the judgment of his father? " 'Well, clear this out now!' said the overseer, and they buried the hunger artist, straw and all." No, it simply is not in the cards for Kafka ever to become *the* Kafka—why, that would be stranger even than a man turning into an insect. No one would believe it, Kafka least of all.

"Only It Ain't No Joke!" II

Tricky Comforts the Nation

From personal and religious beliefs I consider abortions an unacceptable form of population control. Furthermore, unrestricted abortion policies, or abortion on demand, I cannot square with my personal belief in the sanctity of human life —including the life of the yet unborn. For, surely, the unborn have rights also, recognized in law, recognized even in principles expounded by the United Nations.

—RICHARD NIXON
San Clemente, April 3, 1971

1. Tricky Comforts a Troubled Citizen

CITIZEN: Sir, I want to congratulate you for coming out on April 3 for the sanctity of human life, including the life of the yet unborn. That required a lot of courage, especially in light of the November election results.
TRICKY: Well, thank you. I know I could have done the popular thing, of course, and come out *against* the sanctity of human life. But frankly I'd rather be a one-term President and do what I believe is right than be a two-term President by taking an easy position like that. After all, I have got my conscience to deal with, as well as the electorate.
CITIZEN: Your conscience, sir, is a marvel to us all.
TRICKY: Thank you.

The opening two chapters of *Our Gang* (1971), a political satire published in the first term of the Nixon Administration, before the Watergate disclosures.

CITIZEN: I wonder if I may ask you a question having to do with Lieutenant Calley and his conviction for killing twenty-two Vietnamese civilians at My Lai.
TRICKY: Certainly. I suppose you are bringing that up as another example of my refusal to do the popular thing.
CITIZEN: How's that, sir?
TRICKY: Well, in the wake of the public outcry against that conviction, the popular thing—the most popular thing by far—would have been for me, as Commander-in-Chief, to have convicted the twenty-two unarmed civilians of conspiracy to murder Lieutenant Calley. But if you read your papers, you'll see I refused to do that, and chose only to review the question of his guilt, and not theirs. As I said, I'd rather be a one-term President. And may I make one thing more perfectly clear, while we're on the subject of Vietnam? I am not going to interfere in the internal affairs of another country. If President Thieu has sufficient evidence and wishes to try those twenty-two My Lai villagers posthumously, according to some Vietnamese law having to do with ancestor worship, that is his business. But I assure you, I in no way intend to interfere with the workings of the Vietnamese system of justice. I think President Thieu, and the duly elected Saigon officials, can "hack" it alone in the law and order department.
CITIZEN: Sir, the question that's been troubling me is this. Inasmuch as I share your belief in the sanctity of human life—
TRICKY: Good for you. I'll bet you're quite a football fan, too.
CITIZEN: I am, sir. Thank you, sir . . . But inasmuch as I feel as you do about the unborn, I am seriously troubled by the possibility that Lieutenant Calley may have committed an abortion. I hate to say this, Mr. President, but I am seriously troubled when I think that one of those twenty-two Vietnamese civilians Lieutenant Calley killed may have been a pregnant woman.
TRICKY: Now just one minute. We have a tradition in the courts of this land that a man is innocent until he is proven guilty. There were babies in that ditch at My Lai, and we know there were women of all *ages* but I have not seen a single document that suggests the ditch at My Lai contained a *pregnant* woman.
CITIZEN: But what *if*, sir—what *if* one of the twenty-two was a

pregnant woman? Suppose that were to come to light in your judicial review of the lieutenant's conviction. In that you personally believe in the sanctity of human life, including the life of the yet unborn, couldn't such a fact seriously prejudice you against Lieutenant Calley's appeal? I have to admit that as an opponent of abortion, it would have a profound effect upon me.

TRICKY: Well, it's very honest of you to admit it. But as a trained lawyer, I think I might be able to go at the matter in a somewhat less emotional manner. First off, I would have to ask whether Lieutenant Calley was *aware* of the fact that the woman in question was pregnant *before* he killed her. Clearly, if she was not yet "showing," I think you would in all fairness have to conclude that the lieutenant could have had no knowledge of her pregnancy, and thus, in no sense of the word, would he have committed an abortion.

CITIZEN: What if she *told* him she was pregnant?

TRICKY: Good question. She might indeed have tried to tell him. But in that Lieutenant Calley is an American who speaks only English, and the My Lai villager is a Vietnamese who speaks only Vietnamese, there could have been no possible means of verbal communication. And as for sign language, I don't believe we can hang a man for failing to understand what must surely have been the gestures of a hysterical, if not deranged, woman.

CITIZEN: No, that wouldn't be fair, would it.

TRICKY: In short then, if the woman was not "showing," Lieutenant Calley could *not* be said to have engaged in an unacceptable form of population control, and it would be possible for me to square what he did with my personal belief in the sanctity of human life, including the life of the yet unborn.

CITIZEN: But, sir, what if she *was* "showing"?

TRICKY: Well then, as good lawyers we would have to ask another question. Namely: did Lieutenant Calley believe the woman to be pregnant, or did he, mistakenly, in the heat of the moment, assume that she was just stout? It's all well and good for us to be Monday Morning My Lai Quarterbacks, you know, but there's a war going on out there, and you cannot always expect an officer rounding up unarmed civilians to be able to distinguish between an ordinary fat Vietnamese woman and one who is in the middle, or even the late, stages of pregnancy. Now if the pregnant ones would wear maternity clothes, of course, that would be a great help to our boys. But in that they don't, in that all of them seem to go around all day in their pajamas, it is almost impossible to tell the men from the women, let alone the pregnant from the nonpregnant. Inevitably then—and this is just one of those unfortunate things about a war of this kind—there is going to be confusion on this whole score of who is who out there. I understand that we are doing all we can to get into the hamlets with American-style maternity clothes for the pregnant women to wear so as to make them more distinguishable to the troops at the massacres, but, as you know, these people have their own ways and will not always consent to do even what is clearly in their own interest. And, of course, we have no intention of forcing them. That, after all, is why we are in Vietnam in the first place—to give these people the right to choose their own way of life, in accordance with *their* own beliefs and customs.

CITIZEN: In other words, sir, if Lieutenant Calley assumed the woman was simply fat, and killed her under that assumption, that would still square with your personal belief in the sanctity of human life, including the life of the yet unborn.

TRICKY: Absolutely. If I find that he assumed she was simply overweight, I give you my utmost assurance, I will in no way be prejudiced against his appeal.

CITIZEN: But, sir, suppose, just *suppose,* that he *did* know she was pregnant.

TRICKY: Well, we are down to the heart of the matter now, aren't we?

CITIZEN: I'm afraid so, sir.

TRICKY: Yes, we are down to this issue of "abortion on demand," which, admittedly, is totally unacceptable to me, on the basis of my personal and religious beliefs.

CITIZEN: Abortion on *demand?*

TRICKY: If this Vietnamese woman presented herself to Lieutenant Calley for abortion . . . let's assume, for the sake of argument, she was one of those girls who goes out and has a good time and then won't own up to the consequences; unfortunately, we have them here just as they have them over there—the misfits, the bums, the tramps, the few who give the many a bad name . . . but if this woman presented herself to Lieutenant Calley for abortion, with some kind of note, say, that somebody had written for her in English, and Lieutenant Calley, let's say, in the heat and pressure of the moment, performed the abortion, during the course of which the woman died . . .

CITIZEN: Yes. I think I follow you so far.

TRICKY: Well, I just have to wonder if the woman isn't herself equally as guilty as the lieutenant—if she is not more so. I just have to wonder if this isn't a case for the Saigon courts, after all. Let's be perfectly frank: you cannot die of an abortion if you don't go looking for the abortion to begin with. If you have not gotten yourself in an abortion *predicament* to begin with. Surely that's perfectly clear.

CITIZEN: It is, sir.

TRICKY: Consequently, even if Lieutenant Calley did participate in a case of "abortion on demand," it would seem to me, speaking strictly as a lawyer, mind you, that there are numerous extenuating factors to consider, not the least of which is the attempt to perform a surgical operation under battlefield conditions. I would think that more than one medic has been cited for doing less.

CITIZEN: Cited for what?

TRICKY: Bravery, of course.

CITIZEN: But . . . but, Mr. President, what if it wasn't "abortion on demand"? What if Lieutenant Calley gave her an abortion without her demanding one, or even asking for one—or even wanting one?

TRICKY: As an outright form of population control, you mean?

CITIZEN: Well, I was thinking more along the lines of an outright form of murder.

TRICKY *(reflecting):* Well, of course, that is a very iffy question, isn't it? What we lawyers call a hypothetical instance—isn't it? If you will remember, we are only *supposing* there to have been a pregnant woman in that ditch at My Lai to begin with. Suppose there *wasn't* a pregnant woman in that ditch—which, in fact, seems from all evidence to have been the case. We are then involved in a totally academic discussion.

CITIZEN: Yes, sir. If so, we are.

TRICKY: Which doesn't mean it hasn't been of great value to me, nonetheless. In my review of Lieutenant Calley's case, I will now be particularly careful to inquire whether there is so much as a single shred of evidence that one of those twenty-two in that ditch at My Lai was a pregnant woman. And if there is—if I should find in the evidence against the lieutenant anything whatsoever that I cannot square with my personal belief in the sanctity of human life, including the life of the yet unborn, I will disqualify myself as a judge and pass the entire matter on to the Vice President.

CITIZEN: Thank you, Mr. President. I think we can all sleep better at night knowing that.

2. *Tricky Holds a Press Conference*

MR. ASSLICK: Sir, as regards your San Dementia statement of April 3, the discussion it provoked seems now to have centered on your unequivocal declaration that you are a firm believer in the rights of the unborn. Many seem to believe that you are destined to be to the unborn what Martin Luther King was to the black people of America, and the late Robert F. Charisma to the disadvantaged Chicanos and Puerto Ricans of the country. There are those who say that your San Dementia statement will go down in the history books alongside Dr. King's famous "I have a dream" address. Do you find these comparisons apt?

TRICKY: Well, of course, Mr. Asslick, Martin Luther King was a very great man, as we all must surely recognize now that he is dead. He was a great leader in the struggle for equal rights for his people, and yes, I do believe he'll find a place in history. But of course we must not forget he was not the President of the United States, as I am, empowered by the Constitution, as I am; and this is an important distinction to bear in mind. Working *within* the Constitution I think I will be able to accomplish far more for the unborn of this *entire* nation than did Dr. King working *outside* the Constitution for the born of *a single race.* This is meant to be no criticism of Dr. King, but just a simple statement of fact.

Now, of course I am well aware that Dr. King died a martyr's tragic death—so let me then make one thing very clear to my enemies and the enemies of the unborn: let there be no mistake about it, what they did to Martin Luther King, what they did to Robert F. Charisma and to John F. Charisma before him, great Americans all, is not for a moment going to deter me from engaging in the struggle that lies ahead. I will not be intimidated by extremists or militants or violent fanatics from bringing justice and equality to those who live in the womb. And let me make one thing more perfectly clear: I am not just talking about the rights of the fetus. I am talking about the microscopic embryos as well. If ever there was a group in this country that was "disadvantaged," in the sense that they are utterly without representation or a voice in our national government, it is not the blacks or the Puerto Ricans or the hippies or what-have-you, all of whom have their spokesmen, but these infinitesimal creatures up there on the placenta.

You know, we all watch our TV and we see the demonstrators and we see the violence, because, unfortunately, that is the kind of thing that makes the news. But how many of us realize that throughout this great land of ours, there are millions upon millions of embryos going through the most complex and difficult changes in form and structure, and all this they accomplish without waving signs for the camera and disrupting traffic and throwing paint and using foul language and dressing in outlandish clothes. Yes, Mr. Daring.

MR. DARING: But what about those fetuses, sir, that the Vice President has labeled "troublemakers"? I believe he was referring specifically to those who start in kicking around the fifth month. Do you agree that they are "malcontents" and "ingrates"? And if so, what measures do you intend to take to control them?

TRICKY: Well, first off, Mr. Daring, I believe we are dealing here with some very fine distinctions of a legal kind. Now, fortunately *(impish endearing smile)* I happen to be a lawyer and have the kind of training that enables me to make these fine distinctions. *(Back to serious business)* I think we have to be very very careful here—and I am sure the Vice President would agree with me—to distinguish between two kinds of activity: *kicking* in the womb, to which the Vice President was specifically referring, and *moving* in the womb. You see, the Vice President did not say, despite what you may have heard on television, that *all* fetuses who are active in the womb are troublemakers. Nobody in this Administration believes that. In fact, I have just today spoken with both Attorney General Malicious and with Mr. Heehaw at the FBI, and we are all in agreement that a certain amount of movement in the womb, after the fifth month, is not only inevitable but *desirable* in a normal pregnancy.

But as for this other matter, I assure you, this administration does not intend to sit idly by and do nothing while American women are being kicked in the stomach by a bunch of violent five-month-olds. Now by and large, and I cannot emphasize this enough, our American unborn are as wonderful a group of unborn as you can find anywhere. But there are these violent few that the Vice President has characterized, and I don't think unjustly, in his own impassioned rhetoric, as "troublemakers" and "malcontents"—and the Attorney General has been instructed by me to take the appropriate action against them.

MR. DARING: If I may, sir, what sort of action will that be? Will there be arrests made of violent fetuses? And if so, how exactly will this be carried out?

TRICKY: I think I can safely say, Mr. Daring, that we have the finest law enforcement agencies in the world. I am quite sure that Attorney General Malicious can solve whatever procedural problems may arise. Mr. Respectful.

MR. RESPECTFUL: Mr. President, with all the grave national and international problems that press continually upon you, can you tell us why you have decided to devote yourself to this previously neglected issue of fetal rights? You seem pretty fired up on this issue, sir—why is that?

TRICKY: Because, Mr. Respectful, I will not tolerate injustice in any area of our national life. Because ours is a just society, not merely for the rich and the privileged, but for the most powerless among us as well. You know, you hear a lot these days about Black Power and Female Power, Power this and Power that. But what about Prenatal Power? Don't they have rights too, membranes though they may be? I for one think they do, and I intend to fight for them. Mr. Shrewd.

MR. SHREWD: As you must know, Mr. President, there are those who contend that you are guided in this matter solely by political considerations. Can you comment on that?

TRICKY: Well, Mr. Shrewd, I suppose that is their cynical way of describing my plan to introduce a proposed constitutional amendment that would extend the vote to the unborn in time for the '72 elections.

MR. SHREWD: I believe that is what they have in mind, sir. They contend that by extending the vote to the unborn you will neutralize the gains that may accrue to the Democratic Party by the voting age having been lowered to eighteen. They say your strategists have concluded that even if you should lose the eighteen-to-twenty-one-year-old vote, you can still win a second term if you are able to carry the South, the state of California, and the embryos and fetuses from coast to coast. Is there any truth to this "political" analysis of your sudden interest in Prenatal Power?

TRICKY: Mr. Shrewd, I'd like to leave that to you—and to our television viewers—to judge, by answering your question in a somewhat personal manner. I assure you I am conversant with the opinions of the experts. Many of them are men whom I respect, and surely they have the right to say whatever they like, though of course one always hopes it will be in the national interest . . . But let me remind you, and all Americans, because this is a fact that seems somehow to have been overlooked in this whole debate: I am no Johnny-come-lately to the problem of the rights of the unborn. The simple fact of the matter, and it is in the record for all to see, is that I myself was once unborn, in the great state of California. Of course, you wouldn't always know this from what you see on television or read in the papers *(impish endearing smile)* that some of you gentlemen write for, but it happens nonetheless to be the truth. *(Back to serious business)* I was an unborn Quaker, as a matter of fact.

And let me remind you—since it seems necessary to do so, in the face of the vicious and mindless attacks upon him—Vice President What's-his-name was also unborn once, an unborn Greek-American, and proud to have been one. We were just talking about that this morning, how he was once an unborn Greek-American, and all that has meant to him. And so too was Secretary Lard unborn and so was Secretary Codger unborn, and the Attorney General—why, I could go right on down through my cabinet and point out to you one fine man after another who was once unborn. Even Secretary Fickle, with whom as you know I had my differences of opinion, was unborn when he was here with us on the team.

And if you look among the leadership of the Republican Party in the House and the Senate, you will find men who long before their election to public office were unborn in just about every region of this country, on farms, in industrial cities, in small towns the length and breadth of this great republic. My own wife was once unborn. As you may recall, my children were both unborn.

So when they say that Dixon has turned to the issue of the unborn just for the sake of the votes . . . well, I ask only that you consider this list of the previously unborn with whom I am associated in both public and private life, and decide for yourself. In fact, I think you are going to find, Mr. Shrewd, with each passing day, people around this country coming to realize that in this administration the fetuses and embryos of America have at last found their voice. Miss Charmin', I believe you had your eyebrows raised.

MISS CHARMIN': I was just going to say, sir, that of course President Lyin' B. Johnson was unborn, too, before he came to the White House—and he was a Democrat. Could you comment on that?

TRICKY: Miss Charmin', I would be the first to applaud my predecessor in this high office for having been unborn. I have no doubt that he was an outstanding fetus down there in Texas before he came into public life. I am not claiming that my administration is the first in history to be cognizant of the issue of fetal rights. I am saying that we intend to do something about them. Mr. Practical.

MR. PRACTICAL: Mr. President, I'd like to ask you to comment upon the scientific problems entailed in bringing the vote to the unborn.

TRICKY: Well, of course, Mr. Practical, you have hit the nail right on the head with the word "scientific." This is a scientific problem of staggering proportions—let's make no mistake about it. Moreover, I fully expect there are those who are going to say in tomorrow's papers that it is impossible, unfeasible, a utopian dream, and so on. But as you remember, when President Charisma came before the Congress in 1961, and announced that this country would put a man on the moon before the end of the decade, there were many who were ready to label him an impossible dreamer, too. But we did it. With American know-how and American teamwork, we did it. And so too do I have every confidence that our scientific and technological people are going to dedicate themselves to bringing the vote to the unborn—and not before the decade is out either, but before November of 1972.

MR. PRACTICAL: Can you give us some idea, sir, how much a crash program like this will cost?

TRICKY: Mr. Practical, I will be submitting a proposed budget to the Congress within the next ten days, but let me say this: you cannot achieve greatness without sacrifice. The program of research and development such as my scientific advisers have outlined cannot be bought "cheap." After all, what we are talking about here is nothing less than the fundamental principle of democracy: the vote. I cannot believe that the members of the Congress of the United States are going to play party politics when it comes to taking a step like this, which will be an advance not only for our nation, but for all mankind.

You just cannot imagine, for instance, the impact that this is going to have on the people in the underdeveloped countries. There are the Russians and the Chinese, who don't even allow adults to vote, and here we are in America, investing billions and billions of the taxpayers' dollars in a scientific project designed to extend the franchise to people who cannot see or talk or hear or even think, in the ordinary sense of the word. It would be a tragic irony indeed, and as telling a sign as I can imagine of national confusion and even hypocrisy, if we were willing to send our boys to fight and die in far-off lands so that defenseless peoples might have the right to choose the kinds of government they want in free elections, and then we were to turn around here at home and continue to deny that very same right to an entire segment of our population, just because they happen to live on the placenta or in the uterus, instead of New York City. Mr. Catch-Me-in-a-Contradiction.

MR. CATCH-ME-IN-A-CONTRADICTION: Mr. President, what startles me is that up until today you have been characterized, and not unwillingly, I think, as someone who, if he is not completely out of touch with the styles and ideas of the young, has certainly been skeptical of their wisdom. Doesn't this constitute, if I may use the word, a radical about-face, coming out now for the rights of those who are not simply "young" but actually in the gestation period?

TRICKY: Well, I am glad you raised that point, because I think it shows once and for all just how flexible I am, and how I am always willing to listen and respond to an appeal from *any* minority group, no matter how powerless, just so long as it is reasonable, and is not accompanied by violence and foul language and throwing paint. If ever there was proof that you don't have to camp on the White House lawn to get the President's attention away from a football game, I think it is in the example of these little organisms. I tell you, they have really impressed me with their silent dignity and politeness. I only hope that all Americans will come to be as proud of our unborn as I am.

MR. FASCINATED: Mr. President, I am fascinated by the technological aspect. Can you give us just an inkling of how exactly the unborn will go about casting their ballots? I'm particularly fascinated by these embryos on the placenta, who haven't even developed nervous systems yet, let alone limbs such as we use in an ordinary voting machine.

TRICKY: Well, first off, let me remind you that nothing in our Constitution denies a man the right to vote just because he is physically handicapped. That isn't the kind of country we have here. We have many wonderful handicapped people in this country, but of course, they're not "news" the way the demonstrators are.

MR. FASCINATED: I wasn't suggesting, sir, that just because these embryos don't have central nervous systems they should be denied the right to vote—I was thinking again of the fantastic *mechanics* of it. How, for instance, will the embryos be able to weigh the issues and make intelligent choices from among the candidates, if they are not able to read the newspapers or watch the news on television?

TRICKY: Well, it seems to me that you have actually touched upon the very strongest claim that the unborn have for enfranchisement, and why it is such a crime they have been denied the vote for so long. Here, at long last, we have a great bloc of voters who simply are not going to be taken in by the lopsided and distorted versions of the truth that are presented to the American public through the various media. Mr. Reasonable.

MR. REASONABLE: But how then will they make up their minds, or their yolks, or their nuclei, or whatever it is they have in there, Mr. President? It might seem to some that they are going to be absolutely innocent of whatever may be at stake in the election.

TRICKY: Innocent they will be, Mr. Reasonable—but now let me ask you, and all our television viewers, too, a question: what's *wrong* with a little innocence? We've had the foul language, we've had the cynicism, we've had the masochism and the breast-beating—maybe a big dose of innocence is just what this country needs to be great again.

MR. REASONABLE: *More* innocence, Mr. President?

TRICKY: Mr. Reasonable, if I have to choose between the rioting and the upheaval and the strife and the discontent on the one hand, and more innocence on the other, I think I will choose the innocence. Mr. Hardnose.

MR. HARDNOSE: In the event, Mr. President, that all this does come to pass by the '72 elections, what gives you reason to believe that the enfranchised embryos and fetuses will vote for you over your Democratic opponent? And what about Governor Wallow? Do you think that if he should run again, he would significantly cut into your share of the fetuses, particularly in the South?

TRICKY: Let me put it this way, Mr. Hardnose: I have the utmost respect for Governor George Wallow of Alabama, as I do for Senator Hubert Hollow of Minnesota. They are both able men, and they speak with great conviction, I am sure, in behalf of the extreme right and the extreme left. But the fact is that I have never heard either of these gentlemen, for all their extremism, raise their voices in behalf of America's most disadvantaged group of all, the unborn.

Consequently, I would be less than candid if I didn't say that when election time rolls around, of course the embryos and fetuses of this country are likely to remember just who it was that struggled in their behalf, while others were addressing themselves to the more popular and fashionable issues of the day. I think they will remember who it was that devoted himself, in the midst of a war abroad and racial crisis at home, to making this country a fit place for the unborn to dwell in pride.

My only hope is that whatever I am able to accomplish in their behalf while I hold this office will someday contribute to a world in which *everybody,* regardless of race, creed, or color, will be unborn. I guess if *I* have a dream, that is it. Thank you, ladies and gentlemen.

MR. ASSLICK: Thank you, Mr. President.

Tricky's Farewell Speech

My fellow Americans:

I have an announcement to make to you tonight of the greatest national importance. As you know, the Senate has voted this afternoon to remove me from the Office of the President. That, of course, is their right under the Constitution of the United States of America, and as you know, I have not interfered in any way with their deliberations on this matter, as I did not interfere some weeks ago when the House of Representatives arrived at their decision after their own deliberations. They have a right to express their opinion, as does any American, without Presidential interference or pressure of any kind from the Executive branch. That is what is known as the separation of powers. You probably know by now that there were even members of my own political party among those in the Legislative branch who voted to remove me from the Presidency. I consider that to be a vigorous and reassuring sign of their independence of mind, and of their personal integrity. I applaud them for their actions, which can only strengthen the democratic process here at home, and enhance the image of American democracy abroad.

However, according to the doctrine of the separation of powers, the Executive branch has an equal voice in the management

---

A Nixon parody written at the height of the Senate Watergate hearings. It appeared first in *The New York Review of Books* (June 14, 1973) and subsequently in *Reading Myself and Others* (1975).

of government, along with the Legislative and the Judicial branches. That, after all, is only fair. It is what is meant by the "American Way." Moreover, the President has the sole responsibility for safeguarding the security of the nation. That responsibility is spelled out in the oath of Office, which, as you all know, every President takes on Inauguration Day. President Washington, whose picture you see here, took that oath. So did President Lincoln, pictured here. And so did our great President Dwight David Eisenhower, whose grandson has just completed serving his country in the United States Navy and is married to my daughter Julie, whom you see pictured here. My other daughter, Tricia, is pictured here, in her wedding dress. And of course standing beside Tricia is my wife Pat. My fellow Americans, I owe it not only to these great American Presidents who preceded me in this high Office but to my family, and to you and your families, to respect and honor that oath to which I swore on the Holy Bible on my Inauguration Day. To speak personally, I just couldn't live with myself if I went ahead and shirked my duty to safeguard the security of the nation.

And that is why I have decided tonight to remain in this Office. My fellow Americans, though I respect the sincerity and the integrity of those Senators who voted earlier in the day for my removal, I find, after careful study and grave reflection, that to accept their decision would be to betray the trust placed in me by the American people, and to endanger the security and the well-being of this nation.

As you all know, there has never been an American President yet who has stepped down in the middle of his term of Office because of Congressional pressure of any kind. That is something for which there is just no precedent in American history—and let me tell you, straight from the shoulder, I don't intend to break the record my predecessors have established of standing up under fire.

You know, no one, I don't care which party he belongs to, expects this Office to be a bed of roses. If he does he shouldn't run for the Presidency to begin with. As the late President Harry Truman put it—and you remember, Harry Truman didn't always see eye to eye on everything with us Republicans—"If you can't take the heat, you shouldn't be in the kitchen." Well, I happen to pride myself on the amount of heat I've taken over the years—some of it, as you older folks may remember, in a kitchen in the Soviet Union with Premier Khrushchev. But in the name of the American people, I stood up to Premier Khrushchev in that kitchen; and in the name of the American people, I am standing up to the Congress tonight.

Richard Nixon is not going to be the first President in American history to be removed from Office by the Legislative branch. I am sure that is not the kind of President that the American people elected me to be. Frankly, if I were to give in to this Congressional pressure to remove me from Office, if I were to come on television tonight to tell you, yes, President Nixon is quitting because he can't take the heat, well, that to my mind would constitute a direct violation of my oath of Office, and I would in fact *voluntarily* step down from the Presidency, out of a sense of having profoundly failed you, the American people, whose decision it was to place me in Office in the first place.

My fellow Americans, during my years as President I have, as you know, devoted myself to one goal above and beyond all others: the goal of world peace. As I talk to you here tonight, negotiations and discussions are being conducted around the globe by Dr. Kissinger, Secretary Rogers, and key members of the Department of State to bring peace with honor to America, and to all of mankind. These negotiations are taking place at the highest diplomatic level and necessarily in secret—but I am pleased to report to you tonight that we are pursuing them with every hope of success.

Now I am sure that no one in Congress would willingly or knowingly want to endanger the chances of world peace, for us, for our children, and for generations to come. And yet, by calling upon the President to pack up and quit just because the going is a little rough, that is precisely what they are doing. And that is precisely why I will *not* quit. I happen to care more about world peace now and for generations to come than about making myself popular with a few of my critics in the Congress. Oh, I am sure that the easier choice would be to retire to San Clemente and bask there in the honors and tributes that we Americans lavish upon our former Presidents. But I prefer to take the hard road, the high road, if that is the road that leads to the end of warfare and to world peace for our children and our children's children. My fellow Americans, I was raised to be a Quaker, not a quitter.

Now I have to say some things to you that you may not care to hear, especially those of you who try to think the best of our country, as I do myself. But tonight I must speak the truth, unpleasant as it may be; you deserve no less. My fellow Americans, I understand there are going to be those in Congress who will not respect the decision I have announced here tonight, as I respected theirs, arrived at earlier in the day. We have reason to believe that there are those who are going to try to make political capital out of what I have said to you tonight from the bottom of my heart. There are even going to be some who will use my words to attempt to create a national crisis in order to reap political gain for themselves or their party. And, most dangerous of all, there are some elements in the country, given to violence and lawlessness as a way of life, who may attempt to use force to remove me from Office.

Let me quickly reassure you that this Administration will not tolerate lawlessness of any kind. This Administration will not permit the time-honored constitutional principle of the separation of powers to be subverted by a disgruntled, ambitious, or radical minority. This Administration intends to maintain and defend that great American tradition that has come down to us unbroken from the days of the Founding Fathers—the great tradition of a President of the United States, duly elected by the people of the United States, serving out his Office without violent interference by those who disagree with his policies. Disagreement and dissent are, of course, in the great tradition of a democracy like our own; but the violent overthrow of the elected government is something that is repugnant to me, as it is to every American, and so long as I am President, I promise you that I will deal promptly and efficiently with those who advocate or engage in violence as a means of bringing about political change.

In order to discourage those who would resort to violence of any kind, and in order to maintain law and order in the nation and to safeguard the welfare and well-being of law-abiding American citizens, I have tonight, in my constitutional role as Commander-in-Chief, ordered the Joint Chiefs of Staff to place the Armed Forces on a stand-by alert around the nation. The Department of Justice and the Federal Bureau of Investigation have also been advised to take all necessary steps to ensure domestic tranquillity. The National Guard has already been notified, and throughout the fifty states units are being mobilized for duty. Furthermore, state and local police have been encouraged to request whatever assistance they may require, in the way of personnel or equipment, in order to maintain law and order in your communities.

My fellow Americans, I swore upon taking this Office to safeguard this nation and its citizens, and I intend to stand on my word. No one—and that includes your Congressman and your Senator, just as it does the armed revolutionary—is going to tell the American people that they cannot have sitting in the White House the President they have chosen in a free and open election. And I don't care whether that President happens to be myself, President Washington, President Lincoln, or President Eisenhower. I give you every assurance tonight that the President you, the American people, elected for a second four-year term will not permit the votes you cast so overwhelmingly in his favor to have been cast in vain.

God bless each and every one of you.

Good night.

THE '43 MUNDYS

SS Frenchy Astarte
2B Nickname Damur
1B John Baal
C Hothead Ptah
LF Mike Rama
3B Wayne Heket
RF Bud Parusha
CF Roland Agni

P Jolly Cholly Tuminikar
P Deacon Demeter
P Bobo Buchis
P Rocky Volos
P Howie Pollux
P Catfish Mertzeger
P Chico Mecoatl

UT Specs Skirnir
UT Wally Omara
UT Mule Mokos
UT Applejack Terminus
UT Carl Khovaki
UT Harry Hunaman
UT Joe Garuda
UT Swede Gudmund
UT Ike Tvashtri
UT Red Kronos

The Visitors' Line-Up

A distressing chapter wherein the reader is introduced to each member of the 1943 Mundy starting line-up as he steps up to the plate, and comes thus to understand why Americans have conspired to remove all reminders of such a team from the history books; their records recounted more fully than on the back of the bubble gum cards. Containing much matter to vex the ordinary fan and strain his credulity, which is as it must be, in that real life is always running away with itself, whereas imagination is shackled by innocence, delusion, hope, ignorance, obedience, fear, sweetness, et cetera. Containing that which will move the compassionate to tears, the just to indignation, and the cruel to laughter.

"Batting first and playing shortstop, No. 1: FRENCHY ASTARTE. ASTARTE."

Jean-Paul Astarte (TR, BR, 5'10", 172 lbs.), French-Canadian, acquired in unusual deal late in 1941 from Tokyo team of Japan in association with Imperial Japanese Government—the only player ever traded out of his own hemisphere (and the only player ever traded back). Began career in twenties, down in Georgia, thence to Havana in the Cuban League, Santiago in the

---

Chapter 2 of *The Great American Novel* (1973), the story of the Ruppert Mundys, the only homeless big-league baseball team in American history, whose wretched players wander like refugees from one Patriot League city to the next during World War II, dropping deeper and deeper into humiliation, despair, and last place.

Dominican League, finally Caracas. It began to look as though the French-speaking boy out of the freezing North was destined in the end to play for the Equator—but no, misery is never so orderly in its progression; it wouldn't be real misery if it was. Early in the thirties, when baseball boomed in Japan, he was traded to Tokyo by way of the Panama Canal; there he played shortstop for nearly a decade, dreaming day in and day out of his father's dairy farm in the Gaspé. When news reached him in the fall of '41 that he was to be traded once again, he just somehow assumed it would be to Calcutta; he did not understand a word his Japanese owner was telling him (anymore than he had understood his Spanish owner or his American owner when they had called him in to say *au revoir*) and actually started in weeping at the prospect of playing ball next with a bunch of guys talking it up in Hindi and running around the bases in bedsheets. Oh, how he cursed the day he had donned a leather mitt and tried to pretend he was something other, something *more,* than a French-Canadian farmboy! Why wasn't what was good enough for the father good enough for the son? At sixteen years of age, with those powerful wrists of his, he could do a two-gallon milking in five minutes—wasn't that accomplishment enough in one life? Instead he had had dreams (what Canadian doesn't?) of the great stadiums to the south, dreams of American fame and American dollars . . . He boarded the boat with the Japanese ticket in one hand and his bag full of old bats and berets in the other, fully expecting to come ashore in a land of brown men in white dresses, and wound up instead (such was Frenchy's fate) being greeted at the dock by something he could never have expected. "Welcome, *Monsieur!* Welcome to Port Ruppert!" The famous Ulysses S. Fairsmith, the greatest manager in the game! *Mon Dieu!* It was not India he had reached, but America; like Columbus before him, he was a big leaguer at last.

How come? Simple. The Mundy brothers, into whose laps a million tons of scrap metal had dropped, had traded directly with Hirohito, a penny a pound, and (shrewd afterthought) a shortstop to fill the hole that would be left in the Mundy infield when the war started up in December. Yes, there was literally nothing the Mundy brothers didn't have the inside dope on, including the bombing of Pearl Harbor. That's what made them so successful. "Tell you what," they were reported to have said to the eager Emperor of Japan, "throw in the shortstop from the Tokyo club, and you got yourself a deal, Hirohito." Thus did they kill two birds with one stone, and God only knows how many hundreds of American soldiers.

Unfortunately the Most Valuable Player in the Far East found the majors rather different from what he had been imagining during his years of exile. For one thing, he was now thirty-nine, a fact of some consequence when you were hitting against carnivorous two hundred pounders instead of little rice-eaters about the size of your nephew Billy. It was weeks before he got his first Patriot League hit: seven, to be exact. Then there was that throw to first. How come they kept beating out for hits what used to be outs back in Asia? How come the fans booed and hooted when he came to the plate—when they used to cry *"Caramba!"* in Venezuela and *"Banzai!"* in the Land of the Rising Sun? Why, here in the big American leagues of his dreams, he was even more of a foreigner than he had been in Tokyo, Japan! There he was an all-star shortstop, white as Honus Wagner and Rabbit Maranville—white as them and *great* as them. But here in the P. League he was "Frenchy" the freak.

In '42 he batted .200 for the Mundys, just about half what he'd batted halfway around the globe, and he led the shortstops in the three leagues in errors. His specialty was dropping high infield flies. The higher the ball was hit, the longer it gave him to wait beneath it, thinking about Japan and the day he would return to Tokyo and stardom.

It was Frenchy's error in the last game of the '42 season (and the last game ever played in Mundy Park), that sent two Rustler runners scampering home in the ninth, and knocked the Mundys into last. At the time, finishing half a game out of the cellar or right down in it didn't make much difference to his teammates —by the end of that first wartime season, all those old-timers wanted from life was not to have to push their bones around a baseball field for the next six months. And Frenchy too was able to live with the error by thinking of it as a mere one seventy-fifth of the mistakes he had made out on the field that year—until, that is, word reached him in snowbound Gaspé (as strange to him now as steamy Havana once had been, for his father was dead, as were all the cows he used to know there as a boy) that the last-place Mundys had been booted out of Mundy Park and henceforth would be homeless.

Unlucky Astarte! Because of my error, he thought, that made us come in last! Because at that moment, his mind hadn't been on Ruppert finishing seventh in the P. League, but Japan finishing first in the war! Yes, Japan victorious über alles . . . Japan conquering America, conquering Yankee Stadium, Wrigley Field, Mundy Park . . . Yes, waiting beneath what was to have been the last fly ball of the '42 season, he had been envisioning opening day of 1943—Hirohito throwing out the first pitch to a Ruppert team of tiny Orientals, with the exception of himself, the Most Valuable Player in an Imperial Japanese world . . .

Oh, if ever there was a player without a country, it was the Mundy lead-off man, who forever afterwards believed himself and his traitorous thoughts to have caused the expulsion from Port Ruppert. Was Frenchy the loneliest and unhappiest Mundy of them all? A matter of debate, fans. In the end, he was their only suicide, though not the only Mundy regular to meet his Maker on the road.

"Batting second and playing second base, No. 29: NICKNAME DAMUR. DAMUR."

Nickname Damur (TR, BR, 5′, 92 lbs.) could run the ninety feet from home to first in 3.4 seconds, and that was about it. At fourteen he was the youngest player in the majors, as well as the skinniest. The joke was (or was it a joke?) that the Mundy brothers were paying him by the pound; not that the boy cared anything about money anyway—no, all he seemed to think about from the moment he joined the team in spring training, was making a nickname for himself. "How about Hank?" he asked his new teammates his very first day in the scarlet and white, "don't I look like a Hank to you guys?" He was so green they had to sit him down and *explain* to him that Hank was the nickname for Henry. "Is that your name, boy—Henry?" "Nope. It's worse . . . Hey, how about Dutch? Dutch Damur. It rhymes!" "Dutch is for Dutchmen, knucklehead." "Chief?" "For Injuns." "Whitey?" "For blonds." "How about Ohio then, where I'm from?" "That ain't a name." "Hey—how about Happy? Which I sure am, bein' here with you all!" "Don't worry, you won't be for long." "Well then," he said shyly, "given my incredible speed and all, how about Twinkletoes? Or Lightning? Or Flash!" "Don't boast, it ain't becomin'. We wuz all fast once't. So was everybody in the world. That don't make you special one bit." "Hey! How about Dusty? That rhymes too!"

But even when he himself had settled upon the nickname he wouldn't have minded seeing printed beneath his picture on a bubble gum card, or hearing announced over the loud speaker when he stepped up to bat, his teammates refused to address him by it. Mostly, in the beginning, they did not address him at all if they could help it, but just sort of pushed him aside to get where they were going, or walked right through him as though he weren't there. A fourteen-year-old kid weighing ninety-two pounds playing in their infield! "What next?" they said, spitting on the dugout steps in disgust, "a reindeer or a slit?" In the meantime, Damur began tugging at his cap every two minutes, hoping they would notice and start calling him Cappy; he took to talking as though he had been born on a farm, saying "hoss" for horse and calling the infield "the pea patch," expecting they would shortly start calling him Rube; suddenly he began running out to his position in the oddest damn way—"What the hell you doin', boy?" they asked. "That's just the way I walk," he replied, "like a duck." But no one took the hint and called him Ducky or Goose. Nor when he chattered encouragement to the pitcher did they think to nickname him Gabby. "Shut up with that noise, willya?" cried the pitcher—"You're drivin' me batty," and so that was the end of that. Finally, in desperation, he whined, "Jee-zuz! What about *Kid* at least?" "We already got a Kid on this club. Two's confusin'." "But he's fifty years old and losin' his teeth!" cried Damur. "I'm only fourteen. I *am* a kid." "Tough. He wuz here before you wuz even born."

It was Jolly Cholly Tuminikar, the Mundy peacemaker and Sunday manager, who christened him Nickname. Not that Damur was happy about it, as he surely would have been, dubbed Happy. " 'Nickname' isn't a nickname, it's the *name* for a nickname. Hey—how about Nick? *That's* the nickname for nickname! Call me Nick, guys!" "Nick? That's for Greeks. You ain't Greek." "But whoever heard of a baseball player called *Nickname Damur?*" "And whoever heard a' one that weighed ninety-two pounds and could not endorse a razor blade if they even asked him to?"

Indeed, so slight was he, that on the opening day of the '43 season, a base runner barreling into second knocked Nickname so high and so far that the center-fielder, Roland Agni, came charging in to make a sensational diving two-handed catch of the boy. "Out!" roared the field umpire, until he remembered that of course it is the ball not the player that has to be caught, and instantly reversed his decision. The fans, however, got a kick out of seeing Nickname flying this way and that, and when he came to bat would playfully call out to him, "How about Tarzan? How about Gargantua?" and the opposing team had their fun too, needling him from the bench—"How about Powerhouse? How about Hurricane? How about Hercules, Nickname?" At last the diminutive second-sacker couldn't take any more. "Stop it," he cried, "stop, *please,*" and, with tears running down his face, pleaded with his tormentors, "My name is Oliver!" But, alas, it was too late for that.

Nickname, obviously, had no business in the majors, not even as a pinch-runner. Oh, he was swift enough, but hardly man enough, and if it was not for the wartime emergency, and the irresponsibility of the Mundy brothers, he would have been home where he belonged, with his long division and his mom. "How about Homesick?" the sportswriter Smitty whispered into the boy's ear, a month after the '43 season began, and Nickname, black and blue by now and batting less than his own weight, threw himself in a rage upon the famous columnist. But what began with a flurry of fists ended with the boy sobbing in Smitty's lap, in a wing chair in a corner of the lobby of the Grand Kakoola Hotel. The next day, Smitty's column began, "A big league player wept yesterday, cried his heart out like a kid, but only a fool would call him a sissy . . ."

Thereafter the fans left off teasing Nickname about his size and his age and his name, and for a while (until the catastrophe at Kakoola) he became something like a mascot to the crowds. Of course, being babied was the last thing he wanted (so he thought) and so under the professional guidance of Big John Baal, he took to the booze, and, soon enough, to consorting with whores. *They* called him whatever he wanted them to. In sleazy cathouses around the league they called him just about every famous ballplayer's nickname under the sun—all he had to do was ask, and pay. They called him Babe, Nap, Christy, Shoeless, Dizzy, Heinie, Tony, Home Run, Cap, Rip, Kiki, Luke, Pepper, and Irish; they called him Cracker and Country and King Kong and Pie; they even called him Lefty, skinny little fourteen-year-old second baseman that he was. Why not? It only cost an extra buck, and it made him feel like somebody important.

"Batting in third position, the first baseman, No. 11, JOHN BAAL. BAAL."

Big John (TR, BL, 6'4", 230 lbs.), said never to have hit a homer sober in his life, had played for just about every club in the league, including the Mundys, before returning to them in '42, paroled into the custody of their benevolent manager. Baal joined the club after serving two years on a five-year gambling rap—he'd shot craps after the World Series with the rookie of the year, and wiped the boy out with a pair of loaded dice. Not the first time John had walked off with somebody else's World Series earnings, only the first time they caught him with the shaved ivories. In prison Big John had had the two best seasons of his life, earning the ironic appellation (coined, of course, by Smitty) "the Babe Ruth of the Big House." With Big John in the line-up, Sing Sing beat every major prison team in the country, including the powerful Leavenworth club, and went on to capture the criminal baseball championship of America two consecutive seasons after nearly a decade of losing to the big federal pens stocked with hard-hitting bootleggers. Inside the prison walls a Johnny Baal didn't have to put up with the rules and regulations that had so hampered him throughout his big league career, particularly the commandment against taking the field under the influence of alcohol. If a slugger had a thirst around game time, then his warden saw that it was satisfied (along with any other appetite a robust man might develop), because the warden wanted to *win*. But out in society, you couldn't get past the dugout steps without some little old biddy in a baseball uniform sniffing you all over for fear that if you blew on their ball with your sour mash breath, you might pop open the stitching and unravel the yarn. Consequently, aside from his criminal record, the only record Big John held outside of prison was for the longest outs hit in a single season. Christ, he clouted that ball so high that at its zenith it passed clear out of sight—but as for distance, he just could not get it to go all the way, unless he was pickled.

Now, every ballplayer has his weakness, and that was Big John's. If he didn't drink, if he didn't gamble, if he didn't whore and cheat and curse, if he wasn't a roughneck, a glutton and a brawler, why he just wasn't himself, and his whole damn game went to pot, hitting *and* fielding. But when he had fifteen drinks under his belt, there was nobody like him on first base. Giant that he was, he could still bounce around that infield like a kangaroo when he was good and drunk. And could he hit! "Why, one time in that jail up there," Big John told Smitty upon his release from the prison, "I had me a lunch of a case of beer and a bottle of bourbon and got nine for nine in a doubleheader. Yep, every time I come up, I just poked her into the outside world. But this rule they got out here—why it's disgustin'! It ain't for men, it's for lollipops and cupcakes! It's a damn joke what they done to this game—and that there Hall of *Fame* they got, why, that's a bigger joke! Why, if they ever asked me to come up there and gave me one of them poems or whatever it is they give, why I'd just laugh in their face! I'd say take your poem and wipe your assholes with it, you bunch a' powder puffs!"

Big John's contempt for the Hall of Fame (and his antisocial conduct generally) seemed to stem from grievances against Organized Baseball that had been implanted in him by his notorious father, who, in turn, had inherited from *his* notorious father a downright Neanderthal attitude toward the game. John's grandfather was, as everyone knows, *the* Baal, the legendary "Base," who is still mistakenly credited with the idea of substituting sand-filled bags, or bases, for the posts used to mark off the infield in baseball's infancy; in actuality he earned the nickname early in his career because of his behavior on the playing field. If we are to believe the stories, Base Baal played on just about every cornfield and meadow in America before the first leagues were organized, before stadiums were built and men earned a living as players. Like many American boys, he learned the fundamentals in the Army camps of the Civil War. The game in that era consisted of several variants, all of which would be as foreign to the American baseball fan of today as jai alai or lacrosse. This was long before pitchers began to throw overhand, back when the bat was a stick that was narrow at both ends, if it was not a fence post or a barrel stave, back when there would be as many as twenty or thirty players on a team, and when the umpire, chosen from the crowd of spectators, might well be punched in the nose and run off the field if his judgment did not accord with everyone else's. The ball was a bit larger, something like today's softball, and "plugging" or "soaking" was the order of the day—to get the runner out, you had only to "plug" him (that is, hit him with the ball while he was between two bases), for him to be retired (as often as not, howling in pain). Frequently a fielder, or "scout" as he was called in some parts of the country, would wait for the runner to come right up to him, before "plugging" him in the ribs, much to the pleasure of the onlookers. And that was Base's stock in trade. In fact, when the old fellow finally broke into the newly formed four-club Patriot League in the eighties—by which time the game had taken on many of its modern, more civilized characteristics—he apparently "forgot" himself one day and "plugged" a runner heading home from third right in that vulnerable part of a man's anatomy for which he always aimed. He was instantly mobbed and nearly beaten to death by the other team—a bearded giant of a man, close to sixty now—all the while crying out, "But that's out where I come from!"

Base's son, and Big John's father, was the infamous pitcher Spit, who, in the years before wetting down the ball was declared illegal, would serve up a pitch so juicy that by the end of an inning the catcher had to shake himself off like a dog come in from romping in the rain. The trouble with Spit's spitball was, simply, that nobody could hit it out of the infield, if they could even follow the erratic path of that dripping sphere so as to get any wood on it at all. Once it left Spit's hand, carrying its cargo of liquid, not even he was sure exactly what turns and twists it would take before it landed with a wet thud in the catcher's glove, or up against his padded body. As opposition mounted to this spitter that Baal had perfected—it was unnatural, unsanitary, uncouth, it was ruining the competitive element in the game—he only shrugged and said, "How am I supposed to do, let 'em hit it out theirselves?" On hot afternoons, when his salivary glands and his strong right arm were really working, Spit used to like to taunt the opposition a little by motioning for his outfielders to sit back on their haunches and take a chew, while he struck out—or, as he put it, "drownded"—the other side. Angry batsmen would snarl at the ump, "Game called on accounta rain!" after the first of Spit's spitters did a somersault out in front of the plate and then sort of curled in for a strike at the knees. But Spit himself would pooh-pooh the whole thing, calling down to them, "Come on now, a little wet ain't gonna hurt you." "It ain't the wet, Baal, it's the stringy stuff. It turns a white man's stomach." "Ah, ain't nothin'—just got me a little head cold. Get in there now, and if you cain't swim, float."

In the beginning, various conservative proposals were offered to transform the spitter back into what it had been before Spit came on the scene. The citrus fruit growers of America suggested that a spitball pitcher should have to suck on half a lemon in order to inhibit his flow of saliva—fulfilling his daily nutritional requirement of vitamin C in the process. They tried to work up public interest in a pitch they called "the sourball," but when the pitchers themselves balked, as it were, complaining there was not any room for a lemon what with teeth, tongue, and chewing tobacco in there already, the proposal, mercifully, was dropped. A more serious suggestion had to do with allowing a pitcher to use all the saliva he wanted, but outlawing mucus and phlegm. The theory was that what the ballplayers euphemistically called "the stringy stuff" was precisely what made Baal's pitch dance the way it did. A committee of managers assigned to study his motion maintained that Spit was very much like a puppeteer yanking on a web of strings, and that the rules had only to be rewritten to forbid a pitcher blowing his nose on the ball, or bringing anything up from back of the last molar for the problem to be solved, not only for the batsman, but for those fans who happened to be sitting in its path when it was fouled into the stands. It might even bring more of the ladies out to see a game, for as it stood now, you could not even get a suffragette into the bleachers on a day Baal was pitching, so repugnant was his technique to the fair sex. Even the heartiest of male fans showed signs of squeamishness pocketing a foul tip to bring home as a souvenir to the kiddies. But Spit himself only chuckled (he was a mild, mild man, until they destroyed him). "When I go to a tea party, I will be all good manners and curtsy goodbye at the door, I can assure you of that. But as I am facin' two hundred pounds of gristle wavin' a stick what wants to drive the ball back down my gullet, why then, I will use the wax out of my ears, if I has to."

It was not a remark designed to placate his enemies. In fact, the discovery that he *had* used earwax on a ball in the 1902 World Series caused the controversy to spread beyond the baseball world; owners who had come to consider wetting the ball a part of the game—and Spit a gifted eccentric who would have his day and pass into obscurity soon enough—became alarmed by the outrage of a public that had seemed on the brink of accepting baseball as *the* American sport, now that it had grown away from the brutish game, marked by maiming and fisticuffs, played by Spit's Daddy. The editorialists warned, "If baseball cannot cleanse itself at once of odious and distasteful ways that reek of the barnyard and the back alley, the American people may well look elsewhere—perhaps to the game of tennis, long favored by the French—for a national pastime." From all sides the pressure mounted, until at the winter meeting of the Patriot League owners in Tri-City, following the World Series of 1902 in which Baal, by his own admission, had waxed a few pitches with some stuff he'd hooked out of his head, the following resolution was passed: "No player shall anoint the ball with any bodily secretions for any purpose whatsoever. Inevitable as it is that droplets of perspiration will adhere to a ball in the course of a game, every effort shall be made by the players and the umpire, to keep the ball dry and free of foreign substances at all times." And with these words baseball entered its maturity, and became the game to which an entire people would give its heart and soul.

Spit's career ended abruptly on the opening day of the 1903 season, when he scandalized the country by an act in such flagrant violation of the laws of human decency, let alone the new resolution passed in Tri-City the previous winter, that he became the first player ever to be banished from baseball—the first deplorable exception to the Patriot League's honorable record. What happened was this: throwing nothing but bone-dry pitches, Spit was tagged for eight hits and five runs by a jeering, caustic Independence team even before he had anyone out in the first inning. The crowd was booing, his own teammates were moaning, and Spit was in a rage. They had ruined him, those dryball bastards! They had passed a law whose purpose was the destruction of no one in the world but himself! A law against him!

And so before twenty thousand shocked customers—including innocent children—and his own wide-eyed teammates, the once great pitcher, who was washed up anyway, did the unthinkable, the unpardonable, the inexpiable: he dropped the flannel trousers of his uniform to his knees, and proceeded to urinate on the ball, turning it slowly in his hands so as to dampen the entire surface. Then he hitched his trousers back up, and in the way of pitchers, kicked at the ground around the mound with his spikes, churning up, then smoothing down the dirt where he had inadvertently dribbled upon it. To the batter, as frozen in his position as anyone in that ball park, he called, "Here comes the pissball, shithead—get ready!"

For years afterward they talked about the route that ball took before it passed over the plate. Not only did it make the hairpin turns and somersaults expected of a Baal spitter, but legend has it that it shifted gears *four* times, halving, then doubling its velocity each fifteen feet it traveled. And in the end, the catcher, in his squat, did not even have to move his glove from where it too was frozen as a target. Gagging, he caught the ball with a *squish*, right in the center of the strike zone.

"Stree-*ike!*" Baal called down to the voiceless umpire, and then he turned and walked off the mound and through the dugout and right on out of the park. They banished him only minutes afterward, but (not unlike the great Gamesh thirty years later) he was already on the streetcar by then, still wearing his uniform and spikes, and by nightfall he was asleep in a boxcar headed for the Rio Grande, his old stinking glove his pillow and his only pal. When he finally jumped from the train he was in Central America.

There he founded that aboriginal ancestor of Latin American baseball, the hapless Mosquito Coast League of Nicaragua—if you could call it a league, where the players drifted from one club to another for no reason other than whim, and entire teams were known to disappear from a town between games of a double-header, never to be seen again.. The Nicaraguan youths that Spit Baal recruited for his league had no local games of their own comparable in complexity and duration, and few were ever really able to maintain concentration through an afternoon of play in that heat. But they accepted without question that you could rub anything you wanted on a ball before pitching it, and in fact took to the spitball much the way American children take to the garden hose in summertime. Down in the Mosquito Coast League, Spit's native boys played just the sort of disgusting, slimy, unhygienic game that his own countrymen had so wholeheartedly rejected by passing the resolution against a wet or a waxed baseball. The few Americans who drifted to Nicaragua to play were sailors who had jumped ship, and assorted nuts and desperadoes in flight from a sane and decent society; occasionally an unemployed spitballer would come crawling out of the jungle swamp and onto the playing field, in search of a home. Carried from village to village on mules, sleeping in filth with the hogs and the chickens, or in hovels with toothless Indians, these men quickly lost whatever dignity they may once have had as ballplayers and human beings; and then, to further compromise themselves and the great game of baseball, they took to drinking a wretched sort of raisin wine between innings, which altered the pace of the game immeasurably. But the water tasted of rats and algae, and center field in the dry season in Guatemala is as hot as center field must be in Hell—catch nine innings in Nicaragua in the summer, and you'll drink anything that isn't out-and-out poison. Which is just what the water was. They used it only to bathe their burning feet. Indian women hung around the foul lines, and for a penny in the local currency could be hired for an afternoon to wash a player's toes and pour a bucketful of the fetid stuff over his head when he stepped up to bat. Eventually these waterwomen came to share the benches with the players, who fondled and squeezed them practically at will, and it was not unusual for such a woman to attach herself to a team, and travel with them for a whole season.

Because the pitchers—whose life was no bed of roses down there—rinsed their mouths with raisin wine even while out on the mound, going to the jug as often as a civilized pitcher goes to the resin bag, in a matter of innings the ball came to look as though it had been dipped in blood; the bat too would turn a deep scarlet from contact with the discolored ball and the sticky, sopping uniforms—numeraled serapes, really—of the players. The clean white stitched ball that is the very emblem of the game as played in our major leagues, was replaced in the Mosquito Coast League with a ball so darkly stained that if you were on the sidelines peering through the shimmering waves of the heat, you might have thought the two teams were playing with a wad of tar or a turd.

Into this life Big John Baal was born, the bastard offspring of the only pitcher ever to dare to throw a pissball in a major league ball park, and a half-breed who earned a few coins from the players in the on-deck circle by pouring Central American water over their ears and their ankles. By the time Juanito was two or three seasons old, his father no longer even remembered which of the dozens of waterwomen around the league had mothered his little son—to him they all looked the same, dirty, dark, and dumb, but at least they were a step up from the livestock with whom his battery-mate found happiness. A major leaguer had to draw the line somewhere, and Spit drew it at goats. When the child asked him "Mamma? Madre?" Spit wouldn't even bother to wrack his brain (in that heat wracking your brain could bring on the vertigo) but pointed to whichever one happened to be rolling in the dust with the reliever down in the bullpen (where, on some days, there was even a young snarling bull). By the age of eighteen months, John was already big and strong enough to hold a green banana in his ten fat fingers and swing at the pebbles that the native-born players liked to throw at the manager's little boy when his father happened not to be around; and when a few years later he was able to swing a regulation bat, the child was taught by his father the secret to hitting the spitter. John shortly became so adept at connecting with the scarlet spitball (or spic-ball, as the disillusioned and drunken expatriates sneeringly called it among themselves) that by the time he was old enough to leave Nicaragua to go out and take his vengeance on the world, it was like nothing for him to lay into a ball that was both white and dry. Oh, what an immortal he might have been, if only he did not have the morals of someone raised in the primordial slime! Oh, if only he had not come North with a heartful of contempt for the league that had banished his dad, and the republic for which it stood!

"Batting fourth for the Mundys, the catcher, No. 37, HOT PTAH. PTAH."

Hothead, or Hot (for short) Ptah (TR, BR, 5'10", 180 lbs.), far and away the most irritating player in baseball, and the Mundy most despised by the other teams, despite the physical handicap which might otherwise have enlisted their sympathies. Probably his disposition had to do with his not having one of his legs, though his mother back in Kansas maintained that he had always been crabby, even when he'd had both. To the wartime fans, Hot was more a source of amusement than anything else, and they probably got more of a kick out of his angry outbursts than from the foibles and eccentricities of any other Mundy. However, those who had to stand at the plate and listen to that one-legged chatterbox curse and insult them, didn't take to it too well, try as they might. "Okay, Hot, so you ain't got all your legs, that ain't my fault." But he would just keep buzzing like a fly on a window-pane—until all at once the batter would whirl around to the umpire, his eyes welling with tears. "Do you hear that! Did you hear what he just said! Why don't you do something about it!" "*O*-kay, what'd he say now?" the ump would ask, for Hot had a way of pouring the venom directly into the hitter's ear, leaving the umpire out of it entirely. "What'd he *say?* A lot of unkind words about my mother bein' intimate with niggers down in the South, that's what!" "Now you listen here, Ptah—" But by this time Hot would have ripped off his mask and started in pounding it on the plate, till you expected one or the other to be smashed to smithereens—or else he would just hammer with his hand and his glove on his chest protector, like a gorilla in a baseball suit, howling all the while about his "freedom of speech." Hot could go into the craziest song and dance ever seen on a ball field (or anywhere, including the Supreme Court of the United States) about the Constitution, the Bill of Rights, the Declaration of Independence, the Monroe Doctrine, the Emancipation Proclamation, even the League of Nations, in order to defend his right to say what he did into some poor Southern boy's ear. "I know you," Hot would whisper to the batter, starting off low and slow, "and your whole damn family and I know your mother . . ." And then he had the gall to defend himself with the First Amendment. And a hundred more things that most umpires had never even heard of, but that Hot had studied up on in the legal books that he lugged around with him in his suitcase from one hotel to the next. He *slept* with those damn books . . . but then what else could he sleep with, poor gimp that he was? "The Wagner Act! The Sherman Antitrust Act! Carter versus Carter Coal! Gompers versus Buck Stove! The Federal Reserve Act, damn it! And what about the Dred Scott decision? Don't that count for nothing in this country no more? Gosh *damn!*" And here, having baffled and confused everyone involved, having set the fans to roaring with laughter in the stands (which only burned him up more) he would go hobbling back behind the plate, and the umpire would call for play to be resumed. After all, not being lawyers by profession, the umpires could not be expected to know if what Hot was saying made any sense, and so rather than get into a legal harangue that might end up in the courtroom with a litigious catcher like this son of a bitch, they preferred to respect his so-called freedom of speech, rather than send him to the showers. And besides, if he didn't catch for the Mundys, who would —a guy with *no* legs?

To Hot's credit, it should be said that he had as good a throwing arm as any catcher in the league in '43, and he could drill the ball up against the left-field fence when you needed a run driven in; however, having that leg made out of wood caused him to lurch like something on a pogo stick when he came charging after a bunt, and he was not exactly death on fly balls popped back to the screen behind home plate. His doubles and triples were plentiful, only he was never able to get farther than first on them; and his singles, of course, were outs, the right-fielder, or the center-fielder, or the left-fielder to the first-baseman. (If you're scoring, that's 9 to 3, 8 to 3, or 7 to 3.)

Now obviously, in peacetime a one-legged catcher, like a one-armed outfielder (such as the Mundys had roaming right), would have been at the most a curiosity somewhere down in the dingiest town in the minors—precisely where Hot had played during the many years that the nations of the world lived in harmony. But it is one of life's grisly ironies that what is a catastrophe for most of mankind invariably works to the advantage of a few who live on the fringes of the human community. On the other hand, it is a grisly irony to live on the fringes of the human community.

"Batting fifth and playing left field, No. 13, MIKE RAMA. RAMA."

Even before the Mundys had to play day in and day out on the other fellow's terrain, Mike "the Ghost" Rama (TL, BL, 6′1″, 183 lbs.) had his troubles with the outfield wall. Just so long as there was one of them behind him, whether it was in Mundy Park or on the road, sooner or later the Ghost went crashing up against it in do-or-die pursuit of a well-tagged ball. In '41, his rookie year, he had on five different occasions to be removed on a stretcher from the field in Port Ruppert. The fans, of course, were deeply moved by a brilliant youngster so dedicated to victory as to be utterly heedless of his own welfare. It rent their hearts to hear the *konk* resound throughout the ball park when Mike's head made contact with the stadium wall—was he dead this time? and, damn it, had he dropped the ball? But miraculously neither was the case. The umpire who rushed to the outfield to call the play (before calling the hospital) invariably found the baseball lodged snugly in the pocket of the unconscious left-fielder's glove. "Out!" he would shout, and without irony, for he was describing only the status of the batter. Hurray, cried the fans—whereupon the bullpen catcher and the batboy would come dashing onto the field to lift the crumpled hero from the grass onto the stretcher, and thence to the ambulance that could already be heard wailing across Port Ruppert to the stadium. And how that sound sobered and saddened the crowd . . .

Once the solemnity of the moment had passed, the fans did have to wonder if perhaps Mike wasn't a little short on brainpower to be knocking himself out like this every couple of weeks; for it wasn't as though he misjudged the proximity of the wall in his effort to catch the ball, but rather that he seemed completely to forget that such things as walls even existed. He just could not seem to get the idea of a barrier into his head, even after bringing the two into forceful conjunction. Why they came to call him the Ghost was because he appeared to think—if that is the word for it—that what was impenetrable to the rest of us would be as nothing to him: either he did not believe that walls were really walls, or flesh only flesh, or he just was never going to get over having been born and raised in Texas. For down there, where he had been a great high school star, it seemed they did not bother to fence the field in . . . just laid out the bases and let the boys roam like the longhorns.

In Mike's rookie year, Mister Fairsmith would make it his business to be at the hospital first thing in the morning to fetch the Mundy left-fielder once the doctors had put the pieces back together and proclaimed him ready to have another go at life. They would drive directly from the hospital to Mundy Park, where the two would walk out across the manicured diamond onto the outfield grass. With only the groundskeepers looking up from their rakes to watch the oddly touching scene, Mister Fairsmith would lead the rookie all the way from the left-field corner to Glorious Mundy's headstone in furthest center, and then back again. They might walk to and fro like this for half an hour at a stretch, Mike, under Mister Fairsmith's direction, running the tips of his fingers along the wall so as to prove to himself that it was no figment of anybody's imagination.

"Michael," Mister Fairsmith would say, "can you tell me what is going on in your mind when you act like this? Do you have any idea?"

"Sure. Nothin'. I'm thankin' about catchin' the ball, that's all. I ain't havin' no sex thoughts or nothin', Mister Fairsmith, I swear."

"Michael, I am cognizant of the fact that there were no walls surrounding the ball fields in the part of the world where you grew up, but surely, lad, you had walls in your house when you were a boy down there. Or am I mistaken?"

"Oh sure we had walls. We wuz poor, but we wuzn't that poor."

"And did you, as a child, go running into the walls in your house?"

"Nope, nope. But then a' course I wasn't chasin' nothin' then."

"Son, you are going to be held together by clothesline and baling wire before you are even twenty-one, if you do not change your ways. Keep this up and your next fly ball may be your last."

"Gee, I sure hope not, Mister Fairsmith. I live for baseball. I eat, drink, and sleep baseball. It's just about the only thang I ever thank about, is baseball. I see pop flies in my dreams. I can't even sleep sometimes, imaginin' all the different kinds of line drives there are to catch. Baseball is my whole life, I swear."

"And your death too, lad, if you don't start in this minute thinking about *the reality of the wall.*"

But nothing anyone could say was able to implant in Mike Rama a healthy respect for the immovable and the unyielding. To the contrary, as some men are drawn to wine and some to women, so Mike Rama was drawn to that left-field wall. If he could be said to have had a temptress, that was it. "Why, I'll tell you what I think," said Johnny Baal to Smitty, "if that there wall had titties on it, Mike 'ud marry her."

"Batting sixth and playing third base, No. 2, WAYNE HEKET. HEKET."

Kid Heket (TR, BR, 6', 172 lbs.), the oldest Mundy of them all, the oldest major leaguer of them all, a rookie in 1909 and a utility infielder and pinch-runner thereafter, he had become a regular only after the Mundy brothers had sold everybody of value on the great championship team, and just about everything else that was any good in the dugout "exceptin'," as the Kid told it, "me and the water cooler." Of course he was no longer "so fleet afeet," as he'd been in his pinch-running days, but then, as the aging third-sacker asked, "Who is?" Were his reflexes gone, would he say? "I sure would," replied the Kid. And his eyesight? "Dim durin' the day, practically nil at night. Nope, don't see very good at all no more." His strength? He sighed: "Oh, gone with the wind, Smitty. Call me broken down and I won't argue." Why did he stay on in baseball then? "What else is there? This here is just about all that I am fit to do now, and, as you see, I ain't fit for it."

Fortunately, playing for the wartime Mundys was not really as taxing physically as a job on a farm or a factory might have been for a man of fifty-two. And during the winter months the Kid could just sit around down home resting up in the barber shop, enjoying the smell of the witch hazel, the warmth of the stove, and the pictures in the old magazines. During the season itself, in order to conserve what little energy he had, he just played as close as he could to the third-base line, hoping in this way to cut down the extra-base hits, but otherwise granting to the opposition whatever they could poke between him and the shortstop. "The way I see it now, if a feller hits it to my left, he got hisself a single and more power to him. If a' course the Frenchman wants to try and get it, well, that's his business and I don't propose to interfere. His ways is his ways and mine is mine. As I gets older I find myself gettin' more philosophical. I got to ask myself, you see, who am I to say what should be a base hit and what shouldn't, a feller with but four years of schoolin' in his whole life. No, some old folks may do otherwise, but I don't propose to set Wayne Heket up as some kind of judge of others at this late stage of the game." By which he meant the game of life, clearly, for even if it was only the bottom of the first, he paid no mind to what was hit between third and short. "At my age you just got to cut down, no question about it. You just got to give up somethin', so I give up goin' to my left. Let's be honest, Smitty, my runnin' days is over, and there ain't no sense in actin' like they ain't."

When the Mundys came to bat, the Kid always made it his business to catch a quick nap—no sooner did his seat hit the bench but he was out like a light. "That's what I credit my long baseball life to, you know. Them naps. So long as I can catch me some shuteye in that dugout there, there is no doubt that I am a better man for it back on the playing field. A' course, as you can imagine, nobody cherishes more than me them times that we get a little rally goin', and I can really slip off into dreamland. There is no doubt about it—and I tole Mister Fairsmith, right out, too—if we was a better hittin' team, I would be gettin' more sleep. The worst for me is when the fellers start swingin' at them first pitches. What in hell's the hurry, I ask 'em, where's the fire anyhoo? Sometimes my stiff ol' bones has barely stopped throbbin' with pain, when they are shakin' my shoulder, tellin' me it's time to go back on out to the field. Best of all was the other day in Aceldama. It was top of the eighth and I was near to droppin', let me tell you. I was up first, struck out lookin'—or not lookin', I suppose—come back to the bench, expectin' that of the old forty winks I'd be gettin' myself maybe four, if I was lucky. Well, what happens, but that whole darn bunch of hitless wonders catches fire and we don't go out until they have batted all the way around to me. What a snooze I had! Like a top! Unfortunately, the Butchers, they come back with seven in their half of the inning to beat us—but if I had not had that good long nap while we was up, I tell you, I might not have made it all the way through them seven runs of theirs on my feet. As it was, I dozed off a couple times in the field, but then I usually does, when we is changin' pitchers. Tell you the truth, I thought they had scored only four and we was still ahead by one. I didn't find out till the next mornin' when I seen it in the paper down in the lobby that we lost. Must be then that I was out on my feet for three of them runs—not that it makes much difference. You been around as long as me, you seen one run, you seen 'em all. That afternoon, when I run into some of the Butchers on the streetcar goin' out to the ball park, I asked them how come they didn't wake me up in the eighth yesterday when they was roundin' third. You don't find that kind of consideration every day, you know, especially from the other team, which is usually tryin' to hair-ass you, one way or another. I joked 'em—I said, 'What ever got into you boys, bein' so quiet and all comin' round the bag? Don't want to rouse the sleepin' beast or somethin'?' And you know what they tole me? I couldn't believe it. They tole me they come *whoopin'* round that bag, each and ever one of 'em, squawkin' their heads off like a bunch of crows, and I didn't budge one inch. Well, that'll give you a idea of just how tired a feller can get bein' in baseball all his life. Maybe that is what it is like bein' in anything all your life, but I can only speak for myself, you know. And I'm just shot. Why, if this here terrible war goes on too long, and I keep playin' in the regular line-up like this, why, I wouldn't be surprised if one afternoon I will just drop off, you know, and that's that. The other fellers'll come runnin' back in to the bench when the innin' is over and it's our turn to bat, but not me. I'll just be left stooped over out there, with my hands on my knees and a jaw full of tobacco juice, waitin' for the next pitch, only I'll be dead. Well, I only hope it don't happen while the game is in progress, 'cause if the other team finds out, they sure as hell will start droppin' them bunts in down the third-base line. Now, even alive I ain't hardly the man with a bunt I was back before the First World War. But with me dead with rigor mortis, and Hothead havin' only one leg, they could just about bunt us crazy, don't you think? If they was smart, that is."

"Batting seventh and playing right field, No. 17, BUD PARUSHA. PARUSHA."

Bud Parusha (TR, BR, 6′3″, 215 lbs.) was the youngest of the Parusha brothers, two of whom, Angelo and Tony, were all-star outfielders for the Tri-City Tycoons, and until they entered the service boasted the two strongest throwing arms in the majors. A throwing arm no less powerful and accurate was said to belong to the third brother, who surely would have been a Tycoon outfielder too, if it weren't that the throwing arm was the only arm he'd been born with. It was as though Mother Nature—or, to be realistic about it, Mother Parusha—having lavished such gifts upon Angelo and Tony, had run out of steam by the time she got to Bud, and when it came to finishing him off, could not deliver up anything whatsoever, not even a stump, where the mate to the throwing arm should have been. Consequently, when Angelo and Tony went off to the majors, Bud was left to work as best he could as a waiter in his father's restaurant in Bayonne. Then came the war. Angelo and Tony were commissioned and placed in charge of the hand grenade training program for the entire United States Marine Corps, and Bud found himself elevated to the big leagues, not up to the Tycoons of course—they were the P. League champs after all—but across the Jersey marshes, to the team that seemed rapidly to be becoming a haven for the handicapped. Bud moved in with Hothead Ptah, whose averages in the minors he had followed for years in the back pages of *The Sporting News,* and rumor had it that the two would shortly be joined by a one-eyed pitcher from the Blues, a Jewish fellow called Seymour Clops, nicknamed inevitably "Sy." "What about a sword-swallower and a tattooed man, while they're at it!" cried Hothead, who did not at all cotton to the idea of being a freak in a freakshow. "And what about dwarfs! There must be some of them around! Oh, I just can't wait to get up some morning and look over and find I am rooming with a left-handed dwarf, all curled up and sleepin' in my mitt. And a Jew on top of it!" The dwarf, of course, when he came, would be right-handed and a Christian, the pitcher O. K. Ockatur.

For those who never saw Bud Parusha in action during the war years—and after him, Pete Gray, the one-armed outfielder who played for the St. Louis Browns—it will be necessary to explain in some little detail, how, and to what degree, he was able to overcome his handicap on the field.

First off, to catch an ordinary fly ball was no more problem for Bud than for any fielder of major league caliber; however, in that he wore his glove on the end of his throwing arm, it did require an unorthodox maneuver for him to return the ball to the infield. Unlike Gray of the Brownies, who had a stump of a left arm under which he could tuck his glove while he extracted the ball from the pocket, Bud (with no left arm at all) had to use his mouth. He was lucky to have a large one—"that old law of compensation," said the sports announcers—and a strong bite which he had further developed over the years by five minutes of chewing on a tennis ball before going to sleep each night. After fielding a ball, he was able instantly to remove it from his glove with his teeth, and hold it clamped between them while he shook the glove from his hand; then he extracted the ball from his mouth with his bare right hand, and hurled it with Parusha-like speed and accuracy to the infield. All this he accomplished in one fluid, unbroken motion and with such efficiency and even grace that you would have thought that this was the way the outfield was supposed to be played.

In the beginning the fans did not know quite what to make of Bud's singular fielding technique and there were those who laughed at the man in the Mundy outfield who looked from a distance to be giving birth to something through the orifice in his head. There were even those in the bleachers—there always are—who, like children popping out of closets, would shout "Boo!", hoping in that way to startle Bud and cause him to swallow the baseball. Unfortunately there were occasions when in his anxiety not to drop the ball out of his mouth while flinging off his glove, he would take it too far back between his molars, and find himself unable to extricate it unassisted. It happened infrequently, but always in the same tense situation: with the bases loaded. And each time with the same disastrous result: an inside-the-mouth grand-slam home run. Roland Agni would race over from center and Nickname would tear out from second to try to save the day, but not even those two together, performing the play as they had practiced it—Agni kneeling on Bud's chest, forcing open his jaws like a fellow about to stick his head into the mouth of a crocodile, and young Damur, with those quick hands of his, yanking and jiggling at the ball for all he was worth—were able to prevent the four runs from scoring.

Despite his difficulties—and, in part, because of them—kindly, uncomplaining Bud became popular as Hothead, who had been there first, had never even tried to be. While the sluggers and fancy dans were paid to endorse razor blades and hair oil, Bud's beautifully formed signature soon came to adorn the pages of medical magazines, where he was pictured in his gray road uniform with the scarlet piping and insignia, sitting in a wheelchair, or balancing himself on a crutch. Where it was feasible, he would always test a product before giving it his endorsement—more than most of his colleagues bothered to do for items far less compromising to a ballplayer's prestige than oxygen tents and artificial limbs. And when the Mundys had a free day on the road, he never failed to go off to visit the local veterans hospital, where he would promise one of the amputees to get a base hit for him the next time they threw him anything good. He could not dedicate home runs to them, because big as he was he really could not be expected to hit home runs with only one arm, but every six or seven times at bat, he managed to smack a single, and then from the loud speaker there would be the announcement that Bud's hit had been "for" so-and-so in such-and-such a hospital, and the fans would smile and clap.

Around the league he began to build a real following among the handicapped of all ages; sometimes as many as forty or fifty of them would be out there in the stands along the right-field line when the Mundys and Bud came to town. The public address system had only to announce Bud's number for them to begin banging on the railings with their canes and crutches. "Parusha's Clinic" Smitty dubbed the right-field stands, and in Kakoola and Tri-City they even set up ramps out there to make things easier for the handicapped who turned out to see Bud perform. In their excitement some of his supporters occasionally went too far and would try, for instance, to touch him with the tip of a crutch as he came near the stands to field a foul, endangering his three remaining limbs, not to mention his eyesight. Once a woman in a wheelchair attempted to lean forward to pluck Bud's cap off for a souvenir and tumbled out of the stands onto his back. But mostly they were content to just sit there and take heart from the courage and ingenuity that Bud displayed; in Kakoola, in fact, one fan was so inspired by Bud's example that after ten years in a wheelchair, he found himself up on his feet cheering wildly as Buddy made a diving shoestring catch in the bottom of the ninth. It was in a column about this very fellow that Smitty coined the name "Parusha's Clinic." "I'm walking!" the man suddenly cried out, even as Bud was extracting the ball from his mouth to fire it to first to double off the Reaper runner and end the game.

CRIPPLE CURED AS RUPPERTS ROMP

the Kakoola evening paper reported to its readers that night—but then could not resist the sardonic subhead—

TWO MIRACLES IN ONE DAY

"Batting eighth for the Mundys, and playing center field, No. 6, ROLAND AGNI. AGNI."

Roland Agni (TL, BL, 6′2″, 190 lbs.), in '43 a kid of eighteen tapering like the V for Victory from his broad shoulders and well-muscled arms down to ankles as elegantly turned as Betty Grable's—swift on his feet as Nickname Damur, strong as a Johnny Baal, as mad for baseball as Mike Rama, and in his own baby-blue eyes destined to be the most spectacular rookie since Joltin' Joe. One difference: the Yankee Clipper, aside from being four years older than Agni when he entered the majors, had also played a few seasons down in the minors; what was so amazing about Roland, Roland thought, was that he was leaping right from high school to the big time.

Only there was a catch. Upon his graduation the previous June, Roland had turned down forty athletic scholarships in four sports from colleges all around the nation, and offers from twenty-three major league clubs in order to be signed up by his father with the Ruppert Mundys, the only team in the three leagues that had not even bothered to scout him. It was precisely their indifference that had convinced Mr. Agni that the Mundys were the major league team for his son, if major league team there had to be. Not that Mr. Agni, like some fathers, had any objection to baseball as a career; the problem was Roland's pride, which, in a word, was overweening. The boy had been hearing applause in his ears ever since he had hurled a perfect sandlot game at age six, with the result that over the years he had become, in his father's opinion, contemptuous of everything and everyone around him, above all of his family and the values of humility and self-sacrifice that they had tried, in vain, to instill in him. When his father dared to criticize him for his superior attitudes, Roland would invariably storm away from the dinner table, screaming in his high-pitched adolescent voice that he couldn't help it, he *was* superior. "But," asked his mother, using psychology, "do you want the girls to go around whispering that Roland Agni is stuck on himself?" "They can whisper whatever they want—they'd be stuck on themselves too, if they was me!" "But nobody likes a self-centered person, darling, who thinks only of himself." "Oh don't they? What about the forty colleges begging me to enroll there? What about the twenty-three major league teams pleading with me to play ball for them?" "Oh but they don't want you for your character, Roland, *or* for your mind—they want you only for your body." "Well, they *should,* because that's what's so great about me! That's what makes me so phenomenal!" "Roland!" "But it's true! I got the greatest physique of any boy my age in America! Maybe in the whole world!" "Go to your room, Roland! You are just as conceited as all the girls say! What are we going to do with you to make you realize that you are *not* God's gift to the world?" "But I am—to the baseball world that's just exactly what I am! That's just what the scout said from the St. Louis Cardinals! Them very words!" "Well, shame on him, flattering you that way just so they could sign you up! As if you aren't conceited enough! Oh," cried Mrs. Agni, turning to her husband, "what is going to happen to him out in the real world? How will he ever survive the hardships and cruelty of life with such an attitude? Roland, tell me, whatever made you think you were such a hero at seventeen years of age?" "MY BATTING AVERAGE!" screamed the star, his voice echoing off the dozens of trophies in his room.

Roland's father listened politely to the twenty-three fast-talking major league scouts as each tried to outbid the other for his son's services, and then telephoned the Mundy front office in Port Ruppert to announce that the father of the phenomenal Roland Agni was on the line. "Come again?" said the voice at the other end—"the phenomenal who?" No response could have been more heartening to the boy wonder's dad. He gave the Mundy front office a brief account of Roland's high school career: in four years of varsity play he had batted .732 and regularly hurled shutouts when he wasn't in the outfield robbing the other team of extra-base hits. However, Mr. Agni rushed to say, if hired to play for the Ruppert Mundys, his son was to receive no more than the lowest paid member of the team, was to bat eighth in the line-up in his first year, and to rise no more than one notch in the batting order in each succeeding year. It would be more than enough for a boy as self-centered as Roland to leap from high school directly to the majors without making him rich, or clean-up hitter, in the bargain. These, said Mr. Agni, were his only conditions.

"Look," laughed the Mundys' man in Port Ruppert, "what about if we go you one better and don't pay him at all."

Mr. Agni leaped at the suggestion. "In other words, I would just continue to give him his allowance—?"

"Right. And of course his room, board, and supplies."

"In other words, he'd be playing for a professional team but still have his amateur status."

"Correct. Of course, we'd need a deposit from you right off, so's we can keep the eighth slot in the batting order open for him. And room and board we'd have to have in advance. You can understand that."

"Fine. Fine."

"All right, you're on. Now what's that name again? Angry?"

"*Ag*ni."

"First name?"

"Roland."

"Okey-dokey. Spring training begins March 1, Asbury Park, New Jersey—on account of the war. Be cheaper for you anyway than Florida. We'll hold the eighth spot for him until noon that day."

"Thank you. Thank you very much."

"Well, thank *you,* Mr. Angry, and thanks for calling the Mundys," said the fellow, with a chuckle, and hung up, believing that he had just indulged a practical joker, or perhaps a sports-writer having some fun at the expense of the Mundy front office. Maybe even a fella name a' Smitty.

To find himself in the P. League with the Ruppert Mundys, and batting eighth in their line-up—and not even getting paid for it—had something like the humbling effect upon their boy that the Agnis had hoped for. Still, crushed and bewildered as he was by this bizarre turn of events, Roland Agni led the league in batting that year with .362, in hits with 188, in home runs with 39, and in doubles with 44. Of course with the pitcher batting behind him, he hardly scored, unless he hit the ball out of the park, or stole second, third, and then home; after getting on with a hit he was generally cut down at second on a d.p. or left stranded as the pitcher went out on strikes. And given the eight who batted before him he had no chance of doing much of anything in the r.b.i. department.

In the middle of the season he was called for his Army physical and found unfit for service. First the Mundys, now 4F!

It took a team of physicians a whole morning to study his marvelous V-shaped physique, whispering all the while among themselves—in admiration, thought the innocent center-fielder —before arriving at their decision. "Okay, Roland," they asked, slumping wearily to the floor of the examination room after the three-hour ordeal, "what is it? Trick knee? Bad ticker? Night sweats? Nosebleeds? Sciatica?" "What do you mean?" "What's wrong with you, Roland, that you're too ashamed to say?" "Wrong with *me?* Nothin'! Just look," he cried, standing to show himself off in the nude, "I'm perfect." "Listen, Roland," said the doctors, "there's a war on, in case you haven't heard. A *world* war. What happens to be at stake isn't eighth place in the Patriot League but the future of civilization itself. We're doctors, Roland, and we have a responsibility. We don't want somebody going into a battle that may turn the tide of history suddenly coming down with a sick headache and just lying down on the job in the trench. We don't want the lives of an entire platoon endangered just because somebody like you has to stop to scratch his pruritus ani." "But I don't get sick headaches, or the other thing either." "How do you know you don't get 'the other thing,'" they asked suspiciously, "if you don't even know what it is?" "Because I don't get *anything*—I have never even had a cavity, or a pimple. Smell my breath—it's like fresh-cut hay!" But when he blew his sweet odor into their nostrils, it only further infuriated the doctors. "Look here, Agni—we want to know what the hell is wrong with you, and we want to know now. Constipation? Sinusitis? Double vision? Get the shakes, do you? Hot flushes? Or is it the chills, Roland? How about epilepsy, does that ring a bell?" they asked, slamming him up against the white tile wall to have another go at him with their stethoscopes. "No! No! I tell you, I never been sick in my life! Sometimes I even think I am impregnable! And that ain't a boast—it's a fact!" "Oh it is, is it? Then how come according to our records here you are the only unpaid professional athlete in the business? How come your old man is paying them to keep you on the team, rather than the other way around? How come an impregnable boy like you isn't up with the Tycoons, Roland?" "That's what *I* want to know!"

cried Agni, and collapsed onto the examination stool, where he sat weeping into his hands. They let him sob until it appeared he had no more resistance left in him. Then they stole upon him where he sat unclothed and gorgeous and, softly stroking his golden curls, whispered into his ear, "Wet the bed? Sleep with a night light? How come a big strong handsome boy like you, leading the league in base hits and doubles, is still batting eighth for Ruppert, Roland? Don't you like girls?"

"Daddy," Roland shouted into the phone when he was dressed again and back out in the world, "I am unfit for the service now too! I am 4F—ONLY THERE IS NOTHING WRONG WITH ME!"

"Well, there is that pride again, Rollie."

"BUT THE DOCTORS COULDN'T FIND ANYTHING, NOT EVEN THE THREE OF THEM TOGETHER!"

"Well, doctors aren't perfect, anymore than the rest of us. That's the very point I am trying to make to you."

"But I should be 1A, not 4F! And not a Ruppert Mundy, either! Oh, Daddy, what am I doing on that team, where everybody is some kind of crackpot, thinking all the time about his name, or running into the walls, or having to have me sit on his chest to pull the darn baseball out of his *mouth!*"

"In other words, what you are telling me, Roland, is that you are too good for them."

"It ain't sayin' you are too good if you just happen to have all your arms and can stay awake for nine innings!"

"In other words then, you're just 'better' than everybody else."

"On this team, who wouldn't be!"

"And it doesn't occur to you that perhaps your teammates have had hardships in their lives about which you know nothing. Do you ever think that perhaps why you're 'better' is because you were fortunate enough to have all the opportunities in life that they were denied?"

"Sure I think about it! I thank my lucky stars about it! And that's why I don't belong with them, even if I was batting first and gettin' a million dollars!"

"Oh, son, what are we going to do with you, and this unquenchable thirst for fame and glory?"

"Trade me! Trade me away from these freaks and these oddballs! Daddy, they ain't even got a home park that's their own—what kind of major league ball club is that?"

"You mean for the great Roland Agni to be playing with?"

"For *anybody* to be playin' with—but me especially! Daddy, I am leading the league in batting in my rookie year! There's been nobody like me since Joe DiMaggio, and he was twenty-two!"

"And yet you're 4F. Doesn't that mean anything to you at all?"

"No! No! Nothin' means *nothin'* anymore!"

"Batting in ninth position and pitching for the Ruppert Mundys . . ."

The Mundy council of elders: starters Tuminikar, Buchis, Volos, and Demeter; relievers Pollux, Mertzeger, and the tiny Mexican right-hander, Chico Mecoatl—every last one of them flabby in the middle, arthritic in the shoulder, bald on the top. "The hairless wonders," said Jolly Cholly Tuminikar, who had discovered the fine art of self-effacement following the tragedy that destroyed his confidence and his career, "and a good thing too. Ain't a one of us could raise his arm to comb his hairs if he had any. Why, if I go three innings on a windy day, I got to use my other hand the next morning to wipe myself. Don't print that, Smitty, but it's the truth." Yes, has-beens, might-have-beens, should-have-beens, would-have-beens, never-weres, and never-will-bes, Tuminikar and his venerable cohorts managed nonetheless to somehow get the ball the sixty feet and six inches to the plate, which was all the rule book required of them. The ball, to be sure, occasionally arrived on a bounce, or moved so slowly and with so little English on it that the patrons back of home plate would pretend to be reading General Oakhart's signature off the horsehide all the while the pitch was in transit. "What time you say she's due in?" they'd ask, holding up their pocket watches, and on and on, comically, in that vein. There was even one of them, Chico Mecoatl, who on occasion tossed the ball in *underhand.* "How about if he fungoes 'em, Chico, then you won't have to throw at all!" the sadistic hecklers called, heedless of the pain that caused Chico to resort sometimes to a style of pitching that had not been the custom now in baseball since the days of the buffalo and the Indian.

The fans who needled the wretched Mexican were not so plentiful actually as their vociferousness might make it appear. Most people seemed to find it eerie, rather than amusing or irritating, to watch him work in relief. Invariably it was dusk when Chico, the last bald man in the bullpen, would trudge across the darkening field to pitch for the Mundys, already brutally beaten with an inning or two of punishment still to come. By this hour, the hometown fans, filled to the gills on all the slugging they'd seen, would have begun to leave their seats, tugging their collars up against the cool breeze and smiling when they peered for a final time out at the scoreboard to what looked now like the score of a football game. Two, three touchdowns for the home team; a field goal for the visitors, if that . . . So, they would converge upon the exits, a swarm of big two-fisted creatures as drowsy with contentment as the babe whose face has dropped in bloated bliss from the sugary nipple. Ah, victory. Ah, triumph. How it does mellow the bearded sex! What are the consolations of philosophy or the affirmations of religion beside an afternoon's rich meal of doubles, triples, and home runs? . . . But then came Chico out to the mound, and made that little yelp of his as he tossed his single warm-up pitch in the general direction of Hothead's mitt, that little bleat of pain that passed from between his lips whenever he had to raise his arm above his waist to throw the ball. The fans, clustered now in the dark apertures that opened onto the ramps leading down to the city streets, would swing around upon hearing Chico's bleat, one head craning above the other, to try to catch a glimpse of the pitcher with the sorest arm in the game. For there was no one who had a motion quite like Chico's: in order to release the ball with a minimal amount of suffering, he did not so much throw it as push it, with a wiggling sort of straight-arm motion. It looked as though he might be trying to pass his hand through a hoop of flames without getting it burned —and it sounded as though he wasn't quite able to make it. "Eeeep!" he would cry, and there would be the ball, floating softly through the dusk at its own sweet pace, and then the solid retort of the bat, and all the base runners scampering for home.

Probably the fans themselves could not have explained what exactly it was that held them there sometimes five and ten minutes on end watching Chico suffer so. It was not pity—Chico could quit and go back to Mexico if he wanted, and do down there whatever it was Mexicans did. Nor was it affection; he was, after all, a spic, closer even to a nigger than the Frenchman, Astarte. Nor was it amusement, for after three hours of watching the Mundys on what even for them was an off day, you didn't have the strength to laugh anymore. It would seem rather that they were transfixed, perhaps for the first time in their lives, by the strangeness of things, the wondrous strangeness of things, by all that is beyond the pale and just does not seem to belong in this otherwise cozy and familiar world of ours. With the sun all but down and the far corners of the stadium vanishing, that noise he made might have originated in the swaying jungle foliage or in some dark pocket of the moon for the sense of fear and wonder that it awakened in men who only a moment earlier had been anticipating their slippers and their favorite chair, a bottle of beer and the lovely memories they would have forever after of all those runners they'd seen galloping around third that afternoon. "Hear it?" a father whispered to his young son. "Uh-huh," said the little boy, shifting on his little stick legs. "Hear that? It can give you the goose bumps. Chico Mecoatl—you can tell your grandchildren you heard him make that noise. *Hear* it?" "Oh, Poppy, let's go."

So home they went (home, to their homes!), leaving Chico, who hardly ever got anybody out anymore, to fill the bases two times over, and the relentless home team to clear them two times over, before, mercifully, the sun set, the field disappeared, and the disaster being played out now for the sake of no one was called on account of darkness.

Probably the [illegible] couldn't have explained what [illegible] it was that [illegible] to Mexico if he wanted [illegible] the Mexican [illegible] there was no [illegible] you didn't [illegible] to laugh [illegible] the [illegible] of things, the [illegible] and the [illegible] [illegible]

[illegible]

In the Wilderness

One sunny Saturday morning early in August, the Ruppert Mundys boarded a bus belonging to the mental institution and journeyed from their hotel in downtown Asylum out into the green Ohio countryside to the world-famous hospital for the insane, there to play yet another "away" game—a three-inning exhibition match against a team composed entirely of patients. The August visit to the hospital by a P. League team in town for a series against the Keepers was an annual event of great moment at the institution, and one that was believed to be of considerable therapeutic value to the inmates, particularly the sports-minded among them. Not only was it their chance to make contact, if only for an hour or so, with the real world they had left behind, but it was believed that even so brief a visit by famous big league ballplayers went a long way to assuage the awful sense such people have that they are odious and contemptible to the rest of humankind. Of course the P. League players (who like all ballplayers despised any exhibition games during the course of the regular season) happened to find playing against the Lunatics, as they called them, a most odious business indeed; but as the General simply would not hear of abandoning a practice that brought public attention to the humane and compassionate side of a league that many still associated with violence and scandal, the tradition was maintained year after year, much

---

From Chapter 3 of *The Great American Novel.*

to the delight of the insane, and the disgust of the ballplayers themselves.

The chief psychiatrist at the hospital was a Dr. Traum, a heavy-set gentleman with a dark chin beard, and a pronounced European accent. Until his arrival in America in the thirties, he had never even heard of baseball, but in that Asylum was the site of a major league ball park, as well as a psychiatric hospital, it was not long before the doctor became something of a student of the game. After all, one whose professional life involved ruminating upon the extremes of human behavior had certainly to sit up and take notice when a local fan decided to make his home atop a flagpole until the Keepers snapped a losing streak, or when an Asylum man beat his wife to death with a hammer for calling the Keepers "bums" just like himself. If the doctor did not, strictly speaking, become an ardent Keeper fan, he did make it his business to read thoroughly in the literature of the national pastime, with the result that over the years more than one P. League manager had to compliment the bearded Berliner on his use of the hit-and-run, and the uncanny ability he displayed at stealing signals during their annual exhibition game.

Despite the managerial skill that Dr. Traum had developed over the years through his studies, his team proved no match for the Mundys that morning. By August of 1943, the Mundys weren't about to sit back and take it on the chin from a German-born baseball manager and a team of madmen; they had been defeated and disgraced and disgraced and defeated up and down the league since the season had begun back in April, and it was as though on the morning they got out to the insane asylum grounds, all the wrath that had been seething in them for months now burst forth, and nothing, but nothing, could have prevented them from grinding the Lunatics into dust once the possibility for victory presented itself. Suddenly those '43 flops started looking and sounding like the scrappy, hustling, undefeatable Ruppert teams of Luke Gofannon's day—and this despite the fact that it took nearly an hour to complete a single inning, what with numerous delays and interruptions caused by the Lunatics' style of play. Hardly a moment passed that something did not occur to offend the professional dignity of a big leaguer, and yet, through it all, the Mundys on both offense and defense managed to seize hold of every Lunatic mistake and convert it to their advantage. Admittedly, the big right-hander who started for the institution team was fast and savvy enough to hold the Mundy power in check, but playing just the sort of heads-up, razzle-dazzle baseball that used to characterize the Mundy teams of yore, they were able in their first at bat to put together a scratch hit by Astarte, a bunt by Nickname, a base on balls to Big John, and two Lunatic errors, to score three runs—their biggest inning of the year, and the first Mundy runs to cross the plate in sixty consecutive innings, which was not a record only because they had gone sixty-seven innings without scoring earlier in the season.

When Roland Agni, of all people, took a called third strike to end their half of the inning, the Mundys rushed off the bench like a team that smelled World Series loot. "We was due!" yelped Nickname, taking the peg from Hothead and sweeping his glove over the bag—"Nobody gonna stop us now, babe! We was due! We was *over*due!" Then he winged the ball over to where Deacon Demeter stood on the mound, grinning. "Three big ones for you, Deke!" Old Deacon, the fifty-year-old iron-man starter of the Mundy staff, already a twenty-game loser with two months of the season still to go, shot a string of tobacco juice over his left shoulder to ward off evil spirits, stroked the rabbit's foot that hung on a chain around his neck, closed his eyes to mumble something ending with "Amen," and then stepped up on the rubber to face the first patient. Deacon was a preacher back home, as gentle and kindly a man as you would ever want to bring your problems to, but up on the hill he was all competitor, and had been for thirty years now. "When the game begins," he used to say back in his heyday, "charity ends." And so it was that when he saw the first Lunatic batter digging in as though he owned the batter's box, the Deke decided to take Hothead's advice and stick the first pitch in his ear, just to show the little nut who was boss. The Deacon had taken enough insults that year for a fifty-year-old man of the cloth!

Not only did the Deke's pitch cause the batter to go flying back from the plate to save his skin, but next thing everyone knew the lead-off man was running for the big brick building with the iron bars on its windows. Two of his teammates caught him down the right-field line and with the help of the Lunatic bullpen staff managed to drag him back to home plate. But once there they couldn't get him to take hold of the bat; every time they put it into his hands, he let it fall through to the ground. By the time the game was resumed, with a 1 and 0 count on a new lead-off hitter, one not quite so cocky as the fellow who'd stepped up to bat some ten minutes earlier, there was no doubt in anyone's mind that the Deke was in charge. As it turned out, twice in the inning Mike Rama had to go sailing up into the wall to haul in a long line drive, but as the wall was padded, Mike came away unscathed, and the Deacon was back on the bench with his three-run lead intact.

"We're on our way!" cried Nickname. "We are on our God damn way!"

Hothead too was dancing with excitement; cupping his hands to his mouth, he shouted across to the opposition, "Just watch you bastards go to pieces now!"

And so they did. The Deke's pitching and Mike's fielding seemed to have shaken the confidence of the big Lunatic right-hander whose fastball had reined in the Mundys in the first. To the chagrin of his teammates, he simply would not begin to pitch in the second until the umpire stopped staring at him.

"Oh, come on," said the Lunatic catcher, "he's not staring at *you.* Throw the ball."

"I tell you, he's right behind you and he is too staring. Look you, I see you there behind that mask. What is it you want from me? What is it you think you're looking at, anyway?"

The male nurse, in white half-sleeve shirt and white trousers, who was acting as the plate umpire, called out to the mound, "Play ball now. Enough of that."

"Not until you come out from there."

"Oh, pitch, for Christ sake," said the catcher.

"Not until that person stops staring."

Here Dr. Traum came off the Lunatic bench and started for the field, while down in the Lunatic bullpen a left-hander got up and began to throw. Out on the mound, with his hands clasped behind his back and rocking gently to and fro on his spikes, the doctor conferred with the pitcher. Formal European that he was, he wore, along with his regulation baseball shoes, a dark three-piece business suit, a stiff collar, and a tie.

"What do you think the ol' doc's tellin' that boy?" Bud Parusha asked Jolly Cholly.

"Oh, the usual," the old-timer said. "He's just calmin' him down. He's just askin' if he got any good duck shootin' last season."

It was five full minutes before the conference between the doctor and the pitcher came to an end with the doctor asking the pitcher to hand over the ball. When the pitcher vehemently refused, it was necessary for the doctor to snatch the ball out of his hand; but when he motioned down to the bullpen for the left-hander, the pitcher suddenly reached out and snatched the ball back. Here the doctor turned back to the bullpen and this time motioned for the left-hander *and* a right-hander. Out of the bullpen came two men dressed like the plate umpire in white half-sleeve shirts and white trousers. While they took the long walk to the mound, the doctor made several unsuccessful attempts to talk the pitcher into relinquishing the ball. Finally the two men arrived on the mound and before the pitcher knew what had happened, they had unfurled a straitjacket and wrapped it around him.

"Guess he wanted to stay in," said Jolly Cholly, as the pitcher kicked out at the doctor with his feet.

The hundred Lunatic fans who had gathered to watch the game from the benches back of the foul screen behind home plate, and who looked in their street clothes as sane as any baseball crowd, rose to applaud the pitcher as he left the field, but when he opened his mouth to acknowledge the ovation, the two men assisting him in his departure slipped a gag over his mouth.

Next the shortstop began to act up. In the first inning it was he who had gotten the Lunatics out of trouble with a diving stab of a Bud Parusha liner and a quick underhand toss that had doubled Wayne Heket off third. But now in the top of the second, though he continued to gobble up everything hit to the left of the diamond, as soon as he got his hands on the ball he proceeded to stuff it into his back pocket. Then, assuming a posture of utter nonchalance, he would start whistling between his teeth and scratching himself, as though waiting for the action to *begin.* In that it was already very much underway, the rest of the Lunatic infield would begin screaming at him to take the ball out of his pocket and make the throw to first. "What?" he responded, with an innocent smile. "The ball!" they cried. "Yes, what about it?" "Throw it!" "But I don't have it." "You *do!*" they would scream, converging upon him from all points of the infield, "You do too!" "Hey, leave me alone," the shortstop cried, as they grabbed and pulled at his trousers. "Hey, cut that out—get your hands *out* of there!" And when at last the ball was extracted from where he himself had secreted it, no one could have been more surprised. "Hey, the *ball.* Now who put that there? Well, what's everybody looking at *me* for? Look, this must be some guy's idea of a joke . . . Well, Christ, *I* didn't do it."

Once the Mundys caught on, they were quick to capitalize on this unexpected weakness in the Lunatic defense, pushing two more runs across in the second on two consecutive ground balls to short—both beaten out for hits while the shortstop grappled with the other infielders—a sacrifice by Mike Rama, and a fly to short center that was caught by the fielder who then just stood there holding it in his glove, while Hothead, who was the runner on second, tagged up and hobbled to third, and then, wooden leg and all, broke for home, where he scored with a head-first slide, the only kind he could negotiate. As it turned out, the slide wasn't even necessary, for the center-fielder was standing in the precise spot where he had made the catch—and the ball was still in his glove.

With the bases cleared, Dr. Traum asked for time and walked out to center. He put a hand on the shoulder of the mute and motionless fielder and talked to him in a quiet voice. He talked to him steadily for fifteen minutes, their faces only inches apart. Then he stepped aside, and the center-fielder took the ball from the pocket of his glove and threw a perfect strike to the catcher, on his knees at the plate some two hundred feet away.

"Wow," said Bud Parusha, with ungrudging admiration, "now, that fella has a arm on him."

"Hothead," said Cholly, mildly chiding the catcher, "he

woulda had you by a country mile, you know, if only he'd a throwed it."

But Hot, riding high, hollered out, "Woulda don't count, Charles—it's dudda what counts, and I dud it!"

Meanwhile Kid Heket, who before this morning had not been awake for two consecutive innings in over a month, continued to stand with one foot up on the bench, his elbow on his knee and his chin cupped contemplatively in his palm. He had been studying the opposition like this since the game had gotten underway. "You know somethin'," he said, gesturing toward the field, "those fellas ain't thinkin'. No sir, they just ain't usin' their heads."

"We got 'em on the run, Wayne!" cried Nickname. "They don't know *what* hit 'em! Damn, ain't nobody gonna stop us from here on out!"

Deacon was hit hard in the last of the second, but fortunately for the Mundys, in the first two instances the batsman refused to relinquish the bat and move off home plate, and so each was thrown out on what would have been a base hit, right-fielder Parusha to first-baseman Baal; and the last hitter, who drove a tremendous line drive up the alley in left center, ran directly from home to third and was tagged out sitting on the bag with what he took to be a triple, and what would have been one too, had he only run around the bases and gotten to third in the prescribed way.

The quarrel between the Lunatic catcher and the relief pitcher began over what to throw Big John Baal, the lead-off hitter in the top of the third.

"Uh-uh," said the Lunatic pitcher, shaking off the first signal given by his catcher, while in the box, Big John took special pleasure in swishing the bat around menacingly.

"Nope," said the pitcher to the second signal.

His response to the third was an emphatic "N-O!"

And to the fourth, he said, stamping one foot, "Definitely *not!*"

When he shook off a fifth signal as well, with a caustic "Are you kidding? Throw him that and it's bye-bye ballgame," the catcher yanked off his mask and cried:

"And I suppose that's what I want, according to you! To lose! To go down in defeat! Oh, sure," the catcher whined, "what I'm doing, you see, is deliberately telling you to throw him the wrong pitch so I can have the wonderful pleasure of being on the losing team again. Oh brother!" His sarcasm spent, he donned his mask, knelt down behind the plate, and tried yet once more.

This time the pitcher had to cross his arms over his chest and look to the heavens for solace. "God give me strength," he sighed.

"In other words," the catcher screamed, "I'm wrong *again.* But then in your eyes I'm *always* wrong. Well, isn't that true? Admit it! Whatever signal I give is *bound* to be wrong. Why? Because *I'm* giving it! I'm daring to give *you* a signal! I'm daring to tell *you* how to pitch! I could kneel here signaling for the rest of my days, and you'd just stand there shaking them off and asking God to give you strength, *because I'm so wrong and so stupid and so hopeless and would rather lose than win!*"

When the relief pitcher, a rather self-possessed fellow from the look of it, though perhaps a touch perverse in his own way, refused to argue, the Lunatic catcher once again assumed his squat behind the plate, and proceeded to offer a seventh signal, an eighth, a ninth, a tenth, each and every one of which the pitcher rejected with a mild, if unmistakably disdainful, remark.

On the sixteenth signal, the pitcher just had to laugh. "Well, that one really takes the cake, doesn't it? That really took brains. Come over here a minute," he said to his infielders. "All right," he called back down to the catcher, "go ahead, show them your new brainstorm." To the four players up on the mound with him, the pitcher whispered, "Catch this," and pointed to the signal that the catcher, in his mortification, was continuing to flash from between his legs.

"Hey," said the Lunatic third-baseman, "that ain't even a finger, is it?"

"No," said the pitcher, "as a matter of fact, it isn't."

"I mean, it ain't got no nail on it, does it?"

"Indeed it has not."

"Why, I'll be darned," said the shortstop, "it's, it's his thing-amajig."

"Precisely," said the pitcher.

"But what the hell is that supposed to mean?" asked the first-baseman.

The pitcher had to smile again. "What do you think? Hey, Doc," he called to the Lunatic bench, "I'm afraid my battery-mate has misunderstood what's meant by an exhibition game. He's flashing me the signal to meet him later in the shower, if you know what I mean."

The catcher was in tears now. "He made me do it," he said, covering himself with his big glove and, in his shame, dropping all the way to his knees, "everything else I showed him wasn't *good* enough for him—no, he teases me, he taunts me—"

By now the two "coaches" (as they were euphemistically called), who had removed the starting pitcher from the game, descended upon the catcher. With the aid of a fielder's glove, one of them gingerly lifted the catcher's member and placed it back inside his uniform before the opposing players could see what the signal had been, while the other relieved him of his catching equipment. "He provoked me," the catcher said, "he always provokes me—"

The Lunatic fans were on their feet again, applauding, when their catcher was led away from the plate and up to the big brick building, along the path taken earlier by the starting pitcher. "—He won't let me alone, ever. I don't want to do it. I never wanted to do it. I *wouldn't* do it. But then he starts up teasing me and taunting me—"

The Mundys were able to come up with a final run in the top of the third, once they discovered that the second-string Lunatic catcher, for all that he sounded like the real thing—"Chuck to me, babe, no hitter in here, babe"—was a little leery of fielding a bunt dropped out in front of home plate, fearful apparently of what he would find beneath the ball upon picking it up.

When Deacon started out to the mound to pitch the last of the three innings, there wasn't a Mundy who took the field with him, sleepy old Kid Heket included, who didn't realize that the Deke had a shutout working. If he could set the Lunatics down without a run, he could become the first Mundy pitcher to hurl a scoreless game all year, in or out of league competition. Hoping neither to jinx him nor to unnerve him, the players went through the infield warm-up deliberately keeping the chatter to a minimum, as though in fact it was just another day they were going down to defeat. Nonetheless, the Deke was already streaming perspiration when the first Lunatic stepped into the box. He rubbed the rabbit's foot, said his prayer, took a swallow of air big enough to fill a gallon jug and, on four straight pitches, walked the center-fielder, who earlier in the game hadn't bothered to return the ball to the infield after catching a fly ball, and now, at the plate, hadn't moved the bat off his shoulder. When he was lifted for a pinch-runner (lifted by the "coaches") the appreciative fans gave him a nice round of applause. "That's lookin' 'em over!" they shouted, as he was carried from the field still in the batting posture, "that's waitin' 'em out! Good eye in there, fella!"

As soon as the pinch-runner took over at first, it became apparent that Dr. Traum had decided to do what he could to save face by spoiling the Deacon's shutout. Five runs down in the last inning and still playing to win, you don't start stealing bases—but that was precisely what this pinch-runner had in mind. And with what daring! First, with an astonishing burst of speed he rushed fifteen feet down the basepath—but then, practically on all fours, he was scrambling back. "No! No!" he cried, as he dove for the bag with his outstretched hand, "I won't! Never mind! Forget it!" But no sooner had he gotten back up on his feet and dusted himself off, than he was running again. "Why not!" he cried, "what the hell!" But having broken fifteen, *twenty,* feet down the basepath, he would come to an abrupt stop, smite himself on his forehead, and charge wildly back to first, crying, "Am I crazy? Am I out of my *mind?*"

In this way did he travel back and forth along the basepath some half-dozen times, before Deacon finally threw the first pitch to the plate. Given all there was to distract him, the pitch was of course a ball, low and in the dirt, but Hothead, having a great day, blocked it beautifully with his wooden leg.

Cholly, managing the club that morning while Mister Fairsmith rested back in Asylum—of the aged Mundy manager's spiritual crisis, more anon—Cholly motioned for Chico to get up and throw a warm-up pitch in the bullpen (one was enough—one was too many, in fact, as far as Chico was concerned) and meanwhile took a stroll out to the hill.

"Startin' to get to you, are they?" asked Cholly.

"It's that goofball on first that's doin' it."

Cholly looked over to where the runner, with time out, was standing up on first engaged in a heated controversy with himself.

"Hell," said Cholly, in his soft and reassuring way, "these boys have been tryin' to rattle us with that there bush league crap all mornin', Deke. I told you fellers comin' out in the bus, you just got to pay no attention to their monkeyshines, because that is their strategy from A to Z. To make you lose your concentration. Otherwise we would be rollin' over them worse than we is. But Deke, you tell me now, if you have had it, if you want for me to bring the Mexican in—"

"With six runs in my hip pocket? And a shutout goin'?"

"Well, I wasn't myself goin' to mention that last that you said."

"Cholly, you and me been in this here game since back in the days they was rubbin' us down with Vaseline and Tabasco sauce. Ain't that right?"

"I know, I know."

"Well," said the Deke, shooting a stream of tobacco juice over his shoulder, "ain't a bunch of screwballs gonna get my goat. Tell Chico to sit down."

Sure enough, the Deacon, old war-horse that he was, got the next two hitters out on long drives to left. "Oh my God!" cried the base runner, each time the Ghost went climbing up the padded wall to snare the ball. "Imagine if I'd broken for second! Imagine what would have happened then! Oh, that'll teach me to take those crazy leads! But then if you don't get a jump on the pitcher, where are you as a pinch-runner? That's the whole idea of a pinch-runner—to break with the pitch, to break *before* the pitch, to score that shutout-breaking run! That's what I'm in here for, that's my entire purpose. The whole thing is on *my* shoulders —so then what am I doing *not* taking a good long lead? But just then, if I'd broken for second, I'd have been doubled off first! For the last out! But then suppose he hadn't made the catch? Suppose he'd dropped it. Then where would I be? Forced out at second! *Out*—and all because I was too cowardly. But then what's the sense of taking an unnecessary risk? What virtue is there in being foolhardy? None! But then what about playing it too safe?"

On the bench, Jolly Cholly winced when he saw that the batter stepping into the box was the opposing team's shortstop. "Uh-oh," he said, "that's the feller what's cost 'em most of the runs to begin with. I'm afraid he is goin' to be lookin' to right his wrongs—and at the expense of Deacon's shutout. Dang!"

From bearing down so hard, the Deacon's uniform showed vast dark continents of perspiration both front and back. There was no doubt that his strength was all but gone, for he was relying now solely on his "junk," that floating stuff that in times gone by used to cause the hitters nearly to break their backs swinging at the air. Twice now those flutter balls of his had damn near been driven out of the institution and Jolly Cholly had all he could do not to cover his eyes with his hand when he saw the Deke release yet another fat pitch in the direction of home plate.

Apparently it was just to the Lunatic shortstop's liking too. He swung from the heels and, with a whoop of joy, was away from the plate and streaking down the basepath. "Run!" he shouted to the fellow on first.

But the pinch-runner was standing up on the bag, scanning the horizon for the ball.

"Two outs!" cried the Lunatic shortstop. "Run, you idiot!"

"But—where is it?" asked the pinch-runner.

The Mundy infielders were looking skywards themselves, wondering where in hell that ball had been hit to.

"Where *is* it!" screamed the pinch-runner, as the shortstop came charging right up to his face. "I'm not running till I know where the *ball* is!"

"I'm coming into first, you," warned the shortstop.

"But you can't overtake another runner! That's against the law! That's *out!*"

"Then *move!*" screamed the shortstop into the fellow's ear.

"Oh, this *is* crazy. This is exactly what I *didn't* want to do!" But what choice did he have? If he stood his ground, and the shortstop kept coming, that would be the ballgame. It would be all over because he who had been put into the game to run had simply refused to. Oh, what torment that fellow knew as he rounded the bases with the shortstop right on his tail. "I'm running full speed—and I don't even know where the ball is! I'm running like a chicken with his head cut off! I'm running like a madman, which is just what I don't want to do! Or be! I don't know where I'm going, I don't know what I'm doing, I haven't the foggiest idea of what's happening—and I'm running!"

When, finally, he crossed the plate, he was in such a state that he fell to his hands and knees and, sobbing with relief, began to kiss the ground. "I'm home! Thank God! I'm safe! I made it! I scored! Oh thank God, thank God!"

And now the shortstop was rounding third—he took a quick glance back over his shoulder to see if he could go all the way, and just kept on coming. "Now where's *he* lookin'?" asked Cholly. "What in hell does he see that I can't? Or that Mike don't either?" For out in left, Mike Rama was walking round and round, searching in the grass as though for a dime that might have dropped out of his pocket.

The shortstop was only a few feet from scoring the second run of the inning when Dr. Traum, who all this while had been walking from the Lunatic bench, interposed himself along the foul line between the runner and home plate.

"Doc," screamed the runner, "you're in the way!"

"That's enough now," said Dr. Traum, and he motioned for him to stop in his tracks.

"But I'm only inches from pay dirt! Step aside, Doc—let me score!"

"You just stay vere you are, please."

"Why?"

"You know vy. Stay right vere you are now. And giff me the ball."

"What ball?" asked the shortstop.

"You know vat ball."

"Well, I surely don't have any ball. I'm the *hitter.* I'm about *to score.*"

"You are not about to score. You are about to giff me the ball. Come now. Enough foolishness. Giff over the ball."

"But, Doc, I haven't got it. I'm on the offense. It's the *defense* that has the ball—that's the whole idea of the game. No criticism intended, but if you weren't a foreigner, you'd probably understand that better."

"Haf it your vay," said Dr. Traum, and he waved to the bullpen for his two coaches.

"But, Doc," said the shortstop, backpedaling now up the third-base line, *"they're* the ones in the field. *They're* the ones with the gloves—why don't you ask them for the ball? Why me? I'm an innocent base runner, who happens to be rounding third on his way home." But here he saw the coaches coming after him and he turned and broke across the diamond for the big brick building on the hill.

It was only a matter of minutes before one of the coaches returned with the ball and carried it out to where the Mundy infield was now gathered on the mound.

The Deacon turned it over in his hand and said, "Yep, that's it, all right. Ain't it, Hot?"

The Mundy catcher nodded. "How in hell did *he* get it?"

"A hopeless kleptomaniac, that's how," answered the coach. "He'd steal the bases if they weren't tied down. Here," he said, handing the Deacon a white hand towel bearing the Mundy laundrymark, and the pencil that Jolly Cholly wore behind his ear when he was acting as their manager. "Found this on him too. Looks like he got it when he stumbled into your bench for that pop-up in the first."

The victory celebration began the moment they boarded the asylum bus and lasted nearly all the way back to the city, with Nickname hollering out his window to every passerby, "We beat 'em! We shut 'em out!" and Big John swigging bourbon from his liniment bottle, and then passing it to his happy teammates.

"I'll tell you what did it," cried Nickname, by far the most exuberant of the victors, "it was Deacon throwin' at that first guy's head! Yessir! Now that's my kind of baseball!" said the fourteen-year-old, smacking his thigh. "First man up, give it to 'em right in the noggin'."

"Right!" said Hothead. "Show 'em you ain't takin' no more of their shit no more! Never again!"

"Well," said Deacon, "that is a matter of psychology, Hot, that was somethin' I had to think over real good beforehand. I mean, you try that on the wrong feller and next thing they is all of them layin' it down and then spikin' the dickens out of you when you cover the bag."

"That's so," said Jolly Cholly. "When me and the Deke come up, that was practically a rule in the rule book—feller throws the beanball, the word goes out, 'Drag the ball and spike the pitcher.' Tell you the truth, I was worried we was goin' to see some of that sort of stuff today. They was a desperate bunch. Could tell that right off by their tactics."

"Well," said the Deke, "that was a chance I had to take. But I'll tell you, I couldn't a done it without you fellers behind me. How about Bud out there, throwin' them two runners out at first base? The right-fielder to the first-baseman, *two times in a row.* Buddy," said the Deacon, "that was an exhibition such as I have not seen in all my years in organized ball."

Big Bud flushed, as was his way, and tried to make it sound easy. "Well, a' course, once I seen those guys wasn't runnin', I figured I didn't have no choice. I *had* to play it to first."

Here Mike Rama said, "Only that wasn't what *they* was figurin', Buddy-boy. You got a one-arm outfielder out there, you figure, what the hell, guess I can get on down the base line any old time I feel like it. Guess I can stop off and get me a beer and a sangwich on the way! But old Bud here, guess he showed 'em!"

"You know," said Cholly, philosophically, "I never seen it to fail, the hitters get cocky like them fellers were, and the next thing you know, they're makin' one dumb mistake after another."

"Yep," said Kid Heket, who was still turning the events of the morning over in his head, "no doubt about it, them fellers just was not usin' their heads."

"Well, maybe they wasn't—but *we* was! What about Hot?" said Nickname. "What about a guy with a wooden leg taggin' up from second and scorin' on a fly to center! How's that for heads-up ball?"

"Well," said Wayne, "I am still puzzlin' that one out myself. What got into that boy in center, that he just sort of stood there after the catch, alookin' the way he did? What in hell did he want to wait fifteen minutes for anyway, before throwin' it? That's a awful long time, don't you think?"

They all looked to Cholly to answer this one. "Well, Wayne," he said, "I believe it is that dang cockiness again. Base runner on second's got a wooden leg, kee-rect? So what does Hot here do —he *goes.* And that swellhead out in center, well, he is so darned stunned by it all, that finally by the time he figures out what hit him, we has got ourselves a gift of a run. Now, if I was managin' that club, I'd bench that there prima donna and slap a fine on him to boot."

"But then how do you figure that shortstop, Cholly?" asked the Kid. "Now if that ain't the strangest ballplayin' you ever seen, what is? Stickin' the ball in his back pocket like that. And then when he is at bat, with a man on and his team down by six, and it is their last licks 'n all, catchin' a junk pitch like that inside his shirt. Now I cannot figure that out nohow."

"Dang cockiness again!" cried Nickname, looking to Cholly. "He figures, hell, it's only them Mundys out there, I can do any dang thing I please—well, I guess we taught him a thing or two! Right, Cholly?"

"Well, nope, I don't think so, Nickname. I think what we have got there in that shortstop is one of the most tragic cases I have seen in my whole life long of all-field-no-hit."

"Kleptomaniac's what the coach there called him," said the Deacon.

"Same thing," said Cholly. "Why, we had a fella down in Class D when I was just startin' out, fella name a' Mayet. Nothin' got by that boy. Why, Mayet at short wasn't much different than a big pot of glue out there. Fact that's what they called him for short: Glue. Only trouble is, he threw like a girl, and when it come to hittin', well, my pussycat probably do better, if I had one. Well, the same exact thing here, only worse."

"Okay," said Kid Heket, "I see that, sorta. Only how come he run over to field a pop-up and stoled the pencil right off your ear, Cholly? How come he took our towel away, right in the middle of the gosh darn game?"

"Heck, that ain't so hard to figure out. We been havin' such rotten luck this year, you probably forgot just who we all are, anyway. What boy *wouldn't* want a towel from a big league ball club to hang up and frame on the wall? Why, he wanted that thing so bad that when the game was over, I went up to the doc there and I said, 'Doc, no hard feelin's. You did the best you could and six to zip ain't nothin' to be ashamed of against big leaguers.' And then I *give* him the towel to pass on to that there kleptomaniac boy when he seen him again. So as he didn't feel too bad, bein' the last out. And know what else I told him? I give him some advice. I said, 'Doc, if I had a shortstop like that, I'd bat him ninth and play him at first where he don't *have* to make the throw."

"What'd he say?"

"Oh, he laughed at me. He said, 'Ha ha, Jolly Cholly, you haf a good sense of humor. Who efer heard of a first-baseman batting ninth?' So I said, 'Doc, who ever heard of a fifty-year-old preacher hurlin' a shutout with only three days' rest—but he done it, maybe with the help of interference on the last play, but still he done it.' "

"Them's the breaks of the game anyway!" cried Nickname. "About time the breaks started goin' our way. Did you tell him that, Cholly?"

"I told him that, Nickname. I told him more. I said, 'Doc, there is two kinds of baseball played in this country, and maybe somebody ought to tell you, bein' a foreigner and all—there is by the book, the way you do it, the way the Tycoons do it—and I grant, those fellers win their share of pennants doin' it that way. But then there is by hook and crook, by raw guts and all the heart you got, and that is just the way the Mundys done here today.' "

Here the team began whooping and shouting and singing with joy, though Jolly Cholly had momentarily to turn away, to struggle against the tears that were forming in his eyes. In a husky voice he went on—"And then I told him the name for that. I told him the name for wanderin' your ass off all season long, and takin' all the jokes and all the misery they can heap on your head day after day, and then comin' on out for a exhibition game like this one, where another team would just go through the motions and not give two hoots in hell how they played—and instead, instead givin' it everything you got. I told the doc the name for that, fellers. It's called courage."

Only Roland Agni, who had gone down twice, looking, against

Lunatic pitching, appeared to be unmoved by Cholly's tribute to the team. Nickname, in fact, touched Jolly Cholly's arm at the conclusion of his speech, and whispered, "Somebody better say somethin' to Rollie. He ain't takin' strikin' out too good, it don't look."

So Cholly the peacemaker made his way past the boisterous players and down the aisle to where Roland still sat huddled in a rear corner of the bus by himself.

"What's eatin' ya, boy?"

"Nothin'," mumbled Roland.

"Why don'tcha come up front an'—"

"Leave me alone, Tuminikar!"

"Aw, Rollie, come on now," said the sympathetic coach, "even the best of them get caught lookin' once in a while."

"Caught *lookin'?*" cried Agni.

"Hey, Rollie," Hothead shouted, "it's okay, slugger—we won anyway!" And grinning, he waved Big John's liniment bottle in the air to prove it.

"Sure, Rollie," Nickname yelled. "With the Deke on the mound, we didn't need but one run anyway! So what's the difference? Everybody's gotta whiff sometimes! It's the law a' averages!"

But Agni was now standing in the aisle, screaming, "You think I got caught *lookin'?*"

Wayne Heket, whose day had been a puzzle from beginning to end, who just could not really take any more confusion on top of going sleepless all these hours, asked, "Well, wasn't ya?"

"You bunch of morons! You bunch of idiots! Why, you are bigger lunatics even than they are! Those fellers are at least locked up!"

Jolly Cholly, signaling his meaning to the other players with a wink, said, "Seems Roland got somethin' in his eye, boys—seems he couldn't see too good today."

"You're the ones that can't see!" Agni screamed. *"They were madmen! They were low as low can be!"*

"Oh, I don't know, Rollie," said Mike Rama, who'd had his share of scurrying around to do that morning, "they wasn't *that* bad."

"They was *worse!* And you all acted like you was takin' on the Cardinals in the seventh game of the Series!"

"How else you supposed to play, youngster?" asked the Deacon, who was beginning to get a little hot under the collar.

"And you! You're the worst of all! Hangin' in there, like a regular hero! Havin' conferences on the mound about how to pitch to a bunch of hopeless maniacs!"

"Look, son," said Jolly Cholly, "just on account you got caught lookin'—"

"But who got caught lookin'? How could you get caught lookin' against pitchers *that had absolutely nothin' on the ball!"*

"You mean," said Jolly Cholly, incredulous, "you took a *dive?* You mean you throwed it, Roland? *Why?*"

"Why? Oh, please, let me off! Let me off this bus!" he screamed, charging down the aisle toward the door. "I can't take bein' one of you no more!"

As they were all, with the exception of the Deacon, somewhat pie-eyed, it required virtually the entire Mundy team to subdue the boy wonder. Fortunately the driver of the bus, who was an employee of the asylum, carried a straitjacket and a gag under the seat with him at all times, and knew how to use it. "It's from bein' around them nuts all mornin'," he told the Mundys. "Sometimes I ain't always myself either, when I get home at night."

"Oh," said the Mundys, shaking their heads at one another, and though at first it was a relief having a professional explanation for Roland's bizarre behavior, they found that with Roland riding along in the rear seat all bound and gagged, they really could not seem to revive the jubilant mood that had followed upon their first shutout win of the year. In fact, by the time they reached Keeper Park for their regularly scheduled afternoon game, one or two of them were even starting to feel more disheartened about that victory than they had about any of those beatings they had been taking all season long.

Whacking Off

Then came adolescence—half my waking life spent locked behind the bathroom door, firing my wad down the toilet bowl, or into the soiled clothes in the laundry hamper, or *splat,* up against the medicine-chest mirror, before which I stood in my dropped drawers so I could see how it looked coming out. Or else I was doubled over my flying fist, eyes pressed closed but mouth wide open, to take that sticky sauce of buttermilk and Clorox on my own tongue and teeth—though not infrequently, in my blindness and ecstasy, I got it all in the pompadour, like a blast of Wildroot Cream Oil. Through a world of matted handkerchiefs and crumpled Kleenex and stained pajamas, I moved my raw and swollen penis, perpetually in dread that my loathsomeness would be discovered by someone stealing upon me just as I was in the frenzy of dropping my load. Nevertheless, I was wholly incapable of keeping my paws from my dong once it started the climb up my belly. In the middle of a class I would raise a hand to be excused, rush down the corridor to the lavatory, and with ten or fifteen savage strokes, beat off standing up into a urinal. At the Saturday afternoon movie I would leave my friends to go off to the candy machine—and wind up in a distant balcony seat, squirting my seed into the empty wrapper from a Mounds bar.

From *Portnoy's Complaint* (1969), a novel in the form of a psychoanalytic confession. The psychoanalyst is the silent Dr. Spielvogel, the patient Alexander Portnoy, a thirty-three-year-old lawyer, lover, Jew, son, etc.

On an outing of our family association, I once cored an apple, saw to my astonishment (and with the aid of my obsession) what it looked like, and ran off into the woods to fall upon the orifice of the fruit, pretending that the cool and mealy hole was actually between the legs of that mythical being who always called me Big Boy when she pleaded for what no girl in all recorded history had ever had. "Oh shove it in me, Big Boy," cried the cored apple that I banged silly on that picnic. "Big Boy, Big Boy, oh give me all you've got," begged the empty milk bottle that I kept hidden in our storage bin in the basement, to drive wild after school with my vaselined upright. "Come, Big Boy, come," screamed the maddened piece of liver that, in my own insanity, I bought one afternoon at a butcher shop and, believe it or not, violated behind a billboard on the way to a bar mitzvah lesson.

It was at the end of my freshman year of high school—and freshman year of masturbating—that I discovered on the underside of my penis, just where the shaft meets the head, a little discolored dot that has since been diagnosed as a freckle. Cancer. I had given myself *cancer.* All that pulling and tugging at my own flesh, all that friction, had given me an incurable disease. And not yet fourteen! In bed at night the tears rolled from my eyes. "No!" I sobbed. "I don't want to die! Please—no!" But then, because I would very shortly be a corpse anyway, I went ahead as usual and jerked off into my sock. I had taken to carrying the dirty socks into bed with me at night so as to be able to use one as a receptacle upon retiring, and the other upon awakening.

If only I could cut down to one hand-job a day, or hold the line at two, or even three! But with the prospect of oblivion before me, I actually began to set new records for myself. Before meals. After meals. *During* meals. Jumping up from the dinner table, I tragically clutch at my belly—diarrhea! I cry, I have been stricken with diarrhea!—and once behind the locked bathroom door, slip over my head a pair of underpants that I have stolen from my sister's dresser and carry rolled in a handkerchief in my pocket. So galvanic is the effect of cotton panties against my mouth—so galvanic is the *word* "panties"—that the trajectory of my ejaculation reaches startling new heights: leaving my joint like a rocket it makes right for the light bulb overhead, where to my wonderment and horror, it hits and it hangs. Wildly in the first moment I cover my head, expecting an explosion of glass, a burst of flames—disaster, you see, is never far from my mind. Then quietly as I can I climb the radiator and remove the sizzling gob with a wad of toilet paper. I begin a scrupulous search of the shower curtain, the tub, the tile floor, the four toothbrushes—God forbid!—and just as I am about to unlock the door, imagining I have covered my tracks, my heart lurches at the sight of what is hanging like snot from the toe of my shoe. I am the Raskolnikov of jerking off—the sticky evidence is everywhere! Is it on my cuffs too? in my *hair?* my *ear?* All this I wonder even as I come back to the kitchen table, scowling and cranky, to grumble self-righteously at my father when he opens his mouth full of red jello and says, "I don't understand what you have to lock the door about. That to me is beyond comprehension. What is this, a home or a Grand Central station?" ". . . privacy . . . a human being . . . around here *never,"* I reply, then push aside my dessert to scream, "I don't feel well—*will everybody leave me alone?"*

After dessert—which I finish because I happen to like jello, even if I detest them—after dessert I am back in the bathroom again. I burrow through the week's laundry until I uncover one of my sister's soiled brassieres. I string one shoulder strap over the knob of the bathroom door and the other on the knob of the linen closet: a scarecrow to bring on more dreams. "Oh beat it, Big Boy, beat it to a red-hot pulp—" so I am being urged by the little cups of Hannah's brassiere, when a rolled-up newspaper smacks at the door. And sends me and my handful an inch off the toilet seat. "—Come on, give somebody else a crack at that bowl, will you?" my father says. "I haven't moved my bowels in a week."

I recover my equilibrium, as is my talent, with a burst of hurt feelings. "I have a terrible case of diarrhea! Doesn't that mean anything to anyone in this house?"—in the meantime resuming the stroke, indeed quickening the tempo as my cancerous organ miraculously begins to quiver again from the inside out.

Then Hannah's brassiere *begins to move.* To swing to and fro! I veil my eyes, and behold!—Lenore Lapidus! who has the biggest pair in my class, running for the bus after school, her great untouchable load shifting weightily inside her blouse, oh I urge them up from their cups, and over, LENORE LAPIDUS'S ACTUAL TITS, and realize in the same split second that my mother is vigorously shaking the doorknob. Of the door I have finally forgotten to lock! I knew it would happen one day! *Caught!* As good as *dead!*

"Open up, Alex. I want you to open up this instant."

It's locked, I'm *not* caught! And I see from what's alive in my hand that I'm not quite dead yet either. Beat on then! beat on! "Lick me, Big Boy—lick me a good hot lick! I'm Lenore Lapidus's big fat red-hot brassiere!"

"Alex, I want an answer from you. Did you eat French fries after school? Is that why you're sick like this?"

"Nuhhh, nuhhh."

"Alex, are you in pain? Do you want me to call the doctor? Are you in pain, or aren't you? I want to know exactly where it hurts. *Answer me.*"

"Yuhhh, yuhhh—"

"Alex, I don't want you to flush the toilet," says my mother sternly. "I want to see what you've done in there. I don't like the sound of this at all."

"And me," says my father, touched as he always was by my accomplishments—as much awe as envy—"I haven't moved my bowels in a week," just as I lurch from my perch on the toilet seat, and, with the whimper of a whipped animal, deliver three drops of something barely viscous into the tiny piece of cloth where my flat-chested eighteen-year-old sister has laid her nipples, such as they are. It is my fourth orgasm of the day. When will I begin to come blood?

"Get in here, please, you," says my mother. "Why did you flush the toilet when I told you not to?"

"I forgot."

"What was in there that you were so fast to flush it?"

"Diarrhea."

"Was it mostly liquid or was it mostly poopie?"

"I don't look! I didn't look! Stop saying poopie to me—I'm in high school!"

"Oh, don't you shout at *me,* Alex. I'm not the one who gave you diarrhea, I assure you. If all you ate was what you were fed at home, you wouldn't be running to the bathroom fifty times a day. Hannah tells me what you're doing, so don't think I don't know."

She's missed the underpants! *I've been caught!* Oh, *let* me be dead! I'd just as soon!

"Yeah, what do I do . . .?"

"You go to Harold's Hot Dog and *Chazerai* Palace after school and you eat French fries with Melvin Weiner. Don't you? Don't lie to me either. Do you or do you not stuff yourself with French fries and ketchup on Hawthorne Avenue after school? Jack, come in here, I want you to hear this," she calls to my father, now occupying the bathroom.

"Look, I'm trying to move my bowels," he replies. "Don't I have enough trouble as it is without people screaming at me when I'm trying to move my bowels?"

"You know what your son does after school, the *A* student, who his own mother can't say poopie to any more, he's such a *grown-up?* What do you think your grown-up son does when nobody is watching him?"

"Can I please be left alone, please?" cries my father. "Can I have a little peace, please, so I can get something accomplished in here?"

"Just wait till your father hears what you do, in defiance of every health habit there could possibly be. Alex, answer me something. You're so smart, you know all the answers now, answer me this: how do you think Melvin Weiner gave himself colitis? Why has that child spent half his life in hospitals?"

"Because he eats *chazerai.*"

"Don't you dare make fun of me!"

"All right," I scream, "how *did* he get colitis?"

"Because he eats *chazerai!* But it's not a joke! Because to him a meal is an O Henry bar washed down by a bottle of Pepsi. Because his breakfast consists of, do you know what? The most important meal of the day—not according just to your mother, Alex, but according to the highest nutritionists—and do you know what that child eats?"

"A doughnut."

"A doughnut is right, Mr. Smart Guy, Mr. Adult. And *coffee.*

Coffee and a doughnut, and on this a thirteen-year-old *pisher* with half a stomach is supposed to start a day. But you, thank God, have been brought up differently. You don't have a mother who gallavants all over town like some names I could name, from Bam's to Hahne's to Kresge's all day long. Alex, tell me, so it's not a mystery, or maybe I'm just stupid—only tell me, what are you trying to do, what are you trying to prove, that you should stuff yourself with such junk when you could come home to a poppyseed cookie and a nice glass of milk? I want the truth from you. I wouldn't tell your father," she says, her voice dropping significantly, "but I *must* have the truth from you." Pause. Also significant. "Is it just French fries, darling, or is it more? . . . Tell me, please, what other kind of garbage you're putting into your mouth so we can get to the bottom of this diarrhea! I want a straight answer from you, Alex. Are you eating hamburgers out? Answer me, please, is that why you flushed the toilet—was there hamburger in it?"

"I told you—I don't look in the bowl when I flush it! I'm not interested like you are in other people's poopie!"

"Oh, oh, oh—thirteen years old and the mouth on him! To someone who is asking a question about *his* health, *his* welfare!" The utter incomprehensibility of the situation causes her eyes to become heavy with tears. "Alex, why are you getting like this, give me some clue? Tell me please what horrible things we have done to you all our lives that this should be our reward?" I believe the question strikes her as original. I believe she considers the question unanswerable. And worst of all, so do I. What *have* they done for me all their lives but sacrifice? Yet that this is precisely the horrible thing is beyond my understanding—and still, Doctor! To this day!

I brace myself now for the whispering. I can spot the whispering coming a mile away. We are about to discuss my father's headaches.

"Alex, he didn't have a headache on him today that he could hardly see straight from it?" She checks, is he out of earshot? God forbid he should hear how critical his condition is, he might claim exaggeration. "He's not going next week for a test for a tumor?"

"He is?"

" 'Bring him in,' the doctor said, 'I'm going to give him a test for a tumor.' "

Success. I am crying. There is no good reason for me to be crying, but in this household everybody tries to get a good cry in at least once a day. My father, you must understand—as doubtless you do: blackmailers account for a substantial part of the human community, and, I would imagine, of your clientele—my father has been "going" for this tumor test for nearly as long as I can remember. Why his head aches him all the time is, of course, because he is constipated all the time—why he is constipated is because ownership of his intestinal tract is in the hands of the firm of Worry, Fear & Frustration. It is true that a doctor once said to my mother that he would give her husband a test for a tumor—if that would make her happy, is I believe the way that he worded it; he suggested that it would be cheaper, however, and probably more effective for the man to invest in an enema bag. Yet, that I know all this to be so, does not make it any less heartbreaking to imagine my father's skull splitting open from a malignancy.

Yes, she has me where she wants me, and she knows it. I clean forget my own cancer in the grief that comes—comes now as it came then—when I think how much of life has always been (as he himself very accurately puts it) beyond his comprehension. And his grasp. No money, no schooling, no language, no learning, curiosity without culture, drive without opportunity, experience without wisdom . . . How easily his inadequacies can move me to tears. As easily as they move me to anger!

A person my father often held up to me as someone to emulate in life was the theatrical producer Billy Rose. Walter Winchell said that Billy Rose's knowledge of shorthand had led Bernard Baruch to hire him as a secretary—consequently my father plagued me throughout high school to enroll in the shorthand course. "Alex, where would Billy Rose be today without his shorthand? Nowhere! So why do you *fight* me?" Earlier it was the piano we battled over. For a man whose house was without a phonograph or a record, he was passionate on the subject of a musical instrument. "I don't understand why you won't take a musical instrument, this is beyond comprehension. Your little cousin Toby can sit down at the piano and play whatever song you can name. All she has to do is sit at the piano and play 'Tea for Two' and everybody in the room is her friend. She'll never lack for companionship, Alex, she'll never lack for popularity. Only tell me you'll take up the piano, and I'll have one in here tomorrow morning. Alex, are you listening to me? I am offering you something that could change the rest of your life!"

But what he had to offer I didn't want—and what I wanted he didn't have to offer. Yet how unusual is that? Why must it continue to cause such pain? At this late date! Doctor, what should I rid myself of, tell me, the hatred . . . or the love? Because I haven't even begun to mention everything I remember with pleasure—I mean with a rapturous, biting sense of loss! All those memories that seem somehow to be bound up with the weather and the time of day, and that flash into mind with such poignancy, that momentarily I am not down in the subway, or at my office, or at dinner with a pretty girl, but back in my childhood, *with them.* Memories of practically nothing—and yet they seem moments of history as crucial to my being as the moment of my conception; I might be remembering his sperm nosing into her ovum, so piercing is my gratitude—yes, *my* gratitude!—so sweeping and unqualified is my love. Yes, me, with sweeping and unqualified love! I am standing in the kitchen (standing maybe for the first time in my life), my mother points, "Look outside, baby," and I look; she says, "See? how purple? a real fall sky." The first line of poetry I ever hear! And I remember it! A *real fall sky* . . . It is an iron-cold January day, dusk—oh, these memories of dusk are going to kill me yet, of chicken fat on rye bread to tide me over to dinner, and the moon already outside the kitchen window—I have just come in with hot red cheeks and a dollar I have earned shoveling snow: "You know what you're going to have for dinner," my mother coos so lovingly to me, "for being such a hard-working boy? Your favorite winter meal. Lamb stew." It is night: after a Sunday in New York City, at Radio City and Chinatown, we are driving home across the George Washington Bridge—the Holland Tunnel is the direct route between Pell Street and Jersey City, but I beg for the bridge, and because my mother says it's "educational," my father drives some ten miles out of his way to get us home. Up front my sister counts aloud the number of supports upon which the marvelous educational cables rest, while in the back I fall asleep with my face against my mother's black sealskin coat. At Lakewood, where we go one winter for a weekend vacation with my parents' Sunday night Gin Rummy Club, I sleep in one twin bed with my father, and my mother and Hannah curl up together in the other. At dawn my father awakens me, and like convicts escaping, we noiselessly dress and slip out of the room. "Come," he whispers, motioning for me to don my earmuffs and coat, "I want to show you something. Did you know I was a waiter in Lakewood when I was sixteen years old?" Outside the hotel he points across to the beautiful silent woods. "How's that?" he says. We walk together —"at a brisk pace"—around a silver lake. "Take good deep breaths. Take in the piney air all the way. This is the best air in the world, good winter piney air." *Good winter piney air*—another poet for a parent! I couldn't be more thrilled if I were Wordsworth's kid! . . . In summer he remains in the city while the three of us go off to live in a furnished room at the seashore for a month. He will join us for the last two weeks, when he gets his vacation . . . there are times, however, when Jersey City is so thick with humidity, so alive with the mosquitoes that come dive-bombing in from the marshes, that at the end of his day's work he drives sixty-five miles, taking the old Cheesequake Highway—the Cheesequake! My God! the stuff you uncover here!—drives sixty-five miles to spend the night with us in our breezy room at Bradley Beach.

He arrives after we have already eaten, but his own dinner waits while he unpeels the soggy city clothes in which he has been making the rounds of his debit all day, and changes into his swimsuit. I carry his towel for him as he clops down the street to the beach in his unlaced shoes. I am dressed in clean short pants and a spotless polo shirt, the salt is showered off me, and my hair —still my little boy's pre-steel wool hair, soft and combable—is beautifully parted and slicked down. There is a weathered iron rail that runs the length of the boardwalk, and I seat myself upon it; below me, in his shoes, my father crosses the empty beach. I watch him neatly set down his towel near the shore. He places his watch in one shoe, his eyeglasses in the other, and then he is ready to make his entrance into the sea. To this day I go into the water as he advised: plunge the wrists in first, then splash the underarms, then a handful to the temples and the back of the neck . . . ah, but slowly, always slowly. This way you get to refresh yourself, while avoiding a shock to the system. Refreshed, unshocked, he turns to face me, comically waves farewell up to where he thinks I'm standing, and drops backward to float with his arms outstretched. Oh he floats so still—he works, he works so hard, and for whom if not for me?—and then at last, after turning on his belly and making with a few choppy strokes that carry him nowhere, he comes wading back to shore, his streaming compact torso glowing from the last pure spikes of light driving in, over my shoulder, out of stifling inland New Jersey, from which I am being spared.

And there are more memories like this one, Doctor. A lot more. This is my mother and father I'm talking about.

But—but—but—let me pull myself together—there is also this vision of him emerging from the bathroom, savagely kneading the back of his neck and sourly swallowing a belch. "All right, what is it that was so urgent you couldn't wait till I came out to tell me?"

"Nothing," says my mother. "It's settled."

He looks at me, so disappointed. I'm what he lives for, and I know it. "What did he do?"

"What he did is over and done with, God willing. You, did you move your bowels?" she asks him.

"Of course I didn't move my bowels."

"Jack, what is it going to be with you, with those bowels?"

"They're turning into concrete, that's what it's going to be."

"Because you eat too fast."

"I don't eat too fast."

"How then, slow?"

"I eat regular."

"You eat like a pig, and somebody should tell you."

"Oh, you got a wonderful way of expressing yourself sometimes, do you know that?"

"I'm only speaking the truth," she says. "I stand on my feet all day in this kitchen, and you eat like there's a fire somewhere, and this one—this one has decided that the food I cook isn't good enough for him. He'd rather be sick and scare the living daylights out of me."

"What did he do?"

"I don't want to upset you," she says. "Let's just forget the whole thing." But she can't, so now *she* begins to cry. Look, she is probably not the happiest person in the world either. She was once a tall stringbean of a girl whom the boys called "Red" in high school. When I was nine and ten years old I had an absolute passion for her high school yearbook. For a while I kept it in the same drawer with that other volume of exotica, my stamp collection.

Sophie Ginsky the boys call "Red,"
She'll go far with her big brown eyes and her clever head.

And that was my mother!

Also, she had been secretary to the soccer coach, an office pretty much without laurels in our own time, but apparently *the* post for a young girl to hold in Jersey City during the First World War. So I thought, at any rate, when I turned the pages of her yearbook, and she pointed out to me her dark-haired beau, who had been captain of the team, and today, to quote Sophie, "the biggest manufacturer of mustard in New York." "And I could have married him instead of your father," she confided in me, and more than once. I used to wonder sometimes what that would have been like for my momma and me, invariably on the occasions when my father took us to dine out at the corner delicatessen. I look around the place and think, "We would have manufactured all this mustard." I suppose she must have had thoughts like that herself.

"He eats French fries," she says, and sinks into a kitchen chair to Weep Her Heart Out once and for all. "He goes after school with Melvin Weiner and stuffs himself with French-fried potatoes. Jack, you tell him, I'm only his mother. Tell him what the end is going to be. Alex," she says passionately, looking to where I am edging out of the room, *"tateleh,* it begins with diarrhea, but do you know how it ends? With a sensitive stomach like yours, do you know how it finally ends? *Wearing a plastic bag to do your business in!"*

Who in the history of the world has been least able to deal with a woman's tears? My father. I am second. He says to me, "You heard your mother. Don't eat French fries with Melvin Weiner after school."

"Or ever," she pleads.

"Or ever," my father says.

"Or hamburgers out," she pleads.

"Or hamburgers out," he says.

"Hamburgers," she says bitterly, just as she might say *Hitler,* "where they can put anything in the world in that they want—and *he* eats them. Jack, make him promise, before he gives himself a terrible *tsura,* and it's too late."

"I *promise!"* I scream. "I *promise!"* and race from the kitchen—to where? Where else.

I tear off my pants, furiously I grab that battered battering ram to freedom, my adolescent cock, even as my mother begins to call from the other side of the bathroom door. "Now this time don't flush. Do you hear me, Alex? I have to see what's in that bowl!"

Doctor, do you understand what I was up against? My wang was all I really had that I could call my own. You should have watched her at work during polio season! She should have gotten medals from the March of Dimes! Open your mouth. Why is your throat red? Do you have a headache you're not telling me about? You're not going to any baseball game, Alex, until I see you move your neck. Is your neck stiff? Then why are you moving it that way? You ate like you were nauseous, are you nauseous? Well, you ate like you were nauseous. I don't want you drinking from the drinking fountain in that playground. If you're thirsty wait until you're home. Your throat is sore, isn't it? I can tell how you're swallowing. I think maybe what you are going to do, Mr. Joe DiMaggio, is put that glove away and lie down. I am not going to allow you to go outside in this heat and run around, not with that sore throat, I'm not. I want to take your temperature. I don't like the sound of this throat business one bit. To be very frank, I am actually beside myself that you have been walking around all day with a sore throat and not telling your mother. Why did you keep this a secret? Alex, polio doesn't know from baseball games. It only knows from iron lungs and crippled forever! I don't want you running around, and that's final. Or eating hamburgers out. Or mayonnaise. Or chopped liver. Or tuna. Not everybody is careful the way your mother is about spoilage. You're used to a spotless house, you don't begin to know what goes on in restaurants. Do you know why your mother when we go to the Chink's will never sit facing the kitchen? Because I don't want to see what goes on back there. Alex, you must wash everything, is that clear? Everything! God only knows who touched it before you did.

Look, am I exaggerating to think it's practically miraculous that I'm ambulatory? The hysteria and the superstition! The watch-its and the be-carefuls! You mustn't do this, you can't do that—hold it! don't! you're breaking an important law! *What* law? *Whose* law? They might as well have had plates in their lips and rings through their noses and painted themselves blue for all the human sense they made! Oh, and the *milchiks* and *flaishiks* besides, all those *meshuggeneh* rules and regulations on top of their own private craziness! It's a family joke that when I was a tiny child I turned from the window out of which I was watching a snowstorm, and hopefully asked, "Momma, do we believe in winter?" Do you get what I'm *saying?* I was raised by Hottentots and Zulus! I couldn't even contemplate drinking a glass of milk with my salami sandwich without giving serious offense to God Almighty. Imagine then what my conscience gave me for all that jerking off! The guilt, the fears—the terror bred into my bones! What in their world was not charged with danger, dripping with germs, fraught with peril? Oh, where was the gusto, where was the boldness and courage? Who filled these parents of mine with such a fearful sense of life? My father, in his retirement now, has really only one subject into which he can sink his teeth, the New Jersey Turnpike. "I wouldn't go on that thing if you paid me. You have to be out of your mind to travel on that thing—it's Murder Incorporated, it's a legalized way for people to go out and get themselves killed—" Listen, you know what he says to me three times a week on the telephone—and I'm only counting when I pick it up, not the total number of rings I get between six and ten every night. "Sell that car, will you? Will you do me a favor and sell that car so I can get a good night's sleep? Why you have to have a car in that city is beyond my comprehension. Why you want to pay for insurance and garage and upkeep, I don't even begin to understand. But then I don't understand yet why you even want to live by yourself over in that jungle. What do you pay those robbers again for that two-by-four apartment? A penny over fifty dollars a month and you're out of your mind. Why you don't move back to North Jersey is a mystery to me—why you prefer the noise and the crime and the fumes—"

And my mother, she just keeps whispering. *Sophie whispers on!* I go for dinner once a month, it is a struggle requiring all my guile and cunning and strength, but I have been able over all these years, and against imponderable odds, to hold it down to once a month: I ring the bell, she opens the door, the whispering promptly begins! "Don't ask what kind of day I had with him yesterday." So I don't. "Alex," *sotto voce* still, "when he has a day like that you don't know what a difference a call from you would make." I nod. "And, Alex"—and I'm nodding away, you know—it doesn't cost anything, and it may even get me through—"next week is his birthday. That Mother's Day came and went without a card, *plus* my birthday, those things don't bother me. But he'll be sixty-six, Alex. That's not a baby, Alex—that's a landmark in a life. So you'll send a card. It wouldn't kill you."

Doctor, these people are incredible! These people are unbelievable! These two are the outstanding producers and packagers of guilt in our time! They render it from me like fat from a chicken! "Call, Alex. Visit, Alex. Alex, keep us informed. Don't go away without telling us, please, not again. Last time you went away you didn't tell us, your father was ready to phone the police. You know how many times a day he called and got no answer? Take a guess, how many?" "Mother," I inform her, from between my teeth, "if I'm dead they'll smell the body in seventy-two hours, I assure you!" "Don't *talk* like that! God *forbid!*" she cries. Oh, and now she's got the beauty, the one guaranteed to do the job. Yet how could I expect otherwise? Can I ask the impossible of my own mother? "Alex, to pick up a phone is such a simple thing—how much longer will we be around to bother you anyway?"

Doctor Spielvogel, this is my life, my only life, and I'm living it in the middle of a Jewish joke! I am the son in the Jewish joke —*only it ain't no joke!* Please, who crippled us like this? Who made us so morbid and hysterical and weak? Why, why are they screaming still, "Watch out! Don't do it! Alex—*no!"* and why, alone on my bed in New York, why am I still hopelessly beating my meat? Doctor, what do you call this sickness I have? Is this the Jewish suffering I used to hear so much about? Is this what has come down to me from the pogroms and the persecution? from the mockery and abuse bestowed by the *goyim* over these two thousand lovely years? Oh my secrets, my shame, my palpitations, my flushes, my sweats! The way I respond to the simple vicissitudes of human life! Doctor, I can't stand any more being frightened like this over nothing! Bless me with manhood! Make me brave! Make me strong! Make me *whole!* Enough being a nice Jewish boy, publicly pleasing my parents while privately pulling my putz! Enough!

you. Yet how could I expect otherwise? Can I take the [illegible] of [illegible]? [illegible] to pick up a [illegible] is [illegible] [illegible] [illegible] way?

Do not [illegible] this [illegible], [illegible] only [illegible], and I'm living [illegible] the [illegible] [illegible] [illegible] [illegible] [illegible] who [illegible] the third [illegible]

"You Must Change Your Life"

III

Novotny's Pain

In the early months of the Korean War, a young man who had been studying to be a television cameraman in a night school just west of the Loop in Chicago was drafted into the Army and almost immediately fell ill. He awoke one morning with a pain on the right side of his body, directly above the buttock. When he rolled over, it was as though whatever bones came together there were not meeting as they should. The pain, however, was not what had awakened him; his eyes always opened of themselves five minutes before the appearance in the barracks of the Charge of Quarters. Though there was much of Army life that he had to grit his teeth to endure, he did not have to work at getting up on time; it simply happened to him. And when it was necessary to grit his teeth, he gritted them and did what he was told. In that way, he was like a good many of the young men who suffered military life alongside him and had suffered it before him. His sense of shame was strong, as was his sense of necessity; the two made him dutiful.

Also, he was of foreign extraction, and though his family had not as yet grown fat off the fat of the land, it was nevertheless in their grain to feel indebted to this country. Perhaps if they had grown a little fatter they would have felt less indebted. As it was, Novotny believed in fighting for freedom, but because what he himself wanted most from any government was that it should let

First published 1962, in *The New Yorker;* revised 1980.

him alone to live his life. His patriotism, then—his commitment to wearing the republic's uniform and carrying the republic's gun—was seriously qualified by his feelings of confinement and of loss.

When the C.Q. got around to Novotny's bed that morning, he did not shine his flashlight into the soldier's eyes but simply put a hand to his arm and said, "You better get yourself up, young trooper." Novotny was appreciative of this gentleness, and though the pain across his back was momentarily quite sharp as he stepped from his bunk, he met the day with his usual determination. Some mornings, deciding to be determined required that he swallow hard and close his eyes, yet he never decided otherwise: *I am willing.* He did not know if any of those around him had similar decisions to make, because he did not ask. He did not mull much over motive. People were honest or dishonest, good or bad, himself included.

After dressing, he moved off with four others to the mess hall, where it was their turn to work for the day. It was still dark, and back in the barracks the other recruits slept on. The previous day, the entire company had marched fifteen miserable miles wearing full packs, and then, when it was dark, they had dropped down on their stomachs and fired at pinpoints of light flickering five hundred yards away that were supposed to be the gunfire of the enemy. Before they climbed into the trucks that would carry them back to the camp at midnight, they were ordered to attention and told in a high, piercing voice by their captain, a National Guardsman and real-estate broker recently and unhappily called back to duty, that only one out of every fifty rounds they fired had hit the targets. This news had had a melancholy effect upon the weary recruits, and the trucks were silent all the way to the barracks, where it was necessary for them to clean their rifles and scrape the mud from their boots before they flung themselves down for a few hours' rest.

At the mess hall, the K.P.s were each served two large spoonfuls of Army eggs and a portion of potatoes. The potatoes had not been cooked long enough, and the taste was disheartening at such an early hour, with no light outdoors and a cold wind blowing. But Novotny did not complain. For one thing, he was occupied with finding a comfortable position in which to sit and eat —he had pain when he twisted the wrong way. Besides, the food was on his tray to give him strength, not pleasure. Novotny did not skip meals, no matter how ill-prepared they were, for he did not want to lose weight and be unequal to the task assigned him.

Before entering the Army, Novotny had worked for several years as an apprentice printer with a company in Chicago that manufactured telephone books. It turned out to be dull work, and because he considered himself a bright and ambitious young man, he had looked around for a night school where he might learn a job with a future. He settled on television, and for over a year had been attending classes two evenings a week. He had a girl friend and a mother, to both of whom he had a strong attachment; his girl friend he loved, his mother he took care of. Novotny did not want to cause any trouble. On the other hand, he did not want to be killed. With his girl friend, he had been a man of passion; he dreamed of her often. He was thrifty, and had four hundred dollars in a savings account in the First Continental Bank on LaSalle Street in Chicago. He knew for a fact that he had been more adept at his work than anyone else in his television course. He hated the Army because nothing he did there was for himself.

The labors of the K.P.s began at dawn, and at midnight—light having come and gone—they were still at it. The cooks had ordered the men around all day and then at five in the afternoon the Negro mess sergeant showed up, hung his Eisenhower jacket on a hook, rolled back his shirt cuffs, and said, "As there is a regimental inspection tomorrow morning, we will now get ourselves down to the fine points of housecleaning, gentlemens." The K.P.s proceeded to scrub the mess hall from floor to ceiling, inside and out.

A little after midnight, while Novotny was working away at a potato bin with a stiff brush and a bucket of hot, soapy water, the man working beside him began to cry. He said the sergeant was never going to let them go to sleep. He said the sergeant could be court-martialed for keeping them up like this. From exhaustion they could all get weak and sick—they could come down with meningitis. All Novotny knew of the fellow was that his name was Reynolds and that he had been to college. Apparently, the mess sergeant knew only half that much, but that was enough: "College boy," he said, when he came into the storeroom and saw Reynolds weeping into the empty potato bins, "wait'll they get you over in Korea." The sergeant delivered his words standing over them, looking down, and for the moment Novotny stopped feeling sorry for himself.

When the scrubbing job was finished, Novotny and Reynolds had to get the potatoes, which were in garbage cans, and dump them back into the bins. Reynolds began to explain to Novotny that he had a girl friend whom he was supposed to have called at ten-thirty. For some reason, Reynolds said, his not having been able to get to a phone had made him lose control. Novotny had, till then, been feeling superior to Reynolds. For all that he resented the stupidity that had made them scrub the bins out one minute so as to dump dirty potatoes back into them the next, he had been feeling somewhat in league with the sergeant. Now Reynolds' words broke through to his own unhappiness, and he was about to say something kind to his companion when the fellow started crying again. Reynolds threw his hand up to cover his eyes and dropped his end of the can. Novotny's body stiffened; with a great effort he yanked up on the can so that it wouldn't come down on Reynolds' toes. Pain cut deep across the base of Novotny's spine.

Later, he limped back to the barracks. He got into bed and angrily counted up the hours he had spent on K.P. At a dollar and a quarter an hour, he would have made over twenty dollars. Nineteen hours was more night-school time than he had been able to squeeze into three weeks. He had known Rose Anne, his girl, for almost a year, but never had they been together for nineteen consecutive hours. Though once they had had twelve hours . . . He had driven in his Hudson down to Champaign, where she was a freshman at the University of Illinois, and they had stayed together, in the motel room he had rented, from noon to midnight, not even going out for meals. He had driven her back to her dormitory, his shoelaces untied and wearing no socks. Never in his life had he been so excited.

The following week, he had been drafted.

After completing his eight weeks of basic training, Novotny was given a week's leave. His first evening home, his mother prepared a large meal and then sat opposite him at the table and watched him eat it. After dinner, he stood under the shower for twenty minutes, letting the hot water roll over him. In his bedroom, he removed the pins from a new white-on-white shirt and carefully laid it out on the bedspread, along with a pair of Argyles, a silver tie clasp, cuff links, and his blue suit. He polished his shoes—not for the captain's pleasure, but for his own—and chose a tie. Then he dressed for his date as he had learned to dress for a date from an article he had read in a Sunday picture magazine, while in high school, that had been taped ever since to the inside of his closet door. He had always clipped from the papers articles having to do with how to act at parties, or dances, or on the job; his mother never had any reason not to be proud of Novotny's behavior. She kissed him when he left the house, told him how handsome he looked, and then tears came into her eyes as she thanked him for the government checks—for always having been a good son.

Novotny went to a movie with Rose Anne, and afterward he drove to the forest preserve, where they parked until 2 A.M. In bed, later, he cursed the Army. He awoke the following morning to find that the pain, which had not troubled him for some weeks, had returned. It came and went through the next day and the following night, when once again he saw Rose Anne. Two days later, he visited the family doctor, who said Novotny had strained a muscle, and gave him a diathermy treatment. On their last night together, Rose Anne said that if writing would help, she would write not just twice each day, as was already her habit, but three times a day, even four. In the dark forest preserve, she told Novotny that she dreamed about his body; he told her how he dreamed of hers.

He left her weeping into a Kleenex in her dim front hallway, and drove home in a mood darker than any he had ever known. He would be killed in Korea and never see Rose Anne again, or his mother. And how unfair—for he *had* been a good son. Following his father's death, he had worked every day after school, plus

Wednesday nights and Saturdays. When he had been drafted, he had vowed he would do whatever they told him to do, without grievance or resentment. He had kept his mouth shut and become proficient at soldiering. The better soldier he was, the better chance he had of coming out alive and in one piece. But the night he left Rose Anne, he felt he had no chance at all. He would leave some part of his body on the battlefield, or come home to Rose Anne in a box. Good as he had been—industrious, devoted, resolute, self-sacrificing—he would never have the pleasure of being a husband, or a television cameraman, or a comfort to his mother in her old age.

Five days after his return to the post—where he was to receive eight weeks of advanced infantry training, preparatory to being shipped out—he went on sick call. He sat on a long bench in the barren waiting room, and while two sullen prisoners from the stockade mopped the floor around his feet, he had his temperature taken. There were thirteen men on sick call, and they all watched the floor being washed, while holding thermometers under their tongues. When finally Novotny got to see the medic, who sat outside the doctor's office, he told him that every time he twisted or turned or stepped down on his right foot, he felt a sharp pain just above the buttock on the right side of his body. Novotny was sent back to duty with three inches of tape across his back, and a packet of APC pills.

At mail call the following morning, Novotny received a letter from Rose Anne unlike any he had ever received from her before. It was not only that her hand was larger and less even than usual; it was what she said. She had written down, for his very eyes to see, all those things she dreamed about when she dreamed about his body. He saw, suddenly, scenes of passion that he and she were yet to enact, imagined moments even more thrilling than those they had already known. Oh, Rose Anne—how had he found her?

Novotny's company spent the afternoon charging with fixed bayonets—crawling about, jumping up, racing ahead, through wires, over fences, down into trenches—screaming murderously all the while. At one point, leaping from a high wall, Novotny almost took his eye out with his own bayonet; he had been dreaming of his beautiful future.

The next morning, he walked stiffly to sick call and asked to see the doctor. When, in response to a question, he said it was his back that hurt, the medic who was on duty informed him, sourly, "Everybody's back hurts." The medic told Novotny to take off his shirt so that he could lay on some more tape. Novotny asked if he could please see the doctor for just a minute. He was informed that the doctor was only seeing men with temperatures of a hundred or more. Novotny had no temperature, and he returned to his unit, as directed.

On the seventh weekend, with only one more week of training left, Novotny was given a seventy-two-hour pass. He caught a plane to Chicago and a bus to Champaign, carrying with him only a small ditty bag and Rose Anne's impassioned letter. Much of Friday and Saturday, and nearly all day Sunday, Rose Anne wept, until Novotny was more unhappy than he had ever imagined a man could be. On Sunday night, she held him in her arms and he proceeded to tell her at last of how he had been mistreated by the medic; till then he had not wanted to make her any more miserable than she already was. She stroked his hair and he told her how he had not even been allowed to see a doctor. Rose Anne said the medic should be shot. They had no right to send Novotny to Korea if they wouldn't even look after his health here at home. What would happen to him if his back started to act up in the middle of a battle? How could he defend his life, let alone his country? She raised many questions—rational ones, irrational ones, but none that Novotny had not already considered himself.

Novotny traveled all night by train so as to be back at the base for reveille. He spent most of the next day firing a Browning automatic, and the following dawn, when he was to go off on K.P., he could not even lift himself from his bed, so cruel was the pain in his back.

In the hospital, the fellow opposite Novotny had been in a wheelchair for two years with osteomyelitis. Though every few months they shortened his legs, the disease nonetheless continued its slow ascent. The man on Novotny's right had dropped a hand grenade in basic training and blown bits of both his feet off. Down at the end of Novotny's aisle lay a man whom a crate of ammunition had crushed, and the rest of the men in the ward, many of whom were in the hospital to learn to use prosthetic devices, had been in Korea.

The day after Novotny was assigned to the ward, the man whose back the crate had fallen on was wheeled away to be given a myelogram. He came back to the ward holding his head in his hands. As soon as Novotny was able to leave his bed, he made his way over to this fellow and asked him how he was feeling, what a myelogram was, and why he had come back to the ward holding his head. The fellow told him that they had injected a white fluid directly into his spine and then X-rayed him as the fluid moved along the vertebrae, so as to see if the spinal discs were damaged. He told Novotny that it was the stuff injected into the spine that had given him the headache, but then he added that, lousy as he had felt, he still considered himself pretty lucky. He had heard of cases where the needle had slipped. Novotny had himself heard of doctors leaving towels and sponges inside patients, so he could believe it. The man said that all the needle had to do was go off by a hairbreadth and it would wind up in the nerves leading into the spine. Two days later, two damaged discs were cut out of the man's injured back, and three of his vertebrae fused together. All the following week he lay motionless in his bed.

One evening earlier, while Novotny was still restricted to bed, he had been visited by Reynolds. Reynolds had come around to say goodbye before the entire outfit was flown out the next day. Since Reynolds and Novotny hardly knew each other, they fell silent after Reynolds told him what was to happen to him and the others. Finally Reynolds said that Novotny was lucky to have developed back trouble when he did; he wouldn't mind a little himself. Then he left.

When Novotny was up out of bed and walking around, X-rays were taken of his back, and the doctors told him they showed no sign of injury or disease; there was a slight narrowing of the intervertebral space between what were referred to on the pictures as L-1 and L-2, but nothing to suggest damage to the disc—which was what Novotny had worked up courage to ask about. The doctors took him into the examination room and bent him forward and backward. They ran a pin along his thigh and calf and asked if he felt any sensation. They laid him down on a table and, while slowly raising his leg, asked if he felt any pain. When his leg was almost at a ninety-degree angle with his body, Novotny thought that he did feel his pain—he did, most certainly, remember the pain, and remembered the misery of no one's taking it seriously but himself. Then he thought of all the men around him who hobbled on artificial limbs during the day and moaned in their beds at night, and he said nothing. Consequently, they sent him back to duty.

He was shunted into an infantry company that was entering its seventh week of advanced training. Two days before the company was to be shipped out, he awoke in the morning to discover that the pain had returned. He was able to limp to sick call, where he found on duty the unsympathetic medic, who, immediately upon seeing Novotny, began to unwind a roll of tape. Novotny raised an objection, and an argument ensued, which was settled when the doctor emerged from behind his door. He ordered Novotny into his office and had him strip. He told him to bend forward and touch his toes. Novotny tried, but could only come to within a few inches. The doctor looked over Novotny's medical record and then asked if he expected the Army to stand on its head because one soldier couldn't touch his toes. He asked him what he expected the Army to do for him. The doctor said there were plenty of G.I.s with sore backs in Korea. And with worse.

Though the pain diminished during the day, it returned the next morning with increased severity. Novotny could by this time visualize his insides—he saw the bone as white, and the spot where the pain was located as black. At breakfast, he changed his mind three times over, then went off to the first sergeant to ask permission to go on sick call. He decided that if he did not go and have the condition taken care of within the next few days it would simply get worse and worse; there would be no time for medical attention while they were in transit to Korea, and, once in Korea, those in charge would be even more indifferent to his complaints than they were here. The first sergeant asked Novotny what the matter was this time, and he answered that his back hurt. The first sergeant repeated what the medic had said the first day: "Everybody's back hurts." But he let him go.

At sick call, the doctor sat Novotny down and asked what *he* thought was wrong with him. What the suffering soldier had begun to think was that perhaps he had cancer or leukemia. It was to minimize his complaint that he said that maybe he had a slipped disc. The doctor said that if Novotny had slipped a disc he wouldn't even be able to walk around. Novotny found it difficult to breathe. What had he done in life to deserve this? What had he done, from the day he had grown out of short pants, but everything that was asked of him? He told the doctor that all he knew was that he had a pain. He tried to explain that taping it up didn't work; the pain wasn't on the surface but deep inside his back. The doctor said it was deep inside his head. When the doctor told him to go back to duty like a man, Novotny refused.

Novotny was taken to the hospital office of the colonel in charge of orthopedics. He was a bald man with circles under his eyes and a very erect carriage, who looked to have lived through a good deal. The colonel asked Novotny to sit down and tell him about the pain. Novotny, responding to a long-suffering quality in the man that seemed to him to demand respect, told him the truth: he had rolled over one morning during his basic training, and there it had been, deep and sharp. The colonel asked Novotny if he could think of anything that might have caused the pain. Novotny recounted what had happened on K.P. with Reynolds. The doctor asked if that had occurred before the morning he had awakened with the pain, or after it. Novotny admitted that it was after. But surely that must have aggravated the pain. The doctor said that that did not clear up the problem of where the pain had come from in the first place. He reminded Novotny that the X-rays showed nothing. He ordered Novotny to take off his hospital blues and stretch out on the examination table. By this time, of course, Novotny knew all the tests by heart; once, in fact, he anticipated what he was about to be asked to do, and the colonel gave him a strange look.

When the doctor was finished, he told Novotny that he had a lumbosacral strain with some accompanying muscle spasm. Nothing more. It was what they used to call lumbago. Novotny stood up to leave, and the colonel informed him that when he was released from the hospital he would have to appear at a summary court-martial for having refused to obey the doctor's order to return to duty. Novotny felt weak enough to faint. He was suddenly sorry he had ever opened his mouth. He was ashamed. He heard himself explaining to the colonel that he had refused to obey only because he had felt too sick to go back to duty. The colonel said it was for a trained doctor to decide how sick or well Novotny was. But, answered Novotny—hearing the gates to the stockade slamming shut behind him, imagining prison scenes so awful even he couldn't endure them—but the doctor had made a mistake. As the colonel said, he *did* have a lumbosacral strain, and muscle spasm, too. In a steely voice, the colonel told him that there were men in Korea who had worse. It was the line that everyone finally took and to which Novotny had no answer.

When they put him in traction, he had further premonitions of his court-martial and his internment in the stockade. He, Novotny, who had never broken a law in his life. What was happening? Each morning, he awoke at the foot of the bed, pulled there by the weights strapped to his ankles and hanging to the floor. His limbs and joints ached day in and day out from being stretched. More than once, he had the illusion of being tortured for a crime he had not committed, although he knew that the traction was therapeutic. At the end of a week, the weights were removed and he was sent to the physical-therapy clinic, where he received heat treatments and was given exercises to perform. Some days, the pain lessened almost to the point of disappearing. Other days, it was as severe as it had ever been. Then he believed that they would have to cut him open, and it would be the doctor at sick call who would be court-martialed instead of himself. When the pain was at its worst, he felt vindicated; but then, at its worst, he was also most miserable.

He was by himself only when he was in the bathroom, and it was there that he would try to bend over and touch his toes. He repeated this at every opportunity, as though it were a key to something. One day, thinking himself alone, he had begun to strain toward his toes when he was turned around by the voice of the osteomyelitis victim, who was sitting in the doorway in his wheelchair. "How's the backache, buddy?" he said, and wheeled sharply away. Everybody in the ward somehow knew bits of Novotny's history; nobody, nobody knew the whole story.

Now nobody he didn't know liked him; and he stopped liking those he did know. His mother appeared at the hospital two weeks after his admittance. She treated him like a hero, leaving with him a shoebox full of baked goods and a Polish sausage. He could not bring himself to tell her about his court-martial; he could not disappoint her—and that made him angry. He was even glad to see her go, lonely as he was. The following weekend, Rose Anne arrived. Everybody whistled when she walked down the ward. And he was furious at her—but for what? For being so desirable? So perfect? They argued, and Rose Anne went back to Champaign, bewildered. That night, the Negro next to Novotny, who had lost his right leg in the battle of Seoul, leaned over the side of his bed and said to him, with a note in his voice more dreamy than malicious, "Hey, man, you got it made."

The next day, very early, Novotny went to the hospital library and searched the shelves until he found a medical encyclopedia. He looked up "slipped disc." Just as he had suspected, many of his own symptoms were recorded there. His heart beat wildly as he read of the difficulties of diagnosing a slipped disc, even with X-rays. Ah yes, only the myelogram was foolproof. He read on and on, over and over, symptoms, treatments, surgical procedures. One symptom he read of was a tingling sensation that ran down the back of the leg and into the foot, caused by pressure of the herniated disc on an adjacent nerve. The following morning, he awoke with a tingling sensation that ran down the back of his right leg and into his foot. Only momentarily was he elated; then it hurt.

On his weekly ward rounds, the colonel, followed by the nurse and the resident, walked up to each bed and talked to the patient; everyone waited his turn silently, as if in formation and at attention. The colonel examined stumps, incisions, casts, prosthetic devices, and then asked each man how he felt. When he reached Novotny, he asked him to step out of bed and into the aisle, and there he had him reach down and touch his toes. Novotny tried, bending and bending. Someone in the ward broke the silence. "Come on, Daddy, you can do it." Then another voice called, "Push, Polack, *push*"—and then it seemed to him that all the patients in the ward were shouting and laughing, and the colonel was doing nothing to restrain them. "Ah, wait'll they get you in Korea"—and suddenly the ward was silent again, for Novotny was straightening up, his face a brilliant red. "I can't do it, sir," he said. "Does your back feel better?" the colonel asked. "Yes, sir." "Do you think we should send you back to duty?" "I've had a tingling sensation down the back of my right leg," Novotny said. "So?" the colonel asked. The ward was dead silent; Novotny decided not to answer.

In the afternoon, Novotny was called to the colonel's office. He walked there without too much difficulty—but then it was not unusual for the pain to come and go and come back again, with varying degrees of severity. Sometimes the cycle took hours, sometimes days, sometimes only minutes. It was enough to drive a man crazy.

In the colonel's office, Novotny was told that he was going to get another chance. Novotny was too young, the colonel said, not to be extended forgiveness. If he went back to duty, the charges against him would be dismissed and there would be no court-martial. The colonel said that with a war on there was nothing to be gained by putting a good soldier behind bars. The colonel let Novotny know that he was impressed by his marksmanship record, which he had taken the trouble to look up in the company files.

When it was Novotny's turn to speak, he could only think to ask if the colonel believed the tingling sensation in his leg meant nothing at all. The colonel, making it obvious that it was patience he was displaying, asked Novotny what *he* thought it meant. Novotny said he understood it to be a symptom of a slipped disc. The colonel asked him how he knew that, and Novotny—hesitating only a moment, then carrying on with the truth, proceeding in the only way he ever had—said that he had read it in a book. The colonel asked Novotny if he was that afraid of going to

Korea. Novotny did not know what to answer; he had not thought of it that way before. The colonel asked him if he ever broke out in a cold sweat at night. Novotny said no—the only new symptom was the tingling in the leg. The colonel brought a fist down on his desk and told Novotny that the following day he was sending him over to see the psychiatrist. He could sit out the rest of the war in the nuthouse.

What to do? Novotny did not know. It was not a cold but a hot sweat that he was in all through dinner. In the evening, he walked to the Coke machine in the hospital basement, as lonely a young man as he had ever been. A nurse passed him in the hall and smiled. She thought he was sick. He drank his Coke, but when he saw two wheelchairs headed his way he turned and moved up the stairs to the hospital library, where he immediately set about looking through the shelves for a book on psychology. Since he knew as little about psychology as he did about medicine, he had to look for a long time. He did not want to ask for the help of the librarian, even though she was a civilian. At last he was able to locate two books, and he sat down on the floor between the stacks, where nobody could see him.

Much of what he read he did not follow, but once in a while he came upon an anecdote, and in his frustration with the rest of the book, he would read that feverishly. He read of a woman in a European country who had imagined that she was pregnant. She had swelled up, and then, after nine months, she had had labor pains—but no baby. Because it had all been in her imagination. *Her imagination had made her swell up.* Novotny read this over several times. He was respectful of facts, and believed what he found in books. He did not believe that a man would take the time to sit down and write a book so as to tell other people lies.

As he walked to the ward, his back seemed engulfed in flames. It was then that he became absorbed in the fantasy of reaching inside himself and cutting out of his body the circle of pain. He saw himself standing over his own naked back and twisting down on an instrument that resembled the little utensil that is sold in dime stores to remove the core of a grapefruit. In his bed, he could not find a position in which to forget or to ignore the pain.

He got up and went to the phone booth, where he called long distance to Rose Anne. He could barely prevent himself from begging her to get on a plane and fly down to him that very night. And yet, if it wasn't his back that was causing the pain, was it somehow Rose Anne? Was he being punished for being so happy with her? Were they being punished for all that sex? Unlike his mother, he was not the kind of Catholic who believed in Hell; he was not the kind who was afraid of sex. All he wanted was his chance at life. That was all.

In the washroom, before he returned to bed, he tried to touch his toes. He forced himself down and down and down until his eyes were cloudy from pain and his fingers were within an inch of the floor. But he could not keep his brain from working—and he did not know what to think. If a woman could imagine herself to be in labor, then for him, too, anything was possible. He leaned over the sink and looked into the mirror and admitted to his own face that he was frightened of going to Korea. Terribly frightened. But wasn't everybody? He wondered if nothing could be wrong with him. He wondered if nothing he knew was so.

The next day, the psychiatrist asked Novotny if he felt nervous. He said he didn't. The psychiatrist asked if he had felt nervous before he had come into the Army. Novotny said no, that he had been happy. He asked if Novotny was afraid of high places, and if he minded being in crowds; he asked if he had any brothers and sisters, and which he liked better, his mother or his father. Novotny answered that his father was dead. He again asked which parent Novotny had liked better before his father died. Novotny did not really care to talk about this subject, particularly to someone he didn't even know, but he had decided to be as frank and truthful with the psychiatrist as he'd been with everyone—at least, he meant to tell him what he *thought* was the truth. Novotny answered that his father had been lazy and incompetent, and the family was finally better off with him gone. The psychiatrist then asked Novotny about Rose Anne. Novotny was frank. He asked Novotny if his back hurt when he was being intimate with Rose Anne. Novotny answered that sometimes it did and sometimes it didn't. He asked Novotny if, when it did hurt, they ceased being intimate. Novotny dropped his head. It was with a searing sense that some secret had been uncovered, something not even he himself had known, that he admitted that they did not. He simply could not bring himself to tell the psychiatrist what they did do when Novotny's back was at its worst. He said quickly that he planned to marry Rose Anne—that he had always known he would marry her. The psychiatrist asked where the couple would live, and Novotny said with his mother. When he asked Novotny why, Novotny said because he had to take care of her, too.

The psychiatrist had Novotny stand up, close his eyes, and try to touch the tips of his index fingers together. While Novotny's eyes were closed, the psychiatrist leaned forward, and, in a whisper, asked if Novotny was afraid of dying. The weight of all that he had been through in the past weeks was suddenly more than the young soldier could bear. He broke down and admitted to a fear of death. He began to weep and to say that he didn't want to die. The psychiatrist asked him if he hated the Army, and he admitted that he did.

The psychiatrist's office was across the street from the main hospital, in the building the colonel had called the nuthouse. Novotny, full of shame, was led out of the building by an attendant with a large ring of keys hooked to his belt; he had to unlock three doors before Novotny got out to the street. He went out the rear door, just in sight of a volleyball game that was being played within a wire enclosure at the back of the building. To pull himself together before returning to the hostile cripples in the ward, Novotny watched the teams bat the ball back and forth over the net. Then he realized that they were patients who spent their days and nights inside the building from which he had just been released—and that the doctors were going to put him away there too. Not because he was making believe he had a pain in his back—that was why they had been going to put him in the stockade—but because he was *not* making believe. He was feeling a pain for which there was no cause. He had a terrible vision of Rose Anne having to come here to visit him. She was only a young girl, and he knew that it would frighten her so much to be led to him through three locked doors that he would lose her. He was about to begin to lose things.

He pulled himself straight up—he had been stooping—and clenched his teeth and told himself that in thirty seconds the pain could be gone for good, if only he willed it to be so. He counted to thirty, and took a step. He came down upon his right foot with only half his weight, but there was the pain, so sharp that it made his eyes water. The volleyball smashed against the fence through which he was peering, and, trying to walk as he remembered himself walking when he was a perfectly healthy young man with nothing to fear—a man who had not begun to know of all the confusion growing up inside him—he hurried away from the psychopaths and the madmen.

The colonel had Novotny called to his office the following day. The night before, Novotny had got little sleep, but by dawn he had reached a decision. Now, though he feared the worst, he marched to the colonel's office with a plan of action firmly in mind. When Novotny entered, the colonel asked him to sit down, and proceeded to tell him of his own experiences in the Second World War. He had flown with an airborne division at a time when he was only a little more than Novotny's age. He had jumped from a plane over occupied Normandy and broken both his legs, and then been shot in the chest by a French farmer for a reason he still did not understand. The colonel said that he had returned from Korea only a week before Novotny had entered the hospital. He wished that Novotny could see what the men there were going through—he wished Novotny could be witness to the bravery and the courage and the comradery, and the suffering. The misery of our soldiers—and of those poor Koreans. He was not angry with Novotny personally; he was only trying to tell him something for his own good. Novotny was too young to make a decision that might disgrace him for the rest of his life. He told the young soldier that if he walked around with that back of his for a few weeks, if he just stopped *thinking* about it all the time, it would be as good as new. That, in actual fact, it was almost as good as new right now. He said that Novotny's trouble was that he was a passive-aggressive.

Novotny's voice was very thin when he asked the colonel what he meant. The colonel read to him what the psychiatrist had written. Mostly it was the answers that Novotny had given to the psychiatrist's questions, but in the end the report said that Novotny was a passive-aggressive and recommended he be given an administrative separation from the Army, and the appropriate discharge. Novotny asked what that meant. The colonel replied that the appropriate discharge was plain and simple as far as he was concerned. He took down a book of regulations from a shelf behind him, and after flipping past several pages read to Novotny in a clear, unfaltering voice. " 'An undesirable discharge is an administrative separation from the service under conditions other than honorable. It is issued for unfitness, misconduct, or security reasons.' " He looked up, got no response, and so read further. " 'It is recognized that all enlisted personnel with behavior problems cannot be rehabilitated by proper leadership and/or psychiatric assistance. It is inevitable that a certain percentage of individuals entering the service subsequently will demonstrate defective moral habits, irresponsibility, inability to profit by experience—' " He paused to read the last phrase again, then went on—" 'untrustworthiness, lack of regard for the rights of others, and inability to put off pleasures and impulses of the moment.' " He engaged Novotny's eye. " 'Often,' " he said, returning to the regulation, " 'these individuals show poor performance despite intelligence, superficial charm, and a readiness to promise improvement. The effective leader is able to rehabilitate only the percentage of persons with behavior problems who are amenable to leadership.' " He stopped and pushed the book forward on his desk so that it faced Novotny. "Unfitness, soldier," he said, tapping the page. He waited for Novotny to take in the contents, and while he did, the colonel made it clear that such a discharge followed a man through life. Novotny, hardly even raising his head, asked again what a passive-aggressive was. The colonel laid it on the line. "Just another kind of coward."

What Novotny had decided in bed the night before was to request a myelogram. Of course, he still remembered being told that all the needle had to do was be off by a hairbreadth to ruin you for life; he was convinced, in fact, that something like that was just what would happen to him, given the way things had begun to go in his life. But though such a prospect terrified him, he did not see that he had any choice. The truth had to be revealed, one way or the other. But when the colonel finished and waited for him to speak, he remained silent.

"What do you have against the Army, Novotny?" the colonel asked. "What makes you so special?"

Novotny did not mention the myelogram. Why *should* he? Why should he have to take so much from people when he had an honest-to-God pain in his back? He was not imagining it nor making it up. He had practically ruptured himself when Reynolds had dropped the end of the can of potatoes. Maybe he had only awakened with a simple strain that first morning, but trying to keep the can from dropping on Reynolds' foot, he had done something serious to his back. That all the doctors were unable to give a satisfactory diagnosis did not make his pain any less real.

"You are a goddamned passive-aggressive, young man, what do you think of that?" the colonel said.

Novotny did not speak.

"You know how many people in America have low back pain?" the colonel demanded. "Something like fifteen per cent of the adult population of this country has low back pain—and what do you think they do, quit? Lay down on the job? What do you think a man does who has a family and responsibilities—stop supporting them? You know what your trouble is, friend? You think life owes you something. You think something's coming to you. You think everybody else can go to hell, just so long as you have your way. Imagine if those men in Korea gave in to every little ache and pain. Imagine if that was what had happened at Valley Forge, at Okinawa—then where would we all be? My God, the average man, if you threatened him with this kind of discharge, would do just about anything he could to avoid it. But not you. Even if you have a pain, haven't you got the guts to go ahead and serve like everybody else? Well, answer me, yes or no?"

But Novotny would not answer. All he had done was answer people and tell them the truth, and what had it got him? What good was it, being good? What good was it, especially if at bottom you were bad anyway? What good was it, acting strong, if at bottom you were weak and couldn't *be* strong if you wanted to? With the colonel glaring across at him, the only solace Novotny had was to think that nobody knew any more about him than he himself did. Whatever anybody chose to call him didn't really mean a thing.

Within six days, the Army had rid itself of Novotny. It took Novotny, however, a good deal more than six days to rid himself of his infirmity—if he can be said ever to have rid himself of infirmity—or, at least, the threat of infirmity. During the next year, he missed days of work and evenings of night school, and spent numerous weekends laid out on a mattress supported by a bedboard. He went to one doctor who prescribed a set of exercises, and one who prescribed a steel brace. But when he tried the exercises the pain only got worse, and when he tried the brace he found it so uncomfortable that finally he stuck it away in the attic, though it had cost forty-five dollars. Another doctor, who had been highly recommended to him, listened to his story and simply shrugged his shoulders; and still another told Novotny what the colonel had—that many Americans had low back ailments, that they were frequently of unknown origin, and that he would have to learn to live with it.

That, finally, was what he tried to do. Gradually, over the years, the pain diminished in severity and frequency, though even today he has an occasional bad week, and he still gets a cautionary twinge whenever he bends the wrong way or picks up something he shouldn't. He is married to Rose Anne and is employed as a television cameraman by an educational channel in Chicago. His mother lives with him and his wife in Park Forest. For the most part, he leads a quiet, ordinary sort of life, though his attachment to Rose Anne is still marked by an unusual passion. When the other men in Park Forest go bowling on Friday nights, Novotny stays home, for he tries not to put strains upon his body to which he has decided it is not equal. In a way, all the awfulness of those Army days has boiled down to that—no bowling. There are nights, of course, when Novotny awakens from a deep sleep to worry in the dark about the future. What will happen to him? What next? But surely those uncertainties he shares with all mankind, sufferers of low back pain and non-sufferers alike. Nobody has ever yet asked to see his discharge papers, so about that the colonel was wrong.

Martha's Thanksgiving

Sarah Vaughan awakened Martha Reganhart. She twisted around until she had plugged "Tenderly" out of her ears with her sheet and pillow—but then Markie was in bed beside her.

"Where's the turkey?"

"Honey, it's too early. Go color, go back to bed—"

"Sissy's playing records."

"Go tell Sissy to turn them off."

"I don't know how."

"Tell Cynthia to. Markie baby, Mother's beat. Will you just give her five more minutes? Tell Cynthia to tell Sissy to turn down the volume."

"What?"

"The volume. Tell her . . ." She caught sight of the whole family's dirty laundry heaped up in a corner of the gray room, and she almost went under. "Tell her to turn down the phonograph." A bleary eye fell on the electric clock. "It's seven, honey—it's a holiday. Tell Cynthia—"

"Cynthia's talking on the phone."

"What phone?"

"She called the weather."

"Oh Christ, Mark, tell your sister to hang up! Tell Sissy to lower the phonograph. Oh baby, your pants are wet—"

From Part Three ("The Power of Thanksgiving") of the 1962 novel, *Letting Go*. The setting is the environs of the University of Chicago in the mid-fifties.

"It's going to be clouds all day," Mark said.

"Markie—"

You took my lips,
You took my love,
Sooooooooo—

"Sissy! Lower that thing!"

"I can't *hear* you," Sissy shouted back; and a good forty minutes before it was supposed to, Mrs. Reganhart's day began.

Sissy was in her room, wearing a gossamer shorty nightgown and painting her toenails.

"Sissy, where are the oranges? How do you expect my kids to have breakfast without orange juice?"

"I thought they were my oranges."

"How could your oranges be on the top shelf, Sister? Where's your head?"

"I'm sorry."

"Sissy, yesterday I found a bunch of bananas in the refrigerator. My bananas. Ten million dollars' worth of advertising, and it goes right over your head. I'm at the edge with you, Sissy, I really am. Can't you keep that box off in the morning?"

"Jesus, you just got up. What are you coming on so salty for?"

"Please, do me a favor. Let's make a rule. No Sarah Vaughan until ten. There are two kids here, plus me, right? Either let's make this place a house, keep it a house, or else—I don't know. Can't you even close the door when you take a bath?"

"What's eating you, for God's sake? What are you so prissy about all of a sudden? The kid's four years old—"

"Just do me a favor," Martha Reganhart said, "and close the door."

"I'm claustrophobic."

"You're a goddam exhibitionist."

"For four-year-olds?"

"I'm not even talking about Mark. I'm talking about Cynthia. She's a big girl."

"Christ, we're all one sex."

"There's something about the sight of you shaving your legs in the bathtub that I think has a deleterious effect on her. All right?"

"You think she tends to be a little dykey?"

"That's a bad joke—" Martha Reganhart said. "Why don't you take it back?"

"I will. I'm sorry, Martha. I am."

Martha looked out past the window sill full of cigarette butts into the holiday sky: clouds all day. Oh God. In the room, Sissy's underwear was hanging over chair backs, on doorknobs, and on the two end posts of the bed; one brassiere was hooked over an andiron in the unused fireplace. Sissy herself sat on Martha's Mexican rug (the one she had moved into this back bedroom as a come-on for prospective roomers) painting her toenails. Martha decided not to express the whole new rush of irritation she felt toward the girl. The only roomer Martha could put up with anyway was no roomer at all; besides, Sissy's forty a month helped pay the rent. So she smiled at Sissy—who had, after all, behind those pendulous boobs, a big pendulous heart—and sling-shotted a brassiere off the bedstead into Sissy's curly brown hair. It collapsed around her ears.

"It loves you," Martha said.

"You know, I think you're a little dykey too."

"Oh you're a hard girl to fool, Sis." She left the room wondering not how to dispossess Sissy, but simply how to get the Mexican rug back into the children's bedroom.

In the kitchen, she slid the turkey from the refrigerator and found that it had only just begun to unfreeze; she had been so tired when she got home last night that she had gone directly to bed, forgetting to leave the turkey out. "Why do they let these birds get so *hard?*" she said.

"Who?" Mark said.

"Markie, don't you have anything to do? Do you have to walk directly under my feet?"

"Why does that thing have a big hole in it like that?" he demanded.

"Get your arm out of there. Come on, Markie, take your arm out of there, will you?"

"Why does that turkey have a big hole in it?"

She carried it to the sink and turned the cold water on. She rapped on the breast with her knuckle, asking herself why November couldn't have sneaked by without causing a fuss. Holidays were even worse than work days. Couldn't everything, birthdays, Fourth of July, be celebrated at Christmas?

"Why does that turkey have a big—"

"I don't know."

"It's for the sexual organs," Cynthia said.

"Drink your prune juice."

"I don't like prune juice," Cynthia answered. "I like oranges."

"Sissy drank the oranges this morning."

"They weren't hers anyway."

"Yes they were," Martha said.

"You said so yourself," Cynthia replied.

"I made a mistake. I jumped to conclusions." Since her daughter's normal response to people seemed to be distrust, she saw no need to feed her inclinations; perhaps if everybody ignored the trait she would grow out of it. Martha told herself to be more motherly. "Cynthia, are you going to help me with dinner? You want to help stuff the turkey?"

"What's stuff it?" Markie asked.

"Stuffing," Cynthia said.

"How?" he pleaded.

"In the sexual organs."

"Cynthia, what's this sexual organs business?" Martha looked almost instinctively to Sissy's door, which closed (when Martha could convince Sissy to keep it closed) onto the kitchen. Behind it Sissy was singing a duet with Sarah Vaughan and dressing; that is, heavy objects were bouncing off the floor, so if she was not dressing she was bowling.

"That," Cynthia was saying, pointing toward the opening in the turkey.

"No it's not, honey."

"Yes it is, Mother."

"It's where they removed the insides of the turkey. This is a Tom, sweetie," Martha began to explain.

"It's the sexual organs," Cynthia said.

Markie looked from one to the other, with intermittent glances at the bird's posterior, and waited for the outcome; he seemed to be rooting for his mother.

"It *was* the sexual organs," Martha said. "It's where they remove the intestines—"

"Who?" Mark asked.

"Dears, it's very involved and mysterious and not terribly crucial. It's one of those things that one day is very complicated and the next day is very simple. Why don't you wait?"

"Okay," Mark said, but Cynthia complained again about her prune juice.

"Cynthia, why don't you run down to Wilson's and buy the paper for me?"

"Can I stop in the playground to see if Stephanie's there?"

"Stephanie's mother is sick."

"—sexual organs," Mark was saying.

"Markie, forget that, all right? Why don't you go color? Go with Cynthia—"

"I don't want him along!"

"Who cares!" Mark said, and left the kitchen.

"Please don't fight, will you, Cynthia? It's a holiday. Go get the *Times.*"

"Can I stop at Hildreth's?"

"For what? For candy, no."

"To talk to Blair."

"Blair isn't there."

"Blair's always there," said Cynthia, and Sissy laughed behind the door.

"Isn't it enough, honey, to take a walk? Cyn, I'd love to take a walk. I'd just love to take a nice leisurely walk and get the newspaper and bring it home and sit down for about six hours and read it. Can't you do that?"

"No!"

"Then go get the paper and keep quiet."

"Christ!"

"And enough of that," Martha said.

"*You* say it."

"I also work as a waitress—does that interest you?"

"I can't do *any*thing."

Martha took the dime for the paper out of her slacks pocket with wet hands. "Do you know what day this is?" she asked, wrapping her daughter's fingers around the coin.

Cynthia made a bored admission. "It's Thanksgiving."

"Thanksgiving is a very terrific holiday. How about we have a pleasurable day, all right? We're going to have a guest. Well, don't you want to know who?"

"Who?"

She mustered up an air of excitement, a good deal more than she felt. "Sidney Jaffe!"

And all at once the child, thank God, became a child, a little seven-year-old girl. "Goodie! Terrific!" She skipped out of the house after the paper.

There was one wall of the kids' room—before Sissy's arrival it had been Cynthia's alone—that Martha had given up on and come to consider the coloring wall. Now Mark was laying purple on it with considerable force and violence.

"Markie, what is it you want to do?"

"Yes," the boy said, and continued hammering the crayons against the wall.

"What's the trouble?"

He looked up. "Nothing."

"Are you happy?"

"Uh-huh."

She made Cynthia's bed and changed Mark's wet sheets. Crumpling them into a sour wad, she bit her tongue and said nothing. Finally, as though it was simple curiosity that moved her to ask, she said, "Did you have any bad dreams, my friend?"

He looked up at her again. "Who?"

Why did he always say *who* to everything? All the frustrations of the morning—the missing oranges, the frozen bird, Sarah Vaughan—nearly came out on poor defenseless Mark. Everything: Sissy's stupidity and Cynthia's indefatigable opposition and Markie's bed-wetting and her own unconquerable tiredness . . . She was twenty-six and tired right down to the bone. And she was putting on weight. Twenty-six and becoming a *cow!* Somehow the whole general situation would improve, she thought hazily, if she could only get Sissy to pick up her underwear and put it in a drawer. Or move out. Or shut up. But the truth was that she had been dying for a little companionship. When she dragged in from the Hawaiian House at one in the morning, it gave her a small warm rush of pleasure to find Sissy in the kitchen, drinking hot milk—more than likely laced with Martha's brandy—and listening to Gerry Mulligan. Sissy was silly and gossipy and she did not bother to vote, but it seemed better coming home to her than coming home to nothing. Still, why did she have to be a nut? Martha seemed always to be latching on to people just as they were going through some treacherous maturing period in their lives. Her next roomer, she told herself, would not be under eighty—better they should die in her spare room than grow up in it.

She planted a kiss on her son's neck and he drew a purple line across the bridge of her nose. "Bang! Bang!" he shouted into her ear, and she left him to his drawing.

"What's the matter with your nose?" Sissy asked. "You look like you've just been shat upon."

"Could you control your language in my house?"

"What are you coming on so salty again for?"

"I don't want my children saying shat, do you mind? And put on a bathrobe. My son's earliest memory is going to be of your ass."

"Now who's filthy?"

"I happen to be their mother. I support them. Please, Sissy, *don't* walk around here half-naked, will you?"

"Well, you don't have to be so defensive about it." Sissy went into her room, and came out again, robed, and dribbling ashes off her cigarette. Martha turned to the wall above the sink where the wallpaper was trying to crawl down; she gave it a swat, with the result that it unpeeled a little further. And for this, she thought, they raise the rent. During the last six months—since everybody had had the mumps—life had just been zipping along; then they raised the rent, she brought in Sissy, and things were down to normal again. She turned to her roomer and said, "Sissy, I want to ask you a question."

"What?"

"Stop plucking your face and listen to me."

Sissy lowered her mirror and tweezers. "All right, crab, what is it?"

"Do you smoke pot in there?"

The girl crossed her arms over her chest. "Never."

"Because don't. I don't ever want Blair sleeping over here again, *ever*—and I don't want any pot-smoking within ten feet of the kitchen table, where my children happen to eat their breakfast."

"It was Blair, Martha. He won't do it again."

"You're damn right he won't do it again. Why did I rent that room to you, Sister? I keep forgetting."

"I *applied,* you know, like everybody else. I answered the ad. Don't start shifting blame on me."

Martha returned to the turkey; she had popped a seam in the left side of her slacks, and when she bent over the sink it popped open further. "They're going to put me in a circus," she said. "Five nine and six hundred pounds."

"You eat too much. You could knock people's eyes out. You just eat too much."

"I don't eat too much," she said, running scalding water over the leaden turkey, "I'm just turning into a cow. A horse."

"You know what your trouble is?"

"What? What news do you bring from the far-out world? I'm dying to hear a capsule analysis of my character this morning."

"You're horny."

"You sound about as far out as *McCall's,* Sissy."

"Well, when *I'm* horny I'm a bitch."

"Your needs are more complicated than mine. I'm just tired."

"When I was married to old Curtis, I was practically flippy. You say *boo,* and I was halfway out the window. He was the creepiest, gentlest guy, and I was snapping at him all the time."

The tragedy in Sissy's young life was that she had been married for eleven months to a man who was impotent; she had married him, she said, because he struck her right off as being different. Now—in her continuing search for the exotic—she was involved with Blair Stott, who was a Negro about one and a half neuroses away from heroin, but coming up strong; and if he wasn't impotent, he was a flagellator or something in that general area.

"What about that Ivy League guy?" Sissy asked. "Joe Brummel."

"Beau Brummel, Sissy—what about him?"

"Don't you dig him or what?"

"He's in New York," Martha said.

"I thought he was coming for dinner."

"Sid is."

"Oh Jesus. That very buttoned-down guy, I mean he's not bad. He could be turned on with a little work. But old Sidney, I mean like what he digs is *law."*

"Sissy, how do you talk at the hospital? How do you address people when you're not at home?"

"What?"

"Forget it."

"I hate that God damn hospital. Blair says—" And she proceeded to repeat Blair's words in Blair's dialect: "I'm going to get desexized from the X-ray rays."

"Blair's a genius."

"Martha—" Sissy said, leaning forward and setting down her mirror.

"What?"

"I almost did the most far-out thing of my life last night. I was like *close."*

"To what?"

"Turning tricks."

Martha felt the homey familiar enamel of the sink under her hands, and took a good grip on it. *"Here?"* she demanded. "You were going to be a prostitute in *my house? Are you crazy?"*

"No! No—what do you think I am!"

With relief—though by no means total relief—Martha said, "At Suey's."

"At Suey's," Sissy admitted. "Isn't that something? Suey was out getting her hair set, and this guy called to come over for a fast one. I told him Suey was out, and so he said what about you, sweetheart? And I said okay, come on over, you jerk. I told him to come over."

In a vague way, Suey O'Day was tied up with Martha's own

past, but that was not sufficient explanation for the emotions—shame, fear, vulnerability—that Martha felt while Sissy was speaking. Martha and Suey had been freshmen together at the University. Suey had run off one day with a jockey from Washington Park, and Martha had run off and married Dick, and they had gone to Mexico and then she had come back from Mexico with the kids, and Suey was twenty-four and back in town too—as a call girl. Now Suey's future was said to be very bright; at one A.M., with background music by Gerry Mulligan, Sissy had informed Martha that there was a LaSalle Street broker whom Suey was tempted to marry for loot, and there was an instructor in math at the University who was crazy about her and whom she was tempted to marry for love. (The problem here was whether Suey should tell him The Truth About Herself, which the LaSalle Street broker already knew.) Of course Suey was worlds away from Martha, but Sissy wasn't: Sissy was in her house, Sissy was sleeping on her muslin sheets, and it was Sissy's dumb wildness, her endless temptations, that struck in Martha a painful remembered chord.

"What happened?" Martha said.

"I took off. I came home. I got in bed. That's how I was up so early—I was in bed at nine-thirty."

Martha sat down at the kitchen table and lit a cigarette; she caught sight of her hair in Sissy's mirror—another mess to be cleaned up before one o'clock. "Sissy, you're really going to screw up everything. Why don't you wise up? Dump Blair and dump all this hipster crap and do something with yourself. Honey, you can still dig Gerry Mulligan, but you don't have to *kill* yourself."

"Look, I was just going to turn a lousy trick to see what it was like. I wasn't going to jump off a bridge."

"But, Sissy, you don't want to be a call girl. Do you know what's very square, Sis? To want to be a call girl. Honestly, it's like wanting to be an airline stewardess or a nurse."

"Do you think I love being a stinking X-ray technician? Is that a noble calling? Sixty-five bucks a week?"

"Ah-ha, it's a matter of honor. I didn't know. The culture's crowding you in. We ought to set up an interview for you, Sissy, with Erich Fromm."

"Don't come on so motherly with me, Martha. You're about two years older—"

"True—"

"—and your life isn't exactly a model of order."

"You're going to get kicked in the teeth, Sister, so why don't you shut up." Martha pressed out her cigarette just as the janitor came up the back porch, waved at her, tried to catch a peek at some bare corner of Sissy's anatomy, and emptied—very, very slowly—the garbage.

At the sink she held the turkey submerged in hot water. Behind her Sissy began to apologize. "I just *thought* about it, Martha—"

"Who cares what you thought or what you did! Maybe what you ought to think about is moving out."

"I only just moved *in.*"

"That'll make packing easier. Just roll up all your brassieres, scatter those cigarette butts to the wind, and move the hell out."

"You going to throw me out on a morals charge? Because I don't happen to be compulsively neat?"

"I don't want my kids lifting up the phone when your clients start to call—" Yet even as she spoke the whole business tired her. Everything tired her—even thinking about what she would have to do now. Take another ad, answer phone calls, arrange appointments, show the place to dozens of girls and ladies . . . Just the knowledge that after Sissy left she would have to scrub the place again from top to bottom weakened her resolve. Why hadn't she rented to some eager little physics major in the first place? What insanity it had been to think that this jerk was going to be sweet, fun, *laughs!* All she wanted now, really, was for Sissy to crawl back into her grubby room and close the door and ruin her life however she wanted. She said nothing, but there must have been some sagging in her posture that inspired Sissy to be nasty.

"Just because you have sex problems, Martha, don't call somebody who doesn't a nymphomaniac, all right? If you're frigid, or whatever the hell is bugging you, I don't say I'm not going to live in your *house* because of it. You, you're a regular sexual Senator McCarthy, honest to God you are."

"I'm trying to fix a traditional Thanksgiving Day turkey. Why don't you go play records."

"Actually, I think what it is that bugs you is that like Blair's a dinge."

"As far as I'm concerned, friend, you can go down for the whole Nigerian Army and the Belgian Congo Marines. Just leave me alone, all right?"

Sissy picked up her mirror and tweezers and left the room. And Martha Reganhart was sure that never before had she been so compromised and shat upon; never had she been so soft and expedient and unprincipled. Worst of all, never could it have bothered her less. If she had had the energy to be disgusted with herself, the object of her disgust would have been her inability to *care* any more. For nearly four years now she had been pretending to be two parents, and not half a set. Even the strict observance of national holidays had been a conscious noble decision, something she felt the divorced owed their offspring. Three and a half years ago she had made a whole potful of conscious noble decisions: if Cynthia had long legs, she would have ballet lessons; if she had a good head, she would go to the very best schools; Markie was going to learn to be as crazy over the White Sox as any Chicago kid with a full-time father . . . and so on and so on. Today, however, the whole fatuous lie, all that she had *not* done, screamed at her from every wall, door, and closet. With that granite turkey to roast and cranberries to boil and silverware to polish, she felt as though she had run her course. If she had been allowed one more hour of sleep she could doubtless have faced the next four years with an upper lip as stiff as ever. Now, everything foretold her doom—even the popped seam in her slacks, through which anyone who cared to look could see that Martha Reganhart was wearing no underwear.

But what was she supposed to have done? The dilemma she had had to face at seven A.M., before brushing her teeth or drinking her coffee, was whether or not she would be less of a slob, or more of a hundred-percent-American mother, with no pants under her slacks, or dirty ones—for it turned out there were none clean. She had made her choice in a stupor, and was now suffering dismal emotions as a result. Feeling bedraggled made her feel unworthy, and over her sink she closed her eyes to the near and distant future. She thought it might give her some little solace if she could squeeze her hands around the neck of whoever it was who had raised her rent. But it wasn't a person—it was an agency. There wasn't even anybody to shout at really—they only worked here, lady—when you called up to complain.

Shortly thereafter, her daughter came racing through the front door, impervious to the scab on her right knee that was leaking blood down her shin.

"Mommy! Daddy's picture!"

"Daddy's *what?* Cynthia, look at your *knee—*"

"Daddy's picture. *A painting!*"

"Cynthia, what happened to your knee?"

"Nothing. I slipped. Look!" Cynthia had the paper folded to the art column. She jerked it back and forth in front of Martha's face, but did not relinquish it.

"Calm down," Martha said. "I can't see it if you keep moving it, can I? Go wash your knee. Please—do you want to get an infection and turn blue?"

"Daddy's picture—"

"Go wash your knee!"

Cynthia threw the paper to the floor and, crestfallen, went hobbling off to the bathroom; if the knee was going to use her, she would use the knee. "Christ!" she howled, limping down the hallway. "Christ and Jesus!"

With Cynthia gone, it was easier to take a look; she had not wanted a child around to witness whatever shock there might be. She picked up the paper from the floor and sat down with it at the kitchen table. Her heart slowly resumed its normal beat, though it was true, as Cynthia said, that a painting of her father's was actually printed in the *Times.* She recognized it immediately; only the title had been changed. What had once been "Ripe Wife" was now labeled "Mexico." The bastard. She allowed herself the pleasure of a few spiteful moments. Juvenilia. A steal from de Staël. Punk. Derivative. Corny. Literal. Indulgent. She repeated to herself all the words she would like to repeat to him, but all the incantation served to do was to bring back so vividly all that had been: all the awful quarrels, all the breakfasts he had thrown against the kitchen wall, all the times he had walked out, all the times he had come back, the times he had smacked her, the times he had wept, saying he was really a good and decent man . . . All of it lived at the unanesthetized edge of her memory. *Mexico!* Couldn't he have changed it to Yugoslavia? Bowl of Fruit? Anything but rotten Mexico!

Her eye ran up and down the column; she was unable to read it in any orderly way. It was captioned, *Tenth St. Show Uninspired; Reganhart Exception.*

> . . . except for Richard Reganhart. A resident of Arizona and Mexico, Reganhart, in his four paintings, reveals a talent . . .
>
> . . . manages a rigidity of space, a kind of compulsion to order, that makes one think of a fretful housekeeper . . .
>
> . . . especially "Mexico." The dull gold rectangles are played off against a lust and violence of savage purples, blacks, and scarlets that continually break in through the rigid . . .
>
> . . . will alone emerge of the seven young people

Crap! Fretful housekeeper, *crap!* House*breaker!* Weakling! Selfish! Destroyer of her life! She hated him—she would never forgive him. Someday when it suited her purpose, she would get that son of a bitch. It was nearly three years since he had sent a penny to support their children. Three very long years.

She read the article over again from beginning to end.

When Cynthia came out of the bathroom, a bandage over half her leg, the child asked, "Remember when we were in Mexico?"

"Yes," Martha said.

"Can I remember it?"

"I think you were too small."

"I think I can remember it," Cynthia said. "Wasn't it very warm there?"

"Cyn, you know it's warm there. You learned that in school."

Cynthia reached out and Martha handed her back the paper. "See Daddy's name?" Cynthia asked.

"Uh-huh. I didn't mean to take it away from you, sweetie. I only wanted you to wash your knee—"

"I like that picture, don't you?" Cynthia asked.

"I think it's terrific," Martha said. "I think it's very beautiful."

"Can I cut it out and keep it?"

"Sure."

"Can I hang it up?"

"Absolutely."

"Oh boy! Hey Markie—look what Mommy gave *me!*"

"Oh Cynthia, don't start that, will you? Cynthia—" But the little girl was skipping off toward the living room; she met her brother halfway.

"Look what Mommy gave me. I'm going to hang it up!"

"I want it!" he shouted. "What is it?"

"Daddy's picture. Here. Don't touch. Don't *touch.*"

"I want it. Where—where's Daddy's picture?"

"Here, dope. Can't you see?"

"Cynthia—" Martha said, from the doorway to the living room. "Cynthia . . ." But she found herself unable to attach a command, an instruction, a warning, to her child's name. Cynthia, Cynthia, born of sin.

"Who—?" Markie was asking.

"This—" Cynthia said. "It's Daddy's picture!"

Mark didn't get it; his jaw only hung lower and lower. Would he ever learn to read? Lately she had begun to wonder if he might not be retarded. Should she take him in for tests?

"And it's mine. I'm hanging it over *my bed!*" Cynthia cried.

"My bed—" howled Mark, but his sister had already fled on one bare, one bandaged leg—both willowy, both more perfect every day—carrying her prize to some private corner of the house.

It might have been Christmas, and Sid, Saint Nick. He arrived with bottles of Pouilly Fuissé, Beefeater's, Noilly Prat dry vermouth, and a fifth of Courvoisier. "That's for the kids," he said, placing a row of liquor cartons at Markie's feet. "And now for you," and he unwrapped a doll almost three feet tall and a portable basketball set, both of which he deposited in Martha's arms.

"What's for us?" Cynthia demanded.

The sandpapery voice in which Cynthia had addressed him nearly flattened the man on the spot, but, hanging on courageously to what he had doubtless been planning for the last half hour, he said, "Whiskey."

"It's sour!" Markie cried. "It's beer!"

"Oh Mommy," cried Cynthia, "Mommy we didn't get anything—"

And then, just as Sid's good intentions and his bad judgment threatened to plunge all present into despair, Martha swooped into the center of the room, gathered her children in with the armful of presents, and went spinning around in a circle. "Dummies, dummies, this is for *you!*" Spinning, they fell onto the rug, and the two children came up clutching their rightful gifts to their chests. And Sid was down on the floor with them too, clutching Martha's wrist with his hand—and all the laughter and noise seemed to her only a mockery of a real and natural domesticity. Nevertheless, propelled by a seething desire to make the afternoon work, she kissed the faces of her two children and the brow of her gentleman caller. The skirt of her purple suit—an extravagance of her first winter back in Chicago—was above her knees. Sid Jaffe's weighty brown eyes, those pleading, generous orbs, turned liquidy and hot; he tried to engage her in a significant glance, but she quickly began to explain to Markie the rules of basketball, as she understood them.

There had been a scene with Sid the last time, which neither of them could have forgotten. Martha had rushed away from the sofa, trembling, but acting tough: "Stop persevering, will you! What are you—a schoolboy?" "Just the opposite, Martha!" he had said. "I want to sleep with you!" "I don't care *what* you want—*stop trying to cop feels!*" And he had left, she knew, feeling more abusive than abused, an unfair state to have produced in a man forty-one years old. But then Sid could never think of himself as having been in the right for very long anyway. Forceful as he may have been in court, out of it he defended himself with only the rawness of his needs—he seemed so baldly willing to protect others and not himself. Much as this willingness of his sometimes discomfited her, in the end it was for sexual reasons that Martha had sworn she would let him drift out of her life, just as five or six men had had to drift out previously.

It was almost immediately after Sid had left last time that she had called Gabe Wallach and asked *him*—whom she hardly knew—to join her and hers for Thanksgiving dinner. He was a smoothy, though, and had given some excuse about a party for his father in New York. She, whose parents were of an entirely different chapter of her life, had accepted his refusal graciously, if disbelievingly. Since she suspected Wallach of a kind of polished lechery anyway, she almost felt relieved afterward—she might only have been throwing herself back into the struggle from which she had been trying to extricate herself. Yet she knew that Thanksgiving alone with the kids would be a hollow day. You might as well spend Thanksgiving in China if there wasn't a man around to carve. So some days later she had called Sid's office. And the first thing he said to her was that he was sorry, which only re-enforced a belief she had in her ability to emasculate when she put her mind to it. He said he had missed her; he said he had thought about her; he said he had thought about the kids; he said of course that he would come.

In a way Martha had missed him too, or missed the chance he had given her; she almost regretted now not having submitted to his passion and her own stifled, immeasurable itch. Sid was a vigorous man with a bald head and a broken nose, both of which gave him a kind of athletic, trampled-on good looks. His body was exercised and a little thick, like a weight-lifter's, though he was two inches taller than Martha. He was a little too prissy about not running to seed, but that was a minor quibble and hardly the sort that soured lust. Which was fortunate, for it was lust (plus a natural instinct for sharing pleasure, an inability even to see a movie alone) that she would finally have to rely on with Sid. Well of decency that he was, she did not love him and never could. The affection he did inspire made her feel sorry for him, and sorrow had never for a moment produced a single quiver in her loins. Early in life she had allowed herself the luxury of many men, but she had never been swept backwards into bed out of feelings of pity or pathos. For all her genuine humanity the plight that touched her most was her own. She looked up fiercely and demandingly into men's faces, and some of them—those with more staying power than perception—had circulated stories of nymphomania, when what they had witnessed was only simple selfishness, the grinding out of one's own daily bread.

Sid gazed once again into her eyes; thinking to herself, *why not? what's lost?* she gazed back. Then she saw him soften, saw his eyes saying to her that he demanded no more than he deserved. Ah, he was *too* just, *too* kind. It seemed that almost as great as his desire to sleep with her was his desire to pay her bills and get her a steady maid; something he had once said led her to believe that he had already talked over the possibility with his own cleaning lady.

But despite the feelings which washed over and over her through the afternoon, she carried on with the festivities. After Markie had broken the hoop on the basketball set, and Cynthia had spilled Sid's martini—burrowing into his lap whenever he conversed with her mother—they had their dinner.

Martha Reganhart was sure you could tell something about a man's character from the way he carved a turkey. If he twittered and made excuses and finally hacked the bird to bits, he was Oedipal, wilted under responsibility, and considered himself a kind of aristocrat in the first place—*voilà,* Dick Reganhart. If he made a big production out of it, clanging armor and sharpening knives, performing the ritual and *commenting* on it at the same time, he was either egomaniacal or alcoholic, or in certain spectacular cases—her father's, for instance—both. Of course if the man just answered the need, if he stood up, executed his historical function, and then sat down and ate, chances were he was dutiful, steady, and boring. That was her grandfather, who had had to carve through many bleak Oregon Thanksgivings, after her father had packed his valise, looted the liquor cabinet, and left that eloquent, fateful note: "I am going to California or some God damned place where they make the stuff and you can at least sit in the sun and drink it with nobody looking out for your health." He had bequeathed his office and utensils to his father-in-law, a hard-working railroad engineer, and he had left forever.

Grandpa had filled the gap all right—and so too did Sid Jaffe, who freed both drumsticks from their sockets and laid them, one each, on the children's plates. Martha tried not to take any notice of the sinking in her stomach, which she knew to be a sure signal that self-deception is rampant in the body. She tried to ignore the fact that she had not her grandmother's taste: she tried with all her heart to look over at Sid Jaffe, carving away so efficiently there, and melt with love for him. She imagined all the good it would do them if she could only fall for him. She considered the $54 owed these many months to Marshall Field, and the $300 loan from the co-op; she thought of the $36 bled from her by that thief, Dr. Slimmer. (Those she hated in this world and would never forgive were Dick Reganhart, her father, and Dr. Slimmer, the last for knowing nothing and charging double.) She thought of Sissy and the messy room—she heard Sissy, in fact, singing in the bathtub—and she knew that the only sensible thing was to close her eyes, tip forward, and dive down into an easy love. So she went under three times, but each time came bobbing back up to the surface.

"But what's a lawyer *do?*" Markie was asking. "I don't want to be a lawyer."

"There are laws," Sid was explaining, "like not crossing the street when the light is red. That's a law, right?"

"Of course," Cynthia said.

Mark nodded in agreement. He was hoisting a candied sweet potato to his mouth, not with his fork, but wrapped in the center of his fist. Martha waited for the inevitable to happen: sure as hell he would stick it in his eye. But through luck, or instinct, he managed to locate his lips; he had, however, borne down too heavily on the frail potato, and just as it was to slide safely within, most of it made an appearance along the edges of his fingers. Totally absorbed, and confused, by Sid's explanation—"and the lawyer is the person, Markie, who explains to the judge why he thinks the other person, the person who crossed against the light, say"—floundering in the labyrinths of jurisprudence, Markie cleaned his hand on the front of his white shirt.

"Mark!"

Sid stopped short with his lecture; Markie looked up. "Who?"

"Don't you have a napkin?" Martha asked.

He showed her that he did. Sid said, "Markie, when you want to wipe your hands off, use your napkin."

"It's no use. I think he's part Eskimo," Martha said. "I think he's going to grow up and just head north and find a nice Eskimo girl and the two of them are going to sit around for the rest of their lives asking each other *Who?* and ripping blubber apart with their hands. Markie, my baby-love, pay attention to your food, all right?"

After speaking her last words she saw how she had hurt the feelings of her guest. He was being educational—his way of being fatherly—and she had directed the pupil away from his lessons and back to his plate and napkin. She tried to add some joke, but it was limp, and suddenly she felt unable to bear up much longer under Sid Jaffe's good intentions. Why must he feel obliged to try so hard with her children? It made her angry that, as much as he wanted to visit with her, he seemed to want to visit with Cynthia and Mark.

Sissy now traipsed through in her sheer robe. "Excuse me," she said, leaving water prints across the fringe of the floor. "What do you say, counselor? *Comment ça va?*"

Sid, who still could not understand Sissy's presence in the house, mumbled a greeting. Martha had not told him that her rent had gone up for fear he would volunteer to take the case to the Rent Control Board. She felt pre-defeated in the face of administrative bodies, which seemed to her to work in mad ways of their own; and besides, she owed Sid too much that was not money already. She wanted really to work herself free of this lawyer and of those legal maneuverings which she had once believed might get her more just treatment in the world. At a very early point in her misery she had believed in a kind of parliamentarian approach to confusion; now she understood things better.

"Sissy's feet are wet," Cynthia pointed out. "She's leaving a mess again."

"It's only dew, baby," said Martha. After Sissy had departed, she said, "She's part girl, part stripper—" But Sid was wiping his mouth and saying, "Sometimes I don't understand you, honey."

Cynthia leaned over to whisper into Mark's ear, "He called her honey again."

"Who?"

Since Martha had to be at work by five, they had begun dinner early. Now it was not quite three, but with the meal finished and the dishes stacked, though not washed, it seemed to Martha as though it were time for dusk to settle in. In Oregon at this time —or later, at the real dusk—they would be coming back from their tramp in the woods. She would have pebbles in her Girl Scout shoes, and the dust from the red leaves would have caked around her ankles, to be discovered later when she took off her socks for sleep. Her grandfather would be whistling, her grandmother clearing her throat (forever clearing her throat), and her father would be pinching the behind of her mother—poor baffled beautiful woman—and tripping over every rock on the path. "It's hot *toddy* time!" "Oh Floyd, you've had—" "For God's sake, where's your American spirit, Belle? Your old lady here is a matron of the DAR, and where is your American spirit residing, anyway?" "Why don't you go in and nibble on some turkey; why don't you—" "I'll tell you what I want to nibble on, old sweetheart!" "Floyd, the child—" "Martha Lee, who wants a hot toddy, my baby-love? Who's my baby-love? Who's got a collection of women around him could make a sheik's eyes pop? Is that right, Belle, isn't a sheik one of those fellas with the harems? Baby-love, you're in the sixth grade—haven't they mentioned harems?" It was that Thanksgiving, some long, long-gone holiday, when for the first time she had become dreadfully and unexplainably nervous in his presence.

Mark was taking his nap, Sissy had glided out in flat Capezios and black tights, and Cynthia's voice caroled up from the back yard, where she was jumping rope with Barbara, the janitor's daughter.

Sid kissed her. Following the old saw, she leaned back and tried, at least, to enjoy it. His hands were a great comfort, a regular joy—there was a nice easy stirring in her breasts that moved inward through her, picking up speed and power, until it produced at last a kind of groan in her bones down in the lowest regions of her torso. Then she was off the sofa.

"No," she said.

"Martha," Sid said calmly, "this is getting ridiculous. I'm a grown man, you're a grown woman—"

"It's one of those things that's ridiculous and is going to have to be, Sidney."

Sid swam an hour a day at the Chicago Athletic Club; he had been a Marine Corps officer in two wars; at forty-one he wore the same size belt he had at twenty-one—and now he asked, with a nervous display of bravado, if perhaps it was simply that she found him physically repellent.

"I find you nothing of the sort," she said, touched, but not of course impassioned, by the question. "A lot of traffic has moved across this sofa, Sid. I've been living here going on four years, and a lot of men have come through, you know, on their way home from work. I think there's a bus stops in front of our steps, I don't know. Anyway, if I let everybody's hands go traveling down my blouse, what kind of mother would I be?"

"I'd appreciate it, Martha, if you could just be serious for a minute."

He was dead serious, which caused her to feel all the strain of being a joker. She felt dumb and inconsequential and foolish. Here was a man with a hard-on (and all the seriousness that implied) and she wouldn't give him a straight answer. But there she went *again!* She just couldn't sneak out of things by turning phrases all the time. She addressed herself in a stern voice: *Be serious* . . . But if she were to become serious about old Sidney, she knew—why not face it—that she would marry him. Once they had stripped down together, and she had realized that aside from being a father to her children, he could also give her about as much bedroom excitement as any other girl she knew was getting—once she let him prove this, wouldn't she be a goner? Wed once more for wrong and expedient reasons . . . No, there was only one bag to put your marbles in, one basket for your eggs, and that was love. Nobody was going to marry her again out of necessity; nobody was going to marry her for her breasts, her troubles, or her kids. Nor was she going to miss the mark herself. This time she would do it for love.

At bottom, her demands were no more complicated or original than any other girl's.

Sid walked to where she stood running her hand over the bindings of her small and eclectic collection of paperbacks. He said, "I didn't mean that, Martha," whereupon she thought: *What! What are you apologizing for now!* "I understand," he said. "You're in a tricky position. I'm not trying to make things more difficult for you at all. I care for you so much, Martha. You've got a lot of guts, and you've been remarkable, really, in a very awkward situation. I do appreciate just how complicated it's been for you. But, honey, there's such a simple solution. It doesn't have to go on like this at all. I'm going to get you down on the sofa, and you're going to jump up, and there's such a simple and obvious solution."

"And what's that?"

He took her hand, as was appropriate. "Marry me."

Since her return to Chicago, two other proposals had come Martha's way. One was from Andy Ratten, a Rush Street musician much admired by co-eds and their dates, who pretended to be Paul Hindemith to one set of friends and Dizzy Gillespie to another; when Martha turned him down, he had sent in the mail —the measure of his crew-cutted wit and marijuanaed charm— a Sammy Kaye LP. "Your fate, baby," was all the enclosed card had said. The second proposal had come from Billy Parrino, who at the time was the husband of her best friend. On the playground, while soft-faced, bug-eyed, exhausted Billy was watching his three kids—his wife was home cracking up, a phenomenon only recently completed—and Martha was watching her two, he had come right out with it. "Martha, let's just take off." "I think you have a wife named Beverly." "She's so wacked-up it's driving *me* crazy." "Well, I'd love to, Billy, but the kids—" "We'll take them; we'll take them all, and we'll just go somewhere. Paris." "It all sounds too glamorous—you, me, five kids, Paris." "Oh," wailed Billy, "how this life does stink," and he went home.

So a full-hearted, unqualified, sensible proposal from a man as substantial as Sid Jaffe—which now that it was here melted the cartilage in her knees—was a considerable achievement. Sid made $15,000 a year, was neat and clean, and, God knew, his heart was in the right place. Just three weeks before, they had sat by her TV set, and while poor Adlai Stevenson had conceded defeat in measured eighteenth-century sentences, tears had rolled from Sid's eyes. Sid Jaffe was for all the right things; he was decent and just and kind (she would always have her way; she would be in a marriage, imagine it, where she would always have her way) and he was good to children, if somewhat plodding. And even that was mostly eagerness, and would surely have disappeared by the time of their first anniversary—to be celebrated, no doubt, with ten days in the Bahamas . . .

She had really to search for some switch to throw, something to divert the current that was building up to carry her toward an affirmative reply. "My kids, you know, are little Protestant kids. Markie's circumcision was strictly pragmatic, I don't want you to be tricked by that. He's a slow learner, Sid, and it may take him fifteen years to figure out what a Jew *is.* And Cynthia may turn out to be an anti-Semite; she comes home with something new every day. My grandmother, you know, is a flying buttress still of the DAR—" Yet even as her mouth released all this feeble chatter, she remembered her old grandmother's balanced judgment on the men of Zion: "They're tight-fisted ugly little fellas, Martha Lee, but they're good to their wives and children."

"Martha, you don't have to give me an answer in the next sixty seconds."

When it came to honoring the other person's surface emotions, Sid Jaffe was a very sweet considerate man. "Let me think about it, Sid—all right?"

But he had suggested she wait, apparently not expecting she would choose to; he had to turn away to hide the fact that he was crushed. Suddenly Martha had a vision of Sid proposing to girls ever since high school.

And then he was pressing her to him. She was wearing her one other extravagance, her white silk V-neck blouse, and Sid had buried his head in the V. His mouth sent through her an arc, a spasm of passion, and if Markie had not been sleeping in the other room, if Cynthia's jump-rope song had not ceased, if the phone had not all at once begun to ring, Martha Reganhart might have had a far different future.

"Martha, we can just have the most wonderful—" His mouth went down and down and she closed her eyes.

"Wonderful wonderful—"

"—The phone."

"Let it ring."

But it stopped ringing.

"Mommy! It's Daddy!"

"What!" She was racing for the kitchen—racing away, not toward. "What is it, Cynthia? *What?"*

"It's Daddy from New York! For Mrs. Reganhart! You, Mommy! The operator!"

She took the receiver from Cynthia's hands, wondering—among other things—how long the child had been in the kitchen. Couldn't she even get felt up in private? And now this—Dick Reganhart! From where! "Yes? . . . Operator? This is Martha Reganhart."

"It's not Daddy, however," said the voice at the other end.

She sank down in a chair. "Oh, for Christ's sake."

"Shall I hang up?"

"Certainly not—my child's drunk on Mott's apple juice. How are you?"

"Fine."

"Where are you?"

"Daddyland," Gabe Wallach answered. "New York."

"Oh do excuse her. She gets overexcited when she's not in school. I think she's reacting to the company." She lowered her voice, for she saw the company pacing back and forth in the living room. Was he trying to overhear, or was he walking off lust? How unnatural everything was.

Gabe Wallach asked, "Who's there?" He sounded a little demanding, but Thanksgiving was doubtless a strain on everybody.

"An old friend," Martha said. "He stimulates the children."

"And you?"

More demanding yet. She would have been annoyed were it not as though some hand had reached down to pull her out of the fire. "No, no. No—that's true. Listen, I'm sounding tragic. How's your father's party? Is there really a father and a party, or is some tootsie nestled beside you in her underwear?"

"I call in the absence of the latter."

"It's very sweet of you to call. Happy Thanksgiving."

"I'm having a nice unhappy one."

"Mommy!" Cynthia said. "I want to talk to him—I want to—"

"Just a minute, will you?" Martha said into the phone. Then, away from it, "Cynthia, it is not Daddy!"

"It is!"

"It is not! I'm telling you the truth, Cynthia. Go talk to Sid, he's all alone. Cynthia!" The child was threatening to throw a lollipop at her. "Cynthia!"

In tears, the little girl went toward the room where Markie was napping.

"I'm back," Martha said.

"Good," Wallach said.

Good for what? What kind of weak-kneed out was she going to make this into? Surely she couldn't reject a man who had been so good to her through all these rotten years for another with whom she'd eaten one lousy dinner two weeks before? What right had she to use this flukey phone call against Sid—in fact, to use Sid?

She could tell instantly from the voice on the other end that she had hurt the feelings of still another gentleman. "I just wanted to say Merry Thanksgiving to you."

"Thank you . . ." Then she realized that he was about to hang up. "Shall I go ahead," she asked, "and invite you to another meal? Will you eat leftovers when you come back?"

"I'll be back Monday."

"Come then," Martha Reganhart said, "for dinner."

"Yes, I will . . . Who's Sid?"

"He's a man who just asked me to marry him."

"I see."

"You'll come Monday night."

"As long as you're still single," he answered, "I suppose so."

"Single as ever," she said.

"Does that upset you?" Wallach asked.

"Specifically, no; generally, I'm not sure. This is some long-distance conversation."

"Long distance should be outlawed anyway," he said. "Were you expecting a phone call from your husband?"

"My *ex*-husband—from whom I have no expectations whatsoever." A cry went up from Markie's room. "Oh God, my son just hit my daughter with a chair or something. Give my love to the girl in her underwear."

"You give my love to Sidney."

She felt, when he said that, all the strangeness of their conversation; she wouldn't have minded being angry with him. "We can't possibly be jealous over anything," she said, "so we shouldn't really play at it. Should we?"

"I'm a little deranged today, Martha. I'm wondering," he said, in a very forlorn voice, "if we'll ever manage to level with one another."

And then she wanted really *only* to be level—she wanted to be serious, to be normal; she wanted to be soft and feminine; she wanted a love affair that was no jokes, just intensity; and because the man on the other end was practically a stranger, she led herself into thinking that he could service her in just that way. She wanted to be out of what she was inextricably a part of—her own life. "You come Monday, Gabe. I'll be single. They shouldn't outlaw long distance," she said, holding the phone very close to her. "I feel you've saved my life."

And on the other end he was saying, "There is a father and a party, you know. And I look forward to seeing you."

And she was explaining, "Sid is Sid Jaffe—he was my lawyer. He got me my divorce half-price, and I'm very indebted to him, Gabe, and the children are crazy about him, as crazy as they can be about anybody, anyway. And I have to stop talking on your money. Forgive me, please." She hung up, thinking herself her own woman.

But while she changed into her waitress uniform, she heard laughing and chatter from the kitchen. The uproar in the kids' room had been a false alarm, and Markie had gone back to sleep; the two people having such a good time were her daughter and her lawyer. When she emerged in her starchy blue waitress uniform—her Renoir proportions having taken on the angles of a coffin—she saw that Sid had his sleeves rolled up and was washing the dishes. And Cynthia—complainer, beggar, favor-monger, liar, fatherless baby—Cynthia wiped, and wore upon her face the very sweetest of smiles.

Martha leaned against the door to her bedroom and let the tears come.

"My father painted a picture of me that was in the paper," Cynthia was saying.

"Did he?" Sid asked.

"We used to live in Mexico and he drew it down there. It's very hot down there, even in the winters."

"Can I see the picture? Did he make you as pretty as you are? Did he get those blue eyes in it?"

Cynthia, after a quick look around the kitchen, said, "Well, it's not exactly me. It's really all of us in Mexico."

"Martha too, you mean?"

"Everything. All of us."

"I certainly would like to see it," Sid said.

"Would you?"

"Sure, why not?"

"Just a minute!" She dropped her dishtowel where she stood, and took off for the bedroom, which was beside her mother's. "Hi, Mommy!" she said, and skipped into her own room. Instantly, all hell broke loose.

"Christ, Markie," roared Cynthia, "what's the matter with you? Are you nuts?"

"Whaaa? Whooo? Mommy!"

"Mark*ie,*" Cynthia howled. She rushed back into the hall and began to stamp her feet. "That damn kid," she told her mother, "was sleeping with my picture! He wrinkled my whole picture!"

"It's not just your picture, sweetheart," Martha began.

"If he wants a paper," Cynthia shouted, "let him *buy* one!"

At this point the childless couple who lived above them began to hammer on the floor.

"Oh—" Martha cried, grabbing her hair. "What the fuck do they expect! *It's a holiday!*"

She screamed her words in Sid's direction, as though she

wanted to frighten him; he paled, and dove back into the dishes. While she calmed herself and calmed the children, he finished the silverware—and then, in plain sight of her, he reached up into a cabinet and took down the Bon Ami. Oh the Bon Ami—the Bon Ami was just too much. What right had he to twist her arm so? What right had he to be so perfect? She would have sold her soul to the devil, were he able to make her love the man who stood in an apron in her kitchen, shaking the beautiful white cleanser down into the dirty sink.

It is difficult to be casual about the power of Thanksgiving; it produces expectations, and starts ordering around our emotions, and, above all, it takes unfair advantage of our memories. Though Martha Reganhart did not consider herself particularly reverent about celebrations, she nevertheless could not become accustomed to having to earn a living on Thanksgiving Day by waiting on tables. She could work without too much pain on Sundays, Labor Day, Memorial Day, and even the days of Christ's birth, crucifixion, and ascension; but that she had to spend eight hours on the next-to-last Thursday in November taking orders for fried jumbo shrimp was proof that her life had not turned out as she had hoped. She attempted to pay no attention to the direction in which they were headed. Instead of proceeding directly to the Hawaiian House, she suggested they stop first at the playground and let the kids run around.

Mark and Cynthia—and here was one of the mysteries that held their mother's world together—were strolling twenty feet in front, holding hands. Mark was wearing long pants and his blue coat, and Cynthia her red jacket with the hood; above them the sun was a dull light behind the clouds. Cynthia was helping Markie across the street and seeing to it that he did not toss his cap up into the branches of the bare trees. For twenty minutes she had been as well-behaved a child as one could ask for; outside the apartment building she had taken her brother aside and silently buttoned his fly.

"It comes over her," Martha said, "every once in a while. I think she's going to take flight and join God's angels. Maybe it's fresh air that does it."

"She's going to be a knockout," Sid said. "She has those blue eyes, and then she *rolls* them . . ."

"She's a sweet child," Martha said. "She's just a little frantic."

"She'll be all right. They're perfectly decent, lively, charming kids," Sid told her. "Stop worrying."

They were inspiring words, upon which she was willing to lean. Sid himself was looking like something to lean upon—husky in his raglan coat, jaunty in his tweed hat with the green feather. She would have kissed him for his dependability, except that she was supposed to be deciding, even while they walked, whether to marry him for it; she had thought she had already made up her mind, but it appeared—to her own surprise—that she hadn't.

"It looks," Sid said, "as though Dick is coming up in the world." It looked, too, as though he were changing the subject, though he wasn't.

"Yes, doesn't it?" She took his arm as they crossed the street. Memory carried her all the way back to Oregon. "It's a lovely time of day," she said.

"What do you think he's going to do? Will he start sending money?"

She breathed in a good supply of the autumn air. "I don't think he could have made an awful lot from four or five pictures."

"I don't think that's our business. How much is he behind?"

She shrugged.

"Martha, I've asked you to simply keep a record—"

"He's probably going back to Arizona. He's probably as broke as ever."

"Then maybe he ought to stay in New York and get a job."

All she wanted to do now was to point out a house that reminded her of her family's big frame house back in Oregon; she did not care to dilute the day's pleasure any further with talk of her former husband. In 1953, when he had disappeared into the canyons of the Southwest, she had given up on chasing after him for the support payments. It was not only because she could not find him that she chose not to have any papers served. Dick's running off had told her what she had always wanted to know: paying all the bills, every nickel, dime, and quarter, had permitted her to stop condemning herself. She was not mean, bitchy, immoral, selfish, stupid, and dishonest—all the words he had hurled at her when she had fled finally from Mexico with the children; it could not be she who was the betrayer of their children—not so long as she was as harried and unhappy as she was.

Martha said, "He has a job. He's a painter."

"I meant a real job, to meet his obligations."

All she knew about painting was what Dick had taught her; still, it was no pleasure to see the philistine in Sid oozing out. "It's not important," she said. "Please."

"Well, I'll tell you, that painting looked like hell to me, I'll tell you that."

"In black and white it's hard to know."

"Oh yes? Did you like it? Would you like to tell me what it was supposed to be?"

". . . Cynthia had it—it's all of us in Mexico, I suppose. Look, it's a kind of painting I guess you're not in sympathy with. You've got to see a lot of it"—and the voice she heard was not her own, but her ex-instructor's—"before you start to get it."

"What am I supposed to *get?* That's what I'd like to find out."

"Oh Sid, are you asking me to defend that whole God damn bunch of phonies? The guy doesn't have any money—what am I supposed to do, bleed him? He's a pathetic neurotic whom we should really all pity, except that he happens to be a son of a bitch. Sid, he couldn't *get* a regular job. If he worked in a factory or had to pump gas, well, he just couldn't. He's a painter—that's actually what he is, for some unfathomable reason, and there's nothing we can do to make him not one. So let's forget it for today, please."

"What are you so pigheaded for, Martha?"

"I'm not pigheaded. I don't need him." Sharply she added, "They're my children."

But Sid went right on, not figuring her anger to be directed in any way at him. "He's having a success, right? He's obviously made a little money, isn't that so? Then now is the time to open up correspondence. Honestly, honey, now is the time to slap him in court—"

"Why don't we wait? Why don't we just wait and see what he

does, all right?" But when she squeezed his hand, it made it even more obvious that she had trampled once again on his concern for her. "Sid, I appreciate everything you've done—"

He stopped her. "Do you?"

There was no further conversation until they reached the playground, where Stephanie Parrino and her two little brothers were playing on the seesaw while their grandmother, Mrs. Baker, watched over them.

"My father sent me a picture," Cynthia told Stephanie's grandmother, and then went off with Mark to the swings.

Stephanie's grandmother had once been the mother-in-law of Billy Parrino, the man who had sat in this very playground and asked Martha to run off to Paris with five children and himself. Billy had finally divorced Bev, and Bev had tried to drown herself in the toilet. She was now on the ninth floor of Billings receiving shock treatments, though all discussion of her condition was carried on as though she were down with a bad cold.

"How is she feeling?" Martha asked.

"Oh not perfect yet, of course, but coming right along," said Mrs. Baker.

"That's fine."

"She's responding beautifully," Mrs. Baker said, and they all looked off at the children, rising on swings into the gray rough sky, a sky aching to plunge them directly from November to January. On the apartment-house wall directly behind them, some waggish University student had scrawled:

John Keats

½ loves

Easeful Death

The words were enclosed in a heart. It did not strike her (as it might have on a day when there was a little more sun in the sky) as witty at all. Keats had been dropped into his grave at the age of twenty-six. Thinking of the death of Keats, she thought of her own: for three years she had been meaning to scrape together enough to take out $10,000 worth of insurance on her life . . . She suddenly plunged headlong into gloom. Twenty-six.

Mrs. Baker, meanwhile, was saying that every day another kind mother invited Bev's children for lunch. A friend of Mrs. Baker's had sent a basket of fruit from Florida directly to the hospital, and though Bev wasn't quite up to peeling things yet, her mother had brought the oranges home and marked them with nail polish and put them in the refrigerator so Bev could have them when she got out. Tomorrow, Mrs. Baker said, she was taking all the youngsters bright and early down to see Don McNeill's "Breakfast Club."

Martha reached out for Sid's hand. She sat stone still, wondering how much worse off Bev Parrino would be if some doctor up in Billings shot too much juice through her one day and sent her from this impossible life. As they left the little park, silent but for the creaking of the swings, she managed to put down a strange noise that wanted to make itself heard in her throat. Then Markie began to cry that all he had done was push.

Her watch showed twenty-five minutes of holiday remaining; she tried to think of what they could do until five. The kids were moving—had moved—into their late-afternoon crabbiness, and Sid, she knew, was still waiting for her reply to his proposal. Patient, ever-ready, faithful, waiting. Only ten minutes had elapsed since he had thrown his most solid punch of the day. Do you? Do you appreciate me, Martha, your situation—do you see what I can do for you . . . ? And yes, she saw—she had reached out for his hand, and he had been there to give it to her, even if he did not understand for a moment the panic she had found herself enclosed in.

"I didn't swing! I always push!" Mark was crying. "I want something!"

"You'll swing next time, Markie—"

"I want a Coca-Cola! I want to go to Hildreth's! I want—"

For reasons of her own Martha did not want to go to Hildreth's; but she could not go back to the playground either, to confront Mrs. Baker's stiff inhuman smile and consider further Beverly Parrino's condition. So she stood in the middle of Fifty-seventh

Street, while Markie screamed and Cynthia joined in with him, and she might have stood there for the full twenty-five minutes she had coming to her had not Sid taken her hand once again and led the three of them to Hildreth's for a Coke. And fortunately the place was empty; all the students had gone home for the holiday, and the hangers-on—the strays, the outcasts, all the purposeless people she had come to know during the last few years, who could only have put the final depressing touch to her afternoon—were either sleeping or hiding, or, in private and questionable ways, paying homage somewhere to the day.

The four of them sat at one of the booths along the window, Martha and Sid drinking coffee, and the children over their Cokes, stifling and giving in to gaseous burpings. Behind the lunch counter the Negro girl who ladled out the food was preparing an elaborate turkey sandwich for herself; inside the store dreamy dance music came from a radio, and outside, a pleasant, gray, Sunday deadness hung over the street. Everything combined to lull Martha backward—the music, the coffee, the plasticized smell of the booth itself, and of course the street. Aside from Pacific Avenue in Salem, where she had been born and raised, Chicago's Fifty-seventh Street was the thoroughfare of her life. Looking at it, blowy and deserted, touched now by dusk, was like seeing the set of a familiar play without seeing the performers or hearing the lines. But in the dark theater of memory all the old scenes could easily be recollected, all the old heroes and heroines. She could remember this one long store-lined, tree-lined, University-lined street, and so very many Marthas. There, plain as day, was Martha Lee Kraft, buying her Modern Library books in Woodworth's. And there was Martha Kraft taking the I.C. train to the Loop, and having absolutely the most perfect and adult day in Carson's—a solid hour trying on dark cloche hats, and narrowing her eyes at herself in the mirror when the saleslady wasn't around. And there was Martha Kraft, saying to herself, *Why can't I do anything?* and taking her first lover. And Martha Kraft carrying a placard: VOTE FOR HENRY WALLACE. It weaved above her head as she marched clear from Cottage to the Lake, and beside her, carrying his own sign—who was that anyway? Who was that sweet boy with the social consciousness and practically no hips at all? What was his name, the one into whose basement room she moved her guitar and her Greek sandals and her brilliant full skirts and her uncombed extravagant hair? And there was Martha being wooed and won, right in Hildreth's. Richard M. Reganhart of Cleveland, blue-eyed, dark-haired, fierce, wild, a painter, an ex-G.I.—he had not even to cajole her . . . And there was one morning when Martha was sitting in a booth opposite him, the two of them eating that skimpy, sufficient lover's breakfast of juice and coffee and jelly doughnuts, one morning when at the tip of Martha's uterus Cynthia Reganhart was the size of a pinhead, when Cynthia (who is presently dredging at the bottom of her glass through a straw) was hardly bigger than nothing at all.

But—all those prayers and tears to the contrary—she was not nothing at all, and everything that had then to begin, began, and everything that had to end, ended. For five months Fifty-seventh Street was hardly seen, it was only walked upon, blindly; and then there was sunny Mexico, and Dick Reganhart was ripping the shirt off his own back—his fried eggs, lately heaved against the white stucco wall, sliding relentlessly toward the floor.

"I didn't marry you, you gutless bitch—*you* married *me!*"

"I thought you *loved* me—"

"You thought! You were hot, baby, and you itched for it and you got it! *And you made me marry you,* don't you forget that, *ever!* Four years in the Army, four years—and now *this!* I'm in prison! I can't paint! I have nightmares—"

"Then why can't you just *love* me—"

"You are a sly bitch, Martha Lee. You don't love me—you *know* you don't! Oh someday I'll find your ass down in Our Holy Mother of Guadalupe and you'll be crying out to Jesus for help —why did you get such a sonofabitching husband, why-yyy are you afflicted with such a sinful man! Well, you tell Our Holy Mother, the only sin, you conniving bitch, is this fucking prison of a marriage! Why don't you *listen* to me! *Leave that God damn egg alone!*"

"You miserable coward—don't tell me what to do! Everybody in the *world* loves each other! Every rotten secretary loves her boss! Guys fell off our front porch just from loving me, you bastard—*what's the matter with you!*"

"Let's keep it straight, America's Sweetheart—you used my cock! That's the why and wherefore, Martha—"

"Shut up! We have a baby, you filthy beast!"

"I told you, didn't I? I said get a God damn abortion—"

"I'd like to cut your tongue out, you mean pricky bastard! I'll ruin your life like you've ruined—"

"You *hooked* me is what happened, Martha—you hooked me and now you ought to be happy, you selfish, stupid—"

The train moved north, taking almost two whole days to get through Texas, five impossible meals in the State of Texas and innumerable voyages down the car to the toilet; tiny Mark cried and little Cynthia gloomed out at the never-ending brush, and then there was Oklahoma City, there was St. Louis and then Peoria, and now we are back in Chicago, we are back on Fifty-seventh Street, we are in Hildreth's once again, perhaps in that same historic booth. Dick Reganhart is destined to make a fortune painting rectangles, for he is a child of our times, but for Martha Reganhart life is a circle. And if it ends where it begins, where is that? What's next? Where was she going? This was not what she had envisioned for herself while she tweaked her brand-new little nipples and stared up at the ceiling on those rainy, windy, winter nights in Salem, Oregon.

"Blair!" Cynthia screamed. "Hi!"

"My ofay baby! Honey chile! Cynthiapia!"

Cynthia dissolved, not entirely spontaneously, into laughter, and Mark, always a willing victim, doubled up in ecstasy, and hit his head on the table top.

Blair reached into the booth and plucked Markie out of his seat. "Hey, Daddy," he said, jiggling Markie in the air, "you will have dehydration of the ductual glands which corroborate the factation of the tears. Is this the reactionary reaction cogetary to the stimuli, or is you pulling our leg?"

Mark squelched his tears instantly and stared into the mysterious continent of Blair's skin; the man was brown and rangy and undernourished, with Caucasian lips and nose, dark glasses, and a manic potential that could turn Martha's mouth dry. Cynthia went flying out of her seat toward the visitor, and her Coke wobbled across the table; her mother, years of practice behind her, caught it just before it tipped over into Sid's lap. She looked at her companion and found him trying to throw a smile into this big pot of merriment. But then she heard him groan when Blair slid into the seat opposite them, a child in each of his arms.

"Where's your friend?" Martha asked, conversationally.

"She's buying her mayonnaise."

Several seconds passed before either man publicly acknowledged the presence of the other; then Blair peered over the top rim of his sunglasses. "How's the crime business, Your Honor? What's swinging in the underworld?"

"How are you?" Sid asked.

"Oh me, I'm toeing the ethical norm."

"That's fine."

"Man, I make *nothin'* but the super-ego scene."

Mark found the remark very funny; Cynthia curled up in Blair's arms. Sid sat upright in his chair. There was no question about his being a hundred times the man Blair Stott was, and yet Martha discovered she could not stand him at that moment for being so proper and protective; it seemed a crushing limitation on her life.

Partly out of pique with Sid, she cued Blair. "And how's the hipster movement in North America? What's new?" The children looked at her with wide eyes—she was drawing out the funny man for their enjoyment.

"Well, Mrs. Reganhart," said Blair, whose father was a highway commissioner in Pennsylvania, whose mother was a big shot in the NAACP, and whose masks were two: Alabama Nigger and Uppity Nigger, "well, to tell you the facts, we is all of us taking a deserved rest, for we expended a prodigious, a fantastic, a burdensomely amount of laboriousness and energy, as you might have been reading in the various organs, in placing in the White House that Supreme Hipster of them all, the Grand Potentate and Paragon of What Have You, the good general, D.D.E. It was a uphill battle and a mighty venture, and mightily did we deliver unto it. We are pushing presently for a hipster for Secretary of the State, and, of course, for Secretary of the Bread. What we are anxious to see primarily is one of our lads' names on all them dollar bills. You know, this here bill is legal tender, signed,

Baudelaire. Of course, in our moment of spiritual need and necessitation—which we is regularly having biweekly, you know —we are also turning our fond and prodigious efforts and attentions to the Holy Roman Church, and praying on our bended knees, with much whooping and wailing, that it is from amongst our ranks that the next Pontiff-to-be will be selectified. As may be within the ken of your knowledge, sugar, up till the present hour there has been an unquestioning dearth of hipster Popes—one must go a considerable way back down the road to find hisself one. Like since Peter, *nothin'*. The Pope we got now, the thin fella with the glasses—now in my opinion this is a very square Pope, though on the other hand I learn from our sources in Vatican that this same cat was very hip as a cardinal. What we is looking for with fervor and prodigiosity, not to mention piety and love, is someone we can call 'Daddy' and look up to. How many years has it been now since Rutherford B. Hayes?"

"Coolidge," Martha suggested, fearing for the dryness of her children's underwear; both of them were slithering about in fits of laughter.

"Hip, my dear blond bombshell, but no hipster. Markie, do you agree here with the predilections of my predigitation, or what? You sit so silent, man"—Mark was nearly on the floor—"have you no thriving interest in the life political and the heavenly bodies, or is you numb, Dad, with Coca-Colorama?"

"Coke!" Mark erupted, as Sissy made her entrance, swinging within her clinging black tights her healthy behind, and unscrewing the cap on a jar of Hellmann's mayonnaise. She sat down at the booth and offered the jar around; then she dug in while Mark, awe-struck, watched every trip the spoon made from the jar to her mouth. For Martha, his absorption opened up a whole new world of agonies. Sid looked at her. Pleadingly he said, "It's getting late."

She heard herself answer, "It's only five to."

And Cynthia was shouting, "Blair! Blair!"

Oh father-starved child, modulate your voice! But Martha said not a word. Let them enjoy every last Thanksgiving minute.

"Blair! Tell an Army story!"

"A story!" Mark joined in.

"Well, there I was—" Blair said, and the children hushed. "Up to here—no, higher—with dirty dishes and pots and pans laden and encrustated with an umbilicus of grease and various and sundry remnants and remains. I'm speaking of garbage, Markie —do you get the picture?"

"Picture."

"All right, you got it. I don't want no faking now. All right, up to here in muck. It was my duty, you understand, not only to native land, but to the ethical norm and the powers that am and was, to alleviate these crockeries of the burdensome load under which they was yoked by virtue of this delirious scum and dirt which so hid their splendor. Well, cheerily then, I am approaching the task when, coming from another part of the edifice, I smell upon my nostrils' entrance there, some sort of conflagration, and I think unto myself, I think: Slime, Scum, Private Lowlife, where there is conflagration there is smoke. Erstwhile, says I, this here mess hall is perhaps out to be victimized by the dreadness of fire. *Alors!* I am alarmed when into my area I behold a white-glove inspection is moving itself. Great Scott, says I to myself in my characteristic manner, it is a full colonel, a veritable bastion of democracy, and he is headed my way, seeking out signs of filth and dirt and thereby disrespectability and so forth. He is followed up upon, lapped up after, in a manner of speaking, by two captains and a major, and several noncommissioned bastions, patriotic and knowledgeable men one and all. Well, I snap to, heave forth, I take the extreme attitude of attention, sucking in even on my hair, while I continue preparing my hot sudsy water —and yet, in the meantime, this distinct aroma of a conflagration is sweeping up into my olfactory system and presenting to me the idea that we is all in a pericolous state of danger. This idea mushrooms in my head, and at last—for I am myself a kind of bastion of our way of life; I always eat Dolly Madison ice cream whenever there is the choice—and so I say, 'Your Colonelhood, pardon my humble ass—' "

"Blair!" Sissy said.

" 'Pardon my humble bones, suh, my low condition, my dribbilafaction—' you seem puzzled, Cynthia honey—you ain't heard of that?"

"Yes. Oh yes."

" 'Well, pardon all that then, Colonel, my de facto status and all, but I smell—' But I am cut off in the prime of life—from my larynx and general voice box region my warning is untimely ripped—and all the bastions is shouting at me at once and in unison. What we call A Capella. 'Shut your bones, man. Do not address till you is yourself addressed, sealed, and dropped down the slot there.' Me, I suspect them of high wisdom right off, so I sluk off, and cleave unto myself, and oh yes rightly so, for his name's sake. And they too, in a huff, dealt me a parting glance not deficient in informing me of just who I was and why and what for, yes sir, and they were off to the sagitary, a very snappy group could make your eyes water just the sparkle alone. I was left alone—hang on now, Markie, we is edging up on the end—and all alone it was I who had the glorious and untrammeled experience, the delirious and delectafacatory happiness, the supreme and pleasurable moment—I had for myself, young 'uns, a little life-arama and the last laugh, when that there edifice, all that government wood, and all them government nails and shingles, all them dishes and greasy-faced pots and pans, the whole works, my children, came burning right on down and into the good earth. Thanks go to the Wise Old Lord, too, for I fortunately escaped with my life, and I stood out there on that little ol' company street, and I watched that there mess hall expire and groan and puff itself right out. It burned right on down to the ground, children, and into it, amen."

"What did?" Cynthia asked.

"Who?"

"The edifice. Don't you listen when I'm talking here?"

It had been a long tiring day, and Cynthia's bafflement brought her right to the edge of tears, with Mark only a step behind.

"It's a *joke,* sweethearts!" Martha cried. "A funny story!" And the little girl and her brother, relieved of their confusion, were swept away on waves of laughter, far away from the cares and conditions of their lives.

Necessity aside, it took an effort of the will for Martha to leave Hildreth's. She was having a good time; she was liking Blair Stott; by extension, she was even liking Sissy. She remembered now how much she had liked her on that quiet afternoon she had come to look at the room—carefree and silly and, for all her experience, innocent. Now, both Blair and Sissy seemed to her very happy people. From the doorway, Martha turned back to them and waved a fluttery and uncharacteristic farewell. Sissy threw a kiss and Blair called after her, "*Au revoir,* blondie."

Outside Sid was already at the curb, crossing the children. He had warned and warned her about being late, until finally he had stopped whispering his warnings and gotten up and gone ahead. She watched him now as he looked both ways up the street. She started to follow him, but she couldn't. At first it was only that she wanted to turn back into Hildreth's and have one last cup of coffee. But then she wanted more; she wanted him to take her children, not just across the street, but as far as he liked. She wanted all three of them to continue walking, right out of her life. She wanted to be as mindless as a high school sophomore. She wanted to be taken on a date in somebody's father's car. What she wanted were all those years back. She had never had the simple pleasure of being able to think of herself as a girl in her twenties. One day she had been nineteen; tomorrow she would be thirty. For a moment, she wanted time to stop. *I want to paint my toenails and worry about my hair. I want—*

She looked back over her shoulder into Hildreth's window and saw Sissy eating her mayonnaise. Suddenly it was as though her old Fifty-seventh Street had been pulled from beneath her: she was floating, nothing above or below. All her life seemed an emptiness, a loss.

At the door to the Hawaiian House, Sid stood holding Markie's hand. Cynthia was asking him, "Were you in the Army?"

"The Marines," he told her.

"Were you in a war?"

"Two." And he looked at Martha with his most open appeal of the day: *Two. All those years. I have no wife, no child. Don't deny me.*

"Tell us a story," Mark said.

"Children," Martha said, "Sid has to go home. He has some work to do."

"That's okay." His annoyance with her had disappeared. He

spoke softly, setting the scene. It was here and now that she was supposed to say *yes,* kiss him, fall into his arms. He stood waiting in his big raglan coat, a solid and decent man. "I'll stay with them," he said.

"They can stay alone. It's all right, really."

"I don't mind," he said.

"As long as I'm in by one, Cynthia likes to stay alone." She touched her first baby's cheek. "Don't you, lovey? She's the best baby-sitter in Chicago. Barbie's mother looks in every hour or so."

"I can dial the police," Cynthia said, "the fire, the ambulance, Doctor Slimmer, I can dial Mother, I can dial Aunt Bev, I can find out the weather, the time—"

Martha bent down to kiss the children good night; it was four minutes after five. Kissing Cynthia, she said, "You're a very good brave girl. But, baby-love, *don't* call the weather any more, will you? It's tragically expensive. If you want to know how it is just look out the window. Good night, Markie. Are you happy, honey-bunch?"

"Uh-huh," he said, yawning.

"Good night, Sid. Thank you for a merry Thanksgiving."

"Martha, if you want me to sit with them—"

"You have work to do."

"I can work at your place, honey."

Cynthia looked at Markie: *honey.* Martha put her cheek to Sid's and, for a second, kept it there.

"Martha—" he began. However, she chose to misunderstand him; no, no, they could stay alone; it was good for them, it developed character; it destroyed silly fears. But, Cynthia, don't forget, you don't open the door for anybody. Then, feeling no compulsion to say any more, she left the three of them—it was dusk —and went into the Hawaiian House to feed a bunch of strangers their Thanksgiving dinner.

Cynthia's New Life

That morning, when Cynthia rolled over, she found that her brother had climbed the ladder of the double-decker bed and crawled into the upper bunk beside her. Barely awake, she felt she must be floating in the hollow of a bad bad dream, and suddenly, furious, confused, she pushed with violence at the sleeping little boy. He rolled only once and fell from the bed. There was the thud of his head against the wooden floor, then no further sound. It appeared that Markie was going to sleep right through it; he did not even cry.

But when Cynthia leaned out over the top bunk, she noticed something more. At first it seemed to be a red string wedged in the crack between the floor boards—only it was moving toward the wall. Trembling, she waited for her father or June to come through the door and see what she had done. When time passed and no one had entered, she thought she had just better try to fall back to sleep again. And then it became clear to her that it could not be a bad dream she was having, for if it were, she would be trying to wake herself up rather than fall asleep. She rolled toward the wall anyway and closed her eyes. It was then that she began to scream.

Letting Go, from Part Five ("Children and Men"). Cynthia is now eight and Mark is five, and they have recently left Chicago to live with their father and his new wife in the East. Their mother has let them go, hoping a new life will be better for all, and knowing just what an illusion a new life can be.

Later in the morning her father telephoned from Southampton Hospital. Cynthia sat in the sunny living room turning the pages of a large picture book of statues, while in the hallway June whispered into the mouthpiece. Her stepmother hung up the phone and came in to tell her to put on her bathing suit. They would go to the beach; was that all right? The child turned another page, and then June was kneeling down and holding Cynthia to her. She allowed herself to be held. Her stepmother's hair, a sunnier shade than her real mother's hair, was swept up at the back of her head; Cynthia could imagine the way it looked from the way it felt against her cheek. Soft, fine, whirled up—Markie said it was candy. She could see her brother stiffen with pleasure when he drew in his breath and lowered his face right down into the swell of June's hair. June was very thin, and when she wore a bathing suit or a summer dress, all silky and flower-smelling, Cynthia could see that she had no breasts; there was just skin over bone, like a man. All a child could really push his face into was her hair; and though Markie might amuse himself in this way, Cynthia did not think that it was suitable for her. Not that June had ever favored Markie; it was only that her hair had somehow seemed his property from the start. Certainly June had never scolded her when she spilled her milk—and she had spilled it often during the first month she had come to live in New York City. Nor had June ever once been as cross as her real mother had been to her so many times. Even now June's first impulse was not to blame Cynthia for what had happened, which was surely what her old mother would have done. No one, in fact, had had a chance to ask questions or make accusations. Only minutes after she had begun screaming, her father had carried Markie down to the car wrapped in a big towel, and driven him away in the station wagon. Though it had looked comical for a grownup to be backing a car out of a driveway wearing pajamas and a bathrobe, she had managed not to laugh. When the car swerved down into the road, there had been a flash of blood on the front side door, and then any hint of a smile had vanished completely from her face. She had walked back to the house, taken a sculpture book she liked from the shelf, and settled into a chair by the window; she pretended to be absorbed in the book, while above all she was absorbing herself in being quiet. A blind person could not have heard her turn the pages, and her respiration was as silent as the shifting of the tides of her blood—a shifting that seemed to be taking place in the hollow of her throat.

The house was quieter than it had ever been during the daytime. No child was scooting up the stairs, no friend was slamming through the front screen door, no one was arguing with anyone —and that *was* a change. Lately her father and June seemed always to be bickering at one another at breakfast time. Ever since they had come out to Springs, there was something that June kept saying to her father in the mornings that made him angry. One morning he had become so angry that he had picked up his plate and thrown it clear across the breakfast nook to the kitchen. Markie had begun to giggle and point to where the yolk was slipping down the wallpaper onto the enamel of the sink, but she knew enough to keep her eyes on her bowl and continue spooning cereal into her dry mouth. Only June had gotten up to leave the table.

And yet that evening, when the two of them were sitting out in the white garden chairs after dinner, she had seen her father lean over and kiss June's hands and then her hair and her neck —all while Mark went circling around the house on his tricycle, pretending to be a fire engine, until it was time for him to go to bed. Earlier in the summer there had been an evening when she had been asked to go into the house for some ice from the refrigerator; when she had come onto the back steps holding the cold tray, she had seen her father open a button of June's blouse and put a hand to where her breasts should have been. June was thin, but beautiful too, and she had those perfect white teeth that Cynthia saw at that moment, as her stepmother's head went back and her father pulled her to him with his other hand. When her father hugged and kissed June, she knew it was because June was beautiful, and had been a debutante, and was rich, and had gone to Bryn Mawr College. She would be going there too now that she was rich; Martha had not gone there because she had not been rich at all. Markie was to go to Harvard College, June said, which seemed to Cynthia a ridiculous statement—Markie could not read yet, or even count successfully beyond twelve. But June and her father said ridiculous things quite often, her father particularly. In Springs he was thought of as a very funny man, though everyone agreed that Cynthia was his toughest audience. "Come on, Ed Sullivan," he would finally have to say to her, "how about just a giggle, just a little snort—just raise a *lip* even—" Whenever there were people around he would amuse them, unless, of course, he was unhappy, as he had been when June had made him throw his egg.

At night June and her father slept together in their own room in only one bed. Consequently, she knew that June would be having a baby soon. No one had spoken about it yet, but she was aware that there were happenings of which she was not warned in advance. She had figured out that the baby was coming, for she had been able to discover it was the right month. Some time earlier she had found out that a woman could only have a baby if it was the right month. She knew it was the right month because Mrs. Griffin had simply come right out and said so. She had leaned back onto her beach towel and put two wet little pieces of cotton over her eyes, and she had remarked what a perfect month it had been—*it had been just right.*

So she knew—and she did not like it either. She was not anxious to have still another brother or sister around the house. The smaller the child the more adults seemed to like it. At least the bigger she became the less people cared about her. She knew for a fact that all her father's friends in Springs liked Markie better than her. They were always picking him up and putting him down, though she herself did not really weigh that much more. She had even heard her father say to June that though Markie was the same jolly boy he had always been, Cynthia had turned into a very grave child. And whatever that meant, it was not so. She would have told June—if she had thought that June would not have been predisposed in another direction—that it was her father who had changed. Of course he called her his "special baby," and of course he swung her over his head, and whenever June kissed Markie he would march right over and kiss her. Yet whatever he did displeased her; every time she suspected he was about to do something that would make her happy, he did it, and it made her sad. Surely when he kissed her she should be happy

—but she knew that June did not particularly like him to do it, and so even that finally caused discomfort.

Actually June didn't like him to kiss girls at all. That was what they had been arguing over when her father had thrown his egg. He had said that June didn't even want him to *talk* to them, to stand within ten *feet* of them; June said that wasn't so, he said it was, she said it wasn't—and then the two halves of his plate were rattling on the floor and Markie was pointing at the egg sliding into the sink. Looking steadily into her cereal bowl, Cynthia had been able to imagine how it all had happened: on the Griffins' lawn, where the party had been the night before, her father must have gone up to a girl who was there and kissed her. Cynthia was even able to imagine the girl, in a billowy dress and patent leather sandals like her own new Papagallos . . . Now whenever her father kissed her, she believed that partly it was to spite June, and she knew that would make June angry at *her,* make her cross the way her old mother used to be.

So in the Reganhart household, matters of affectionate display became complicated for a while: first June would kiss Markie, then her father would come over to kiss Cynthia, and Cynthia would have to run out of the room, or up the beach, or to the far end of the garden to get away from him. Which made her *father* angry with her. For the time being she did not want to be kissed by anyone. She had not, however, pushed Markie from her bunk because June preferred to kiss him, or because she had thought her little brother had himself wanted to kiss her. She had pushed him out because he did not belong there in the first place. He was going to do something to her. She had not had to explain to anybody why she had pushed him, because nobody as yet had asked what had happened. Nobody had scolded her and nobody so far had said what the punishment was to be.

When she was being driven to the beach in June's convertible, her stepmother asked her, "Did you see it, Cynthia?"

"See what?"

After a moment June said, "See Markie fall."

And Cynthia replied, "I was sleeping." And then she knew that what she had begun to suspect was not—as usually happened—simply what she was beginning to hope for. She knew that she was not to be punished at all. June had taken one hand from the steering wheel and put it on top of Cynthia's head, gently.

No one knew what had happened. Only Markie, and he didn't know either. He couldn't, for the same reason that he couldn't have been going to do something to her—he had been sleeping. But of course she didn't *know* that anything really had to be done. If it was the right month and a man got into bed with a lady, that was that. Her father had a penis like Markie's, and she, June, her mother, and Mrs. Griffin all had vaginas. All men had penises. They were what gave you the babies.

At Barnes Hole, where the beach was touched by an endless silver bay, she decided that she did not even want to get out of the car.

"Don't you feel well, dear?" June was asking.

"I don't want to go here." She had a sense of some new power that was hers; but now that she was at the bay, at the brink of a regular day, the familiarity of the landscape and the routine was not the comfort she had been expecting it would be.

"Where would you prefer to go?" June removed her sunglasses. While she rubbed her eyes Cynthia had to turn away—their redness embarrassed her. "Would you like to visit somebody?"

"I just don't want to go here, I'll tell you that."

"Well, how about the ocean beach?"

"I suppose so."

"Honey, where would you *like* to go?"

"Oh, the ocean beach is okay."

She did not look up to see what the effect had been of the little snarl in her voice. But looking down she saw that June's slender suntanned hand, the one with the pretty blue ring, had curled over hers again. In a moment the car had turned and they were headed for the ocean. The wind blew her hair—a delightful cool feminine feeling—and she could not help herself: she was smiling. It was because she had had to look straight into Markie's blood that she was receiving so much care and attention; she knew this, but she continued smiling anyway. The truth was that she deserved special attention; the sight of the red blood creeping down the floor boards had nearly turned her stomach. She had cried and become hysterical, and she had screamed and screamed. She remembered now what it was she had screamed: "Markie fell! Markie fell out!"

And hadn't he? Well, hadn't he? If not, then June would be punishing her now instead of rewarding her with kindnesses. If anyone at all *had* pushed Markie it was God, who had seen that it was a sin for her stupid little brother to get in bed with her when they weren't married.

They were driving along the road that led between the trees to Amagansett. "Don't you like Barnes any more?" June asked.

"The water's dirty."

"I thought it was so clean—"

"I don't like it there! I'm not going there!"

"Nobody's making you," June said, and that, she thought happily, was the case. At the edge of Springs they approached the small grocery store with the gas pump out in front. June pulled the car over and parked by the steps that led up to the store. She went inside to make a phone call, while Cynthia waited in the car and spelled out the sign over the doorway.

H. Savage—Groceries and Gas
Barnes Hole Rd, Springs

It had turned out, of course, that there was no hole at Barnes at all. She had looked for it during the first week of her stay. By herself she had walked the long stretch of beach, and then she had even enlisted Markie, but he was no help because he kept seeing holes, virtual abysses, that weren't even there. At low tide she went off alone, dragging her legs through the receding waters, but with no luck; at last she had to come back up to the blanket, her nose wet and the ends of her hair damp, and ask June where the hole was. June explained to her that it was only a name given to the place—officially it was called Barnes Landing. But all the ladies continued to smile and she realized that it was something a child wasn't supposed to know. And she was right—that same afternoon a boy with large ears had let her hang on to his tube with him, and he seemed so helpful she had decided to ask him where the hole was. He had pointed between her legs and then ducked her under the water.

She looked up the steps. Nobody in the dark store was near enough to see her; all she could make out were June's white sandals and one hand holding a Kleenex. She slid down into the crevice of the front seat of the convertible. Pushing her bathing suit aside, she put her finger a little way inside herself. So far, no baby.

Soon June emerged into the sunlight, but her expression was impossible to figure out. She had on dark glasses and was wearing her big straw coolie hat—the one Markie used to like to parade around in—and a blue jumper over the top of her bathing suit. Cynthia thought she looked like a man, but then she came down off the little porch swinging herself like a lady, and got into the car.

"May I turn the radio on?"

June nodded and they started away.

"Is it okay if I listen to music?"

"That's fine," June said.

Turning all the knobs, she asked, "Did you call the hospital?"

"I spoke to your father. Markie's resting—Cynthia, could you tune it down just a little?"

"Is he unconscious?" She had heard earlier that he was.

"That just means he's getting a good rest, Cynthia. It's the body's way of making sure we get a good rest."

"Will he be all right then?"

"Of course—" June said. "Cynthia, *please* lower the radio—"

"But then I won't be able to *hear* it—"

June did not answer. Cynthia listened to the music, her concentration not so intense that she did not notice the tears moving down June's cheeks. "Well, when he comes home," Cynthia said, her hair blowing wonderfully out behind her again, "we'll have to teach him not to fall out like that any more. He was never very careful. Even my mother will tell you that."

Only four other cars were parked at the end of the street leading down to the ocean beach; it was not yet noon. Cynthia raced around to help June take the blanket and folding chair out of the trunk. From the trough in which the spare tire sat, she unwedged her pail and shovel, which she had hardly played with all summer. She grabbed Markie's pail and shovel too, and dragged both pails along the pebbles of the parking area. Then she waited for June to tell her to put Markie's pail back where it belonged. Instead, her stepmother reached out and smoothed the top of the child's hair.

They spread the blanket out where the beach began its slope toward the water. A wave had rolled in a moment before, and the four or five people floundering in the sudsy wake were all laughing and calling to one another. To Cynthia the waves looked large and unfriendly. She carried her pails down to where the sand was wet and started to dig, turning regularly to see what June was doing behind her. A book was open on her stepmother's lap, though she did not seem to be reading it. She did not seem really to be doing anything.

When her sand castle had been washed away, she looked back to see that her stepmother was talking with Mr. Siegel. Pretending to hunt for seashells, she cut a zigzag path up toward the blanket. By the time she was close enough to hear, they had stopped saying anything.

"Hi, Cindy Lou," Mr. Siegel said.

She ran to where he knelt in the sand beside June. "We saw your television program the other night, Mr. Siegel," she said.

"Well, let's hear the dark news," he said. "What's my rating, friend?" She knew that he was one of the people who liked to pick up Markie all the time. Markie, however, was in the hospital this particular morning.

"Oh I loved it!"

"Come on," he said, "you're kidding me." He tossed a handful of sand at her feet. "I understand you're a skeptic about TV. Your father tells me you're an intellectual, that you spend your mornings looking through books on Brancusi."

"I like TV though," she said. She had not quite gotten the sense of all he had said to her. "It was really funny when that old grandfather started slicing up that turkey and then it fell right in his lap. Boy, did I begin to laugh—didn't I, June?"

June smiled, barely.

"Hey, does anybody want to go in the water?" Cynthia asked.

"Water?" said Mr. Siegel. "What water?"

Cynthia's laughter was uproarious.

"Not right now, honey," June said.

She knew that Mr. Siegel and June were anxious to resume their conversation, and she knew what they had been talking about. "When are you going to write another program, Mr. Siegel?"

"Now I know you're on my side, I'm going to get right home and start one this afternoon."

"For me?"

"Absolutely."

"Wow!"

"This time *two* grandfathers and *two* turkeys!"

"That's *great!*" she said, and she went skipping down to the water. She heard June calling after her, "Be careful—" with the result that she skipped right on down to the edge, as though she hadn't heard at all. A wave was rising a little way out, and the sight of it unnerved her. But she took a step directly forward, into the sea—and waited. She did not have to wait very long.

"Cynthia—*please—*"

The child turned. She had been able to get June up off the blanket; she had even been able to move her some five or six feet toward the water.

"Okay," Cynthia said, and she hopped on one leg up to where her pails lay, and flopped down in the sand beside them.

"Please, be careful, Cyn, please," June called, and just at that moment she heard Markie's head hitting the floor. A little sound came out of her mouth, but then she saw that it hadn't been Markie's head at all, only a wave collapsing onto the flat blue surf. It made her think, however. When Markie came out of the hospital he would have to wear a bandage. She decided she would be very generous to him then. She would tie his shoelaces for him and put his toys away without anybody asking.

Though the hit on the head would probably knock some sense into that kid.

She spoke these words out loud; when she tried them a second time, they made her giggle. The hit on the head will probably knock some sense into that kid. Boy, that little kid didn't know anything . . . What she knew for sure and didn't need anyone to tell her, was that she was much smarter than her brother. She was an exceptional child—that was what the teachers at her new school said. She had the mentality of a ten-year-old, which made her *five* years older than Markie. She had reason to be proud of herself. When she was an adult she would be more intelligent than others. They would all have to come to her to ask what the best thing was for them to do.

Cynthia suddenly felt herself so full of pep, so convinced that life was made for pleasure, her pleasure, that she jumped up and went racing toward her stepmother. Because she had seen Markie's blood she knew she could finally get June to agree to take her in the water. She wanted to walk right into the ocean holding June's hand. She left Markie's pail and shovel where they were and went flying to the blanket—but there was a man walking down the beach in her direction. She was momentarily stilled by the familiarity of his gait. Everything about him was so familiar, though at first she could not think what his name was. It did not take her very long, however, to remember, or to stop being able to forget. But where was Mommy? Mommy had come with him to see Markie in the hospital! Mommy would find out that she had pushed him! Well, she hadn't—he fell! That's what he got for committing a sin.

"June," she called, "can we go—"

But Gabe had already seen her. He had come to catch her for her mother. All she could do now was scream and run into her room, but they were not even in the house. They were on the wide beach, under the bright sun, and he was so big that wherever she fled he would find her and bring her back.

In the second before he removed his sunglasses, she wondered if she might not be mistaken. Then his hand reached out—and yes, oh yes, oh what would happen—

"Hi, Cynthia. Hello."

June looked to see who it was. Cynthia thought of making believe that he was a strange man, for she was not supposed to speak to strange men. But when her mother appeared, it would be evident to everyone that she had been lying—and then they would know for sure that she had pushed her brother.

"Hello," Cynthia said.

"You remember me?"

"Uh-huh. Gabe."

"Well, how are you? You look brown as a berry—you look healthy and grown-up and—"

"I'm fine."

"Where's your little brother?"

Cynthia shrugged.

June was standing. "I'm Mrs. Reganhart."

Gabe extended his hand. "I'm Gabe Wallach. How do you do? I'm a friend of Martha Reganhart's. From Chicago."

Now Cynthia looked up to where the cars were parked. She recognized Gabe's car as soon as she saw it—and inside she could make out the figure of her mother; she was crouching in the back, spying on her. This was not the first time that the child had had occasion to suspect her mother of spying. When she had first arrived at her new school in New York, she had been certain that her teacher, Mrs. Koplin, was actually her mother in disguise. Then one rainy afternoon Mrs. Koplin's husband had come to pick her up; he had been carrying an umbrella, and Mrs. Koplin had called him Herb, and she had said that before they went home they must stop first at the A&P on Twelfth Street. And when she said that, Cynthia had known that Mrs. Koplin wasn't her mother after all. Yet she had been so certain . . . Now, however, she could actually see who the woman was, crouched in the back of the car. Cynthia started to whistle and to look up at the sky and to kick her toes into the sand. She was being watched and she did not intend to do a single thing wrong. If she could manage, she wanted it to seem as though she were having a very good time.

"—in the hospital—"

"—how long?"

"—he'll be all right, of course—"

Cynthia turned so that her mother could see only her back. Turning, she saw Markie's pail bobbling up and down at the water's edge. It was just about to be washed away, and if it was washed away who would they blame but her! They would blame her, and then they would start asking questions— Fast as she could, she started down the beach, her arms outstretched toward the pail.

"Cynthia—"

"Cynthia, *what—"*

"Cyn—" Just as she got hold of the handle, somebody grabbed her arm. It was Gabe; behind him stood June, her mouth open, her hand up to her pale cheek.

"Cynthia—oh Cynthia," June said, "what are you doing? Never—"

"Getting Markie's pail." She did not know whether it would help any to cry.

"Oh . . . Oh, Cynthia, that's a good girl, that's fine—oh honey, don't go near the water alone—not today." It was June who seemed as though she were about to weep.

"I won't," she said, and she hoped her mother had seen just how much June worried about her and took care of her. They all started up the beach, and while June moved off ahead, Cynthia asked Gabe, "Why doesn't Mommy come out of the car?"

He smiled. "Martha's not in the car, Cynthia. She's in Chicago."

"What's that?" she said.

"You mean that, in the back seat? That's a beach umbrella. That's my father's beach umbrella."

"Yes?" She took another look. She felt as she had when Mrs. Koplin had called her husband Herb.

"Martha's in Chicago," he said. "She has to work. I'm visiting with my own father in East Hampton. I thought I'd come over and say hello. Your mother wanted me to."

"How did you find me?"

"Oh I just asked anybody on the streets, you know, where Cynthia Reganhart was, and they said you were down here by the ocean."

"We don't even usually come here."

"Then I suppose I was very lucky. I expected to see Mark too."

"Well, he's in the hospital."

"When you see him will you tell him I was here to visit?"

"Okay. He has to learn not to fall out of his bed, that's all."

June was standing by the blanket; she had closed her book. "Mr. Wallach," she said, "could I ask you a favor? Will you be here awhile?"

"A little while, yes—"

"Could you stay a few minutes with Cynthia? Do you mind?"

"No, no, I'd like to—"

"Do you want me to come with you?" Cynthia said.

"No, dear. You stay with Mr. Wallach. All right? I just have to phone."

But it wasn't all right! He would start to ask questions, just as her father had. When she answered, he would become angry. Her father, she remembered, had turned red in the face; she had heard him tell June that Martha was irresponsible beyond imagining, that she just had hot pans. Cynthia had wanted to say that hot pans weren't dangerous so long as you kept the handle in toward the pilot light, but she had not dared say anything. She had, in fact, liked his being angry with Martha, only it frightened her, and that made her think that perhaps she didn't like it. Finally she had asked June if she had done something to anger her father too; and June had explained. Usually, she said, you slept in bed with somebody after you were married and not before, though different people did, certainly, have different beliefs. June said she wanted it clear to Cynthia that her father was angry with her mother and not for a moment with Cynthia herself. Then she had gone on to say that this was natural too; divorced people often had differing opinions—it was what generally decided them to be divorced and live separately.

Now that Gabe had her alone, she knew that he would ask her questions too. He would ask if she had told. She wanted to go off in the car with June, but June was running up the beach, and Gabe was sitting on the blanket as though he belonged there.

"Well," he was saying, looking up at her, "how do you like New York, Cynthia? It's a big city, isn't it?"

"It's okay."

"Are you having a pleasant summer?"

"It's okay."

"Well, you really take things in your stride. Just okay?"

She took a quick look down at him. "Uh-huh." Maybe he wasn't going to ask if she had told about him and Martha sleeping in the same bed—but then she knew from experience that adults did not always ask what they wanted to know right off.

Gabe was leaning back on his elbows, and he did not say anything more. He seemed to be thinking about himself. He was wearing a blue shirt and white trousers and his feet were bare. She kept wanting to look at his feet, but she was afraid he would catch her.

"Is your father still a dentist?" she asked.

"He still is," he said. "You remember?"

"You know," she said, "my mother didn't take very good care of my teeth."

"Didn't she?"

"I had four cavities when I got here."

"All kids have cavities," Gabe said. "I used to have cavities, and my father was a dentist, with an office right in our house."

"Markie didn't have any," she said.

"Mark's too small probably. Little children his age just naturally don't get cavities. I think Martha took care of your teeth, Cynthia. Didn't she take you to Dr. Welker?"

She chose not to answer. He would take Martha's side in anything; they had slept in bed together, so he had to. "Well, it wasn't funny when they had to start drilling," she said.

"I'll bet it wasn't. Are you all right now? Let me see?"

"I suppose so," she said. She wouldn't let him look in her mouth; it was none of his business. "Except where I hurt myself this morning."

"Where?"

"My elbow. Right here."

When he leaned over to look, she knew he would see that she hadn't hurt herself at all; it was Markie who had fallen. He tried to touch her and she jumped. "Oww! Watch it."

He looked at first as though he was going to be mad at her; then he was bending his own arm up and down from the elbow. "Just move it like this," he said. "That should make it feel better."

She bent it up and down once. It did feel better; *she* felt better.

"Does that help any?" Gabe asked.

"Yes, I think so." She bent it twice more. "Oh yes," she said. "Would you like to make a sand castle?"

He looked at his watch. "I don't think so, Cynthia."

"Would you like to watch me make one?"

He smiled.

"What's the matter?" she asked. "Do you have to go home?"

To this he shrugged. "Cynthia, I really don't know."

She did not understand him. Did he or didn't he? He leaned back again and was no fun. No one was. Except sometimes Markie. She would tickle her brother until he couldn't hold it in any longer, and then, with that funny look on his face, he would give in and wet his pants—and then he'd start to cry. But he didn't even get punished for it. June would come in and pick him up and hug him, even though his legs were all wet. Cynthia would sit on the lower bunk and watch until little Mark was promised something or other that would make him stop crying. He liked to be tickled, but when it was over and his pants were changed, he would say that she had made him do it. She wondered if he had come up into her bunk this morning just to be tickled. Well, it wasn't her fault—he wasn't supposed to climb that ladder to her bed anyway. If he fell it was his own fault. She didn't want anybody in her bed with her at all. It was irresponsible. Probably Markie thought he was going to give her a baby because she wasn't married. That's what could happen, of course. June said that one of the most important reasons for getting into bed with somebody was to have a baby; that was why her father felt it was only for married people. Otherwise, her father said, it was a damnshame. And a damnshame, she knew, was the same as a sin—and a sin, for example, was leaving hot pans around on which children could burn themselves. It showed no regard for your children, that was for sure.

She turned on her belly and looked up at the parking lot. Yes, it was still a beach umbrella in the back seat. She found herself wondering if June was going to come back—not in a few minutes, but at all. It might be that all the adults were going to make a switch; maybe that was why Gabe was here. Maybe it had all been arranged beforehand, even Markie's falling out of the bed. June and Markie and her father would go one way, and then she and Gabe would have to move back to Chicago and live with her real mother once again. Then she could get to see Stephanie. And Barbie. That might even be fun. And she wouldn't have to sleep in a double-decker bed any more, so there'd be no accidents to worry about. She could sleep in her old bed and her mother could read to her from that *Charlotte's Web* book. They would get to have dinner at the Hawaiian House, and her mother would bring extra-thick milk shakes to their table because she worked there and knew the cook personally. She could see Blair and Sissy in Hildreth's. She knew that Sissy was probably going to have a baby from sleeping in bed with Blair; she knew they slept in bed together because one night she had seen them, before her mother had made Sissy move out. If they were all in Chicago then Markie wouldn't be in the hospital right now. She wondered if Markie would ever stop being unconscious.

"Markie's unconscious," she said.

"Is he?" She could not tell whether or not he had known.

"He just lay there, and then I screamed and my dad came. I didn't see him fall. I was sleeping."

"Well," said Gabe, "he'll be all right, Cyn. I don't think you have to worry."

"I'm not. I think he was sleeping anyway. I don't think he was unconscious. He's not even supposed to be in my bed anyway, you know."

He looked down at the blanket. Didn't he believe her? "Well, he's not! Ask anybody!" she said. He would always take her mother's side against her father, so how could he know anything!

"I want to go in the water!" She could not think of anything else to say.

"Yes?"

"But," she said wearily, "somebody has to take me, and nobody ever will." That was a lie; her father took her—but Gabe couldn't know that either. She waited, but he did not even answer; he always seemed to be thinking about himself.

Finally he asked, "Would you like me to?"

"To what?"

"Take you into the water."

"You can't. You have pants on."

"Want to see a trick?" he said, standing.

"What?"

He began to unzip his trousers. She couldn't bear to watch; she wanted to close her eyes, to bury her head in the sand. Oh she didn't want to see! He was so big and he would have one just like

Markie's, and it would look so awful. But she could not bring herself to close her eyes; she could not even move them away, let alone cover them with sand.

What she saw was a tan bathing suit. "And now I'm ready to go swimming," Gabe said. He threw his trousers onto the blanket and reached down and offered her a hand. His legs were all covered with hair, she got a good look at them as he pulled her to her feet.

"Aren't you going to take your shirt off?" she asked.

"Don't you want to just play at the edge?"

When he said that, there was a wild pounding in her chest, a surging, something akin to happiness, but more violent and sudden. "Uh-uh," she said. "I want to go all the way in—if you hold me."

"Do you usually do that? It's getting a little rough."

"I do, though. If there's a grownup."

She waited for him to take off his shirt. "Okay," he said, and when he took her hand and they started down the beach, the sea was so sparkling and blue that there seemed to be no boundary between the affection she felt for those waters and for the companion who walked beside her. Both filled her with delight. She began to wish that Gabe was her father and June was her mother—she especially wanted June to be her mother if she was going to keep touching her hair the way she had all day. Her real mother and father could have Markie, and then everything would be even; no one would be gypped.

By the time she reached the water's edge, she was not sure that she wanted to go through with it. Under the waves, which rushed toward her, it would be black and cold. But there were the people, ten or fifteen of them now, being knocked down and swept backwards, and all of them laughing and having a good time. The sunlight on all the wet heads made them look polished.

"Let's go out there," she said. "Okay?" She pointed to where the bathers were.

"Well, okay—"

"Can you carry me in? I don't like the shock."

"Of what?"

"The cold water shock. Carry me?"

Gabe put his hands under her arms. "Here we *go—*" and he lifted her up. "Now hold on," and he began to wade out.

When he stopped the first time, she said, "Hey, further."

"Wow, what a brave girl you are, Cynthia Reganhart."

"Come on, further—"

"Hang on tight."

"Okay."

"Hang on now—"

"Oh oh oh—" she yelped into his ear. "Oh—keep going—oh oh *look—*"

"Hang on—hang on—" Gabe called.

"Whooo!" she yelled.

"Ready, get set—"

"Heeeeere—"

"Wheee—"

She was looking straight up as it came curling over their heads. Gabe squeezed her to him, and she pressed her arms around his neck, and the wave was hanging over them, as though it would never break. She closed her eyes, held her breath, and *crash!* It came flowing down all over them, and she felt the two of them floating, and then their heads rose above the water, and Gabe's hair was hanging in his eyes.

"You look funny!" she shouted.

"So do you!" They were in water only as high as Gabe's knees, and the other bathers were rubbing their eyes and some were blowing their noses right into the ocean.

"I wasn't even scared," she said into his ear.

"Fine. Hang on. There's another one coming."

"This is fun—"

"Close your mouth, you dope!"

"Then I can't *taaaalk—*" she screamed, and the wave rolled in and over. Gabe held her tight and they came up right through the foam.

"Whew!" he said. "Are you all right?"

"Uh-huh." Gabe was wiping her nose off with a handful of water. Oh she didn't just like him—she loved him! She wondered when he was going to kiss her.

"Do you have to go back to Chicago?" she asked.

"I think so, Cynthia."

"To*day?*"

"No, not today—"

"Will you come play with me?"

"Well, we'll see—here comes one!"

"Oh it's a big—"

"Hang on tight!"

"Ooohhh—"

Oh she was glad Markie was unconscious! Oh what a good time! What a tall tall wave! It teetered over their heads and she pushed her face into Gabe's neck, and she waited—and then something collided with them. She felt herself and Gabe tumbling, and then Gabe was gone and she was still tumbling, but alone. Her feet were up and her head was down, and the water wouldn't let her rise. She tried to stand but there was no bottom for her feet. She was rolling, away across the sea, and she swore, oh she swore that she loved everybody. She swore it, but no hand reached down to pick her up. I love Markie Mommy Daddy June Gabe everybody —*Please, Markie, I'm sorry*—

Her head was in the sunlight. She had thought that she was way out beyond the buoys, but when she looked up she saw she was almost up on the dry beach. Sand was beneath her hands, and a big fat man was sitting in the water next to her. He was breathing very loud, and when he saw her sitting there, he said, "Some wave, kid, huh?" His belly hung over the top of his suit, and all the time he was getting up he kept saying, "Whew! Whew!" He started up the beach, and then Cynthia saw Gabe running toward her through the low water.

"Are you all right?" he called. "Cynthia, hey, come here—give me your hand. What's the matter? Are you okay?"

"You let me go," she said.

"We got knocked into, honey. Come on, give me your hand. Are you all right? What is it—?"

She allowed herself to be helped up. But she refused to cry. She knew that he had let her go. She started up toward the blanket by herself.

Then it was dark again and she was in bed. Downstairs Mrs. Griffin was reading a book. Cynthia had not seen her father all day, and a little while ago June had gone off to the hospital too. She had left directly after dinner, when Mrs. Griffin had come to sit with Cynthia. June had said she was only going to kiss Markie good night and then would be back. The drive to the hospital was fourteen miles; for herself Cynthia did not believe that kissing anybody good night was that essential. It was mostly for babies. Gabe had used to kiss her good night in Chicago, and that was because he thought of her as some sort of baby who could be tricked by a kiss; she had never liked that. She had never liked *him;* now she remembered. He had made her mother unhappy. If it hadn't been for him, her mother would have married her father again. But he took her mother into the bedroom and closed the door and made her get into bed with him and say she wouldn't marry Cynthia's father. Whenever Gabe was nice it was only a trick. Today was a perfect example—he had wanted to get back at her for what she had told her father. He would probably try to get his hands on Markie too, and drown him; she had better warn her little brother about that.

She leaned her head over the side of the bunk so that it would be upside-down and make Markie laugh. "Hey, Markie—look at me, booo-aaaa!"

His pillow was puffed up, but he wasn't there. He was still in the hospital—how could she forget that? His bed had been made for him and the floor had been mopped up too. The sight of his pillow, all ready for his bleeding head, gave her the shivers; it almost made her cry, but she wouldn't allow it to. It wasn't her fault that he had fallen. He had no right to get in bed with her. She did not want to marry him. She did not want to marry anybody. When she had a baby she didn't want to have a strange baby that she didn't even know; she wanted the baby to be her. Little Cynthia. She would have a lot of regard for her baby. When the baby wanted to cry she would hold it so that it could put its head on her breasts. By then she would have them . . . She picked up her pillow, doubled it over, and sank her own head down into it. The pillow was a mother . . . And then she couldn't help it, she was crying. She was all in a jumble. She missed her mother. She really did. She wanted to see her, to put her head right into her mother's breasts—and yet two days later, when all the adults had returned to the house from the funeral, Cynthia had her chance and did not even use it. She sat beside June all through the afternoon, and it pleased her that her mother saw when June reached out and smoothed her hair back for her.

Lucy's Will

She passed out twice in the second week of November, first in a booth in The Old Campus Coffee Shop, and the afternoon following, upon rising from her seat at the end of English class. At the student health center, a barracks building that had been converted into the infirmary, she told the doctor that she believed she might be suffering from anemia. Her skin had always been on the pale side, and in winter the tips of her toes and fingers went white and icy when it got very cold.

After the examination she dressed and sat in a chair the doctor had pulled back for her in his office. He said that he did not believe the problem was with the circulation in her extremities. Looking out the window, he asked if she had been having any trouble lately with her periods. She said no, then she said yes, and then, clutching her coat and her books in her arms, she rushed out the door. In the narrow corridor she felt her-

---

From Part II of the novel *When She Was Good* (1967). The time is 1949, in the Middle West. The characters are: Lucy Nelson, who has grown up most unhappily in Liberty Center, and sees in Fort Kean College for Women her first real haven from the humiliations of being the daughter of an alcoholic father (Duane "Whitey" Nelson) and a defenseless mother (Myra); Roy Bassart, a young ex-G.I., just entering a Fort Kean photography school, and the hometown beau whom Lucy had also hoped to escape at college; Daddy Will Carroll, her mother's father, with whom the Nelsons have had to live since Lucy's early childhood; Roy's father, Lloyd Bassart, a high-school teacher in Liberty Center; and Roy's favorite uncle, Julian Sowerby, a Liberty Center businessman, who for a time looked to Lucy to have the manly know-how lacking in a Whitey Nelson, or a Roy Bassart.

self spinning, but this time the sensation lasted only a second.

As soon as she pulled shut the door of the phone booth in the coffee shop she realized that Roy would be in class. His landlady, Mrs. Blodgett, answered, and Lucy hung up without even speaking. She thought of dialing the school and having him called to a phone; but what would she say to him? The strange sensation she began to have—as the first wave of confusion gave way to a second, even more severe—was that it did not have anything to do with him anyway. She found herself thinking like a child who does not know the facts of life, who thinks that pregnancy is something that a woman does to herself, or that simply happens to her if she wishes hard enough.

In her room she looked at all the ridiculous markings on her calendar. Just the previous Saturday, after Roy had driven her back to the dormitory from the movies, she had drawn a thick black ring around Thanksgiving Day. Suddenly she felt dreadful; she went and stood with her mouth open over the toilet, but all she could cough up were some brownish strands of liquid. The dread remained.

That evening she did not answer when the on-duty girl rapped on the door to her room and said that a Roy was on the phone.

At eight in the morning, the other girls drifting down to the dining hall or running off to class, Lucy rushed back to the infirmary. She had to wait on a bench in the corridor until ten, when the doctor finally arrived.

"I was here yesterday," she said. "Lucy Nelson."

"Come in. Sit down."

Before she began to speak he came around to the door and pushed it shut all the way. When he returned to his desk, she told him that she did not want a baby.

He pushed his chair back a little and crossed one leg over the other. That was all he did.

"Doctor, I'm a freshman. A first-semester freshman."

He said nothing.

"I've been working for years to go to college. At night. In a soda fountain. Up in Liberty Center. That's where I'm from . . . And summers too—three whole summers. And I have a Living Aid Scholarship. If I hadn't gotten in here I might not even have been able to go to school at all—because of money." But she did not want to plead poverty, or even helplessness. What he had to know was that she was not weak, she was strong, she had undergone many hardships, and much suffering—she wasn't just another eighteen-year-old girl. It wasn't merely that she needed his help; she *deserved* it. "This is my first real experience away from home, Doctor. I've been waiting for it all my life. Saving for it. It's all I've had to look forward to for years."

He continued to listen.

"Doctor, I'm not promiscuous, I swear it. I'm just eighteen! You've got to believe me!"

Until then the doctor had sat there with his glasses pushed up on his forehead. Now he adjusted the spectacles down onto the bridge of his nose.

"I don't know what to do," she said, trying to regain her self-control.

His face remained immobile. He had soft gray hair and kind eyes, but he only scratched the side of his nose.

"I don't know what to do," she said again. "I really don't."

He crossed his arms. He rocked a little in his chair.

"Doctor, I never had a boy friend before. He was my first one. That's the truth—it really is."

The doctor swung the chair around and looked out the window, toward "The Bastille," as the girls called the main building. He had pushed his glasses up again, and now he began rubbing at his eyes. Maybe he had been out on an emergency all night and was tired. Maybe he was thinking of what to say. Maybe he wasn't even listening. He came out to the school four mornings a week for two hours, so what did he care? He had a practice of his own to worry about; this was just so much extra cash. Maybe he was only letting time pass before he sent her away to deal with her own mess.

He turned back to her. "And where is the young man?" he asked.

". . . Here."

"Speak up, Lucy. Where?"

She felt herself becoming meek. Or was it protective? "In Fort Kean."

"And now that he's had his fun, that's it, I suppose."

"What?" she whispered.

He was rubbing at his temples with the tips of his fingers. He *was* thinking. He was going to help! "Don't you girls know what they're up to?" he asked in a soft and unhappy voice. "Can't you imagine what they'll be like when something like this happens? A bright and pretty little girl like you, Lucy. What were you thinking about?"

Her eyes welled with tears at the sound of her name. It might have been the first time she had ever heard it spoken. *I'm Lucy. I'm bright. I'm pretty.* Oh, her life was just beginning! So very much had happened to her in the last year alone—in the last month. Already there was a girl on her floor who knew a boy she wanted to fix Lucy up with. Only there had never once been an opportunity to meet him, what with Roy coming around every single night, if only to stop off and say hello. She was away from home at long long last—and starting to be pretty! Why, why had she gotten involved with him to begin with? Because he called her Angel? Because he took those pictures? Because he sang all those stupid songs into her ear? That big goon hadn't the faintest idea what she was all about. All summer long he'd acted as though she were some kind of girl she wasn't—as though she were some sort of Monkey Littlefield. And she had let him. She had let him have his stupid way! And now this! Only, *this* was what happened to farm girls, to girls who didn't study, who quit school, who ran away from home. To Babs Egan, but not to her. Hadn't enough happened to her already?

"Doctor, I don't *know* what I was thinking about." She began to cry, despite herself. "All I mean is, lately I don't even know what I'm doing sometimes." She covered her face with her fingers.

"And what about the boy?"

"The boy?" she said helplessly, rubbing her tears away.

"What does he plan to do about all this? Run off to the South Seas?"

"Oh no," she moaned, sadder than ever, "no, he'd marry me tomorrow," and an instant too late she realized that she had said the wrong thing. It was the truth, but it was the wrong thing to have said.

"But you don't want to." The doctor was speaking to her.

She looked up from her lap, partly. "I didn't say that."

"I have to have it straight, Lucy. Just as it is. He wants to, but you don't want to."

She rose from her seat. "But I'm not even here three whole months! I'm a first-semester freshman!"

He was moving his glasses up again. He had such a big, wrinkled, friendly face—you just knew he had a family he loved, and a nice house, and a calm and pleasant life. "If the young man wants to marry you—"

"What of it? What if he does?"

"Well, I think that's something that must at least be taken into consideration. Don't you?"

Blankly she said, "I don't understand." And she didn't.

"His feelings are something that have to be taken into consideration. His love for you."

Dumbly she sat there shaking her head. He didn't love her. He just sang those stupid songs into her ear.

"—what he wants," the doctor was saying, "what he expects, too."

"But he doesn't *know* what he wants."

"You say he wants to marry you."

"Oh, that isn't what I mean. He says things, but he doesn't even know what! Doctor—please, you're right, I don't want to marry him. I don't want to lie to you. I hate liars and I don't lie, and that's the truth! Please, hundreds and hundreds of girls do what I did. And they do it with all different people!"

"Perhaps they shouldn't."

"But I'm not bad!" She couldn't help herself, it was the truth: "I'm good!"

"Please, you must calm down. I didn't say that you were bad. I'm sure you're not. You mustn't jump at everything I say before I finish saying it."

"I'm sorry. It's a habit. I'm terribly sorry."

"They shouldn't," he began again, "because most of them aren't old enough to pay the price if they lose. If they get into trouble."

"But—"

"But," his voice rose over hers, "they're old enough to want the love. I know."

The tears moved again into her eyes. "You do understand. Because that's what happened to me, just what you said. That's exactly it."

"Lucy, listen to me—"

"I am, Doctor. Because that *is* what happened—"

"Lucy, you're not alone in this."

At first she thought he meant that there were other girls in school in the same fix—perhaps even in the infirmary rooms along the corridor beyond his office.

"There is a young man," the doctor said.

"But—"

"Listen to me, Lucy. There is a young man, and there is your family. Have you spoken to your family about this yet?"

She looked into her plaid skirt, where her fingers were clutched at the big safety pin.

"You do have a family?"

"Yes. I suppose."

"I think you have to forget your embarrassment and take this problem to your family."

"I can't."

"Why not?"

"I have a terrible family."

"Lucy, you're not the first eighteen-year-old girl to think her family is terrible. Surely you've discovered that since you've been at school."

"But my family *is* terrible. I don't think it—it's true!"

He said nothing.

"I ignore them. I have nothing to do with them. They're inferior, Doctor," she added when he still didn't seem to believe her.

"In what way?"

"My father drinks." She looked him straight in the eye. "He's a drunkard."

"I see," he said. "And your mother?"

Helplessly she was weeping again. "She's too good for him."

"That doesn't sound inferior," the doctor said quietly.

"Yes, but she should have left him years and years ago, if she had any sense. Any self-respect. She should have found a man who would be good to her and respect her." Like you, she thought. If you had met my mother, if she had married you . . . She heard herself saying, "Some people think, someone said once, she looks like Jennifer Jones. The actress."

He handed her a tissue and she blew her nose. She mustn't ask to be pitied; she mustn't whimper; she mustn't fall to pieces. That's what her mother would do.

"Lucy, I think you should go home. Today. Maybe she understands more than you imagine. Maybe she won't be angry. I would think from what you say that she wouldn't be."

She did not respond. He was trying to get out of it. That's exactly what he was beginning to do.

"You seem to love her. Probably she loves you too."

"But she can't help, Doctor. Love has nothing to do with it. Love is what's *wrong* with her. She's so weak. She's so insipid!"

"My dear, because you're upset now—"

"But, Doctor, *they can't help!* Only you can help," she said, standing. "You must!"

He shook his head. "But I can't, I'm afraid."

"But you have to!"

"I'm terribly sorry."

Could he mean it? Could he understand the situation as he did, and then turn around and say he wasn't going to help? "But this isn't *fair!"* she cried.

The doctor nodded his head. "It isn't."

"So then what are you going to *do* about it? Sit there pushing your glasses up and down? Sit there being wise to me? Call me 'my dear'!" Instantly she sat back down in her chair. "Oh, I'm sorry. I didn't mean that. But why are you . . . ? I mean, you see what happened. You understand." She felt now that she had to plead with him, to convince him that he was right. "You *do* understand, Doctor. Please, you're an intelligent person!"

"But there are limits. On all of us. People may want things, that doesn't mean that we can give them."

"Please," she said angrily, "don't tell me what I know in that tone. I am not a child."

A moment passed. He stood.

"But what's going to happen to me? If you don't help . . ."

He came around to the side of his desk.

"Don't you care?" she asked. "What about my whole life!"

For the first time she sensed his impatience. Then he spoke. "You cannot expect me, young lady, to save your life."

She rose; she faced him where he was standing at the door. "Please do not lecture me in that superior tone! I refuse to be lectured to by a perfect stranger who doesn't know the first thing about all I have had to put up with in my life. I am not just another eighteen-year-old girl, and I won't take your lectures!"

"And what will you take instead?" he said sourly.

"What?"

"I'm asking what you expect, Lucy. You're interesting," he said, "in your expectations. You're perfectly right—you are not just another eighteen-year-old girl." He opened the door.

"But what about my life? How can you be so cruel to me!"

"I hope you come upon someone you can listen to" was his answer.

"Well, I won't," she said in a low, fierce tone.

"That would be too bad."

"Oh," she said, buttoning her coat, "oh, I hope—I hope you're happy, Doctor, when you go home to your nice house. I hope you're happy with all your wisdom and your glasses and your doctor's degree—and being a coward!"

"Goodbye," he said, blinking only once. "Good luck."

"Oh, I won't rely on luck, Doctor. Or on people either."

"On what, then?"

"Myself!" she said, and marched through the open door.

"Good luck," he said softly as she brushed by him, and then shut the door behind her.

"You coward," she moaned as she went rushing off to the coffee shop; "you weakling," she wept as she carried the phone book into the booth at the back of the store; "you selfish, heartless, cruel—" as she drew her finger down the list of physicians in the yellow pages of the directory, imagining them one after another saying to her, "You cannot expect me, young lady, to save your life," and seeing herself dragging from one office to another, humiliated, ignored, and abused.

On Thanksgiving Day they all sat down to the turkey and she told her family that she and Roy Bassart had decided to get married. "What?" her father said. She repeated herself. "Why?" he demanded to know, and slammed down the carving instruments.

"Because we want to."

Within five minutes the only one still at the table was her grandmother. She alone ate right through to the mince pie while overhead various members of the family, in various ways, tried to get Lucy to unlock her door. Berta, however, said she was sick and tired of disorder and tragedy, and refused to allow every single pleasant moment to be destroyed by one person or another, year in and year out.

Roy phoned at four in the afternoon. She came out of her bedroom to take the call, but would not speak until the kitchen was cleared of adults. Roy said that he couldn't get away to see her before nine. But what had they said when he told them? Nothing. He hadn't told them yet.

At nine-thirty he telephoned from the Sowerbys', saying that he had decided to wait until he was back in his own house, alone with his parents, before he broke the news. "Well, when will that be, Roy?" "I don't know exactly. Well, how can I know exactly? Later." But he was the one who had wanted to call them a week ago from Fort Kean; he was the one, she said, who had thought there was nothing that wrong with having to get married, so long as you were a couple who was going to marry anyway, probably, sooner or later. He was the one—

"Here," he said, "Ellie wants to talk to you."

"Roy!"

"Hi," Ellie said. "Hi, Lucy. Sorry about not writing."

"Hello, Eleanor."

"It's just been work, work, work. You can imagine. I'm going crazy in this science course. Hey, we're all rolling on the floor listening to Roy's adventures in that Britannia school. What a place! And I'm actually drinking. Hey, come over."

"I have to stay home."

"I hope it's not hard feelings, or anything, about not writing . . . Is it?"

"No."

"Well, I'll see you tomorrow. Have I got things to tell you. I've met somebody *marvelous,*" Ellie whispered. "I almost sent you his picture. I mean, he's perfect."

At midnight she came out of her bedroom to call Roy at his home. "Did you tell them?"

"Listen, what are you doing? Everybody's sleeping."

"Didn't you *tell* them?"

"It was too late."

"But I told mine!"

"Look, my father's shouting down the stairs asking who it is."

"Well, tell him!"

"Will you please stop instructing me on what to do every minute?" he said. "I'll do it when I'm—" Suddenly he hung up.

She dialed again. Mr. Bassart picked up the phone. "Just who is this?" he asked.

She didn't breathe.

"Look, no pranks at this hour, whoever you are. If it's one of you boys in my fifth-period class, don't think I'm not going to find out who."

In the morning she telephoned again.

"I was going to call *you,*" Roy said.

"Roy, when are you going to tell them?"

"It's only eight in the morning. We haven't had breakfast, even. My Aunt Irene's coming over."

"Then you *did* tell them."

"Who said that?"

"That's why your aunt's coming to your house!"

"How can you say that? How do you know that's even true?"

"Roy, what are you hiding from me?"

"*Nothing.* Can't you just let things settle for a few hours? My God."

"Why is your aunt coming over at eight o'clock in the morning? Who even called her?"

"Oh, look, okay," he said suddenly, "if you have to know—"

"I do! Know what!"

"Well, my father wants me to wait till June."

"Then you did tell them!"

". . . When we came home."

"Then why didn't you say that last night!"

"Because it just so happened that I wanted to give you good news, Lucy, not bad. I was trying to spare you, Lucy, *but you won't stop pushing me against my own timetable!*"

"Timetable? Roy, what are you talking about? How can we wait until June!"

"But he doesn't *know* about that!"

"And don't you tell him either, Roy!"

"I have to hang up. She's here."

At noon he called to say that he wasn't driving back to Fort Kean until Monday, so perhaps she had better plan to take the bus down on Sunday night.

"I'm calling from a booth, Lucy. I'm on my way to Mr. Brunn's to pick up something for my father. I have to hurry—"

"Roy, please explain instantly what this means."

"I'm trying to take care of some things and iron them out, all *right? Do you mind?*"

"Roy! You can't do this! I have to see you, right now!"

"I'm hanging up, Lucy."

"No!"

"Well, I am. I'm sorry. So get ready."

"If you hang up, I'm coming over to your house this minute. Hello? Do you hear me?"

But the line had been disconnected.

She called Eleanor's house.

"Ellie, it's Lucy. I have to talk to you."

"Why?"

"Oh, not you too?"

". . . Me too, what?"

"Ellie, you had to talk to me once—now I have to talk to you. I have to know what's going on, Ellie. I'll come right over."

"Now? Lucy, you better not—right now, I mean."

"Is anybody home?"

"No. But they're all—going crazy."

"Why?"

"Well, Roy says you want to marry him."

"He wants to marry *me!* Didn't he say that?"

"Well, yes . . . Well, sort of. He says he's thinking about it

. . . But, Lucy, they think you're making him— Uh-oh, somebody's pulling into the driveway. Everybody's been driving back and forth all morning . . . Lucy?"

"Yes."

". . . Are you?"

"What?"

"Well, making him."

"No!"

"Then—why?"

"Because we want to!"

"You do?"

"Yes!"

"But—"

"But what, Eleanor!"

"Well . . . you're so young. We all are. I mean, it's a surprise. I guess I just don't know what I mean, really."

"Because you're a dope, Ellie! Because you're a stupid, insipid, self-centered, selfish dope!"

In the early evening she took a bus back to Fort Kean. The doors to The Bastille were chained shut, and she had to walk all around the cold campus before she found the watchman. He led her over to the Buildings and Grounds Office in Barracks Number Three, sat her down in a chair, and took out his spectacles to look for her name in the student directory.

And all those names printed in the register made her think: *Run away.* Who would ever find her?

In her room she beat her fists on the pillow, on the headboard, on the wall. It was awful. It was horrible. Every other college girl in America was home right now, having a good time with her friends and her family. Yet her mother had begged, her grandfather had begged, even her father had asked her to stay. They said that it was just that they were stunned by the news. Wouldn't she agree, they reasoned through the door, that it was a little unexpected? They would try to get used to it, if only she wouldn't run off like this on a holiday weekend. They were shocked at first, and had maybe lost their heads. It was, after all, only the first semester of that college life she had been dreaming about for so long. But probably she knew what she was doing, if her mind was made up the way it sounded that it was. So wouldn't she stay through Monday? When she was fifteen years old and on her own decided on Catholic as her religious preference, had they stood in her way? No, she had insisted that it was what she wanted, and they had decided to let her go ahead. And later, when she had changed her mind, and turned back to Presbyterian again, well, that too had been her own decision, made on her own, without interference from any person in the family. And the same with the snare drum. Another decision made on her own, that they had honored and respected, until finally she decided to give that up too.

Of course they weren't meaning to draw any comparison between taking up the snare drum and taking a husband for life; but their attitude had been that if she preferred beating the drums to resuming piano (which, they reminded her, she had dropped at ten, her own decision once again), or beginning something like accordion, which had been Daddy Will's compromise suggestion, they had no choice but to let her have her way. Their house was not a dictatorship; it was a democracy, in which every person had his ideas—and was respected for them too. "I may not believe what you say," said Daddy Will through the door, "but I will fight for your right to say it." So wouldn't she reconsider and not rush off now to some lonely, empty school? Why didn't she stay and talk it over? After all, Grandma had been baking all week, and for her. "For Thanksgiving," said Lucy. "Well, honey, that's not much different, when you think about it. It's your first big weekend home from college, there isn't one of us doesn't realize . . . Lucy? Are you listening to me?"

But what about her father acting as though the whole thing was a monumental tragedy? Since when did anything having to do with her sacrifices, her suffering, bring tears to his eyes? She could not bear the pretense. And who said she was quitting college? He kept wandering around the house, crying, "I wanted her to go to college," but who had said she wasn't? All she had said was that she was getting married to Roy . . . Or did they know why without her explaining further? Were they content to accept what she told them, simply to avoid the humiliation of confronting the truth? She picked up her French grammar and threw it clear across the room. "They don't even *know,"* she said aloud, "and still they're letting me do it!"

If only they'd say *no.* NO, LUCY, YOU CANNOT. NO, LUCY, WE FORBID IT. But it seemed that none of them had the conviction any longer, or the endurance, to go against a choice of hers. In order to survive, she had set her will against theirs long ago—it was the battle of her adolescence, but it was over now. And she had won. She could do whatever in the world she wanted—even marry someone she secretly despised.

When Roy returned to Fort Kean on Monday evening, and switched on the light in his room, he found Lucy sitting in a chair by the window.

"What are you doing here?" he cried, dropping his suitcase. "The shades are up!"

"Then pull them down, Roy."

Instantly he did. "How did you get inside?"

"How do I always get inside, Roy? On all fours."

"Is she home?"

"Who?"

"My landlady!" he whispered and, without another word, slipped out the door and into the hallway. She heard him whistling his way up the stairs and into the bathroom. *You sigh, the song begins, you speak and I hear . . .* Overhead she even heard him flush the toilet. Then he was sliding into the room again. "She's out," he said, shutting the door. "We better turn off the lights."

"So you won't have to look at me?"

"So she doesn't *find* you here, if she comes home. Well, she just might come home. Well, what's the matter with you?"

She rose and clutched her stomach. "Take a guess!"

"Shhhh."

"But she's out."

"But she'll be back! We *always* have the lights out, Lucy."

"But I want to talk to you, and face to face, not on a phone, Roy, where you can—"

"Well, I'm sorry, but the lights are going off. So get ready."

"But are we getting married or aren't we? Tell me, so I know what to do next, or where to go, or God knows what."

"Well, at least let me take my coat off, will you, please?"

"Roy, yes or no."

"Well, how can I give you a yes or no answer when it's not a yes or no question?"

"But that's exactly what it *is.*"

"Will you calm down? I've been driving for two hours."

While he was hanging his coat in the closet, she came up behind him and stood on her toes. *"Yes or no, Roy!"* up toward his ear, which was still a foot above her.

He ducked away from her. "Now, first, I'm turning the lights off. Just to be safe. Well, look, Lucy, I agreed when I rented here not to have girls in my room."

"But you had me, Roy, and plenty."

"But *she* doesn't know about it! Oh, darn it. Here go the lights," and without pausing to hear an objection, he turned them off.

"Okay, now you don't have to look at me, Roy. Tell me what happened over your long Thanksgiving holiday. While I was down here in an empty dormitory all by myself for two whole days."

"First off, I didn't tell you to go back to any empty dorm. Second, I'm going to sit down, if you don't mind. And why don't you sit, too?"

"I'll stand, thank you."

"In the dark?"

"Yes!"

"Shhhh!"

"Begin," she said.

"Well, let me get settled . . . Okay."

"What?"

"I've got them to come around part way."

"Continue."

"Oh, sit *down,* will you?"

"What's the difference? You can't see me."

"I do too see you! Hanging over me. Sit down, *please.*"

She had been waiting for over an hour. It wasn't sitting she wanted, it was sleep. She lowered herself onto the edge of the bed and closed her eyes. *Go to Mr. Valerio. Run away.* But neither idea made sense. If she should see anyone, it was Father

Damrosch. But what would he do? That was precisely his trouble: he couldn't *do* anything. He was about as much help as Saint Teresa, or Jesus Christ. He looked so strong, and listened to everything she said, and said such beautiful things himself . . . but it wasn't beautiful things she needed to hear. Something had to be *done.*

"First off," he was saying, "don't think it was easy for me. It was hell, actually."

"What was?"

"Pretending you weren't pregnant, Lucy, when everybody kept asking me over and over again *why.*"

"And did you tell them?"

"No."

"Are you sure?"

"Yes! *Shhhhh!*"

"You're the one who's shouting."

"Well, you make me."

"You might be shouting because you're lying, Roy."

"I did not tell them, Lucy! Will you stop accusing? Actually, I keep wondering why I don't. Why can't I just speak the simple truth? If we're going to be married anyway."

"Are we?"

"Well, we would be . . . if I told them, I mean."

"You mean if you don't, we're *not?*"

"Well, that's the point. That's what's so confused. I mean, they had so many arguments for why we should at least wait until June."

"And?"

"And, well, they're all good arguments. I mean, it's just hard to argue against a good argument, that's all."

"So you said you'd wait."

"I said I'd *think* about it."

"But how *can* we?"

"Look, I had to get out of the house, didn't I? I've missed a whole day of school already."

"You have a car, you can drive—"

"But I couldn't leave it the way it was! Don't you understand anything!"

"Why couldn't you? Why didn't you?"

"Why should they all be furious at me, Lucy, and so confused about everything? I'm not doing anything wrong. The opposite, in fact, the very opposite! Why don't we just tell *the truth?* I don't have to lie to my parents, you know."

"I don't have to lie to mine either, Roy, if that's what you mean."

"But you are."

"Because I want to!"

"Why?"

"Oh, why won't you be a man about this! Why are you acting this way!"

"But you're the one who's hiding the simple fact that would make them all understand the whole thing!"

"Roy, do you honestly believe they will all love and adore me when they hear that I'm going to have a baby?"

"They'd *understand* is all I'm saying."

"But only two people have to understand—you and me."

"Well, maybe that's all you think . . . with your family."

"And what's wrong with my family that isn't with yours, Roy? Look, you, if you don't want to marry me," she said, "because someone has begun to tell you that I'm not good enough for you, well, believe me, you don't have to."

A moment passed. And another.

"But I do want to," he said at last.

"Roy, I think you really don't." She buried her head in her hands. "That's the truth, isn't it? 'Trust me, trust me'—and that's the real truth."

"Well . . . no . . . Well, you certainly haven't been acting these last few days like the kind of person someone would like living in the same house with particularly, I'll tell you that . . . Suddenly you're so—"

"So what? Lower class?"

"No," he said. "No. Cold."

"Oh, am I?"

"Well, sort of, recently, yes, as a matter of fact."

"And what else am I?"

"Well, all kidding aside, Lucy, you're just acting so angry."

"You might be a little angry too, if you had agreed beforehand with someone—"

"But I don't mean normal angry!"

"What?"

"Well—practically crazy!"

"You honestly think because I'm angry I'm *insane?*"

"I didn't say *I* did. I didn't say insane."

"Who did say it then?"

"No one."

"Who?"

"No one!"

"Maybe," she said after a moment, "you *make* me insane, Roy Bassart."

"Then why do you want to marry me so much?"

"I *don't* want to!"

"Oh, then don't do me the favor, you know."

"I don't think I will," she said. "Because that's really what it would be."

"Oh, sure. And what will you do instead? Marry somebody else?"

"Do you know something, you? I've been getting rid of you since July, Roy. Since the day you took this room because it had a long bed in it, you—you baby!"

"Well, you sure are a slow worker, I'll say that for you."

"I'm not slow! I have sympathy for you! I felt *sorry* for you."

"Oh, sure."

"I was afraid you'd give up photography if I hurt your little feelings. But I was going to do it, Roy—on Thanksgiving Day of all days, and I would have, too, if I didn't have to marry you instead."

"Oh, don't feel you have to, you know."

"I thought when you collapsed, at least you'd be in Liberty Center, where you could go eat your Hydrox cookies."

"Well, don't worry about my crying, if I can put in my two cents. I don't cry that easy, for one thing. And as for Hydrox cookies, that's irrelevant to anything. I don't even know what it's supposed to mean, in fact. Besides," he said, "if you wanted to drop somebody, don't worry, you'd drop him. You wouldn't bother too much about their crying either."

"No?"

". . . Because you don't have emotions like other people."

"Don't I? And who said that?"

"Lucy? Are you crying?"

"Oh, no. I don't have emotions like other people. I'm a piece of pure stone."

"You *are* crying." He came over to the bed, where she was stretched out, her face still in her hands. "Don't. Please, I didn't mean it. Really."

"Roy," she said, "who said I was insane to you? Who said I didn't have emotions?"

"Ordinary emotions. Nobody."

"Who was it, Roy? Your Uncle Julian?"

"No. Nobody."

"And you believed him."

"I didn't. He didn't say it!"

"But I could tell you about him too! Tell you plenty. The way your Uncle Julian looks at me! How he kissed me at your party!"

"This summer, you mean? But that was a joke. You kissed him back. Lucy, what are you even saying?"

"I'm saying that you're blind! You're blind to how awful people are! How rotten and hateful they are! They tell you I'm lower class and don't have ordinary emotions, and you believe them!"

"I don't!"

"And all on the basis of what? Why, Roy? Say it!"

"Say *what?*"

"My father! But I didn't put him in jail, Roy!"

"I didn't say you did."

"He put himself there! That was years ago, and it's over, and I am not beneath you or them, or anyone!"

The door opened; the light went on over their heads.

In the doorway stood the widow from whom Roy rented his room: Mrs. Blodgett, a thin, nervous, and alert woman with a little coin-slot mouth and a great capacity for expressing disapproval by merely reducing the thing in size. She did not speak right off; she did not have to.

"Well, just how did you get in here?" Roy asked, as though he were the one who was outraged. He had moved instantly between Lucy and the landlady. "Well, how, Mrs. Blodgett?"

"With a key, Mr. Bassart. How did *she* is a better question. Stand up, you hussy."

"Roy," whispered Lucy. But he continued to hide her behind him.

"I said get up from that bed," said Mrs. Blodgett. "And get out."

But Roy was intent upon making his point. "You're not supposed to use a key in another person's door, for one thing, you know."

"Don't tell me the things I'm not supposed to do, Mr. Bassart. I thought *you* were an Army veteran, or so you said."

"But—"

"But what, sir? But you don't know the rules of this house, is that what you're going to have the gall to tell me?"

"You don't under*stand,*" said Roy.

"Understand what?"

"Well, if you'd calm down, I'll tell you."

"You just tell me, whether I'm calmed down or not, which I happen to be anyway. I've had others like you, Mr. Bassart. One in 1937, and another right on his heels in 1938. They look all right, but the looks is about the whole of it. Underneath they're all the same." Her mouth became invisible. "Crooked," she said.

"But this is different," said Roy. "She's my fiancée."

"Who is? You just let her out, so I can see her."

"Roy," Lucy pleaded. *"Move."*

At last he did, smiling all the while. "This is Mrs. Blodgett, my landlady, who I mentioned to you. Mrs. Blodgett"—he rubbed his hands together, as though he had been awaiting this pleasure for a long time—"this is my fiancée. Lucy."

"Lucy what?"

Lucy stood, her skirt finally covering her knees.

"Why were the lights off and all that shouting?" asked Mrs. Blodgett.

"Shouting?" said Roy, looking around. "We were listening to music. You know I love music, Mrs. Blodgett."

Mrs. Blodgett looked at him in such a way as to openly admit to skepticism.

"The radio," he said. "We just turned it off. That was the noise, I guess. We just drove down from home. We were resting. Our eyes. That's how come the lights were dim."

"Off," said the tiny mouth, disappearing.

"Anyway," said Roy, "there's my suitcase. We did just get back."

"Who gave you permission, young man, to bring girls into my house against the rules? This is a dwelling place. I told you that when you first arrived, did I not?"

"Well, as I said, we just drove down. And I thought since she was my fiancée, you wouldn't mind if we rested." He smiled. "Against the rules." No answer. "Since we're getting married."

"When?"

"Christmas," he announced.

"Is that so?"

Lucy was the one being asked.

"It's the truth, Mrs. Blodgett," said Roy. "That's why we came down late from home. Making plans," he said with another big smile; then he turned somber and penitent. "I may have broken a rule about bringing Lucy in here, and if I did, I'm sorry."

"There are no ifs about it," said Mrs. Blodgett. "Not that I can see."

"Well then, I'm sorry then."

"Lucy what?" asked the landlady. "What's your last name, you?"

"Nelson."

"And where are you from?"

"The women's college."

"And is this true? Are you marrying him, or are you just some girl?"

"I'm marrying him."

Roy raised his hands. "See?"

"Well," said Mrs. Blodgett, "she could be lying. That's not unheard of."

"Does she look like a liar?" asked Roy, putting his hands in his pockets and shuffling over toward Lucy. "With this face? Come on, Mrs. Blodgett," he said winningly. "She's the girl next door. Actually, she practically is, you know."

The landlady did not smile back. "I had a boy in 1945 who had a fiancée. But *he* came to me, Mr. Bassart—"

"Yes?"

"—and told me his plans. And then brought the young lady around on a Sunday to be properly introduced."

"A Sunday. Well, that's a good idea, all right."

"Let me finish, please. We then arranged that she might come here to visit until ten in the evening. I did not even have to make it clear that the door to the room was to be left open. He understood that much."

"I see," said Roy with considerable interest.

"Miss Nelson, I am not a close-minded person, but where I have my rules I am strict. This happens to be my dwelling place, and not some fly-by-night person's hotel. Without rules it would go to rack and ruin inside of a month. Maybe you'll understand how that happens when you're older. I certainly hope you do, for your sake."

"Oh, we understand now," said Roy.

"Don't ever try to trick me again, Mr. Bassart."

"Oh, now that I know the ten o'clock setup—"

"And I know your name, young lady. Lucy Nelson. S-o-n or s-e-n?"

"S-o-n."

"And I know the dean over at your school. Miss Pardee, correct? Dean of Students."

"Yes."

"Then don't you ever try to trick me either."

She started for the door.

"So then," said Roy, following her, "at least we're all squared away, anyway."

When Mrs. Blodgett turned to show him what she thought of that last remark, Roy smiled. "I mean, we're all forgiven and everything, right? I know innocence of the law is no—"

"You are not innocent, Mr. Bassart. My back was turned. You are guilty as sin."

"Well, I suppose in a manner of speaking . . ." And he shrugged.

"Now the rules, Mrs. Blodgett—just so I'm sure I've got them straight."

"So long, sir, as the door is left open—"

"Oh, absolutely, wide open."

"So long as she is out of here at ten o'clock—"

"Oh, out she'll be," said Roy, laughing.

"So long as there is no shouting—"

"That was music, Mrs. Blodgett, really—"

"And so long, Mr. Bassart, as there is a marriage, Christmas Day."

For a moment he looked dumbfounded. Marriage? "Oh, sure. Good day, don't you think? Christmas?"

Mrs. Blodgett went out, leaving the door ajar.

"Bye," said Roy, and waited until he heard the door to the back parlor being closed before he fell into a chair. "Wow."

"Then we *are* getting married," said Lucy.

"Shhhhh!"—rising up out of the chair. "Will you—*yes,*" he said all at once, for the parlor door had opened, and Mrs. Blodgett was headed back to the stairs. "Mom and Dad feel—oh, hi, Mrs. Blodgett." He tipped an imaginary hat. "Have a nice sleep now."

"It is nine forty-eight, Mr. Bassart."

Roy looked at his watch. "Right you are, Mrs. Blodgett. Thanks for reminding me. Just finishing up talking over our plans. Night, now."

She started up the stairs, her anger not much abated, it seemed.

"Roy—" Lucy began, but in two steps he was at her side; one hand he pressed to the back of her head, the other to her mouth.

"So," he said loudly, "Mom and Dad felt that for the most part your suggestion—"

Her eyes stared wildly at him, until the bedroom door could be heard closing overhead. He took his wet hand from her lips.

"Don't you ever—ever—" she said, so enraged that she could hardly speak, "do that again!"

"Oh, golly," he said, and threw himself backward onto his bed. "I'm actually going off my *rocker* with you! What do you expect, when she was on the *stairs,* Lucy?"

"I expect—!"

"Shhhhh!" He shot up on the bed. "We're getting married!" he whispered hoarsely. *"So shut up."*

She was suddenly and completely baffled. She was getting married. "When?"

"Christmas! *Okay?* Now will you *stop?"*

"And your family?"

"Well, what about them?"

"You have to tell them."

"I will, I will. But just lay *off* for a while."

"Roy . . . it has to be now."

"Now?" he said.

"Yes!"

"But my mother is in bed, *and quiet down!"* After a moment he said, "Well, she is. I'm not lying. She goes to bed at nine and gets up at five-thirty. Don't ask me why. That's how she does it, Lucy, and how she's always done it, and there's nothing I can do to change her at this stage of the game. Well, that's the truth. And furthermore, Lucy, I have had it for tonight, really."

"But you must make this official. You just can't keep me living this way. It's a nightmare!"

"But I'll make this official when I think it should be!"

"Roy, suppose she calls Dean Pardee! I don't want to be thrown out of school! I don't need that in my one life, too."

"Well," he said, smacking the sides of his head, "I don't want to be thrown out either, you know. Why else do you think I told her what I did?"

"Then it is a lie and you don't mean it *again!"*

"It's not! I *do!* I always have!"

"Roy Bassart, call your parents, or I'll do something!"

He jumped off the bed. "No!"

"Keep your hands away from my mouth, Roy!"

"Don't scream, for God's sakes! That's *stupid!"*

"But I am pregnant with a human baby!" she cried. "I'm going to have your baby, Roy! And you won't even do your duty!"

"I will! I am!"

"When?"

"Now! Okay? *Now!* But don't scream, Lucy, don't throw a stupid fit!"

"Then call!"

"But," he said, "what I told Mrs. Blodgett—I had to."

"Roy!"

"Okay," and he ran from the room.

In a few minutes he returned, paler than she had ever seen him. Where the hair was clipped short at his neck, she could see his white skin. "I did it," he said.

And she believed him. Even his wrists and hands were white.

"I did it," he mumbled. "And I told you, didn't I? I told you she'd be sleeping. I told you he'd have to wake her up and get her out of bed. Well, didn't I? *I wasn't lying!* And I wouldn't be thrown out of school. Why did I say *that!* I'd only be thrown out of this room—and what difference does that make anyway? Nobody else cares about my self-respect anyway, so why should I worry about it? *He* doesn't worry about it! *She* doesn't worry about it! And you—you were going to *scream!* My self-respect, oh, the heck with that, all you want to do is scream and confuse people. That's your way, Lucy—to confuse people. Everybody's way. Confuse Roy—why not? Who's he, anyway? But that's over! Because I'm not confused, Lucy, and from here on out that's the way things are going to be. We're getting married, you hear me—on Christmas Day. And if that doesn't suit people, then the day after—but that's it!"

The door opened upstairs. "Mr. Bassart, there is that shouting again! That is not music, that is clear shouting, and it will not be tolerated!"

Roy stuck his head out into the hallway. "No, no, just saying good night to Lucy here, Mrs. Blodgett—finishing up the old wedding plans."

"Say it then! Don't shout it! This is a dwelling place!" She slammed her door shut.

Lucy was crying.

"Now what are the tears for?" he asked. "Huh? *Now* what hundred thousand things did I do wrong? Really, you know, maybe I've had just about enough complaining and criticizing of me, you know—from you included, too. So maybe you ought to stop, you know. Maybe you ought to have a little consideration for all I've been through, *and just stop, damn it!"*

"Oh," she said, "I'll stop, Roy. Until you change your mind again—!"

"Oh, brother, I'll make that bargain. *Gladly.*"

Whereupon, to his surprise, she threw open the window, and out of anger, or spite, or habit left the room as she had entered it. Roy rushed into the hallway to the front door. Noisily he opened it—"Good night," he called. "Good night, Lucy"—and noisily he closed it, so that upstairs Mrs. Blodgett would continue to believe that everything was really on the up-and-up, even if a little too loud.

Tuesday, Aunt Irene for lunch at the Hotel Thomas Kean.

Wednesday, his mother and father for dinner at The Song of Norway.

Thursday, Uncle Julian, a drink in the taproom of the Kean, lasting from five in the afternoon until nine in the evening.

At nine-thirty Roy dropped into a sofa in the downstairs living room of The Bastille. The corner in which Lucy had chosen to wait for him was the darkest in the room.

"And I haven't eaten," he said. "I haven't even eaten!"

"I have some crackers in my room," she whispered.

"They're not going to treat me like this," he said, glaring down his legs at the tips of his Army shoes. "I won't sit by and listen to threats, I'll tell you that."

". . . Do you want me to get the crackers?"

"That isn't the point, Lucy! The point is, pushing me around! Thinking he could make me sit there! Just *make* me, you know? Well, I don't need them that bad, I'll tell you that. And I don't want them either, not if they're going to take this kind of attitude. What an attitude to take—to me! To somebody they're supposed to care about!"

He got up and walked to the window. Looking out at the quiet street, he banged a fist into his palm. "Boy!" she heard him say.

She remained curled up on the sofa, her legs back under her skirt. It was a posture she had seen the other girls take while talking to their boy friends in the dormitory living room. If the house mother came into the living room, it would seem as though nothing unusual were going on. So far no one in the dorm knew anything; no one was going to, either. In her two and a half months at school Roy hadn't left her alone enough to make any close friends, and even those few girls she had begun to be friendly with on the floor, she had drawn away from now.

"Look," said Roy, coming back to the sofa, "I've got the G.I. Bill, haven't I?"

"Yes."

"And I've got savings still, right? Other guys played cards, other guys shot crap—but I didn't. I was waiting to get out. So I saved! Purposely. And they should know that! I told them, in fact—but they don't even *listen.* And if worst ever came to worst, I'd sell the Hudson, too, even with all the work I put in it. Do you believe me, Lucy? Because it's true!"

"Yes."

Was this Roy? Was this Lucy? Was this them together?

"But they think money is everything. Do you know what he is, my Uncle Julian? Maybe I'm just finding out—but *he's* a materialist. And what a vocabulary! It's worse than you even think it is. What respect for somebody else!"

"What did he say? Roy, what kind of threats?"

"Oh, who cares. *Money* threats. And my father—him too. You know, by and large, whether he knew it or not, I used to respect him. But do you think he has any emotional respect for me, either? He's trying to treat me like I'm in his printing class again. But I just got out of serving my time in the Army. Sixteen months in the Aleutian Islands—the backside of the whole goddamn world. But my uncle says—you know what he says? 'But the war was over, buster, in 1945. Don't act like you fought it.' See, *he* fought it. He won a medal. And what's that have to do with anything anyway? Nothing! Oh—up his."

"Roy," warned Lucy, as some senior girls came into the living room.

"Well," he said, plopping down next to her, "they're always telling me I should speak up for myself, right? 'Make a decision and stick to it, Roy.' Isn't that all I heard since the day I got home? Isn't my Uncle Julian always shooting off about how you have to be a go-getter in this world? That's his big defense of capitalism, you know. It makes a man out of you, instead of just hanging around waiting for things to come your way. But what does he know about Socialism anyway? You think the man has ever read a book about it in his life? He thinks Socialism is Communism, and what you say doesn't make any difference at all. None! Well, I'm young. And I've got my health. And I sure don't care one way or the other about ever being in the El-ene washing-machine business, I'll tell you that much. Big threat that is. I'm going to photography school anyway. And you know something else? He doesn't know right from wrong. That's the real pay-off. That in this country, where people are still struggling, or unemployed, or don't have the ordinary necessities that they give the people in just about any Scandinavian country you can name—that a man like that, without the slightest code of decency, can just bully his way, and the hell with right and wrong or somebody's feelings. Well, I'm through being somebody he can toss his favors to. Let him keep his big fourteen-dollar cigars. Up his, Lucy—really."

The next morning, when the alarm rang at six-thirty, she went off to the bathroom to stick a finger down her throat before the other girls started coming in to brush their teeth. This made her feel herself again, provided she skipped breakfast afterward, and avoided the corridor back of the dining hall, and forced soda crackers down herself from time to time during the morning. Then she could get through the day's classes pretending that she was the same girl in the same body, and in the same way too—alone.

But what about last night? And the night before that? The fainting spells had stopped two weeks back, and the nausea she could starve to death every morning, but now that Roy's body seemed to be inhabited by some new person, the truth came in upon her as it never had before: *a new person was inhabiting hers as well.*

She was stunned. Her predicament was *real.* It was no plot she had invented to bring them all to their senses. It was no scheme to force them to treat her like flesh and blood, like a human being, like a girl. And it was not going to disappear either, just because somebody besides herself was at long last taking it seriously. It was real! Something was happening which she was helpless to stop! Something was growing inside her body, and without her permission!

And I don't want to marry him.

The sun wasn't even above the trees as she ran across Pendleton Park to downtown Fort Kean.

She had to wait an hour in the station for the first bus to the north. Her books were in her lap; she had some idea that she could study on the way up and be back for her two-thirty, but then she had not yet a clear idea of why she was suddenly rushing up to Liberty Center, or what would happen there. On the bench in the empty station she tried to calm herself by reading the English assignment she had planned to do in her free hour before lunch, and during lunch, which she didn't eat anyway. "Here you will have a chance to examine, and then practice, several skills used in writing effective sentences. The skills presented are those—"

She didn't want to marry him! He was the last person in the world she would ever want to marry!

She began gagging only a little way beyond Fort Kean. When he heard the sounds of her distress, the driver pulled to the side of the road. She dropped out the back door and threw her soiled handkerchief into a puddle. Aboard again, she sat in the rear corner praying that she would not be ill, or faint, or begin to sob. She must not think of food; she must not even think of the crackers she had forgotten in her flight from the dorm; she must not think of what she was going to say, or to whom.

What *was* she going to say?

"Here you will have a chance to examine, and then practice, several skills used in writing effective sentences. The skills presented are those used by writers of the models in the Description Section—" Years ago there was a farm girl at L.C. High who took so large a dose of castor oil to try to make the baby come out that she blew a hole in her stomach. She contracted a terrible case of peritonitis, and lost the baby, but afterward, because she had come so close to dying, everyone forgave her, and kids who hadn't even noticed her before— "Here you will have a chance to examine, and then practice, several skills used in writing—" Curt Bonham, the basketball star. He had been a year ahead of her. In March of his last term he and a friend had tried to walk home across the river one night while the ice was breaking up, and Curt had drowned. His whole class voted unanimously to dedicate the yearbook to him, and his graduation photograph appeared all by itself on the opening page of *The Liberty Bell.* And beneath the black-bordered picture was written—

Smart lad, to slip betimes away
From fields where glory does not stay . . .
ELLIOT CURTIS BONHAM
1930–1948

"What is it?" her mother asked when she came through the front door. "Lucy, what are you doing here? What's the matter?"

"I got here by bus, Mother. That's how people get from Fort Kean to Liberty Center. Bus."

"But what is it? Lucy, you're so pale."

"Is anyone else home?" she asked.

Her mother shook her head. She had come running from the kitchen, carrying a small bowl in her hand; now she had it thrust up to her chest. "Dear, your coloring—"

"Where is everyone?"

"Daddy Will took Grandma over to the market in Winnisaw."

"And he went to work? Your husband?"

"Lucy, what is it? Why aren't you in school?"

"I'm getting married Christmas Day," she said, moving into the parlor.

Sadly her mother spoke. "We heard. We know."

"How did you hear?"

"Lucy, weren't you going to tell us?"

"We only decided Monday night."

"But, dear," said her mother, "today is Friday."

"How did you hear, Mother?"

". . . Lloyd Bassart spoke to Daddy."

"Daddy Will?"

"To your father."

"Oh? And what came of that, may I ask?"

"Well, he took your side. Well, that's what came of it. Lucy, I'm answering your question. He took your side and without a moment's hesitation. Despite our not having been properly told by our own daughter, the day of her own wedding—"

"What did he say, Mother? Exactly."

"He told Mr. Bassart he couldn't speak for Roy, of course . . . He told Mr. Bassart we feel you are mature enough to know your own mind."

"Well—maybe I'm not!"

"Lucy, you can't think everything he does is wrong just because he does it. He *believes* in you."

"Tell him not to, then!"

"Dear—"

"I'm going to have a baby, Mother! So please tell him not to!"

"Lucy—you are?"

"Of course I am! I'm going to have a baby and I hate Roy and I never want to marry him or see him again!"

She ran off to the kitchen just in time to be sick in the sink.

She was put to bed in her room. "Here you will have a chance . . ." The book slid off the bed onto the floor. What was there to do now but wait?

The mail fell through the slot in the door and onto the hall welcome mat. The vacuum cleaner started up. The car pulled into the driveway. She heard her grandmother's voice down on the front porch. She slept.

Her mother brought her tea and toast. "I told Grandma it was the grippe," she whispered to her daughter. "Is that all right?"

Would her grandmother believe that she had come home because of the grippe? Where was Daddy Will? What had she told him?

"He didn't even come inside, Lucy. He'll be back this afternoon."

"Does he know I'm home?"

"Not yet."

Home. But why not? For years they had complained that she acted contemptuous of everything they said or did; for years they complained that she refused to let them give her a single word of advice; she lived among them like a stranger, like an enemy even, unfriendly, uncommunicative, nearly unapproachable.

Well, could they say she was behaving like their enemy today? She had come home. So what were they going to do?

Alone, she drank some of the tea. She sank back into the pillow her mother had fluffed up for her and drew one finger lightly round and round her lips. Lemon. It smelled so nice. Forget everything else. Just wait. Time will pass. Eventually something will have to be done.

She fell asleep with her face on her fingers.

Her grandmother came up the stairs carrying a wet mustard plaster. The patient let her nightgown be unbuttoned. "That'll loosen it up," said Grandma Berta, pressing it down. "The two important things, rest and heat. Plenty of heat. Much as you can possibly stand," and she piled two blankets more onto the patient.

Lucy closed her eyes. Why hadn't she done this at the start? Just gotten into bed and left it all to them. Wasn't that what they were always wanting to be, her family?

She was awakened by the piano. The students had begun to arrive for their lessons. She thought, *"But I don't have the grippe!"* But then she drove the thought, and the panic that accompanied it, right from her mind.

It must have begun snowing while she was asleep. She pulled a blanket off the bed, wrapped it around her, and, at the window, put her mouth on the cold glass and watched the cars sliding down the street. The window began to grow warm where her mouth was pressed against it. Breathing in and out, she could make the circle of steam on the glass expand and contract. She watched the snow fall.

What would happen when her grandmother found out what really was wrong with her? And her grandfather, when he got home? And her father!

She had forgotten to tell her mother not to tell him. Maybe she wouldn't But then would anything happen?

She scuffed with her slippers across the old worn rug and got back into her bed. She thought about picking up her English book from the floor to work a little on those sentences; instead she got way down under the blankets and, with her faintly lemony fingers under her nose, slept for the sixth or seventh time.

Beyond the window it was dark, though from where she sat propped up in the bed the snow could be seen floating down through the light of the street lamp across the street. Her father knocked on her door. He asked if he could come in.

". . . It's not locked" was her response.

"Well," he said, stepping into the room, "so this is how the rich spend their days. Not bad."

She could tell that his words had been prepared. She did not look up from the blanket, but began to smooth it out with her hand. "I have the grippe."

"Smells to me," he said, "like you've been eating hot dogs."

She did not smile or speak.

"I tell you what it smells like. Smells like Comiskey Park, down in Chicago."

"Mustard plaster," she finally said.

"Well," he said, giving the door a push so that it closed, "that's one of your grandmother's real pleasures in life. That's one," he said, lowering his voice, "and the other is . . . No, I think that about covers it."

She only shrugged, as though she had no opinions on people's habits, one way or the other. Was he clowning because he knew, or because he didn't know? She saw from the corner of her eye that the pale hairs on the back of his hands were wet. He had washed before coming into her room.

The smell of dinner cooking down below caused her to begin to feel ill.

"Mind if I sit at the foot here?" he said.

"If you want to."

She mustn't be sick, not again. She mustn't arouse in him a single suspicion. No, she did not want him to know, ever!

"Let's see," he was saying. "Do I want to or don't I want to? I want to."

She yawned as he sat.

"Well," he said, "nice and cozy up here."

She stared straight ahead into the snowy evening.

"Winter's coming in with a rush this time," he said.

She glanced quickly over at him. "I suppose."

By looking instantly out the window, she was able to collect herself; she could not remember the last time she had looked directly into his eyes.

"Did I ever tell you," he said, "about the time I sprained my ankle when I was working over at McConnell's? It swelled way up and I came home, and your grandmother just lit up all over. Hot compresses, she said. So I sat down in the kitchen and rolled up my trouser leg. You should have seen her boiling up the water on the stove. Somehow it reminded me of all those cannibals over in Africa. She can't see how it can be good for you unless it hurts or smells bad."

Suppose she just blurted out the truth, to him?

"A lot of people like that," he said . . . "So," and gave her foot a squeeze where it stuck up at the end of the bed, "how's school going, Goosie?"

"All right."

"I hear you're learning French. Parlez-vous?"

"French is one of my subjects, yes."

"And, let's see . . . what else? You and me haven't had a good conversation in a long time now, have we?"

She did not answer.

"Oh, and how's Roy doing?"

Instantly she said, "Fine."

Her father took his hand off her foot at last. "Well," he said, "we heard, you know, about the wedding."

"Where's Daddy Will?" she asked.

"I'm talking to you right now, Lucy. What do you want him for while I'm talking to you?"

"I didn't say I wanted him. I only asked where he was."

"Out," her father said.

"Isn't he even going to have dinner?"

"He went out!" He rose from the bed. "I don't ask where he goes, or when he eats. How do I know where he is? He's out!" And he left the room.

In a matter of seconds her mother appeared.

"What happened now?"

"I asked where Daddy Will is, that's all," Lucy answered. "What's wrong with that?"

"But is Daddy Will your father or is your father your father?"

"But you told him!" she burst out.

"Lucy, your voice," said her mother, shutting the door.

"But you did. You told him! And I didn't say you should!"

"Lucy, you came home, dear; you said—"

"I don't want him to know! It's not his business!"

"Now stop, Lucy—unless you want others to know too."

"But I don't care who knows! I'm not ashamed! And don't start crying, Mother!"

"Then let him talk to you, *please.* He wants to."

"Oh, does he?"

"Lucy, you have to listen to him. You have to give him a chance."

She turned and hid her face in the pillow. "I didn't want him to *know,* Mother."

Her mother sat on the bed, and put her hand to the girl's hair.

"And," said Lucy, moving back, "what was he going to say, anyway? Why didn't he just say it out, if he had anything to say?"

"Because," her mother pleaded, "you didn't give him the chance."

"Well, I'm giving *you* a chance, Mother." There was a silence. "Tell me!"

"Lucy . . . dear . . . what would you think . . . What would you say—what would you think, I mean—of going for a visit—"

"Oh, no."

"Please let me finish. Of going to visit your father's cousin Vera. In Florida."

"And is that his idea of what to do with me?"

"Lucy, till this is over. For the little while it will take."

"Nine months is no little while, Mother—"

"But it would be warm there, it would be pleasant—"

"Oh," she said, beginning to cry into the pillow, "very pleasant. Why doesn't he ship me off to a home for wayward girls, wouldn't that be even easier?"

"Don't say that. He doesn't want to send you anywhere, you know that."

"He wishes I'd never been born, Mother. He thinks I'm why everything is so wrong with *him."*

"That's not *so."*

"Then," she said, sobbing, "he'd have one less responsibility to feel guilty about. If he even felt guilty to begin with."

"But he does, terribly."

"Well, he should!" she said. "He is!"

Some twenty minutes after her mother had run from the room, Daddy Will knocked. He was wearing his lumber jacket and held his cap in his hands. The brim was dark where the snow had dampened it.

"Hey. I hear somebody's been asking for me."

"Hullo."

"You sound like death warmed over, my friend. You ought to be outside and feel that wind. Then you'd really appreciate being sick in bed."

She did not answer.

"Stomach settle down?" he asked.

"Yes."

He pulled a chair over to the side of the bed. "How's about another mustard plaster? Berta called me at the Erwins' and on the way home I stopped and bought a whole fresh packet. So just say when."

She turned and looked at the wall.

"What is it, Lucy? Maybe you want Dr. Eglund. That's what I told Myra . . ." He pulled the chair right up close. "Lucy, I never saw anything like the change in him this time," he said softly. "Not a drop—not a single solitary drop, honey. He is taking this whole decision of yours right in his stride. You set a date and it was just fine with him. Fine with all of us—whatever you think is going to make you and Roy happy."

"I want my mother."

"Don't you feel good again? Maybe the doctor—"

"I want my mother! My mother—and not him!"

She was still looking at the wall when her door was opened.

"Myra," her father said, "sit over there. Sit, I said."

"Yes."

"All right, Lucy. Turn over." He was standing by the side of the bed. "Roll over, I said."

"Lucy," her mother begged, "look at us, please."

"I don't have to see that his shoes are shined and his jaw is set and what a new man he is. I don't have to see his tie, or him!"

"Lucy—"

"Myra, be *quiet.* If she wants to act like a two-year-old at a time like this, let her."

She whispered, "Look who's talking about two-year-olds."

"Listen, young lady. Your backtalk doesn't faze me one way or the other. There have always been smart-aleck teen-agers and there always will be, especially this generation. You just listen to me, that's all, and if you're too ashamed to look me right in the eye—"

"Ashamed!" she cried, but she did not move.

"Are you or are you not going to visit Cousin Vera?"

"I don't even *know* Cousin Vera."

"That isn't what I'm asking."

"I can't go off alone to someone I don't even know—and what? Make up filthy lies for the neighbors—?"

"But they wouldn't be lies," said her mother.

"What would they be, Mother? The truth?"

"They would be *stories,"* her father said. "That you have a husband overseas, say, in the Army."

"Oh, you know all about stories, I'm sure. But I tell the truth!"

"Then," he said, "just what do you intend to do about getting in trouble with somebody who you say you can't even stand?"

She turned violently from the wall, as though she intended to hurl herself at him. "Don't you take such a tone with me. Don't you dare!"

"I am not taking any tone!"

"Because I am not ashamed—not in front of you I'm not."

"Now watch it, you, just watch it. Because I can still give you a licking, smart as you think you are."

"Oh," she said bitterly, "can you?"

"Yes!"

"Go ahead, then."

"Oh, wonderful," he said, and walked to the window, where he stood as though looking outside. "Just wonderful."

"Lucy," said her mother, "if you don't want to go to Cousin Vera's, then what do you want to do? Just tell us."

"You're the parents. You were always dying to be the parents—"

"Now look," said her father, turning to face her once again. "First, Myra, you sit down. And stay down. And you," he said, waving a finger at his daughter, "you give me your attention, do you hear? Now there is a crisis here, do you understand that? There is a crisis here involving my daughter, and I am going to deal with it, and it's going to be dealt with."

"Fine," said Lucy. "Deal."

"Then be still," her mother pleaded, "and let him talk, Lucy." But when she made a move to sit on the bed, her husband looked at her and she retreated.

"Now either I'm going to do it," he said to his wife, speaking between his teeth, "or I'm not. Now which is it?"

She lowered her eyes.

"Unless of course you want to call your daddy in," he said.

"I'm sorry."

"Now," said her father, "if you wanted to marry that Roy Bassart—such as we understood you did, Lucy, till just today, and backed you up on all the way—that would be one thing. But this is something else entirely. Who he is I see pretty clear now, and the less said about him the better. I understand the whole picture, so there is just no need for raising voices. He was older, back from service, and just thought to himself he could come back here and take advantage of a young seventeen-year-old high school girl. And that's what he did. But he is his father's business, Lucy, and we will have to leave it to his high and mighty father, the big schoolteacher, to teach something into that boy's hide. Oh, his father thinks he is very superior and all in his ways, but I guess he is going to have another guess coming now. But my concern is with you, Lucy, and what is uppermost to you. Do you understand that? My concern is your going to college, which has always been your dream, right? Now, the question is this, do you still want your dream, or don't you?"

She did not favor him with a reply.

"Okay," he said, "I am going to go ahead on my assumption that you do, just as you always did. Now, next—to give you your dream I am going to do anything I can . . . Are you listening to me? Anything that is going to give it to you, do you follow me? Because what that so-called ex-G.I. has done to you, which I would like to put my hands around his throat for, well, that is not going to just take away your dream, lock, stock, and barrel . . . Now, anything," he went on. "Even something that isn't usual and ordinary, and that might to some folks seem very—out of the question." He came closer to the bed so that he could speak without being heard outside the room. "Now do you know what *anything* means, before I go to the next step?"

"Giving up whiskey?"

"I want you to go to college, it means! I have given up whiskey, for your information!"

"Really?" she asked. "Again?"

"Lucy, since Thanksgiving," her mother began.

"Myra, you be still."

"I was only telling her—"

"But *I* will tell her," he said. "*I* will do the telling."

"Yes," his wife said softly.

"Now," he said, turning back to Lucy. "Drink is neither here nor there. Drink is not the issue."

"Oh no?"

"No! A baby is!"

And that made her look away.

"An illegitimate baby is," he said again. "And if you don't *want* that illegitimate baby"—his voice had fallen almost to a whisper now—"then maybe we will have to arrange that you don't have it. If Cousin Vera's is still something you are going to consider out of the question—"

"It absolutely is. I will not spend nine months lying. I will not get big and pregnant and lie!"

"Shhh!"

"Well, I won't," she muttered.

"Okay." He wiped his mouth with his hand. "Okay." She could see where the perspiration had formed above his lip and on his forehead. "Then let's do this in order. And without voice-raising, as there are other people who live in this house."

"We're the other people who live here."

"Be still!" he said. "Everybody knows that without your back-talk!"

"Then just what are you proposing to me? Say it!"

Her mother rushed to the bed at last. "Lucy," she said, taking hold of her hand, "Lucy, it's only to help *you*—"

And then her father took hold of the other hand, and it was as though some current were about to pass through the three of them. She closed her eyes, waited—and her father spoke. And she let him. And she saw the future. She saw herself seated between her two parents as her father drove them across the bridge to Winnisaw. It would be early morning. The doctor would only just have finished his breakfast. He would come to the door to greet them; her father would shake his hand. In his office the doctor would seat himself behind a big dark desk, and she would sit in a chair, and her parents would be together on a sofa, while the doctor explained to them exactly what he was going to do. He would have all his medical degrees right up on the wall, in frames. When she went off with him into the little white operating room, her mother and father would smile at her from the sofa. And they would wait right there until it was time to bundle her up and take her home.

When her father had finished, she said, "It must cost a fortune."

"The object isn't money, honey," he said.

"The object is you," said her mother.

How nice that sounded. Like a poem. She was just beginning to study poetry, too. Her last English composition had been an interpretation of "Ozymandias." She had only received the paper back on Monday morning—a B-plus for the first interpretation she had ever written of a poem in college. Only on Monday she had thought it was going to be her last. Before Roy had finally returned to Fort Kean that night, her recurring thought had been to run away. And now she didn't have to, and she didn't have to marry him either. Now she could concentrate on one thing and one thing only—on school, on her French, her history, her poetry . . .

The object isn't money,
The object is you.

"But where," she asked softly, "will you get it all?"

"Let me do the worrying about that," her father said. "Okay?"

"Will you work?"

"Wow," he said to Myra. "She sure don't pull her punches, your daughter here." The red that had risen into his cheeks remained, even as he tried to maintain a soft and joking tone. "Come on, Goosie, what do you say? Give me a break, huh? Where do you think I've been all day today, anyway? Taking a stroll on the boulevard? Playing a tennis game? What do you think I've been doing all my life since I was eighteen years old, and part-time before that? Work, Lucy, just plain old work, day in and day out."

"Not at one job," she said.

"Well . . . I move around . . . that's true . . ."

She was going to cry: they were talking!

"Look," he said, "why don't you think of it this way. You have a father who is a jack of all trades. You should be proud. Come on, Goosie-Pie, how about a smile like I used to get back in prehistoric times? Back when you used to take those 'yumps.' Huh, little Goose?"

She felt her mother squeeze her hand.

"Look," he said, "why do you think people always hire Duane Nelson, no matter what? Because he sits around twiddling his thumbs, or because he knows every kind of machine there is, inside and out? Now which? That's not a hard question, is it, for a smart college girl?"

. . . Afterward she would read in bed. She would have her assignments mailed up to her while she recuperated in her bed. Yes, a college girl. And without Roy. He wasn't so bad; he wasn't for her, that was all. He would just disappear, and she could begin to make friends at school, friends to bring home with her when she came to visit on the weekend. For things would have changed.

Could that be? At long last those terrible days of hatred and solitude, over? To think, she could begin again to talk to her family, to tell them about all the things she was studying, to show them the books she used in her courses, to show them her papers. Stuck into her English book, right there on the floor, was the essay she had written on "Ozymandias." B-plus and across the front the professor had written, "Excellent paragraph development; good understanding of meaning; good use of quotations; but please don't stuff your sentences so." And maybe she *had* overdone the main topic sentence somewhat, but her intention had been to state at the outset all those ideas that she would later take up in the body of the essay. "Even a great king," her paper began, "such as Ozymandias apparently had been, could not predict or control what the future, or Fate, held in store for him and his kingdom; that, I think, is the message that Percy Bysshe Shelley, the poet, means for us to come away with from his romantic poem 'Ozymandias,' which not only reveals the theme of the vanity of human wishes—even a king's—but deals also with the concept of the immensity of 'boundless and bare' life and the inevitability of the 'colossal wreck' of everything, as compared to the 'sneer of cold command,' which is all many mere mortals have at their command, unfortunately."

"But is he clean?" she asked.

"A hundred percent," her father said. "Spotless, Lucy. Like a hospital."

"And how old?" she asked. "How old is he?"

"Oh," her father said, "middle-aged, I'd say."

A moment passed. Then, "That's the catch, isn't it?"

"What kind of catch?"

"He's too old."

"Now what do you mean 'too old'? If anything, he's real experienced."

"But is this all he does?"

"Lucy, he's a regular doctor . . . who does this as a special favor, that's all."

"But he charges, you said."

"Well, sure he charges."

"Then it's not a special favor. He does it for money."

"Well, everybody has got bills to meet. Everybody has got to be paid for what they do."

But she saw herself dead. The doctor would be no good, and she would die.

"How do you know about him?"

"Because—" and here he stood, and hitched up his trousers. "Through a friend," he finally said.

"Who?"

"Lucy, I'm afraid maybe that's got to be a secret."

"But where did you hear about him?" Where *would* he hear about such a doctor? "At Earl's famous Dugout of Buddies?"

"Lucy, that's not necessary," said her mother.

Her father walked to the window again. He cleared a pane with the palm of his hand. "Well," he said, "it's stopped snowing. It's stopped snowing, if anybody cares."

"All I meant—" Lucy began.

"Is *what?*" He had turned back to her.

"—is . . . do you know anybody who he's ever done it to, that's all."

"Yes, I happen to, for your information."

"And they're alive?"

"For your information, yes!"

"Well, it's my life. I have a right to know."

"Why don't you just trust me! I'm not going to kill you!"

"Oh, Duane," her mother said, "she *does.*"

"Don't speak for me, Mother!"

"Hear that?" he cried to his wife.

"Well, he might just be some quack drinking friend who says he's a doctor or something. Well, how do I know, Mother? Maybe it's even Earl himself in his red suspenders!"

"Yeah, that's who it is," her father shouted. "Earl DuVal! sure! What's the *matter* with you? You think I don't mean it when I say I want you to finish college?"

"Dear, he does. You're his daughter."

"That doesn't mean he knows whether a doctor is good or not, Mother. Suppose I die!"

"But I told you," he cried, shaking a fist at her, "you won't!"

"But how do *you* know?"

"Because she didn't, did she!"

"Who?"

No one had to speak for her to understand.

"Oh, no." She dropped slowly back against the headboard.

Her mother, at the side of the bed, covered her face with her hands.

"When?" said Lucy.

"But she's alive, isn't she?" He was pulling at his shirt with his hands. "Answer the point I'm making! I am speaking! She did not die! She did not get hurt in any way at all!"

"Mother," she said, turning to her, "when?"

But her mother only shook her head. Lucy got up out of the bed. "Mother, when did he make you do that?"

"He didn't make me."

"Oh, Mother," she said, standing before her. "You're my mother."

"Lucy, it was the Depression times. You were a little girl. It was so long ago. Oh, Lucy, it's all forgotten. Daddy Will, Grandma, they don't know," she whispered, "—don't have to—"

"But the Depression was over when I was three, when I was four."

"What?" her father cried. "Are you kidding?" To his wife he said, "Is she kidding?"

"Lucy," her mother said, "we did it for you."

"Oh yes," she said, moving backward onto her bed, "for me, everything was for me."

"Lucy, we couldn't have another baby," said her mother. "Not when we were so behind, trying so to fight back—"

"But if only he did his job! If he only stopped being a coward!"

"Look," he said, coming angrily at her, "you don't even know when the Depression was, or what it was, either—*so watch what you say!*"

"I do too know!"

"The whole country was behind the eight ball. Not just me! If you want to call names, you, call the whole United States of America names!"

"Sure, the whole *world.*"

"Don't you know history?" he cried. "Don't you know anything?" he demanded.

"I know what you made her do, you!"

"But," her mother cried, "I *wanted* to."

"Did you hear that?" he shouted. "Did you hear what your mother just said to you?"

"But you're the man!"

"I am also a human being!"

"*That's no excuse!*"

"Oh, what am I arguing with *you* for? You don't know *a* from *z* as far as life is concerned, and you never will! You wouldn't know a man's job if I did it!"

Silence.

"Hear, Mother? Hear your husband?" said Lucy. "Did you hear what he just said, right out in the open?"

"Oh, hear what I *mean,*" he cried.

"But what you *said—*"

"I don't care! Stop trapping me! I came in here to solve a crisis, but how can I do it when nobody lets me even begin? Or end! You'd rather trap me—throw me in jail! That's what you'd rather do. You'd rather humiliate me in this whole town, and make me looked down on as the town joke."

"Town *drunk!*"

"Town drunk?" he said. "Town *drunk?* You ought to *see* the town drunk. You think *I'm* the town drunk? Well, you ought to just see a town drunk, and then think what you're saying twice before you say it. You don't know what a town drunk is. You don't know what anything is! You—you just want me behind bars—that's your big wish in life, and always has been!"

"It's not."

"It is!"

"But that's *over,*" cried Myra.

"Oh, sure it's over," said Whitey. "Sure, people just forget how a daughter threw her own father in jail. Sure, people don't talk about that behind your back. People don't like to tell stories on a person, oh no. People are always giving other people a chance to change and get their strength back. Sure, that's what this little scene is all about too. You bet it is. Oh, she's got me fixed, boy—and that's the way it's going to be. That's how brilliant she is, your so-called college girl scholarship daughter. Well, go ahead, so-called daughter who knows all the answers—solve your own life. Because I'm not good enough for a person like you, and never have been. What am I anyway? The town drunk to her."

He pulled open the door and went loudly down the stairs. They could hear him bellowing in the parlor. "Go ahead, Mr. Carroll.

You're the only one can solve things around here. Go ahead, it's Daddy Will everyone wants around here anyway. I'm just extra anyway. I'm just along for the ride, we all know that."

"Shouting won't help anything, Duane—"

"Right, right you are, Berta. Nothing will help anything around here."

"Willard," said Berta, "tell this man—"

"What's the trouble, Duane? What's the fuss?"

"Oh, nothing you can't fix, Willard. Because you're the Big Daddy, and me, I'm just along for the ride."

"Willard, where is he going? Dinner is all ready."

"Duane, where are you going?"

"I don't know. Maybe I'll go down and see old Tom Whipper."

"Who's he?"

"The town drunk, Willard! That's who the town drunk is, damn it—Tom Whipper!"

The door slammed, and then the house was silent except for the whispering that began downstairs.

Lucy lay without moving on the bed.

Her mother was crying.

"Mother, why, *why* did you let him make you do that?"

"I did what I had to," said her mother mournfully.

"You didn't! You let him trample on your dignity, Mother! You were his doormat! His slave!"

"Lucy, I did what was necessary," she said, sobbing.

"That's not always right, though. You have to do what's *right!*"

"It was." She spoke as in a trance. "It was, it was—"

"It wasn't! Not for you! He degrades you, Mother, and you let him! Always! All our lives!"

"Oh, Lucy, whatever we say, our suggestions, you refuse."

"I refuse—I refuse to live your life again, Mother, that's what I refuse!"

Roy's best man was Joe Whetstone, home from the University of Alabama, where he had kicked nine field goals and twenty-three consecutive extra points for the freshman football team. The maid of honor was Eleanor Sowerby. Unbeknownst to Joe, Ellie had fallen in love at Northwestern. She simply had to tell Lucy, though she made her promise to speak of it to no one, not even Roy. She would shortly be having to write Joe a letter, and she would just as soon not have to think about that during her vacation; it would be difficult enough at the time.

Either Ellie had forgiven Lucy for calling her a dope at Thanksgiving, or else she was willing to forget it during the wedding. All through the ceremony tears coursed down her lovely face, and her own lips moved when Lucy said, "I do."

After the ceremony Daddy Will told Lucy that she was the most beautiful bride he had seen since her mother. "A real bride," he kept saying, "isn't that so, Berta?" "Congratulations," her grandmother said. "You were a real bride." That was as far as she would go; she knew now that it was not the grippe that had caused Lucy to be sick in the kitchen sink.

Julian Sowerby kissed her again. "Well," he said, "I suppose now I get to do this all the time." "Now *I* do," said Roy. Julian said, "Lucky you, boy, she's a cutie-pie, all right," in no way indicating that he had once lectured Roy for four solid hours in the taproom of the Hotel Kean on the evils of becoming her husband.

Nor did Irene Sowerby indicate that secretly she believed Lucy had unusual emotions. "Good luck to you," she said to the bride, and touched her lips to Lucy's cheek. She took Roy's hand and held it for a very long time before she was ready to speak. And then she was unable to.

Then her own parents. "Daughter," was all she heard in her ear; so stiff was she in his embrace that perhaps it was all he said. "Oh, Lucy," her mother said, her wet lashes against Lucy's face, "be happy. You can be if only you'll try. You were the happiest little girl . . ."

Then both Roy's parents stepped forward, and after a moment in which each seemed to be deferring to the other, the two Bassarts lunged at the bride simultaneously. The mix-up of arms and faces that ensued at long last gave everyone present something to laugh about.

Lloyd Bassart was the adult who had finally gotten behind the young couple and supported them in their desire to be married at Christmas—sooner than Christmas if it could be managed.

This sharp change of attitude had occurred one night early in December when Roy broke down over the phone and in tears told *his* parents—who had been pouring it on, once again—to stop. "I can't take any more!" he had cried. "Stop! Stop! Lucy's pregnant!"

Well. Well. It had required only the two "wells." If what Roy had just confessed was the actual situation as it existed, then his father did not see that Roy had any choice but to take the responsibility for what he had done. Between a man doing the right thing and a man doing the wrong thing, there was really no choice, as far as Mr. Bassart could see. Weeping, Roy said it was more or less what he had been thinking to himself all along. "I should certainly hope so," said his father, and so that, finally, was that.

Chez Claire

Upon returning from our travels through the beautiful cities—after I dreamed in Prague of visiting Kafka's whore, we flew the next morning to Paris, and three days later to Bruges, where at a conference on modern European literature I read the paper entitled "Hunger Art"—we decide to split the rent on a small house in the country for July and August. How better to spend the summer? But once the decision is made, all I can think about is the time I last lived in daily proximity to a woman, the tomb-like months just before the Hong Kong fiasco, when neither of us could so much as bear the sight of the other's shoes on the floor of the closet. Consequently, before I sign the lease for the perfect little house that we've found, I suggest that probably it would be best not to sublet either of our apartments in the city for the two months—a small financial sacrifice, true, but this way there will always be a place to retreat to if anything untoward should happen. I actually say "untoward." Claire—prudent, patient, tender Claire—understands well enough what I mean as I jabber on in this vein, the pen in my hand, and the agent who drew up the lease casting unamused glances from the other end of his office. Raised by heavyweight battlers from the day she was born until she was able to leave for school and a life of her own, an independent young woman now since the age of seventeen, she has no

---

The closing section of *The Professor of Desire.* In the novel it follows immediately after the chapter entitled here "The Professor in Prague" (see pp. 111–45).

argument against having a nest to fly off to, as well as the nest that is to be shared, for so long as the sharing is good. No, we won't rent our apartments, she agrees. Whereupon, with the solemnity of the Japanese Commander-in-Chief sitting down aboard MacArthur's battleship to surrender an empire, I affix my signature to the lease.

A small, two-storied white clapboard farmhouse, then, set halfway up a hillside of dandelions and daisies from a silent, untraveled rural road, and twenty miles north of the Catskill village where I was raised. I have chosen Sullivan County over Cape Cod, and that too is fine with Claire—proximity to the Vineyard and to Olivia seems not to matter to her quite the way it did just the year before. And for me the gentle green hills and distant green mountains beyond the dormer windows take me back to the bedroom vista of my childhood—exactly my view from the room at the top of the "Annex"—and augment the sense I already have with her that I am living at last in accordance with my true spirit, that, indeed, I am "home."

And for the spirit what a summer it is! From the daily regimen of swimming in the morning and hiking in the afternoon we each grow more and more fit, while within, day by day, we grow fat as our farmer neighbor's hogs. How the spirit feasts on just getting up in the morning! on coming to in a whitewashed sunlit room with my arms encircling her large, substantial form. Oh, how I do love the size of her in bed! That *tangibility* of hers! And the weight of those breasts in my hands! Oh, very different, this, from all the months and months of waking up with nothing to hold on to but my pillow!

Later—is it not yet eleven? *really?* we have eaten our cinnamon toast, taken our dip, stopped in town to buy food for dinner, brooded over the newspaper's front page, and it is only ten-fifteen?—later, from the rocker on the porch where I do my morning writing, I watch her toil in the garden. Two spiral notebooks are arranged beside me. In one I work at planning the projected book on Kafka, to be called, after my Bruges lecture, *Hunger Art,* while in the other, whose pages I approach with far greater eagerness—and where I am having somewhat more success—I move on to the substance of the lecture whose prologue

I had begun composing in the hotel café in Prague, the story of *my* life in its most puzzling and maddening aspects, *my* chronicle of the iniquitous, the ungovernable and the thrilling . . . or (by way of a working title), "How David Kepesh comes to be sitting in a wicker rocker on a screened-in porch in the Catskill Mountains, watching with contentment while a teetotaling twenty-five-year-old sixth-grade teacher from Schenectady, New York, creeps about her flower garden in what appear to be overalls handed down from Tom Sawyer himself, her hair tied back with a snip of green twister seal cut from the coil with which she stakes the swooning begonias, her delicate, innocent Mennonite face, small and intelligent as a raccoon's, and soil-smudged as though in preparation for Indian night at the Girl Scout jamboree—and his happiness in her hands."

"Why don't you come out and help with the weeds?" she calls—"Tolstoy would have." "He was a big-time novelist," I say; "they have to do that sort of thing, to gain Experience. Not me. For me it's enough to see you crawling on your knees." "Well, whatever pleases," she says.

Ah, Clarissa, let me tell you, all that *is* pleases. The pond where we swim. Our apple orchard. The thunderstorms. The barbecue. The music playing. Talking in bed. Your grandmother's iced tea. Deliberating on which walk to take in the morning and which at dusk. Watching you lower your head to peel peaches and shuck corn . . . Oh, nothing, really, is what pleases. But what nothing! Nations go to war for this kind of nothing, and in the absence of such nothing, people shrivel up and die.

Of course by now the passion between us is no longer quite what it was on those Sundays when we would cling together in my bed until three in the afternoon—"the primrose path to madness," as Claire once described those rapacious exertions which end finally with the two of us rising on the legs of weary travelers to change the bed linens, to stand embracing beneath the shower, and then to go out of doors to get some air before the winter sun goes down. That, once begun, our lovemaking should have continued with undiminished intensity for almost a year—that two industrious, responsible, idealistic schoolteachers should have adhered to one another like dumb sea creatures, and, at the moment of overbrimming, have come to the very brink of tearing flesh with cannibalized jaws—well, that is somewhat more than I ever would have dared predict for myself, having already served beyond the call of duty—having already staked so much and lost so much—under the tattered scarlet standard of His Royal Highness, my lust.

Leveling off. Overheated frenzy subsiding into quiet physical affection. That is how I choose to describe what is happening to our passion during this blissful summer. Can I think otherwise—can I possibly believe that, rather than coming to rest on some warm plateau of sweet coziness and intimacy, I am being eased down a precipitous incline and as yet am nowhere near the cold and lonely cavern where I finally will touch down? To be sure, the faintly brutal element has taken it on the lam; gone is the admixture of the merciless with the tender, those intimations of utter subjugation that one sees in the purplish bruise, the wantonness one thrills to in the coarse word breathed at the peak of pleasure. We no longer *succumb* to desire, nor do we touch each other everywhere, paw and knead and handle with that unquenchable lunacy so alien to what and who we otherwise are. True, I am no longer a little bit of a beast, she is no longer a little bit of a tramp, neither any longer is quite the greedy lunatic, the depraved child, the steely violator, the helplessly impaled. Teeth, once blades and pincers, the pain-inflicting teeth of little cats and dogs, are simply teeth again, and tongues are tongues, and limbs are limbs. Which is, as we all know, how it must be.

And I for one will not quarrel, or sulk, or yearn, or despair. I will not make a religion of what is fading away—of my craving for that bowl into which I dip my face as though to extract the last dram of a syrup I cannot guzzle down fast enough . . . of the harsh excitement of that pumping grip so strong, so rapid, so unyielding, that if I do not moan that there is nothing left of me, that I am stupefied and numb, she will, in that stirring state of fervor bordering on heartlessness, continue until she has milked the very life from my body. I will not make a religion of the marvelous sight of her half-stripped. No, I intend to nurse no illusions about the chance for a great revival of the drama we would seem very nearly to have played out, this clandestine, uncensored, underground theater of four furtive selves—the two who pant in performance, the two who pantingly watch—wherein regard for the hygienic, the temperate, and the time of day or night is all so much ridiculous intrusion. I tell you, I am a new man—that is, I am a *new* man no longer—and I know when my number is up: now just stroking the soft, long hair will do, just resting side by side in our bed each morning will do, awakening folded together, mated, in love. Yes, I am willing to settle on these terms. This will suffice. No more *more.*

And before whom am I on my knees trying to strike such a bargain? Who is to decide how far from Claire I am going to slide? Honored members of Literature 341, you would think, as I do, that it would, it should, it must, be me.

Late in the afternoon of one of the loveliest days of August, with nearly fifty such days already stored away in memory and the deep contentment of knowing that there are still a couple dozen more to come, on an afternoon when my feeling of well-being is boundless and I cannot imagine anyone happier or luckier than myself, I receive a visit from my former wife. I will think about it for days afterward, imagining each time the phone rings or I hear the sound of a car turning up the steep drive to the house that it is Helen returning. I will expect to find a letter from her every morning, or rather a letter about her, informing me that she has run off again to Hong Kong, or that she is dead. When I awaken in the middle of the night to remember how once I lived and how I live now—and this still happens to me, too regularly—I will cling to my sleeping partner as though it is she who is ten years my senior—twenty, thirty years my senior—rather than the other way around.

I am out by the orchard in a canvas lounge chair, my legs in the sun and my head in the shade, when I hear the phone ringing inside the house, where Claire is getting ready to go swimming. I have not yet decided—of such decisions are my days composed—whether I'll go along with her to the pond, or just stay on quietly doing my work until it is time to water the marigolds and open the wine. Since lunch I have been out here—just myself, the bumblebees, and the butterflies, and, from time to time,

Claire's old Labrador, Dazzle—reading Colette and taking notes for the course known by now around the house as Desire 341. Leafing through a pile of her books, I have been wondering if there has ever been in America a novelist with a point of view toward the taking and giving of pleasure even vaguely resembling Colette's, an American writer, man or woman, stirred as deeply as she is by scent and warmth and color, someone as sympathetic to the range of the body's urgings, as attuned to the world's every sensuous offering, a connoisseur of the finest gradations of amorous feeling, who is nonetheless immune to fanaticism of any sort, except, as with Colette, a fanatical devotion to the self's honorable survival. Hers seems to have been a nature exquisitely susceptible to all that desire longs for and promises—"these pleasures which are lightly called physical"—yet wholly untainted by puritan conscience, or murderous impulse, or megalomania, or sinister ambitions, or the score-settling rage of class or social grievance. One thinks of her as egotistic, in the sharpest, crispest sense of the word, the most pragmatic of sensualists, her capacity for protective self-scrutiny in perfect balance with the capacity to be carried away—

The top sheet of my yellow pad is spattered and crisscrossed with the fragmentary beginnings of a lecture outline—running down one margin is a long list of modern novelists, European as well as American, among whom Colette's decent, robust, bourgeois paganism still seems to me unique—when Claire comes out of the kitchen's screen door, wearing her bathing suit and carrying her white terry-cloth robe over her arm.

The book in her hand is Musil's *Young Törless,* the copy I'd just finished marking up the night before. How delighted I am with her curiosity about these books I will be teaching! And to look up at the swell of her breasts above the bikini's halter, well, that is yet another of this wonderful day's satisfactions.

"Tell me," I say, taking hold of the calf of her nearest leg, "why is there no American Colette? Or could it be Updike who comes the closest? It's surely not Henry Miller. It's surely not Hawthorne."

"A phone call for you," she says. "Helen Kepesh."

"My God." I look at my watch, for all the help that will give.

"What time would it be in California? What can she want? How did she find me?"

"It's a local call."

"Is it?"

"I think so, yes."

I haven't yet moved from the chair. "And that's what she said, Helen *Kepesh?"*

"Yes."

"But I thought she'd taken her own name back."

Claire shrugs.

"You told her I was here?"

"Do you want me to tell her you aren't?"

"What can she *want?"*

"You'll have to ask her," says Claire. "Or maybe you won't."

"Would it be so very wrong of me just to go in there and put the phone back on the hook?"

"Not wrong," says Claire. "Only unduly anxious."

"But I *feel* unduly anxious. I feel unduly *happy.* This is all so perfect." I spread ten fingers across the soft swell of flesh above her halter. "Oh, my dear, dear pal."

"I'll wait out here," she says.

"And I *will* go swimming with you."

"Okay. Good."

"So wait!"

It would be neither cruel nor cowardly, I tell myself, looking down at the phone on the kitchen table—it would just be the most sensible thing I could do. Except, of the half-dozen people closest to my life, Helen happens still to be one. "Hello," I say.

"Hello. Oh, hello. Look, I feel odd about phoning you, David. I almost didn't. Except I seem to be in your town. We're at the Texaco station; across from a real-estate office."

"I see."

"I'm afraid it was just too hard driving off without even calling. How are you?"

"How did you know I was staying here?"

"I tried you in New York a few days ago. I called the college, and the department secretary said she wasn't authorized to give out your summer address. I said I was a former student and I was sure you wouldn't mind. But she was adamant about Professor Kepesh's privacy. Quite a moat, that lady."

"So how did you find me?"

"I called the Schonbrunns."

"My, my."

"But stopping off here for gas is really just accidental. Strange, I know, but true. And not as strange, after all, as the truly strange things that happen."

She is lying and I'm not charmed. Through the window I can see Claire holding the unopened book in her hand. We could already be in the car on the way down to the pond.

"What do you want, Helen?"

"You mean from you? Nothing; nothing at all. I'm married now."

"I didn't know."

"That's what I was doing in New York. We were visiting my husband's family. We're on our way to Vermont. They have a summer house there." She laughs; a very appealing laugh. It makes me remember her in bed. "Can you believe I've never been to New England?"

"Well," I say, "it's not exactly Rangoon."

"Neither is Rangoon any more."

"How is your health? I heard that you were pretty sick."

"I'm better now. I had a hard time for a while. But it's over. How are *you?*"

"My hard time is over too."

"I'd like to see you, if I could. Are we that far from your house? I'd like to talk to you, just for a little—"

"About what?"

"I owe you some explanations."

"You don't. No more than I owe you any. I think we'd both be better off at this late date without the explanations."

"I was mad, David, I was going crazy—David, these are difficult things to say surrounded by cans of motor oil."

"Then don't say them."

"I have to."

Out on my chair, Claire is now leafing through the *Times.*

"You better go swimming without me," I say. "Helen's coming here; with her husband."

"She's married?"

"So she says."

"Why *was* it Helen 'Kepesh' then?"

"Probably to identify herself to you. To me."

"Or to herself," says Claire. "Would you rather I weren't here?"

"Of course not. I meant I thought you'd *prefer* going swimming."

"Only if *you* prefer—"

"No, absolutely not."

"Where are they now?"

"Down in town."

"She came all this way—? I don't understand. What if we hadn't been at home?"

"She says they're on their way to his family's house in Vermont."

"They didn't take the Thruway?"

"Honey, what's happened to you? No, they didn't take the Thruway. Maybe they're taking the back roads for the scenery. What's the difference? They'll come and they'll go. You were the one who told *me* not to be unduly anxious."

"But I wouldn't want you to be hurt."

"Don't worry. If that's why you're staying—"

Here suddenly she stands, and at the edge of tears (where I have never before seen her!) she says, "Look, you so *obviously* want me out of the way—" Quickly she starts toward where our car is parked on the other side of the house, in the dust bowl by the old collapsing barn. And I run after her, just behind the dog, who thinks it is all a game.

Consequently we are beside the barn, waiting together, when the Lowerys arrive. As their car makes its way up the long dirt drive to the house, Claire slips her terry-cloth robe on over her bathing suit. I am wearing a pair of corduroy shorts, a faded old T-shirt, battered sneakers, an outfit I've probably had since Syracuse. Helen will have no trouble recognizing me. But will I recognize her? Can I explain to Claire—should I have?—that really, all I want is to *see* . . .

I had heard that, on top of all her debilitating ailments, she had gained some twenty pounds. If so, she has by now lost all that weight, and a bit more. She emerges from the car looking exactly like herself. She is paler-complexioned than I remember—or rather, she is not pale in the cleansed, Quakerish way to which I am now accustomed. Helen's pallor is luminous, transparent. Only in the thinness of her arms and neck is there any indication that she has been through a bad time with her health, and, what is more, is now a woman in her mid-thirties. Otherwise, she is the Stunning Creature once again.

Her husband shakes my hand. I had been expecting someone taller and older—I suppose one usually does. Lowery has a close-cropped black beard, round tortoiseshell glasses, and a compact, powerful, athletic build. Both are dressed in jeans and sandals and colored polo shirts and have their hair cut in the Prince Valiant style. The only jewelry either wears is a wedding ring. All of which tells me practically nothing. Maybe the emeralds are home in the vault.

We walk around as though they are prospective buyers who have been sent up by the real-estate agent to look at the house; as though they are the new couple from down the road who have stopped by to introduce themselves; as though they are what they are—ex-wife with new husband, someone now meaning nothing, artifact of relatively little remaining historical interest uncovered during an ordinary day's archaeological excavation. Yes, giving her the directions to our so perfect lair turns out to have been neither a foolish nor, God knows, a *dangerous* mistake. Otherwise, how would I have known that I have been wholly de-Helenized too, that the woman can neither harm me nor charm me, that I am unbewitchable by all but the most loving and benign of feminine spirits. How right Claire was to caution me against being unduly anxious; before, of course, she went ahead and—doubtless because of my own confusion upon hanging up the phone—became unduly anxious herself.

Claire is up ahead now with Les Lowery. They are headed toward the blackened, ruined oak tree at the edge of the woods. Early in the summer, during a dramatic daylong storm, the tree was struck by lightning and severed in two. While we all walked together around the house and through the garden, Claire had been talking, just a little feverishly, about the wild thunderstorms of early July; a little feverishly, and a little childishly. I had not imagined beforehand just how ominous Helen would seem to her, given the tales of her troublemaking that I have told; I suppose I had not realized how often I must have told them to her in the first months we were together. No wonder she has latched on to the quiet husband, who does in fact seem closer to her in age and spirit, and who, it turns out, is also a subscriber to *Natural History* and the *Audubon Magazine.* Some minutes earlier, on the porch, she had identified for the Lowerys the unusual Cape Cod seashells arranged in a wicker tray in the center of the dining table, between the antique pewter candlesticks that were her grandmother's gift upon her graduation from college.

While my mate and her mate are examining the burned-out trunk of the oak tree, Helen and I drift back to the porch. She is telling me all about him, still. He is a lawyer, a mountain climber, a skier, he is divorced, has two adolescent daughters; in partnership with an architect he has already made a small fortune as a housing developer; lately he has been in the news for the work he has been doing as investigating counsel for a California State Legislature committee unraveling connections between organized crime and the Marin County Police . . . Outside I see that Lowery has moved past the oak tree and onto the path that cuts up through the woods to the steep rock formations that Claire has been photographing all summer. Claire and Dazzle appear to be headed back down to the house.

I say to Helen, "He looks a bit young to be *such* a Karenin."

"I'm sure I'd be sardonic too," she replies, "if I were you and thought I was still me. I was surprised you even came to the phone. But that's because you are a nice man. You always were, actually."

"Oh, Helen, what's going on here? Save the 'nice man' stuff for my tombstone. You may have a new life, but this lingo . . ."

"I had a lot of time to think when I was sick. I thought about—"

But I don't want to know. "Tell me," I say, interrupting her, "how was your conversation with the Schonbrunns?"

"I spoke to Arthur. She wasn't home."

"And how did he take hearing from you after all this time?"

"Oh, he took it quite well."

"Frankly I'm surprised he offered assistance. I'm surprised you asked him for it. As I remember, he was never a great fan of yours —nor you of theirs."

"Arthur and I have changed our minds about each other."

"Since when? You used to be very funny about him."

"I'm not any more. I don't ridicule people who admit what they want. Or at least admit to what they don't have."

"And what does Arthur want? Are you telling me that all along Arthur wanted *you?*"

"I don't know about all along."

"Oh, Helen, I find this hard to believe."

"I never heard anything easier to believe."

"And what exactly is it I'm supposed to be believing, again?"

"When we two got back from Hong Kong, when you moved out and I was alone, he telephoned one night and asked if he could come over to talk. He was very concerned about you. So he came from his office—it was about nine—and he talked about your unhappiness for nearly an hour. I said finally that I didn't know what any of it had to do with me any more, and then he asked if he and I might meet in San Francisco for lunch one day. I said I didn't know, I was feeling pretty miserable myself, and he kissed me. And then he made me sit down and he sat down and he explained to me in detail that he hadn't expected to do that, and that it didn't mean what I thought it meant. He was happily married still, and after all these years he still had a strong physical relationship with Debbie, and in fact he owed her his whole life. And then he told me a harrowing story about some crazy girl, some librarian he had almost married in Minnesota, and how she had once gone after him with a fork at breakfast and stabbed his hand. He'd never gotten over what might have happened to him if he had caved in and married her—he thinks it actually might have ended in a murder. He showed me the scar from the fork. He said his salvation was meeting Debbie, and that he owes everything he's accomplished to her devotion and love. Then he tried to kiss me again, and when I said I didn't think it was a good idea, he told me I was perfectly right and that he had misjudged me completely and he still wanted to have lunch with me. I really couldn't take any more confusion, so I said yes. He arranged for us to eat at a place in Chinatown where, I assure you, nobody he knew or I knew or *anybody* knew could possibly see us together. And that was it. But then that summer, when they moved East, he began writing letters. I still get them, every few months or so."

"Go on. What do they say?"

"Oh, they're awfully well-written," she says, smiling. "He must write some of those sentences ten times over before he's completely satisfied. I think they may be the kind of letters the poetry editor of the college magazine writes late at night to his girl friend at Smith. 'The weather, as clear and as sharp as a fish spine,' and so on. And sometimes he includes lines from great poems about Venus, Cleopatra, and Helen of Troy."

" 'Lo, this is she that was the world's desire.' "

"That's right—that's one of them. I thought it was a bit insulting, actually. Except I suppose it can't be because it's so 'great.' Anyway, he always somehow or other lets me know that I don't have to answer; so I don't. Why are you smiling? It's really rather sweet. Well, it's *something.* Who'da thunk it?"

"I smile," I say, "because I've had my own Schonbrunn letters —from her."

"Now, *that's* hard to believe."

"No, not if you saw them. No great lines of poetry for me."

Claire is still some fifty or so feet away, yet both of us stop speaking as she makes her way back to the house. Why? Who knows why!

And if only we hadn't! Why didn't I just talk nonsense, tell a joke, *recite* a poem, *anything* so that Claire hadn't to come through the screen door into this conspiratorial silence. Hadn't to come in to see me sitting across from Helen, charmed in spite of myself.

Immediately she becomes stony—and reaches a decision. "I'm going swimming."

"What's happened to Les?" asks Helen.

"Took a walk."

"You sure you don't want some iced tea?" I ask Claire. "Why don't we all have some iced tea?"

"No. Bye." That single adolescent syllable of farewell for the guest, then she's gone.

From where I am sitting I am able to watch our car pass down the hill to the road. What does Claire think we are plotting? What *are* we plotting?

Says Helen, when the car is out of sight, "She's terribly sweet."

"And I'm a 'nice man,' " I say.

"I'm sorry if I upset your friend by coming here. I didn't mean to."

"She'll be all right. She's a strong girl."

"And I mean you no harm. That isn't why I wanted to see you."

I am silent.

"I did mean you harm once, that's true," she says.

"You weren't solely responsible for the misery."

"What you did to me you did without wanting to; you did because you were provoked. But I think now that I actually set out to torture you."

"You're rewriting history, Helen. It's not necessary. We tormented each other, all right, but it wasn't out of malice. It was confusion, and it was ignorance, and it was other things too, but had it been malice, we wouldn't have been together for very long."

"I used to burn that fucking toast on purpose."

"As I remember, it was the fucking eggs that were burned. The fucking toast never got put in."

"I used to not mail your letters on purpose."

"Why are you saying these things? To castigate yourself, to somehow absolve yourself, or just to try to get a rise out of me? Even if it's true, I don't want to know it. That's all dead."

"I just always hated so the ways that people killed their time. I had this grand life all planned out, you see."

"I remember."

"Well, that's all dead too. Now I take what I can get, and I'm grateful to have it."

"Oh, don't overdo the 'chastened' bit, if that's what this is. Mr. Lowery doesn't sound like the scrapings to me. He doesn't look it, either. He looks like a very forceful person who knows what he's about. He sounds like somebody to conjure with, taking on the Mafia *and* the police. He sounds like a rather courageous man of the world. Just right for you. It certainly looks like he agrees with you."

"Does it?"

"You look terrific," I say—and am sorry I said it. So why then do I add, "You look marvelous."

For the first time since Claire came onto the porch, we fall silent again. We look unflinchingly at one another, as though we are strangers who dare, finally, to stare openly and unambiguously—the prelude to leaping precipitously into the most shameless and exciting copulation. I suppose there is no way we can avoid a little—if not a little more than a little—flirtation. Maybe I ought to say that. And then again, maybe I ought not. Maybe I ought just to look away.

"What were you sick with?" I ask.

"Sick with? It seemed like everything. I must have seen fifty doctors. All I did was sit in waiting rooms and have X-rays taken and blood taken and have cortisone injections and wait around drugstores to have prescriptions filled, and then bolt down the pills, hoping they'd save me on the spot. You should have seen my medicine chest. Instead of Countess Olga's lovely creams and lotions, vials and vials of hideous little pills—and none of them did a thing, except to ruin my stomach. My nose wouldn't stop running for over a year. I sneezed for hours on end, I couldn't breathe, my face puffed up, my eyes itched all the time, and then I began breaking out in horrible rashes. I'd pray when I went to sleep that they'd just go away the way they came, that they'd be gone for good in the morning. One allergist told me to move to Arizona, another told me it wouldn't help because it was all in my head, and another explained in great detail to me how I was allergic to myself, or something very like that, and so I went home and got into bed and pulled the covers over my face and daydreamed about having all the blood drawn out of me and replaced by somebody else's blood, blood I could get through the rest of my life with. I nearly went crazy. Some mornings I wanted to throw myself out the window."

"But you did get better."

"I began seeing Les," Helen says. "That's how it seems to have happened. The ailments all began to subside, one by one. I didn't know how he could bear me. I was hideous."

"Probably not so hideous as you thought. It sounds as though he fell in love with you."

"After I got well I got frightened. I thought that without him I'd start getting sick again. And start drinking again—because somehow he even got me to stop that. I said to him the night he first came to pick me up, looking so strong and cocky and butch, I said, 'Look, Mr. Lowery, I'm thirty-four years old, and I'm sick as a dog, and I don't like to be buggered.' And he said, 'I know how old you are, and everybody gets sick some time, and buggering doesn't interest me.' And so we went out, and he was so marvelously sure of himself, and he fell in love with me—and of course in love with rescuing me. But I didn't love him. And I wanted time and again to be finished with him. Only when it was over, when it should have been over, I got so frightened . . . So we were married."

I don't reply. I look away.

"I'm going to have a baby," she says.

"Congratulations. When?"

"Soon as I can. You see, I don't care any more about being happy. I've given that up. All I care about is not being tortured. I'll do anything. I'll have ten babies, I'll have twenty if he wants them. And he might. There is a man, David, who has no doubts about himself at all. He had a wife and two children even while he was in law school—he was already in the housing business in law school—and now he wants a second family, with me. And I'll do it. What else *can* she do, who was once the world's desire? Own a smart little antique shop? Be one of those fading beauties? Take a degree and go out and run something? Be one of those fading beauties?"

"If you can't be twenty years old and sailing past the junks at sunset . . . But we have had that discussion. It's no longer my business."

"What about your business? Will you marry Miss Ovington?"

"I might."

"What holds you back?"

I don't answer.

"She's young, she's pretty, she's intelligent, she's educated, and under that robe she seemed quite lovely. And as a bonus there's something childlike and innocent that I certainly never had. Something that knows how to be content, I would think. How do they get that way, do you know? How do they get so *good?* I wondered if she wouldn't be like that. Bright and pretty and good. Leslie is bright and pretty and good. Oh, David, how do you stand it?"

"Because I'm bright and pretty and good myself."

"No, my dear old comrade, not the way they are. They come by it naturally, naïvely. Resist as you will, it's not quite the same, not even for a master repressive like yourself. You're not one of them, and you're not poor Arthur Schonbrunn, either."

I don't reply.

"Doesn't she drive you even a little crazy being so bright and pretty and good?" asks Helen. "With her seashells and her flower bed and her doggie, and her recipes tacked up over the sink?"

"Is this what you came here to tell me, Helen?"

"No. It isn't. Of course it isn't. I didn't come here to say *any* of these things. You're a bright fellow—you know very well why I came. To show you my husband. To show you how I've changed, for the better, of course; and . . . and other assorted lies. I thought I might even fool myself. David, I came here because I wanted to talk to a friend, strange as that may sound right now. I sometimes think of you as the only friend I've got left. I did when I was sick. Isn't that odd? I almost called you one night—but I knew I was none of your business now. You see, I'm pregnant. I want you to tell me something. Tell me what you think I should do. Somebody has to. I'm two months pregnant, and if I wait any longer, well, then I'll have to go ahead and have it. And I can't stand him any more. But then I can't stand anyone. Everything everyone says is somehow wrong and drives me crazy. I don't mean I argue with people. I wouldn't dare. I listen and I nod and I smile. You should see how I please people these days. I listen to Les, and I nod and I smile, and I think I'll die of boredom. There's nothing he does now that doesn't irritate me nearly to death. But I can't be sick alone like that ever again. I couldn't take it. I can take loneliness, and I can take physical misery too, but I can't take them together like that ever again. It was too horrid and too relentless, and I haven't courage any more. I seem to have used it all up; inside me I feel there's no courage left. I have to have this baby. I have to tell him I'm pregnant—and have it. Because if I don't, I don't know what will happen to me. I can't leave him. I'm too terrified to be sick again like that, itching to death, unable to breathe—and it doesn't help to be told it's all in one's head, because that doesn't make it go away. Only he does. Yes, *he* made it all go away! Oh, this is all so crazy. None of this had to be! Because if that wife of Jimmy's had been run down when he had it all arranged, that would have been it. I would have had what I wanted. And I wouldn't have thought twice about her, either. Like it or not, that's the truth about me. I wouldn't have had a moment's stinking guilt. I would have been happy. And she would have gotten what she deserved. But instead I was good—and she's made them *both* miserable. I refused to be terrible, and the result is this terrible unhappiness. Each night I toss in my bed with the nightmare of how much I don't love *anybody.*"

At last, at long last, I see Lowery coming out of the woods and descending the hill toward the house. He has removed his shirt and is carrying it in his hand. He is a strong and handsome young man, he is a great success in the world, and his presence in her life has somehow restored her to health . . . Only it is Helen's bad luck that she cannot stand him. Still Jimmy—still those dreams of what might and should have been, if only moral repugnance had not intervened.

"Maybe I'll love the baby," she says.

"Maybe you will," I say. "That happens sometimes."

"Then again, I may despise my baby," says Helen, sternly rising to greet her husband. "I would imagine that happens sometimes too."

After they leave—just like the new couple from down the road, with smiles and good wishes all around—I get into my bathing suit and walk the mile along our road to the pond. I have no thoughts and no feelings, I am numb, like someone at the perimeter of a terrible accident or explosion, who gets a brief, startling glimpse of a pool of blood, and then goes on his way, unharmed, to continue with the ordinary activities of the day.

Some small children are playing with shovels and pails at the edge of the pond, overseen by Claire's dog and by a mother's helper, who looks up and says "Hi." The girl is reading, of all things, *Jane Eyre.* Claire's terry-cloth robe is on the rock where we always put our things, and then I locate Claire, sunning herself out on the raft.

When I pull myself up beside her I see that she has been crying.

"I'm sorry I acted like that," she says.

"Don't be, don't be. We were both thrown way off. I don't believe those things can ever work out very well."

She begins to cry again, as noiselessly as it is possible to cry. The first of her tears that I've seen.

"What is it, lovely, what?"

"I feel so lucky. I feel so privileged. I love you. You've become my whole life."

"I have?"

This makes her laugh. "It frightens you a little to hear it. I guess it would. I didn't think it was true, till today. But I've never been happy like this before."

"Clarissa, why are you still so upset? There's no reason to be, is there?"

Turning her face into the raft, she mumbles something about her mother and father.

"I can't hear you, Claire."

"I wanted them to visit."

I'm surprised, but say, "Then invite them."

"I did."

"When was that?"

"It doesn't matter. It's just that I thought—well, I didn't think."

"You wrote them? Explain yourself, please. I'd like to know what's wrong."

"I don't want to go into it. It was foolish and dreamy. I lost my head a little."

"You telephoned them."

"Yes."

"When?"

"Before."

"You mean after you left the house? Before you came down here?"

"Down in town, yes."

"And?"

"I should never phone them without warning. I never do. It never works and it never will. But at night when we're having dinner, when we're so content and everything is so peaceful and lovely, I always start to think about them. I put on a record, and start cooking dinner, and there they are."

I hadn't known. She never speaks of what she does not have, never lingers for so much as a moment upon loss, misfortune, or disappointment. You'd have to torture her to get her to complain. She is the most extraordinary ordinary person I have ever known.

"Oh," she says, pushing up to a sitting position, "oh, this day will be fine when it's over. Do you have any idea when that will be?"

"Claire, do you want to stay out here with me, or do you want to be alone, or do you want to swim, or do you want to come home and have some iced tea and a little rest?"

"They're gone?"

"Oh, they're gone."

"And you're all right?"

"I'm intact. An hour or so older, but intact."

"How was it?"

"Not all that pleasant. You didn't take to her, I know, but the woman is in a bad way . . . Look, we don't have to talk about this now. We don't have to talk about it ever. Do you want to go home?"

"Not just yet," says Claire. She dives off the edge of the raft, remains out of sight for a long count of ten, and then surfaces by the ladder. When she sits back down beside me, she says, "There's one thing we'd better talk about now. One more thing I had better say. I was pregnant. I wasn't going to tell you, but I will."

"Pregnant by whom? When?"

A wan smile. "In Europe, love. By you. I found out for sure when we got home. I had an abortion. Those meetings I went to —well, I went to the hospital for the day."

"And the 'infection'?"

"I didn't have an infection."

Helen is two months pregnant, and I am the only person who knows. Claire has been pregnant, by me, and I've known nothing. I sense something very sad, all right, at the bottom of this day's confidences and secrets, but what it is I am too weak right now to fathom. Indeed, worn down more than I had thought from all that has surrounded Helen's visit, I am ready to think it is something about me that makes for the sadness; about how I have always failed to be what people want or expect; how I have never quite pleased anyone, including myself; how, hard as I have tried, I have seemed never quite able to be one thing or the other, and probably never will be . . . "Why did you do this alone?" I ask her. "Why didn't you tell me?"

"Well, it was just at the moment you were letting yourself go, and I thought that had to happen by itself. You were surrendering to something, and it always had to be clear to both of us exactly what it was. Is *that* clear?"

"But you did want to have it."

"The abortion?"

"No, the child."

"I want to have a child, of course. I want to have one with you —I can't imagine having anyone else's. But not until you're ready to with me."

"And when did you do all this, Claire? How could I *not* know it?"

"Oh, I managed," she says. "David, the point is that I wouldn't even *want* you to want it until you know for certain that it's me and my ways and this life that you can be content with. I don't want to make anybody unhappy. I don't want to cause anyone pain. I never want to be anyone's prison. That is the worst fate I can imagine. Please, let me just say what I have to—you don't have to say anything about what you would have said or wouldn't have said had I told you what I was doing. I didn't want any of the responsibility to be yours; and it isn't; it can't be. If a mistake was made, then I made it. Right now I just want to say certain things to you, and I want you to hear them, and then we'll go home and I'll start supper."

"I'm listening to you."

"Sweetheart, I wasn't jealous of her; far from it. I'm pretty enough, and I'm young, and thank God, I'm not 'tough' or 'worldly,' if that's what that's called. Truly, I wasn't afraid of anything she could do. If I were that uncertain I wouldn't be living here. I did get confused a little when you wanted to shoo me out of the way, but I came back to the house only to get my camera. I was going to take some pictures of the two of them together. All in all, I thought it was as good a way to get through that visit as any. But when I saw you sitting alone with her, I suddenly thought, 'I can't make him happy, I won't be able to.' And I wondered suddenly if anyone could. And that stunned me so, I just had to go. I don't know if what I thought was true or not. Maybe you don't either. But maybe you do. It would be agony leaving you right now, but I'm prepared to do it, if it makes sense. And better now than three or four years down the line, when you're absolutely in every breath I draw. It's not what I want, David; it's not anything I am even remotely proposing. Saying these kinds of things you take a terrible risk of being misunderstood, and, please, please, don't misunderstand me. I'm proposing nothing. But if you do think you know the answer to my question, I'd like to be told sometime soon, because if you can't be truly content with me, then let me just go to the Vineyard. I know I could get through up there with Olivia until school begins. And after that I can manage on my own. But I don't want to give myself any further to something that isn't going to evolve someday into a family. I never had one that made the least bit of sense, and I want one that does. I have to have that. I'm not saying tomorrow, or even the day after tomorrow. But in time that's what I want. Otherwise, I'd just as soon tear the roots up now, before the job requires a hacksaw. I'd like us both to get away, if we can, without a bloody amputation."

Here, though the bright sun has baked her body dry, she shudders from head to foot. "I think that's everything I have the energy left to say. And you don't have to say a word. I wish you wouldn't, not just now. Otherwise, this will sound like an ultimatum, and it isn't. It's a clarification, that's all. I didn't even want to make it, I thought *time* would make it. But then it's time that just might do me in. But, please, it doesn't require reassuring sounds to be made in response. It's just that suddenly everything seemed as though it might be a terrible delusion. It was so frightening. Please, don't speak—unless there's something you know that I should know."

"No, there isn't."

"Then let's go home."

And last, my father's visit.

In the letter profusely thanking us for the Labor Day weekend invitation extended to him on the phone, my father asks if he may bring a friend along, another widower whom he has grown close to in recent months and whom he says he wants me in particular to meet. He must by now have discarded or used up the paper and envelopes bearing the name of the hotel, for the request is written on the back of stationery imprinted at the top with the words JEWISH FEDERATION OF NASSAU COUNTY. Imprinted beneath is a brief, pointed epistle to the Jews whose style is as easily recognizable to me as Hemingway's or Faulkner's.

> Dear
>
> I am enclosing your pledge card from the Jewish Federation of Nassau County. I, as a Jew, am making a personal appeal. There is no need to recite our commitment to maintain a Jewish homeland. We need the financial aid of every Jew.
>
> Never again must we allow a holocaust! No Jew can be apathetic!
>
> I beg of you, please help. *Give before it hurts.*
>
> Sincerely,
> Abe Kepesh
> Garfield Garden Apartments
> Co-Chairman

On the reverse side is his letter to Claire and myself, written with a ball-point pen and in his oversized scrawl, though no less revealing than the printed message calling for Jewish solidarity (in those childlike hieroglyphics, all the more revealing) of the fanatically lavish loyalties that, now, in his old age, cause him to be afflicted throughout the waking day with the dull ache and shooting pain of wild sentiment ensnared.

The morning we get his letter I telephone him at my Uncle Larry's office to tell him that if he does not mind sharing our smallish guest room with his friend Mr. Barbatnik, he is of course welcome to bring him along.

"I hate like hell to leave him here alone on a holiday, Davey, that's the only thing. Otherwise I wouldn't bother you. See, I just didn't think it through," he explains, "when I rushed to say yes so quick like that. Only it's got to be no inconvenience for Claire, if he comes. I don't want to burden her, not with school starting up, not with all the work she must have to do to get ready."

"Oh, she's ready, don't worry about that," and I hand the phone over to Claire, who assures him that her school preparations were finished long ago and that it will be a pleasure to entertain the two of them for the weekend.

"He's a wonderful, wonderful man," my father quickly assures her, as though we actually have reason to suspect that a friend of his might turn out to be a rummy or a bum, "somebody who has been through things you wouldn't believe. He works with me when I go collecting for the UJA. And, I tell you, I need him. I need a hand grenade. Try to get money out of people. Try to get *feelings* out of people and see where you wind up. You tell them that what happened to the Jews must never happen again, and they look at you like they never heard of it. Like Hitler and pogroms are something I am making up in order to fleece them out of their municipal bonds. We got one guy in the building across the way, a brand-new widower three years older than me, who already made himself his bundle years ago in the bootleg business and God only knows what else, and you should get a load of him since his wife passed away—a new chippie on his arm every month. Dresses them up in expensive clothes, takes them in to see Broadway shows, wouldn't be caught dead driving them to the beauty parlor in anything but a Fleetwood Caddie, but just try to ask him for a hundred dollars for the UJA and he is practically in tears telling you how bad he has been hit on the market. It's a good thing I can control my temper. And between you and me, half the time I can't, and it is Mr. Barbatnik who has to call me off before I tell this s.o.b. just what I think of him. Oh, this one guy, he really gets my goat. Every time I leave him I have to go get a phenobarb from my sister-in-law. And I'm somebody who don't even believe in an aspirin."

"Mr. Kepesh," Claire says, "please feel free to bring Mr. Barbatnik with you."

But he will not say yes until he has extracted a promise that if they both come she will not think that she has to cook them three meals a day. "I want a guarantee that you are going to pretend that we're not even there."

"But what fun would that be? Suppose instead I take the easy way out and just pretend that you are."

"Hey, listen," he says to her, "you sound like a happy girl."

"I am. My cup runneth over."

Even though Claire is holding the phone to her ear across the kitchen table from me, I clearly hear what comes next. This results from the fact that my father approaches long-distance communication in much the way that he approaches so many of the riddles that elude his understanding—with the belief that the electrical waves transmitting his voice may not make it without his wholehearted and unstinting support. Without *hard work*.

"God bless you," he calls out to her, "for what you are doing for my son!"

"Well—" beneath her tan, she has reddened—"well, he's doing some nice things for me."

"I wouldn't doubt that," my father says. "I'm delighted to hear it. But still and all he has practically gone out of his way to bring trouble into his life. Tell me, does he realize how good he has got it with you? He is thirty-four years old, a grown man already, he can't afford any longer to go around wet behind his ears. Claire, does he know enough by now to appreciate what he's got?"

She tries laughing the question off, but he insists on an answer, even if finally he must give it himself. "Losing your bearings no one needs—life is confusing enough. You don't stick a knife in your own gut. But that is just what he did to himself with marrying that glamour girl, all dressed up like Suzie Wong. Oh, about her and those outfits of hers the less said the better. And those

French perfumes. Pardon my language, but she smelled like a God damn barber shop. And what was he up to living in that sublet apartment with red walls made out of cloth, and with whatever else went on there, that I will never be able to fathom. I don't even want to think about it. Claire dear, listen to me, you at last are somebody worthwhile. If only you can get him to settle into a real life."

"Oh, my," she says, not a little flustered by all the emotion that is flowing her way, "if it were any more settled around here . . ."

Before she can quite figure out, at the age of twenty-five, how to conclude that sentence, my father is roaring, "Wonderful, wonderful, that is the most wonderful news about him since he finished that fellowship to be a gypsy in Europe and came back on that boat in one piece!"

In the lot behind the general store in town, he steps cautiously down from the high front step of the New York bus, but then, despite the scalding heat—despite his advanced age—*surges* forward, and not toward me, but on the wings of impulse, to the person who is no relation of his quite yet. There were those few evenings when she served him a meal in my new apartment, and then, when I gave my public lecture from *Man in a Shell* in the Scholar Series at the university, it was Claire who escorted him and my aunt and uncle into the library and sat beside him in the little auditorium there, identifying at his request which gentleman was the department chairman and which the dean. Nonetheless, now when he reaches out to embrace her, it is as though she is already pregnant with the first of his grandchildren, as though she is in fact *the* genetrix of all that is most estimable in that elite breed of creatures to which he is joined by blood and for which his admiration is overbrimming . . . if and when, that is, the membership does not go around shamelessly showing its fangs and its claws and leaving my father fit to be tied.

Seeing Claire swallowed up by this stranger, Dazzle begins leaping crazily around in the dust at his mistress's sandals—and, though my father has never had all that much trust, or found much to admire, in members of the animal kingdom who breed out of wedlock and defecate on the ground, I am surprised to see that Dazzle's display of unabashed dogginess in no way seems to deflect his attention from the girl he is holding in his arms.

At first I do have to wonder if what we are witnessing is not designed in part at least to put Mr. Barbatnik at ease about visiting a human couple who are not legally wed—if perhaps my father intends, by the very intensity with which he squeezes her body to his, to put his own not entirely unexpected misgivings on that score to rest. I cannot remember seeing him so forceful and so animated since before my mother's illness. In fact, he strikes me as a little nuts today. But that is still better than what I expected. Usually when I call each week there is, in just about every upbeat thing he says, a melancholy strain so transparent that I wonder how he finds the wherewithal to keep going on, as he will, about how all is well, wonderful, couldn't be better. The somber "Yeah, hello?" with which he answers the phone is quite enough to inform me of what underlies his "active" days—the mornings helping my uncle in his office where my uncle needs no help; the afternoons at the Jewish Center arguing politics with the "fascists" in the steam room, men whom he refers to as Von Epstein, and Von Haberman, and Von Lipschitz—the local Goering, Goebbels, and Streicher, apparently, who give him palpitations of the heart; and then those interminable evenings soliciting at his neighbors' doors for his various philanthropies and causes, reading again column by column through *Newsday,* the *Post,* and the *Times,* watching the CBS News for the second time in four hours, and finally, in bed and unable to sleep, spreading the letters from his cardboard file box over the blanket and reviewing his correspondence with his vanished, cherished guests. In some cases more cherished, it seems to me, now that they have vanished, than when they were around and there was too little barley in the soup, too much chlorine in the pool, and never enough waiters in the dining room.

His letter writing. With each passing month it is getting harder for him to keep track of who among the hundreds and hundreds of old-timers is retired and in Florida, and thus capable still of writing him back, and who is dead. And it isn't a matter of losing his faculties, either—it's losing all those friends, "non-stop," as he graphically describes the decimation that occurred in the ranks of his former clientele during just this last year. "I wrote five full pages of news to that dear and lovely prince of a man, Julius Lowenthal. I even put in a clipping that I've been saving up from the *Times* about how they ruined the river over in Paterson where he had his law practice. I figured it would be interesting to him down there—this pollution business was made to order for the kind of man he was. I tell you"—pointing a finger—"Julius Lowenthal was one of the most civic-minded people you could ever want to meet. The synagogue, orphans, sports, the handicapped, colored people—he gave of his time to everything. That man was the genuine article, the *best.* Well, you know what's coming. I stamp and seal the envelope and put it by my hat to take to mail in the morning, and not until I brush my teeth and get into bed and turn out the light does it dawn on me that my dear old friend is gone now since last fall. I have been thinking about him playing cards alongside a swimming pool in Miami—playing pinochle the way only he could play with that legal mind of his—and in actuality he is underground. What is even left of him by now?" That last thought is too much, even for him, especially for him, and he moves his hand angrily past his face, as though to shoo away, like a mosquito that is driving him crazy, this terrible, startling image of Julius Lowenthal decomposing. "And, unbelievable as it may sound to a young person," he says, recovering most of his equilibrium, "this is actually becoming a weekly occurrence, right down to licking the envelope and pasting on the stamp."

It will be hours before Claire and I are finally alone together, and she is able at last to unburden herself of the enigmatic decree issued by him into her ear while we four stood grouped in the fumy wake of the departed bus. The sun is softening us like so much macadam; poor confused Dazzle (barely grown accustomed to this rival) continues carrying on in the air around my father's feet; and Mr. Barbatnik—a short leprechaunish gentleman, with a large, long-eared Asian face, and astonishing scoop-like hands suspended from powerful forearms mapped with a body builder's veins—Mr. Barbatnik hangs back, as shy as a schoolgirl, his jacket folded neatly over his arm, waiting for this living, throbbing valentine, my father, to make the introductions. But my father has urgent business to settle first—like the messenger in a classical tragedy, immediately as he comes upon the stage he blurts out what he has traveled all this way to say. "Young woman," he whispers to Claire, for so it would seem he has been envisioning her, allegorically, as all that and only that, "young woman," commands my father out of the power vested in him by his daydreams—"don't let—don't let—please!"

These, she tells me at bedtime, were the only words that she could hear, pinned as she was against his massive chest; most likely, I say, because these are the only words he uttered. For him, at this point, they say it all.

And having thus ordained the future, if only for the moment, he is ready now to move on to the next event in the arrival ceremonies he must have been planning now for weeks. He reaches into the pocket of the nubby linen jacket slung across *his* arm—and apparently finds nothing. Suddenly he is slapping at the lining of the jacket as though performing resuscitation upon it. "Oh Christ," he moans, "it's lost. My God, it's on the bus!" Whereupon Mr. Barbatnik edges forward and, as discreetly as a best man to a half-dazed bridegroom, says in a soft voice, "Your pants, Abe." "Of course," my father snaps back, and reaching (still with a little desperation in the eyes) into the pocket of his houndstooth trousers—he is dressed, as they say, to the nines—extracts a small packet that he places in Claire's palm. And now he is beaming.

"I didn't tell you on the phone," he says to her, "so it would come as a total surprise. Every year you hold on to it I guarantee it will go up in value ten percent at least. Probably fifteen, and maybe more. It's better than money. And wait till you see the wonderful skill that goes into it. It's fantastic. Go ahead. Open it up."

So, while we all continue to cook away in the parking lot, my affable mate, who knows how to please, and loves pleasing, deftly unties the ribbon and removes the shiny yellow wrapping paper, not failing to remark upon its prettiness. "I picked that out too," my father tells her. "I thought that color would be up your alley—didn't I, Sol," he says, turning to his companion, "didn't I say I'll bet she's a girl who likes yellow?"

Claire takes from its velvet-lined case a small sterling-silver paperweight engraved with a bouquet of roses.

"David told me how hard you work in the garden you made, and the way you love all the flowers. Take it, please. You can use it on your desk at school. Wait till your pupils see it."

"It's beautiful," she says and, calming Dazzle with just a glance, kisses my father on the cheek.

"Look at the handiwork," he says. "You can even see the little thorns. Some person actually did that, by hand. An artist."

"It's lovely, it's a lovely gift," she says.

And only now does he turn and embrace me. "I got you something too," he says. "It's in my bag."

"You hope," I say.

"Wise guy," and *we* kiss.

At last he is ready to introduce his companion, dressed, I now realize, in the same spanking-new, color-coordinated outfit, except where my father is in shades of tan and brown, Mr. Barbatnik wears silver and blue.

"Thank God for this man," my father says as we drive slowly out of town behind a farmer's pickup truck bearing a bumper sticker informing the other motorists that ONLY LOVE BEATS MILK. The bumper sticker on our car, affixed by Claire in sympathy with the local ecologists, reads DIRT ROADS ARE DOWN TO EARTH.

Excited and garrulous as a small boy—much as *I* used to be when *he* was doing the driving around these roads—my father cannot stop talking now about Mr. Barbatnik: one in a million, the finest person he has ever known . . . Mr. Barbatnik, meanwhile, sits quietly beside him, looking into his lap, as humbled, I think, by Claire's buoyant, summery fullness as by the fact that my father is selling him to us much the way, in the good old days, he used to sell the life-lengthening benefits of a summer in our hotel.

"Mr. Barbatnik is the guy who I tell you about from the Center. If it wasn't for him I would absolutely be a voice in the wilderness there about that son of a bitch George Wallace. Claire, pardon me, please, but I hate that lousy cockroach with a passion. You shouldn't have to ever hear the kinds of things so-called decent people think in their private thoughts. It's a disgrace. Only Mr.

Barbatnik and me, we make a team, and we give it to them, but good."

"Not," says Mr. Barbatnik philosophically, in heavily accented English, "that it makes much difference."

"And, tell me, what could make a difference with those ignorant bigots? At least let them hear what someone else thinks of them! Jewish people so full of hatred that they go out and vote for a George Wallace—it's beyond me. *Why?* People who have lived and seen a whole lifetime as a minority, and the suggestion that they make in all seriousness is that they ought to line up the colored in front of machine guns and let them have it. Take actual people and mow them down."

"This of course isn't everybody that says that," Mr. Barbatnik puts in. "This is just one particular person, of course."

"I tell them, look at Mr. Barbatnik—ask him if that isn't the same thing that Hitler did with the Jews. And you know what their answer is, grown men who have raised families and run successful businesses and live in retirement now in condominiums like supposed civilized people? They say, 'How can you compare niggers with Jews?' "

"What's eating this particular person, and the group that he is the leader of—"

"And who appointed him leader, by the way? Of anything? Himself! Go ahead, Sol, I'm sorry. I just wanted to make clear to them what kind of a little dictator we're dealing with."

"What's eating them," Mr. Barbatnik says, "is that they owned homes, some of them, and businesses, and then came the colored, and when they tried to get out what they put in, they took a licking."

"Of course it's all economics when you get down to it. It always is. Wasn't it the same with the Germans? Wasn't it the same in Poland?" Here, abruptly, he breaks off his historical analysis to say to Claire and me, "Mr. Barbatnik only got here after the war." Dramatically, and yes, with pride, he adds, "He is a victim of the Nazis."

When we turn in the drive and I point out the house halfway up the hillside, Mr. Barbatnik says, "No wonder you look so happy, you two."

"They rent it," my father says. "I told him, he likes it so much, why don't he buy it? Make the guy an offer. Tell him you'll pay him cash. At least see if you get a nibble."

"Well," I say, "we're happy enough renting for now."

"Renting is throwing money down the drain. Find out from him, will you? What can it hurt? Cash on the barrelhead, see if he bites. I can help you out, Uncle Larry can help you out, as far as that goes, if it's a straight money deal that he's after. But definitely you ought to own a little piece of property at your stage of the game. And up here, you can't miss, that's for sure. You never could. In my time, Claire, you could buy a little place like this for under five thousand. Today that little house and—and how far does the property go? To the tree line? All right, say four, say five acres—"

Up the dirt drive and in through the kitchen door—and right past the blooming garden he has heard so much about—he continues with his realtor's spiel, so delighted is the man to be back home in Sullivan County, and with his only living loved one, who by all outward appearances seems finally to have been plucked from his furnace and plunked down before the hearth.

Inside the house, before we can even offer a cold drink, or show them to their room or to the toilet, my father begins to unpack his bag on the kitchen table. *"Your* present," he announces to me.

We wait. His shoes come out. His freshly laundered shirts. His shiny new shaving kit.

My present is an album bound in black leather containing thirty-two medallions the size of silver dollars, each in its own circular cavity and protected on both sides by a transparent acetate window. He calls them "Shakespeare Medals"—a scene from one of the plays is depicted on the face side, and on the other, in tiny script, a quotation from the play is inscribed. The medals are accompanied by instructions for placing them in the album. The first instruction begins, "Put on a pair of lint-free gloves . . ." My father hands me the gloves last of all. "Always wear the gloves when you handle the medals," he tells me. "They come with the set. Otherwise, they say that there can be harmful chemical effects to the medals from being touched by human skin."

"Oh, this is nice of you," I say. "Though I don't quite know why now, such an elaborate gift—"

"Why? Because it's time," he answers, with a laugh, and, too, with a wide gesture that encompasses all the kitchen appliances. "Look, Davey, what they engrave for you. Claire, look at the outside."

Centered within the arabesque design that is embossed in silver and serves as a border to the album's funereal cover are three lines, which my father points out to us, word by word, with his index finger. We all read the words in silence—all except him.

FIRST EDITION STERLING SILVER PROOF SET
MINTED FOR THE PERSONAL COLLECTION OF
PROFESSOR DAVID KEPESH

I don't know what to say. I say, "This must have cost an awful lot. It's really something."

"Isn't it? But, no, the cost don't hurt, not the way they set it up. You just collect one medal a month, to begin with. You start off with *Romeo and Juliet*—wait'll I show Claire *Romeo and Juliet*—and you work your way up from there, till you've got them all. I've been saving for you all this time. The only one who knew was Mr. Barbatnik. Look, Claire, come here, you gotta look up close—"

It is a while before they can locate the medallion depicting *Romeo and Juliet,* for in its designated slot in the lower left-hand corner of the page labeled "Tragedies" it seems he has placed *Two Gentlemen from Verona.* "Where the hell is *Romeo and Juliet?"* he asks. The four of us are able to discover it finally under "Histories" in the slot marked *The Life and Death of King John.* "But then where did I put *The Life and Death of King John?"* he asks. "I thought I got 'em all in right, Sol," he says to Mr. Barbatnik, frowning. "I thought we checked." Mr. Barbatnik nods—they did. "Anyway," says my father, "the point is—what was the point? Oh, the *back.* Here, I want Claire to read what it says on the back, so everyone can hear. Read this, dear."

Claire reads aloud the inscription: " '. . . and a rose by any other name would smell as sweet.' *Romeo and Juliet,* Act Two, Scene Two."

"Isn't that something?" he says to her.

"Yes."

"And he can take it to school, too, you see. That's what's so useful. It's something not just for the home, but that he can have ten and twenty years from now to show his classes. And just like yours, it is sterling silver, and something that I guarantee will keep abreast of the inflation, and long after paper money is as good as worthless. Where will you put it?" This last asked of Claire, not me.

"For now," she says, "on the coffee table, so people can see. Come into the living room, everybody; we'll put it there."

"Wonderful," says my father. "Only remember, don't let your company take the medals out, unless they put on the gloves."

Lunch is served on the screened-in porch. The recipe for the cold beet soup Claire found in *Russian Cooking,* one of her dozen or so manuals in a Time-Life series on "Foods of the World" shelved neatly between the radio—whose dial seems set to play only Bach—and the wall hung with two of her sister's calm watercolors of the ocean and the dunes. The cucumber and yogurt salad, heavily flavored with crushed garlic and fresh mint from the herb garden just beyond the screen door, is out of the same set, the volume on the cuisine of the Middle East. The cold roast chicken seasoned with rosemary is a long-standing recipe of her own.

"My God," says my father, "what a spread!" "Excellent," says Mr. Barbatnik. "Gentlemen, thank you," says Claire, "but I'll bet you've had better." "Not even in Lvov, when my mother was cooking," says Mr. Barbatnik, "have I tasted such a wonderful borscht." Says Claire, smiling, "I suspect that's a little extravagant, but thank you, again." "Listen, my dear girl," says my father, "if I had you in the kitchen, I'd still be in my old line. And you'd get more than you get being a schoolteacher, believe me. A good chef, even in the old days, even in the middle of the Depression—"

But in the end Claire's biggest hit is not the exotic Eastern dishes which, in her Clairish way, she has tried today for the first time in the hope of making everybody—herself included—feel instantaneously at home together, but the hearty iced tea she brews with mint leaves and orange rinds according to her grandmother's recipe. My father cannot seem to get enough, cannot stop praising it to the skies, not after he has learned over the blueberries that Claire takes the bus to Schenectady every month to visit this ninety-year-old woman from whom she learned everything she knows about preparing a meal and growing a garden, and probably about raising a child too. Yes, it looks from the girl as though his renegade son has decided to go straight, and in a very big way.

After lunch I suggest to the two men that they might like to rest until the heat has abated somewhat and we can go for a little walk along the road. Absolutely not. What am I even talking about? As soon as we digest our food, my father says, we must drive over to the hotel. This surprises me, as it surprised me a little at lunch to hear him speak so easily about his "old line." Since moving to Long Island a year and a half ago, he has shown no interest whatsoever in seeing what two successive owners have made of his hotel, barely hanging on now as the Royal Ski and Summer Lodge. I had thought he would be just as happy staying away, but in fact he is boiling over again with enthusiasm and, after a visit to the toilet, is pacing the porch, waiting for Mr. Barbatnik to awaken from the little snooze he is enjoying in my wicker easy chair.

What if he should drop dead from all this fervor in his heart? And before I have married the devoted girl, bought the cozy house, raised the handsome children . . .

Then what am I waiting for? If later, why not now, so he too can be happy and count his life a success?

What am I waiting for?

Down the main drag and through every last store still there and open for business my father leads the three of us, he alone seemingly oblivious to the terrific heat. "I can remember when there were four butchers, three barbershops, a bowling alley, three produce markets, two bakeries, an A&P, three doctors, and three dentists. And now, look," he says—and without chagrin; rather with the proud sagacity of one who imagines he actually knew to get out when the getting was good—"no butchers, no barbers, no bowling alley, just one bakery, no A&P, and unless things have changed since I left, no dentists and only one doctor. Yes," he announces, avuncular now, taking the overview, sounding a little like his friend Walter Cronkite, "the old, opulent hotel era is over—but it was something! You should have seen this place in summertime! You know who used to vacation here? You name it! The Herring King! The Apple King!—" And to Mr. Barbatnik and to Claire (who does not let on that she already made this same sentimental journey some weeks ago at the side of his son, who had explained at the time just what a herring king *was*) he begins a rapid-fire anecdotal history of his life's major boulevard, foot by foot, year by year, from Roosevelt's inauguration right on up through L.B.J. Putting an arm around his sopping half-sleeve shirt, I say, "I bet if you set your mind to it you could go back before the Flood." He likes that—yes, he likes just about everything today. "Oh, could I! This is some treat! This is *really* Memory Lane!" "It's awfully hot, Dad," I warn him. "It's nearly ninety degrees. Maybe if we slow down—" "Slow *down?*" he cries and, showing off, pulls Claire along on his arm as he breaks into a crazy little trot down the street. Mr. Barbatnik smiles and, mopping his brow with his handkerchief, says to me, "He's been hoping a long time."

"Labor Day weekend!" my father announces brightly as I swing into the lot next to the service entrance of the "main building." Aside from the parking lot, which has been resurfaced, and the tumescent pink the buildings have all been painted, little else seems to have been changed as yet, except of course for the hotel's name. In charge now are a worried fellow only a little older than myself and his youngish, charmless second wife. I met them briefly on the afternoon in June when I came down with Claire to conduct my own nostalgic tour. But there is no nostalgia for the good old days in these two, no more than those clutching at the debris in a swollen stream are able to feel for the golden age of the birch-bark canoe. When my father, having sized up the situation, asks how come no full house for the holiday—a phenomenon utterly unknown to him, as he quickly makes only too clear—the wife goes more bulldoggish even than before, and the husband, a hefty boyish type with pale eyes and pocked skin and a dazed, friendly expression—a nice, well-meaning fellow whose creditors, however, are probably not that impressed by plans extending into the twenty-first century—explains that they have not as yet been able to fix an "image" in the public mind. "You see," he says uncertainly, "right now we're still modernizing the kitchen—"

The wife interrupts to set the record straight: young people are put off because they think it is a hotel for the older generation (for which, it would seem from her tone, my father is to blame), and the family crowd is frightened away because the fellow to whom my father sold out—and who couldn't pay his bills by August of his first and only summer as proprietor—was nothing but a "two-bit Hugh Hefner" who tried to build a clientele out of "riffraff, and worse."

"Number one," says my father before I can grab an arm and steer him away, "the biggest mistake was to change the name, to take thirty years of good will and wipe it right off the map. Paint outside whatever color you want, though what was wrong with a nice clean white I don't understand—but if that's your taste, that's your taste. But the point is, does Niagara Falls change its name? Not if they want the tourist trade they don't." The wife has to laugh in his face, or so she says: "I have to laugh in your face." "You what? *Why?*" my outraged father replies. "Because you can't call a hotel the Hungarian Royale in this day and age and expect the line to form on the right, you know." "No, no," says the husband, trying to soften her words, and meanwhile working two Maalox tablets out of their silver wrapping, "the problem is, Janet, we are caught between life-styles, and that is what we have to iron out. I'm sure, as soon as we finish up with the kitchen—" "My friend, forget about the kitchen," says my father, turning noticeably away from the wife and toward someone with whom a human being can at least have a decent conversation; "do yourself a favor and change back the name. That is half of what you paid for. Why do you want to use in the name a word like 'ski' anyway? Stay open all winter if you think there's something in it—but why use a word that can only scare away the kind of people who make a place like this a going proposition?"

The wife: "I have news for you. Nobody wants today to take a vacation in a place that sounds like a mausoleum." Period. "Oh," says my father, revving up his sarcasm, "oh, the past dies these days, does it?" And launches into a solemn, disjointed philosophical monologue about the integral relationship of past, present, and future, as though a man who has survived to sixty-six *must* know whereof he speaks, is *obliged* to be sagacious with those who follow after—especially when they seem to look upon him as the begetter of their woes.

I wait to intercede, or call an ambulance. From seeing his life's work mismanaged so by this deadbeat husband and his dour little wife, will my overwrought father burst into tears, or keel over, a corpse? The one—once again—seems no less possible to me than the other.

Why am I convinced that during the course of this weekend he is going to die, that by Monday I will be a parentless son?

He is still going strong—still going a little crazy—when we climb into the car to head home. "How did I know he was going to turn out to be a hippie?" "Who's that?" I ask. "That guy who bought us out after we lost Mother. You think I would have sold to a hippie, out of my own free will? The man was a fifty-year-old man. So what if he had long hair? What am I, a hard-hat, that I hold something like that against him? And what the hell did she mean by 'riffraff' anyway? She didn't mean what I think she meant, did she? Or did she?" I say, "She only meant that they are going under fast and it hurts. Look, she is obviously a sour little pain in the ass, but failing is still failing." "Yeah, but why blame *me?* I gave these people the last of the golden geese, I gave them a good solid tradition and a loyal clientele that all they had to do was stick to what was *there.* That was *all,* Davey! 'Ski!' That's all my customers have to hear, and they run like hell. Ah, some people, they can start a hotel in the Sahara and make a go of it, and others can start in the best of circumstances and they lose everything." "That's true," I say. "Now I look back in wonder that I myself could ever accomplish so much. A nobody like me, from nowhere! I started out, Claire, I was a short-order cook. My hair was black then, like his, and thick too, if you can believe it—"

Beside him Mr. Barbatnik's sleeping head is twisted to one

side, as though he has been garrotted. Claire, however—amiable, tolerant, generous, and willing Claire—continues to smile and to nod yes-yes-yes as she follows the story of our inn and how it flourished under the loving care of this industrious, gracious, shrewd, slave-driving, and dynamic nobody. Is there a man alive, I wonder, who has led a more exemplary life? Is there an ounce of anything that he has withheld in the performance of his duties? Of what then does he believe himself to be so culpable? My derelictions, my sins? Oh, if only he would cut the summation short, the jury would announce "Innocent as a babe!" without even retiring from the courtroom.

Only he can't. Into the early evening his plea streams forth unabated. First he follows Claire around the kitchen while she prepares the salad and the dessert. When she retires to shower and to change for dinner—and to rally her forces—he comes out to where I am preparing to cook the steak on the grill behind the house. "Hey, did I tell you who I got an invitation to his daughter's wedding? You won't guess in a million years. I had to go over to Hempstead to get her blender fixed for your aunt—you know, the jar there, the top—and who do you think owns the appliance store that services now for Waring? You'll never guess, if you even remember him." But I do. It is my conjurer. "Herbie Bratasky," I say. "That's right! Did I tell you already?" "No." "But that's who it was—and can you believe it, that skinny *paskudnyak* grew up into a person and he is doing terrific. He's got Waring, he's got G.E., and now, he tells me, he is getting himself in with some Japanese company, bigger even than Sony, to be the sole Long Island distributor. And the daughter is a little doll. He showed me her picture—and then out of the blue two days ago I get this beautiful invitation in the mail. I meant to bring it, damn it, but I guess I forgot because I was already packed." Already packed two days ago. "I'll send it," he says; "you'll get a real kick out of it. Look, I was thinking, it's just a thought, but how would you and Claire like to come with me—to the wedding? That would be some surprise for Herbie." "Well, let's think about it. What does Herbie look like these days? What is he now, in his forties?" "Oh, he's gotta be forty-five, forty-six, easy. But still a dynamo—and as sharp and good-looking as he was when he was a kid. He ain't got a pound on him, and still with all his hair—in fact, so much, I thought maybe it was a rug. Maybe it was, come to think of it. And still with that tan. What do you think of that? Must use a lamp. And, Davey, he's got a little boy, just like him, who plays *drums!* I told him about you, of course, and he says he already knew. He read about when you gave your speech at the school; he saw it in the *Newsday* calendar of what's happening around the area. He said he told all his customers. So how do you like that? Herbie Bratasky. How did you know?" "I took a guess." "Well, you were right. You're psychic, kiddo. Whew, that's some beautiful piece of meat. What are you paying up here by the pound? Years ago, a sirloin cut like that—" And I want to enfold him in my arms, bring his unstoppable mouth to my chest, and say, "It's okay, you're here for good, you never have to leave." But in fact we all must depart in something less than a hundred hours. And—until death do us part—the tremendous closeness and the tremendous distance between my father and myself will have to continue in the same perplexing proportions as have existed all our lives.

When Claire comes back down to the kitchen, he leaves me to watch the coals heat up, and goes into the house "to see how beautiful she looks." "Calm down . . ." I call after him, but I might as well be asking a kid to calm down the first time he walks into Yankee Stadium.

My Yankee puts him to work shucking the corn. But of course you can shuck corn and still talk. On the cork bulletin board she has hung over the sink, Claire has tacked up, along with recipes out of the *Times,* some photographs just sent her from Martha's Vineyard by Olivia. I hear them through the kitchen's screen door discussing Olivia's children.

Alone again, and with time yet before the steak goes on, I at last get around to opening the envelope forwarded to me from my box at the university, and carried around in my back pocket since we went into town hours ago to pick up the mail and our guests. I hadn't bothered to open it, since it wasn't the letter I have been expecting daily now, from the university press to which I submitted *Man in a Shell,* in its final revised version, upon our return from Europe. No, it is a letter from the Department of English at Texas Christian University, and it provides the first truly light moment of the day. Oh, Baumgarten, you are a droll and devilish fellow, all right.

Dear Professor Kepesh:

Mr. Ralph Baumgarten, a candidate for the position of Writer in Residence at Texas Christian University, has submitted your name as an individual who is familiar with his work. I am reluctant to impose on your busy schedule, but would be most grateful if you would send me, at your earliest convenience, a letter in which you set forth your views on his writing, his teaching, and on his moral character. You may be assured that your comments will be held in the very strictest confidence.

I am most grateful for your help.

Cordially yours,
John Fairbairn
Chairman

Dear Professor Fairbairn, Perhaps you would like my opinion of the wind as well, whose work I am also familiar with . . . I stick the letter back into my pocket and put on the steak. *Dear Professor Fairbairn, I cannot help but believe that your students' horizons will be enormously enlarged and their sense of life's possibilities vastly enriched . . .* And who next, I wonder. When I sit down at my place for dinner, will there be an extra plate at the table for Birgitta, or will she prefer to eat beside me, on her knees?

I hear from the kitchen that Claire and my father have got around finally to discussing her parents. "But *why?*" I hear him ask. From his tone I can tell that whatever the question, the answer is not unknown to him, but rather, wholly incompatible with his own passionate meliorism. Claire replies, "Because they probably never belonged together in the first place." "But two beautiful daughters; they themselves college-educated people; the two of them with excellent executive positions. I don't get it. And the drinking: *why?* Where does it get you? With all due respect, it seems to me stupid. I myself of course never had the advantages of an education. If I had—but I didn't, and that was that. But my mother, let me tell you, I just have to remember her to get a good feeling about the whole world. What a woman! Ma, I would say to her, what are you doing on the floor again? Larry and I will give you the money, you'll get somebody else in to wash the floors. But no—"

It is during dinner that, at last, in Chekhov's phrase, the angel of silence passes over him. But only to be followed quickly by the shade of melancholia. Is he teetering now at the brink of tears, having spoken and spoken and spoken and still not having *quite* said it? Is he at last about to break down and cry—or am I ascribing to him the mood claiming me? Why should I feel as though I have lost a bloody battle when clearly I have won?

We eat again on the screened-in porch, where, during the days previous, I have been making every effort, with pen and pad, to speak *my* it. Beeswax candles are burning invisibly down in the antique pewter holders; the bayberry candles, arrived by mail from the Vineyard, drip wax threads onto the table. Candles burn everywhere you look—Claire has a passion for them on the porch at night; they are probably her only extravagance. Earlier, when she went around from holder to holder with a book of matches, my father—already at the table with the napkin drawn through his belt—had begun to recite for her the names of the Catskill hotels that had tragically burned to the ground in the last twenty years. Whereupon she had assured him that she would be careful. Still, when a breeze moves lightly over the porch, and the flames all flicker, he looks around to check that nothing has caught fire.

Now we hear the first of the ripe apples dropping onto the grass in the orchard just beyond the house. We hear the hoot of "our" owl—so Claire identifies for our guests this creature we have never seen, and whose home is up in "our" woods. If we are all silent long enough, she tells the two old men—as though they are two children—the deer may come down from the woods to graze around the apple trees. Dazzle has been cautioned about barking and scaring them away. The dog pants a little at the sound of his name from her lips. He is eleven and has been hers since she was a fourteen-year-old high school girl, her dearest pal ever since the year Olivia went off to college, the closest thing to her, until me. Within a few seconds Dazzle is peacefully asleep, and once again there is only the spirited September finale by the tree toads and the crickets, most popular of all the soft summer songs ever heard.

I cannot take my eyes from her face tonight. Between the Old Master etchings of the two pouched and creased and candlelit old men, Claire's face seems, more than ever, so apple-smooth, apple-small, apple-shiny, apple-plain, apple-fresh . . . never more artless and untainted . . . never before *so* . . . Yes, and to what am I willfully blinding myself that in time must set us apart? Why continue to cast this spell over myself, wherein nothing is permitted to sift through except what pleases me? Is there not something a little dubious and dreamy about all this gentle, tender adoration? What will happen when the *rest* of Claire obtrudes? What happens if no "rest of her" is there! And what of the rest of me? How long will *that* be sold a bill of goods? How much longer before I've had a bellyful of wholesome innocence—how long before the lovely blandness of a life with Claire begins to cloy, to pall, and I am out there once again, mourning what I've lost and looking for my way!

And with doubts so long suppressed voiced at last—and in deafening unison—the emotions under whose somber portentousness I have been living out this day forge themselves into something as palpable and awful as a spike. *Only an interim,* I think, and as though I have in fact been stabbed and the strength is gushing out of me, I feel myself about to tumble from my chair. Only an interim. Never to know anything durable. Nothing except my unrelinquishable memories of the discontinuous and the provisional; nothing except this ever-lengthening saga of all that did not work . . .

To be sure, to be sure, Claire is still with me, directly across the table, saying something to my father and Mr. Barbatnik about the planets she will show them later, brilliant tonight among the distant constellations. With her hair pinned up, exposing the vulnerable vertebrae that support the stalk of her slender neck, and in her pale caftan, with its embroidered edging, sewn together early in the summer on the machine, and lending a tiny regal air to her overpowering simplicity, she looks to me more precious than ever, more than ever before like my true wife, my unborn offspring's mother . . . yet I am already bereft of my strength and my hope and my contentment. Though we will go ahead, as planned, and rent the house to use on weekends and school vacations, I am certain that in only a matter of time—that's all it seems to take, just time—what we have together will gradually disappear, and the man now holding in his hand a spoonful of her orange custard will give way to Herbie's pupil, Birgitta's accomplice, Helen's suitor, yes, to Baumgarten's sidekick and defender, to the would-be wayward son and all he hungers for. Or, if not that, the would-be *what?* When this too is gone in its turn, what then?

I can't, for the sake of us all, fall out of a chair at dinner. Yet once again I am overcome by a terrible physical weakness. I am afraid to reach for my wineglass for fear that I will not have sufficient strength to carry it the distance to my mouth.

"How about a record?" I say to Claire.

"That new Bach?"

A record of trio sonatas. We have been listening to it all week. The week before, it had been a Mozart quartet; the week before that, the Elgar cello concerto. We just keep turning over one record again and again and again until finally we have had enough. It is all one hears coming and going through the house, music that almost seems by now to be the by-product of our comings and goings, compositions exuded by our sense of well-being. All we ever hear is the most exquisite music.

Seemingly with a good reason, I manage to leave the table before something frightening happens.

The phonograph and speakers in the living room are Claire's, carried up from the city in the back seat of the car. So are most of the records hers. So are the curtains sewed together for the windows, and the corduroy spread she made to cover the battered daybed, and the two china dogs by the fireplace, which once belonged to her grandmother and became hers on her twenty-fifth birthday. As a child on her way home from school she used to stop and have tea and toast with her grandmother, and practice on the piano there; then, armed at least with that, she could continue to the battlefield of her house. On her own she decided to have that abortion. So I would not be burdened by a duty? So I could choose her just for herself? But is the notion of duty so utterly horrendous? Why didn't she tell me she was pregnant? Is there not a point on life's way when one yields to duty, *welcomes* duty as once one yielded to pleasure, to passion, to adventure—a time when duty is the pleasure, rather than pleasure the duty . . .

The exquisite music begins. I return to the porch, not quite so pale as when I left. I sit back down at the table and sip my wine. Yes, I can raise and lower a glass. I can focus my thoughts on another subject. I had better.

"Mr. Barbatnik," I say, "my father told us you survived the concentration camps. How did you do it? Do you mind my asking?"

"Professor, please let me say first how much I appreciate your hospitality to a total stranger. This is the happiest day for me in a very long time. I thought maybe I even forgot how to be happy with people. I thank you all. I thank my new and dear friend, your wonderful father. It was a beautiful day, and, Miss Ovington—"

"Please call me Claire," she says.

"Claire, you are beyond your years and young and adorable as well. And—and all day I have wanted to give you my deep gratitude. For all the lovely things you think to do for people."

The two elders have been seated to either side of her, the lover directly across: with all the love he can muster, he looks upon the fullness of her saucy body and the smallness of her face above the little vase of asters he plucked for her on his morning walk; with all the love at his command, he watches this munificent female creature, now in the moment of her fullest bloom, offer a hand to their shy guest, who takes it, grasps and squeezes it, and without relinquishing it begins to speak for the first time with ease and self-assurance, at last at home (just as she had planned it, just as she has made it come to pass). And amid all this, the lover does, in fact, feel more deeply implicated in his own life than at any moment in memory—the true self at its truest, moored by every feeling to its own true home! And yet he continues to imagine that he is being drawn away by a force as incontrovertible as gravity, which is no lie either. As though he is a falling body, helpless as any little apple in the orchard which has broken free and is descending toward the alluring earth.

But instead of crying, either in his mother tongue or with some rudimentary animalish howl, "Don't leave me! Don't go! I'll miss you bitterly! This moment, and we four together—this is what should be!" he spoons out the last of his custard and attends to the survival story that he has asked to hear.

"There was a beginning," Mr. Barbatnik is saying, "there has to be an ending. I am going to live to see this monstrosity come to an end. This is what I told myself every single morning and night."

"But how was it they didn't send you to the ovens?"

How do you come to be here, with us? Why is Claire here? Why not Helen and our child? Why not my mother? And in ten years' time . . . who then? To build an intimate life anew, out of nothing, when I am forty-five? To start over again with everything at fifty? To be forever a beweeper of my outcast state? I can't! I won't!

"They couldn't kill everybody," says Mr. Barbatnik. "This I knew. Somebody has to be left, if only one person. And so I would tell myself, this one person will be me. I worked for them in the coal mines where they sent me. With the Poles. I was a young man then, and strong. I worked like it was my own coal mine inherited from my father. I told myself that this was what I wanted to do. I told myself that this work I was doing was for my child. I told myself different things every single day to make it just that I could last till that night. And that's how I lasted. Only when the Russians started coming so quick all of a sudden, the Germans took us and at three in the morning started us off on a march. Days and days and days, until I stopped keeping track. It went on and on, and people dropping every place you looked, and sure, I told myself again that if one is left it is going to be me. But by then I knew somehow that even if I made it to the destination where we were going, when I got there they would shoot whoever of us was left. So this is how come I ran away after weeks and weeks of marching without a stop to wherever in

God's name it was. I hid in the woods and at night I came out and the German farmers fed me. Yes, that's true," he says, as he stares down at his large hand, in the candlelight looking very nearly as wide as a spade and as heavy as a crowbar, and enfolding within it Claire's thin, fine fingers with their delicate bones and knuckles. "The individual German, he isn't so bad, you know. But put three Germans together in a room and you can kiss the good world goodbye."

"And then what happened?" I ask, but he continues looking down, as though to contemplate the riddle of this one hand in the other. "How were you saved, Mr. Barbatnik?"

"One night a German farm woman said to me that the Americans are here. I thought she must be lying. I figured, don't come back here to her, she's up to something no good. But the next day I saw a tank through the trees, rolling down the road, with a white star, and I ran out, screaming at the top of my lungs."

Claire says, "You must have looked so strange by then. How did they know who you were?"

"They knew. I wasn't the first one. We were all coming out of our holes. What was left of us. I lost a wife and two parents, my brother, two sisters, and a three-year-old daughter."

Claire groans, *"Oh,"* as though she has just been pierced by a needle. "Mr. Barbatnik, we are asking you too many questions, we shouldn't . . ."

He shakes his head. "Darling, you live, you ask questions. Maybe it's why we live. It seems that way."

"I tell him," says my father, "that he should make a book out of all he went through. I can think of some people I'd like to give it to read. If they could read it, maybe they would shake their heads that they can be the way they are, and this man can be so kind and good."

"And before the war started?" I ask him. "You were a young man then. What did you want to be?"

Probably because of the strength of his arms and the size of his hands I expect to hear him say a carpenter or a mason. In America he drove a taxi for over twenty years.

"A human being," he answers, "someone that could see and understand how we lived, and what was real, and not to flatter myself with lies. This was always my ambition from when I was a small child. In the beginning I was like everybody, a good cheder boy. But I personally, with my own hands, liberated myself from all that at sixteen years. My father could have killed me, but I absolutely did not want to be a fanatic. To believe in what doesn't exist, no, that wasn't for me. These are just the people who hate the Jews, these fanatics. And there are Jews who are fanatics too," he tells Claire, "and also walk around in a dream. But not me. Not for a second since I was sixteen years old and told my father what I refuse to pretend."

"If he wrote a book," says my father, "it should be called 'The Man Who Never Said Die.' "

"And here you married again?" I ask.

"Yes. She had been in a concentration camp also. Three years ago next month she passed away—like your own mother, from cancer. She wasn't even sick. One night after dinner she is washing the dishes. I go in to turn on the TV, and suddenly I hear a crash from the kitchen. 'Help me, I'm in trouble.' When I run into the kitchen she is on the floor. 'I couldn't hold on to the ditch,' she says. She says 'ditch' instead of 'dish.' The word alone gave me the willies. And her eyes. It was awful. I knew then and there that she was done for. Two days later they tell us that cancer is already in her brain. And it happened out of nowhere." Without a trace of animus—just to keep the record straight—he adds, "How else?"

"Too terrible," Claire says.

After my father has gone around to each candle to snuff out the flame—blowing even at those already expired, just to be sure—we step into the garden for Claire to show them the other planets visible from the earth tonight. Talking toward their upturned eyeglasses she explains about the Milky Way, answers questions about shooting stars, points out, as she does to her sixth-graders—as she did with me on our first night here—that mere speck of a star adjacent to the handle of the Little Dipper which the Greek soldiers had to discern to qualify for battle. Then she accompanies them back into the house; if they should awaken in the morning before we do, she wants them to know where there is coffee and juice. I remain in the garden with Dazzle. I don't know what to think. I don't want to know. I want only to climb by myself to the top of the hill. I remember our gondola rides in Venice. "Are you sure we didn't die and go to heaven?" "You'll have to ask the gondolier."

Through the living-room window I see the three of them standing around the coffee table. Claire has turned the record over and put it back on the turntable to play. My father is holding the album of Shakespeare medals in his hands. It appears that he is reading aloud from the backs of the medallions.

Some minutes later she joins me on the weathered wooden bench at the top of the hill. Side by side, without speaking, we look up again at the familiar stars. We do this nearly every night. Everything we have done this summer we have done nearly every night, afternoon, and morning. Every day calling out from the kitchen to the porch, from the bedroom to the bath, "Clarissa, come see, the sun is setting," "Claire, there's a hummingbird," "Sweetheart, what's the name of that star?"

For the first time all day she gives in to exhaustion. "Oh, my," she says, and lays her head on my shoulder. I can feel the air she breathes slowly filling, then slowly leaving her body.

After inventing a constellation of my own of the sky's brightest lights, I say to her, "It's a simple Chekhov story, isn't it?"

"Isn't what?"

"This. Today. The summer. Some nine or ten pages, that's all. Called 'The Life I Formerly Led.' Two old men come to the country to visit a healthy, handsome young couple, brimming over with contentment. The young man is in his middle thirties, having recovered finally from the mistakes of his twenties. The young woman is in her twenties, the survivor of a painful youth and adolescence. They have every reason to believe they have come through. It looks and feels to both of them as though they have been saved, and in large part by one another. They are in love. But after dinner by candlelight, one of the old men tells of his life, about the utter ruination of a world, and about the blows that keep on coming. And that's it. The story ends just like this: her pretty head on his shoulder; his hand stroking her hair; their owl hooting; their constellations all in order—their medallions all in order; their guests in their freshly made beds; and their summer cottage, so cozy and inviting, just down the hill from where they sit together wondering about what they have to fear. Music is playing in the house. The most lovely music there is. 'And both of them knew that the most complicated and difficult part was only just beginning.' That's the last line of 'Lady with a Lapdog.' "

"Are you really frightened of something?"

"I seem to be saying I am, don't I?"

"But of what?"

Her soft, clever, trusting, green eyes are on me now. All that conscientious, schoolroom attention of hers is focused upon me—and what I will answer. After a moment I tell her, "I don't know really. Yesterday at the drugstore I saw that they had portable oxygen units up on the shelf. The kid there showed me how they work, and I bought one. I put it in the bathroom closet. It's back of the beach towels. In case anything should happen to anyone tonight."

"Oh, but nothing is going to happen. Why should it?"

"No reason. Only when he was going on like that about the past with that couple who own the hotel, I wished I had brought it along in the car."

"David, he isn't going to die just from getting heated up about the past. Oh, sweetheart," she says, kissing my hand and holding it to her cheek, "you're worn down, that's all. He gets so worked up, he *can* wear you to a frazzle—but he means so well. And he's obviously still in the best of health. He's fine. You're just exhausted. It's time for bed, that's all."

It's time for bed, that's all. Oh, innocent beloved, you fail to understand and I can't tell you. I can't say it, not tonight, but within a year my passion will be dead. Already it is dying and I am afraid that there is nothing I can do to save it. And nothing that you can do. Intimately bound—bound to you as to no one else!—and I will not be able to raise a hand to so much as touch you . . . unless first I remind myself that I must. Toward the flesh upon which I have been grafted and nurtured back toward something like mastery over my life, I will be without desire. Oh, it's stupid! Idiotic! Unfair! To be robbed like this of you! And of this life I love and have hardly gotten to know! And robbed by whom? It always comes down to myself!

And so it is I see myself back in Klinger's waiting room; and despite the presence there of all those *Newsweeks* and *New Yorkers,* I am no sympathetic, unspectacular sufferer out of a muted Chekhov tale of ordinary human affliction. No, more hideous by far, more like Gogol's berserk and mortified amputee, who rushes to the newspaper office to place a maniacal classified ad seeking the return of the nose that has decided to take leave of his face. Yes, the butt of a ridiculous, vicious, inexplicable joke! Here, you therapeutic con man, I'm back, and even worse than before! Did all you said, followed every instruction, unswervingly pursued the healthiest of regimens—even took it on myself to study the passions in my classroom, to submit to scrutiny those who have scrutinized the subject most pitilessly . . . and here is the result! I know and I know and I know, I imagine and I imagine and I imagine, and when the worst happens, I might as well know nothing! You might as well know nothing! And feed me not the consolations of the reality principle! Just find it for me before it's too late! The perfect young woman is waiting! That dream of a girl and the most livable of lives! And here I hand to the dapper, portly, clever physician the advertisement headed "LOST," describing what it looked like when last seen, its real and sentimental worth, and the reward that I will offer anyone giving information leading to its recovery: "My desire for Miss Claire Ovington—a Manhattan private-school teacher, five feet ten inches tall, one hundred and thirty-eight pounds, fair hair, silvery-green eyes, the kindest, most loving and loyal nature—has mysteriously vanished . . ."

And the doctor's reply? That perhaps it was never in my possession to begin with? Or that, obviously, what has disappeared I must learn to live without . . .

All night long, bad dreams sweep through me like water through a fish's gills. Near dawn I awaken to discover that the house is not in ashes nor have I been abandoned in my bed as an incurable. My willing Clarissa is with me still! I raise her nightgown up along the length of her unconscious body, and with my lips begin to press and tug her nipples until the pale, velvety, childlike areolae erupt in tiny granules and her moan begins. But even while I suck in a desperate frenzy at the choicest morsel of her flesh, even as I pit all my accumulated happiness, and all my hope, against my fear of transformations yet to come, I wait to hear the most dreadful sound imaginable emerge from the room where Mr. Barbatnik and my father lie alone and insensate, each in his freshly made bed.

The Breast

It began oddly. But could it have begun otherwise, however it began? It has been said, of course, that everything under the sun begins oddly and ends oddly, and *is* odd. A perfect rose is "odd," so is an imperfect rose, so is the rose of ordinary rosy good looks growing in your neighbor's garden. I know about the perspective from which all that exists appears awesome and mysterious. Reflect upon eternity, consider, if you are up to it, oblivion, and everything becomes a wonder. Still, I would submit to you, in all humility, that some things are more wondrous than others, and that I am one such thing.

It began oddly—a mild, sporadic tingling in the groin. During that first week I would retire several times a day to the men's room adjacent to my office in the humanities building to take down my trousers, but upon examining myself, I saw nothing out of the ordinary, assiduous as was my search. I decided, halfheartedly, to ignore it. I had been so devout a hypochondriac all my life, so alert to every change in body temperature and systemic regularity, that the reasonable man I also was had long found it impossible to take seriously all my telltale symptoms. Despite the grim premonitions of extinction or paralysis or unendurable pain that accompanied each new ache or fever, I was, at thirty-eight, a man of stamina and appetite, six feet tall with good posture and a trim physique, most of my hair and all of my teeth, and no

First published 1972; revised 1980.

history of major illness. Though I might rush to identify this tingling in my groin with some neurological disease on the order of shingles—if not worse—I simultaneously understood that it was undoubtedly, as always, nothing.

I was wrong. It was something. Another week passed before I discerned a barely perceptible pinkening of the skin beneath the pubic hair, a blemish so faint, however, that I finally instructed myself to stop looking; it was no more than a minor irritation and certainly nothing to worry about. After another week—making, for the record, an incubation period of twenty-one days—I glanced down one evening while stepping into the shower and discovered that through the hectic day of teaching and conferences and commuting and dining out, the flesh at the base of my penis had turned a shade of pale red. Dye, I instantly decided, from my undershorts. (That the undershorts at my feet were light blue meant nothing in that panic-stricken burst of disbelief.) I looked *stained,* as though something—a berry of some sort—had been crushed against my pubes and the juices had run down onto my member, raggedly coloring the root.

In the shower I lathered and rinsed my penis and pubic hair three times, then coated myself carefully from thighs to navel with a thick icing of soap bubbles that I proceeded to massage into my flesh for a count of sixty; when I rinsed with hot water—burning hot this time—the stain was still there. Not a rash, not a scab, not a bruise or a sore, but a deep pigment change that I associated at once with cancer.

It was just midnight, the time when transformations routinely take place in horror stories—and a hard hour to get a doctor in New York. Nonetheless, I immediately telephoned my physician, Dr. Gordon, and despite an attempt to hide my alarm, he heard the fear easily enough and volunteered to dress and come across town to examine me. Perhaps if Claire had been with me that night instead of back at her own apartment preparing a curriculum-committee report, I would have had the courage of my terror and told the doctor to come running. Of course on the basis of my symptoms at that hour it is unlikely that Dr. Gordon would have rushed me then and there into a hospital, nor does it appear from what we now know—or continue not to know—

that anything could have been done in the hospital to prevent or arrest what was under way. The agony of the next four hours I was to spend alone might perhaps have been alleviated by morphine, but nothing indicates that the course of the disaster could have been reversed by any medical procedure short of euthanasia.

With Claire at my side I might have been able to cave in completely, but alone I suddenly felt ashamed of losing control; it was no more than five minutes since I'd discovered the stain, and there I was, wet and nude on my leather sofa, trying vainly to overcome the tremolo in my voice as I looked down and described into the phone what I saw. *Take hold,* I thought—and so I took hold, as I can when I tell myself to. If it was what I feared, it could wait until morning; if it wasn't, it could also wait. I would be fine, I told the doctor. Exhausted from a hard day's work, I had just been—startled. I would see him in his office at —I thought this brave of me—about noon. Nine, he said. I agreed and, calmly as I could, said good night.

Not until I hung up and examined myself yet again under a strong light did I remember that there was a third symptom—aside from the tingling groin, and the discolored penis—that I had failed to mention to the doctor; I had taken it, until that moment, for a sign of health rather than of disease. This was the intensity of local sensation I had experienced at sex with Claire during the preceding three weeks. To me it had signaled the resurgence of my old desire for her; from where or why I did not even care to question, so thrilled—and so relieved—was I to have it back. As it was, the strong lust her physical beauty had aroused in me during the first two years of our affair had been dwindling for almost a year now. Until lately, I would make love to her no more than two or three times a month and, more often than not, at her provocation.

My cooling down—my coldness—was distressing to both of us, but as we both had endured enough emotional upheaval in our lives (she as a child with her parents, I as an adult with my wife), we were equally reluctant to take any steps toward dissolving our union. Dispiriting as it surely was for a lovely and voluptuous young woman of twenty-five to be spurned night after night,

Claire displayed outwardly none of the suspicion or frustration or anger that would have seemed justified even to me, the source of her unhappiness. Yes, she pays a price for this equanimity—she is not the most expressive woman I have ever known, for all her sexual passion—but I have reached the stage in my life—that is, I *had*—where the calm harbor and its placid waters were more to my liking than the foaming drama of the high seas. Of course there were times—out in company, or sometimes just alone over our dinner—when I might have wished her livelier and more responsive, but I was far too content with her dependable sobriety to be disappointed in her for lacking color. I had had enough color, thank you, with my wife.

Indeed, during the course of three years, Claire and I had worked out a way of living together—which in part entailed living separately—that provided us the warmth and security of each other's affections, without the accompanying dependence, or the grinding boredom, or the wild, unfocused yearning, or the round-the-clock strategies of deception and placation which seemed to have soured all but a very few of the marriages we knew. A year back I had ended five years of psychoanalysis convinced that the wounds sustained in my own Grand Guignol marriage had healed as well as they ever would, and in large part because of my life with Claire. Maybe I wasn't the man I'd been, but I wasn't a bleeding buck private any longer, either, wrapped in bandages and beating the drum of self-pity as I limped tearfully into the analyst's office from that battlefield known as Hearth and Home. Life had become orderly and stable—the first time I could say that in more than a decade. We really did get on so easily and with so little strain, we liked each other so much that it seemed to me something very like a disaster (little I knew about disaster) when, out of the blue, I began to take no pleasure at all in our lovemaking. It was a depressing, bewildering development, and try as I might, I seemed unable to alter it. I was, in fact, scheduled to pay a visit to my former analyst to talk about how much this was troubling me, when, out of the blue again, I was suddenly more passionate with her than I had ever been with anyone.

But "passion" is the wrong word: an infant in the crib doesn't feel passion when it delights in being tickled playfully under the chin. I am talking about purely tactile delight—sex neither in the head nor the heart, but excruciatingly in the epidermis of the penis, sex skin-deep and ecstatic. It was a kind of pleasure that made me writhe and claw at the sheets, made me twist and turn in the bed with a helpless abandon that I had previously associated more with women than with men—and women more imaginary than real. During the final week of my incubation period, I nearly cried with *tears* from the sheer tortuous pleasure of the friction alone. When I came I took Claire's ear in my mouth and licked it like a dog. I licked her hair. I found myself panting, licking my own shoulder. I had been saved! My life with Claire had been spared! Having lain indifferently beside her for nearly a year, having begun to fear the worst about our future, I had somehow—blessed mysterious somehow!—found my way to a pure, primitive realm of erotic susceptibility where the bond between us could only be strengthened. "Is this what is meant by debauchery?" I asked my happy friend whose pale skin bore the marks of my teeth; "it's like nothing I've ever known." She only smiled, and closed her eyes to float a little more. Her hair was stringy with perspiration, like a little girl's from playing too long in the heat. Pleasured, pleasure-giving Claire. Lucky David. We couldn't have been happier.

Alas, what has happened to me is like nothing *anyone* has ever known: beyond understanding, beyond compassion, beyond comedy. To be sure, there are those who claim to be on the very brink of a conclusive scientific explanation; and those, my faithful visitors, whose compassion is seemingly limitless; and then, out in the world, those—why shouldn't there be?—who cannot help laughing. And, you know, at times I am even one with them: I understand, I have compassion, I too see the joke. Enjoying it is another matter. If only I could sustain the laughter for more than a few seconds—if only it weren't so brief and so bitter. But then maybe more laughs are what I have to look forward to, if the medical men are able to sustain life in me in this condition, and if I should continue to want them to.

I am a breast. A phenomenon that has been variously described to me as "a massive hormonal influx," "an endocrinopathic catastrophe," and/or "a hermaphroditic explosion of chromosomes" took place within my body between midnight and 4 A.M. on February 18, 1971, and converted me into a mammary gland disconnected from any human form, a mammary gland such as could only appear, one would have thought, in a dream or a Dali painting. They tell me that I am now an organism with the general shape of a football, or a dirigible; I am said to be of spongy consistency, weighing one hundred and fifty-five pounds (formerly I was one hundred and sixty-two), and measuring, still, six feet in length. Though I continue to retain, in damaged and "irregular" form, much of the cardiovascular and central nervous systems, an excretory system described as "reduced and primitive," and a respiratory system that terminates just above my mid-section in something resembling a navel with a flap, the basic architecture in which these human characteristics are disarranged and buried is that of the breast of the mammalian female.

The bulk of my weight is fatty tissue. At one end I am rounded off like a watermelon, at the other I terminate in a nipple, cylindrical in shape, projecting five inches from my "body" and perforated at the tip with seventeen openings, each about half the size of the male urethral orifice. These are the apertures of the lactiferous ducts. As I am able to understand it without the benefit of diagrams—I am sightless—the ducts branch back into lobules composed of the sort of cells that secrete the milk that is carried to the surface of the normal nipple when it is being suckled, or milked by machine.

My flesh is smooth and "youthful," and I am still a "Caucasian." The color of my nipple is rosy pink. This last is thought to be unusual because in my former incarnation I was an emphatic brunet. As I told the endocrinologist who made this observation, I find it less unusual than certain other aspects of the transformation, but then I am not the endocrinologist around here. Embittered wit, but wit at last, and it must have been observed and noted.

My nipple is rosy pink—like the stain at the base of my penis the night this all happened to me. Since the apertures in the nipple provide me with something like a mouth and vestigial ears —at least it has seemed to me that I am able to make myself heard through my nipple, and, faintly, to hear through it what is going on around me—I had assumed that it was my head that had become my nipple. But the doctors conclude otherwise, at least as of this month. For one thing, my voice, faint as it is, evidently emanates from the flap in my mid-section, even if my sense of internal landscape doggedly continues to associate the higher functions of consciousness with the body's topmost point. The doctors now maintain that the wrinkled, roughened skin of the nipple—which, admittedly, is exquisitely sensitive to touch like no tissue on the face, including the mucous membrane of the lips—was formed out of the glans penis. The puckered pinkish areola encircling the nipple is said to have metamorphosed from the shaft of the penis under the assault of a volcanic secretion from the pituitary of "mammogenic" fluid. Two fine long reddish hairs extend from one of the small elevations on the rim of my areola. "How long are they?"

"Seven inches exactly."

"My antennae." The bitterness. Then the disbelief. "Will you pull one, please?"

"If you like, David, I'll pull very gently."

Dr. Gordon wasn't lying. A hair of mine had been tugged. A familiar enough sensation—indeed, so familiar that I wanted to be dead.

Of course it was days after the change—the "change"!—before I even regained consciousness, and another week after that before they would tell me anything other than that I had been "very ill" with "an endocrine imbalance." I keened and howled so wretchedly each time I awoke to discover anew that I could not see, smell, taste, or move that I had to be kept under heavy sedation. When my "body" was touched, I didn't know what to make of it: the sensation was unexpectedly soothing, but far away, and reminded me of water lapping at a beach. One morning I awakened to feel something new happening to me at one of my extremities. Nothing like pain—rather more like pleasure—yet it felt so strange just to *feel* that I screamed, "I've been burned! I was in a fire!"

"Calm yourself, Mr. Kepesh," a woman said. "I'm only washing you. I'm only washing your face."

"My face? Where is it! Where are my arms! My legs! Where is my mouth! *What happened to me?"*

Now Dr. Gordon spoke. "You're in Lenox Hill Hospital, David. You're in a private room on the seventh floor. You've been here ten days. I've been to see you every morning and night. You are getting excellent care and all the attention you require. Right now you're just being washed with a sponge and some warm soapy water. That's all. Does that hurt you?"

"No," I whimpered, "but where is my face?"

"Just let the nurse wash you, and we'll talk a little later in the morning. You must get all the rest you can."

"What happened to me?" I could remember the pain and the terror, but no more: to me it had felt as though I were being repeatedly shot from a cannon into a brick wall, then marched over by an army of boots. In actuality it was more as though I had been a man made of taffy, stretched in opposite directions by my penis and my buttocks until I was as wide as I had once been long. The doctors tell me that I couldn't have been conscious for more than a few minutes once the "catastrophe" got going, but in retrospect, it seems to me that I had been awake to feel every last bone in my body broken in two and ground into dust.

"If only you'll relax now—"

"How am I being fed!"

"Intravenously. You mustn't worry. You're being fed all you need."

"Where are my arms!"

"Just let the nurse wash you, and then she'll rub some oil in, and you'll feel much better. Then you can sleep."

I was awakened like this every morning, but it was another week or more before I was sufficiently calm—or torpid—to associate the sensations of washing with erotic excitement. By now I had concluded that I was a quadruple amputee—that the boiler had burst beneath the bedroom of my parlor-floor apartment, and I had been blinded and mutilated in the explosion. I sobbed almost continuously, giving no credence whatsoever to the hormonal explanations that Dr. Gordon and his colleagues proposed for my "illness." Then one morning, depleted and numb from my days of tearless weeping, I felt myself becoming aroused—a mild throbbing in the vicinity of what I still took to be my face, a pleasing feeling of . . . engorgement.

"Do you like that?" The voice was a man's! A stranger's!

"Who are you? Where am I? What is going on?"

"I'm the nurse."

"Where's the other nurse!"

"It's Sunday. Take it easy—it's only Sunday."

The next morning the regular nurse, Miss Clark, returned to duty, accompanied by Dr. Gordon. I was washed, under Dr. Gordon's supervision, and this time, when I began to experience the sensations that accompany erotic fondling, I let them envelop me. "Oh," I whispered, "that does feel nice."

"What is it?" asked Dr. Gordon. "What are you saying, David?"

The nurse began to rub in the oil. I could feel each one of her fingers kneading that face no longer a face. Then something began to make me tingle, something that I soon realized was only the soft palm of her hand slowly moving in caressing circles on that faceless face. My whole being was seething with that exquisite sense of imminence that precedes a perfect ejaculation. "Oh, my God, this is so wonderful." And then I began to sob so uncontrollably that I had to be put back to sleep.

Shortly thereafter, Dr. Gordon came with Dr. Klinger, who for five years had been my psychoanalyst, and they told me what it is I have become.

I was washed gently but thoroughly every morning and then smeared with oil and massaged. After I heard the truth about myself—after learning that I live now in a hammock, my nipple at one end, my rounded, bellied underside at the other, and with two velvet harnesses holding my bulk in place—it was several months before I could take even the remotest pleasure in these morning ablutions. And even then it was not until Dr. Gordon consented to leave me alone in the room with the nurse that I was again able to surrender wholly to Miss Clark's ministering fingers. But when I did, the palpations were almost more than could be borne, deliciously "almost"—a frenzy akin to what I had experienced in those final weeks of lovemaking with Claire, but even more extreme, it seemed, coming to me in my state of utter helplessness, and out of nothingness, and from this source dedicated solely to kindling my excitement. When the session was over and Miss Clark had retired from my room with her basin of warm water and the vials of oil (I imagined colored vials), my hammock would sway comfortingly to and fro, until at last my heaving stopped, my nipple softened, and I slept the sleep of the sated.

I say the doctor consented to leave us alone in the room. But how do I know anyone has ever left me alone, or that this is even a room? Dr. Gordon assures me that I am under no more surveillance than any other difficult case—I am not on display in a medical amphitheater, am not being exposed to closed-circuit television . . . but what's to prevent him from lying? I doubt that in the midst of this calamity anybody is watching out for my civil liberties. That *would* be laughable. And why do I even care if I am not alone when I think I am? If I am under a soundproof glass dome on a platform in the middle of Madison Square Garden, if I am on display in Macy's window—what's the difference to me? Wherever they have put me, however many may be looking in at me, I am really quite as alone as anyone could ever wish to be. Best to stop thinking about my "dignity," regardless of all it meant to me when I was a professor of literature, a lover, a son, a friend, a neighbor, a customer, a client, and a citizen. If ever there was a time to forget about propriety, decorum, and personal pride, this is it. But as these are matters intimately connected to my idea of sanity and to my self-esteem, I am, in fact, troubled now as I wasn't at all in my former life, where the style of social constraint practiced by the educated classes came quite easily to me, and provided real satisfaction. Now the thought that my morning sessions with Miss Clark are being carried live on intra-hospital TV, that my delirious writhings are being observed by hundreds of scientists assembled in the galleries overhead . . . well, that is sometimes almost as unbearable as the rest of it. Nonetheless, when Dr. Gordon assures me that my "privacy" is being respected, I no longer contradict him. I say instead, "Thank you for that," and in this way I am able at least to pretend to them that I think I am alone even if I'm not.

You see, it is not a matter of doing what is right or seemly; I can assure you that I am not concerned with the etiquette of being a breast. Rather, it is doing what I must, to continue to be me. For if not me, who? Or what? Either I continue to be myself or I go mad—and then I die. And it seems I don't want to die. A surprise to me too, but there it is. I don't foresee a miracle either, some sort of retaliatory raid by my anti-mammogenic hormones, if such there be (and God alone knows if there are in someone made like me), that will undo the damage. I suspect it's a little late for that, and so it is not with this hope springing eternally in the human breast that the human breast continues to want to be. Human I insist I am, but not that human. Nor do I believe the worst is over. I get the feeling that the worst is yet to come. No, it is simply that having been terrified of death since the age of two, I have become entrenched in my hatred of it, have taken a personal stand *against* death from which I seem unable to retreat because of This. Horrible indeed This is; but on the other hand, I have been wanting not to die for so long now, I just can't stop doing it overnight. I need time.

That I have not died is, as you can imagine, of great interest to medical science. *That* miracle continues to be studied by microbiologists, physiologists, and biochemists working here in the hospital and, I am told, in medical institutions around the country. They are trying to figure out what makes me still tick. Dr. Klinger thinks that no matter how they put the puzzle together, in the end it could all come down to those old pulpit bromides, "strength of character" and "the will to live." And who am I not to concur in such a heroic estimate of myself?

"It appears then that my analysis has 'taken,' " I tell Dr. Klinger; "a tribute to you, sir." He laughs. "You were always stronger than you thought." "I would as soon never have had to find out. And besides it's not so. I can't live like this any longer." "Yet you have, you do." "I do *but I can't.* I was never strong. Only determined. One foot in front of the other. Good grades in all subjects. It goes back to handing homework in on time and carrying off the prizes. Dr. Klinger, *it's hideous in here.* I want to quit, I want to go crazy, to go spinning off, ranting and wild, *only I can't.* I sob. I scream. I touch bottom. I lie there on that bottom! But then I come around. I make my mordant little jokes. I listen to the radio. I listen to the phonograph. I think about what we've said. I restrain my rage and I restrain my misery—and I wait for your next visit. But this is madness, my coming around. To be putting one foot in front of the other is madness—*especially as I have no feet!* This ghastly thing has happened, and I listen to the six o'clock news! This incredible catastrophe, and I listen to the weather report!" No, no, says Dr. Klinger: strength of character, the will to live.

I tell him that I want to go mad, he tells me that it's impossible: beyond me, *beneath* me. It took This for me to find that I am a citadel of sanity.

So—I may pretend otherwise, but I know they are studying me, watching as they would from a glass-bottomed boat the private life of a porpoise or a manatee. I think of these aquatic mammals because of the overall resemblance I now bear to them in size and shape, and because the porpoise in particular is said to be an intelligent, perhaps even rational, creature. Porpoise with a Ph.D. Associate Porpoise Kepesh. Oh, really, it is the silliness, the triviality, the *meaninglessness* of life that one misses most in a life like this. For quite aside from the monstrous, ludicrous fact of me, there is the intellectual responsibility that I seem to have developed to this preposterous misfortune. WHAT DOES IT MEAN? HOW COULD IT HAVE HAPPENED? IN THE ENTIRE HISTORY OF THE HUMAN RACE, WHY PROFESSOR KEPESH? Yes, it is clever of Dr. Klinger to keep to what is ordinary and familiar, to drone on about strength of character and the will to live. Better these banalities than the grandiose or the apocalyptic; for citadel of sanity though I may be, there is really only so much that even I can take.

As far as I know, my only visitors other than the scientists, the doctors, and the hospital staff, have been Claire, my father, and Arthur Schonbrunn, formerly my department chairman and now the Dean of Arts and Sciences. My father's behavior has been staggering. I don't know how to account for it, except to say that I simply never knew the man. Nobody knew the man. Aggressive, cunning, at his work tyrannical—with us, the little family, innocent, protective, tender, and deeply in love. But this self-possession face to face with such horror? Who would have expected it from the owner of a second-class South Fallsburg hotel? A short-order cook to begin with, he rose eventually to be the innkeeper himself; retired now, he "kills time" answering the phone mornings at his brother's booming catering service in Bayside. Once a week he comes to visit and, seated in a chair that is drawn up beside my nipple, tells me all the news about our former guests. Remember Abrams the milliner? Cohen the chiropodist? Remember Rosenheim with the card tricks and the Cadillac? Yes, yes, I think so. Well, this one is near death, this one has moved, this one's son has gone and married an Egyptian. "How do you like that?" he says; "I didn't even know they would allow that over there." It is an awesome performance. Only is it performance? Is he the world's most brilliant actor, or just a simpleton, or just completely numb? Or has he no choice other than to go on being himself? *But doesn't he get what has happened? Doesn't the man understand that some things are more unusual even than a Jew marrying an Egyptian?*

One hour, and then he leaves for home—without kissing me. Something new for my father, leaving without that kiss. And that is when I realize he is no simpleton. It *is* a performance—and my father is a great and brave and noble man.

And my excitable mother? Mercifully for her she is dead; if she weren't, this would have killed her. Or am I wrong about her too? She put up with alcoholic bakers and homicidal salad men and bus boys who still wet the bed—so who knows, maybe she could have put up with me too. *Beasts,* she called them, *barnyard animals,* but always she went back to the kettles, back to the cleanser and the mops and the linens, despite the *angst* she endured from Memorial Day weekend to Yom Kippur because of the radical imperfection of our help. Isn't it from my mother that I learned determination to begin with? Isn't it from her example that I learned how one goes on from summer to winter to summer again, in spite of everything? So, still more banality: I am able to bear being a mammary gland because of my upbringing in a typically crisis-ridden Catskill hotel.

Claire, whose equanimity has from the first been such a tonic to me, a soothing antidote to the impulsiveness of my former wife, and I suppose even to my mother's palpitations and all the hotel-kitchen crises—Claire, oddly, was not nearly so good as my father at quelling her anguish right off. What was astonishing wasn't her tears, however, but the weight of her head on my midsection when she broke down and began to sob. *Her face on this flesh? How can she touch me?* I had been expecting never to be handled again by anyone other than the medical staff. I thought, "If Claire had become a penis . . ." But that was just too ridiculous to contemplate—inasmuch, that is, as it hadn't happened. Besides, what had happened to me had happened to me and no one else because it could not happen to anyone else, and even if I did not know why that was so, *it was so,* and there must be reasons to make it so, whether I was ever to know them or not. Perhaps, as Dr. Klinger observed, putting myself in Claire's shoes was somewhat beyond the call of duty. Perhaps; but if Claire *had* become a five-foot-nine-inch male member, I doubt that I would be capable of such devotion.

It was only a few days after her first visit that Claire consented to massage my nipple. Had she wept from a safe distance, I could never have been so quick to make the suggestion; I might never have made it at all. But the very moment I felt the weight of her head touch down upon me, *all* the possibilities opened up in my mind, and it was only a matter of time (and not very much of that) before I dared to ask for the ultimate act of sexual grotesquerie, in the circumstances.

I must make clear, before going further, that Claire is no vixen; though throughout our affair she had been wonderfully aroused by ordinary sexual practices, she had no taste, for instance, for intercourse *per anum,* and was even squeamish about receiving my sperm in her mouth. If she performed fellatio at all, it was only as a brief antecedent to intercourse, and never with the intention of bringing me off. I did not complain bitterly about this, but from time to time, as men who have not yet been turned into breasts are wont to do, I registered my discontent—I was not, you see, getting all I wanted out of life.

Yet it was Claire who suggested that she would play with my nipple if that was what I most desired.

This was during her fourth visit in four days. I had described to her for the first time how the nurse ministered to me in the mornings. I planned—for the time being anyway—to say this and no more.

But Claire immediately asked, "Would you like me to do what she does?"

"Would you—do that?"

"Of course, if you want me to."

Of course. Cool, imperturbable girl!

"I do!" I cried. "Please, I do!"

"You tell me what you like then," she said. "You tell me what feels best."

"Claire, is anyone else in the room?"

"No, no—just you and me."

"Is this being televised, Claire?"

"Oh, sweetheart, no, of course it isn't."

"Oh, then squeeze me, squeeze me hard!"

Once again, days later, after I made incoherent conversation about my nurse for nearly an hour, Claire said, "David dearest, what is it? Do you want my mouth?"

"Yes! Yes!"

How could she? How can she? Why does she? Would *I?* I say to Dr. Klinger, "It's too much to ask. It's too awful. I have to stop this. I want her to do it all the time, every minute she's here. I don't want to talk any more. I don't want her to read to me—I don't even listen. I just want her to squeeze me and suck me and lick me. I can't get enough of it. I can't stand it when she stops. I shout, I scream, "Go on! More! Go on!" But I'll drive her away, I will, I know, if I don't stop. And then I'll have no one. Then I'll have the nurse in the morning—and that's all I'll have. My father will come and tell me who died and who got married. And you will come and tell me about my strong character and my will to live. *But I won't have a woman!* I won't have Claire or sex or love ever again! Oh, Doctor, I want her to take her clothes off—but how can I ask? I don't want to drive her away, it's bizarre enough now—but I want her clothes off, all of them off, at her feet, on the floor. I want her to get up on me and *roll* on me. Oh, Doctor, I want to fuck her! With my nipple! But if I even say it, it will drive her away! She'll run and never return!"

Claire visits every evening after dinner. During the day she teaches fourth grade at the Bank Street School here in New York. She is a Phi Beta Kappa graduate of Cornell; her mother is principal of a school in Schenectady, divorced now from her father, an engineer with Western Electric. Her older sister is married to an economist in the Commerce Department, and lives with him and four little children in Alexandria, Virginia. They own a house on the South Beach of Martha's Vineyard, where Claire and I visited them on our way to a week's vacation in Nantucket last summer. We argued politics—the Vietnam war. That done, we played fly-catcher-up with the kids down on the beach and then went off to eat boiled lobsters in Edgartown; afterward we sat in the movies, big, hearty, hairy carnivores, reduced in the cozy dark to nothing more than wind-burned faces and buttered fingers. Delicious. We had a fine time, really, "square" as were our hosts—I know they were square because they kept telling me so. Yet we had such a good time. She is something to look at on the beach, a green-eyed blonde, tall and lean and full-breasted. Even with desire on the wane, I still liked nothing better than to lie in bed and watch her dress in the morning and undress at night. Down in the hollow of the dunes, I unclip the top of her bikini and watch it drop away. "Imagine," she says, "where they'll be at fifty, if they droop like this at twenty-five." "Can't," I say, "won't," and drawing her to her knees, I lean back on the hot sand, dig down with my heels, shut my eyes, and wait with open lips for her breast to fill my mouth. Oh, what a sensation, there with the sea booming below! As though it were the globe itself—suckable soft globe!—and I Poseidon or Zeus! Oh, nothing beats the pleasures of the anthropomorphic god. "Let's spend all next summer by the ocean," say I, as people do on the first happy day of vacation. Claire whispers, "First let's go home and make love." It's been some time—she's right. "Oh, let's just lie here," I say—"Where is that strange thing? Oh, again, again." "I don't want to cut off your air. You were turning green." "With envy," I say.

Yes, I admit openly, that is what I said. And if this were a fairy tale instead of my life, we would have the moral now: "Beware preposterous desires—you may get lucky." But as this is decidedly *not* some fairy tale—not to me, dear reader—why should a wish like that have been the one to come true? I assure you that I have wanted things far less whimsically in my life than I wanted on that beach to be breasted. Why should playful, loverly words —spoken on the first day of our idyllic vacation!—become flesh, while whatever I have wanted in deadly earnest I have been able to achieve, if at all, only by putting one foot in front of the other over the course of thirty-eight years? No, I refuse to surrender my bewilderment to the wish-fulfillment theory. Neat and fashionable and delightfully punitive though it may be, I refuse to believe that I am this thing because this is a thing that I wanted to be. No! Reality is just a little grander than that. Reality has *some* style.

There. For those who prefer a fairy tale to life, a moral: "Reality," concludes the embittered professor who for reasons unbeknown to himself became a female breast, "has style." Go, you sleek, self-satisfied Houyhnhnms to whom nothing disgusting has yet happened, go and moralize on that!

It was not to Claire that I made my "grotesque" proposal then, but to my female nurse. I said, "Do you know what I think about when you wash me like this? Can I tell you what I am thinking about right now?"

"What is that, Professor Kepesh?"

"I would like to fuck you with my nipple."

"Can't hear you, Professor."

"I get so excited I want to fuck you! I want you to sit on my nipple—with your cunt!"

"I'll be finished with you now in just a moment . . ."

"Did you hear me, whore? Did you hear what I want?"

"Just drying you down now . . ."

By the time Dr. Klinger arrived at four I was one hundred and fifty-five pounds of remorse. I even began to sob a little when I told him what I had done—against all my misgivings and despite his warning. Now, I said, it was recorded on tape; for all I knew, it would be on page one of tomorrow's tabloids. A light moment for the straphangers on their way to work. For there certainly was a humorous side to it all; what is a catastrophe without its humorous side? Miss Clark—as I had known all along—is a short, stocky spinster, fifty-six years old.

Unlike Dr. Gordon, Claire, and my father, who continually assure me that I am not being watched other than by those who announce their presence, Dr. Klinger has never even bothered to dispute the issue with me. "And? If it is on page one? What of it?"

"It's nobody's business!" Still weeping.

"But you certainly would like to do it, would you not?"

"Yes! Yes! But she ignored me! She pretended I'd asked her to hurry up and be done! I don't want her any more! I want a new nurse!"

"Have anyone in mind?"

"Someone young—someone beautiful! Why not!"

"Someone who will hear you and say yes."

"Yes! Why not! It's insane otherwise! I should have what I want! This is no ordinary life and I am not going to pretend that it is! *You* want me to be ordinary, you *expect* me to be ordinary— in this condition! I'm supposed to go on being a sensible, rational man—in this condition! But that is crazy of you, Doctor! I want her to sit on me with her cunt! And why not! I want Claire to do it! What makes that 'grotesque'? To be denied my pleasure in the midst of this—*that* is the grotesque! I want to be fucked! Why shouldn't I be fucked? Tell me why that shouldn't be! Instead you torture me! Instead you prevent me from having what I want! Instead I lie here being sensible! And there's the madness, Doctor—being sensible!"

I do not know how much of what I said Dr. Klinger even understood; it is difficult enough to follow me when I am speaking deliberately, with concentration, and now I was sobbing and howling with no regard for the TV cameras or the spectators up in the stands . . . Or is that *why* I was carrying on so? Was I really so racked by the proposal I'd made that morning to Miss Clark? Or was the display largely for the benefit of my great audience, to convince them that, appearances aside, I am still very much a man—for who but a man has conscience, reason, desire, and remorse?

This crisis lasted for months. I became increasingly lewd with the stout, implacable Miss Clark, until finally one morning I offered her money. "Bend over—take it from behind! I'll give you anything you want!" How I would get the money into her hands, how I would go about borrowing if she demanded more than I had saved in my account I tried to figure out during my long, empty days. Who would help me? I couldn't very well ask my father or Claire, and they were the only two people by whom I was willing to be seen. Ridiculous perhaps, given how sure I was that my image was being mercilessly recorded by television cameras and my daily progress publicized in the *Daily News,* but then I am not arguing that since my transformation I have been a model of Mature Adult Responsible Behavior. I am only trying to describe, as best I can, the stages I have had to pass through on the way to the present phase of melancholy equilibrium . . . Of course to assist me—to get hold of the money, to make the financial arrangements, either with Miss Clark or, if need be, with some woman whose profession is not circumscribed by a nurse's ethical outlook—I could easily have called upon a young bearded colleague, a clever poet from Brooklyn who is no prude and whose sexual adventurousness has made him somewhat notorious in our English Department. But then neither was I a prude, and once upon a time I had had a taste for sexual adventure no less developed than my young friend's. You must understand that it was not a man of narrow experience and suffocating inhibitions who was being tormented by his desires in that hammock. I had experimented with whores easily enough back in my twenties, and during a year as a Fulbright student in London, I had for several months carried on a thrilling, overwrought affair with two young women—students my age on leave together from university in Sweden, who shared a basement bedroom with me—until the less stable of the pair tried halfheartedly to pitch herself under a lorry. No, what alarmed me wasn't the strangeness of my desires in that hammock, but the degree to which I would be severing myself from my own past—and kind—by surrendering to them. I was afraid that the further I went the further I would go—that I would reach a point of frenzy from which I would pass over into a state of being that no longer had anything to do with who or what I once had been. It wasn't even that I would no longer be myself—I would no longer be anyone. I would have become craving flesh and nothing more.

So, with Dr. Klinger's assistance, I set about to extinguish—and if not to extinguish, at least (in Klinger's favorite word) to *tolerate*

—the desire to insert my nipple into somebody's vagina. But with all my will power—and, like my mother's, it can be considerable when I marshal my forces—I was helpless once that bath began. Finally it was decided that nipple and areola should be sprayed with a mild anesthetic before Miss Clark started preparing me to meet the day. And this in fact did sufficiently reduce sensation so as to give me the upper hand in the battle against these impractical urges—a battle I won, however, only when the doctors decided, with my consent, to change my nurse.

That did the trick. Inserting my nipple into either the mouth or the anus of Mr. Brooks, the new male nurse, is something I just can't imagine with anything like the excitement I would imagine my nipple in Claire, or even in Miss Clark, though I realize that the conjunction of male mouth and female nipple can hardly be described as a homosexual act. But such is the power of my past and its taboos, and the power over my imagination of women and their apertures, that I am able now—temporarily anesthetized and in the hands of a man—to receive my morning ablutions like any other invalid, more or less.

And there is still Claire, angelic imperturbable Claire, to "make love" to me, with her mouth if not with her vagina. And isn't that sufficient? Isn't that incredible enough? Of course I dream of MORE, dream of it all day long—but what good is MORE to me anyway, when there is no orgasmic conclusion to my excitement, but only this sustained sense of imminent ejaculation in which I writhe from the first second to the last? Actually I have come by now to settle for less rather than MORE. I think I had better if I don't want Claire to come to see herself as nothing but the female machine summoned each evening to service a preposterous organism that once was David Kepesh. Surely the less time she spends at my nipple, the greater my chances of remaining something other to her (and to myself) than that nipple. Consequently, it is only for half of her hour-long visits that we now engage in sex—the rest of the time we spend in conversation. If I can, I should like to cut the sex play by half yet again. If the excitement is always at the same pitch, neither increasing nor decreasing in intensity once it's begun, what's the difference if I experience it for fifteen rather than thirty minutes? What's the difference if it is for only *one* minute?

Mind you, I am not yet equal to such renunciation, nor am I convinced that it is desirable even from Claire's point of view. But it is something, I tell you, simply to entertain the idea after the torment I have known. Even now there are still moments, infrequent but searing, when I have all I can do not to cry out, while her lips are rhythmically palpating my nipple, "Fuck on it, Ovington! With your cunt!" But I don't, I don't. If Claire were of a mind to, she would have made the suggestion herself already. And, after all, she is still only a fourth-grade teacher at the Bank Street School, a girl brought up in Schenectady, New York, and Phi Beta Kappa at Cornell. No sense causing her to consider too carefully the grotesqueries she has already, miraculously, declared herself willing to participate in with the likes of me.

Sometime between the first and the second of the two major "crises" I have survived so far here in the hospital—if hospital it is—I was visited by Arthur Schonbrunn, Dean of Arts and Sciences at Stony Brook, and someone I have known since Palo Alto, when he was *the* young hot-shot Stanford professor and I was there getting my Ph.D. It was as the chairman of the newly formed comparative-literature department that Arthur brought me from Stanford to Stony Brook eight years ago. He is nearly fifty now, a wry and charming gentleman, and for an academic uncommonly, almost alarmingly, suave in manner and dress. It was his social expertise as much as our long-standing acquaintanceship that led me (and Dr. Klinger) to settle finally on Arthur as the best person with whom to make my social debut following the victory over the phallic cravings of my nipple. I also wanted Arthur to come so that I could talk to him—if not during this first visit, then the next—about how I might maintain my affiliation with the university. Back at Stanford I had been a "reader" for one of the enormous sophomore classes he lectured in "Masterpieces of Western Literature." I had begun to wonder if I couldn't perform some such function again. Claire could read aloud to me the student papers, I could dictate to her my comments and grades . . . Or was that a hopeless idea? It took Dr. Klinger several weeks to encourage me to believe that there would be no harm in asking.

I never got the chance. Even as I was telling him, a little

"tearfully"—I couldn't help myself—how touched I was that he should be the first of my colleagues to visit, I thought I could hear giggling. "Arthur," I asked, "are we alone—?" He said, "Yes." Then giggled, quite distinctly. Sightless, I could still picture my former mentor: in his blue blazer with the paisley lining tailored in London for him by Kilgore, French; in his soft flannel trousers, in his gleaming Gucci loafers, the diplomatic Dean with his handsome mop of salt-and-pepper hair—giggling! And I hadn't even made my suggestion about becoming a reader for the department. Giggling—not because of anything ludicrous I had proposed, but because he saw that it was true, I actually *had* turned into a breast. My graduate-school adviser, my university superior, the most courtly professor I have ever known—and yet, from the sound of it, overcome with the giggles *simply at the sight of me.*

"I'm—I—David—" But now he was laughing so, he couldn't even speak. Arthur Schonbrunn unable to speak. Talk about the incredible. Twenty, thirty seconds more of uproarious laughter, and then he was gone. The visit had lasted about three minutes.

Two days later came the apology, as elegantly done, I'd say, as anything Arthur's written since his little book on Robert Musil. And the following week, the package from Sam Goody's, with a card signed, "Debbie and Arthur S." A record album of Laurence Olivier in *Hamlet.*

Arthur had written: "Your misfortune should not have had to be compounded by my feeble, unforgivable performance. I'm at a loss to explain what came over me. It would strike us both as so much cant if I even tried."

I worked on my reply for a week. I must have dictated easily fifty letters: gracious, eloquent, forgiving, lighthearted, grave, hangdog, businesslike, arch, vicious, wild, literary—and some even sillier than the one I dispatched. "Feeble?" I wrote Arthur. "Why, if anything it is evidence of your earthy vitality that you should have laughed yourself sick. I am the feeble one, otherwise I would have joined in. If I fail to appreciate the enormous comedy of all this, it is only because I am really more of an Arthur Schonbrunn than you are, you vain, self-loving, dandified prick!" But the one I finally settled on read simply: "Dear Debbie and Arthur S.: Thanx mucho for the groovy sides. Dave 'The Breast'

K." I checked twice with Claire to be sure she had spelled thanks with that *x* before she went ahead and mailed my little message. If she mailed it. If she even took it down.

The second crisis that threatened to undo me and that I appear —for the time being—to have weathered might be called a crisis of faith. As it came fully a month after Arthur's visit, it is hard to know if it was in any way precipitated by that humiliation. I am long since over hating Arthur Schonbrunn for that day—at least I continue to work at being long since over it—and so I tend now to agree with Dr. Klinger, who thinks that what I had to struggle with next was inevitable and can't be blamed on my three minutes with the Dean. Evidently nothing that has happened can be blamed on anyone, not even on me.

What happened next was that I refused to believe I had turned into a breast. Having brought myself to relinquish (more or less) my dreams of nippled intercourse with Claire, with Miss Clark —with whoever would have me—I realized that the whole thing was impossible. A man cannot turn into a breast other than in his own imagination.

It had taken me six months to figure this out.

"Look, this isn't happening—it can't!"

"Why can't it?" asked Dr. Klinger.

"You know why! Any child knows why! Because it is a physiological and biological and anatomical impossibility!"

"How then do you explain your predicament?"

"It's a dream! Six months haven't passed—that's an illusion, too. I'm dreaming! It's just a matter of waking up!"

"But you are awake, Mr. Kepesh. You know very well that you're awake."

"Stop saying that! Don't torture me like that! Let me get up! Enough! I want to wake up!"

For days and days—or what pass for days in a nightmare—I struggled to wake myself up. Claire came every evening to suck my nipple and talk, my father came on Sunday to tell me the latest news, Mr. Brooks was there every morning, rousing me from sleep with a gentle pat just at the edge of my areola. At least I imagined that he had just awakened me by touching the edge of my areola. Then I realized that I had not been awakened from a real sleep, but from the sleep that I slept within the nightmare itself. I wasn't an awakening breast—I was myself, still dreaming.

Oh, how I cursed my captors—though, to be sure, if it was a dream I was only cursing captors of my own invention. *Stop torturing me, all of you! Somebody help me get up!* I cursed the spectators in the gallery I had constructed, I cursed the technicians on the television circuit I had imagined—*Voyeurs!* I cried, *heartless, ogling, sadistic voyeurs!*—until at last, fearing that my battered system might collapse beneath the emotional strain (yes, those were the words of concern that I put into their lying mouths), they decided to place me under heavy sedation. How I howled then!—*Cold cunt of a Claire! Idiot, ignoramus of a father! Klinger you quack! Klinger you fraud!*—even as the drug enfeebled me, a sedating drug somehow administered to the dreamer by himself.

When I came around, I at last realized that I had gone mad. I was not dreaming. I was crazy. There was to be no magical awakening, no getting up out of bed, brushing my teeth, and going off to teach as though nothing more than a nightmare had interrupted my ordinary and predictable life; if there was ever to be anything at all for me, it was the long road back—becoming sane. And of course the first step toward recovering sanity was this realization that my sense of myself as a breast was the delusion of a lunatic, the realization that rather than being slung in a hammock following an endocrinopathic catastrophe unlike any the endocrinologists had ever known before, I was, more than likely, simply sitting, deluded, in a room in a mental hospital. And that is something we know can and does happen to all too many people, all the time. That I could not see, that I could not taste, that I could not smell, that I could only faintly hear, that I could not make contact with my own anatomy, that I experienced myself as speaking to others like one buried within, and very nearly strangulated by, his own adipose tissue—were these symptoms so unusual in the trance-world of psychosis?

Why I had lost my sanity I couldn't understand, however. What could have triggered such a thoroughgoing schizophrenic collapse in someone seemingly so *well?* But then whatever might have caused such a breakdown was undoubtedly so frightening that I would have *had* to obliterate all memory of it . . . Only why then was Dr. Klinger—and that it was Dr. Klinger with whom I was talking I was sure; I had to be sure of something if I was to make a start, so I clung to his mildly accented English, to his straightforward manner and his homely humor as proof that at least *this* in my experience was real—why then was Dr. Klinger telling me to *accept* my fate, when clearly the way back to sanity was to *defy* this absolutely crazy conception of myself? The answer was obvious—should have been all along! *That wasn't what Klinger was saying.* My illness was such that I was taking his words, simple and clear as they were when he spoke them, and giving them precisely the opposite meaning.

When he came that afternoon, I had to call forth all my famous strength of character in order to explain, as simply and clearly as *I* could, my incredible discovery. I sobbed when I was finished, but otherwise was as inspired in speech as I have ever been. When teaching, one sometimes hears oneself speaking in perfect cadences, developing ideas into rounded sentences, and combining them into paragraphs full to brimming, and it is hard then to believe that the fellow suddenly addressing his hushed students with a golden tongue and great decisiveness could have made such a muddle of his notes only the hour before. Well, harder still to believe that the measured tones in which I had just broken the good news to Dr. Klinger came from the vituperous madman who had to be sedated only the day before by his keepers. If I was still a lunatic—and still a breast, I was still a lunatic—I was now, at least, one of the more lucid and eloquent on my floor.

I said, "Curiously, it's Arthur Schonbrunn's visit that convinces me I'm on the right track. How could I ever have believed that Arthur would come here and *laugh?* How could I take that blatantly paranoid delusion for the truth? I've been cursing him for a month now—and Debbie too, for those idiotic records—and none of it makes any sense at all. Because if there is one person in the world who simply *couldn't* lose control like that, it's Arthur."

"He is beyond the perils of human nature, this Dean?"

"You know something? The answer to that is yes. He is beyond the perils of human nature."

"Such a shrewd operator."

"It isn't that he's so shrewd—that's going at it the wrong way round. It's that I've been so mad. To think that I actually made all that up!"

"And his note, which you answered so graciously? The note that made you so livid?"

"More paranoia."

"And the recording of *Hamlet?*"

"Ah, *that's* Mr. Reality. That is real—and right up Debbie's alley. Oh yes, I can feel the difference now, even as I talk I can sense the difference between the insane stuff and what's truly happened. Oh, I do feel the difference, *you must believe me.* I've gone mad, but now I know it!"

"And what do you think has caused you, as you put it, to 'go mad'?" Dr. Klinger asked.

"I don't remember."

"Any idea at all? What could have drawn someone like you into such a fully developed and impenetrable delusion?"

"I'm telling you the truth, Doctor. I don't have the least idea. Not yet, anyway."

"Nothing comes to mind? Nothing at all?"

"Well, what comes to mind, if anything—what came to mind this morning—"

"Is what?"

"I'm grasping at straws—and I know how whimsical it seems in the circumstances. But I thought, 'I got it from fiction.' The books I've been teaching—they put the idea in my head. I'm thinking of my European Literature course. Teaching Gogol and Kafka every year—teaching 'The Nose' and 'Metamorphosis.' "

"Of course, many other literature professors teach 'The Nose' and 'Metamorphosis.' "

"But maybe," said I, the humor intentional now, "not with so much conviction."

He laughed.

"I *am* mad, though—aren't I?" I asked.

"No."

I was set back only momentarily. I realized that I had inverted his meaning as easily, and as unconsciously, as we turn right side up the images that flash upon the retina upside down.

"I want to tell you," I calmly explained, "that though you just answered yes when I asked whether I was mad, I heard you say no."

"I did say no. You are not mad. You are not suffering from a delusion—or certainly haven't been, up till now. You are a breast, of sorts. You have been heroic in your efforts to accommodate yourself to a mysterious misfortune. Of course one understands the temptation: this is all just a dream, a hallucination, a delusion—even a drug-induced state of mind. But, in fact, it is none of these things. It *is* something that has happened to you. And the best way to go mad—do you hear me, Mr. Kepesh?—*the way into madness* is to start to pretend otherwise. The comfort of that will be short-lived, I can assure you. I want you right now to disabuse yourself of the notion that you are insane. You are not insane, and to pretend to be insane will only bring you to grief. Insanity is no solution—neither imagined insanity nor the real thing."

"Again I heard everything reversed. I turned the sense of your words completely around."

"No, you did not."

"Does it make any sense to you to think of my delusion as somehow fueled by years of teaching those stories? I mean, regardless of the trauma that triggered the breakdown itself."

"But there was no trauma, not of a psychological nature; and as I have told you, and tell you now again, and will continue to tell you: *this is no delusion."*

How to press on? How to break through this reversing?

With an artfulness that pleased me—and bespoke health! health!—I said, "But if it were, Dr. Klinger—since I again understood you to say just the opposite of what you said—*if* it were, would you *then* see any connection between the kind of hallucination I've embedded myself in and the power over my imagination of Kafka or Gogol? Or of Swift? I'm thinking of *Gulliver's Travels,* another book I've taught for years. Perhaps if we go on speaking hypothetically—"

"Mr. Kepesh, enough. You are fooling no one but yourself—if even yourself. There has been shock, panic, fury, despair, disorientation, profound feelings of helplessness and isolation, the darkest depression and fear, but through it all, quite miraculously, quite marvelously, no delusions. Not even when your old friend the Dean showed up and had his laughing fit. Of course that shocked you. Of course that crushed you. Why shouldn't it have? But you did not imagine Arthur Schonbrunn's unfortunate behavior. You have not made up what has happened to you, and you did not make up what happened here to him. You didn't have to. You are pretending to be a naïf, you know, when you tell me that such a reaction is simply out of the question for a man in Arthur Schonbrunn's position. You are a better student of human nature than that. You've read too much Dostoevsky for that."

"Will it help any if I repeat to you what I thought I heard you say?"

"No need. What you thought you heard, you heard. That is known as sanity. Come off the lunatic kick, Mr. Kepesh—and the sooner the better. Gogol, Kafka, and so on—it is going to get you into serious trouble if you keep it up. The next thing you know you will have produced in yourself genuine and irreversible delusions exactly like those you now claim to want to be rid of. Do you follow me? I think you do. You are a highly intelligent man and you have a remarkably strong will, and I want you to stop it right now."

How exhausting to hear it all backwards! How ingenious insanity is! But at least now I *knew.* "Dr. Klinger! Dr. Klinger! Listen to me—I won't let it drive me crazy any more! I will fight myself free! I will stop hearing the opposite! I will start hearing what you are all saying! Do you hear *me,* Doctor? Do you understand *my* words? I will not participate any longer in this delusion! I refuse to be a part of it! You *will* get through to me! I *will* understand what you mean! Just don't give up! Please," I pleaded, "don't give me up for lost! I will break through and be myself again! I am determined! With all my strength—with all my will to live!"

Now I spent my days trying to penetrate the words I heard so as to get through to what actually was being said to me by the doctors, and by Claire, and by Mr. Brooks. The effort this required was so total, and so depleting, that by nightfall I felt it would take no more than a puff from a child's lips to extinguish for good the wavering little flame of memory and intelligence and hope still claiming to be me.

When my father came for his Sunday visit, I told him everything, even though I was sure that Claire and Klinger would have let him know by phone the day it happened. I babbled like a boy who'd won a trophy. It was true, I told him—I no longer believed I was a breast. If I had not yet been able to throw off the physical sense of unreality, I was daily divesting myself of the preposterous psychic delusion; every day, every hour I sensed myself slowly turning back into myself, and could even begin to see through to the time when I would again be teaching Gogol and Kafka rather than experiencing vicariously the unnatural transformations they had imagined in their famous fictions. Since my father knows nothing of books, I told him how Gregor Samsa awakens in the Kafka story to discover that he has become an enormous beetle; I summarized for him "The Nose," recounting how Gogol's hero awakens one morning missing his nose, how he sets out to look for it in St. Petersburg, places an ad in the newspaper requesting its return, sees "it" walking on the street, one ridiculous encounter after another, until in the end the nose just turns up again on his face for no better reason than it disappeared. (I could imagine my father thinking, "He teaches this stuff, in a college?") I explained that I still couldn't remember the blow that had done me in; I actually became deaf, *could not hear,* when the doctor tried to get me to face it. But whatever the trauma itself may have been—however terrifying, horrifying, repellent—what I knew was that my escape route was through the fantasy of physical transformation that lay immediately at hand, the catastrophe stories by Kafka and Gogol that I had been teaching my students only the week before. Now, with Dr. Klinger's assistance, I was trying to figure out just why, of all things, I had chosen a breast. Why a big brainless bag of dumb, desirable tissue, acted upon instead of acting, unguarded, immobile, hanging, *there,* as a breast simply hangs and is *there?* Why this primitive identification with *the* object of infantile veneration? What unfulfilled appetites, what cradle confusions, what fragments out of my remotest past could have collided to spark a delusion of such classical simplicity? On and on I babbled to my father, and then, once again, joyously, I wept. No tears, but I wept. Where *were* my tears? How soon before I would feel tears again? When would I feel my teeth, my tongue, my toes?

For a long while my father said nothing. I thought that perhaps he was crying too. Then he went into the weekly news report: so-and-so's daughter is pregnant, so-and-so's son has bought himself a hundred-thousand-dollar home, my uncle is catering Richard Tucker's younger brother's son's wedding.

He hadn't even heard me. Of course. I may have broken through the *idea* that I was a breast, but I still seemed required virtually to give a recitation, as from a stage, if I wanted to make myself understood. What I believed was a normal conversational tone tended, apparently, to come out sounding like somebody muttering across the room. But this wasn't because my voice box was buried in a hundred-and-fifty-five-pound mammary gland. My body was still a body! I had only to stop whispering! I had only to speak out! Could that be part of the madness? That when I believed I was speaking aloud, I was speaking only to myself? Speak up then!

And so I did. At the top of my lungs (my two good lungs!) repeated to my father the story of my breakthrough.

And then it was time to take the next step. One foot in front of the other. "Dad," I said, "where are we? You tell me."

"In your room," he answered.

"And tell me, have I turned into a breast?"

"Well, that's what they say."

"But that's not true. I'm a mental patient. Now tell me again —what am I?"

"Oh, Davey."

"What am I?"

"You're a woman's breast."

"That's not true! What I heard you say is not true! I'm a mental patient! In a hospital! And you are visiting me! Dad, if that's the truth, I just want you to say yes. Listen to me now. You must help me. I am a mental patient. I am in a mental hospital. I have had a severe mental breakdown. Yes or no. *Tell me the truth."*

And my father answered, "Yes, son, yes. You're a mental patient."

"I heard him!" I cried to Klinger when he came later in the day. "I heard my father! I heard the truth! I heard him say I'm a mental patient!"

"He should never have told you that."

"I heard it! I'm not imagining it either! It didn't get reversed!"

"Of course you heard it. Your father loves you. He's a simple man and he loves you very much. He thought it would help if he said it. He knows now that it can't. And so do you."

But I couldn't have been happier. My father had gotten through to me. I could be gotten through to! It would follow with the others soon enough. "I heard it!" I said. "I'm not a breast! I'm mad!"

How I strain in the coming days to be my sane self again! How I dredge at the muck of my beginnings, searching for what will explain—and thus annihilate—this preposterous delusion! I have returned, I tell the doctor, to the dawn of my life, to my first thousand hours after the eons of hours of nothing—back to when all is oneself and oneself is all, back to when the concave is the convex and the convex the concave . . . oh, how I talk! How I work to outsmart my madness! If I could only remember my hungering gums at the spigot of love, my nose in the nourishing globe—! "Oh, if she were alive, if she could tell me—" "Yes? Tell you what?" asks Klinger. "Oh," I moan, "how do *I* know?" But where else to begin but there? Only there there is nothing. It is all *too* far back, back where I am. To dive to that sea bottom where I began—to find in the slime this secret! But when I rise to the surface, there is not even silt beneath my fingernails. I come up with nothing.

Perhaps, I say, perhaps, I tell him, it is all a post-analytic collapse, a year in the making—the most desperate means I could devise to cling to Klinger. "Have you ever thought what fantasies of dependence bloom in your patients merely on the basis of your name? Have you realized, Doctor, that all *our* names begin with K, yours and mine and Kafka's? And then there is Claire—and Miss Clark!" "The alphabet," he reminds me, a language teacher, "only *has* twenty-six letters. And there are four billion of us in need of initials for purposes of identification." "But!" "But what?" "But *something!* But *anything!* Please, a clue! If I can't—then *you.* Please, some clue, some lead—I have to get out!"

I go over with him again the salient moments in my psychological development, once again I turn the pages in the anthology of stories that we two had assembled as text for the course conducted by us, three times a week for five years, in "The History of David Alan Kepesh." But in fact those stories have been recounted and glossed so exhaustively so many times that they are as stale to me as the favorite literary chestnut of the most retrograde schoolteacher in America. My life's drama, as exciting in the early years of therapy as *The Brothers Karamazov,* has all the appeal now of some tenth-grade reader beginning with "The Necklace" and running through to "The Luck of Roaring Camp." Which accounts for the successful termination of analysis the year before.

And *there,* I thought, is my trauma! Success itself! There is what I couldn't take—a happy life! "What is that?" asks Dr. Klinger, quizzically. "What was it you couldn't take?" "Rewards—instead of punishment! Wholeness! Comfort! Pleasure! A gratifying way of life, a life *without—*" "Wait just a minute, please. Why couldn't you take such things? Those are wonderful things. Come off it, Mr. Kepesh. As I remember, you could take happiness with the best of them." But I refuse to listen, since what I hear him saying isn't what he's saying anyway. That is just my illness, turning things around to keep me insane. On I go instead, talking next about what patients will talk about sooner or later—that imaginary friend they call My Guilt. I talk about Helen, my former wife, whose life, I have been told, is no better now than when we suffered together through five years of that marriage. I remember I couldn't help but gloat a little when I heard about Helen's continuing unhappiness from an old San Francisco friend, who had come to dinner with me and my lovely, imperturbable Claire. Good for the bitch, I thought . . . "And now," Klinger asks with amusement, "you believe you are punishing yourself in this way for such ordinary, everyday malice?" "I'm saying that my happy new life was too much for me! It's why I lost my desire for Claire—it was all too good to last! So much satisfaction seemed—seemed unjust! Compared to Helen's fate, seemed somehow iniquitous! My Guilt!" I plead. "My dear sir," he replies, "that is analysis right out of the dime store—and you know it as well as I do." "Then if not that, *what?* Help me! Tell me! *What did it?*"

"Nothing 'did it.' "

"Then why in God's name am I mad?"

"But you're not. And you know that too."

The next Sunday, when he comes to visit, I again ask my father if I am a mental patient—just to be sure—and this time he answers, "No."

"But last week you said yes!"

"I was wrong."

"But it's the truth!"

"It's not."

"I'm reversing again! I've lost it now with you! I'm back where I was! I'm reversing with everyone!"

"You're not at all," said Dr. Klinger.

"What are you doing here? This is Sunday! My father is here, not you! You're not even here!"

"I'm here. With your father. Right beside you, the two of us."

"This is getting all crazy again! I don't want to be crazy any more! Help me! Do you hear me? Am I being heard? Help me, please! I need your help! I cannot do this alone! Help me! Lift me! Tell me only the truth! If I am a breast, where is my milk! When Claire is sucking me, where is the milk! Tell me *that!"*

"Oh, David." It was my father, his unshaven cheek on my areola! "My son, my poor sonny."

"Oh, Daddy, what's happened? Hold me, Poppy, please. What's really happened? Tell me, please, *why did I go mad?"*

"You didn't, darling," he sobbed.

"Then where is my milk? Answer me! If I am a breast I would make milk! Hold milk! Swell with milk! And that is too crazy for anybody to believe! Even me! THAT SIMPLY CANNOT BE!"

But evidently it can be. Just as they are able to increase the milk yield of cows with injections of the lactogenic agent GH, the growth hormone, so it has been hypothesized that I very likely could become a milk-producing mammary gland with appropriate hormonal stimulation. If so, there must be those out in the scientific world who would jump at the chance to find out. And when I have had my fill of all this, perhaps I will give it to them. And if I am not killed in the process? If they succeed and milk begins to flow? Well, then I will know that I am indeed a wholly authentic breast—or else that I am as mad as any man has ever been.

In the meantime fifteen months have passed—by their calendar—and I live for the moment in relative equanimity. That is, things have been worse and will be again, but for now, for now Claire still comes to visit every day, does not miss a single day, and still, for the first half hour of each hour, uncomplainingly and without repugnance attends to my pleasure. Converts a disgusting perversion into a kindly, thoughtful act of love. And then we talk. She is helping me with my Shakespeare studies. I have been listening of late to recordings of the tragedies. I began with the Schonbrunns' gift, Olivier in *Hamlet.* The album lay for months here in the room before I asked Mr. Brooks one morning to break the cellophane wrapper and put a record on the phonograph. (Mr. Brooks turns out to be a Negro; and so, in my mind's eye—a breast's mind's eye, to be sure—I imagine him looking like the handsome black Senator from Massachusetts. Why not, if it makes This cozier for me?) Like so many people, I have been meaning ever since college to sit down someday and reread Shakespeare. I may even once have said as much to Debbie Schonbrunn, and she bought the record album because she realized that I now had the time. Surely no satire was ever intended, however much I may have believed otherwise when the *Hamlet* arrived the week after Arthur's three-minute visit. I must remember that aside from the more obvious difficulties occasioned by my transformation, I am no longer the easiest person in the world to buy a present for.

For several hours every morning and again sometimes in the afternoons when there is nothing better to do, I listen to my Shakespeare records: Olivier playing Hamlet and Othello, Paul Scofield as Lear, *Macbeth* as performed by the Old Vic company. Unable to follow with a text while the play is being spoken, I invariably miss the meaning of an unfamiliar word, or lose my way in the convoluted syntax, and then my mind begins to wander, and when I tune in again, little makes sense for lines on end. Despite the effort—oh, the effort, minute-by-minute this effort!—to keep my attention fixed on the plight of Shakespeare's suffering heroes, I do continue to consider my own suffering more than can be good for me.

The Shakespeare edition I used in college—Neilson and Hill,

The Complete Plays and Poems of William Shakespeare, bound in blue linen, worn at the spine by my earnest undergraduate grip, and heavily underlined by me then for wisdom—is on the table beside the hammock. It is one of several books I have asked Claire to bring from my apartment. I remember exactly what it looks like, which in part is why I wanted it here. In the evenings, during the second half hour of her visit, Claire looks up for me in the footnotes words whose usage I long ago learned and forgot; or she will slowly read aloud some passage that I missed that morning when my mind departed Elsinore Castle for Lenox Hill Hospital. It seems to me important to get these passages clear in my head—my brain—before I go off to sleep. Otherwise it might begin to seem that I listen to *Hamlet* for the same reason that my father answers the phone at my Uncle Larry's catering establishment—to kill time.

Olivier is a great man, you know. I have fallen in love with him a little, like a schoolgirl with a movie star. I've never before given myself over to a genius so completely, not even while reading. As a student, as a professor, I experienced literature as something unavoidably tainted by my self-consciousness and all the responsibilities of serious discourse; either I was learning or I was teaching. But responsibilities are behind me now; at last I can just listen.

In the beginning I used to try to amuse myself when I was alone in the evenings by imitating Olivier. I worked with my records during the day to memorize the famous soliloquies, and then I performed for myself at night, trying to approximate his distinctive delivery. After some weeks it seemed to me that I had really rather mastered his Othello, and one night, after Claire had left, I did the death-scene speech with such plaintive passion that I thought I could have moved an audience to tears. Until I realized that I had an audience. It was midnight, or thereabouts, but nobody has given me a good reason yet why the TV camera should shut down at any hour of the day or night—and so I left off with my performance. Enough pathos is enough, if not, generally, too much. "Come now, David," said I to myself, "it is all too poignant and heartbreaking, a breast reciting 'And say besides, that in Aleppo once . . .' You will send the night shift home in tears." Yes, bitterness, dear reader, and of a shallow sort, but then permit my poor professorial dignity a little rest, won't you? This is not tragedy any more than it is farce. It is only life, and I am only human.

Did fiction do this to me? "How could it have?" asks Dr. Klinger. "No, hormones are hormones and art is art. You are not suffering from an overdose of the great imaginations." "Aren't I? I wonder. This might well be my way of being a Kafka, being a Gogol, being a Swift. They could envision the incredible, they had the words and those relentless fictionizing brains. But I had neither, I had nothing—literary longings and that was it. I loved the extreme in literature, idolized those who wrote it, was virtually hypnotized by the imagery and the power—" "And? Yes? The world is full of art lovers—so?" "So I took the leap. Made the word flesh. Don't you see, I have out-Kafkaed Kafka." Klinger laughed, as though I meant to be only amusing. "After all," I said, "who is the greater artist, he who imagines the marvelous transformation, or he who marvelously transforms himself? Why David Kepesh? Why me, of all people, endowed with such powers? Simple. Why Kafka? Why Gogol? Why Swift? Why anyone? Great art happens to people like anything else. And this is my great work of art! Ah," but I quickly added, "I must maintain my sane and reasonable perspective. I don't wish to upset you again. No delusions—delusions of grandeur least of all."

But if not grandeur, what about abasement? What about depravity and vice? I could be rich, you know, I could be rich, notorious, and delirious with pleasure every waking hour of the day. I think about it more and more. I could call my friend to visit me, the adventurous younger colleague I spoke of earlier. If I haven't dared to invite him yet, it isn't because I'm frightened that he'll laugh and run like Arthur Schonbrunn, but rather that he'll take one look at what I am—and what I could be—and be all too eager to help; that when I tell him I have had just about enough of being a heroically civilized fellow about it all, enough of listening to Olivier and talking to my analyst and enjoying thirty minutes every day of some virtuous schoolteacher's idea of hot sex, he won't argue, the way others would. "I want to get out of here," I'll say to him, "and I need an accomplice. We can carry with us all the pumps and pipes that sustain me. And to look after my health, such as it is, we can hire the doctors and nurses to come along—money will be no problem. But I am sick and tired of worrying about losing Claire. Let her go and find a new lover whose sperm she will not drink, and lead with him a normal and productive life. I am tired of guarding against the loss of her angelic goodness. And between the two of us, I am a little tired of my old man too—he bores me. And, really, how much Shakespeare do you think I can take? I wonder if you realize how many of the great plays of Western literature are now available on excellent long-playing records. When I finish with Shakespeare, I can go right on to first-rate performances of Sophocles, Sheridan, Aristophanes, Shaw, Racine—but to what end? To what end! That *is* killing time. For a breast it is the bloody *murder* of time. Pal, I am going to make a pot of money. I don't think it should be difficult, either. If the Beatles can fill Shea Stadium, why can't I? We will have to think this through, you and I, but then what was all that education for, if not to learn to think things through? To read more books? To write more critical essays? Further contemplation of the higher things? How about some contemplation of the lower? I will make hundreds of thousands of dollars—and then I will have girls, twelve- and thirteen-year-old girls, three, four, and five at a time, naked and giggling, and all on my nipple at once. I want them for days on end, greedy wicked little girls, licking me and sucking me to my heart's content. And we can find them, you know that. If the Rolling Stones can find them, if Charles Manson can find them, then with all our education we can probably find a few ourselves. And women. There will also be women quite eager to open their thighs to a cock as new and thrilling as my nipple. I think we will be happily surprised by the number of respectable women who will come knocking at the dressing-room door in their respectable chinchillas just to get a peek at the tint of my soft hermaphroditic flesh. Well, we will have to be discriminating, won't we, we will have to select from among them according to beauty, good breeding, and the lewdness of their desire. And I will be deliriously happy. *And I will be deliriously happy.* Remember Gulliver among the Brobdingnags? How the maid-servants had him strolling out on their nipples for the fun of it? He didn't think it was fun, poor lost little man. But then he was a humane English physician, a child of the Age of Reason, a faithful follower of the Sense of Proportion trapped on a continent of outlandish giants; but this, my friend and accomplice, is the Land of Opportunity, this is the Age of Self-Fulfillment, and I am the Breast, and will live by my own lights!"

"Live by them or die by them?"

"It remains to be seen, Dr. Klinger."

Permit me now to conclude my lecture by quoting the poet Rilke. As a passionately well-meaning literature teacher I was always fond of ending the hour with something moving for the students to carry from the uncontaminated classroom out into the fallen world of junk food and pop stars and dope. True, Kepesh's occupation's gone—*Othello,* Act III, Scene 3—but I haven't lost entirely a teacher's good intentions. Maybe I haven't even lost my students. On the basis of my fame, I may even have acquired vast new flocks of undergraduate sheep, as innocent of calamity as of verse. I may even be a pop star now myself and have just what it takes to bring great poetry to the people.

("Your fame?" says Dr. Klinger. "Surely the world knows by now," I say, "excepting perhaps the Russians and Chinese." "In accordance with your wishes, the case has been handled with the utmost discretion." "But my friends know. The staff here knows. That's enough of a start for something like this." "True. But by the time the news filters beyond those who know and out to the man in the street, he tends by and large not to believe it." "He thinks it's a joke." "If he can take his mind off his own troubles long enough to think anything at all." "And the media? You're suggesting they've done nothing with this either?" "Nothing at all." "I don't buy that, Dr. Klinger." "Don't. I'm not going to argue. I told you long ago—there of course were inquiries in the beginning. But nothing was done to assist anyone, and after a while these people have a living to make like everybody else, and they move right along to the next promising misfortune." "Then no one knows all that's happened." "All? No one but you knows it all, Mr. Kepesh." "Well, maybe I should be the one to tell all then." "Then you *will* be famous, won't you?" "Better the truth than tabloid fantasy. Better from me than from the chattering madmen and morons." "Of course the madmen and the morons will chatter anyway, you know. You realize that you will never be taken on your own terms, regardless of what you say." "I'll still be a joke." "A joke. A freak. If you insist on being the one to tell them, a charlatan too." "You're advising me to leave well enough alone. You're advising me to keep this all to myself." "I'm advising you nothing, only reminding you of our friend with the beard who sits on the throne." "Mr. Reality." "And his principle," says Klinger.)

And now to conclude the hour with the poem by Rainer Maria Rilke entitled "Archaic Torso of Apollo" written in Paris in 1908. Perhaps my story, told here in its entirety for the first time, and with all the truthfulness that's in me, will at the very least illuminate these great lines for those of you new to the poem—particularly the poet's concluding admonition, which may not be so elevated a sentiment as appears at first glance. Morons and madmen, tough guys and skeptics, friends, students, relatives, colleagues, and all you distracted strangers, with your billion different fingerprints and faces—my fellow mammalians, let us proceed with our education, one and all.

We did not know his legendary head,
in which the eyeballs ripened. But
his torso still glows like a candelabrum
in which his gaze, only turned low,

holds and gleams. Else could not the curve
of the breast blind you, nor in the slight turn
of the loins could a smile be running
to that middle, which carried procreation.

Else would this stone be standing maimed and short
under the shoulders' translucent plunge
nor flimmering like the fell of beasts of prey

nor breaking out of all its contours
like a star: for there is no place
that does not see you. You must change your life.

[illegible]

And now to conclude the [illegible]

[illegible]

We did not know [illegible]
in which [illegible]
the [illegible]
in which [illegible]

Both [illegible]
[illegible]
of the [illegible]
to that [illegible] which [illegible]

[illegible]
[illegible]
[illegible]

[illegible]
like a [illegible]
that does not [illegible]